THE
MERICAN

UNLAWFUL MEN BOOK #5

Chapter 1

BRAD

Red. It's everywhere.

Eyes open, eyes closed.

Red.

Blood, pain, gunshots.

Her hair.

Red.

I duck, the sound of guns firing, bullets flying.

But I still see red.

And then . . . green.

Green eyes looking up at me full of relief. Of hope. I tell her she's going to be okay. She nods. It's weak, it's jerky.

Red.

This time, it's not blood I see. It's not vibrant, glossy, shoulder-length waves.

It's a red mist.

Anger.

She looks down at the crook of her arm, and I follow her eyes to the needle hanging out. Then up the pipe toward a bag. There's a hair tie halfway up, knotted around the tube, blocking the flow of drugs to her veins. Her jaw tenses, and she yanks it out. Blood sprays the mattress, and I look over my shoulder, seeing Danny hauling a blonde girl up from another bed. Goldie is watching the door, James has another girl in one arm, a gun in the other, and Ringo is carrying a brunette. Every taste in women is covered. *Sick bastards.*

"We have one more," I yell. The weight of the other unconscious girl on my shoulder becomes heavier. "Fuck." I jerk my arm, shifting her up more as I round the bed. "She's awake," I call. *Smart.* She's smart. And so fucking young. I ask the girl—because that's what she is, a girl—if she can walk. She gives me another jerky, strained nod as I offer a hand, and her delicate, pale limb reaches for me. She holds on to me so tightly as I help her up off the dirty mattress, the strain on her face painful to watch. The strap of her tank slips off her shoulder.

Purple. Yellow. Black.

So much fucking red, I'm forced to blink back the mist clouding my vision, anger crippling me. Her hand feels for the strap of her tank, missing it, her movements clumsy and disorientated. "Here." I wince, lifting it back into place, covering her bruised breast. My teeth grind. *What the fuck did they do to her?* I hold out my hand again, but she doesn't take it. I look at her. She looks at me. And for a moment, I'm lost, no longer dodging bullets and running for my life. Instead, I'm tumbling into a gaze so expressive. So hopeful.

So fucking beautiful.

Falling.

Just staring.

I feel my forehead furrow and shake my head mildly, trying to realign my focus. But her eyes. I'm a prisoner to them. I need to get her out of here.

And yet for all the will in the fucking world, I can't move. Can't even feel the weight of the other girl on my shoulder anymore.

Bang!

It takes that gunshot to break the spell. The girl startles, and I blink my vision clear of the red, looking back. More gunshots ring out, and mumbled yells of panic come from the young women who are drugged up to their eyeballs. "Fuck. We've got to go, sweetheart." She's quickly tucked into my side, clinging to my torso, both arms wrapped around me to hold herself up as she staggers along beside me. "You okay?" I ask, checking on her constantly, as well as our surroundings. James is raining bullets with no mercy or break, a machine gun in each hand, his face a picture we're all used to.

Murderous.

We make it outside, and James holds the door while he and Danny have a brief argument over whether he blocks the Polish from making it through or comes with us. We all know Danny will lose. James isn't moving from that door. Not until we get all the girls on the boat. So I keep jogging, knowing Danny will soon be following. My shoulder is burning, my muscles screaming. "Jesus." I check on the girl still clinging to me, her weight hanging off my side as she trips and staggers along beside me.

"Brad, you good?" Danny yells, obviously seeing the other girl on my shoulder slipping. He takes the redhead from my side, allowing me to reposition the girl on my shoulder.

"We need to up our game in the gym," I say, taking the redhead back and picking up my pace, hearing the sound of bullets hitting metal behind us. Fuck me, I hope James can hold that door for long enough.

I look down at the uneven, rocky pathway, catching sight of the girl's bare feet as I do. If I could be sure it wouldn't slow me down enough and get us all killed, I'd pick her up.

I look at her as she looks up at me, and once again I'm momentarily lost. No longer running for my life. *Fucking hell.* I tear my eyes away, seeing the broken, old jetty up ahead. I concentrate on getting her onto the boat before easing the other girl off my shoulder, rolling it a few times, wincing.

"You go," I hear Danny say.

I turn, seeing him checking the magazine of a Beretta. "What?" I stand tall, ready for the fight. "No." There is not a fucking chance in hell he's going back, not without me.

"Go," he grates, his face lethal.

Couldn't give a fuck.

There's always been one rule between Danny and me—never leave the other behind. *Ever.* He's not only my cousin, he's my best friend. Plus, I have the added bonus of promised death from his wife if I ever go home without him. Unlucky for Danny, I'm more afraid of Rose than I am of him. So yeah, not going anywhere.

I take a step and meet some resistance, something grabbing my hand and holding me back. I look down.

Red.

Her green eyes are scared. Lost. "I'll be back in a minute," I promise her, flexing my fingers in her hand, her hold tight. I manage to break away with some effort, collecting a rifle as I head back to Danny, ignoring his lethal expression. I check the chamber as I pass. "Say one word," I warn him, "and I'll fucking shoot you." This dickhead—my cousin—has developed a habit of taking senseless risks. It started when he took Rose Cassidy from the enemy as collateral. *Fatal.* Since then, he's made some really stupid fucking decisions. Can't lie, I've become rather attached to Danny's now wife. I quite love James's other half too. They're like sisters to me. So, yeah, I'm invested.

Getting on the jet ski, I wedge the rifle between my legs and start it up, making the engine scream as I roar away from the shore. I follow Danny around the cove, bouncing across the waves. "I'm out," James yells when he sees us racing toward him, tossing his guns aside and forcing his weight back into the door. I look at Danny turning his ski, giving James the rear end, and then turn my eyes back onto James, seeing he's got the gist. "Fuck me," I breathe, locking, loading, and aiming. "So we're stuntmen now, are we?"

James eases off the door, telling me not to miss. I laugh. He runs. And I fire.

Bang, bang, bang, bang, bang.

I watch as each of my targets catapults back, until I'm firing . . . nothing. I'm out. James sprints toward the sea, launching himself off the edge of the rocks toward the back of Danny's jet ski. I toss the gun into the water and scan the vicinity, circling my jet ski, making sure we're clear before I slam down on the throttle, catching up with Danny at the next curve on the coastline. But James isn't on the back of his jet ski. *Fuck.* I search the jet stream for any sign of him, looking over my shoulder through the spray of water, hearing nothing but the roar of engines.

My body jolts.

"Fuck." I cough, losing my grip of the handlebar, a wicked pain shooting through my shoulder. I frown and look down, seeing a perfect hole in my wetsuit by my collarbone. And when I slow down, I look over my back. Another hole. I puff out my cheeks, swallowing, gritting my teeth. *Jesus fucking Christ.*

I blink my vision clear, slowing, and the moment I see Danny's panicked eyes scanning the water, my stomach falls into my ass. I start searching with him, my pain forgotten. *Where the fuck is he?*

"We go back," Danny yells, taking the words out of my mouth.

I turn my jet ski, still searching the water, damning the stupid fuck to hell and back. Jesus Christ, I do not want to be in Beau's path when she sees James isn't with us when we get back to the boatyard. "Come on," I whisper, searching the ocean.

"Dan—"

A surge of water rises, and James breaks the surface. "Motherfucker," he bellows, shaking the water from his eyes, as I fold over the handlebars of my jet ski in relief.

"Jesus," I breathe.

"Were you worried about me?" James asks, casual. Unaffected.

"Fuck you," Danny wheezes, mirroring my pose, slumped over the handlebars, exhausted, relieved, and everything in between.

Couldn't have said it better myself. Yes, I was worried, and I won't lie and claim it's because I don't want to explain his death to his girlfriend who will likely shoot me for losing him. Fact is, I care about the murdering sicko. Since the day he walked into my club and told me my best friend wasn't actually dead, I knew James Kelly would be around for a long time. I also knew Danny would be resurrected and shit would fly far and wide. And it has. It's been nothing but fun and games.

I laugh, rubbing at my forehead, gritting my teeth, as Danny helps him onto the back of his jet ski.

"How many are left?" James asks me.

"I saw three drop." I roll my shoulder.

"So two, assuming the hits were fatal?" he says, and I nod my confirmation. I'm a good shot. I aimed for their heads but bobbing on a jet ski on the ocean isn't a marksman's friend. "You okay?" Danny asks, looking me up and down.

"Dandy, but I really need a drink." I squeeze the throttle and wince again, blinking back the haze. Not red, not anger.

Pain.

My stomach turns as I watch Danny maneuver the ski, heading back to Byron's Reach, and the moment he's turned away from me, I give in to the nausea, throwing up into the sea. "Shit," I curse, watching Danny and James getting farther away. I peek down at my wetsuit, feeling at the hole, hissing. Blood spurts out. I'm no doctor, but the rate of loss isn't reassuring. I shake my head, my vision clears, and I hit the throttle, squeezing the seat with my thighs, holding on for dear life as I zoom across the water.

It's the longest fucking journey of my life. The shore seems to get closer before drifting away again, the people in the distance close but miles away.

I eventually pull up onto the shore, faster than I should, wedging my jet ski into the seabed, and I slide off. "Fuck," I mutter, reaching back with my good hand and pulling down the zip of my wetsuit, swaying, blinking, my legs heavy as I walk through the water, trying to make it onto the beach. I see two of everything. Danny, James, Beau, Otto, and Ringo. Hear nothing but slow, undistinguishable words that sound like groans as I pull the top of my wetsuit down. The pressure of it squeezing my body is making me feel sick.

The relief is instant.

Before the pain flares, my stomach turns, and I black out.

Red.

Chapter 2

BRAD

"Fucking hell," I breathe as I catapult up in bed, drenched in sweat. The moment I register where I am, I breathe out my relief and fall back to the pillow, my shoulder throbbing. But I don't close my eyes.

No red today.

Fuck me, it's been six months, and every single fucking night, the same damn dream. Sometimes daydreams too. And when will this pain fuck off? I roll my shoulder, looking down at the scar, and throw the covers back, angry, getting up and pulling my cell off charge. It's not even six. I went to bed precisely two hours ago. I don't know how much longer I can take this deprivation.

And yet . . . I can't fucking sleep.

I need to have a word with the contractors who are turning my apartment from a bomb site—literally—to an apartment again. Danny's dirty great big mansion—my temporary accommodation—is like a pressure pot. And so fucking busy.

Pulling on some shorts and sneakers, I rake a hand through my hair and make my way down to the gym, stopping off in the kitchen. I absentmindedly go through the motions of making a coffee, focusing on the sounds of the birds tweeting, watching the sun rising over the tall trees that line the boundary wall of the mansion. Another day. "Another dollar," I muse, lifting the black liquid to my lips, sipping.

I spot the dogs in the distance, rounding the side of the pool. They're excited, running back and forth.

Red.

"Fuck." I blink, catching sight of Pearl in the distance following Cindy and Barbie, tossing a ball and catching it as they circle her legs, begging her to throw it. Bare legs. My eyes climb them, my cup at my lips, until I'm looking at the beacon of fire-red hair. Except this morning it's tied back, revealing her dainty neck. Her bare lips are stretched, her smile wide. It's a stark contrast to the girl I found beaten on a dirty mattress in a hangar waiting to be sold.

I swallow and relax where I stand, lowering my cup, having a stern word with myself. *You're old enough to be her fucking father.* "Remember that, Brad," I say to myself, unable to tear my eyes away. I don't think I've ever met a woman so robust. And yet I saw her let her walls down briefly when she held my hand. When I looked into her eyes.

What's her story?

I hate myself for being curious.

"Remember what?"

I jerk and spin, spilling my coffee all over my hand. "Fuck." Steam rises from my skin, my flesh instantly pink. "Fuck, fuck, fuck." I discard my cup and shake my hand as Beau snatches a tea towel off the stove handle—expertly hung there by Esther, no doubt—and holds it under the cold faucet, before laying it over my burning limb. "Fuck, that's sore."

"Stop whining," she says, smiling down as she holds the cold cloth over the wound. I wrinkle my nose and grunt an apology as I stare at Beau's heavily scarred arm. I should not be bitching about a small scold in front of a woman who is scarred for life by fire. "Who were you talking to?" she asks.

"Myself," I admit, relaxing back on the counter.

She peeks up at me. I hate the knowing in her eyes. "You look like shit."

"Thanks."

"What time did you get in from the club?" She lifts the cloth and inspects the damage.

"Four."

"Brad, come on. You need more than two hours' sleep."

You tell my mind that.

Beau leaves me by the counter and goes to the cupboard, pulling out a box and some cream. "How much longer can you go on like this?"

Until I can be sure I can close my eyes and not see red. "I'm fine."

"Seriously?" She squeezes some cream onto my hand and rubs it in, and I try my fucking hardest not to hiss. "You need to speak to Doc."

"Doc can't help me."

Looking up at me, she sighs her annoyance, and her hand comes forward, reaching for my shorts. I watch on a frown as she dips into my pocket—*fuck*—and pulls out a small plastic bag full of white powder, her head tilting accusingly.

I don't appreciate it. I swipe it out of her grasp and stuff it back in my pocket. The Florida snow is in case of emergencies. *Like every day right now.*

"Well, I spoke to Doc," she says. "He said he might be able to help."

"You talked to Doc about me?"

Her eyes narrow, angry. I know she's worried. She needn't be. Holding up a pot, she tilts her head. "Sleeping pills." She doesn't give me an opportunity to reject them, slipping them into my pocket.

With the cocaine.

"Haven't you got other things to worry about?" I ask, turning to the coffee machine to top off my cup. "A nursery to paint, a husband's kink to suppress?"

"God, you're a dick sometimes."

"Better than a pussy-whipped killer who's under the thumb." I smile at the machine, waiting for it. She doesn't disappoint. I get an elbow in the back, making me grunt and fold a little. "Coffee?" I ask.

"I'm not allowed coffee."

I look over my shoulder, seeing her in the fridge. She pulls out some of James's signature green slop and grins around the rim before she swigs some back. I grimace and head out of the kitchen. James has more than a short leash on Beau these days. No one can blame him after what they've been through. I'm surprised he hasn't actually wrapped her and his unborn baby in cotton wool.

"When are you going on your honeymoon?" I ask over my shoulder.

"Good question."

I stall at the door and look back. Her head is tilted again. Fucking hate it. I know Beau well enough to know when her cop instincts are buzzing, and they've been buzzing for the past six months since Danny walked out of this mansion on the warpath to chase that Russian fucker Sandy down. What a fucking shock that was. No man wants to find out the guy he's about to do business with, albeit illegal business, is the man who raped his wife when she was fourteen. *Jesus fucking Christ.* No one could have anticipated *that* twist. Unfortunately, Danny's reckless pursuit of Sandy led to him being shot. Three times. The jerk also returned, on his knees, and told his wife the man who's haunted her for the past fourteen years was dead. *He isn't.* Sandy, the cunt, sped away in his Bentley, and no one has heard from him since. Or found the fucker. It's not through lack of trying. Between Danny, James, me, and the others, we've turned Miami inside out. Pushed out to New York, where Sandy was supposedly moving in on. Nothing. It's eerily quiet these days. The Bear's dead, along with most of her army. But are we relaxing?

Never.

"For some reason," Beau goes on, lowering her puke juice to the counter. "We can't go until . . ." Her eyebrows rise. "What?"

"What?"

"I don't know, you tell me."

"Tell you what?"

"Why I can't go on my honeymoon."

Because James won't dare to leave Miami in case all fucking hell breaks loose, which is likely when Danny finds Sandy. "No idea."

One eye narrows on me. Fucking hell, I feel cornered. "I did a little investigating," she says, and my walls fly up.

"I'm late for the gym." I turn.

And walk straight into someone.

Red.

So much fucking red.

All I can see is red.

I clench my eyes closed and breathe in and out, composing myself, getting my thoughts under control before I face her. The vibrancy before me is too much at this hour of the day. At *any* hour of the day. "Mind where you're going," I snap, sidestepping her and stalking away.

"Wanker," Pearl mutters to my back, and I don't argue with her. I'm a first-class cunt these days.

I make it to the gym and push my way inside, slamming the door behind me. "Fuck."

"What?" Danny shoots up from the weights bench, startled, disorientated.

And slips off the leather, hitting the gym mat with a thud. "Fuck."

I look down at him on his back, making no attempt to get up, probably because he's not got the energy. Now here is a man who will understand my sleep deprivation. Not that I can tell him I'm deprived of sleep. Poor guy is fucking knackered.

"Another rough night?" I ask, sipping some coffee before setting it on the towel cabinet.

His head drops to the side, his tired, red-rimmed eyes looking me up and down. "I'm so tired, Brad," he breathes, and I laugh.

"Don't ever say that in front of Rose."

He hums, closing his eyes, staying exactly where he is, on his back, on the mat, in the gym. I lower to the bench on the other side of the room, smiling to myself. The Angel-faced Assassin, The Brit, Danny Black, put on his ass by a newborn baby. Uncle Carlo would turn in his fucking grave. And that's another thing. Where the fuck is his body? I'm sure Danny will beat that information out of Sandy when he finds him.

I fall to my back and look up at the weights. They look really heavy this morning. *Really* fucking heavy. I close my eyes, resting them for just a moment, thinking someone around here needs to get better coffee. I need just a few minutes. I sigh, my back melding into the leather.

Red.

Fuck!

I shoot up.

And smack my head on the pole. "Shit." I blink, dazed, glancing around. Danny's still on the mat, mouth open, catching flies. "Fucking hell."

"What the fuck are you two doing?"

James is in the doorway, looking between Danny and me, one lethal eyebrow lifted in amusement. "What's the time?" I ask, feeling around on the floor for my cell.

"Eight."

"No shit." What a result. Another two hours in the bag. Maybe I'll only need two grams of coke today. *For fuck's sake.* I dodge the pole, sitting up, rubbing at my forehead. "I need to get to the club."

"We need to have a conversation," James counters.

That's worrying. "What about?"

"Beau." He paces over to Danny and toes him with his boot. "Wake up, Sleeping Beauty."

"Daddy's tired," he mumbles. "Please, darling, go to sleep."

I chuckle, and James smiles, pulling his foot back and booting Danny in the thigh. "Wake up."

Danny opens one eye. Snarls. "Do you want to die today?"

"Do *you*?" James counters, making me straighten, focused. "What's going on?"

"I had a call from Higham," James says, and both Danny and I visibly tense. It's a matter of days before our FBI friend retires. Poor guy can't stand the heat. "Beau's digging."

"Oh, for fuck's sake," I breathe, resting my elbows on my knees, looking at the screen of my cell, seeing a missed call from Nolan. "Can't you control that woman?" I thumb the button to call him back.

"Do *you* want to die too?"

"Death's probably better than my current torture," I mumble, ignoring James's questioning look, lifting my cell to my ear. His big mouth is probably why Beau's giving me looks like that too. I'll never fold under the pressure to confirm whatever they think they know. Because they *don't* know. "What's up?" I say when Nolan answers.

"Leon's here to pick up some beer for the café. How much am I giving him?"

"Wait there," I say, putting my phone on my shoulder. "Leon's at the club to pick up. How much?"

"A million. All in twenties." Danny struggles to sit up, scrubbing his palms down his face. "Tell him to put it in the bunker for now."

"Did you get that?" I ask, my cell back at my ear.

"I heard."

"I'll be in later." I hang up and stand, stretching. "So what's Higham said?" I ask, collecting my coffee and downing it, my nose wrinkling. It's cold. But it's caffeine.

James opens the door and peeks out before closing it again. Makes sense, since Beau is the gym's most frequent visitor, and that won't change now she's expecting Baby Enigma. "The report in the paper the day after Danny went after Sandy all those months ago detailed the bodies of four men."

"And?" I ask.

James looks at me tiredly. "Don't you think Beau would have counted the number of men that were with Sandy when they arrived at the house before Danny chased them down and went all Die Hard on them, Brad?"

"Fuck," Danny breathes.

"Fuck," I mimic. That woman is a pain in our fucking asses. She's also really fucking useful. So she knows one Russian bastard walked away from that particular shootout. "You think she's suspicious?"

"Beau's suspicious of everything. It's innate." James lowers to a bench. "We all know she won't stop with Higham. The last thing you need is her finding out Sandy is still alive."

Because she'll tell Rose.

"He won't be alive soon," Danny growls, the scar on his face glowing, his hand rubbing across his thigh where Sandy and his men buried a bullet in The Brit. Pray for Sandy.

"We've turned the city upside down," I remind him. "And New York is silent."

"Do you think he's going to slip away into the night and that will be that? Give me a fucking break." Danny's jaw ticks. "He tried to kill Beau when James took his brother out. He turned his back on Volodja and The Bear."

Danny's right. And, actually, I don't think Sandy had any intention of leaving us to rule Miami while he moved in on the Italians in New York. I look at James. "You need to take Beau on your honeymoon."

He huffs. "Don't you know my wife at all?"

Admittedly, not as much as James, obviously, but I know her. "Seriously. She needs to concentrate on being married and pregnant."

James looks as if he could quite easily lay me out. "Don't you think I know that? *Want* that? But as long as we have people to kill, Beau will be on high alert. And let's not forget, Sandy isn't the only one we're looking over our shoulders for."

"The Mexicans," Danny grunts, falling to his back again. "Fuck, I don't have the brain power for this right now."

The Mexicans. That'll teach us for recanting on the deal with them, but we didn't really have much choice at the time when we had endless shit flying at us. "I've got to get to the club." I head for the door. "We're hiring."

"Hiring?" James asks. "You just took on Pearl and Anya."

I stop and look back, a sarcastic smile on my face. Don't I fucking know it. "We hired them as bartenders. I don't think it would be in good taste to ask the girls we saved from sex slavery if they'd like to strip in our money-laundering joint."

Danny chuckles on the floor, his eyes still closed, ending his amused fit with a sigh.

I curl a lip at him, even though he can't appreciate it. "When the fuck will the salon be ready?" I ask, irritated.

"It's a beauty spa," James reminds us, failing to hide his smile.

"Who the fuck knows," Danny says, eyes still closed, fingers now laced and resting on his chest. "I just handed over another five hundred grand."

To be honest, I don't care how much it's costing. I need it to be finished so Pearl can work for Rose ASAP. Because it's awkward. "Are you purposely stalling the completion?" I ask, suspicious.

"Don't know what you're talking about, darling."

"Sure you don't." Rose will kick his fucking ass if she cottons on. I pull the door open, and James follows me out, leaving Danny to grab a few more winks. "What are you doing today?" I ask as we walk side by side down the corridor.

"Taking Beau to the condo I bought and hoping I can convince her that the second bedroom will make an amazing nursery."

I laugh. "You're tempting her with a renovation project?"

"I need to keep her busy."

I hear him perfectly well. Beau asking questions about the roadside shootout six months ago with Sandy isn't the only fuck-fest we need to distract our resident ex-cop from. Her mother's death is playing on everyone's mind. Or, less her mother's death, but *how* she died.

A gunshot wound to the head.

And Beau pulled the trigger.

It was James or her mother.

She didn't need to think about it too much. I don't suppose a man could ask for better proof of commitment. The fact that Jaz Hayley was The Bear—the person responsible for the deaths of James's family's, Beau's ex-fiancé, *and* her father—knocked us all sideways. But Beau?

Destroyed.

She was distracted for five months arranging their wedding. Now I know James is hoping the pregnancy will distract her for another five months. I also know he's hoping in vain. The mystery was solved. Beau's demons were supposed to be put to bed.

But this is Beau. She will never be able to let go of her need to question . . . everything. It's what made her a brilliant cop.

"Good luck with that," I say as we cross the foyer. I look up the stairs and see Tank and Fury descending, both fastening their ties, ready to take the kid to school. Then Ringo and Goldie appear, both stoic, but as relaxed as I've ever seen them. Then from the garden, Otto and Esther walk in, laughing. *So* fucking busy.

I walk into the kitchen and stop on the threshold when I find Lawrence brewing coffee, telling Anya and Pearl, who are at the breakfast bar, about his act last night. Pearl looks over her shoulder at me, both hands wrapped around a mug, the cuffs of her hoodie pulled down, covering her palms, protecting her from the hot china. Her smile falters.

Red.

I look away and head upstairs, passing through the middle of every-fucking one. I need to get out of here.

Chapter 3

Pearl

I return my attention to the breakfast bar, feeling Anya's eyes on me. "What?" I whisper, as Lawrence grinds some beans, apparently blissfully unaware of the dramatic change in temperature. Ice. As always when Brad and I are in the same room. Same house. Same club. Same bloody planet. And yet . . .

"Nothing." She shrugs, getting up. "I'm going to shower."

"Okay." I release the cuffs of my jumper from my palms and roll up my sleeves. Because . . . heat. It's anger, I'm sure of it. The man is an arsehole. His anger makes no sense to me. I don't know why the hell he bothered saving me—he looks at me like he wants to kill me most of the time.

"Morning," Beau sings, appearing in her yoga kit, James not far behind. I can't help but smile when I look at them. And Danny and Rose. The love, the fire, the passion.

"Will you back off?" Beau says over her shoulder, prompting a displeased scowl from James. "You're crowding me."

"I've always crowded you." He ignores her demand and sweeps her off her feet, sitting her on a nearby stool and getting up in her face. "Have you had your morning juice?"

I grin around my coffee cup as Beau looks at Lawrence, like . . . *please, help me.* Her uncle, who doubles as an aunt when in drag, shakes his head, moving his rainbow kimono from under his arse so he doesn't sit on the silk when he takes a seat. "Darling, you chose to marry an over-the-top, protective assassin, so you can deal with it."

Beau snorts, returning her attention to her husband. He's half-smiling. Relaxed. I know his history. It's nasty. Dark. Beau's is as bad. And yet together, they're . . . light.

I fall into thought as I watch the comings and goings of the kitchen, everyone stopping by to collect coffees, bagels, or one of Esther's famous cups of tea. Since I'm British, I can attest. They're really fucking good. Remind me of home. I flinch that thought away. *Home.*

I'd rather be in hell.

I stare down into my coffee, watching the brown liquid swirl.

• • •

"Careful, darling," Mother says as I kneel on one of the chairs, leaning across the table to help her set out the delicate fine china decorated with white wisteria and lilac butterflies. The handle is so tiny, not nearly big enough for Father to get his fat finger through, so he'll wrap his big hand over the rim and drink from Mother's fine bone china with much less grace. That's if he stops by during her afternoon tea, which he probably won't. The men will be in the drawing room smoking fat cigars and drinking amber liquid from Father's crystal-cut short glasses. They'll laugh loudly. The ladies will not. They will sip tea and chat quietly. They'll wear two-piece frocks.

I hit the cup on the saucer.

"Darling!" Mother scurries around the table and checks the cup for chips, and the moment she gasps, I know she's found one.

"I'm sorry, Mother," I whisper, slipping down from the chair and moving away from the table.

"What are you sorry for?" Father appears at the large wooden double doors, his rugged face frowning.

I inhale, taking one more step away from the table.

"Nothing," Mother places the cup down, turning it so the chip is facing away from him. "Upstairs now, darling," she says, taking my shoulders and walking me out of the room. I look back at Father, hoping he doesn't check the cup. They're expensive and were a gift to Mother for her birthday. He doesn't check the cup, but he does tweak Mother's arrangement, taking the little silver spoons she's placed on the table and setting them where he prefers. On the saucer. "Here," Mother says, holding her hand out discreetly in front of me. There's a sugar lump in her palm. I grin and quickly snatch it, popping it in my mouth and sucking it until it's nothing, looking up at her and smiling. She winks. "Our little secret," she whispers.

• • •

I startle when the coffee cup is removed from my hand and Esther replaces it with a cup of tea on a small smile, giving my cheek a fond stroke before returning to faffing around the giant kitchen. I love her.

She's the mother I lost. She's never pressed further on what I've told her, no one ever has, but Esther seems to have a motherly instinct that detects there's . . . something. I worry my time shirking my story will soon be over.

I bite the corner of my lip where the hole remains, a constant reminder of my past, and reach up to my hair, feeling it skimming my shoulders. It's an inch or two too long. That needs to be fixed. I get up and finish my tea as I walk to the sink, placing my mug neatly on the side above the dishwasher. "Thank you." I give Esther a kiss on the cheek, halting her conversation with Otto.

"Where are you going?" she calls after me.

"Just a few errands to run before my shift at the club." I make it out into the lobby, seeing Rose coming down the stairs in workout clothes, cradling the baby in her arms. Not that she'll be working out. How the hell can a woman look this amazing a month after giving birth? Her body has snapped back into shape, no workouts required. "Morning," I say, greeting her with a kiss before fussing over the newest addition to the family.

"Morning," she chirps, smiling down at her daughter. I won't ask if it was a good night; I could hear the cries. "Have you seen Danny?" she asks.

"I assumed he was still in bed."

"I'll try his office." Rose carries on her way, looking back. "Want a walk around the garden soon? Go for coffee?" She smiles, and it's a lovely sight. Coffee dates—just leaving the mansion on a whim to sit in a coffee house—are not a normal thing in Rose's life. Obviously, Danny has to know her every move, but she can at least move. A giant, hairy guy following aside. It's freedom. I can appreciate her appreciation.

"I have a few things I need to do." I take the stairs, feeling her curious look on my back. I won't feed it. I smile as I jog down the corridor, googling local salons as I go, my mind sub-consciously counting the doors as I pass them until I'm at Anya's and my room. I walk right on in, reading the reviews of a place downtown as I do. "I'm going to get my hair cut," I declare to Anya as I look up, all smiles. "And my—" My eyes widen. "Brad?" He's standing in the middle of my room, a towel held on his wet hair, butt naked. My eyes fall down his prime chest to . . .

Oh Lord.

It's—

I quickly shoot my eyes to his, all kinds of weird shit happening between my thighs. I'm pulsing. Throbbing. I gulp as I stare at him, and he stares right back. No apologies. Not bothering to cover himself. He's not looking at me like he wants me dead now. He looks . . . shell-shocked.

"What are you doing in here?" I say on a breathy gasp.

He slowly lowers the towel from his head, but he still doesn't cover himself. *Cover yourself!* "This is *my* room, Pearl."

I move my eyes left. Right. Look past him at the curtains. *Oh shit.* I take one step back into the corridor, craning my neck and counting the doors to this one. *Idiot.* I close my eyes briefly and take a breath. "I didn't mean—"

"Sure." The door slams in my face, and my mouth falls open. *What the hell?* I throw the wood the filthiest look, hoping it burns through and burns *him. Wanker.*

It's an effort not to barge back in and give him a piece of my mind, but I resist, going to my room—the right room—and pushing my way in. I fall against the wood and look to the ceiling. What the hell is his problem? I've heard he's moving as soon as his burnt-out apartment is restored to its former, bachelor pad glory. I wish the builders would hurry the hell up. Being civil toward one of the bosses is getting harder by the day. With one word, he could have me out on my arse.

And I'll be found faster than Brad Black can draw his gun and fire, and I've heard that's pretty fucking fast.

· · ·

The salon I find has the best reviews. I'm no expert in hairdressing, although I have completely put myself up shit's creek by claiming I studied it at college back home. I wish. But what else could I tell them? The truth? I was scrambling for something, anything to share that would mean I could avoid the truth. Because the truth could have me killed, either by Brad, Danny, or James for lying, or by the monsters who'll find me when I'm inevitably thrown out. But I'm in a different country. I have to keep reminding myself of that.

But back to my more immediate problem: I'm no hairdresser,

and Rose thinks I am. The closest I got to any kind of education after I turned ten was the library where I'd lose myself for hours in various books. No one else read them. That library wasn't there for reading. It was a status symbol. And it came with the ridiculous house my father bought.

I study the stylist in the mirror as she pulls chunks of my thick red hair out with a comb, one eye closing, measuring, snipping, until my chin-length bob is back, just long enough to tie back if I want to. She puts some waves through with the straighteners and spiritizes it with some gloss spray. It's my first proper haircut in over eleven years. I pay with my own money, smiling as I do, then I walk across the road for my next appointment, taking a deep breath as I push my way through the door.

• • •

Des and Drake eye me with an edge of curiosity as I wriggle out of my denim jacket. "Pearl?" Des asks, his chin lifting a little. "What you doing putting holes in your face, girl?"

"You've no need to worry." I pat his suit-covered arm. "Unless they're bullet holes."

"That's not funny."

I smile and wander into the club, finding it surprisingly quiet for . . . I look down at my phone. Eleven. "Where is everyone?" I ask Mason. He's checking the glasses, holding them up to the light before slipping them onto the shelves behind the bar.

"I was told to limit staff this afternoon as there are some interviews."

I dump my bag and coat on the bar. "I didn't know we were hiring."

"Dancers."

"Oh . . ." I press my lips together and lower until I'm crouching on the floor, my black knee-length jersey dress stretching to allow it. "I might audition." Mason looks over the bar at me, his eyebrows high. I'm always mystified when he does that. How can he lift them with so many rings through them? "Did you get another piercing?" I ask, rising.

"Did you?"

I pout, nibbling at my lip ring, feeling the clink of metal on my teeth. "It's old but new." I smile mildly, swallowing discreetly.

Mason smiles, jerking his head. "Come on, help me with these glasses."

I leave my jacket and bag on the bar and round it, grabbing a towel and a highball. I won't ask him why the other staff aren't here but I am. Turns out I'm rather good at this bar malarky. Or perhaps my initiative and willingness is simply because this is my first job and my enthusiasm is off the charts. I'm happy here. Safe. "What time do the interviews start?" I ask, closing one eye and holding the glass up.

"Any minute."

"You had a haircut, girl?" Drake says as he passes.

"I have, indeed, had a haircut." And it feels so much better. Swishier. Thicker. And much neater than when I hacked it off myself with blunt scissors. "You like?" I feel at my nape.

"You got a fella?"

"What?"

"A man?" Drake smiles.

"No, why?"

"Show me your hands." He makes it to the bar, nodding at my hands, and Mason chuckles beside me. "Show me."

"Show him," Mason adds.

I sigh, placing the glass and towel down, holding out my hands and wriggling my fingers. "There."

He sniffs, looking at me in question. "No nail polish."

"I don't do polish." My father wouldn't allow it. So maybe I should get a manicure and fix that. "Are we done?" I collect my glass and towel.

"We're done," Drake says, wandering off to join Des. "As you were," he adds in the worst British accent I've ever heard.

I laugh and get back to business, and I don't stop smiling. All these men, they're like endless big brothers looking out for me. It's new, if strange. Addictive. I've never felt so safe immersed in such danger, surrounded by deadly men.

Nolan comes from the corridor that leads to the office. "You have to find a way to keep me," I say, leaning on the bar.

He laughs. "Pearl, babe, what Rose wants, she gets, and she wants you at the salon when it's done."

"It's a beauty spa." How many times do these men need telling?

"I love working here," I add. It doesn't involve qualifications that I *don't* have, and everyone is so friendly and protective. It's a novelty. I get back to polishing, my eyes naturally moving up to the secret office. Everyone except *him*. But I can avoid him.

"Listen, Pearl," Nolan says, pulling my attention his way.

"I'm listening." Always listening.

He gets on a stool, giving a nod to Mason. I don't ask. There are so many nods happening around this place, the mansion, and the boatyard. I'm surrounded by Churchill dogs. "I don't want to lose you."

I smile and reach across the bar, placing my hand on his. "I don't want to lose you either, Nolan."

Mason lets out a bark of laughter, and Nolan chuckles under his breath. Then he frowns. "Did you get a haircut?"

"God, you men are so observant." Something catches my eye across the club. "Oh, I think this is one of your applicants." A young woman struts in on heels that defy the law of balance, and I watch in wonder as she dials up the sex appeal, firing the men at the bar—not me—a toothy, wide, and definitely seductive smile. She's stunning. *Really* stunning. "Never lose an opportunity of seeing anything beautiful," I muse, "for beauty is God's handwriting."

"Emerson?" Mason asks, surprising me.

I look at him, interested. "Yeah."

"Did you study him?"

I nod, lying. Or is it lying? I *did* study Emerson, just not in a school, college, or university. "You're familiar with his work?" I ask, seeing Nolan greet the woman in my peripheral vision.

"For my finals." He grins. "I gave up philosophy and poetry to manage a bar and help launder money for the mafia. It pays better."

I chuckle, but it dries up when Brad appears across the club, fixing the lapels of his suit jacket. He spots me. His lip definitely curls a little. I quickly break the staring deadlock, raising a glass and inspecting the sparkles.

"What the fuck's the deal with you two?" Mason asks.

"I don't think Mr. Black appreciates appreciation." I lower the glass, seeing he's on his way over. So it's time for me to vacate the vicinity.

"What?" Mason says as I drop my towel and collect the keys for the store cupboard. I'll clean the toilets. Anything. It beats hanging around this ice box.

"I'll be in the restrooms," I say, leaving the men to hire the flesh.

"The cleaners have sorted the restrooms already," Mason calls.

Damn it. "I'll hoover the office."

"They did that too."

Bloody hell. "I'll check the stock."

"I did it, Pearl."

I sigh, exasperated, and face him. "There must be *something* I can do other than . . ." I shut up when I feel Brad close behind me, and I give Mason a pleading look. He doesn't catch it.

"I don't pay you to stand around looking like a spare part," Brad snipes, brushing my arm as he passes.

"I was just—"

"Do some fucking work."

I flinch, holding my tongue. *I must not retaliate. I must not retaliate.* I tell myself every time he riles me. Sometimes I succeed, sometimes I don't. I have to start succeeding *every* time. "I know your meanness isn't because you dislike me," I say to his back, my mouth speaking words while my mind is telling me to shut the hell up. "It's because you dislike *yourself*." Again, I wonder what the hell his problem is. Have done for the past six months. He's so . . . angry. Why?

Brad slows to a stop and faces me, and the temperature plummets once more. His chiseled jaw ticks. His chest rolls. "I don't like women with smart mouths."

That's bullshit. I know he loves Beau and Rose, and they both have *very* smart mouths. "Then you had better shut me up." *What the hell are you doing, Pearl?*

"Don't tempt me," he growls lowly, his cold stare adding another layer of freezing to the room. "Now get some fucking work done before I fire your ass."

"I have an *arse*, Mr. Black." I smile sweetly and walk past him. "And you can kiss it."

Mason coughs, Nolan balks, and the woman—I'm yet to learn her name—looks between us all, bemused. I'm asking for bloody trouble, I know it, and yet he's unearthed the fight in me that was knocked out of me—*literally*—many years ago. And maybe my smart mouth is being unleashed because I know deep down these men don't hurt women.

Mason and Nolan follow my path back to behind the bar, eyes cautious, and I pick up another glass and my towel, ready to get polishing again. But no sooner has the cloth met the side of the tumbler, I'm on my way back out from behind the bar, virtually being dragged.

"A word," Brad growls, hauling me across the club by my elbow, my hands still full. I don't fight him, of course I don't fight him. Giving the boss a bit of lip is one thing. Giving him a right hook to the face is another matter entirely. I wish I could, though. I've experienced fear of unthinkable levels. Brad Black doesn't scare me. Besides, like I said, these men don't hurt women.

"This doesn't feel like a *word*, Mr. Black," I breathe. "This feels more like physical assault."

He laughs, but it sounds demented, and I look up at him, seeing he looks quite demented too. "You have no idea," he snaps, pushing me into the office and slamming the door. I have no idea? The fucking idiot.

Roughly releasing me, he gets up in my face, forcing me to take some backward steps. "Don't you *ever* talk to me like that in front of my staff again."

Fuck off. "What about when you're *not* in front of your staff?"

"Ever!" he roars, knocking me back slightly with the force.

"Okay," I say, quickly finding my senses. It's hard amid the absolute disbelief I'm feeling, which is coupled with something else entirely unrecognizable.

Brad recoils, stepping back, his expression fleetingly unsure. But he soon finds his rage again. "Fucking apologize," he hisses, back up in my face.

I look him directly in the eye, not wavering, not melting under the heat of his hard, blazing stare, his breath, and anger. "I'm sorry." *I'm sorry you're such a wanker. I'm sorry I tried to be grateful for saving me. I'm sorry you don't like me. And I'm sorry I find you insanely attractive even though you're a complete arsehole to me.* "I'm sorry," I whisper again.

Another recoil, this time faint. It's as if he wasn't expecting me to comply. His eyes dart across my face. "Why aren't you crying?" he asks, his voice rough. Deep.

I shift on the spot, uncomfortable with the sensation of my blood heating. What the hell is that? "I only cry when I'm scared."

"You're not scared?"

"Of you?" I ask. "Do you *want* me to be scared of you?" Because it really feels like it. He's a bloody conundrum. He saved me. Reassured me. Calmed me. Cared for me. And then when I tried to thank him, he was a complete and utter bastard. What the hell am I supposed to make of this? *And* the feelings he's provoking? It's such a strange concoction of anger and . . . desire? Is that what this is? *Jesus Christ.*

He frowns, and his body softens, as if he's relaxing. "Of course I don't want you to be scared of me."

I'm shocked by my mental revelation. *Desire.* Is that what this buzzing inside me is? No. Surely not. He celebrated his thirty-fifth birthday months ago. And how did he celebrate? He took off to a fancy hotel and bought himself a mountain of cocaine and a few hookers. That is not the kind of man I should feel anything for but contempt. I was so disappointed in him, which is really bloody ridiculous. Who am I, a twenty-one-year-old woman, to be disappointed in a mass-murdering member of the mafia? He's attractive. God, he's attractive. Well-built, strong, loyal. Apparently quite funny, too, although I've never seen that side of him. But he's also a lot older than I am. I don't even know what the hell it is that's drawing me toward him. I frown to myself. Because he saved me? Give me a bloody break. I am no damsel in distress, and he is no knight in shining armor. I flinch again.

I *was* a damsel in distress. I needed help. I needed saving, and he was so kind. So handsome. But he didn't accept my gratitude. He ignored my thank-you. I don't know what the hell I've done wrong, but he's made it easy to dislike him. Ignore him. But this weird flutter in my tummy isn't so easy to ignore. *Ignore him.*

"Excuse me." I push past him, needing some breathing space, but I don't make it very far. His large, capable hand wraps around my slight wrist, and I look back, coming face to face with him again. Handsome. So, *so* handsome. Typically handsome, with lazy eyes, and a flawless, evenly stubbled, cut jaw. I bet if he smiles, that handsomeness accelerates. Will I ever see him smile?

He stares at me, and before I know what's happening, he's taking the glass and towel out of my limp hands, holding my arms, and walking me backward. My breathing becomes strained. My muscles tense. "What are you doing?" I ask on a breathy whisper, certain my body language and face must be spelling out my secrets. My attraction.

"What's your story?" he asks, his stare concentrated and unmoving, as if he's worried he'll miss a clue. "Where did you come from?"

I've told Rose and Beau this endless times—so many times I know my story by heart. "I was taken from a hostel," I whisper. "I've already shared that."

"When?"

"What?"

"How?"

"Brad, I—"

"Who took you?" He gets closer and closer, close enough to smell the lies. "Come on, Pearl." Nose to nose. "Talk."

I look into his eyes, frozen. He blinks slowly. Looks at my lips. Scowls mildly. "Brad," I whisper, starting to shake with the effort to remain standing.

"Pearl," he breathes. "Talk to me."

I don't want to talk. Right now, I want to kiss him.

Oh my God.

No.

I raise my hands, ready to shove him away, but the door swinging open distracts me, and Brad flies around. Nolan stands on the threshold, looking between us. "Everything all right?"

I don't answer, and I don't give Brad a chance to either. I collect my glass and towel and rush out, feeling the pressure easing from my shoulders as I hurry to the restrooms. As soon as I'm alone, I fight to catch my breath. "Shit," I whisper, falling against the wall and sliding down to my arse. *What the hell was that?*

Chapter 4

BRAD

Nolan watches her dash off before slowly turning a questioning stare my way. Can't say I like it, and I truly hope my deadly glare warns him not to say a fucking word. *Don't you fucking dare.* I already know this is fucked up. I don't need him, or anyone, telling me *how* fucked up. James was wary. Danny too. I soon put that to bed. I know the others have wondered. So, yeah, I need to stay away from Pearl and ensure *any* suspicions remain squashed. "I'll be out in a minute," I say, and he nods, backing out and closing the door quietly.

The moment he's gone, I bury my fist in a wall and fire a few fucks. I'd fire a gun if I had one within reach.

Right in my temple.

I shake my fist and drop into the chair, raking my good hand through my hair before slamming my head back. "Fucked up, Brad. Really fucking fucked up." I pull the drawer open, grab the Marlboros, and light up, exhaling loudly. A few deep breaths. Closing my eyes for a few minutes. Just . . . breathing. Smoking.

Doesn't work.

I'm so fucking exhausted, lacking the energy I really need right now.

To ignore her.

To resist her.

I stub out my smoke and dip into my inside pocket, pulling out my savior, racking up a line on the desk, before rolling a note and snorting it. I drop back in my chair, the hit instant. *Yes.* I feel every muscle unravel, my mind clearing.

That. Will. Do.

I push myself up, swipe off the remnants of white stuff from the desk and head out, significantly calmer than five minutes ago. More in control. By the time I make it onto the club floor, the first of three girls interviewing is on the stage, the pole in her hand. I keep my eyes away from the bar and lower to a chair. "Get on with it," I say to Nolan.

He quickly goes to the foot of the stage, and the girl, an attractive blonde, crouches in her killer platforms, her generous chest more or less pressed into Nolan's face. It's a tactic I'm familiar with. It never works. Has with Nolan, though. Once. He won't be snared by that net again.

I'm a Slave 4 U by Britney Spears kicks in—fuck my life—Nolan returns to the table, and the girl starts to dance. She's good. Got all the moves, the expressions, the sultry, magnetic appeal most men like. But I can't appreciate any of it, my shoulders constantly rolling, uncomfortable.

My mind focuses elsewhere.

On her.

Chapter 5

ROSE

Where the hell is he? I've searched this entire house, all bazillion rooms, walked the gardens, and found no sight nor sound of my husband. In a past life, I would have been out of my mind. Now? Now, there are no enemies to kill. No mysteries to solve. So, again, where the hell is he?

"Did you scare him away?" I whisper, nuzzling down into Maggie's cheek, getting a hit of her magnificent baby scent. I'll never get enough of it. The gym is the last room I search, because, poor love, why would he be in the gym? He's been too beat to work out since our daughter was born a month ago. I find it empty and back out, but a noise makes me still, the door ajar. On a frown, I push my way back in and scan the space. "Oh my God," I breathe when I see a bare foot poking out at the end of a weights bench. I walk over, rocking Maggie when she whimpers, and peek over the bench. I can't help my smile. He's flat on his back, arms and legs splayed, mouth hanging open. My deadly killer, who looks fit for nothing. It's almost a shame to wake him. *Almost.*

I move around the bench and toe him with my Ugg slipper. "Time to wake up, Daddy."

Danny murmurs, hums, exhales, flapping a hand at thin air, like he's searching for the snooze button on an alarm clock. "Two minutes."

"No, not two minutes." I need a shower, my hair is in desperate need of a wash, and I need . . . some pruning. I haven't waxed in places a woman should wax regularly for weeks. "Come on, Danny," I breathe, crouching, poking him. "I have to shower." There are a dozen people in this house who would fly to my aid and watch Maggie. But none of them are her father, and it's been nice having him at my beck and call recently.

I look down at Maggie. She's wide awake, her blue eyes showing all the signs of being as piercing as her father's. She has his bone structure too. "Just typical that I went through the agony of birth and you come out looking like your daddy." Although, I can't lie, I'm pretty sure Danny was in immeasurable pain at points during Maggie's birth too. I apologized each time I scratched him, grabbed him, smacked him.

I negotiate Maggie in my arms, making sure she's bundled up nicely, and place her on Danny's scarred chest. Cuts. Bullet holes. How will we ever explain them to her as she's growing up? Where she's come from.

I tentatively let her go and watch as her weight there slowly brings my husband back to life. His hand instinctively holds her in place as he breathes in, sending her up a little before he exhales and she sinks into his chest. He opens one eye. Looks down at her. My wonder seeing him look at her like this will never fade. She is literally life to him. He kisses the top of her head and lifts her a little higher, enjoying what I was enjoying moments ago. Her smell.

"It's the robber of sleep," he murmurs, closing his eyes again. "The crusher of my sex life."

I laugh, but on the inside, I grimace. The thought of penetration makes me shudder. And my boobs feel like they could explode for ninety percent of the day, so there's no fun to be had there, either. Poor guy.

"What are you doing in here?" I ask.

He doesn't open his eyes. "I came to work out, fell, and hit my head."

I roll my eyes and stand. "Come on, I need to go out." I turn and head for the door.

"What? Go out? Where?"

I smile to myself, not looking back. He's not been left alone with her yet. And he's not being left alone now. The house is full, and Esther is here. He has an army of helpers on hand. "I'm going to the spa to see how the reno is coming along, and then I'll pick Daniel up from school." I swing the door open and pass through.

"Rose!" Danny yells.

I peek over my shoulder as I pace down the corridor, seeing him scrambling to his feet, Maggie safe in the crook of his muscly arm. Panic. It's a rare expression on my husband. He's capable. Confident. What the hell is he stressing about? I head to the kitchen with Danny in pursuit and go to the fridge. "Morning," I sing to Esther's ass as I pass her bending over the dishwasher.

"Morning," she replies, not looking up. "What kind of night did you have?"

"Long." God help me, every hour she woke up and wanted feeding. And now she will sleep all day. I swear, she's nocturnal. I open the fridge and grab the OJ, drinking straight from the carton.

Esther, smiling, pops up from the dishwasher and flaps her arms, exasperated.

"What?"

"Why does everyone around here insist on slurping from the carton?" She searches my arms. She doesn't get a chance to ask. Danny falls into the kitchen, Maggie held to his chest with one spade of a hand. It is the most incredible sight. My tall, built, scarred, murdering, mafia boss husband handling something so delicate. His sex appeal has tripled, which means my husband is one scorching-hot male. Even if he looks like he could fall asleep standing. I wince, still feeling the tenderness between my legs. I feel like my insides could fall out at any moment. *So* sexy.

"Here she is," Esther coos, forgetting everything and going to Danny. God damn it. "Do you want me to take her for a bath?"

"No," I pipe up quickly, going to the island as Esther swings around, a little injured and slightly indignant. I tilt my head, feeling Danny's laser stare on me. "Maggie needs some daddy time."

"Oh, right, yes, of course." Esther nods, understanding. "Daddy time."

"I have to go to work," Danny grates.

"Work? But everyone is dead, darling." I smile sweetly. "So there is no work to do." I go back to the fridge, opening the door and returning the OJ before taking a bottle of breast milk out. I turn and present it to Danny. His face. His scar is glowing. It's not glowed for a while. I've missed it. "Freshy pumped."

His eyes drop to my chest. "She prefers to drink from the source."

I laugh loudly, and Esther takes that as her cue to get back to the dishwasher. "Like her daddy," I say, going to him, reaching up and kissing his rough chin. "Mummy has business to see to." What a novelty. Me seeing to business and not Danny. Legal business. I push the bottle into his limp hand and kiss Maggie's head. "There's more in the fridge." Plenty, because it seems I've turned into a cow. "Have a lovely day." I leave them in the kitchen.

"You're taking Tank."

"Standard," I sigh, climbing the stairs. No danger, no enemies, at least none on the hunt for us, and yet I still have to take a Viking. If I wasn't so fond of Tank, I'd complain, but he's good company and, actually, a really useful carrier of bags.

"Rose, come on," Danny pleads, coming after me.

"What are you so worried about?"

"I'm not worried."

"You don't think you can do it?" I know he can do it.

"Of course I can do it."

I turn at the top of the stairs and face him. I don't like his filthy look. It's a look of defense. "Is there a problem?" I ask, head tilted, eyes lasers on him. Or something he's not telling me?

"There's no problem."

"You seem a bit too worried about me, considering all the enemies are dead."

"I'll never stop worrying about you."

I smile mildly. "I'll see you both later." Leaving Danny behind, I go to our room and take a shower. And it's glorious. What's not so glorious is how overgrown I am. Everywhere. I rinse the conditioner out of my hair and brush the water out of my face, dreading the thought of letting anyone near me with wax strips. God damn my husband. I step out of the stall and reach for my cell on the vanity, calling Beau.

"Why does Danny look like he wants to kill?" she asks when she answers.

"Oh, he does?" I say, smiling to myself. "I've missed that look on him."

She chuckles. "Where are you?"

"In the shower." It's a long shot—I know my husband is passionate about it, but I'm desperate. "Do you have a razor?" Silence. It's probably unreasonable of me, but I roll my eyes. "So I can shave," I go on. I can't even be annoyed that I need to explain. Because why else would I want a razor? "I don't think I can face waxing."

"Danny banned all razors from the house," Beau reminds me, as if I need fucking reminding. The men around here go to the salon for trims and tidies more than the women.

This is my best friend. Breaker of rules. "I know he banned them. That wasn't my question." I look down at my puckering skin. Cold. "My question was, do you have one?" Beau doesn't get waxed, I know that for certain, and I'm hedging my bets that she doesn't use hair removal cream, so—

"I'll be there in a minute."

I smile. "Thanks."

She hangs up and I get back under the hot spray, soaping myself down—gritting my teeth while on my boobs.

"If he asks, this was nothing to do with me." Beau appears, holding out a Gillette Venus.

"Thank you," I gasp, plucking it out of her fingers. "You might need a new blade once I've finished cutting through this hedge." I look down, wondering where the hell to start.

Beau laughs and sits on the vanity unit. "Your boobs, though, Rose."

I shake my head, exasperated by the melons currently weighing me down and causing me so much discomfort. But I will persevere. Doc's assured me they'll calm down soon, and I'm living for that day. Throughout this pregnancy and birth, I've been truly astonished by what the female body is capable of. I never could appreciate it when I had Daniel. I was too young. Too stressed. Too scared. I look up at Beau, smiling. It's tinged with a little sadness for me and Daniel, for missing the first ten years of his life.

"Okay?" she asks, crossing one ripped jean leg over the other, her baggy shirt fastened with one button, her Birkenstocks dangling from her toes. She looks so relaxed. The most relaxed I've ever seen her, and I know she isn't faking it like she has in the past. Her demons have been crushed. Her tragic story had to get more tragic before she could truly heal, and now she's healing. Healing and growing a baby in her belly. Of course there are Doc's daily checkups by James's orders. Of course he's wrapped her in cotton wool. Of course he's watching her like a hawk.

"Yeah, I'm fine." Since I completely ruined their wedding by going into labor, we haven't really spent any time together. Understandable, what with Maggie only a month old and Beau being a newlywed. I miss her. "When are you going on your honeymoon?"

"Good question." She laughs, but it dries up and she nods at my chest. "You're leaking."

"What?" I peek down and see my nipples oozing. "Oh, for God's sake, I just expressed." I grab a face cloth and wipe myself.

"Where are you going, anyway?" she asks, seeming content to be missing a honeymoon. Maybe James doesn't want her to travel. Maybe he's taking unnecessary precautions. We all know Beau can fly, but after what they've been through, I dare anyone to tell James he's being overprotective. Anyone except Beau.

"To the spa." I grab a sponge and get a lather worked up. "It's been weeks since I checked in on the remodel. Want to come?"

She wedges her hands into the wood of the vanity and uses them as an anchor to lift her ass and swing off the unit. "Would love to, but—"

"Why do you lie to me?" I ask over a laugh, working the sponge into my legs. I'll start there. It looks less daunting.

"Trust me, I would love to, but my husband has other plans."

"Like what?"

"The apartment he bought."

I straighten. "What about it?" I hate the mild wave of panic that comes over me. The apartment that James said he was selling because it was a mistake buying it? Because he realized he and Beau would be happier here, surrounded by their family and friends who could support her through the trauma of having to kill her mom or let her mom kill James? And that was *before* Beau found out she was pregnant.

"Exactly. What about it?" Beau pouts. "I think he wants us to have our own space."

"This house is enormous, Beau."

"And so is the occupancy," she says, laughing. "Speaking of own space . . ." She lowers to the toilet seat. "I'm worried about Brad."

"Yeah, me too," I admit. He's not been right since he was shot. He doesn't crack many jokes anymore, doesn't play much, doesn't get involved. "I was talking to Doc." God love the lack of patient/doctor confidentiality around here. "I'm worried he has post-traumatic stress."

"You think?" Beau doesn't look convinced.

"What else . . ." I pause, realizing where her thoughts are. "Pearl,"

I breathe. "You still think it's got something to do with Pearl?" He can't even be in the same room as her.

Beau pulls a face, eyebrows high. Pearl was definitely asking too many questions about Brad after her ordeal when he was laid up. "Maybe."

"Whatever crush Pearl had is dead in the water," I say. "Especially since she found out about his adventure at the Four Seasons with too many hookers and too much cocaine."

She hums, apparently not convinced.

"Beau?" James voices comes through the wood, and I instinctively hold a palm over my bits.

"I'm naked!" I yell. "And it isn't pretty." Good grief, I think I'm hairier than Otto, Mason, *and* The Vikings right now. Combined.

"I'm in here." Beau chuckles, getting up and going to the door, nodding back at the razor in my hand. "If that doesn't work, call me and I'll have the gardener bring up the hedge trimmer."

I gasp, disgusted, and throw my soggy face cloth over the screen. It slaps the door, just as Beau's amused face disappears behind it. "Cheeky bitch." I look down again. She has a point though. I take a deep breath and get to work.

• • •

Airy. It's an odd sensation as I step out onto the terrace, my skirt swishing with the breeze. Lowering to the lounger, I slip my sandals on, smiling as I look around. My eyes land on an ashtray. What can I do to make him quit?

"Hey, Rose!"

I frown and get up, going to the edge of the terrace, looking down onto the garden. Beau's there, her face a picture of delight. "I'm coming to the spa."

"I thought you were going to the apartment?"

She shakes her head. It's a win. He's letting her out of his sight? It's the small, simple things, I think, as I tie my hair into a ponytail. "I'm coming." I knot the tails of my silk blouse, slip on some bangles, and snatch up my purse, excited to be spending some time with my *other* girl. As I pass Anya and Pearl's room, I knock. "Anya, we're heading to the spa, do you want to come?"

The door opens, and she smiles, her almond eyes sparkling. "I'll be ready in a few minutes, will you wait?"

"Of course." I dig through my purse and get my cell. "I'll call Pearl to see if she wants to meet us there. See you downstairs." I dial and make my way down to Beau, hearing the sound of my baby crying coming from the kitchen. I wince, my heart squeezing, telling myself they'll be fine as I take the handle of the front door and pull it open. "God damn it." I cut my call to Pearl and breathe in, going to the kitchen. Danny's on a stool, bottle in one hand, baby in the other. Esther spots me but Danny is too focused on Maggie, his smile both fond and worried as he teases her lips with the teat.

"Go," Esther mouths, flapping a shooing hand at me.

I back away and quickly turn, hurrying out before I give in to the urge to take over, dialing Pearl again.

"Hello?" she says.

"Are you working?"

"Just wrapping up before I go on a break."

"What time do you have to be back?"

"In a few hours."

"We're going to the spa."

"Fab, on my way." She hangs up, and I break out into the sunshine, slipping on my shades. Tank and Fury are propped up against one of the Range Rovers. "Where's James?" I ask Beau.

"He's gone to the club."

"Why? It's early-afternoon." Nothing happens at the club in the day. Not even shootouts anymore.

Beau shrugs. "I don't know, but I'm here and isn't that what matters?"

I grin and go to her, letting her wrap an arm around my shoulder.

"How's it feeling down below?" she asks.

"Breezy."

Beau bursts into fits of laughter, as do I, and it feels so good. Loud, unapologetic laughter. And, thankfully, no pee escapes. Pelvic floor exercises are a woman's friend, Doc said. Don't I know it.

"It's the interviews today," Fury says from the car.

We both shut up, looking at him in question.

"At the club," he goes on. "New dancers. Interviews today."

"Interviews?" I question. "You mean auditions?"

He shrugs, and Tank chuckles, the sound deep and earth shaking.

"Great," Beau breathes. "We get freedom, and our husbands get a pass to watch women strip."

I laugh and go to the car. If there is one thing in this world that I am sure of, it's my husband's fidelity, and I know Beau feels the same. But . . . I'm hardly meeting Danny's needs right now. I miss him. I miss *us*. Does he? On cue, my boobs twinge, reminding me of their purpose right now, and it's not my husband's pleasure. "Anya's coming and Pearl's meeting us there." I slip into the back and Beau gets in beside me, shuffling up so she's in the middle, leaving the door open for Anya as she comes dancing down the steps, wrapping a light scarf around her neck.

My mind goes back to the club. Strippers. Many willing women whose bodies are young and tight.

I shake my head to myself. I'm being ridiculous. That's sleep deprivation for you.

• • •

I stand in the middle of the spa with the fattest smile on my face as the contracts manager, Alan, talks me through the updates. "We had to move the washing stations a fraction this way," he says, indicating some plumbing work. "Because your ceiling drops here and if you want the floating ceiling with illumination, we've got to start a foot farther away."

I nod, reaching up and straightening my hard hat. "And the pedicure stations?"

"Could you lose one?" he asks, walking to the far side. "It would make the space less tight around each chair."

I ponder that. "Sure." I don't want clients feeling like they're on top of each other. "And the million-dollar question," I say, smiling, hoping to charm the right answer out of him rather than adopting my husband's tactic and terrorizing it out of him. "When can the decorators start?"

"Well, Mrs. Black," he says, gazing around the space. "There's been a few unexpected problems along the way which have hindered the schedule."

I narrow a suspicious eye. "Like?"

Alan suddenly can't look at me, and he's mute, unable to list the unexpected problems.

Something tells me The Brit's been poking his nose in. "The owner of the spa"—let's remind him of that—"would like to open by the first."

Alan balks. "That's four weeks."

"Correct. And two weeks for you to finish." It's been five months since we bought the salon. Three since the remodel started. "Let's get things moving." I leave Alan with his completion date and wander over to the girls, who are looking over the mood board I stuck to the wall when the works started, a reminder of what we're working toward. Lots of green, lots of plants, lots of . . . calm. Perfect.

"Did I hear you just tell him two weeks?" Beau asks.

"Yes." I ignore her surprise. "They built Byron's in that time, so if anyone tells me it can't be done . . ." I don't need to finish that statement.

"But the contractors aren't even finished."

"They will be in two weeks."

"Then you've got to decorate."

"It's all going to be fine," I say, smiling brightly at her. "Besides, I know an amazing decorator, and I also happen to know she's available right now."

"Who?" Pearl and Anya ask in unison, as Beau sighs.

"Me." She shakes her head. "Good luck convincing my husband I'm fit for work."

"We'll help. It'll be so much fun!" I clap my hands. "We should go for cocktails and mocktails." I check my phone again. No word from Danny. I can't lie, I'm surprised. "Then I need to collect Daniel from school." There's a reason we should go for drinks, and Beau catches it when I nod to Pearl. She seems a little subdued. I link arms with her, Beau on the other side, Anya joins the line, and we all walk out onto the street. "I see palm trees here and here," I say, nodding to the new glass doors. "And a living wall just inside by the reception."

"We need to think about marketing," Anya says.

"You're in charge of that," I tell her. She's young, probably a whizz on social media. I look at Pearl. "Love the lip."

She smiles, biting at it.

"And the hair."

"Thanks."

"Anything you want to talk about?"

"Yes, when am I starting at the spa?" she asks, suddenly super keen.

I raise my brows, studying her. "Anyone would think you don't like your current job."

She smiles, awkward, and I feel Beau nudge me. See? If there was anything between Brad and Pearl—and, again, their contempt toward each other is quite conclusive—why would she be so keen to get away from the club?

My cell rings, and when I see Barney's dad calling, I feel myself tense.

"Oh, it's the hot, single banker," Beau chimes. "There could still be some murdering yet."

I roll my eyes and answer. "Lennox, hi."

"Hey, have you had a call from the school?" he asks, just as my phone declares another incoming call.

I look down, and my heart drops. "They're calling me now. What's happened?"

"You'd better take it."

"Okay," I squeak, hanging up and answering to the school, my heart beating double time. "Hello?"

"Mrs. Black, it's Principal Tucker."

"Hi, Principal Tucker," I say, pulling all of the girls eyes my way. "Is everything okay?"

"First of all, Daniel is fine."

I sag, relieved. "Thank God," I breathe, and Beau, Pearl, and Anya all deflate too, feeding off my energy.

"But I do need you to come in, Mrs. Black. There's been an incident. The police have been called."

"The police?" I blurt.

"Yes, Mrs. Black."

Oh shit. This isn't good. Not for Daniel *or* his dad. "I'm on my way. And, Principal Tucker?"

"Yes?"

"Do *not* call Daniel's father."

"I already tried calling him."

"Fuck." I wince. "I mean, darn."

"He *is* the primary contact."

"Is he?" Why didn't I know that?

"He didn't answer." *Fucking hell.* "I'll call him now," I say, hurrying to the car. "I'm on my way." I head to the passenger door, looking back at Fury as Tank automatically slips into the driver's seat. "Can you call Len to bring another car?"

He nods, and Beau rushes over. "Do you want me to come?"

"No, it's fine," I assure her, although I am positively stressed, not just because Daniels's in trouble, but because Danny is going to flip out. "I'll see you back at the hou— No, wait. You should definitely come." Beau might know the cops, therefore may be able to sweet-talk them should any sweet-talking be required.

Better than letting my husband loose. But what the hell has happened?

· · ·

Lennox is waiting on the steps outside when we pull up, and I'm out of the car fast, dialing Danny again. God damn it, why the hell isn't he answering? Neither is Esther. "Hey," I say, stuffing my cell in my purse. "You've met Beau," I say as we approach Lennox.

"On one of the many drop-offs and pick-ups." He smiles at Beau, looking far more relaxed than I feel. "Nice to see you again."

"You too."

"Let's find out what our boys have been up to, shall we?" Lennox sweeps out a hand in gesture, and I lead the way, my erratic heartbeats continuing. Yes, let's. I throw a quick prayer to the heavens, hoping it's something trivial and won't get my son thrown out of this amazing school. I remember the day we came to visit—like a proper family. I was smiling like an idiot the whole time, constantly straightening Daniel's shirt when the principal wasn't looking, so much so, Danny started pulling me back every time he detected an opportunity for me to fuss. But I really wanted Daniel to come here. It's an impressive facility, the security is second to none, and even Lennox sent Barney here when he decided to relocate back to Miami.

I press the buzzer and we're let through the gates and met at the door by Mrs. Carnaby, the friendly receptionist. She always offers smiles and coffees. Not today. Today, we only get offered a seat before she returns to her desk.

When Principal Tucker swings his door open, I hate the look on his face. He means business. And when I see Daniel sitting in his office, head bowed, I fear the worst. Shame. It's rampant. Oh, God, what's he done? My fear isn't helped when I see two cops enter the reception area.

"Do you know them?" I ask Beau, and she shakes her head.

"Please, come in." Principal Tucker opens the way.

"I'll wait here," Beau says. "But if you need me . . ."

I nod and like two naughty children, Lennox and I stand, silent and pensive. "Just Mrs. Black," he says, as Barney emerges, looking sheepish.

I feel Lennox look down at me. "Are you okay?"

"Yeah." I pretend within an inch of my life, entering and sitting, my eyes on Daniel, silently demanding him to look at me. He doesn't. I peek over my shoulder when the two officers join us, my heart now pounding. *Fucking hell.*

"Actually, if you don't mind," Lennox says, appearing at the doorway behind them. "I'm going to sit in." He looks back at Barney, pointing to a chair, and he sits obediently.

"And me," Beau says, pushing her way in too. I can't hide my relief. No one likes to feel outnumbered, and I was feeling beyond outnumbered.

They all pile in, and Principal Tucker takes his throne. He's a tall man, gangly, gray, and wise looking. "I'm afraid there has been a very serious allegation made against Daniel," he says.

"But it's just an allegation," Lennox replies.

"A serious one."

"Serious or not, it's an allegation," I say, looking at the cops. They look grave too. Like Daniel's guilty without any evidence needed. What is this madness? "To be proven, I assume."

"Yes," Principal Tucker says, casting his eye across to Daniel.

Whatever happened to innocent until proven guilty? They're treating my son like a criminal, and they don't even know if he's guilty of the crime he's supposedly committed. Which is what? I look at Beau. She appears as equally annoyed. Daniel is a good boy. Decent, kind. What crime, damn it? "And what is the allegation?" I ask, getting worked up, the lioness in me racing to the surface.

"He threatened to stab a fellow student with his dad's gold letter opener."

I choke on thin air, and Beau coughs. *Oh fuck.* I look at Daniel as he cautiously peeks up at me, and I know, I just *know*, he absolutely did that. "What the hell?" I blurt at him.

He remains guiltily silent, and Lennox shifts in his seat next to me. His hand's positioned by his mouth, his body slipping down the chair. Embarrassed? And then it occurs to me. He's trying to make himself smaller. It's body language 101. He doesn't want the police to think he's associated with such scum. Oh God, will he stop Barney seeing Daniel? Will my son lose his friend too because of some stupid words? He wouldn't follow through on his threat, of course he wouldn't, he hasn't a violent bone in his body. But what if he develops some? What if he wants to be like Danny? Feared? A criminal? A murderer?

I inhale, looking over my shoulder to the police. That's why they're here. They know who Daniel's father is. They're not here to question Daniel. This is hearsay bullshit, not worthy of police intervention. But because Daniel is The Brit's son?

How long has Principal Tucker known?

"And what part did Barney play in this?" Lennox asks.

"He did nothing," Daniel cries.

He's wrong. Barney's associated with The Brit's son, making him guilty too. "I'll be taking Daniel home now," I say, standing, mortified and disappointed. I'm not waiting around to be thrown out. No. We had planned on Maggie to come here, too as they have an amazing kindergarten. Not now. We'll be banished forever, not just because of Daniel's silly, weightless threats, but because of who we are. The Brit's family.

I collect my idiot son from the chair and lead him out by his elbow. "I cannot believe what you've done."

"I didn't do anything, Mom, I *said* it."

And he gives me cheek? "Why the hell would you even *say* that?" I squeeze his arm a little, just so he can appreciate just how pissed off I am. "You've just thrown away so many opportunities, opportunities we fought hard for so you can have the best of everything." I walk him outside where Tank is waiting, "Get in the car." Daniel trudges toward Tank, looking up at him, probably hoping to get some sympathy. My dark look tells Tank to back off, stalling his huge hand from giving Daniel's hair a ruffle. Instead, he opens the back door for him, looks over his head, and Daniel slips in without a word. "Fucking hell," I curse.

Beau joins me, but she doesn't try to make me feel better, she just gives me a small, sympathetic smile.

"He's grounded forever," I bark, looking down at my cell, wondering why the hell Danny hasn't called me back. Doesn't he know there's an emergency?

"Rose," Lennox calls, coming out of the door, Barney in his grasp.

I can't face him. I bet he's all kinds of horrified. I'm sure Principal Tucker has—out of a duty of care, I suppose—told Lennox who my husband is and what he does. What he *used* to do. God damn it, he might not have killed anyone in the past few months, but that's only because there's no one left to fucking kill. He still launders money and runs guns.

Good lord. No one left to kill? I look at the school. Principal Tucker may be in grave danger right now.

"Rose, wait."

I don't, hurrying to the car.

"Rose!"

For God's sake. I swing around and collide with Lennox, and pain radiates through my chest. Fuck, my boobs. I cry out, and Lennox, alarmed, makes a grab for my arm to steady me. But he misses my arm and scuffs my breast. "Fuck!"

"Fuck," he parrots. "Shit, I'm sorry, I didn't mean to—"

"It's fine," I assure him, wincing, feeling the need to shield them, hold them. "Look, I'm sorry Barney's been caught up in this whole mess. I don't know why Daniel would—"

"Come on, Rose." Lennox laughs. "Do you think I don't know who your husband is?"

I still, my eyes wide, my skin a certain shade of telling. "What?"

He rolls his eyes. "Daniel's a great kid. I wouldn't take a friend away from Barney. The boy's lost too much."

His mom. He means his mom. "Really?"

"Really." He frowns and looks down at my chest, then proceeds to scan the floor. "Did I make you spill a drink?"

Confused, I look down, seeing two huge wet patches on my silk blouse. Oh my God, this day gets worse. "I better get Daniel home."

And myself, where my leaking boobs are safe from public eyes.

Realization dawns on Lennox and he becomes unbearably embarrassed, unable to look at me. "Will you let me know if you plan on enforcing consequences?"

I nod and go to the car, my eyes brimming, emotion creeping up on me. Unreasonable? I don't think so. I must be the stupidest woman alive to think our lives could ever be normal.

Chapter 6

DANNY

I hit my phone on the steering wheel, trying to get some service. "What the fuck is going on with this thing?" I snap. Then quickly apologize for my bad language when I remember who's riding with me today.

I cast my eyes over to the back seat. Silence. It's fucking golden. I've been sitting outside the club for half an hour, scared to move, scared to wake her up, because who the hell knows when she might decide to give us some peace again? What I do know is, it won't be tonight. Little thing seems to love burning the midnight oil. And the one-a.m. oil. And the two-a.m. oil. And the three . . .

I sigh and rest my head back, closing my eyes, sinking farther down in my seat. Peace. Quiet. The only sound is the cars passing. When she sleeps, *we* should sleep. That's what Doc said.

So I will.

Knock, knock, knock.

I shoot up, startled, and turn to the driver's window, recoiling when I find Nolan's face pressed up against the glass. "What the fuck?" I breathe, just as all hell seems to break loose in the back of the car, the shocked, high-pitched screams of Maggie piercing my ears. My nostrils flare, and I look at Nolan like I'm going to kill him.

Because I am.

He appears confused for a moment, his brow furrowed as he looks into the back of the car. Then he realizes. Backs up.

I swing the door open, get out, pull my gun, and shove it under his chin.

"Fuck, fuck, fuck," he whispers. "I'm sorry, I'm sorry, I'm sorry."

"There's no fucking point whispering now, you stupid cunt. She's a-fucking-wake!"

His hands up, he leans back, getting as far away from me as possible while I have his jacket bunched in my fist. "You've been out here for forty minutes. I came out to see if you're okay."

"I was fine," I rant. "Fucking blissful, actually, and you've just blown the peace to bits, Nolan." I shove him away, stuff my gun in the back of my jeans, and swing the back door open, fucking savage. "Hey, my beautiful," I coo quietly, unclipping her belt and scooping her out of the infant car seat, hushing her, bouncing her, kissing her head. All while glaring at Nolan.

I walk up and down by the car, persistent with my strategy, until she finally calms, her cries morphing into quiet sobs until she's quiet again, just the odd sniffle. That was a proper cry. A truly upset cry. I'm learning to recognize the various degrees of distress. Hunger, tiredness, shitty nappy. "There," I whisper, peeking down at her nestled in the crook of my arm, her hand now in her mouth. Look at her. Just fucking look at her. The most beautiful thing I've ever set eyes on. And the loudest. How can something so disruptive offer such an incredible sense of peace too? My nose wrinkles, probably making my scar deepen.

"I need your help." I reach into the car and pull out the baby carrier. It's bespoke. Handmade. Tried and tested.

Bulletproof.

And today is its maiden voyage. Problem is, it didn't come with any instructions. I hold up the contraption and Nolan stares at it, wary. "What is that?"

"A bulletproof baby carrier."

His eyes shoot to mine. "You're not joking, are you?"

I shake my head. "Any idea how these things work?"

He takes it, turns it one way, then another. "Where did you get it?"

"Chaka."

He laughs. "Of course you did." A few more turns and frowns. "I'd call him."

"I can't call him." I reach into my pocket and pull out my phone. "Something's wrong with it."

"I'll call him." Nolan dials and hands me his phone, and I accept, putting it to my ear and getting back to walking up and down.

"It's Danny."

"Black," Chaka rumbles. "Don't tell me you need more guns."

I huff. Definitely not. The bunker is full to the rafters and we have no one to sell to right now, since we pissed off the Mexicans and they'd likely want to use their new purchases on us. And Sandy—fuck that rapist cunt—has disappeared after I chased the fucker down and got shot a few times for my trouble. So, yeah, we're what you could call well-armed right now. "No guns," I say, just as Maggie yells. I quickly refocus on bouncing her in my arm, walking up and down again. "I need advice, Chaka."

He laughs, making the phone vibrate in my hand. "Babies? I have fifteen children, Black, and I still wouldn't recommend asking me for advice on babies."

"Fifteen?" My mind bends. *Jesus Christ.* "This thing you had made for Maggie. How the fuck does it work?"

"Ah, let me put you on to the manufacturer."

I frown. "There's a manufacturer for bulletproof baby carriers?"

"Yes, my wife."

I let out a bark of laughter. "You mean, even with fifteen kids, she still has time for other shit?"

"Didn't you know, Black? Women are wonders."

"Yeah, I know." I look down at Maggie. See Rose in my mind's eye. Smile. "Can I speak to your wonder woman?"

"Make it quick, Black. She's busy." A woman comes on the line, laughing loudly, and in just two sentences, she tells me exactly what I need to do before she hangs up. I look down at the phone, handing it to Nolan.

"Well?" he asks, the carrier dangling from his grasp.

I take it, slip one arm through, shift Maggie into my other arm, slip my right arm through, and turn. "Do me up. The straps need to cross over. Make it tight. But not too tight." I lift Maggie and lower her legs through the holes, pulling the two straps as per Chaka's wife's instruction. "Snug as a bug," I muse, tapping the back pad. Or back shield. It clangs. "And as safe as houses."

"Looks the same as any other," Nolan says, impressed, giving the back of the carrier a small knock too. "Nifty."

I grab the baby bag, sling it over my shoulder, and cross the road. "Go inside and turn off the music."

"But Brad's doing auditions."

I stop and look at Nolan. I don't need to say a word. Off he goes, while I check my phone again, holding it up to the sky to find some service. Nothing. "Fuck's sake." I hear the track playing in the club cut abruptly so I make my way inside.

"Are you fucking joking?" Brad asks, standing from a chair that's in front of the stage. "Seriously, Danny, it's bad enough I live in a house full of women and kids, now you're bringing them to work?"

"Shut up, you miserable fuck." I sling the bag down and nod to Mason, Des, and Drake at the bar. "And there're only two kids in the house. Three if you include Anya. Four if you include Pearl." I raise a brow, and Brad snarls. God, he's being a dick lately. "What's up with you?"

"Nothing."

"This got anything to do with Pearl?" I ask, watching for his reaction. I'm still not convinced that matter is dead in the water.

"Fuck off, Danny."

"Where is she anyway?"

"Are we talking business or pussy?"

So she's pussy? "Or kids." I smile, earning myself another snarl.

"How the fuck would I know where she is?"

"Because she works here."

"Don't I fucking know it," he mutters.

I've known Brad since I was ten. He's the first to crack a joke. The first to alleviate the tension. The most easygoing deadly man I've ever known and ever likely to know. But since his brush with death— or, more to the point, the arrival of Pearl—he's changed. I can't say I appreciate it. I know exactly what's wrong with him. He wants to fuck a female he shouldn't want to fuck, because the female is barely a woman, and Brad isn't getting any younger. What I can't figure out is if his beef is purely age related, or simply because a member of the opposite sex has gotten under his skin, and women *never* get under Brad Black's skin, least of all one nearly half his age.

"I can't believe you brought the baby to Hiatus," he grumbles.

"Her name's Maggie. You want to hold her? You've not held her yet." Hardly even looked at her. "Here." I start unfastening the straps on the carrier, and Brad backs up, alarmed.

"No, thanks."

I falter in my movements. He looks truly terrified. "What the hell is going on?" I ask, leaving Maggie exactly where she is, safe against my chest. This reaction, the mood, all just feels over the top for a simple case of having the hots for someone you shouldn't have the hots for. Do I need to take him for a drink? I know I've been absent recently. Distracted. Really fucking tired. But . . . I look down at my chest. She's awake. Awake and quiet. It's a fucking miracle.

"I'm fine," Brad grunts. "The interviews are over." An impatient hand gets thrown up in the air. "You were all shit."

I look across the bar, noticing for the first time a line of young women sitting on the edge of the stage. All eyes on me. Or my chest, and not for the same reasons I'm used to. It's swoon central, apparently, as they all move in. I wrap my arms around Maggie and get us the fuck out of there. "Where's Otto?" I ask Brad over my shoulder.

"Upstairs with James."

James is here? "He's not with Beau?"

"Beau's with Rose at the salon," he calls.

I stop at the entrance of the office, looking back at him. "You coming?"

He holds up a hand, his phone going to his ear. I leave him, entering the office, and Nolan swings around, startled. Could be me, but he looks guilty as he puts something in his pocket. "All right?" I ask, suspicious.

The smile he slaps on his face is epic. Fake. Nervous as shit. "Good, boss."

I scowl at him, assessing his disposition. I don't like it, but Brad walks in behind me before I can pin the fucker down and grill him.

"Leon's gonna pick up some more stock later," Nolan says.

"Got it." Brad punches in the code at the door that leads up to the secret office and looks back at me impatiently, like *hurry the hell up.* "May as well give Maggie the full tour."

I rip my wary eyes off Nolan. "Want to see where we hide some of the cash, Maggie?" I ask. "Just don't tell your mummy."

"Oh, for God's sake." Brad shakes his head in despair. Couldn't give a fuck. She's still quiet. "I think I've nailed this babysitting business."

"It's not babysitting when it's your daughter, you jerk."

Daughter. Still weird. I climb the stairs and enter with Brad, finding James with his feet kicked up on the desk, looking bored out of his mind, and Otto hunched over a laptop. I'm staggered every time I see Otto like this. What the fuck does he do on that fucking laptop all the fucking time?

"Your phone's been bugged," he says, so casual, without even looking up. Brad and I stop halfway across the office and look at each other, just waiting, and James drops his feet, sitting up in his chair. *Whose phone?* Otto eventually turns his eyes onto me. "So I've cut the line."

"What?" I ask, slightly squeaky. "What the hell do you mean, bugged?"

"I mean what I say, and I said your phone was bugged."

"Who the fuck would want to bug me?" All I've done recently is try to sleep—*try* being the operative word. The only thing they'll have heard is Maggie crying in the background while I cried down the line to Doc, begging him for some miracle cure for my nocturnal baby. "And how? I've hardly left the house for weeks."

Otto snaps the lid of his laptop shut. "I'm looking into it."

Brad's phone rings and he dips into his pocket. "Higham," he says, his attention on the screen, as if the caller's name might change if he stares at it long enough.

I take one step back as James rises from the chair, like he's been resurrected. Like this is what he's been waiting for. I know he won't leave the city until we know exactly what the deal is with Sandy. Can't say I'm all too fond of the feeling in my stomach. I agreed to leave Higham alone if he covered up Detective Collins's murder for us after Nolan got a bit trigger-happy at the club and shot her. The kid's capable, yes. Dependable, yes.

Really fucking dumb sometimes, yes.

Why the fuck is Higham calling?

Brad clicks the call to loudspeaker. "We have a situation," Higham says, pulling us all closer to the phone.

"Is this something to do with Beau poking around?" James asks.

"I can handle your wife, Kelly."

My eyebrows shoot up. I'm not sure that's true, and judging by James's rolling eyes and Brad's huff of laughter, they agree. "So what's the situation if it's not Beau?" I ask.

"And by *we*, do you mean we, you and your colleagues," James says, a veil of darkness falling. "Or *we*, as in you and us?"

"I mean the whole fucking city."

On collective inhales, we all lean back, eyes darting to each other. "Can it wait?" Brad points to me. "The Angel-faced Assassin is babysitting right now."

I see a familiar twinkle in Brad's eyes as James chuckles, along with Otto, and I smile. There he is. The sarcastic fucker who I fucking adore. I peek down at Maggie. She looks so cute wrapped up in her armor. It's fucking heavy, though.

"I'm on my way over," Higham says tiredly and unamused, hanging up.

"Well," I say, going to the couch and lowering, taking a load off, absolutely raging with curiosity. I hardly want to admit it, but I can feel something coming to life inside. It's been an odd few months. The women busier than the men. Out more than the men. More to do than the men. "I always thought peace was overrated, anyway." And right on cue, Maggie starts wailing, forcing me to my feet again. "Shhhh," I whisper, starting to bob where I stand.

"You look so deadly," Brad says, pouring himself a drink and knocking it back.

"While you're there." I nod to an empty glass behind him, and he huffs a burst of laughter.

"Drinking on the job?" he asks.

"It's not a job when it's your daughter." I smile, reaching back to unclip the catch and lowering Maggie onto the desk, pulling her out of the carrier. "Now get me a fucking drink. *Pur . . . lease.*"

"My pleasure."

The door opens and Ringo enters, looking entirely wrong without Goldie somewhere nearby. She was in Venice last we heard. Enjoying her freedom.

Ringo's eyes fall to the crook of my arm and the big, ugly fucker smiles, ironically making him even uglier. "Can I?" he asks.

I find myself stepping back. "You want to hold her?"

"Yeah, I want to hold her." He moves in, and I'm suddenly moving farther back with Maggie. "What the fuck's wrong with you?" he asks. "Don't you trust me?"

"Thing is, Ringo, she's quiet at the moment, and the second she sees your ugly mug, she's gonna scream to high fucking heaven."

"Fuck off, you cunt." He helps himself to my daughter, and I look at James, not surprised to see his eyes on Maggie. I have this weird feeling in my bones that Beau's carrying a girl. *Two* girls? Fuck me, all these men—capable men—around them growing up? They'll be the most protected girls to walk the planet.

Ringo takes Maggie over to the glass window to look down on the club, and I lower to the desk, accepting a drink from Brad before he plonks himself in the chair. I look around the room. James is on his phone, probably texting Beau, Otto gets up and leaves the room, probably to take a leak, Brad is daydreaming into his Scotch, and Ringo is having a full-blown conversation with Maggie. "Jesus, we really are a force to be reckoned with."

"What?" James asks, looking up from his phone.

"Nothing."

Ringo turns from the window, pointing down at the club. "Why the fuck has Higham just walked into the club?"

Nolan bursts through the door looking panicked. "Higham's here."

Well, he certainly didn't waste any time. I'm curious as to what the big problem is and why it's brought our FBI friend dashing to Hiatus. I slowly stand, going to Ringo and reclaiming my daughter. "Nolan, her pram is in the trunk. Go get it."

He leaves and we all make our way down to the other office — the office we're comfortable hosting an FBI agent in. Because it's not harboring millions in laundered cash. Everyone takes their seats, and I abandon my drink in favor of breast milk for Maggie. Her mouth fumbles around the teat, her little nose wrinkling, her hands thrashing. "Come on," I whisper, glancing up when Higham strolls in. He looks smart in a tuxedo. Fresh. Less beaten. "Now I know you didn't get all dressed up just for me."

"I have a date," he says, prompting me to look at the clock on the wall. It's midafternoon. "A gala for the charity my wife and I support."

"Your wife? So it didn't work out with the journalist?" I smile. Natalia Potter was one hundred percent with Higham for information and nothing else.

"It didn't." He shifts, irritated. "I'm making amends."

"So I could have killed her after all?"

He rolls his eyes and looks at my arms. "You recruit young, Danny."

"Let's be clear, Higham," I say, looking down, silently willing Maggie to take the milk. "This is the only time you'll ever meet my daughter." She's gonna be a good girl. Rose will kill me if she isn't. "So what can we do for you?" Maggie finally latches on, and I exhale my relief, relaxing.

"As ever, Danny, it isn't what you can do for me, but what I can do for you."

Oh? "Did I miss the part when I came to you for help right now?" I won't lie, my heart is clattering with anticipation. None of us have forgotten the small matter of my wife seeing red and shooting my ex-fuck Amber. Problem is, Oliver Burrows moved the body before we could get rid of it. And the further problem is, Oliver Burrows is now dead, courtesy of Beau's mother, so we can't ensure the body of my ex-fuck is never found, therefore I can't guarantee my wife is safe from prosecution. So . . . is that why he's here? Has Amber's body turned up?

Higham looks at the less well-stocked bar. "Mind?" he asks, helping himself before getting a nod. I look at Brad. Brad looks at James. James looks at Ringo. Ringo looks at Otto. It's a Mexican wave of concerned expressions. Higham seems like he really needs that drink.

And then he flops down into a chair and exhales. I don't like this.

As ever, Danny, it isn't what you can do for me, but what I can do for you.

"Talk, Higham." Brad takes the words right out of my mouth, and James moves in closer, adding a presence. His hands are twitching. They haven't murdered anyone for quite some time.

Higham looks between all of us in turn, like he can't decide which one of us he wants to be farthest away from right now. He must decide I'm the lesser of three evils—I'm assuming Maggie in my arms is playing a part in that—because Higham gets up and comes to the desk. Reaching into his inside pocket as he necks the last of his drink, he slaps a bunch of photographs down. Everyone moves in, crowding the wood, looking down, and I tentatively reach forward and disturb the pile.

My stomach turns, and I instinctively pull Maggie in closer to my chest, shielding her from the horror on my desk. A horror I recognize.

"What the fuck?" Brad breathes, seeing what I'm seeing. As expected, James and Otto look pretty clueless, the men in the pictures are just two more dead, mutilated bodies, and, frankly, James has made far worse messes of men before. Ringo, however, has been around my family long enough to know what we're staring at.

Brad looks up at me. His face. I expect mine is a similar shade of *Jesus Christ.* I feel my nostrils flaring, rage brewing. Not ideal when I have my baby daughter in my arms. Maggie loses her grip of the teat, starting to get frustrated, and I stand, walking off some of the stress as I battle to help her get hold of it again. But for all the will in the world, she's not taking it. "For fuck's sake," I hiss quietly, as frustrated as she is. "Come on, darling. You can do it."

"Will someone tell me why the fuck the temperature in here just went from comfortable to icy?" James asks, his tall, built body stiff. Charged. "Who are those men?"

"I don't know," I say, as Maggie goes all out demonic and starts screaming. "No, no, no, baby, it's okay." I lift her to my shoulder, patting at her back, focusing on her wind. Not the rage. "Daddy's here, don't cry."

"Then what the fuck's the problem?"

"The problem," Brad says loudly, to be heard over Maggie. "Is the emblem carved into their chests." I look across to Brad, his finger on the top picture. "That's the Black family emblem."

"And there are only two members of the Black family alive," I add.

James takes a wary step away, looking between Brad and me. AKA: the only two members of the Black family still alive. "When did these men die?" He turns his attention to Higham.

"At a guess, within the past week."

"Fuck."

"Shhhh," I hush, fighting with Maggie, my mind sprinting, question after question turning over in my head. Who did this? What does it mean? My ears are starting to ring. Nolan smacks the door open with Maggie's pram.

He reads the room in an instant. "What?" he asks, looking at us all while Maggie continues on her mission to bring the fucking roof down with her cries. Fuck, I can't think. But who the fuck carved that emblem on those chests and why isn't my priority right now. I go to Nolan and claim the pram, laying Maggie down. I catch a whiff of what may be the problem. "Where's her bag?"

"Here." Pearl appears, holding up Maggie's changing bag.

"Everything okay?" she asks, obviously sensing the tension, the bag lowering.

"You shouldn't be in here," Brad snaps, taking her arm and guiding her out of the office. She doesn't protest. She should. In fact, if I were her, I'd punch the fucker on the nose. I can't even blame his mood on this shocking revelation. This is just Brad lately and, unfortunately for Pearl, she seems to be a trigger.

"You're such a fucking dick," I say to him as I push Maggie out of the office. "No one says a word about those pictures until I'm back." I slam the door, not that you can hear it over Maggie's cries, and wheel her down the corridor to the restrooms. I pass a sheepish-looking Pearl. "You free?"

"Yeah," she breathes, bringing the bag.

"Ignore him," I tell her over my shoulder, reaching over Maggie's pram and pushing the door open, wheeling her in.

"I'm trying," she says quietly, looking back at the office. "I don't know what his problem is."

I laugh under my breath. "You don't want to."

"What?"

"Nothing. Pass me her changing mat."

"What's happened?"

"Nothing for you to worry about. This floor been cleaned?"

"Yes, a few hours ago."

I accept the mat and roll it out on the floor. It's not ideal, but baby-changing facilities aren't the norm in a strip joint. I lay Maggie down and pull the poppers of her sleepsuit open, pulling her legs out. "I thought you were with Rose."

"She got a call from the school."

I look up, stalling in my task. Rose got a call? But I'm the first contact. And then I remember. My phone's dead. Because it's been bugged. More questions. "Tell me Tank went with her."

Pearl smiles. "And Beau."

I nod, not feeling particularly reassured—what the fuck's happened?—and get back to the business of Maggie's shitty nappy. And boy is it shitty. "Jesus Christ," I mumble, wiping her up. "Where the hell does it come from?"

Pearl laughs and passes me the cream. "Do you want me to watch her for a while?"

"I'd say yes, but her mother would tear me to shreds if she found out I'd palmed her off on anyone." I give Pearl a raised brow. "Besides, aren't you supposed to be working? Let's not give Brad any more reason to be a grumpy arsehole." I notice a gold ring in the corner of Pearl's lip, and she reaches for it, fiddling with the delicate piece of jewelry.

"I had it re-pierced."

"Because they removed it," I say, swallowing, and she nods, only very mildly. The hell Rose went through, what happened to Pearl. I look down at Maggie. She's suddenly quiet now, looking up at me. Her blue eyes are so clear. No hurt, no damage, no comprehension of the world she's been born into. Fucking hell, I have a whole new level of disgust and anger now. It's bad enough my wife became a victim of that darkness. My daughter? My stomach turns, and I once again wonder how many of the fuckers are still out there. Gangs like that don't just disappear.

I accept the nappy Pearl's holding out to me and get Maggie in it, wrestling with her little legs to get them back in the sleepsuit. "Can I ask you something?"

"Depends what it is?" Pearl gets up onto the counter, waiting.

I fasten the last popper and pick Maggie up, and she burps, her whole little body relaxing, as does mine, the relief immeasurable. "Good girl," I breathe, offering her the bottle again. This time, she takes it, no fight or drama. "What was so terrible back home that makes living here in Miami with mafia and danger around every corner so appealing?" Not to mention the fact that Brad's a complete arsehole toward her. Who the fuck would stick around to be treated like that?

She nibbles at the gold ring in her lip, apprehensive. "My parents were murdered."

"I know," I say automatically, my tone lacking any empathy. "And that made you skip the country?"

"I couldn't stay in my parents' house anymore. Not after that."

So she left and went traveling, and then traffickers took her in Romania. "You're scared," I say. She nods. And now she feels safe here. It's ironic, really. "Were you there when it happened?"

She shakes her head.

"So you found—"

Brad bursts in, looking all impatient, his mouth open and loaded ready to fire some fucks. It snaps shut when he sees Pearl.

She starts to shift uncomfortably on the counter. "Would you like me to watch Maggie while you deal with whatever needs dealing with?" she asks.

"That would be helpful, thanks." This is not palming my daughter off. This is protecting her ears from what I'm afraid I'm about to hear.

Pearl slips down, and I hand over my baby, astonished when she somehow manages to hold her, wheel the pram out, *and* keep the bottle in her mouth. Incredible. Brad pretty much plasters himself to the door as she passes. He closes his eyes too. And is he holding his breath? For fuck's sake.

As soon as Pearl has gone, he visibly deflates. I have *never* seen him like this. It's worrying. I completely understand the attraction. Pearl's a beaut—red hair, green eyes, creamy skin. But, again, she's barely a woman. "Brad," I say quietly, knocking him out of his trance.

He blinks and looks at me. "What?"

"This has to stop." And I don't mean his callousness. There is no happy ending here. We all know Brad isn't interested in long-term, least of all with a twenty-one-year-old, so the moment he succumbs to this insanity, he'll be making a whore of Pearl. As well as probably breaking her heart, and the girl has been through enough.

He laughs, with no humor. In fact, it's almost psychotic. I swear, if he asks me what I'm talking about, I'm going to punch him so fucking hard. "Fuck," he hisses, slamming his head back against the door. He's a mess.

"What is it about her?" I've got to ask.

He pushes his fingertips into his sockets and rubs hard before looking at me, serious. "You mean other than the fact that I can't stop thinking about her?"

Shit. I mean, I kind of knew, yes, but hearing him say it? "You can't fuck her." Not if he wants to keep his balls, and Rose and Beau will certainly cut them off.

He laughs again, and this time it's an easy laugh. "Yeah, Danny, I know that. And since that's all I'm capable of, I guess I'm going to have to suffer."

"Or fuck someone else." *Anyone* else.

"Yeah, easy as that," he breathes, pushing himself off the door with his shoulder blades. "Maybe I'll get a room at the Four Seasons." His look darkens. "No raiding and shoving a gun in my face this time."

Hands up, I smile. "Promise." Anything if it'll solve this little problem. I'm a fucking dick. We've been there before, Brad in a hotel room, fucking his way through women, right after the rescue when he was shot and Pearl arrived. It didn't work then, and I'm not sure it will work now. "Look—"

The door swings open and James appears, his face as straight as it always was before Beau's and his nightmare ended. It's nice to see him looking like his old self. "The anticipation is fucking killing me," he says, taking a swig of the clear liquid from the tumbler in his hand.

"Come on, we have shit to deal with." And I need to call Rose and find out why the fuck she's been called by the school. I take Brad's shoulder and guide him back to the office, listening for the sound of Maggie crying. Nothing.

I close the door, let everyone settle, and look to Higham to kick things off. "Both Mexican," he says, pointing to the image of two dead men. "Men of Luis."

"Fuck," Ringo mutters, as I drop my head back, looking at the ceiling.

"So whoever did this wants Luis, who is already pissy with us for not supplying his last delivery of guns, to believe we killed his men." Bottom line, someone is trying to start a fucking war.

"Russian," Brad says. "This will be Sandy's doing."

"Afraid not." Higham goes to the photos and moves them around, revealing one at the bottom. "These two were found at the scrapyard off Biscayne Bay Docks."

We all lean in. Two more bodies. Both also with our family emblem carved into their chests.

"You're going to tell me they're Russian, aren't you?" Brad asks, going to the cabinet and refilling.

"Fucking hell." James holds his hand out to Brad, who promptly obliges, pouring him more vodka.

I stare down at the pictures in utter disbelief. "Well," I say, laughing but not laughing. "Some fucker out there certainly has it in for us." Not Mexican. Not Russian. But whoever it is has given Luis and Sandy another really solid good reason to vie for our blood. "Any ideas?" I ask, looking around the room. No offers. "And there we were thinking this wonderful calm and peace was our lives now." Not true. Like I said, men like Luis and Sandy don't just disappear, although it would be really fucking handy if they did, especially Sandy, since my wife thinks the sick fucker who raped her—and who, unfortunately, is also Daniel's biological father—is dead. What a fucking mess.

"Bet you wish you'd gone on that honeymoon now," Brad says to James, a hint of the familiar Brad making an appearance again. Maybe he doesn't need a whore after all. Just alternative action.

Like a killing spree.

"Jesus, the girls are going to go spare." I put my hands over my face. This means we're going back to heavily guarding, and that's going to go down like a concrete balloon. And how the fuck do we protect them and keep the fact Sandy is still alive under wraps until we can find him and do the job properly? I can't tell Rose. She's settled. Calm. I don't want to raise old ghosts.

"Yeah, good luck with them." Brad laughs.

Cunt. I look at Higham, who's on his second drink. "How did you know it wasn't us?" I ask, my head cocked. Higham could have turned up here with backup and a warrant and put all our arses behind bars. The evidence is all over this desk.

He points at the pictures with his glass. "Those emblems were carved by someone who is left-handed."

"How the fuck do you know that?"

"An old case. Learned a thing or two. So whoever you're looking for is left-handed, and I don't believe anyone in this room is left-handed." Higham casts his eyes around, and everyone looks at their hands. "The Brit, The Enigma, and The American was theirs," he says, almost wistful. "So, naturally, the officer leading the case was thrilled to hear my verdict that proved you three get to live another day."

I laugh under my breath. "The American," I muse, casting my eyes over to Brad. "They only started calling you that because of me. You know, what goes with The Brit?" I smile. "The American."

"You got a hard-on?" he asks, unimpressed.

"I'll see myself out." Higham goes to the door and opens it, looking back. "Obviously you'll keep me in the loop."

I smile. It's dark. "Obviously."

The door closes and my smile drops. "Fuck." I slam my fist down on the desk.

"We need to find out where someone would go if they couldn't get guns from us." Brad goes to the door and opens it, looking up and down the corridor to make sure Higham's gone.

"You'd go to Bernard King," Otto says, pulling stunned looks from everyone.

"What?" I murmur. Bernard King is based in London. If you're in the States, you do not go to Britain for guns. "Are we talking about the same Bernard King?" I ask.

"The savage who cuts off his enemies dicks and feeds them to his hellhounds?" Brad asks. "The beast who eats fingers like chicken dippers?"

I laugh, head thrown back, and Brad smiles. Pops told us the story more than once. Bernard King is a savage, double-crossing bastard with absolutely no scruples. The message was clear. *Never* do business with Bernard King. The stories are endless. "The man who—when in the armed forces—survived on an artic mountain top for five weeks because he ate the rest of the platoon?"

"That's the one," Otto says. "The one who also flew into Miami a few months ago."

"Say what?" I murmur.

"Are you telling me a Brit is moving in on another Brit's turf?" Brad laughs through his question.

"He's *a* Brit," I seethe. "I'm *The* Brit."

"God, you're a diva."

James lowers to a chair, looking shell-shocked. "He went after my father." He glances at Otto. "Is he still in the game? What is he, sixty?"

"Fifty-nine." Otto turns the screen of his laptop, revealing an ox of a man. "And still a beast."

"Isn't he just?" I lean in. The man has muscles on muscles on muscles. "Why'd he go after your dad?"

"Ego," James says, thoughtful. "My dad was a businessman. King's only ever been a thug."

"So does that mean King thinks you're dead?" I ask. Fucking hell, this could get even messier.

The Enigma is suddenly in the room, and I can't say I'm

particularly happy to see him. "I doubt it," James says. "Everyone on our side of the world knows who I am and where I've come from."

"James," Brad says quietly, placing a daring hand on his shoulder, while I watch Otto observing James with a quiet wariness I hate. "Is there something you want to tell us?"

Why do I get the feeling I'm not going to like what I'm about to hear? Otto looks nervous. I *feel* nervous. We all wait, bracing ourselves, pensive, really fucking worried. "Nothing at all," he eventually says. Is he telling us or himself? "I need to get back to Beau." He leaves sharpish, and I look at Otto for an answer. I don't get one. But I do get handed a new phone. How the fuck does he do that?

"Thanks."

"I'll let you know if I find anything on the old one."

I slip it into my pocket. "What did Bernard King do, Otto?"

Pouting through his massive beard, he pulls his T-shirt up, revealing a long, jagged scar. "This. James's dad had a matching one."

"Oh fuck." I stare at the old wound as Brad moves in and inspects the damage.

"Damn," he mutters. "But at least you weren't on the mountain with him."

My laughter is instant and intense, and my cheeks balloon to try and stem it. *Fail.* Air gushes out of me and, thank God, Otto chuckles too, letting his T-shirt down. "I've told your mother I was in a motorcycle accident."

What a way to kill the fucking buzz. Remind me that my mother has seen his aging chest. I'm being spiteful, of course. Otto is a prime specimen of an older man. But no son wants to imagine their mother going there. "Anything else?" I ask, as Brad continues to chuckle to himself.

"Yeah." Otto heads toward the door. "I need to talk to you about something."

"What?"

"I'll speak to you later." The door slams, and I stand.

"I'm busy later," I yell, still not over the fact that my mum and that hairy beast are a thing. "In fact, I'm busy forever."

"You really need to take your head out of your ass," Brad says. "He's fucking your mom."

"I'll be fucking you *up* in a minute." I bury my fists in the wood of the desk. "Leave you fucking brain-dead, Brad. What do you say? That'll solve your little problem of thinking about things you shouldn't be thinking about, won't it?"

He rolls his eyes and gets us both a drink. "Sit down, you animal."

I snatch the drink from his hand and drop to the seat. "Thanks."

"I get it, Danny." He takes a chair opposite. "But I kind of don't either."

"What are you talking about? My mum? Otto? Pearl?"

He rolls his eyes. "Pearl is a non-issue."

"If you say so."

"I fucking say so."

"Okay, okay." I submit, a hand up in surrender. He looks adamant about that. Good.

"You didn't know my mom very well," Brad goes on.

I vaguely remember her. A tall woman, with platinum-blond hair and a curvy body. She died a couple of years after Carlo Black brought me to Miami. Not much was said about it. Brad already lived at the house with her, and things seemed to carry on like normal after she was gone. I know nothing about his father, though.

"Carlo killed my dad," Brad says, and I lean back in my chair, trying not to show my shock.

"Why?"

"For making her sad."

"What?"

"He cheated on her. Constantly. But she loved him, so she stayed." He shrugs, like it's nothing, and I know it really isn't. "She was a bombshell. Uncle Carlo told me he was constantly batting the men off, warning them away." He smiles fondly. "She looked just like Marilyn Monroe."

I smile too. Yeah, she really did.

"She met my dad, fell head over heels, and there was nothing Carlo could do about it. Not until he wronged her. Mom knew Uncle Carlo would butcher my dad if he found out, so she protected him. She slowly became less vivacious, less happy, less alive. Then one day when I was eight, I walked in on Dad fucking the maid, and I ran out the house. Uncle Carlo found me on the docks. I told him what had happened. Mom begged Carlo to leave things alone, but he knew she'd never leave him. Weak. Uncle Carlo didn't like weak, so he removed the thing that was making someone he loved weak." He smiles again, but now it's sad. "He told Mom my dad had left town, but we knew. Of course we knew."

Fuck. Me.

Brad doesn't want to be his father. He doesn't want to hurt a good woman. Makes fucking sense now. He doesn't trust himself.

"Why have you never told me?"

He shrugs. "What was the point? Dad was gone, then she was gone."

Gone. "Your mum didn't die in a boating accident, did she?" I ask. *She fucking killed herself?*

"It was sweet of Uncle Carlo to try and cover it up."

"Fucking hell, Brad."

He stands. "Danny, Uncle Carlo was more of a man and father than my dad ever was. You have your mom. Appreciate that. If I could have made mine happy, don't you think I would have done anything?"

I blink, my heart squeezing. Pops was *trying* to make Brad's mum, his sister, happy. He must have hated himself. Blamed himself. For the first time in forever, I don't see Brad, my cousin, The American. I see an abandoned child. "Point taken," I say quietly.

"I've got some shit to deal with at my apartment."

"It's finished?"

"Nowhere fucking near." He leaves, and I try to process what Brad's divulged. Pops was trying to protect Aunty Betty. I get it. No joke, I will kill every boy/man who comes near Maggie. It would be instinctive. "Fuck." I look down at my mobile when it rings. And frown. "Alan?"

"Yeah, hi, I've been trying to get hold of you all afternoon."

"Problem?"

"You could say that. Mrs. Black stopped by today to check on the work at the spa. She wants us done and out in two weeks."

I laugh. "She's something else, right?"

He laughs too, but it's nervous. He thinks I might reinforce that. I won't. In light of the bugged phones and bodies turning up all over the city with the Black family emblem carved into them, I'm even more passionate about the spa's delayed completion. "You just keep going at the pace we agreed, Alan. I'll drop the next payment round next week."

"Thanks, Danny."

"Welcome." I hang up and dial Rose.

"Finally," she breathes down the line. "I need you home. Now."

She doesn't need to ask me twice. I get up and head for the door to track down my baby. "Is everyone okay?"

"We're fine. I just need you to come home."

"I'm on my way."

• • •

I walk through the door and listen. I'm not sure what for. "Rose?" She appears from the kitchen, a glass of wine in her hand. "I thought you couldn't do that while breast feeding?" I lower Maggie to the floor in her car seat and take my jacket off.

"It's small, and I really need it."

"Why?"

"Daniel's been thrown out of school."

"Why?"

"He threatened to stab a kid with your fancy gold letter opener."

I laugh. "What?" How the fuck does he know about Pops's letter opener?

"It's not funny, Danny."

"No, it's not." I turn, jacket in hand, and leave the house again.

"Where are you going?" she yells.

"To solve the problem." The fucker. He throws my kid out, after all the money I've invested into that school? I've paid for new flood lights, new sports equipment, landscaping. I can't say it was all completely selfless.

"Danny, for Christ's sake, you can't go around threatening principals."

"Watch me."

My arm is grabbed, and I'm hauled back. Rose gasps. "Ouch, fuck, ouch!"

I look her up and down, alarmed. "What? What is it?"

She holds a palm over a boob. "It's nothing. Lennox walked into me earlier and knocked one of them."

"Excuse me?"

"I'm fine."

"Maybe, but I'm not." What the fuck? Lennox doesn't do a very good job of hiding his attraction to my wife. I get it. She's a showstopper, but he should take a leaf out of every other man's book and abstain from admiring, or risk being bludgeoned.

"Oh, shut up," Rose snaps. "And you need to have a word with Alan at the spa. Make sure he's finished in two weeks." She takes my arm and manhandles me back into the house.

How the fuck did this turn around on me? "I've had a word with Alan. It's not possible."

She swings a disgusted look my way. "So you can get an underground bunker big enough to serve the US military finished in two weeks, but I can't get a few sinks plumbed in a few days?"

I shrug, collecting Maggie and making my way to the kitchen. I find Mum over the stove, doing her favorite thing—feeding people. "You just can't get the staff these days," I say, dropping a kiss on Mum's cheek and handing over Maggie. "I appreciate you, Mum," I say, surprising her. "I just want you to know that."

"Are you okay?"

"Wonderful." I face my wife with a big smile. "Date night?"

She recoils. "Now?"

"Yes, now."

"No, Danny. Did you not hear what I said?"

"Yes, but you won't let me go to the principal and have a discussion, so we may as well go out for dinner."

"You need to talk to Daniel."

She's right, I do, but after today, actually, I'd rather either kill a principal or fuck my wife brutally. And I'm being blocked on both. "If I talk to Daniel, can we go out for dinner?"

Her smile is small and coy, and I swoop in, looping an arm around her waist, tugging her close, but not so close I put pressure on her chest. My dick sings its happiness.

"Well?" I grind into her subtly, mindful of my daughter and her grandma behind us. "I promise not to kill anyone for appetizers or mains." I kiss the corner of her mouth, tasting the wine. "And maybe we can take dessert at home."

Her anticipation is being breathed all over my face. "Okay."

Fuck, yes. I brush our noses, rub my hardening cock into her groin, and kiss her hard. "Be ready in half an hour."

I leave on quick feet, going straight up the stairs to Daniel's room. He's on his bed. No phone. "Confiscated?" I ask, shutting the door.

His head drops to the side. "And my console, and my iPad, and my whole damn life."

I go to the bed and get on, resting against the headboard next to him. "What happened, kid?"

"He said you were a murderer."

Oh? He did, did he? But what can I say? Whoever *he* is, he's right. "Sticks and stones and all that, kid."

"And he said his dad's going to lock you up forever, and I won't have a dad anymore."

Say what, now? "Who the fuck said that?"

"Preston Bean. His dad's a cop. So I told him to shut his stupid mouth or I'd stab him in the eye with my murdering dad's favorite gold letter opener."

My eyes widen, my cheeks puff out. Fuck. Rose really did need that wine. *Daniel knows.* "Kid, you can't go around saying shit like that."

"Well, I did, and I'm not sorry, so don't try to make me apologize. Preston Bean is a jerk."

I agree. As for his dad? I think he and I need to have a little chat. Fuck me, this morning my list of men to kill was sparse. Now I can't decide who I want to slaughter first. I'm almost chuckling on the inside with glee. "I'll sort it out, okay?"

"What are you going to do?"

I hate the curiosity I see. *Hate* it. "That's not your concern. What you need to do is get your head down and study your arse off, do you hear me?"

"I hear you."

"Good. I'll go get your phone, but if I find out you've had any contact with that Preston Bean brat, you'll be sorry. Say you hear me, kid."

"I hear you, Mister."

"Good."

"And what about Mom?"

"I'll handle your mother." I give his head a ruffle and go to the door as I text Otto, telling him to look for a cop called Bean.

When I make it back to our room, I find Rose on the bed and Maggie on her boob, and just one look at my wife tells me there will be no date night tonight. She looks exhausted. Cozy. Glorious with our daughter feeding from her. I sigh, accept what needs to be accepted, and go to the bed, climbing on and settling my head on her tummy, just under Maggie. Rose's hand finds my hair and strokes. "I hate you," she whispers, and I smile. She really might when she finds out I lied about Sandy being dead.

Chapter 7

BRAD

I walk past the bar, my focus set forward, my body tense—like I've run a gauntlet.

"I've let Pearl go home," Mason says as I pass.

Every muscle relaxes as I slow to a stop. But— "Why?"

"She didn't look very good. Said she felt sick." Mason moves back, indicating to a man down the bar to yell his order. "It's not too busy," he goes on. "I have Anya, and Des offered a hand."

"Des works the door." I look toward the door. "So Drake's out there alone?" Always, always, *always* at least two on the door. It's mandatory. Mason knows that, and now the whole fucking club is at risk because Pearl feels sick? I've felt sick for months. Still here.

"No," Mason says, focusing on the beer he's pulling. "Rose is home with Danny, so I pulled in Tank."

"Right." I have no argument now. But still. It's inconvenient. And not only for Tank. After checking my apartment, I was planning on listening to Beau and going home to try and get an early night. Give the sleeping pills Doc's prescribed a go. Something has *got* to give. I'm walking fucking dead right now. "I'll be in my office."

I don't have the energy to climb the stairs to the secret office that looks over the club, so I dump myself in a chair in the shitty office downstairs, looking down at my watch. And sigh. It's not even eight. I have to spend another fuck knows how many hours pretending I'm indispensable. Needed around here. I reach into my inside pocket and pull out one of the pictures that Higham left us, resting back and staring down at the Black family emblem. I've seen it endless times, mostly carved by Uncle Carlo. A few from Danny. One or two from me. But the last time was Danny, and it was nearly four years ago in an alley Downtown. Some fucker who bullied Danny as a kid. Cut his face. Unfortunately for that poor fucker, the kid he preyed on became The Brit. But, again, that was years ago, and as far as Blacks go, there's only my cousin and me. Danny didn't do this. I didn't do this.

So who the fuck did?

Someone wants us out of their way. The question is, who? Not the Mexicans, not Sandy. What fuckers have we got to end now? I ponder that while I close my heavy eyes, letting my head fall back, my breathing slowing.

Red.

The door to the office opens, and I startle, sitting up straight. Nolan strides in. "For fuck's sake, go home."

Yeah. Can't do that. I look down at my watch. Eight thirty. Will Pearl be home by now? Asleep? In her room, out of my way? "I'm sorting the . . ." I gaze around the desk for something to be doing.

"Boss, seriously, you look wrecked."

I narrow my eyes as Nolan takes a seat opposite me. "Did I ask for your concern?" I slip the photograph back in my pocket. "No. So shut the fuck up, stand the fuck up, and get the fuck out of my office." I get up and fetch myself a drink, leaving Nolan still sitting at my desk. Unfazed. Immune to my shitty mood. "Who's on tonight?"

"Ella and Francine. Do you want me to check over the applicants again and arrange some more auditions?"

"No, get the girls from earlier back for a second shot."

"I thought you said they were all shit."

"I've changed my mind." I didn't see them dance. I was in a trance. Unfocused. "The blonde was up to scratch."

"Okay, boss."

"Now you can fuck off," I grunt, necking a Scotch and looking at my watch again, mentally running through my phone contacts. Who can I call? Who can I fuck?

Nolan gets up and leaves. "Just go home," he says, just before the door meets the jamb. Another look at my watch. It's been a day. More has happened in twenty-four hours than in six fucking months. I can't go home. Don't want to sit here all night. I'm hungry. Horny. "Fuck it." I pull out my cell and dial the first female I come across. The same one I called last week. And the week before. Because it's easy. No effort. I'll call, she'll come. And an added bonus, she's not a hooker. Just some classy chick I met at the bar in the hotel. This won't rid me of my problem, but it certainly alleviated some of the . . . pressure. "It's me," I say when she answers. "Busy?"

"No."

"Meet me at the Four Seasons in an hour."

"See you there."

I hang up and get my ass out of the club, waving to Nolan and Mason as I pass.

When I make it outside, I pull my Marlboros out and light up as I text Jeeves, telling him to give Allison the key to the presidential suite when she arrives. I'll fuck her, maybe twice, make my excuses for her to leave, and get myself a good night's sleep. It'll cost me ten grand, but right now, I'd pay a million just to feel better than I do.

I slip my cell into my pocket, pulling on my cigarette. Drake's a statue next to me, hands joined behind his back, and Tank's eyes are unmoving, focused on something down the street.

"What's up?" I ask, following his stare to an Escalade parked a few hundred yards away.

"That car," he says, nodding subtly. "Been there for an hour. No one's got out."

I pull a drag and exhale, just as the headlights come on and the engine starts. "And suddenly there's somewhere it needs to be." *Or someone it's waited for.* I flick my scarcely smoked cigarette away and walk into the road. "You loaded?" I ask Tank over my shoulder as I reach into the back of my trousers.

"Fully."

"Stay where you are, Drake." My pace picks up, my walk turning into a jog down the center of the road, my gun rising. I'm in no mood to fuck about. And neither, it seems, is the Escalade. It comes at me, tires spinning, engine roaring, and I aim and fire, putting two bullets through the windshield, one in a headlight.

And it still comes.

"Brad," Tank rumbles from behind, keeping up with my pace. "Move."

I veer off to the left slightly, giving Tank line of sight to the vehicle, and he proceeds to empty his magazine, and yet the Escalade keeps coming. I slow my jog until I come to a stop, aiming again.

"Brad, get off the road."

I don't move.

"Brad, for fuck's sake!"

Close one eye.

"Brad!"

Squeeze the trigger.

"Brad!"

Bang!

Tank knocks me from the path of the Escalade, and I feel the right wing of the car catch my arm as he pulls me out of the way, sending my gun flying out of my hand. "Fucking hell, Brad," Tank pants, out of breath. The Escalade sails past, my eyes focused on the windows. But they're blacked out. And then it slows down. Comes to a stop. The windows start to lower.

"Fuck," I whisper as the reverse lights come on. I search the ground for my gun, seeing it's slid halfway across the road. Not happening.

"Boss?" Tank asks in question as the car starts to reverse.

I'm out of options, and when I see the head of a machine gun pointed out of the window, I wonder if I've finally run out of lives too. But the vehicle suddenly stops again, the reverse lights go off, and the driver puts his foot down, pulling away fast. *The fuck?* I'm a sitting duck here, and they didn't take me out? And who the fuck are *they*?

Tank's expressing a similar questioning face. "That's weird, right?" I ask, as the Escalade takes the corner up the street, disappearing.

"Weird as fuck," Tank agrees, tucking away his gun as I head across the road to pick mine up. I put it in my trousers and feel in my pocket for my cigarettes, lighting up again. And I plan on finishing this one. I blow out the smoke, shaking my head, suddenly wide awake. A brush with death will do that.

"Here," Drake says, holding out his phone, showing me an image of the rear of the Escalade. The license plate's blurred. But nothing Otto can't fix. "Send it to me." I give his shoulder a slap. "Good work." I back up, ready to head to my car, but a cop car at the end of the road catches my eye, cruising leisurely. Or conveniently?

"I think we might be looking at the reason why they fucked off," Tank muses, eyes on the cop car.

"A lookout?" Drake says, glancing up and down the street, searching.

"Definitely." I put my cigarette between my lips and straighten out my suit jacket as the cop car roll up beside us. "Evening," I say with a smile through my cigarette. "Anything I can help you with?"

The officer gives each of us a moment of his eyes, his partner leaning across to get his fill too. "Brad Black," the driver says. It's not a question. It's a statement. There's not a cop in the state of Florida who doesn't know who I am. Who Danny is. Who James is.

"The American one," his partner muses.

"You sure about that, old chap?" I say in a British accent both the boys would crucify me for, blowing my smoke toward the car.

"There was a report of gunshots."

"Here? I didn't hear any gunshots." I look back to Tank and Drake. "Did you hear any gunshots?"

"No gunshots," Tank says as Drake shakes his head.

I return my attention to the cops and smile. "Definitely no gunshots."

Both look like they're chewing wasps, their eyes narrowing to slits. "Good night."

"Farewell, *gents*."

The driver shifts the car into gear and drives away, and I trudge back into the club, needing a drink. I sit on a stool at the bar and wave Mason over as I text Otto the license plate number, Paul Kalkbrenner's *No Goodbye* booming.

"I thought you were leaving." Mason pulls down a tumbler and grabs a bottle, pouring neat.

"I was. Then an Escalade tried to pull a drive-by on me."

"What?" Nolan hops on the stool next to me, looking me up and down. "You okay?"

"Fine." I click send and accept my drink, knocking it back. "Make sure the footage isn't available if the police come calling. They were sniffing around outside just now."

"Got it." Nolan's off promptly, and Mason leans on the bar, twisting a tuft of his beard as he looks past me.

"What?" I ask, looking over my shoulder.

"One of the girls."

"What about them?"

"I walked into the dressing room earlier without knocking."

I look at him tiredly.

"I know," Mason relents. "In my defense, no one's shift had started so I didn't think anyone was here."

"Is there a point to this, other than you copping a bonus look at the tits you see every day?"

He leans on the bar, lowering his voice. "She was startled."

"I would be too if a hairy, pierced fucker like you walked in on me getting dressed." I slide my empty across to him in instruction to fill. "Get to the point."

"She was on a cell. Nothing unusual. Except her cell was on the dressing table."

My eyebrows jump up. "Two cells?"

Mason nods. "I heard Danny's phone was bugged. I also heard some Mexicans and Russians have shown up dead. And you just got shot at outside." He rises, taking another glass down and pouring himself some water. "I think now is the time to question everything, right?"

"Right," I say, looking over my shoulder. "Which one?"

"Ella."

One of the newer girls. She and Erica are popular. I nod, watching the Amazonian-looking beauty grind down on the stage, her long, straight black hair skimming the floor with her pussy. "How long is left of her set?"

"Fifteen minutes."

I get up and head to the dressing rooms, knocking, listening, and entering when I get no indication that anyone is in there. I pull out my car keys, get the master for the lockers and open Ella's, pulling out a backpack. I dump it on the chair nearby and open, going in. I find one phone. Dig a little deeper. And find another.

Both are iPhones, one newer than the other. Both have the same screen saver. A golden retriever. Cute. I pocket both the phones and put her bag back, securing the locker and returning to the club.

I give Mason a nod, silently telling him to expect a complaint from staff about missing belongings, and neck the last of my drink, checking the time. I have fifteen minutes to make it to the Four Seasons. I'm not worried. She'll wait.

I text Danny and James as I leave.

We need to talk

• • •

I get in my Mercedes, looking up and down the street as I do, wondering if today is the day we stop moving around alone again. Wondering if we're vulnerable again. I pull off, driving sensibly, in no rush to get to the hotel. My head is reeling with so much, and I'm at a massive disadvantage right now, without the brain power to process the unexpected developments today—the killings, the emblems, Danny's bugged cell, the drive-by, the dancer with two phones.

I come to a stop at a set of lights and take the opportunity to be courteous and text Allison to let her know I'm ten minutes away. As I slip my phone back into my inside pocket and look up at the lights, something over the road catches my attention.

Red.

My heart begins to beat dangerously fast as I watch Pearl move in on an ATM, a can of soda in her hand. The shape of her body in that black dress. Her ass.

Fuck.

No.

I curse that curvy ass off to hell and back for being so fucking reckless. Alone. This time of night. Using a fucking ATM. And I thought she was ill. If she's sick, she should be at home in bed.

A horn sounds, surprising me, and I look up to see the lights have turned green. "Fuck it," I hiss, pulling away, staying in my lane, rather than indicating and moving across toward the sidewalk to stop. She's not my concern. Danny and James can deal with this.

I cruise past the ATM, eyes forward, hands holding the steering wheel tightly, thinking of the pussy waiting for me. The distraction. No complications. No pissed off Rose and Beau. No conscience. Because all I can offer is an emotionless fuck.

I can't rescue her from the clutches of traffickers and then violate her.

Breathe in. Breathe out.

"Shit." I release one hand from the wheel and hit the screen on my dash, pulling up my recent calls. I dial Len.

"Brad," he says.

"Were you asked to pick Pearl up after her shift tonight?"

"Yeah, she called and said she didn't feel well and was getting a cab home. Didn't want to wait for me to come from the boatyard."

"Right."

"Everything all right?"

"Fine."

"Am I getting Anya at the normal time?"

"Please." I hang up and notice the flash of red getting smaller in the rearview mirror. *Keep driving, keep driving.* My knuckles begin to turn white on the wheel. My shirt starts to stick to my back. "Jesus Christ, Brad," I mutter, indicating and cutting across the traffic to the side of the road, earning myself a collection of angry horns. I get out and stride up the sidewalk toward the ATM, looking at the endless potential threats to a young woman in central Miami at this time of night. I'm fucking livid.

With her.

With me.

I see Pearl pull some bills from the machine and slip them into her purse as she backs away from the ATM, and then she lights up—I fucking hate that she smokes—and when she looks up and sees me stalking toward her, she stops dead in her tracks, her lips—those fucking lips—parting, her chest rising.

An inhale.

My vision fogs for a moment, a red haze blinding me. I'm putting it down to anger. I should be fucking my way to a clear conscience. Instead, I'm chasing stupid little girls around town. "What the fuck are you doing?" I yell as I approach, my skin burning.

Anger.

Pearl backs up, wary, the can of soda she's holding pulled closer into her chest, the cigarette limp between her fingers. "What are you doing here?"

"You don't look very ill to me."

She blinks, frowns, looks completely caught off guard. "I'm—"

"And why the fuck did you tell Len you're getting a cab?"

"I wa—"

"And cash at this time of night? For what?"

"I—"

"Get in the fucking car." I throw my arm back, indicating my Mercedes down the street.

She recoils. "Excuse me?"

"Now."

"Fuck you, Brad," she whispers angrily. "Go fuck some whores in a hotel and shove some coke up your fucking nose." She tosses her can of soda in a nearby trashcan with anger and accuracy—that pisses me off too—then storms past me, taking a long drag of her smoke, and I turn with her, watching her go. *Fuck you?*

No, fuck *you*.

She doggedly marches straight past my Mercedes, and to add insult to injury, flips me the bird.

"The fuck?" I go after her, my ego ruling me. She is one brave woman, and I'm a killer in a foul mood. "I said, get in the fucking car."

"And I said, fuck you."

"Get in the fucking car!" I grab her bare arm and yank her to a stop, and she swings toward me, her creamy skin taking on a fiery blush.

"Get the fuck off me!"

I get up in her face, enraged, heaving like a bull, and she doesn't back down, getting up in my face too, her green eyes blazing.

But I'm suddenly at a loss for words.

Forgotten why I'm here.

Angry.

Pissed off.

Losing my fucking mind.

Fuck.

The smell of lavender mixed with nicotine hits me like a bulldozer and electricity sizzles between our close chests. She stares up at me, toe to toe, waiting. My eyes move to her lips. The new gold ring. She bites at it.

Jesus Christ.

My dick pounds against the back of my pants, and that just inflames the anger more. What the fuck is my body doing? These reactions? "Get in the fucking car, Pearl, or God help me, I will put you in there myself."

"Try it," she says calmly, and it's all I need. I move my hold to her elbow, marching her toward the car, and she fights me with a strength that surprises me. "Get the fuck off me."

"Your language is foul for a young woman." Who the fuck am

I, her father? I flinch. "And you shouldn't be doing this." I take the cigarette from between her fingers and toss it on the ground.

"Brad, for God's sake!"

"Hey, dude," someone yells, making me look back. I see a guy coming at us, his face a picture of disgust. I do *not* need a law-abiding, do-gooder, pillar of the community stepping in and playing hero. Not now. Or maybe I do. *Maybe* if someone else saves her, she'll become their problem and do us both a favor.

But—

I stop, pull my gun, and aim it at the man. "Turn and walk away," I say calmly, feeling anything but.

"Brad!" Pearl gasps, reaching for my wrist and pushing the gun down.

And, weirdly, I let her, watching the guy back off promptly, hands up. I look down at her dainty hand around my wrist, holding it. Feel the heat. Smell the sweet scent of her perfume. Taste the desire between us. Our eyes meet. Pearl releases my wrist and takes a step back, as I absorb every one of her exquisite features before letting my gaze drift across the black dress clinging to her body. Every curve. Small waist, generous hips, lavish tits, shapely legs. Pearl must have a starring role in every man's wet dream. She's *all* woman.

Beautiful. Wise. Brave. Smart. Fiery.

But . . .

Only.

Twenty.

One.

I blink and look up at her slightly parted lips. What the fuck am I thinking? "I can't do this," I say, my mouth out of control. I can't stand the pull. Don't think I can resist it for much longer. She's fire, and I am playing way too close to the burning flames.

I turn away from her, raking a hand through my hair, and go back to my car, getting behind the wheel and starting the engine, fighting the urge inside. An urge that I have no idea how to deal with.

Drive away. Leave.

Go fuck Allison.

I slip my car into drive, check my mirrors, and ease off the brake, pulling away.

And quickly stop again, punching the steering wheel. I can't save a woman's life then leave her on the streets of Miami waiting to be mugged, raped, or murdered. "Fuck," I bellow, letting my head meet the wheel, hitting it a few times before looking at the ceiling and yelling my frustration.

No amount of random fucking will eliminate my problem.

I'm screwed.

Pearl isn't going anywhere, and I can't either. So what? I must sustain this torture forever?

Beaten, I let my head drop. My eyes focus past the windshield.

My vision is invaded by red.

She's in the road at the foot of the hood, watching me having a complete meltdown. Her face is straight—no attitude, no amusement, no *anything*.

Still fucking beautiful.

I'm out of fight. My resistance has snapped. What the fuck am I doing? I stare at her as she stares at me.

I don't need to tell her. She comes to the passenger side and gets in the car.

Quiet.

Eyes away from me, looking out of the window.

I take a moment, breathe in and out discreetly, clear my vision, and pull out, calmer than I'm feeling. But definitely more settled now she's actually in my car. The alarm starts beeping, telling me she's not put her seatbelt on. I don't know what comes over me. I reach across, my attention split between my task and my driving, and pull it across her body, my face disturbingly close to hers. I catch her eye as I'm pushing in the clip. She doesn't stop me. She doesn't protest. But she does swallow, her gaze dropping to my mouth as I pull away and return my attention to the road.

The car is suddenly ringing, and Allison's name comes up on the screen. I stare at it for a few moments before turning my eyes Pearl's way, seeing she's staring at the screen too.

I connect the call. "Something's come up," I say flatly. And then hang up, focusing on the road.

The silence is screaming, and in an effort to kill it, I hit the screen on the dashboard and select my recent tracks, feeling her eyes burning into my profile. Feeling my heart smashing in my chest.

Bokka's *Town of Strangers* comes through the speakers, the track sounding as moody as I'm feeling. Pearl reaches for the volume control, turning it up, obviously needing more noise.

I look out the corner of my eye, shifting in my seat, feeling the heat rising in the car, so I crank up the air con. Pearl watches me. I pull a button of my shirt open. She watches me do that too. Then she turns the volume up some more. I cast my eyes across to her again. She looks directly at me.

Speaking without speaking.

Understanding.

I inhale deeply, my chest swelling, the tension thick. I look at her when she's not looking at me. She looks at me when I'm not looking at her. Glances being stolen constantly. The track ends. She starts it again. And the cycle continues. Looks. Pressure. Desire so fucking intense, the car is pulsing.

It feels like years waiting for the gates to open when we arrive at the house. I drive through, shifting in my seat, raking a hand through my hair, noticing Pearl tucking hers behind her ear, giving perfect sight to her profile. Once I've turned off the engine, I remain in my seat, the music continuing to play. One more look at Pearl before I get out.

I walk up the steps to the house, removing my suit jacket, and push my way through the door, turning right and heading to the office.

I enter.

Take my phone out of my jacket pocket and drape it on the couch.

Go to the chair.

Lower.

I pull my music app up and put the track back on, my eyes on the door.

Patient.

But not.

Will she come?

I sink deeper into my seat, strung, hard, my elbow wedged into the armrest, the knuckle of my index finger brushing over my top lip.

Fighting my conscience. Holding my breath.

I release it when she appears, and every tiny piece of her calls for me.

Goodbye conscience.

Our eyes glued, she steps in and closes the door. I don't have to tell her to lock it. I push the chair away from the desk, and she visibly gathers the strength she clearly thinks she needs by inhaling, slow and long.

I do the same, again calling upon the sense I need to stop what I know is happening. But all I can tell myself in this moment is that I need to get this out of my system. Fuck her. Scratch the itch. Damn the consequences. A woman has never grinded me down before, and Pearl has done it with little effort. I want her. Fuck, I want her so bad.

"Come to me," I say, my voice hoarse and dry, slowly patting my lap. She drops her purse to the floor and wanders over, slow but sure, rounding the desk.

And her eyes never leave mine.

The moment she's close enough, I reach for her, hooking an arm around her waist and tugging her to between my legs. I slide my palms onto her hips and search her eyes as I fill my lungs. Wait for her to stop this.

She doesn't.

Instead, she slips a hand into my hair and clenches a fistful. A suppressed groan rumbles in my throat. My dick throbs in my pants. My hearing distorts, the music sounding louder than it actually is. I take the bottom of her dress, pulling it up her legs, standing as I do, and once it's past her ass, I encourage her to sit on the desk. Her arms raise into the air, her eyes never wavering from mine, watching me as I pull the material over her head. Her hair catches in the neck and swishes around her face. She pushes one side over her ear. Bites her lip.

Fuck.

Tossing her dress aside, I pull her shoes off, drop them to the floor, and then focus on her full, lace-covered tits, her nipples visible through the soft pastel blue material. I reach forward and pull the cups down, breathing in. No bruises. My eyes drift up to her collarbone where her hair skims, and I push it back, stroking the flesh over the bone. Watching her chest expand. Hearing her sharp intakes of breath. Seeing her constantly nipping at the ring in her lip.

My eyes stick to that one sweet spot, and I dip slowly, bracing myself, and kiss the corner of her lips, moving gently across, feeling her open up to me, tasting the relief. The pleasure.

"Jesus," I whisper, letting my tongue enter her mouth, meeting hers, and they swirl languidly, blood pumping in all the right places, charged, ready. One palm slips onto her nape, the other down her thigh between her legs. I feel her stiffen, losing the rhythm of her kiss. "Okay?" I ask quietly, withdrawing, my hand stilling where it is. I look at her. *Really* look at her. It's not the first time, but it's the first time I've allowed her to see me studying her. She doesn't answer, so I push. "Do you want this?" Want *me?*

She holds my gaze, nodding mildly, but she doesn't move beyond that. If she's anything like me right now, she'll be close to being paralyzed by anticipation. So I gently stroke her thigh, hoping to loosen her up, silently marveling at the smoothness of her skin. Young, soft skin, under my older, rough hands. Hands that kill.

Not today.

Today, they caress. Today, they're gentle. Today, they take something they shouldn't have.

I massage her nape, move in closer, tilt her head back, and drop my mouth onto hers again as I push past the seam of her panties and get my first feel of her condition. A low growl vibrates in my throat, a small whimper in hers. But despite my want, hers too, my kiss remains tender. My touch gentle.

Experiencing this.

Savoring this.

I encourage her down to the desk, kissing her until she's lying down, and trail my mouth across her chest, taking a nipple deep, sucking gently, brushing my tongue over the peak until it's stiff. *Jesus.* I feel delirious with pleasure, repeating on the other as I stroke between the wet lips of her pussy, looking up constantly to see her watching me work her. Pleasure her. I've got to taste her. Kiss her everywhere.

I drop to my knees, drag her panties down, and breathe in deeply, eyes on that special place, my mouth watering. *This. This is what I've wanted. This. Her.* I move in slowly, kiss the inside of her thigh, feel her writhe, her hands grabbing the edge of the desk. She says my name. Over and over, each time sounding more desperate.

She's throbbing before my eyes as I let my tongue slowly glide up her thigh onto her heat. She jacks off the desk and cries out, and I moan, my eyes closing in bliss, my tongue plunging inside her, licking her, kissing her, biting her. She yells at the ceiling—eager, desperate—and I retreat before she gets carried away and comes too soon.

The moment she settles, I start again, kissing her thigh, slowly moving toward her sweet pussy, gorging on her flesh, relishing her quiet sounds of pleasure.

And pull away once again when her back arches.

"Brad," she says, breathless. "Brad, please."

One more delicate kiss on her clit, and I rise, my eyes now feasting on her naked body laid out on the desk as I unbutton my shirt before tackling my pants. I let them fall to the ground, but I don't step out of them—my shoes won't allow it—and I am in no position to take a break and kick them off.

I slip my hand past the waistband of my boxers and take hold of my raging erection. Her eyes are fixed there, waiting, and when I pull it out, she sucks back air. I put on a condom under her watchful eye, rolling it down my dick to the root as I move in and positioning myself at her opening. Taking her thighs, I watch as she reaches over her head and clings to the side of the desk. My heart's pumping. Blood's burning. Muscles aching.

I push in slowly, a million curses loaded ready to be spat out. *Fuck*. My knees tremble, my fingertips dig into her flesh as my cock sinks deeper.

Fuck . . . ing . . . hell.

I can't describe the feeling. Incredible. Extraordinary. Beautiful. What makes this pussy different to the hundreds of others? I close my eyes for a moment, remaining still, holding tight.

Moving will put me on my ass.

Red.

I feel her hands rest over mine on her thighs and open my eyes. Her face is unbelievably impassive. Her pussy gloriously tight. "What is it, gorgeous?"

"I really want to be here." She strains the words, breathing heavily.

I tilt my head in question, stumped, and Pearl squeezes my

hands before returning them to the edge above the desk, closing her eyes, breathing in, arching her back. "You want me to move?" I ask, remaining stock-still. It's an effort, my cock screaming for friction. She nods into her darkness and brings the heels of her feet onto the desk.

So exposed.

Wide open for me.

I'm in no fit state to play the game of power. Make her wait or beg. I roll my hips, she whimpers, and I lower my torso to hers, starting to thrust lazily, work us up slowly, savoring the feel of her walls squeezing my dick beautifully, every inch of her touching every inch of me. Her eyes remain closed. I've never looked at a woman too closely when I've fucked her. This is unprecedented. And in this moment, when I'm high on pleasure and wonder, I'm incapable of questioning my actions.

I instinctively reach for Pearl's face and stroke her cheek, silently telling her to open her eyes, my moves unhindered, my pace consistent and smooth.

Her lids flicker, her thick, dark lashes fluttering. Her eyes open. See me.

She releases the desk and reaches for my face, holding it, moving with me, accepting every inch of me, pulling me back into her each time I retreat. I don't think I've ever seen anything so beautiful in my life. Her face while I'm inside her. Gorgeous. Perfect.

Her hands go back to the desk. Come back to my face. She bites her lip. Writhes beneath me.

It's coming. For both of us.

I wedge my fists into the wood and lift my chest from hers, getting better leverage, working us calmly. Her eyes become glossy, shine madly, her body squirms, and it's incredible to watch her expression change as her release creeps up. Her pussy squeezes me tighter. My cock pounds. My heart bucks.

"Brad," she gasps.

"I've got you." I grind hard and slow, and she jerks, blinks, and I come hard but calmly, my shakes instant as I explode. Pearl yells, bracing her hands on my forearms, tensing everywhere, waves of shudders rippling through her body with the pleasure.

Her eyes are wild, and I gasp, dropping to my forearms, my head on her chest. I pant, exhausted.

And the pleasure stays.

So much pleasure, so much peace, I can't even muster the energy to regret what I've done.

Yet.

But once I've come down from my high?

Chapter 8

PEARL

It was stupid, maybe. Inevitable, yes. I feel so incredibly full as he pulses inside me, his face hiding in my chest. The tingles are still intense. The euphoria incredible. His skin on mine.

Wanted.

Appreciated.

Safe.

But what now?

I know this is going nowhere—I know who Brad is, what he does. I know I'm just a number to him, a pussy. And I'm completely fine with that. He's solved a problem for me and, really, the tension was unbearable. Will it be gone now that he's scratched his itch?

I'm breathless, looking up at the ceiling, his weight a comfort I'm not used to. The guilt flames. But all I can think is, if I give it to someone, at least no one can take it from me.

I shift, disturbed by my thoughts, and Brad lifts his head and looks up at me. I search for regret. I search for shame. I find none. His eyes are clear—the swirl of anger I'm so used to gone. But what hasn't disappeared is the inexplicable want I'm feeling now that I've admitted, *and* acted on, the pull I feel toward him. I should get dressed. Leave. Go to my room.

Hide.

But under his soft gaze, I'm capable of nothing except soaking up the unfamiliar warmth of both his body and his eyes. It's . . . unexpected.

He's the first to move, peeling his chest from mine. He takes my hands and pulls me up to sitting, and I automatically look between my legs expecting to see blood. "Are you okay?" he asks as he pulls the condom off and knots it.

I smile down at my thighs as I tug the cups of my bra up. "You keep asking me that."

"You've not said much." He pulls his trousers up and slips the condom in his pocket before pulling the two sides of his shirt together and buttoning it up.

"Neither have you." I search the floor for my knickers, spotting them on top of my dress, but before I can slide off the desk to collect them, Brad's dipped and picked up the bunch of clothes.

He separates my knickers from my dress, hands me my dress, and slips my knickers into his pocket. I shoot him a surprised look.

"We're not done yet, Pearl."

"We're not?" I don't know how I feel about that. Scratch the itch, and the itch is scratched. Obviously, I'm completely lying to myself. But taking more will make this whole situation even worse.

"Here." Brad gathers my dress by the neck and slips it over my head. "Arms." I lift them as instructed and watch him with interest as he dresses me. This isn't good. I gravitated toward him when he was a cold arsehole. I don't need him being all attentive and considerate. *All the things I'm not used to.* And yet I can't stop myself taking his hand when he offers it and letting him help me down from the desk where I just let him fuck me. He keeps hold of me as he collects my bag and his jacket and leads us out of the office, apparently unconcerned by being seen by any one of the people who live here. He leads me up the stairs, down the corridor, and opens the door.

To his room.

I stop on the threshold as he stops just inside, turning on the lights, his back to the door to hold it open. Looking at me. *Oh God, oh God, oh God.* I shouldn't enter this room. I should not go to bed with him. But to have that feeling of uninhibitedness again? To feel that warmth, that . . . affection?

I step inside on a deep breath and gaze around the room, and the door shuts behind me. I hear a thud, my bag and his jacket dropping to the floor, and my shoulders rise when I feel him move in behind me, pressing his front to my back. His groin into my arse. That heavy, persistent pulse drops to between my thighs again. Electricity sizzles and sparks around us. My body is flaming hot. It's almost unbearable, and I know—fear—there's only one way to cool it.

Looking down, I see his arm slide around my waist, easing me back gently, his hips rolling, showing me his condition. He's hard again already? Then he starts walking forward, forcing my steps, the bed our destination. The sheets are strewn, unmade. He takes my dress and pulls it up over my head, forcing my arms up, and then unfastens my bra. Taking the straps, he drags it down my arms, his mouth falling to my shoulder, kissing me.

And I'm gone, at the mercy of his tenderness. My head falls back onto his shoulder and he moves in on my neck, working my throat, up to my chin, encouraging my face toward him. A brief look into my eyes before he claims my mouth, his hand sliding over my tummy, over my pubic bone, and into the wetness, his other hand cupping a breast. My short nails bite into the flesh of his forearms—my grip fierce—as he kisses the daylights out of me, and I try to keep up with his tongue's attack while dealing with the onslaught of pleasure.

I bend on a whimper, the pressure building immediately, flames and sparks ruling me. My hips roll, my body quakes, he tugs at the ring in my lip, scissors his fingers over my pulsing clitoris.

Gasping, I come all over his hand, cry out into his mouth, scratch desperately at his arms, forcing my body back into his. I'm given mere seconds to gather myself before I'm being pushed down to the bed front first. My knees sink into the mattress, my arse high, my chest and face flat on the sheets. I look across the bedroom, calm but apprehensive, hearing him unfasten his trousers. Remove his shirt. The rip of a condom wrapper. He takes my arms and holds them by my wrists at the top of my backside. The feel of him pushing against me cools the need slightly, and I close my eyes, dazed, accepting him, taking it all, slowly and surely, until I'm full to the hilt. I squeeze my eyes closed, dealing with the mild discomfort, as he holds himself deep, breaking me in gently, his spare hand stroking my arse cheek. His breathing is loud. My body screaming for movement is louder. But I'm too scared to speak again. To allow the wrong words to fall out in the throes of passion, to lose control of my mouth.

I really want to be here.

So I say nothing and simply listen to his breathing. My eyes ping open when I feel the pad of one of his fingers meet the nape of my neck. Covering the scar there. I wait for him to ask, my manufactured reason for the mar ready.

But he says nothing and drags that fingertip down my spine slowly, and with each inch it covers, I relax. He starts to roll his hips, not thrust or pump, just roll—firm and slow—and only when the pain eases does he pull out and drive forward again, like he's sensed I'm ready for it.

My skin prickles, my body naturally following his movements, instinctively pushing back as he thrusts forward. I let my lips part, flex my hands where they're secured, try to urgently catch air and fill my lungs.

He slips in and out.

In and out.

Slowly.

My blood simmers in my veins, rushing to my head.

In and out.

Measured.

My heart beats its way into my throat.

In and out.

Meticulous.

He grunts, and I feel him pause for a moment, feel his shakes. Controlling himself. He slips back in, the wet, hot friction on my insides cooling the burn but at the same time enflaming the want.

"Fuck," he curses, pulling out, taking my hips and turning me onto my back. And I'm hit with the sight of a six-foot-two-inch god—naked and ready—eyes hooded, lips wet and parted, his perfect face covered in beads of sweat. I've never seen such a perfectly fine-tuned form. And the way he's looking at me?

Pulsing.

Ready.

Hungry.

He kneels on the end of the bed, slips an arm beneath my lower back, and moves me up the mattress. Then settles on his forearms, eyes level with mine, his hips held up. And we're back in that place of gazing. Scanning each other's faces. Silent. It's as if we both know not to talk. We don't want talking. But do we want this level of intimacy? It's too intense. Is this still scratching an itch? *I don't know.* But he definitely hasn't fucked me yet.

He should. He should fuck me, because that's what he does, and that is what I expected from him. With that in mind, I reach down between us, braving taking the lead, and take him in my hand, encouraging him to me.

"Pearl," he whispers, eyes clenching shut as he circles and plunges deep.

I cry out and lift, burying my face in the crook of his neck, taking the pleasure and pain and nothing else. My muscles tense, gripping him inside of me, and I suck his neck, tasting his salty skin, biting at him. His moves become more urgent, and I welcome every drive, my body accepting all of him and the complete mindfuck that is this situation. But for the life of me, I could never stop it. He's given me two orgasms, and a third is on the way. It's a new feeling, a feeling of raw abandon, when I can focus on nothing else except the pleasure about to consume me and rock me to my core, sate me, calm me, leaving my lungs drained and my heart pounding.

Brad growls when I latch onto his neck, my knees bending, my heels wedging into his arse, my nails scratching at his back. My body is on auto pilot. Coming. He pumps harder, faster.

Fucking.

Our wet flesh slips and slides together, our breathing becomes louder, our bodies tighter. He curses, I yell, and he lifts his chest from mine, forcing me out of my hiding place.

Looking down at me, he bites his lip. Beads of sweat drip down on me.

And then silence. Eyes locked.

My muscles draw him in, squeeze, and the pressure releases, draining the air from my lungs. I'm knocked out by the untold pleasure that rips through me, shaking uncontrollably beneath him, watching as his face strains, his chest expands, and his jaw ticks. He swells inside me, exhales loudly, his braced arms shaking as he comes calmly but hard. It's fascinating. The strain, the form of his body when he climaxes, every muscle tightening before my eyes.

My gaze falls to the wound on this shoulder, the scar pink against his tan skin, and before I can stop myself, I've reached for it, stroking gently across the small area with my fingertip as he continues to throb inside me, and I continue to constrict around him.

"Does it still hurt?" I ask quietly.

He looks down, watching me touch him. "It aches from time to time." He sighs and lowers to his forearms, his head dropped, my body still full of him. I'm content, without the energy or inclination to move, despite feeling stifling hot. It's too peaceful.

I drift off, and for the first time in as long as I remember, it's without the fear that the monsters will find me while I sleep.

Chapter 9

BRAD

I suck on the cigarette hard, like I might be able to suck some sense into me. Too late. I don't want to admit that I slept well for the first time in months. What's more, without help from alcohol, drugs, or a hooker to exhaust myself in.

What the fuck have I done?

I look over my shoulder to the open doors into my room. She's fast asleep, her naked body tangled up in the sheets. It took everything out of me not to sink my cock back into her when I woke up next to her. Everything I had and more.

I bring my cigarette to my lips and take another drag, exhaling the smoke with a sigh as I rip my eyes away and sink deeper into the chair, looking across the grounds. There was too much of that last night. Looking. Watching. Studying. And definitely not enough words to ensure we both knew this was nothing more than scratching that fucking insatiable itch. I roll my shoulder, my skin tingling. Too gentle. Too careful. Too fucking greedy.

"Fuck's sake." I drop my head back and stare at the early morning sky, puffing my way through the rest of my smoke. I stub it out and wedge my hands into the arms of the chair, pushing myself up. I enter the room and collect up the strewn clothes, draping them on the chair with her purse, and then I go to the bed. Lower to the edge. I should throw her out. Be cold. Cruel. Make sure she doesn't come back for more.

I really want to be here.

God damn me, I reach for a lock of her blindingly bright hair, pushing it off her face. "Pearl," I whisper, glancing at the clock on the nightstand. I need to get her back to her own room before the house wakes up. "Pearl, wake up."

Her lashes flutter, her eyes opening. There's a fleeting moment of confusion on her face when she sets eyes on me, her chest lifting from the bed, her head craning to check where she is. *Yes, gorgeous, somewhere you definitely shouldn't be.* Even now I'm fighting the urge to crawl on top of her again. I intended to fuck her. It didn't quite work out that way. I tried to pull it back when we moved from the office to my bed, told myself repeatedly to bang her hard, treat her like I've treated them all, with little courtesy and less tenderness. I couldn't. It's fucking with my head. But I couldn't fuck her. Her age? The circumstances? I can't save her from those fuckers and then treat her like an object.

So I should have left her well alone.

"Morning," she croaks awkwardly, pulling the sheets in as she sits up.

"Hi." *Hi?* I roll my eyes to myself, searching my head for the right words. There are none. She's in my bed butt naked, I'm sitting here fighting the blood from surging into my dick, and I give her a *hi*. "It's—"

Knock, knock.

My body freezes, but my heart clatters, as I look over my shoulder to the door. "Brad, are you awake?" Beau calls through the wood.

"Fuck," I whisper, ready to push Pearl down under the sheets, but when I face the bed again, she's not there. I see her fly into the bathroom, slamming the door, just as Beau pushes her way in. She looks at me sitting on the edge of the bed, naked, my palm over my dick as I pull a sheet onto my lap. Then she looks at the bathroom door, obviously having heard it slam. "Why do you bother knocking if you're going to walk right in anyway?" I ask irritably.

Eyebrows high and interested, Beau sends a scornful look my way. "I thought we didn't have . . ." She pauses, thinks, obviously trying to muster a more appealing word than what I know she was going to say. "Lady friends back at the house anymore." Her frown deepens. "In fact, you've *never* had lady friends back at the house."

Yes. Always hotels. Never my apartment and never the mansion. My apartment was my peaceful place. The mansion was a place for an in-house whore. I never utilized the in-house whore, always sourced my own. How admirable of me. "Beau, it's five thirty in the fucking morning, for Christ's sake. What do you want?"

Not easing up on the questioning in her eyes, she holds up a pot of something. "Try this." And tosses it at me. "Lawrence said it works wonders with restlessness."

"Restlessness?" I look down at the label. I'm not restless. I'm fucked. "What is it?"

"Some magic potion. Lavender, chamomile—this, that, and something else."

Lavender. Fuck me. "And you thought you'd drop it off now?"

"Well, you're usually awake at this time of day." Her eyes fall to the bathroom door again. "And alone."

"Go away."

She pouts, backing up. "I'll be in the gym if you'd like to talk about it."

"There's nothing to talk about." I shift, uncomfortable, mindful that Pearl can probably hear every word being said. And . . . "Should you be working out in your condition?"

"I'm pregnant, Brad. I don't have a condition."

"Still, he's happy with that, is he?"

"*He* was a little distracted last night." She takes the handle of the door. "What happened at the club?"

Yeah, not telling her that. "Time to go," I say, standing with my sheet and walking toward her, effectively forcing her out. "Take it easy in the gym."

"Or else?"

I scowl, letting her catch it before the door meets the jamb. And I smile, because that look on Beau—the serene, chilled, light one—is beautiful on her. She's waited a long time for that, and not even the new unrest can take it away from her. The Bear's dead.

She's free.

Now, back to *my* problem. I go to the bathroom door and knock lightly. "She's gone," I call through the wood. I get no answer. "Pearl?" I listen. Nothing, no words, no movement. So I back off, going outside for another smoke, collecting my cell as I pass the bed when it rings and leaving the lavender potion in its place. I answer to James. "Are you cool with your wife working out?" I ask in answer, lowering to the chair, lighting up.

"Brad, let me teach you a thing or two about women."

"I don't need to learn *anything* about women." I smile, remembering the day James Kelly walked into Hiatus again. The Enigma. On the warpath. And now, married with a kid on the way. Under the thumb like The Brit.

"What do you need to talk about?" he asks.

"What?"

"I got a text from you."

I feel like my brain has short-circuited. Last night. Red. Creamy flesh. The sweet smell of lavender. It's holding poll position, and that's a problem all by itself.

"Brad?"

The Escalade. I gather myself and stand, walking to the edge of the terrace. "There was a drive-by."

"What?"

"Outside the club. Drake got the license plate number. I've sent it to Otto." I'm not mentioning the dancer with two phones until I need to. *If* I need to. I need to get those phones to Otto.

"What the fuck's going on?" The tone of his voice has changed dramatically. It's got The Enigma all over it.

"I don't know, but I do know you're gonna be short one ballbag if you don't take Beau on a honeymoon soon."

"Is that humor I hear, Brad?"

Twice in one morning. I smile. It drops the second I remember what's currently hiding in my bathroom. "No." I take one last drag of my smoke and stub it out. "Your empty apartment," I say, wondering why I haven't thought of it before.

"What about it?"

"Can I move in until the work on mine is done?"

"I was thinking Beau and I should move in there."

I still, caught off guard. "Since when?"

"Since this house started bursting at the seams with people."

"Tell me about it," I mutter, looking back at the bedroom again. "But given the intel we learned yesterday, haven't you changed your mind?" There's no way James will leave Beau in an apartment alone.

"All the reason why you shouldn't be out on your own too. Are you trying to avoid someone, Brad?"

I laugh—not in humor—as I peek down at my arm. At the scratches and marks she's left behind. "What are you talking about?"

A long, loud sigh. "There's not a chance in hell any of us are moving out of this mansion until the new shitstorm has passed. I'm heading for the boatyard to stock up. Might have a run out on the water while I'm there."

Stock up. We'll all be stocking up, now it's confirmed we all need to be. The bunker won't be jam-packed for much longer. "Beau going?" I ask tentatively. I need to plan whatever bullshit I'm spewing to the men when they find out a woman was in here, because I'm sure as shit Beau will be telling James.

"No, she's got a meeting with a lawyer. I'm banished."

"What for?"

"Something to do with her mother. It's a sore subject."

I flinch. Yeah, I can imagine. "She's taking Fury, right?"

"Don't ask stupid fucking questions, Brad." He hangs up. The girls will not be happy. Bye-bye easygoing, relaxed killer husbands. At least until we find out who the fuck's fucking with us.

I hear the bathroom door open behind me, reminding me of another problem. "Fuck." I head back inside, just catching sight of Pearl dipping out quietly and closing the door. "Pearl," I call, going after her. I pull the door open and search the corridor. No Pearl. But I do find Otto.

"What's up?" he asks, looking me up and down.

"Nothing."

He raises curious eyebrows as he keeps walking.

"Wait," I call, backing up and going to my jacket, pulling out the phones I found in Ella's backpack. I hand them to Otto. "See what you can find from these. And don't mention it to anyone else."

"Sure." He doesn't ask any questions, going on his way.

I shut the door, looking at the chair where my clothes are. I dip my trousers and pull out the used condom. And Pearl's knickers. *I'm not done with you yet.* I should never have gone there in the first place.

I shake my head to myself and head to the bathroom, but stall, frowning at the bed. I move in closer.

Red.

"Fuck," I whisper, taking in the bloody sheets.

And there's me, being so careful not to hurt her.

There's the proof.

I'm incapable.

And not just physically.

Chapter 10

Pearl

I drop to the end of the bed and fall to my back. "Bloody hell," I murmur, wincing at the soreness between my legs. My insides feel like they're swollen, throbbing, and raw. To be expected, I suppose, given Brad was hardly at the back of the queue when God gave out—

"Where have you been?"

I lift my head off the bed, my mind scrambled, as Anya observes me from the bathroom doorway. *Think.* "I fell asleep in the TV room," I blurt, getting up, avoiding her eyes, as I pass her and go to the bathroom.

"Do you feel better?"

"Not really." *Worse.* I go to the mirror, cringing as I get out of my dress.

Fucked.

Ruined.

I reach between my thighs, wincing, seeing the dried blood staining my skin. I sigh. I can't go back now, only forward. Problem is, I don't know where to head. Having sex in the office was one thing. Having sex in his room and staying the night, now that's another thing altogether.

Isn't it? My palm meets my forehead, my eyes squeezing shut.

He took me to bed.

What do I do with that?

• • •

After showering and throwing on a white shift dress—no makeup, because I'm ill—I brave leaving the room, sure it's now safe to do so. He won't be here. Hardly ever is, and I can't imagine that's changed now. I wander down the corridor, still tense, and as I descend the stairs, I see Daniel coming up them. "Hey, kid," I say, taking in his forlorn expression. "What's the matter?"

"I'm grounded," he grunts, passing me. "Well, Mom says I'm

grounded. Dad says I'm not."

I laugh. "Then you're definitely grounded, kid." Rose certainly has the power over her capable, murdering husband. She's fearless.

"Yeah, I know."

I check the time on my phone. He should be getting ready for school. "Does grounded mean you don't go to school? Because that sounds like a great kind of grounded to me." I turn at the bottom of the stairs and watch Daniel trudge up them.

"Principal Tucker has thrown me out."

My eyes widen. "Why?"

"Because I said something dumb, but Preston Bean was asking for it."

"Oh. What did Preston Bean do?"

"Called Dad a murderer. His dad's a cop."

Oh shit. I wouldn't want to be Preston Bean's dad right now. Or Principal Tucker. "Chin up, I'm sure your dad will sort it out." I see plenty of threats heading their way. Stupid men.

Daniel mumbles and moans as he climbs the stairs, and Rose appears, Maggie in her arms, crossing the hallway to the kitchen. "Hey," she says, head tilted. "Okay?"

I nod, turning with her and going to the kitchen. "Daniel just told me about the school."

"Nightmare," she says, shaking her head. "Back to homeschooling, unless I want my husband to fix it."

I smile. "What are you doing today?" I ask, joining Anya at the island.

"Maggie has a checkup with Doc, and *I* will be convincing the contractors at the spa that I'm scarier than my husband."

Esther laughs. "That shouldn't be hard," she says, putting a cup of tea in my hand. I smile my thanks. "Are you feeling better?"

I don't need to ask how she knows. The answer is sitting next to me chomping her way through some toast.

"Oh, you're ill?" Rose asks, rearranging the muslin cloth on her shoulder and holding Maggie there, starting to pat her back.

"A little." I nibble at the corner of the croissant, hoping the questioning stops there.

"You should see Doc."

"Who should?"

I turn and find Doc behind us, dressed in his usual sharp tweed suit. "I'm fine," I assure him. Except for the soreness between my legs. And the feeling of dread in my tummy. I don't expect him to have a cure for either.

He doesn't listen, coming at me with his palm and laying it over my forehead. "You're hot."

Yes, because I still haven't cooled down after last night.

Beau saves me, breezing in *without* a towering assassin following her for once. She's a little breathless, her skin damp, and her hand rests on her small bump. "I'm starving." She leans past me and plucks a pastry from the pile. God, what would she say if she knew it was me in Brad's bathroom this morning? "You okay?" she asks, looking at me curiously as she takes a huge bite.

I feel myself getting hotter again. "I'm fine."

Anya pushes the croissant to my mouth. "You should eat," she says, and I smile, pacifying my friend by taking another small bite. My stomach protests, but I swallow, fighting to keep it down, my anxiety threatening to force it up.

Yesterday at the club was a flashback, nothing more, a silly something that was triggered by Anya crunching some ice. It caught me off guard. I couldn't stop the blood draining from my face, and Mason didn't miss it. It was easy to say yes when he asked if I felt unwell. Easier than telling him the truth. I needed air, to walk off the anxiety. So I left the club. *And ended up in The American's car.*

"Morning, darlings!" Zinnea breezes in, her dress wafting behind her. "I'm out for the day. And maybe the night too." She puts her tongue in her cheek. "If I'm lucky."

"When will we get to meet Quinton officially?" Beau asks, lifting onto a stool next to me. I pour her some of the green juice James insists she drinks, and she air-kisses me, her mouth full again as she accepts.

"Bring him back here?" Zinnea asks, helping herself to a coffee. "To the Munsters house? Really, darling? He'll run a mile."

"You're ashamed of us?" Rose gasps, bobbing on the spot, now rubbing Maggie's back.

"I'm not ashamed. I'm merely ensuring he's in love with me and could never possibly leave me before I introduce him to my dysfunctional family."

I laugh into my tea as I take a sip. Dysfunctional, yes. It's also amazing, and as I gaze around the kitchen now, I feel a horrible, deep ache in my stomach. I never want to leave, and not only because I feel safe here. I don't want to leave because I've grown attached to everyone. Or most of them, anyway. What happened last night could wreck this. Or my truths could. I hate lying to them, especially the girls. What would they do if I told them? Kick me out? Send me back? The men, maybe, but the girls?

"You going to eat that?"

"Pardon?" I look at Beau, seeing her pointing to the croissant I've hardly touched. "Oh, no." I push the plate her way. "You have it." I can't eat. I'm too sidetracked.

Torn.

"Do you feel well enough to work today?" Anya asks, dusting of the flaky pastry from her hands.

I'm not relishing it, being there is an odd mixture of relief and stress. "Yes, what time are you starting?"

"Two."

"I'm six, so I'll see you later?" I get up and drop a kiss on Anya's cheek first, then Beau's. Now it's time to find somewhere private to quietly regret sleeping with one of the bosses. "Cindy and Barbie are waiting to play fetch." And I need some air. "See you later."

Beau smiles over her shoulder at me, but I see the questions in her eyes. In the six months I've been here, we have become close, but I've never shared where I've really come from with her. I would rather pretend it never happened. I take my cup to the sink and set it on the counter, just as Esther flips the tap on.

The sound of rushing water fills the room.

• • •

"Mum?" I call, following the sound of water. "Mum, where are you?" I creep down the landing, constantly checking behind me, making sure I'm not found out of bed at this hour. Is he even home? "Mum?" I call, nearing the far end of the house, the noise getting louder. "Mum?" I take the gold doorknob of the bathroom door. "Mum, are you in there?" I stand on the threshold, pushing the door. It creaks open.

• • •

"Pearl?"

I jolt, blinking, staring at the violent rush of water whooshing out.

"God damn it, this tap needs replacing," Esther mutters, fiddling with the handle. "The pressure's knackered."

The water shuts off.

I try to control my shaking hands, try to breathe easy.

"Pearl?" Beau says, slipping off her stool.

"Just feeling a little hot." I smile meekly. "Some fresh air will help." I leave everyone in the kitchen and head out into the garden, replying to Mason's text as I make my way past the pool, telling him I'm feeling much better and I'll be at work later. Once I've shaken off this unease. I tuck my phone in my dress pocket and scoop up a half-chewed tennis ball, whistling. The ground shakes with the pounds of their chunky paws as they run from wherever they are to find me. I smile when they come flying around the corner, galloping like horses, their tongues hanging out and flapping up the sides of their faces. "Hey, girls," I coo, tossing the ball in my hand as they leap up and down, excited. "Ready, ready, ready, ready, ready . . ." I launch the ball as far as I can, which is probably a pathetic effort by their standards, but they shoot off, barking, the competition fierce between them to get there first. Cindy wins. Always Cindy. Which means I'll end up holding her collar to give Barbie a head start, just so she can win once or twice. They come bounding back. "Drop," I order. Cindy obediently releases, and I scoop it up, walking on with them flanking me either side, looking up eagerly, begging me to chuck it again. I throw it toward the garden house and take a seat on the bench under a willow tree. Hidden. But the dogs still sniff me out. Always do.

Cindy drops the ball in my lap, and I grimace, wiping the drool off my dress. "Yum." I take her collar and throw the ball again, giving Barbie a few yards advantage before releasing Cindy. She pelts off, kicking up some tufts of grass.

A rustle behind me pulls my eyes back. And my heart stops in my chest and starts again, pumping faster. Brad dips through a few branches, and everything inside that was beginning to relax becomes tense again. My eyes fall to his navy suit, his open-collared shirt. His hands are in his pockets, relaxed. Good for him. I return forward when I feel something land in my lap. Barbie pants up at me, looking extremely pleased with herself, oblivious to the sudden pivot of my disposition.

I thought he'd left.

"Morning," he says, his voice getting closer.

"Hi," I reply, frowning down at the soggy ball in my lap. He appears in my peripheral vision, lowering to the bench, his hands still in his pockets. I look at him. He looks at me. And I quickly turn away before I can fall victim to his lazy gaze again.

"Do you feel better?" he asks.

I pick up the ball and throw it, sending the dogs off. Brad must have wondered what was bad enough to send me home early from work that wasn't bad enough to stop me taking my clothes off for him. Or letting *him* take them off. "I do, thanks."

"So you'll be at work?"

"At six. In case you needed to avoid me." I turn a small smile his way, desperately not wanting things to be awkward. Desperately not wanting him to make it impossible for me to stay. I can't lie to myself—last night was the most incredible thing I've ever experienced. It truly sucks that I'll never have that again, but I can accept that so long as I can stay. It'll be hell, seeing him every day, knowing he'll never see me as anything other than a fuck but, again, I'll endure it so I can stay.

He huffs a little bit of laughter. "Pearl, listen, last night—"

"Shouldn't have happened, I know."

He recoils, surprised, gazing at me with those fucking take-me-to-bed eyes. "Right," he breathes, and I turn away, clenching my eyes closed, mortified.

My God, he's told himself he needs to pacify the child. Make sure I understand that he's a man, a real man, and one who is good at only one thing. Fucking. Did he think I'd built a fairy tale around him? Mentally married him, had his babies, lived happily ever after in his mafia world? God, he's going to be disappointed. I learned long ago not to dream of fairy tales. And last night? It needed to happen. For Brad *and* for me.

And yet, I can't ignore the sting of disappointment.

"You thought I'd expect more."

"I thought . . ." He clears his throat, shaking his head, his eyes becoming more hooded, searching mine. "I thought it was a pleasant evening."

"Pleasant?"

"Nice."

I laugh. "That's even worse than pleasant, Brad." God, he looks annoyingly comfortable while he tells me that I was okay in bed. I don't suppose I can grumble. He's had more experience than I have. *Way* more experience. "Let's just forget it ever happened and go back to—"

"Hating each other?" he says.

I roll my eyes, exasperated. "Yeah, let's do that. It's what people are used to from us."

"I don't think I can do that, Pearl."

I shoot him a look, something inside shifting, and I don't know what. What is he saying? His lips become straight, and he pulls a hand out of his pocket, a packet of cigarettes and lighter held in his grasp. He lights up. I need one of those too.

"Not after last night," he adds quietly.

I remain silent, scared to talk, and watch as he puts his free hand on his knee, palm up, flexing his fingers. I read him, tentatively placing my hand in his, and he wraps his fingers around mine, looking at our joined hands.

"So can we at least be civil?"

And that feeling I couldn't recognize? I realize, as unwarranted disappointment engulfs me, that it was hope. "Yeah," I say softly, breaking our joined hands—I can't bear the heat. "I'll see you later." I stand and walk away.

"Pearl?" he calls, and I look back. I hate the expression on his face. I hate how handsome he is. *I hate that I'm twenty-one.* "I'm sorry if I hurt you."

"Hurt me?" I ask, confused, as he rises to his feet. "Like, broke my heart?"

"No, Pearl. The blood on the bed."

I feel my face drop, and there's nothing I can do to stop it, despite my best efforts. *Shit.* My cheeks become hot, my tongue thick in my mouth. "You didn't hurt me." I should *not* have said that. "It's fine." I bumble on. "I—" I tuck my hair behind my ear. "I'll see you later." I get my arse out of there before I give myself away. *Fucking hell, just tell him you came on your period!*

"Whoa, wait," Brad calls. I clench my eyes closed, keeping up my pace. "Pearl," he yells, his tone changing, along with his mood. "Pearl, stop where the fuck you are."

On a quiet curse, I stop, and Brad rounds me, his eyes no longer hooded. They're worried. "Please tell me . . ." A swallow. "Jesus, don't say . . ."

I feel my shoulders drop, defeated. "It's no big deal."

"You're a virgin?" he breathes.

Embarrassment claims me. "*Was*, Brad. I *was* a virgin." A pure, perfect, untouched, unbroken, *expensive* virgin.

"Fucking hell." He sucks on his cigarette and puffs out the smoke on a few more fucks for good measure. I didn't want him to know. The aftermath is bad enough without that thrown into the mix. "Why the fuck didn't you tell me?"

I look at him like he's stupid, because in this moment he is. "I'm sorry, should I have put that on my résumé?"

He winces like he's been slapped.

"Are all your fucks obliged to state their sexual experience before you stick your cock in them?"

Snarling, he gets up in my face. "You have a mouth like a fucking sewer."

Is he really taking the moral high ground? "Are you telling me off?" This is better. Anger. No disappointment, only anger. He's acting like he's some kind of fucking angel and I've just robbed his halo.

Taking my face in his grip, Brad squeezes my cheeks. Livid. And then . . . not. His eyes fall to my lips. *Oh shit.* My body responds, buzzing, begging for the electric energy consuming me again. He moves in, his lips skimming mine. I taste his cigarette. Sex. My anger dissipates and every tiny thing I felt last night while he worshipped me returns.

"Fuck," he hisses.

I'm suddenly not in his hold anymore, struggling to stand on my own two feet.

"Fuck, fuck, fuck." He stalks away, and I stagger a pace or two, catching myself, as I watch him throw down his cigarette and yell his frustration.

Regret.

There it is.

Chapter 11

DANNY

I gaze around the racking system in the bunker. Guns, grenades, harpoons, every weapon known to man, is stored, stacked high to the ceiling, on the table in the middle of the room, and in crates on the floor. "What the fuck are we going to do with them all?" I ask as I lift an AK47 and blow across the top of the hand guard. They are literally collecting dust.

"Use them." James tidies a box of bullets on the back shelf, gazing along the line of handguns next to it. "It sounds like that peace you begged for isn't going to be around for much longer."

"You wanted it too," I remind him. "Ready to hit the water?"

"Yeah," he says slowly, looking toward the stairs that lead up to the container. "You heard from Brad?"

"No, why?"

"Beau said he had a guest in his room this morning."

He's taken my advice? "Good." Hopefully whoever it was rode his bad mood away. And the temptation. Wandering towards the stairs, I pull my wetsuit up my chest, tripping up a box as I go. "Fuck it."

James laughs—the wanker—pulling out his phone when it chimes. "Otto's calling us up to the café."

I pause with one arm in a sleeve. "Did he say what for?"

"That cop you asked him to look into." James passes me, taking the stairs out of the bunker, his bare, scarred back pulsing. "He's talking about things he shouldn't be talking about." He disappears, leaving me behind with a frown.

"Like what?" I ask, pulling my arm back out of the sleeve and going after him.

"You."

I make it into the container that hides the entrance into the bunker and dip to help James lift the iron hatch into place. "I already know he's talking about me. That's why Daniel's now excluded from school." And also why this Bean cop's going to lose the use of his legs very soon.

We push the table into place. "It's *who* he's talking to." James opens the door of the container and light streams in, blinding me.

I step outside to the roar of jet skis flying across the water. Our jet skis are on the shore, waiting for us to give them a run. I've been on the water more in the past six months than in the past six years. Something tells me that's going to change. I nod to Leon and collect my Marlboros off a nearby wall, lighting up as James heads toward the café. "Who's he talking to?"

"Nolan."

"The fuck?" I blurt, going after him. He has a bad habit of doing that. Dropping bombs and fucking off to avoid the flying shrapnel. "Nolan?" Fuck, this isn't good.

James looks over his shoulder, eyebrows high. "Yeah, Nolan."

I feel what I see on James. Dread. We've all grown fond of the dipshit, Brad more than most of us. I pick up my feet and get my arse up the steps to the café, spotting Otto on the decked veranda nearest the water, his face in his laptop, his fingers twisting a tuft of his beard as he concentrates. What the fuck does my mother see in him? If I didn't appreciate him, and—for my sins—actually like the hairy brute, I might kill him. He's clever. *Loyal.* That's been proven beyond doubt in the light of the connection with Bernard King.

I narrow my eyes as I collect a bottle of water, holding it up to the server as I pass. "I'll put it on your tab," she says, tapping at the cash register.

"Thanks."

I make it to the table and drop to a chair opposite Otto, James next to him. Otto looks up and turns his screen toward me. "I'm not going to see any lovey-dovey messages pop up from my mum, am I?" I ask before I look at the screen. It wouldn't be the first time.

"Disabled," he says, as James chuckles in his chair. "But remind me to talk to you about something."

That's the second time he's mentioned talking. "Is my mum okay?" I saw her a couple hours ago looking as happy as a pig in shit doing her thing in the kitchen.

"She's fine." He points to the screen. "Officer Richard Bean."

I turn my eyes to the laptop. And recoil. "Fuck, he's nearly as ugly as Ringo."

"Who is?" We all look up and find the man himself gazing around the table at us.

"Him." I point at the screen.

Ringo grimaces at the picture of Bean. "He's definitely uglier than I am."

"I don't agree," someone else says—someone who's not at the table. "You're way uglier."

I lean back in my chair at the sound of the voice, as James sits up straight and Otto turns his head slowly. Goldie looks between us all, tugging down the sleeves of her suit jacket.

"Don't all rush to welcome me back at once."

I slowly turn my eyes onto James, assessing his disposition. It's as I expected. He doesn't look happy. "What the hell are you doing here?" he asks, rising. "You're supposed to be on holiday, walking in the park, eating ice-fucking-creams, enjoying freedom."

Freedom from James's demons. That's what he means. We all knew Goldie wouldn't break away until whoever killed James's family was taken care of, and it was taken care of the day Beau killed her mother.

"I heard some dead bodies turned up." Goldie pulls out a chair, unfazed by James's grumpy vibes. "I also heard Bernard King's name thrown into the mix." Her eyes drop to Otto's stomach.

"Heard from who?" James glares at Ringo accusingly, and he shrugs, unperturbed. I smile. I know the ugly fuck missed our she-warrior. I think perhaps Goldie missed Ringo too. And here they are. Reunited. Let the banter commence.

"Can we get back to the matter at hand?" I ask, reminding James that we have bigger issues to worry about. Besides, I get the feeling Goldie's holiday wasn't all she thought it was going to be. I look between her and Ringo, wondering . . .

"Who is it, anyway?" Ringo asks, sitting, motioning to the screen.

"Officer Richard Bean," I explain, taking a drag of my forgotten cigarette before it burns out. I flick it into the sea. "His kid, Preston, attends the same school as Daniel. They had a few words and Daniel's been thrown out."

"Basically," James says, "Bean's been saying things he shouldn't have been saying to Bean junior, and Bean junior's been antagonizing the kid."

"Fuck me, was that a tongue twister?" I ask over a laugh.

James eyes me, his expression irked. "Otto's been doing some digging and found Bean's been talking—"

Ringo starts sniggering. "I can't take this seriously."

"Bean *has* been—"

"No." Ringo chuckles, falling back in his chair. "Doesn't work."

Otto throws his hands up, exasperated.

"The cop," I say. "Let's just call him the cop."

"The cop has been in contact with Nolan," Otto finishes, and doesn't that shut Ringo the fuck up. Yeah. My thoughts exactly.

"Does Brad know?" Goldie asks, frowning. "And where is he, anyway?"

"Probably hanging out the back of a hooker," I murmur, rubbing at my forehead.

"Seriously, Danny." Goldie's face is pure disgust. "So he's still a moody bastard?"

"Affirmative." James eyes are on me, obviously thinking the same thing. *Pearl.* He's moody because of Pearl. And it was hard seeing him so torn up in the club yesterday—admitting he's struggling. Acknowledging the problem. *He won't fuck her.* I know that much. And she seems pretty disgusted by him. Plus, there was a woman in his room this morning. Which means what? I blink, my head hurting.

"No one mentions to Brad that Bean's been talking to Nolan." Funnily enough, no one laughs this time. "I'll handle it."

"What the fuck are you going to do?" James asks. "Put a bullet in Nolan's head and hope Brad doesn't notice he's gone missing?"

I'm hoping it doesn't come to any bullets anywhere, but I have a horrible feeling in my stomach. I haven't forgotten how shifty Nolan was yesterday. "No one mentions this to Brad," I affirm.

"And the cop?" Goldie asks. "The last thing you want is to make an enemy of a cop."

"Because they aren't all enemies already?" I ask.

"I'm talking about personal vendettas," she says.

"Bean made it personal when he let his son hear shit he shouldn't have heard. We managed to keep who we are and what we do well away from Daniel and his education until Bean came along." I can't hand on heart say that's true, given the kid's retaliation. Pops's gold letter opener. But still . . . "Now, my kid is out of school." I unscrew the

cap of my water and take a slug. "I promise I'll handle it delicately."
I'll use a shotgun instead of a rocket launcher.

"And the principal?" James asks.

"Will be having a civilized conversation with the barrel of my
gun."

"Rose will be delighted." Goldie laughs.

"Rose won't know," I grate, raising my eyebrows at her. "Will
she?"

Otto drags his laptop back to his side of the table. "Heads-up."
He nods past me, and I turn to see Brad's arrived. Looking like he
wants to kill something.

"Jesus Christ," Ringo breathes. "Who shat in his cornflakes?"

"Well, it wasn't you, Ringo," I say, scrubbing a hand down my
face, "because you only shit in the evenings, don't you?"

"Fuck off."

Goldie falls apart, and it's a lovely sight. Bugged phones, the
Black family emblem, dead Russians and Mexicans, a moody bastard
cousin, a wife, baby, the kid. Trouble around here is like buses in
London—you don't see one for hours then ten of the fuckers show
up at once. But, and I hardly want to admit it, I've missed this.
Brainstorming. Picking things apart, putting the puzzle pieces
together.

Brad swipes an orange juice from the fridge when he passes and
swigs it down as he walks over, dropping heavily into a chair.

"All right?" I ask, getting ready to duck to miss his swing. What
the fuck's wrong with him now? Clearly his *guest* last night hasn't
loosened him up.

"Fine. What did I miss?"

I humor his need to swerve my question. "Nothing," I say, giving
everyone around the table a warning look. For fuck's sake. Nolan?
"Otto was just about to update us on—"

"The Escalade outside the club?" Brad asks.

"Yes, that. What's the deal with you playing kamikaze?" I saw
the footage. Brad walked right into that, the prick.

"What the fuck did you expect me to do?"

"Call for backup."

"I was busy dodging bullets, Danny."

Or more likely trying to alleviate his stress in another way.

Looking for a fight. A way to release the pressure, and I, of all people, know how much calm can be found in a kill. I snarl at Brad as he drags my cigarettes toward him. "Help yourself."

"Fuck off." He slips one between his lips and lights up, pulling hard and long and flopping back in his chair. "What are you doing back?" he asks Goldie. "Full up on ice cream or did you miss Ringo?"

I roll my eyes. The antagonistic prick. "Let's have a little recap, shall we?" *Make sure everyone is up to speed.*

"I love your recaps." James gets comfortable in the chair, which doesn't look very comfortable at all, his big body bent and awkward on the small wooden seat. I can attest. I grimace and shift, wondering where to start. "Your phone," James prompts.

"Bugged," I say, pulling a rare expression of surprise from Goldie. "Any news on that?"

Otto shakes his head. "I've got a feeling it's something to do with the cops hanging around outside Hiatus."

"What cops?" Goldie asks.

"The ones that scared off the Escalade that pulled a drive-by on Brad." I chuckle, hearing the words aloud. We've dealt with so much more, sure, but . . . I don't know. Maybe it's the sleep deprivation. My brain doesn't seem to want to work and help me out with how to solve this puzzle. "That was after Higham showed up and presented us with a few photographs of dead Russians and Mexicans with the Black family emblem carved into their chests."

Goldie's frown is monstrous. "And I'm assuming you didn't carve the emblems?" She nods at me and then Brad.

"Correct," Brad confirms, looking blankly into thin air.

"Correct," I murmur, studying him. He's here but not here. This is fucking important. "Brad," I snap, irritated.

He blinks and looks at me. "What?"

I can't deal with him right now. For fuck's sake. "We also have a cop called Bean who's been shooting his mouth off and, consequently, had Daniel thrown out of school."

Goldie slides down her chair. "Oh."

"Yeah, oh." And then we have Nolan talking to the Bean cop. Can't mention that in Brad's company. Not that he'd hear me.

"So in summary," Brad speaks up, eyeing me with a curled lip. He takes a drag of his smoke and exhales, making Goldie cough and call him a few choice words. "Two Mexicans and two Russians turned up dead with our family emblem etched into their chests. One would assume either Danny or I did that, but Higham, smart and observant fucker that he is, has identified that whoever scratched the Black emblem into the chests was left-handed, and neither Danny nor I are left-handed. So whoever did it has failed in their attempts to get the FBI on our backs. They haven't, however, failed to get the Mexicans and Russians on our backs. They'll be gunning for us. On top of that, Danny's phone's been bugged, and I was shot at outside Hiatus." Brad slips his Marlboro between his lips and holds it there while he pulls at his tie, eyeing me again, like . . . see? I'm here. I'm present. "The police conveniently showed up as whoever was in the Escalade aimed a machine gun at me, scaring them off," he continues. "On top of that, Beau's suspicious. She knows one Russian fucker walked away from the shootout when Dumb Fuck here"—he points his Marlboro at me—"went after Sandy alone."

"And there was me thinking you're unfocused," I say, slightly stunned.

"I'm perfectly focused." He pulls his tie from the collar of his shirt and exhales smoke, still holding it between his lips. "The Bean cop obviously has an ax to grind and has dragged the kid into it—big mistake—and I would hazard a guess that he also has something to do with the cops loitering around outside Hiatus."

So the fuck he had last night worked after all? Good. I feel reassured by that. He needs to be on the ball. "You missed one point."

"What's that?"

Two, actually but, again, can't mention Nolan. "I've hardly left the house for weeks, and if I have, I've only been here or to Hiatus."

"So whoever bugged your phone is in the fold," Brad says, popping open the top two buttons of his shirt as everyone hums their thoughts on that, everyone looking around the table to each other before looking out to the yard, thoughtful. Brad's wondering who. Everyone else at the table thinks Nolan has some explaining to do. "And there's nothing on the bug?"

"Nothing." Otto closes the lid of his laptop, frustrated. "It's got to be government issued."

"How sure are you?" Because if that's the case, it means we have the cops on our arses, although why the fuck we have the cops on our arses is a fucking mystery since we've all been rather good recently. A bunker full of firearms and a club full of illegal cash aside, of course. The point is, we're inactive. And someone's clearly trying to change that. Fuck me, Nolan? Are they blackmailing him? Do they have something on him?

James is clearly thinking the same, given his expression. And then we both look at Brad, wondering how the hell we deal with this. He's now undoing his trousers, standing from his chair, cigarette still hanging out of his mouth as he wriggles out of them before finishing on his shirt. And we all just watch as he strips down to his boxers.

"Tell me you're going out on the water," James says, just as Leon hurries in with Brad's wetsuit.

"I'm going out on the water."

"I thought you were quitting to join the girls on the stage at Hiatus."

Brad pinches the Marlboro between his thumb and index finger, gyrating his hips. I laugh lightly, happy to see the Brad we know and love, as he takes the wetsuit, flicks his cigarette away, and turns away from us, walking off in his boxers, giving everyone in the café an eyeful of his sharp physique.

And the red, angry scratches all over his back. *Jesus.* "I think he's cured," I murmur. "His back's nearly as gross as yours." I look at James. He doesn't retaliate.

"Ready for the water?" he asks.

I check my watch. God damn it, I've missed my opportunity. "Nope. I have a meeting."

James's face is a picture of indignation. "With whom?"

I get up, scoop my Marlboros off the table, and walk away from him. "Beau."

"What?"

I smile as a few clatters and bangs ring around the terrace, a sign of James getting up from his chair quickly. "Your wife owns Winstable," I say over my shoulder. "And I'm going to buy it from her." It'll be back in the family—the original boatyard. I'm smiling when I hear Otto and Goldie's collective curses.

"Why the hell don't I know about this?" James asks, as I join Brad on the steps, getting a closer look at the red marks decorating his back. And his arms too. *Ouch.*

"That's some damage you've got there," I say, ignoring James.

"What?" Brad frowns, his wetsuit halfway up his body.

"Your back. Your arms."

"Danny," James presses, putting himself between us, unimpressed and uninterested in Brad's war wounds. "Why the fuck didn't I know about it?"

"It's between me and Beau."

"Fuck that. I should have known."

"From me or Beau?"

"Both of you."

Brad bats his eyes between us, interested, almost goading. "Are we getting on the waves today or are you two bitches gonna carry on bitching over your bitches?"

We turn to Brad, both of us ready to rip his head off. Until we see there's no need. Absolutely no need at all. I feel a smile pull at the corners of my mouth as the dumb fuck gets his arms into his wetsuit with a shit-eating grin plastered all over his face. Something tells me this is a show. Don't tell me that with the addition of a few vicious fingernails he's cured and his winning, irritating-as-fuck personality is back. I'm not buying it. But, whatever. He's about to have his arse handed to him on a plate.

Brad looks between us, his smile slowly falling, and I follow James's lead, folding my arms over my chest.

"What?" he asks.

I help him out, nodding my head in indication.

He looks over his shoulder. "Oh."

"Bitches?" Beau asks.

"Bitches?" Rose mimics, disgusted.

My eyes bounce back and forth between Brad and the girls, James's too, both of us amused. Beau moves in, and I see James's body engage. "Beau," he warns, but he's too late. She dips, spins, and swipes Brad's feet from beneath him, sending him to his back on a wince-worthy thud.

"Fuck," Brad gasps, winded, as Rose cackles and James shakes his head, annoyed but satisfied.

Beau moves in and stands over him, her jaw rolling. "Who was in your room this morning?"

"Fuck off." He gets to his feet and grimaces. "What the hell are you doing? You can't be going all Lara in your condition."

James grunts his agreement, his grievance with Brad now redirected at his wife. She rolls her eyes. Worse thing she could do. "I'm fine."

"I'm taking you home," James declares, taking her elbow.

"I can't go home." She wriggles out of his hold. "I have a meeting with The Brit." She looks at Brad. "And you."

I'm falling apart on the inside. Until something occurs to me. I find Rose. "What are *you* doing here?"

My wife, God love the front on that woman, raises her nose, a certain edge of superiority emerging I'm sure I don't like. "I'm here in an official capacity."

"What?"

"I'm Beau's advisor." She swans past, pulling out a note pad. A fucking note pad. "Where's the meeting being held?"

"In a torture chamber," I growl. Brad's now the one laughing. *Wanker.* "Why'd you bring her?" I ask Beau as I look back at Rose. "And where's our baby?"

"With her grandmother."

"Oh, so it's okay for *her* to pull in resources, but not me?"

"Quit bitching." Beau smiles and passes, looking James up and down. "Are you going out on the water?"

He starts wrestling his arms back out of the wetsuit, going after her. "No, I'm joining this fucking meeting."

"Yes, you are." I narrow my eyes on my wife's back before casting them over to Beau. "Since you have a wingman, I'll take one too."

"You already have Brad," she calls back.

"For what fucking use he is," I mutter, trudging after the girls, frowning down at my bare chest. I feel the need for a suit all of a sudden. This was supposed to be a relaxed, straight-forward meeting, and something tells me I'm going to be sorely disappointed. "So I'm taking The Enigma," I add to myself, entering the café and seeing Rose setting up a table in the far corner. Three chairs on one side, two on the other. I smile on the inside, not the outside, at her breasts forcing against the material of her blouse. *Fuck.* My restrained dick twitches. Not ideal when she's off limits. Jesus Christ, how much longer do I need to abstain? My balls are ready to burst.

I gather myself and lower to a chair slowly, eyes on Rose as she fixes a pile of papers. What the fuck is she doing? So she wants to play business? Let's do it.

She peeks up at me. I raise my brow. She wants to smile. Won't. She looks so fucking hot. "Okay?" I ask as she shifts in her chair.

"Never better."

Good. So she'll let me fuck her later. "You look a little . . ." I lick my lips, and her eyes follow my tongue. "Flustered."

"Focus," Beau says as she takes a seat next to Rose.

"Right, yes." Rose rips her eyes away from me and realigns her attention on the paperwork, as Brad and James take up their seats on either side of me. The girls on one side of the table, the boys on the other. Beau clears her throat, peeking at James. He does *not* look happy.

"Come on, then," Brad presses. "My jet ski's waiting for me."

"We're just waiting for one more person," Beau says, looking across the café. "Oh, here she is." She gets up and pulls another chair over, and all three of our heads turn toward the door as Pearl hurries across the café. But she comes to a startled—very fucking suspicious—stop when she clocks Brad at the table. Her face is full of horror. Her disposition awkward as fuck. Brad's jaw is tight, his earlier light and breezy mood turning to dust. Doesn't matter that it was feigned. He clearly can't keep it up in front of Pearl.

Pearl corrects herself and forces a smile as she walks calmly over and lowers quietly to the seat. "Sorry, that took longer than I expected," she says, taking something out of her bag, a file, and sliding it across the table to Rose.

"What did?" I ask, eyes on that file.

"What the hell is going on?" James growls.

"So." Beau straightens her shoulders. "As you know, Jaz's estate has been dismissed from the investigation and I'm now free to sell off her assets."

Emphasis on *Jaz*. She refuses to accept that woman, The Bear, was her mother.

"No, I didn't know that," James snaps, "because you haven't fucking told me." He snatches a bottle of water off the table and glugs it down.

Beau ignores him. "And Winstable is now for sale."

"And my offer of fifteen million is on the table," I say slowly, my eyes constantly passing between the three women. I don't like this. It feels scarily like an ambush.

Beau nods. "A very generous offer."

"I agree," I say, resting my stare on my wife, certain I don't like the look on her face. It's between smugness and nervousness. "Advisor?" I ask.

Her lips twitch. "And competition."

"What?"

"Rose has offered twenty million," Beau says, making James and Brad cough and me twitch.

I glare at Rose. "What the fuck are you playing at?"

"I'm extending my business portfolio."

"With *my* fucking money?"

"But, darling." She smiles. "It's *my* money, remember?"

"Jesus Christ," Brad breathes.

Fuck this. I give my attention to Beau, hoping she sees the threat in my expression. Wasted threat. "I'll give you thirty." The club is bursting at the seams with cash. *Fuck you, Rose.* She thinks she has me backed into a corner? She better think again.

Beau shakes her head. "This has to be a legit sale."

"And you only have dirty cash," Rose pipes up.

My fist balls and slams onto the table. "Don't push me, baby. Why the fuck do you want Winstable? It's acres of barren land with a fucking hangar in the middle of it."

"Like I said, I'm extending my business portfolio." Her lips press together. "It'll be a beach club."

"What?"

"Yes, what?" Brad asks. James, however, remains quiet, sulking.

"A beach club. Cabanas, jetties, cocktails, music. Pearl will run the bar, Beau will—"

"*Not* be involved," James snaps, incensed.

"I'm being employed on a consultation basis," Beau says.

"Are you now?"

"Yes."

Brad leans forward, eyes precisely held on Rose. "And you think you're poaching my staff?"

"Pearl was going to work at the spa anyway," Rose says over a laugh. "Stop being petty."

"I didn't approve her move to the spa. I need her at the club."

"I've quit," Pearl says quietly, and Brad recoils like he's been shot.

"Since when?" he asks.

Pearl bites at her lip piercing, nervous. "Since I gave Mason my notice an hour ago."

"Your notice should come to me."

"Right," Pearl breathes, tucking her hair behind her ear. "Then please accept this as my official resignation."

Poor Brad looks like he's been stung. He should be accepting keenly. She'll be out of his way, and I know he wants that. "I don't need notice. You're fired."

For fuck's sake. He sounds like a brat.

"Great." Pearl shrugs. "Either works for me."

I get us back to the matter at hand, giving my wife daggers. "Rose, there's no beach there."

"Oh, I know, darling." Every time her smile stretches that little bit more, my snarl does too. She's got an answer for every-fucking-thing, and I know she has a solution for that too. "We'll make one. Pearl has found an amazing company that creates beautiful, golden *sandy* beaches."

I turn my glare onto Pearl, and she wilts a little, smiling in apology. "They worked on the Palms in Dubai," she says quietly. "Apparently."

"Handy," I mutter. A fucking beach club? It's not even what she's making it, more that she's exacting power, and I'm not at all comfortable with Rose galivanting off around town, especially now.

"So thank you for your offer, Danny," Beau says, standing, "but I will graciously decline."

"How good of you." I look at James. "This is *not* acceptable."

He ignores me, his attention on Beau, quietly seething. "We're married. We're supposed to discuss things."

Planting her hands on the table, she leans in. "Let's discuss why we can't go on our honeymoon."

James's big body wilts in the chair, while I heave in mine, furious. Rose stands and gathers her things, stuffing them into her handbag. "Excuse me, I have to check on the spa." She breezes off, and I'm up fast, going after her.

I rest my palm on her neck from behind, walking with her, squeezing threateningly.

"You don't scare me, Danny Black."

I laugh at the irony, because she fucking terrifies me. "You'll be punished for this." I slide my hand into her hair and clench a fistful and, true to my wife, she jars her head, forcing the pull.

"Can't wait."

"Tomorrow night, we're going out." I've got to tell her about Sandy to be graced with her compliance. I'm not looking forward to it, expecting fireworks.

But bottom line, the girls' freedom is going to be curbed again, and that's going to go down as well as a pot of puke.

Chapter 12

Brad

Rose leaves, Danny leaves, Beau leaves, and James leaves. I, however, can't move. Every muscle's tense, my fists are balling on the table, and my jaw's about to snap. She quit. I should be thrilled. Especially considering her accidental revelation. A fucking virgin. *How?*

My back stings, my shoulder blades pulling in to try and curb it. Curb the reminder of being buried inside her. The quietness, the calm, the stillness in that moment. Every minute of my life has been full throttle. Fast paced. From work to bed. *In* bed too. Hard, fast, and furious. With Pearl, there was an undercurrent of concord I never knew I needed and, fuck my life, I understood for a brief moment why Danny and James yielded to their women. The release of pressure. The escape. The appreciation and adoration for a strong woman.

Fuck.

Pearl reaches for her hair and tucks it behind her ear, and I watch, mentally yelling at myself not to. But her delicate fingers. The creaminess of her flesh against the vivid red of her hair. Those intense green eyes.

I wrench my stare away and frantically search for something to focus on, unable to do what I need to do and leave the table. My legs are rigid. I find a bottle of water and snatch it up, guzzling it down. Parched. The atmosphere is thick. Worse than it ever was. I watch the lid of the bottle as I slowly screw it on, working on convincing myself to stand. I can't, and the longer I sit here, I get more and more worked up, wishing Pearl would do what I can't seem to do.

Leave.

I'm a glutton. I must be, because I look at her. She's writing on the file, appearing relaxed, comfortable, oblivious to my presence. It stokes the frustration. "You should have told me."

Her writing hand stills, her eyes remaining on the file. "Why?" She doesn't look up.

"You owed me that."

Laughing sardonically under her breath, she clicks the end of the pen. And then she looks up. Worst thing she could do. "You want an explanation?" she asks. "Maybe *I* want one."

"What the fuck for?"

"For saving my life and for being a complete arsehole since you did."

She does *not* want an explanation for that. But does she really fucking need one after last night? *Fuck this.* "A man should know if he's a woman's first."

Her head cocks in interest. "So they can be gentle?" she asks, resting the pen down and her body back in the chair.

"No, so they can bail."

She flinches but tries to hide it. And then she laughs again. I can't blame her. Nothing would have stopped me in that moment, but I'll never admit it. "I'm sorry I didn't tell you," she says, placid and calm, like she truly means it, then gathers the file and stands. My eyes lift with her. "Let's just forget it ever happened."

I choke on my cough of disbelief. Forget? Not fucking likely. "Shouldn't be too hard," I mutter like a jerk, and she appears injured for a moment. I hate myself for it, but it's for the best. Once was a mistake. Twice? Fucked up. "And since I've fired you, we don't have to endure each other at work." Listen to me. Just fucking listen to me.

I expect a fully deserved slap, any kind of retaliation. I get nothing. Just a smile as she inhales long and steadily. I hate how together she is. How unaffected. How fucking *mature.* "Excuse me." She turns and weaves her way through the tables.

Just like that.

Done.

Gone.

Fuck.

I wanted a slap. Anything to show she cares. It's fucked up on so many levels, because a cavalier Pearl is the best outcome. Did she use me? And if so, why the fuck do *I* care? But I do care. I really fucking care that she appears indifferent. Calm. I can't stop fucking thinking about her.

That's your problem, Brad. Not hers.

I'm out of my chair fast, going after her. I'm not done. She fucking used me?

I barge into the female changing rooms and am greeted by a collection of shocked gasps, a couple of women scrambling to cover their chests with towels or clothes, whatever they can lay their hands on. But I don't turn away. I don't leave. Pearl's halfway to getting her tank off, revealing her black bra, and her denim shorts are undone, showing a flash of her black panties. She looks between me and the other two women as she slowly continues pulling her tank up over her head. Her hair gets caught up in the material, falling down and swishing around her face. "Brad?" she questions, dropping it to the bench.

The other two women appear frozen. Shocked? Awed? Both? I can't speak, so I flash them a look that tells them it's time to leave before I turn away and give them some privacy to dress, at the same time scrubbing a hand down my face, willing myself to leave too. I hear the door open and close.

And my skin prickles. My cock throbs. "The fuck?" I breathe to myself.

"Pardon?"

Leave.

Leave, leave, leave.

"Nothing." I face her. *Do. Not. Look. At. Her. Chest.*

"Do you want something?" she asks, sliding her hands into the tops of her shorts.

I blink, looking away from that too. Do I want something? I laugh on the inside. *Oh Pearl, do not ask me stupid fucking questions.* I need to pull this back before I confirm beyond all doubt that I'm fucked up. "This stays between us," I say, closing my eyes to escape the sight of her pushing her shorts down her shapely legs.

"Do you think I'm going to call a sleepover with all of my girlfriends and talk about how good of a kisser you are?" she asks. "Tell them every detail of my first time and giggle while I do?"

My teeth clench as I lift my eyes but not my head. "I don't need your sarcasm, Pearl."

"Then what do you need?" she asks as she reaches behind her and unfastens her bra. It pings and falls away from her chest, the straps hanging from the crook of her arms.

"I need you to stop fucking undressing," I grate.

"Why?" It falls to the floor.

"Pearl," I warn, clearing my throat, forcing my eyes away from her tits—and my body to turn—while I beg my dick to pipe down. "What the hell are you doing?"

"Me?" she asks. "I'm getting ready to go out on the water. What are *you* doing, Brad?"

Dying on the inside.

But—

Wait.

She's never been out on the water.

I turn and find her panties around her ankles. "Jesus Christ, Pearl," I blurt, slapping a hand over my eyes.

"What?" She laughs. "I haven't got time to wait around for you to decide what the hell you're doing in here. Leon's waiting for me."

Leon? My back straightens. Hot, surfer dude, pot smoking, *younger* Leon? "Are you decent?" I ask, getting a bit hot.

"No."

I turn anyway, inhaling when I find her still gloriously naked. I'm going to hell. "You've never been out on the water before," I point out.

Her green eyes sparkle excitedly, her smile demure but small. "It seems to be a standard skill to have around here, so I thought I'd better pull my finger out and learn."

So she's asked Leon to teach her? No one knows a jet ski like I do around here. Maybe Danny does, but that's not the point. The point is, she's a newbie and Leon is . . . young. Which means his *young* arms will be wrapped around her *young* body and *that's* fucking acceptable.

Except it isn't.

In fact, it's really fucking *un*acceptable.

Pearl turns toward the wetsuit hanging on the locker, giving me her ass. A sweat breaks across my brow. Perfect, pert. *Young.* I groan under my breath when she reaches up on tiptoes to unhook it from the hanger, every piece of her becoming taut.

Along with my cock.

She pulls some bikini bottoms on and then sits on the bench, getting the wetsuit at her feet. "Are we done?" she asks, feeding her legs through, looking up through a veil of red hair that's fallen over her face.

I don't have a chance to answer. The door knocks and opens immediately, and Leon appears.

"B-Boss?" he says in question.

My mouth falls open, astounded. Is he for real? I look over my shoulder to Pearl. My half-*naked* Pearl. "What's the point in fucking knocking if you're gonna walk right in?" He's obviously picking up bad habits from Beau. "Anyone could have been in here." I walk forward and push a palm into his chest, forcing him out.

"I saw Pearl go in and the other ladies leave," Leon says, laughing nervously. I don't like it. His nerves. "I didn't see you go in," he goes on, craning his neck to look past me to Pearl. I look back too. She's standing now, pulling the wetsuit up her body, her tits out and proud. *What the fuck?*

"Out," I hiss, shoving him through the door and slamming it. So he came in here thinking she was alone? And . . . what then? I shouldn't care.

Problem is, I fucking do. I really fucking do.

My fist bunches, and I push it into the wood to stop myself from punching the door. "Are you decent?" I ask through my teeth, refusing to give my eyes what they want.

"I'm decent," she confirms quietly, so I slowly face her, just as the zip of her wetsuit passes her breastbone. I smile, unable to stop myself. "What?" she asks, looking down her front. "What did I do?"

"It's back to front," I tell her, waving a finger up and down her body. "The zipper should be at the back."

Her frown is huge. "Oh." Then she proceeds to pull it down again, and I realize I've just completely fucked myself over.

"Pearl, wait," I say, holding a halting hand up, making her pause midway to wriggling her arms out.

"I'm waiting," she says. "But what for?"

"For me to leave."

"Then leave," she says, easy as that, as if it *is* as easy as that.

"I'm fucking trying. Really trying, Pearl."

"But you can't?"

Fuck. "Did you use me?" I blurt.

"Use you?"

"To . . ." I can't say it. "To . . ." So I stutter and stammer all over my words. I'm a grown fucking man, for Christ's sake. Listen to me.

"To get the matter of my virginity out of the way?" she asks in utter disbelief. "Yes, Brad. I did that." Her nostrils flare, all light and breezy leaving the building. "I used you." She's mad. Good. I'm with her. "Now can you just fuck off so I can take this fucking thing off and put it on the right fucking way?"

I flinch, wince, and cringe. Her English accent makes swearing sound proper. It still sounds awful on her, though. "Will you stop cussing?"

"No!" she snaps petulantly, her face becoming red.

Knock, knock, knock.

"What?" we both yell in unison at the door.

"Umm, I have another lesson in an hour," Leon calls through the wood. "Just sayin'."

"I'm coming," Pearl calls, pushing the wetsuit to her feet. "Just give me a second." She wrestles her legs out of the rubber, and I'm back to square one. Dizzy. Cross-eyed. Dumping her ass on the bench, she flips the wetsuit and stuffs her feet in the leg holes again. "I don't mean to inflate your ego, Brad Black, but if I was going to use a man to be rid of my virginity, I'd pick one that's not a murdering arsehole who likes hookers, cocaine, and who *doesn't* have a cock that's likely to split me in half."

I blink. "Excuse me?"

"Just fuck off, Brad."

I growl and stomp over, pulling her to her feet, getting up in her face. "Do I need to wash your mouth out with soap?"

She pushes her forehead to mine. "What are you, my—"

I stop her before she can finish, slamming my mouth onto hers and swallowing down the words I don't want to hear. And she's in the game with me, now seemingly unbothered by my old habits and big cock, kissing me ferociously, whimpering, her naked boobs pushing into my chest. My fists are in her hair, the burn inside is being dowsed and cooled. *Jesus Christ.*

I. Am. Fucked.

"No," she gasps, pulling away. "No, I can't do this."

What? "Why?" I gasp, breathless.

"Because it's wrong," she grates, shoving me back. "Because you're—"

"I'm what?" *Old?*

"You!" she yells, high-pitched, laughing, hurrying into her wetsuit. "You're you, Brad, and I'm just me." Getting her arms into the sleeves, she squirms around, straightening the material. "Young, stupid, and naïve." She walks away, leaving me standing dumbstruck, my lips sore, as she feels around behind her for the zip, muttering her frustration. "This is stupid. The front was easier."

I'm . . . *me.*

Hookers. Cocaine. A killer.

The American.

Thirty-five.

A heartbreaker.

Old.

I sigh, exhausted by myself, and approach her, resting my hands on her shoulders. She stills. "Let me." I reach for the pull and tug it up halfway before taking her hand and leading it to the fastener so she can do it herself, hiding the bare skin of her back from me. It's for the best. "You'll get the hang of it."

And I hope I get the hang of resistance too. It's not my place to teach her . . . anything. Not to jet ski, not to . . . what? Fuck? "Be careful on the water." I pass her and leave, keeping my eyes off Leon, who's waiting outside, afraid he might see the threat in my eyes. *Keep your hands off her.* But I know a young lad like Leon is the best option for Pearl.

And undoubtedly for me too.

I make my way to the end of the jetty, not now bothered for the water. I can see James and Danny in the distance, The Brit and The Enigma riding at each other, spinning, spraying. Being total fucking kids. I need that too. Respite from—

Fuck . . . me.

Respite from the trials and tribulations of a woman.

I lower to the wood and hang my legs off the end, lighting up, squinting at the sunlight bouncing off the water as I breathe in steadily. I'm all good. Thinking reasonably. I'm helped along the path of rationality when my cell rings.

"Allison." I say her name on the exhale of smoke, nipping at a flake of tobacco on my lip and flicking it away.

"You stood me up."

"Something came up." I watch as James races toward me,

standing, his conviction obvious. I don't move. I'm a sitting duck. He turns at the last minute, sending a fan of water into the air, drenching me. "You fucker," I mutter, shaking the wet from my hair.

Allison laughs down the line. "Charming."

"Not you." I hold up my smoke. The flame's been extinguished. If only. And then the soggy stick slowly starts to droop, flopping down. I laugh at the irony. Yeah. *If only.* "You free later?" I ask.

"Depends. Are you going to show up this time?"

"Yeah, I'll show up."

"Good. I missed you."

I frown. She missed me while I fucked a girl in her place, and then kept her in my bed. All fucking night. *Not* missing Allison. "Eight o'clock. Four Seasons." I hang up and drop my useless cigarette into the sea as James chugs past, now sitting in the seat.

"Come on, Brad." His eyes say things his mouth never will. He knows. Danny knows. "Come out on the water."

I nod, raking a hand through my wet hair. "I thought you'd have marched Beau home."

He laughs. "How's your back?" he asks, reminding me that no one tells Beau what to do. Or Rose, these days. Somehow, I think that might change imminently.

I roll my shoulders and get a sharp reminder of Pearl's fingernails scraping at my flesh. "Letting her enjoy her freedom before lockdown?"

He smirks. "She knows it's coming."

"Did you tell her?"

His eyebrows rise, and he pulls his shades down from his head, covering his eyes. He doesn't need to answer. Of course he didn't tell her. Beau's an ex-cop, has retained that sixth sense, and we all need to remember that. James rarely needs to tell her trouble's afoot. She just knows. "Come on." He races away, and Danny falls into the stream behind him, both heading out of the bay area. That's what I need. Chaos on the water instead of in my head. Danger on the waves. The taste of salt on my tongue to rid the lingering taste of Pearl's pussy, the ear-piercing roar of the engine drowning out my thoughts and her moans. The smell of the ocean instead of lavender.

And then a good fuck with Allison. And it would be really fucking handy if Otto came up with some names so I can put a bullet in someone. That should sort me out. "And these are a few of my favorite things," I sing to myself as I walk back up the jetty, slowing to a stop when I see Leon sitting on a jet ski, Pearl behind him, pushed close into his back. She's laughing. Leon looks like a pig in shit. I divert my eyes to the wood beneath my bare feet. Out of sight, out of mind. But not out of earshot.

"Hold tight," Leon says, and I look up as Jerry pushes them away from the shore.

"I'm holding." Pearl rests her cheek on his back. Arms around his waist. Thighs squeezing his ass. *Breathe. Keep walking.*

"I mean, you don't need to hold *that* tight," Leon says over his laugh. "But I'll take it."

"Sorry."

"Don't be sorry. I like it."

Pearl smiles, but it falls when she finds me on the jetty. She quickly looks away. Tenses. I see every bit of her body tighten, which means her hold of Leon does too.

And the look on his face?

Yeah, I'm not okay with that.

"Get off," I say before I can stop myself, hopping off the jetty into the shallow water. "Now."

Pearl's eyes widen, and Leon looks this way, frowning. "B-Boss?" he questions, his forehead bunched.

"It's too choppy out there to take a beginner." I take Pearl's arms and physically remove them from around Leon's waist as the poor kid looks between the lunatic jostling Pearl, and the very still ocean. Pearl is momentarily stunned. Quiet. My head is screaming.

Stop.

"What the bloody hell are you doing?" she asks as I lift her off the jet ski and place her on her feet.

"I told you, it's too choppy out there. Dangerous."

She looks down at the calm water lapping our ankles. "I actually think it's more dangerous on dry land." Lifting her head, she searches my eyes as I gaze into hers, spellbound. "It's okay, Leon," she says, eyes not leaving mine. "Another day."

"Sure." He sounds disappointed, but I hear the jet ski pull away.

"What are you doing, Brad?" she asks calmly.

"I don't know," I admit through my gritted teeth. "But I can't seem to stop fucking doing it."

"You mean hassling me?"

I snort, taking her arm and manhandling her around the back of a container, out of sight. "Get the hell off me," she snaps, wrenching her arm out of my grip.

"Did. You. Use. Me?"

She comes close, head tilted back to look up at me. "Yes. I used you. And now it's done, so you don't have to worry about me becoming all needy or falling in love with you." A condemning sneer curls her lip. "I actually think you're unlovable. Or perhaps one of your hookers will fall. Or a whore. But never me."

"You're not a whore?"

"I don't think you can call a virgin a whore."

"But you're not a virgin anymore."

"You bastard," she hisses.

I don't see it coming. The fist. But boy do I feel it. The crunching sound of my nose rings in my ears and my eyes burst with water. "Fuck," I breathe, bending, blinking, watching the blood drip down onto the ground in fat, heavy drops.

"Oh shit," Pearl whispers.

I brace my hands on my knees and look up at her, my nose streaming. I see regret. It's not a consolation, because I don't want her to be sorry. I don't want her to apologize. Feel remorse. And as if she's read me, she steps back, her shoulders straightening in an act of strength. Resilience. Where the fuck did she learn to swing like that?

"Ouch," I say flatly, making her lips press together. Is she restraining a laugh? God help me, I want to strangle her. *Better than wanting to fuck her.* There aren't many people in the world who would get away with socking me one to the face. Lucky for Pearl, I deserved it.

And then she delivers a fatal blow. "I'm sorry," she whispers.

No. I shake my head and wipe my face with the sleeve of my wet suit, wrinkling my nose on a hiss of pain. *Motherfucker.* "Just stay away from me."

"You pulled me off the jet ski," she blurts, half laughing, half outraged. "I was looking forward to my lesson."

"He wants you," I yell, startling both of us.

She backs up. "And that's a problem?"

"Yes! No!" *Fuck!*

"Oh, I can't deal with you." She pivots and walks off, patting at her neck, feeling for the cord.

"Do *not* take that off out here," I warn, mentally seeing her naked body beneath.

"Fuck off." She finds the pull and yanks it down, revealing her bare back.

"Pearl!"

Her arms come out next. What the fuck is she doing? I find myself going after her, disgusted, and jostling her to face me, squishing her to my front. "Get off me," she protests, as I scan the area around us for watching eyes. Lucky for me, and not just because Pearl's half naked, there's no one around.

"Now you're just being ridiculous." I lift her from her feet and walk her around the container, back into the cabin, sniffing back the flowing blood. I back into the changing room and release her. "You can't walk around flaunting yourself, Pearl. It's beneath you." I've seen endless women using their assets as a weapon. Pearl isn't one of them, and I won't let her be.

"I can do whatever the hell I want."

"Not on my watch," I growl, bending to make sure she sees the unbridled rage, wiping my still-bleeding nose. "If you're in this family, you do as you're damn well told, no questions asked."

"Fuck off."

"I'd love to, but unfortunately for both of us, neither of us are going anywhere." Except me. To hell.

Her eyes drop to my lips.

I see it in the heated depths immediately. Intention. We stare, breathe—a mix of anger and desire. And both move at the same time, our mouths coming together fast and hard, lips clashing, tongues thrashing. I push her into the lockers, slamming a door loudly, the sound of metal crashing together deafening. Grabbing her thigh under her ass, I pull her leg up to my hip, kissing her like some kind of depraved crazy man.

"I didn't use you," she says around my mouth, going at me hell for leather.

"Don't say that," I warn, grabbing a breast, squeezing. "Fuck, don't say that."

"Why?"

What are you, my—

I wrench myself away, panting, looking down at one of my hands on her boob, another on the back of her thigh. *What am I doing?* No. Not again. I drop her and move back, resisting the pull. I need to get my kicks elsewhere. Relieve the pressure by other means. Means that won't fuck with my conscience.

Leave.

I avoid her eyes and stalk out the changing room to seek solace somewhere else, and with *someone* else.

I fall into my car. Stare at the windshield.

Jump out of my fucking skin when someone raps on the window.

Danny's murderous face is pushed up against the glass. "Otto found some info on the Escalade outside Hiatus."

I lower the window, seeing James pacing behind. His persona tells me he's already privy to this information. And I definitely do not like his thoughtful, scowling face. "What?"

"It's registered to a Johnathan Dresden."

"Who the fuck is Johnathon Dresden?"

"An ex-cop."

"Say what?"

"Living in Lake Harbor."

I get out of my car. "That's a bit far, isn't it? To swing by for a drive-by?"

Danny frowns. "What the fuck happened to your nose?"

"I walked into a locker." I wipe it again. "So you're telling me an ex-cop tried to kill me?"

"I'm telling you what I know," Otto says. "And I know that vehicle is registered to a retired cop. Johnathon Dresden."

"And what are we going to do about this?" *Please say kill.*

"We think, that's what. No guns blazing." Danny laughs at the irony of that statement. "For once. Who the fuck was in your bed this morning?"

"Fuck off." What's with the twenty fucking questions?

"Te—" His phone rings, and he looks down at the screen briefly before returning his attention to me. "Tell m—" A frown. Another look at his phone. Then he holds it up, and James moves in too, both of us looking at the screen flashing.

I don't like the sudden tension. Danny answers, holding his cell between us. Doesn't speak.

The Russian accent has each one of us scowling.

"You killed my men."

Danny's eyes are instantly insane. "You raped my wife."

Sandy laughs. "Oh, it's coming back to me now. She was good. A nice, *tight* pussy."

Jesus fucking Christ. Rose was a child. Fourteen. Probably a *virgin.* I step back, out of the range of the imminent explosion, nervous. Fuck, Sandy does *not* want to play that game.

The evil I know and only sometimes love spreads across Danny's face, deepening his scar, his knuckles turning white around the phone. "I'll find you, Sandy. And torture you until you squeal for your momma."

He chuckles, enjoying himself, and the line goes dead. I quickly pry the cell from Danny's hand before it crumbles, taking his shoulder, massaging, working him down. "You gotta keep it together, Danny."

He moves away from my touch, his eyes fucking crazy, and stalks toward the water, wrestling his wetsuit up his arms. He's going out on his jet ski. It's probably best. It's open space, the chances of someone getting in his way small. "Fucking hell."

"He needs to tell Rose." James follows our loose cannon, pulling a stressed hand through his hair as he goes.

I pace after them, feeling the pressure inside building. I can't even appreciate the distraction. It's all too fucking messy.

"Hey, B-Boss," Leon says, falling into stride beside me.

"What?"

"So Pearl mentioned she's quit the club."

Eyes still on Danny's stalking form as he wades into the water toward his jet ski, I slow to a stop, feeling that pressure heightening. "And?"

"Well"—he kicks his beaten converse, shifting nervously—"we can always do with a few extra hands around here."

I fucking bet. My throat is tight and my skin prickles. I look over my shoulder, feeling her eyes on me. She's in a bikini. I look away. "You're welcome to her." I march on through a group of men getting ready to go out on the water, arms everywhere as they pull their wetsuits up. One of them catches my shoulder.

"Watch it, you jerk," he says, hostile.

I stop.

Turn my eyes onto him. He must realize who he's giving lip to, because he backs up. He has a red flame logo on his wetsuit.

Red.

I can still feel her watching me. I close my eyes. *Breathe.* Feel her nails in my back. *Breathe.*

The pressure pot that is my head releases, and I swing, putting the mouthy fucker on his ass. He hits the deck with a thud.

I feel no better. The pressure hasn't released. "Fuck!" I yell, seeing the same red flame on a nearby jet ski. I snarl at it and search the vicinity. There's a hammer on a nearby rock along with a bunch of other tools. I swipe it up.

"Brad," James warns, coming back toward me.

"Fuck off." I swing and smash into the front of the jet ski, putting a hole through the bow. And I don't stop there, pulling back and swinging, taking off the throttle, hitting the handlebar. I roar, smashing into the side panel, hole after hole, destroying the machine and yelling my way through it.

By the time I'm done, it's in pieces, some of it floating away, the crowd behind me silent. I'm sweating. Heaving. I drop the hammer and look down at the water around my feet. Then slowly drag my eyes to my right.

Pearl backs up, folding her arms over her chest, and turns, walking away.

The sun hits her hair and fires shards of light this way.

Blinding me.

Fucking. Red.

Chapter 13

ROSE

We're in the kitchen, it's quiet, and Esther has set up all the breakfast things as per usual. I sip my coffee. "Sleek." I smile down at the mood board as Beau tweaks a few pictures. The ideas we have, the excitement inside. It's a big project but God, it'll be amazing when it's finished. The go-to destination in Miami. I feel so incredibly excited, a new zest for life—a life with no constraints—blooming. An enthusiasm for business. I know my husband thinks I should be at home playing mom, and I absolutely will, but I need a purpose beyond that. I've never earned my own money. I went from being abused to being worshipped. But always kept. This new power I feel? I love it. I want more. Besides, it'll take a few years to achieve this vision, so my husband has nothing to worry about. I'll be the mom both he and I want me to be. Maggie will be starting kindergarten before we know it, and then what? I sit around this big mansion waiting for school drop-offs and pick-ups? Wait for my husband to get home from *work*? No. "Do you think they'll approve the plans?"

Beau pouts at her design. "We could talk to the mayor," she says, looking up with a crafty smile. "No bribing, just a friendly chat."

"Monroe Metcalfe doesn't look like the kind of man who could be bribed anyway."

"Which means our boys have less chance of messing this up for us."

I hum. "But they could threaten death. Blackmail him." And I bet they'll try, if only to get the power back. For God's sake, they have Byron's Reach. They don't need more land for their jet ski/gun business, especially now that there are no enemies.

We both look up when Anya walks into the kitchen, her face lighting up when she spots the plans on the island.

"Come see," I say, waving her over. "This will be the restaurant area, here's the beach loungers, with waiter service, of course, and this here is the massage emporium." I smile down at the drawings.

"I can't wait." Anya jumps on a stool and pulls the papers closer. "I was thinking of taking an aromather . . . arom . . . aromat . . ."

"Aromatherapy," Beau says, smiling.

"Yes!" She beams at us before going back to the plans. "I can work at the club at nighttime, and at the beach club in the daytime."

"You can tell Brad," I mumble out the corner of my mouth for only Beau to hear.

"What?" Anya asks, looking up.

"Nothing." I smile and collect my breast pump off the table, pulling down the strap on my tank and unclipping my bra as I check the baby monitor, seeing Maggie sound asleep in her crib. "Where's Pearl?" I ask, attaching the pump to my aching boob. "I want her to see these."

"She's upstairs. She's . . . quiet."

Beau and I both caught the stench of tension at our *meeting* when she walked in. Brad looked like he was about burst a blood vessel. "Quiet," I muse, exhaling my relief when the pressure subsides in my boob. Anya gives us a telling look. She's sensed it too. I don't know about the men. They were so busy focusing their fury on us and our intended transformation of Winstable to notice much else. Since Danny told Pearl about Brad's hooker and cocaine binge, the dreadful atmosphere that fell every time they were in each other's orbit got worse.

"Maybe she found out about the woman Brad had in his room the other night," Beau says.

I don't know if I should be happy his attention is focused elsewhere. And perhaps that really is why Pearl is quiet. Upset? God, this isn't good. "We need to set Pearl up with someone." Someone her own age. Someone who isn't guaranteed to fuck her up, because that's Brad. She's been through enough—her parents' murders, being taken to be sold.

"We might not need to." Beau wriggles her eyebrows and goes to Anya, pushing a lock of her long, dark hair out of her eye. She smiles her thanks. "Leon's got his eye on her."

I gasp, jerking, and as a result my breast pump disconnects from my boob. "Fuck." Milk dribbles down my tank as I reattach it. "Leon?" I ask.

"Leon?" Anya parrots. "He doesn't seem Pearl's . . ." She pouts, thinking.

"Type?" Beau prompts, pulling a jug from the fridge.

"Yes, type."

"Well." I laugh. "A killer wasn't my type until he kidnapped me."

Beau snorts. "And an assassin wasn't mine until he . . ." She darts her eyes, a little red in the face. "Never mind."

I chuckle, amused, as Anya's eyes widen. They'd fall out of her head if Beau finished. I know exactly what happened between Beau and James. It involved restraints. And her ass.

"What's your type, Anya?" I ask, relieving Beau of the attention.

"My type?"

"Yes, who w—" I stop, my brain reminding me that whatever happened to Anya in her past life means she wanted to stay here with us rather than go home like the rest of the girls. The rest, except Pearl too. "Shit, I'm sorry."

She waves a hand, dismissing my apology. "It is okay." She comes to me, smiling. "I need to take a shower."

"Okay."

She drops a kiss on my cheek then Beau's before leaving, and we watch her go, both of us thoughtful. "I can't help but wonder," I say.

"Me neither."

"About what?" Esther asks, coming in with hands full of laundry.

"The girls," I answer, perching on a stool and checking the expressing situation. "Where they've come from, what they've been through." Does it matter? They're both thriving here. Well, Anya's thriving. It would be fair to say Pearl's struggling. But perhaps Leon can fix that. "You need to give that goofball some wooing advice," I say to Beau.

"Yeah, when he's not stoned I might try."

"Leon?" Esther says, dropping the pile by the laundry room door.

"How'd you guess?"

Esther comes to the island and rests her elbows on the marble, looking between me and Beau.

"What?" I ask.

"What?" Beau mimics.

"I sense unrest," Esther says, and both Beau and I laugh. Esther rolls her eyes. "How did they take it?"

"Terribly, as you'd expect." I smile wide at my mother-in-law. "Your son looked like he wanted to strangle me."

"Standard," she muses. "Am I still babysitting tonight?"

I falter answering, not just because I'm nervous for both Danny and me to leave Maggie for our date night. "I'm not sure it's safe to be alone with him."

Beau chuckles, making me give her a tired look. "Sorry."

"Why don't you and James come?" A foursome. Take the pressure off. And the heat.

"Because Danny already told us we're not invited."

"Great," I murmur. "So I'm a sitting duck."

"The only thing Danny wants to do with you is fu—"

"Beau!" Esther yells, horrified, and Beau puts her hands up, laughing.

"I'm saying it how it is."

"I'll be in the laundry room," Esther mutters, disappearing hastily.

"The poor guy is desperate."

"Jesus, Beau, pile on the pressure, why don't you?" My boobs throb some more, and my internal muscles twinge, reminding me they're still a bit tender. I pout to myself. The thought of sex thrills me, I'm desperate for him to have his hands all over me, reinforcing his attraction, his love. It also fills me with dread. I know he can be gentle. But he's also desperate right now, and I know my husband when he's desperate.

Ouch.

I relieve my boob of the pump.

Just as Brad bowls in. "Jesus Christ, Rose." He swings away, and Beau is off again, laughing. I grimace, throwing her another dirty look. I cannot wait for her to have all these problems.

"Sorry," I grumble, fixing myself. "It's safe now, Brad." Anyone would think he's not seen a breast in his life, and we all know that's not true. I bet he's seen the most of all the men—every shape, size, and variety. Beau slips onto a stool next to me and hands over an orange juice.

"You look smart today," she says, swigging, eyes on Brad's suited form as he braves facing the room. I'm pleasantly surprised. Not that

Brad doesn't always look smart, but his sallow skin seems brighter. Did he actually get some sleep last night?

Splitting his attention between the two of us, he raises his brows, amused by our close inspection.

"What?" I ask, laughing. "It's just an observ—" My words stall when someone walks in behind him. A woman. Smart. Tall. Sexy as hell.

"This is Allison," Brad says, all casual, like this isn't fucking weird. "Allison, Rose and Beau." He walks past us, leaving us staring like goldfish at the woman on the threshold of the kitchen. Speechless. So this is who was in his bathroom the other morning when Beau walked in?

"Hi," Allison says, approaching, holding her hand out to Beau first. "Lovely to meet you." Beau shakes, before Allison offers it to me. I take it limply and let her do all the shaking. Her smile is bright. Her makeup perfect. Not a hair on her head out of place. Yes, she's pure power in a woman, but that aside, what the hell is she doing in the house?

"Pleasure," I say, returning her smile. "I love your jacket." I gesture to the cream tailored piece with impressive shoulder pads and beautiful gold buttons.

"Oh, thanks. Armani, I think. Or Vivian. I forget." She smiles, friendly, and brushes the front down.

"What do you do, Allison?" I look over my shoulder to see Brad at the coffee machine, him looking back too, interested, smiling. I have not a fucking clue what to make of this, and judging by Beau's wide eyes and shocked face, she doesn't either. She lifts her green juice to her lips, her attention fixed on the beauty before us, as wowed as I am.

"I'm an attorney."

Beau snorts, sending green slop shooting out of her nose, and my cheeks balloon, not just at the state of Beau, but . . . an attorney? Is this real? "Oh cool," I say like a chump. "Criminal or family law?"

Allison frowns at Beau. "Criminal."

Another cough from Beau, and I want the ground to swallow us both whole. "I'm so sorry," Beau says, holding up her juice. "This is really sharp."

"Looks . . . appetizing." Allison turns her frown onto the green slop.

"It's actually not bad." Beau gets herself together. "My husband insists."

"Beau's pregnant," Brad says, joining us, nodding at Beau's stomach, prompting Beau to feel at her tummy on a smile.

A criminal attorney?

"Oh, congratulations." Allison beams at Beau.

"And Rose recently gave birth," he adds.

"Oh, you noticed that?" I ask seriously, earning a narrowed eye from Brad. What is this, speed friending?

"Oh, how wonderful," Allison says. "Boy or girl?"

"Girl. Maggie. She's a month, and my son is fourteen."

"Wow, you don't look old enough."

I smile, an edge of sadness to it, inevitably. "Unfortunately, I am."

"Come on," Brad says, collecting Allison's elbow, obviously eager to get her away from us. Then why the hell did he bring her here in the first place? This isn't how Brad does things. He fucks in hotel rooms, usually hookers, albeit high-class hookers, and Allison clearly isn't a hooker. She's a fucking attorney. "I'll walk you out to the cab."

"It was lovely meeting you," Allison says, letting Brad lead her away.

"And you," Beau and I sing in unison.

"What the hell has Brad told her he does for a living?" Beau whispers.

I shrug. I'm stumped. "Maybe they don't do much talking."

Brad looks back, and both of us show our palms to the ceiling, silently asking for an explanation. He shakes his head, as if exasperated. He has a nerve. I want every little detail.

The moment they're gone, Beau and I scramble up and dash to the window that looks out over the drive, searching for Allison's cab.

"Well," Beau breathes. "That was interesting."

"Wasn't it just?" I say, as James wanders in, not looking where he's going, his neck craned, obviously seeing Brad and Allison go.

He faces us, his expression bewildered. "Who the hell was that?" he asks.

"A criminal lawyer," Beau says, making James's mouth drop open. "You didn't know about her?"

"No, I didn't know about her. Did you?"

"Only when she breezed on in here this morning and introduced herself."

"Who introduced herself?" Esther asks, returning to the kitchen.

"Oh my God, you missed it."

"Missed what?"

"The criminal lawyer."

Her back straightens, worry plaguing her. "A criminal lawyer? Here in the house? Why?" She scans the doorway, obviously wondering if she needs to find her son and hide him.

"Brad's *guest*," I say, getting up and collecting my breast pump, unscrewing the bottle and taking it to the fridge.

"What?" Esther's face is a picture of confusion. Join the club.

"She stayed the night."

"A criminal lawyer?" she gasps. "What the hell is he playing at?"

I shrug, as Beau turns her attention onto James. "What's he playing at?"

James laughs, then places his hand on his chest. "Why'd you think I'd know? I have no idea what the fuck's going on in that man's head these days."

"He's lost his mind," Beau grumbles, smiling sarcastically as she hands James her empty glass of green. "I'm taking a shower."

He soon discards the glass. "I'll join you."

"Oh, so you're talking to me now?"

He scowls. "I don't need to talk while I fuck you."

"Oh my God!" Esther cries, disappearing back into the laundry room.

I grab the baby monitor and laugh my way out of the kitchen to go check on Daniel and feed Maggie, Beau and James following. "Anyone seen my husband?" I ask over my shoulder.

"Asleep in the gym," Brad answers, his hand on the front door handle.

"Oh, you're still here." I smile at Allison. "See you again soon." Will we? Is this a thing? Christ, a lawyer? How will that go down? Danny can't possibly know about her.

Brad, obviously still amused, pulls the door open for Allison.

"Tell Danny I'll see him at the club after I—" His attention lifts to the top of the stairs, a veil of contempt falling. Frowning, I follow his stare, along with Beau and James.

"Oh shit," James whispers as Pearl, looking casually glorious in an old worn pair of jeans and a baggy white tee, stutters to a stop at the top. The silence is excruciating. Brad is staring, eyes narrowed, jaw tight. Beau is chewing her lip nervously. James's eyes are on Brad. Pearl looks like a deer caught in the headlights. And Allison, obviously confused, is smiling mildly, scanning our faces, wondering what the problem is.

"Hi," Allison eventually squeaks, stepping toward the stairs, looking up at Pearl.

Pearl looks at me. For guidance? I don't know. And has Brad really done this to be a jerk? It's worked. He's a full-blown asshole right now. My lips straighten as Pearl turns to Beau, obviously looking for some help.

"This is Allison," Beau blurts, and I cringe. "She's . . . umm . . ." She can't say it. Can't say the words that'll confirm what Pearl is thinking. Can't deliver the blow. I throw a filthy look at Brad. The immature piece of shit.

"I'm a friend of Brad's," Allison says, full of diplomacy. "Nice to meet you . . ."

"Pearl," she replies, forcing a smile, coming down the stairs toward Allison's offered hand. "Nice to meet you."

Allison laughs. "Do you all live here?"

Jesus. "Not all," I say, watching as James rubs at his forehead, stressed. We're not the only ones who are going to kill Brad. A horrible silence falls once again. Unbearable. I speak to Brad through my filthy glare, ordering him to get Allison out of here. The bastard. Pearl's held herself beautifully, but I can see the hurt in her eyes. We were right to be worried.

"Your cab's waiting." Brad collects Allison, slipping an arm around her waist—again, *bastard*—and walks her out of the house. Oxygen only returns to the space when the door closes behind them. But the silence remains.

Until Daniel comes bounding down the stairs. "Hey, who was that woman coming out of Uncle Brad's bedroom?"

If I cringe anymore this morning, I'm going to need Botox pronto.

Or a fucking face lift. Pearl's eyes widen slightly before she corrects it. "That, kid, was your uncle Brad finally getting his shit together." She smiles and takes the rest of the stairs down, passing through the middle of us, our stunned stares following. "I've found some great pieces online that'll work amazingly at the beach club so I'm going to check them out at the store."

Oh. I look at Beau, who appears as perplexed as I am. Maybe we're wrong. Pearl seems . . . absolutely fine.

"You can take Fury," James calls to Pearl, making her slow to a stop and look back.

"Why?"

"Yes, why?" Beau asks, a million questions in her eyes.

"Yes, why," I ask too, my alarm bells ringing.

James, obviously feeling ambushed, takes on an edge of scary. It's an obvious attempt to try and force us to back off. It would perhaps work with Pearl. With Beau and me? Not a chance. It does with Daniel, though. He scrams, racing into the TV room.

"No TV or Xbox until you've done your schoolwork!" I yell after him.

"I already did."

"Damn it," I hiss. "Why, James? Why does Pearl need to take Fury?"

"Because I said so."

"Not good enough," Beau interjects, confronting him, toe to toe. James's face switches from James to The Enigma in a heartbeat. I can't say I'm pleased to see him. "What's going on?" she presses.

I watch, interested, as James searches for an answer under the watchful eyes of three women. "Just do what you're damn well told for once," he snaps.

"You've not told me to do anything," Beau retorts. "Why does Pearl need Fury?"

James takes Beau's arm and starts guiding her up the stairs. "We're taking a shower."

"Not on your life." She shrugs him off and returns to the bottom of the stairs.

Poor man looks flummoxed. Then mad. He points up the stairs. "I'm going to take a shower. Don't leave me waiting." Off he stomps, moody, and Beau snorts her disgust.

"The man is deluded."

"I'm worried," I admit.

"Should I be worried?" Pearl asks, looking between us.

"Not at all." I shake my head, scolding myself for instilling apprehension into her. But is it unwarranted? "Fury's great company."

Pearl nods, obviously not convinced, and backs up into the kitchen. I don't miss the fleeting flick of her eyes to the front door before she disappears. I'm so confused by the whole situation this morning but, worryingly, we have bigger concerns right now. What the hell is going on?

"I'm going to find Danny," I say, marching off toward the gym, pumped up on determination to get some answers. I fling the door open, making it crash into the plaster behind it. "Oh," I say, surprised to find him wide awake in the middle of some bench presses.

He rests the bar in the holder, using his stomach muscles to sit up, every one of them glistening and rippling as he rises to sit. My mind turns to mush.

Sex. On. Legs.

Then I remember why I'm here. I just don't know which grievance to begin with. "James is making Pearl take Fury to town."

He grabs a towel and wipes his brow, one eyebrow arched. "Morning, baby," he says quietly. "Sleep well?"

What a stupid question. Neither of us are sleeping well at the moment. We're lucky if we sleep at all. I smile sweetly. "Morning, dear. Now answer my question."

Danny rises from his ass, giving me his full physique in all its sweaty glory. His black shorts hang low on his hips. His thigh muscles swell. I'm close to dribbling.

Never gets old.

He's a fine specimen.

And currently horny as hell. And I'm unable to sate his needs.

I rip my longing eyes away from his beautiful body and find his face. Dripping. His icy eyes are narrowed to slits. His scar deep. I know my husband better than I know my name. I'm about to encounter The Brit. "Change your tone." he says, his voice low. Quiet. But not lacking any threat. Doesn't mean I'll heed the warning.

"No," I say over a sarcastic laugh. "What's going on?"

He approaches me, slowly, intimidatingly, and I can't deny it, it both turns me on and fills me with dread. Pressing his body to mine, he reaches for my hair, takes a fistful, and pulls my head back so he can look down at me. "It's not even nine a.m., Rose. I didn't sleep, I've not even had a fucking coffee this morning, and I'm still reeling after your bombshell at the *meeting*. I suggest you be wise and think *very* carefully about how you approach me today."

"What are you going to do?" I say, snapping my head hard so he yanks my hair. "Slap me? Fuck me brutally?"

His lip quirks, fire fighting through the ice in his eyes. Burning. I'm with him. My mind is capable. Can withstand anything he throws at me. My body, however, is delicate. I could cry. "Maybe both," he whispers hoarsely, brushing his lips across mine gently. My insides explode. I'm done for. My mind scrambles, my grievances are forgotten, and pleasure takes over the discomfort. I grab his neck and haul him onto my mouth, and he's ravenous. Starving. The baby monitor tumbles to the floor and my hand goes straight for his shorts. I gasp into his mouth. Iron. Huge.

I'm walked back into the door and pushed up against the wood, his tongue exploring deeply, his growls animalistic, his kiss wild.

Desperate.

He pushes into my body a little too much.

"Fuck," I gasp, throwing my head back. Pain sails through my boobs. It's suddenly all I can focus on, not the desire, the pleasure, or the need.

Danny rips his mouth from my neck, gasping, and searches me out. "What is it?" His hand cups me between my legs.

And I feel nothing.

Just pain.

And then he frowns, looking down at my chest. "Oh fuck," he breathes. "You're leaking."

And I burst into tears.

"Oh, baby," he says, sighing, taking my dropped chin and lifting my face to his. "Don't cry. It doesn't suit you." He places a small, soft kiss on the corner of my mouth, so obviously concentrating on ensuring his torso doesn't touch mine. "Come on. Stop it."

But I can't. My fists ball on his chest, and I hide there, sobbing my heart out, wondering where this emotion has come from. I miss our intimacy. I miss raw, carnal sex with my husband. I miss him kissing me like he's going to eat me. I want it all, but my damn body won't let me take it. The spa, the beach club, they're great additions to my life, but Danny's and my physical connection is the essence of us. And its absence is beginning to scream at me. How much longer will it take for my body to adapt? For my boobs to settle? For my internal muscles to stop hurting? And how long can Danny wait? What if he gets tempted elsewhere? What if he needs to release the pressure? What if he gives himself to another woman? My thoughts increase my emotions, my sobs racking my body.

And he holds me, hugs me as best he can without causing pain. "I love you, Rose," he whispers, forcing me out of his chest, looking into my eyes as he wipes the tears away. "I love you harder than I can hate, and you know how hard I can hate."

I laugh over a sob, sniffling. "What if you get tired—"

His finger meets my lips, silencing me. "When I'm tired of us, I'll be dead."

"Don't say that."

"It's the truth." Another kiss. "You're my soul, Rose Lillian Black. My love, my hate, and everything in between. Sore boobs aren't going to change that." His nose wrinkles. "Understand?"

I swallow.

"Tell me you understand."

I need to beat back those words of fear. Listen to my husband.

I love you harder than I can hate . . . You're my soul, Rose Lillian Black.

I need to focus on his love and loyalty. He would die for me. Quite literally. There's no greater love than that. I nod again. "I understand."

"Good. Now tell me what you're wearing for our date tonight."

"What do you want me to wear?" I reach up to his scar and trace the length of it.

"Not red. Not tonight." Dipping, he collects the monitor off the floor and slips his arm around my shoulders, walking us out. I won't push on the Fury situation right now—I'll save it for our date tonight—but Brad?

"Did you know that a woman stayed here again last night?"

"What woman?"

"Allison. And did you know she's a criminal attorney?"

Danny jars to a stop, looking down at me with wide, what-the-fuck eyes. I nod, confirming it. "The fuck?"

"Yes. Pearl walked down as Brad was seeing Allison out. It all felt a bit . . . odd."

"Odd, how?"

"I don't know if she was bothered. But I do know I want to slap Brad."

"Surely it's a good thing he's focused his attention elsewhere."

I look up at him. "Has he said something to you about Pearl?"

"Not a thing."

"He's never brought a woman to the house, you know that. Never to his place either."

"Always hotels," Danny muses, thoughtful.

"Yes, so why now is he flaunting women around the house?"

"Trying to get the message across to Pearl?"

"Well, it achieved that." I wince for her.

"Listen, Brad knows better than anyone that he would hurt her, so this is for the best."

"Yeah, I know," I breathe. Rip the Band-Aid off. Be cruel to be kind. But again, Pearl didn't seem bothered.

We make it up to the bedroom, just as Maggie's stirring. Danny goes straight to her crib and gets her out, cradling her in his bare arm, smiling down at her as he shuffles onto the bed and rests against the headboard. I join him, laying my head on his arm, stroking Maggie's cheek.

"She hungry?" he asks.

"She'll soon tell you if she's hungry."

He gasps. "Oh fuck."

I startle, sitting up. "What?"

He's staring down at our daughter, his eyes fixed, searching.

"Danny, what is it?" My heart starts beating fast.

"She smiled."

"No, she didn't," I say, laughing. "It was probably gas."

"I'm telling you, Rose, she smiled at me." He pushes his face closer to Maggie's "Didn't you, girl? Go on. Smile for Daddy."

We both watch, as Maggie's arms flail and she makes a few

snorty sounds.

And then it happens. Only small, only brief.

But she smiles.

"That's the most beautiful thing I've ever seen in my life," Danny says quietly, mesmerized. "Fuck, I love you, girl." Kissing her forehead, he settles back, lifting an arm for me to join him, and I watch, awed, as he talks all the smiles out of our little girl.

So deadly.

Chapter 14

Pearl

I hear the distant sound of a car pulling down the driveway. Allison. Perfectly dressed, precisely groomed, flawless makeup, hair like she's literally stepped out of a salon.

Not a bed.

Brad's bed.

The bed I was in a few nights ago.

I flinch, taking my pen to my mouth, chewing the end. That whole situation was so contrived. Everyone knows Brad doesn't have company at the house. Was he actually trying to prove a point? Make me jealous? Jesus, and they say women are complex creatures. He kisses me, he curses me. He pulls me close, he pushes me away. He looks at me like he wants to jump me *and* kill me.

Obviously he's struggling, and I hate that I understand why. He might see me as a child—for fuck's sake—but he's the one behaving like one. Regardless, I need to give Brad Black a wide berth. I'm not deluded. He's incapable of anything beyond sex and killing.

It would be awkward.

He might send me away.

And that alone is enough reason for me to resist, and since Brad's clearly adverse to me, we should be good. Does it sting that he ran from me to someone completely out of my league? Sure. But I will guard my emotions, the ones that have felt exploited and mistreated—because that's what I learned to do many years ago. Protect. Hide. Be safe.

Brad Black will no longer be on my radar. Allison is welcome to him.

I spread the catalogs out on the table and open my laptop, pulling up my spreadsheet and clicking my pen as I scroll through sites I've bookmarked to show Rose and make a note of the stores to visit. This project is a lifesaver. Something to do that doesn't involve being at the club. Or thinking about—

I shake my head and start making notes in my journal, chewing the end of my pen, screenshotting endless images of sun loungers, design ideas, and lighting. This place is going to look incredible.

Someone enters the kitchen, and I lift my face from the screen of my laptop, smiling, ready to greet whoever it is.

My smile drops.

And so do my eyes to my laptop. What the hell is he doing back here? "Morning." I force the word, clicking my way across the screen.

"Morning," he grunts.

The only sound in the room is me tapping at the mousepad on my laptop. The atmosphere is heavy. Horrible. For God's sake. I close my eyes briefly, swallow, take a breath, and face him. "Allison seemed lovely."

Brad blinks a few times before his brow furrows just a fraction. I hate that he expects a hissy fit from me. A reaction. But I'm at a point I can actually control my urge to smash his stupid face in or give him a piece of my mind. Yesterday at the boatyard was traumatic, and for the first time, Brad Black scared me. Not his anger, or what he's capable of. The twinge of need inside scared me. I should never have let him kiss me. Although he was determined. Strong. Angry. There was no avoiding it. Whatever, I definitely shouldn't have told him I didn't use him.

"Yeah," he finally murmurs. "Really lovely."

We stare at each other, as I click the pen, feeling awkward, smiling a little, throwing off friendly vibes. "Was there something else?" I ask his static, unmoving form.

His frown deepens. "No, nothing."

"Do you mind if I continue?" I ask, pointing at my screen. "I wouldn't want you to think I was being rude."

Poor man looks absolutely flummoxed as he glances between me and the laptop. "Sure." He stuffs his hands into the pockets of his trousers. "What are you doing?"

He wants to chitchat? "Researching for the beach club." I turn my attention onto the website showing me endless luxury sunbeds, my hair falling across my face, forcing me to tuck it behind my ear on one side.

He snorts. "Right. Because you work for Rose now, not me."

My shoulders drop, my eyes lifting but not my head. He's lost his confusion and has found irritation. He's goading me. Wants a reaction. "It's for the best."

"Agreed." He walks past me, sneering as he does. Another attempt to get a reaction from me. I breathe deeply, telling myself repeatedly that no matter what he does, I will not rise to it. *Fucking child.* I hear the clang of coffee cups behind me, feeling really fucking vulnerable when I can't see him. My shoulders roll back, my head tilting from side to side, the pressure inside growing, more so when a waft of his cologne finds me. I try to cut off my sense of smell, holding my breath. Then I still. Gulp. I feel his breath move in on my ear, and I close my eyes, trying to discreetly inhale. "If you ever," he whispers on an angry hiss, "flaunt your naked body in public again, I will—"

"What, Brad?" I turn my head so we're nose to nose. "What will you do?" I ask quietly, scanning his angry eyes. "Smack my bottom? Put me on the naughty step? Or ground me?"

He inhales, his lip curling, and pushes himself up. I return his filthy look, but my phone ringing relieves Brad of my distain. I pick it up, my thumb about to hit the green icon. But I falter. A withheld number.

My blood runs cold, my body solidifying, while Brad remains looming over me, heaving. I reach for the lid of my laptop and snap it shut, gathering my things and standing, forcing Brad back a few steps. I don't look at him. "Have a lovely day," I say quietly, escaping.

I leave the house by the side door and as soon as I'm around the corner and out of sight, I jog through the gardens, Barbie and Cindy finding me, yapping and jumping, thinking I'm about to play.

I pass the pool and dip, collecting a rock, then look over my shoulder to make sure I'm alone. Once I reach the summer house, I put my things on a bench and place my phone on the ground.

Then smash it to smithereens, lifting and ploughing the rock into it over and over, suppressing my yells. By the time I'm done, I'm exhausted. I fall onto my arse and welcome Cindy and Barbie close, hiding my face between their heads, scratching their ears. Letting a few stressed tears escape. I rootle through my bag and pull out my cigarettes, lighting up and dragging in nicotine urgently.

Not today.

He doesn't find me today.

• • •

As I round the house, I see Brad's car pulling out of the gates. Relief makes me that little bit shakier. "Hey, you okay?" Rose asks, coming down the steps with Daniel, followed by Tank who's got Maggie in her car seat.

"Great." I force a smile and lift my laptop. "Research. Where are you going?"

"Daniel needs some new cleats, and I need a new outfit for my date tonight."

Beau struts out with James, Goldie, Otto, and Ringo following, the house emptying—everyone going to *work*. James points a finger at Beau, a warning, before slipping into a Range Rover with the others and pulling away.

"Did anyone figure out why I have to take Fury?" I ask. The men all seem . . . how would I put it? *Active?* And Goldie's back. Suited. Okay, the Vikings always accompany Rose and Beau and the kid, but me? Anya? Never. So, yes, something is definitely off.

"No," Beau says quietly, watching her husband pull off down the driveway.

"I'll get it out of him if it kills me," Rose says as a cab pulls through the gates.

"Who's this?" I ask. Good grief, don't tell me Allison has forgotten something and come back? I don't know if I can hold up this front for much longer.

"Good question." Beau steps forward, her palms pointing back toward us, like stay back. I'm sure she forgets she's pregnant. Fury must be thinking along the same lines because he steps forward and puts his massive frame in front of Beau.

We all watch the cab pull up. The door opens. A silver sparkly stiletto appears. "Darlings!"

I exhale my relief when Zinnea appears, dressed to the nines, but her makeup is far from perfect. I smile.

Beau's wide eyes follow her aunt's tall body across the driveway. "That's right. You do the walk of shame."

"I don't walk, darling," Zinnea says, flicking her hair over her shoulder. "I sashay."

"You do the sashay of shame." Rose giggles.

"You bet your ass I will!" Zinnea stops, kicks a leg up, her head back, and goes into catwalk mode, taking the steps in style as we all laugh behind her.

"Does this mean we get to meet Quinton now?" Beau calls.

"We're only at oral, darling. Give it time."

"Jesus Christ," Tank grunts, shaking his head, and all the girls chuckle.

Zinnea stops at the front door and braces a hand on each side, posing. "Where are you gorgeous chops going?"

"Shopping. You coming?"

"Do The Brit and The Enigma murder on mass?"

I shake my head, bemused, and hold up my laptop. "I'm going to get my jacket. Where's my bodyguard?"

"Here," Fury grunts. He looks thrilled.

"Ready for some shopping?"

"No."

"Fabulous. Give me five minutes." I call my goodbye to the others as I dash up the steps past Zinnea, heading to our room, excited for my outing. *Distraction.* I refuse to look at Brad's door as I pass.

I let myself in and go to the bathroom. "Hey, Anya, you in there?"

There are a few bangs, a collection of knocks, and the sound of frantic movements. "Yes!" she yelps.

I step back from the wood. "Are you okay?"

The door opens and Anya appears, rubbing her head. "I hit my head."

"Ouch," I say, wincing. "Let me see." She removes her hand and I have a quick check. "There's no cut. Might be a bump though. I'm heading into town. Coming?"

She moves past me and opens the wardrobe, rubbing at her head again. "I need to go to work."

"And I don't," I muse quietly, slipping my things into my bag and grabbing my jacket. "See you later."

Chapter 15

BRAD

I kill most of my day in my old apartment just sitting on the floor in the corner. Alone. Letting my mind turn in circles, driving myself crazy. Fucking Allison didn't have the desired effect. Nowhere close. Taking her back to the house? Don't ask me what the fuck I was doing. Being a jerk? Stirring shit when I should be letting it settle? Not that it matters. Pearl was unfazed by my childish stunt. I feel used. Abused. Injured. It's fucking ridiculous. Allison rode me like her life depended on it last night, screaming, crying out, thrashing her head around. Her effort was commendable. And fucking pointless. I couldn't come. Chased the fucking release for hours and got nowhere close. Then I relented to all that is fucked up, blanked out Allison, put Pearl on my lap instead, and came on a bark of frustration, tossing Allison aside and taking myself onto the terrace to smoke my way through the rest of the night. Again, no sleep.

I laugh under my breath as I stub out my smoke in a used paint can. It's a shell. Weeks away from being finished. Which means I'm weeks away from escaping. I pull my cell out of my inside pocket when it rings and sigh at the screen. "Allison," I say with no warmth or happiness.

"Hey, handsome."

I close my eyes and let my head rest back against the wall. "What can I do for you?" Stupid question. Allison had the time of her life last night. She's an intelligent woman. Confident. She couldn't have missed my absence.

"Last night was fun."

Deluded?

"Yeah," I breathe non-committedly. "Fun." I should go back to Leonora for my kicks. My regular never called me, I always called her. But I haven't touched a hooker since Danny found Leonora riding me like a horse, tits bouncing, pleasure singing. Not surprisingly, she hasn't called to find out why I've not been in touch. She likely thinks I'm dead after Danny waved his gun around the hotel room. There's plenty of other paid pussy available. I could go there. If it didn't feel so wrong. Depraved.

But fucking a twenty-one-year-old virgin is fine, yes?

I flinch, cursing under my breath. I can't claim Pearl didn't look that young. I knew she was that young. And now I think about how incredibly tight she was, I should have fucking clicked. And yet despite all that, I still can't resist the pull. Despite her underhanded stunt, keeping me in the dark about something I should have fucking known, I still fucking want her. Every fucking minute of the fucking day, I want her. Think about her. Hear her. Fucking smell her.

"Brad?"

I blink, looking around the empty room. "What?"

"I said, are you free tonight?"

Two nights in a row? Don't tell me Allison thinks this is more than it is, which is basically me using her as a distraction. A distraction that isn't working. So what's the fucking point?

"I thought we could have dinner," she goes on.

My shoulders drop, my chin hitting my chest. She does. She thinks this is more. *Wants* more. Allison is a woman of a certain age. Of course she wants more. I should have walked away when she gave me eyes in the bar at the Four Seasons. Should have taken my ass up to the room and called one of my old regulars. "Sure," I say, because I haven't the energy to say anything else.

"Are you okay?" The concern in her voice adds another layer to my worry. I've given her no reason to catch feelings. I've fucked her. *Invited her back to the house.*

"Tired." So fucking tired.

"Me too," she replies, an edge of coyness in her tone. "I have to go, my client is here. Call me later." She hangs up, and I drop my cell to the floor.

Fucking hell.

• • •

I walk into the club at six. It's busy already, Mason, Anya, and the rest of the staff flying up and down the bar, delivering drinks fast. Anya spots me and immediately abandons serving a customer to pour me a Scotch. I take it on a smile of thanks and knock it back.

"That kind of day?" Mason asks as he pulls a pint.

"Yeah." I don't want to talk about my day. It's been fucking long and painful doing sweet fuck all. Except torture myself. "Any backlash from Ella?"

"I've told her I'll check the CCTV. I'm stalling her."

"Good." How long does it fucking take to get into a couple of cells? "Where's Nolan?"

Mason nods, indicating behind me, and I turn to see him coming from the office, suited and booted, a shit-eating grin plastered across his face. "What are you so happy about?" I ask as he approaches.

"You loo—"

"Shut your fucking face, Nolan." If anyone passes comment on how fucking exhausted I look again, I'll happily introduce them to the end of my gun. I slide my glass onto the bar, and Anya's quick to refill it. I look up and down the length of wood, to all the bodies behind it, staff serving. No Pearl. No red.

"Here's Leon," Nolan says, reversing his steps.

"What the fuck is he doing here?" I ask as our resident stoned surfer dude approaches with caution.

"Picking up some stock."

"B-Boss," Leon says, a world away from his usual loud, dopey self.

I should apologize. Should. *Won't.* "Stock pickups are always done when we're closed," I point out.

"Yeah, sorry about that, B-Boss."

"So why are you late?"

"I was fixing—" He stops, peeking at Mason and Nolan. "I was fixing something."

"What the fuck were you fixing?"

"A jet ski."

"This is more fucking important than fixing a fucking jet ski, Leon." I get up in his face, trying not to let my other grievance with him cloud how I handle this. But he knows. He knows pickups and drop-offs are done outside club hours. He knows the actual jet skis come last to everything else.

"Well, thing is, B-Boss," Leon says, fidgeting. "I didn't think you'd want the police sniffing around the boatyard."

"Why the fuck would the police be sniffing around the boatyard if you *don't* fix a fucking jet ski?"

"Because if I didn't fix the jet ski, the sheriff's son would have reported you for assault and vandalism."

I recoil, my anger shrinking along with my body. *Fuck it.* "You should have sent the fucker to me and I would have put a bullet in his fucking head."

"Yeah, I didn't think that was a good idea either, given who he is."

Initiative. Loyalty. Leon's got it all. And the hots for my girl. *The fuck, Brad?* "Get on with it," I snap. "And use the rear entrance."

"Already parked there, B-Boss." Leon and Nolan leave, and I turn, placing my empty on the bar.

"Another?" Anya asks.

"No." I take a stool, seeing Otto walk into the club.

"The phones you gave me to look into?" he says, pulling one out. *Finally.*

"This is what I found."

I look at the screen. "Jesus, Otto." I turn away from the footage of a woman bent over—"Wait, is that my desk?" I brace myself and look again. "That's my fucking desk." I point, ignoring the sight of a man's ass driving forward and retreating.

"Recognize the arse?"

My eyes widen in disgust as I study the bare cheeks. "Nolan," I murmur. "I'll fucking kill him."

"She has a lot of messages and calls from someone in particular."

"Who?"

"Someone called Cody. But it's on this phone." He holds up the other cell. "Boyfriend?"

"For fuck's sake." I take down Cody's number, handing that phone back to Mason before pocketing the other.

"I'm going home." Otto leaves.

"Where the fuck is he?" The little fucker. Hasn't he learned? I start to rise, ready to go reinforce a few lessons, but a man approaching the bar catches my eye. I look him up and down and *don't* like what I see. He's got a cocky air about him. And trouble written all over his pumped-up, muscled body. His neck's thicker than my thighs, his lip in a constant sneer.

My beef with Nolan is momentarily forgotten. I get comfortable, and Mason doesn't miss my observations.

"What can I get you?" he asks the guy.

"Rum and Coke."

Mason eyes me as I raise my brows, tapping the top of my glass. I think I'll stay for another after all. He takes care of the *customer* first. Then me. I lift my drink to my lips as the guy settles and waves Mason over again, reaching into his pocket. He pulls something out and slaps it on the bar. "I'm looking for this girl."

My glass pauses at my lips, and I crane my neck, trying to catch a glimpse of whoever's in the picture. Red invades my vison. My glass lowers. My stomach turns.

What the fuck?

Who the fuck is he?

Mason stares at the picture, playing it cool, and then discreetly looks out the corner of his eye to me. I mildly shake my head and set my glass down, willing my heart to stop beating so hard and fast. "Never seen her," Mason says, taking a towel and wiping his hands.

"You sure?"

"I'm sure." Mason looks at him, face straight, serious.

"I heard she was seen around here," he presses, scanning up and down the bar area. Looking for Pearl.

Mason's jaw rolls. He's getting worked up. I'm with him. "You heard wrong," he says, his voice tight. He's gonna lose his shit soon. I flatten my hand on the bar and lift and lower slowly, telling him to dial it down.

"Like I said, never seen her before," Mason says calmly, hearing me. "The drink's twelve bucks." Translated: shut up and drink before I break your legs.

I watch as the guy picks up his glass and slowly tips it back, eyes on Mason, goading him. Dumb fuck. He drains the glass and calmly sets it back on the bar. Pushes it calmly toward Mason. Leisurely reaches for the photograph. Drags it at a snail's pace across the wood, slipping it back into his pocket. It's all so very passive-aggressive. And really fucking stupid.

He doesn't pay for his drink but turns his back on Mason and has a long, thorough look around the club, not showing any interest in the dancers, before he turns back to the bar. "Don't mind if I use your facilities before I leave, do you." It's not a question.

Mason looks at me out the corner of his eye again, and I nod down at my empty. "Sure thing," he says. "Down the corridor across the back of the club."

He doesn't thank Mason, and still doesn't pay, wandering slowly off, his beefy body rocking as he walks. I follow him with my eyes, eventually turning on my stool when I can't twist my neck anymore.

"What the fuck was all that about?" Mason asks.

I ignore him, obviously, not letting my eyes leave the guy's back. "Make sure no one uses the men's." I get up and follow the guy to the restrooms, my mind spinning, my blood boiling. The brazen fucker walks into my club and thinks a bit of passive-aggressiveness will go down well?

I push my way through the door, finding him—name to be determined—with his dick in his hand taking a leak. He looks across to me, eyes running up and down my body. He nods. I nod in return and unzip my fly as I wander to the urinals, discreetly checking the stalls for anyone else in here. No one.

I pull out my dick. Stare at the tiles before me as I piss. I feel him look down at my cock, so I slowly turn my attention his way, face straight. He quickly returns his stare forward, and I smile on the inside. The big scary fucker has a complex about his small dick?

I've just found the outlet I need right now, since fucking Allison last night wasn't effective.

"You're looking for someone," I say flatly.

He glances at me, taking me in, up and down. "And you are?"

"Doesn't matter who I am." I finish and tuck myself away while this guy, whoever the fuck he is, keeps on pissing. "Who the fuck are *you*?"

He snorts, dismissing me, continuing his merry, long piss. Brave man.

"I asked you a question."

He laughs. "Fuck you."

I grab the back of his fat head and smash it into the tile wall, cracking a few, leaving a smudge of blood on the porcelain. He squeals like a fucking pig, falling back to his ass, still fucking pissing all over the place. "What the fuck?"

I kneel, fisting his jacket and yanking him close. "Who. Are. You?"

He dribbles and coughs, the blood coming from his forehead, his mouth, his nose. "Go fuck yourself."

I shove him to his back and straddle his lump of a body, pulling back my fist and letting loose. Punch after punch, I feel some of the stress leave my body, powering my blows, not giving him a moment to blink in between each one. I smash into his face until he's no longer yelling, his body limp, and clench his jacket in my fists and yank him up, getting my face up in his. "Fucking talk or every glass in this club will be sunken into your flesh."

He coughs up some blood, the reflex bringing him back round. Then he spits a few teeth out. I shove him back to the ground and stand, looking down at his pants on a sneer, his limp dick hanging out of the zipper. I dip into his pocket and pull out a phone, waking up the screen. The dumb fuck tries to knock me out of the way, so I lift my boot and slam it into his groin, and he yells his agony. I pull my gun and aim it at his head, keeping him perfectly still on the ground.

"Passcode," I say, crouching, pressing the end of my Heckler into his forehead.

His eyes widen. "Four, eight, three, six, two, nine."

"Well done." I go into the settings and change the code to something I'm not going to forget. "Wasn't so hard, was it?" He shakes his head. "Who the fuck are you?"

"I was hired to find a girl."

What's left of the air in my lungs leaves. "By whom?"

He shakes his head again. "I don't know. They email me."

I look down at the phone briefly. Then back up at him. "You should have turned the job down." I pull the trigger and turn away from the spray of blood, pushing through my legs to stand as I open the email app on the cell. There's nothing. I open the call log. Nothing. My heart beats a bit faster. Messages. Nothing. "Fuck," I bellow, throwing it at the wall.

The door crashes open behind me and Nolan scans the mess I've made. "Oh fuck," he whispers.

Poor Nolan. He's come at the perfect time for me, the worst time for him. "What the fuck are you doing?" I yell, getting him up against the tile wall. "Fucking Ella? I've fucking told you."

"Brad, please, wait," he says, looking utterly terrified. It would usually tug at my heartstrings. Not today. I wedge my gun under his chin. "You've completely disregarded my orders. And on my desk?

And why the fuck does she have two phones?"

"It's her boyfriend, he—"

"Cody, yes, I know."

"He's an asshole."

"So are you, Nolan. What the fuck are you doing? You fancy yourself as a bit of a porn star, huh?"

"It was just—"

I press the end of my gun harder under his chin. "A *bit of fun?*"

"No, not just a bit—"

"Shut up."

"I can explain."

"Does now look like a good fucking time?" I release him and point at the body. "For fuck's sake, Nolan."

I get my phone out and take a picture of my victim's mashed-up face. "Clean it up," I bark, picking up the pieces of the cell and pocketing them. "And not a fucking word to anyone." I walk to the door and stop, looking back. "I mean anyone, Nolan. Not Danny, not James, no one." The last thing I need is them pressing for information on the dead dude in the restrooms, or why the hell he's looking for Pearl. "And maybe I won't share your shenanigans with Ella in the office." Fuck me, we'll be another dancer down, and I haven't got time for that shit. "Whatever the fuck's going on between you and her, end it." I leave the restroom—ironically feeling worse—and dial Pearl, lifting my phone to my ear, passing Mason. "If anyone asks, nothing happened."

He nods, getting me a drink and a wet towel. I check my knuckles. Split. My suit. Splattered. I frown when I get an automated voicemail, swigging back my drink before wiping my suit over and dabbing at my bloody hand. I need a smoke. "All right, boss?" Des asks as I stalk past, pulling out my Marlboros.

I can't speak. I light up and pull hard, taking the nicotine hit deep into my lungs and breathing out long and slowly.

Who's looking for her? Her parents are dead, so who the fuck is she hiding from?

I dial her again and roar when it goes to voicemail *again*, swinging my fist into the wall. Cursing. *Fuck, that hurts.* I shake it out and call Esther, hardly wanting to admit that I'm worried. Really fucking worried. Where the fuck is she? Why is her phone off? "And who the fuck is looking for her?" I yell, pacing up and down.

"Brad?" Esther says in answer.

"Are you at home?" I try to calm my voice. Try. Don't succeed.

"Where else would I be?"

"Who's there?"

"What?"

"Just answer the question, Esther."

"Would you like to change your tone?"

I breathe in, close my eyes, and look at the dusky sky. "I'm just checking in on everyone."

"Has something happened?" she asks, sounding worried.

I laugh on the inside. So fucking much. "Nothing's happened."

"Then why do you sound like it has?"

For fuck's sake. "You're getting as bad as Beau and Rose. Can you please just answer my question?" I haven't the capacity to locate some bullshit reason for my impatience and interrogation right now. "Who's home?"

"Just me and the kids. Otto's popped to the club. Len's on the gate. James has taken Beau to the boatyard, out on the jet skis, I think. Danny and Rose have gone for dinner, Zinnea's on another date, and Ringo and Goldie are heading to the club with Tank." She pauses for a beat, and I will her to get to the person I *actually* want to know about. "Anya's at work and Pearl's out."

I still. "Pearl's out? Where?"

"Shopping I think. She took Fury."

I relax, if only a little. "Thanks." I hang up and dial Fury. He answers in two rings.

"Boss?"

"Where are you?"

"I don't fucking know. Some plant shop on Lincoln with Pearl."

Every muscle in me liquifies, my back meeting a nearby wall. I exhale, feeling lightheaded. "You've got eyes on her?"

"Yes, I've got eyes on her." He sounds insulted. I can't blame him. Tank and Fury are indispensable. Crucial. They're also the only reason the girls are allowed out of Danny's and James's sight when shit's flying around town. And now the only reason why I'll allow Pearl out of *my* sight. "Something I should know?" he asks.

I take a drag of my Marlboro, looking up to see Drake hovering nearby, looking vigilant. "Nothing you don't know already. Just . . ." How do I say it without raising questions? I might have killed the fucker, but I don't know who he was, who hired him, what they want, and until I do, I won't settle. He came to the club looking for Pearl. Knew she's been here. Where did he get that information? "Just stay close, okay? Pearl wasn't too happy about having you tailing her."

Fury laughs. "Beau felt the same. Look at us now."

I allow myself to smile and hang up, pushing off the wall with my shoulder blades. I need another fucking drink.

I give Drake a nod of appreciation and get my ass back in the club. CamelPhat & Elderbrook *Cola* plays, and every pole in the joint has a set of long legs wrapped around it. I see Nolan across the way drying his hands. He gives me a nod, and I turn my stare onto Ella. She's at the front of the stage, tits out, hips grinding. What the fuck was he thinking?

Anya slips a drink in front of me. "Thanks," I say, sipping now, as opposed to downing.

"Well," Mason muses, slamming the cash register drawer shut, looking past me. "This one sticks out like a sore thumb."

I look over my shoulder and see a woman, maybe mid-thirties, in come-fuck-me stilettos, a sharp trouser suit, with a fancy purse and layered blond hair. "Doesn't she just," I say quietly, watching her approach the bar. She leans over, asking Anya something. Anya looks down the bar to me before smiling at the woman and shaking her head. Mason moves in. Talks to her for a few moments. Gives her a glass of wine.

She sits on a stool and faces the stage, and Mason comes back down my end. "She's asking after you."

"Name?"

"Elsa Dove."

I frown, thinking. "Why does that ring a bell?"

"Because she owns the Pink Flamingo." Mason's pierced brows rise as I shoot him a surprised look.

"Isn't the Pink Flamingo the club James stormed six months ago with a few guns and found the Leprechaun?"

"The one and only." Mason chuckles. "He left a body behind too. Do you think she's here for an apology?"

"I don't know, but I'm really fucking curious." I get up and wander down the bar, putting myself in front of Elsa Dove. She's attractive. Oozes confidence. I hold my hand out. "Brad Black."

"The American," she muses, her head tilting, her eyes falling down my still damp-suited form. "Elsa Dove." She shakes, gripping hard. "Pull a stool over, Brad."

I raise a surprised brow but do exactly that, lowering and kicking a foot up on to the footrest. "What can I do for you?"

"I have a problem."

"And you came to me?"

"The American, The Brit, and The Enigma. You work together, right?"

I don't entertain her observations. "What's the *problem*, Elsa Dove? I'm kinda busy." I need to speak to Otto and somehow get him to run the dead dude's face through the system without raising too many questions that I don't want to answer until I actually *have* some answers. I also need him to see what he can get out of the empty, smashed phone.

"I fired the guy who runs my club."

I look at Mason. "Des Stanton," he prompts around a small smile, looking at Elsa.

Ah, that's right. I remember James mentioning him at some point after he'd got trigger-happy at the Pink Flamingo. "This isn't your HR department, Ms. Dove."

She clears her throat, and I can see it so very fucking clearly. How much she hates asking for help. "Des was inviting some unsavory characters into my establishment." Like The Leprechaun—now dead, courtesy of James. "He had to go. It's not the kind of crowd I want to attract." She leans into me, and I instinctively move back. "If you know what I mean." Her eyes drop to my lips. "I need to ensure they stay out of my club."

"So you came to me?"

"I can make it very worth your while."

"Can you now?" I look up and down her expensive body as she sips some wine, eyes burning into mine. She's obviously a pro at getting what she wants.

"I have information you might welcome."

My ears prick, and I feel Mason nearby, interested too. "About what?"

She stands. "Mind if I use the restroom?"

Oh? So she's aiming for delayed gratification, is she? Extending my anticipation? I silently motion the way and watch her strut off in her heels, her efforts to hold my attention on her ass quite commendable. And successful. It's a nice ass. "What are you thinking?" I ask Mason.

"I'm thinking she clearly has the hots for you, stud." Mason places another inch of Scotch down and I laugh, nodding to Anya when she looks down the bar to me. Good job. Always check.

"And we have another one," Mason muses, nodding toward the door.

"What?"

"When did we become a hangout for thirty-something designer, preened, businesswomen?" Mason asks.

I look back again, my neck beginning to feel achy. "Oh fuck," I breathe, watching as Allison, smiling seductively, breezes through my club.

"Hey," she sings, coming straight in for a kiss. I naturally freeze. There are a few things wrong right now. One, she said to call her. I haven't. Two, I've not told her what club I own. Just a bar owner. Minimal information. So, she's been doing a bit of digging.

"I thought I was calling you," I say, stoic, as she puts herself on Elsa's stool. She doesn't notice the half-drunk glass of wine with red lipstick on the rim.

"Well, I was passing, so thought I'd drop in and catch you."

"I didn't tell you I was here," I say. "Or where *here* is."

Her cheeks fill with color. I can't say I take any pleasure from calling her out. She's an all right woman. All right in bed. There's not much pillow talk, if any. And now—stupid me—because I've taken her back to the house, we're serious?

Allison laughs. "Yeah, you did."

"No," I reply quickly, shaking my head. "I didn't."

I glance past Allison when Elsa Dove appears, looking as indignant as fuck. "Excuse me, that's my seat."

I inhale deeply, bracing myself, as Allison looks over her shoulder to Elsa. Both women look each other up and down, and both appear completely offended. "And you are?" Allison asks.

"That's none of your business, sweetheart," Elsa retorts, nodding to the glass of wine on the bar. "You're in my seat."

"And this is my boyfriend," Allison barks back.

I balk, surprised. "Am I?" I say automatically, and Elsa laughs. Allison appears outraged. Jesus Christ, it's designer purses at dawn. This is comical. Fuck me, does Allison think Elsa here is responsible for the endless claw marks on my back and arms? Because, naturally, the question was asked. And I ignored it. "I'm no one's boyfriend." I stand. "And I have shit to do." I walk away, pulling my cell out, dialing Danny.

"What the fuck are you playing at bringing lawyers into the house?" he barks.

I roll my eyes. I could never explain. "You'll never guess who just walked into the club."

Muffled sounds come down the line, probably Danny removing himself from his wife's vicinity. "I'm assuming they're not Russian or Mexican or I'd be hearing gunfire," he whispers.

"Not even men."

"If you say Amber—"

"She's dead."

"There's no body, Brad."

I laugh with no humor at all. "It's not Amber." Shit, that's a bitch of a situation. No one wants proof that Amber is actually dead because proof will also provide evidence that Rose did it.

"Spit it out," Danny presses, impatient. "Rose is at the table wondering who I'm talking to and why."

"Elsa Dove."

"Who?"

"Pink Flamingo."

"Ohhhh," he breathes. "And what the fuck does *she* want?"

"What does anyone who comes to us want?" I ask. "Let me give you a clue. The answer begins with *pro* and ends with *tection*."

"You're a fucking dick sometimes."

For once, I agree with him. "She said she has information."

"I'm on my way."

Chapter 16

DANNY

Fuck my life, we've not long arrived. I look through the window into the restaurant and see Rose at the table. She's looking this way, watching me as I hang up to Brad. Worried. I can't say I was looking forward to telling her the man who raped her and haunted her for years is still alive. That I didn't kill him. That I lied to her. But it needs to be done.

Things are about to change around here again, and she needs to understand why. I dial Brad back, taking the handle of the door and pulling it open. "Can it wait an hour?"

"What? No, it can't wait. Allison's turned up too. I'm outnumbered."

Dick. What was he thinking inviting a woman back to the house? And not just a woman, but a fucking lawyer. "Brad," I say quietly, stopping by the door. Rose sits up in her chair, her wine halfway to her lips, her expression apprehensive. Hopeful. It fucking kills me. I give her a small, reassuring smile. She returns it. "I'm looking at my wife's face across the restaurant right now wondering how the fuck I tell her I didn't kill Sandy."

"Fuck."

"Yeah." I blow out my cheeks, once again amused by the fact that there is nothing in this world that terrifies me more than my wife. Will she get up and walk out? Leave me? Throw a drink in my face? Yell at me, hit me? All will be actions resulting from fear. I vowed she would never be scared again.

"Take your time," Brad says, soft and understanding. "And a heads-up."

"What?"

"Elsa Dove's obviously a woman who gets what she wants."

I smile. "A flirt?"

"Massive."

"It's a good job you're not married then, eh?"

"Tell that to Allison," he mutters. "She and Elsa haven't exactly hit it off."

I laugh, hanging up, and slip my phone into my pocket, taking a deep breath and bracing myself. Rose's eyes follow me the entire way to the table and down when I lower to the seat. I take the bottle of wine and top us both up, smiling when the waiter arrives at the table. "Mr. Black, wonderful to have you again."

Rose chuckles as she picks up her menu, undoubtedly thinking about the time I made a mess of a table with Gordon Blinks's brain. I give her a wry smile. "Good to see you, Francesco."

"Mrs. Black." He nods to Rose.

"Francesco," she says, smiling down at her menu. "Can you give us five minutes?"

"Sure, sure." Hands up, he backs away, and I sink back in my chair, scissoring my fingers around the stem of my wine glass, watching my wife. Waiting for the questions. But while I wait, I don't mind just sitting here and admiring her. She reaches back and pulls her hair over one shoulder, running her fingers through the ends while she reads the menu, lips pouting in contemplation. I smile to myself. She's pretending she's not curious about me leaving the table to take Brad's call. Pretending she's not worried. My eyes drop down her front to the black silk blouse that's tucked into black leather pants. Black to disguise any leakage. Pants to hold her tummy in. She has no tummy, she's just being self-conscious. She's a walking sex bomb. I just can't have sex with her right now and, can't lie, it's killing me. I won't pretend I was hopeful tonight would be the night to break the drought. Not when I'm breaking bad news. The last thing I'm expecting after ruining date night is sex.

"Is everything okay?" she asks her menu, sounding blasé.

I take some liquid courage. "Not really, baby."

She looks up sharply, her blue eyes anxious. "What's happened?" she asks with a wobbly voice.

I glance around the busy restaurant, counting the number of spectators we'll have when Rose flies off the handle. Too many. Reaching up, I rub into the corner of my eye. Here we go. "Before I tell you, I want you to remember something."

She stares at me, quiet, but I can see her mind spinning, running over all the things I could throw at her. I bet she doesn't for a moment consider what I *actually* have to confess.

"Talk, Danny," she says, as she rests back in her chair, setting her menu back down.

"Remember I love you."

Her head tilts, her lips straight. "I said, talk."

"And I'll do whatever it takes to make it right." Like find the fucker and *really* kill him this time.

"Oh my God," she breathes, taking her wine and throwing it back. "You fucking bastard." She slams her empty down, raging. "How could you?"

I recoil, completely confused, running back over my words. Did I tell her and miss it?

She shoots up from her chair and slams her hands down on the table, making the silverware jump and clang. I feel all eyes on us. "I fucking hate you."

"I love you too, baby," I murmur, frowning at her fuming form.

"My body has been ravaged from carrying your daughter, I'm in fucking agony most the time, I have stretchmarks and a battered fucking pussy, and you thank me by sticking your cock in another woman?"

What the fuck?

"Who was it?" she yells. "What dirty little whore did you fuck, you betraying, selfish fuck head? One of the girls from the club?" She pours herself more wine, but she doesn't drink it. Oh no. She throws it in my face. I still, closing my eyes. *My fucking God.* Where the fuck has she got *that* from?

I reach for the napkin and slowly wipe it down my face, my blood simmering. She actually thinks I'd do that? I look up at her, my jaw about to snap, and she withdraws at the sight of the beast rising.

"Sit the fuck down," I order, my voice brittle.

Her mouth drops open. She's shocked? *Join the fucking club, baby.* "Fuck you, Black." She swipes up her clutch bag and marches to the door, and I'm up fast going after her, slamming a palm into the wood over her shoulder, forcing the door shut again. "This is weirdly reminiscent," I whisper in her ear, seeing her shoulders rise, fighting off the tingles.

"Fuck you."

"Wouldn't that be nice?" I roll my hips into her arse. I'm turned on. That's what weeks without release will do to a man.

"Fuck off."

"Oh, baby, there will be no fucking *off*." I reach around the front of her and clench her cheeks, directing her face to mine. Her eyes fall to my scar. I can feel it pulsing. "I suggest you get your arse back to the table."

"Else *what*?"

"I'm already close to a killing spree, baby. Don't make that happen in this lovely restaurant in front of these lovely people."

Eyes wide, Rose glances around the silent room. All attention's on us.

"Are you okay, ma'am?" a man asks over the sound of his seat being pushed out. I keep my eyes on my wife. The alternative won't work out well for the man.

"I'm fine," Rose says, smiling, before returning her blue gaze to mine. I back up, releasing her from the door. I don't need to tell her again. Whether that be to save the bystander or herself, I couldn't give a fuck. She walks back through the silent restaurant and calmly lowers to the chair.

I not so calmly dump my arse down on my seat. Not surprisingly, the waiter keeps his distance. "You think I'd put my dick in another woman?"

"You said—"

"That I put my dick in another woman? No, Rose. You told *yourself* I put my dick in another woman."

She wilts before my eyes, peeking around the restaurant. It's still quiet. Could not give a fuck. In fact, I hope Mr. Do-Gooder speaks up again because I've got the urge to hit something. I slam my fist on the table. "I would never put my dick in another fucking woman, Rose." I grab the napkin again and roughly wipe myself down as she shrinks farther and farther into her chair. I slam that onto the table too, my temper showing no signs of cooling. She actually thinks I could do that? I stand, cup myself, and thrust forward. "This cock is yours, Rose. It'll only ever be in your mouth. Only ever in your cunt."

She coughs over her surprise, having another look around the restaurant. "Okay," she says, willing me to sit down.

"Tell me you understand," I demand, oblivious to our crowd, my hand still holding myself. "Now."

She looks me directly in the eye. "I understand."

"Good. Don't ever question me again." I sit and neck my wine. Fuck it. It couldn't get any worse than my wife thinking I could betray her like that. Let's get this over with. "Sandy's not dead." I sneer at her as she balks at me. "I told you I'd killed him because I didn't want you to worry."

"What?"

"You fucking heard me, Rose."

I see the temperature in her cheeks rising. "What?" she yells.

Oh goody. Here comes round two. I hold up my wine glass. "More wine please, Francesco."

"Are you fucking joking?"

"No, baby. I'm deadly serious." About the wine *and* Sandy. "He's still alive, and I don't know where the fuck he is, but when I find him, I'm going to slice him open with a blunt, rusty razor blade and let him bleed out slowly." I snatch the wine off Francesco and drink straight from the bottle, gasping for air once I've swallowed. "Well, this is going well, isn't it?"

Her nostrils flaring, she stands. "I fucking hate you." And stomps off, leaving me fighting to rein myself in.

Can't.

I dive up and stalk after her, armed with my wine, catching her at the door again. I don't see this one coming, maybe because the red mist is hampering my vision. She turns, swings, and cracks me straight on the nose, and blood bursts from it. "Fuck," I hiss, dropping the bottle and clenching my nose. I can't even tell her that was uncalled for. She heaves before me, displaying no remorse whatsoever. I feel psycho. She *looks* psycho. Two fucking psychos. I wrap a hand around her throat and push her up against the door, getting up in her face. "I think we both need to calm the fuck down before our kids end up orphans."

"Fuck you," she hisses, holding my hand on her throat, squeezing. Goading. *Standard.*

I get my face closer and rub my nose up her cheek. "You—" I feel a pair of hands on my shoulders, and I'm suddenly hauled back, the sharp move jarring Rose, making her cough when my hand yanks on her neck. I hit the deck, back first, and choke on impact, thoroughly winded.

Fuck.

Blinking up at the ceiling, disorientated, I hear the echoing of gasps ringing around the restaurant. "What the fuck?" I wheeze, craning my head to find Rose. She looks worried.

"I think that's enough." A man appears above me, dusting off his hands. He actually dusts off his hands. "I'm placing you under citizen's arrest."

I burst out laughing, hysterical. Or psychotic. My stomach aches. My nose continues to bleed. Water hampers the red mist further, forcing me to wipe my eyes. I find Rose by the door again. She takes one look at my eyes and pulls it open, leaving.

Because she knows what's coming.

But the sight of her walking out chases away my amusement and I am livid once again. Unfortunately for Mr. Do-Gooder, he's my outlet. I look up at him, just as another man steps in, flanking him. And another on the other side. Three beefy pricks who want to save the day. I feel my lip curling and inject all of my rage into my limbs, taking the one on the right down with a kick of my leg. Naturally, in response, the other two pounce, throwing their bodies onto me and trying to pin me down, like two wannabe wrestlers. For fuck's sake. I don't have time for this. I have a woman on the loose and being out there alone is *not* ideal. The thought ramps up the anger, and I use it as my fuel, roaring as I heave them off me, getting to my feet and kicking each of the fuckers in the stomach, not neglecting the other guy on the floor. If I didn't need to get to Rose, these men would all be in for a very real lesson. I pull my gun out and aim it between the three of them, raising my voice so they can hear me over the panicked gasps. "Get up, get back to your table, and eat your fucking dinner." Not surprisingly, they all look at each other in question.

"Get the fuck up!" I bellow, searching for Rose out of the window. My patience and sanity lost, I start kicking them up, and practically boot them all back to their tables. "Now sit down, shut up, and eat." I grab a handful of one of the guy's pasta and ram it in his face. "And next time, think very carefully before you step into *my* discussions with *my* wife." I shove my gun in my trousers and stalk out of the restaurant, raking a hand though my hair as I look up and down the street. "Rose!" I yell, walking to the corner, searching. "Rose!" I pull out my phone and dial her. It rings off. "Rose!" I pace back up the street, breaking out into a run to the other corner, looking left and right. Nothing. "Fuck." I dial her again as I rush back to my car, falling into the seat. I get her voicemail, so I leave her a loving message. "I swear to God, Rose, ring me back or—" What the fuck will I do? I slump in my seat. "Baby, please. Don't leave me here worrying about you. Tell me where you are. Let me pick you up. We can sort this out." I start the car and pull away, my eyes searching the streets for her.

My heart pounding anxiously.

• • •

I drive around for an hour with one of Maggie's muslin cloths held at my nose, trying to stop it bleeding. *Definitely* broken. I call Mum to check if she's gone home. "What's going on?" she asks. "I've had Brad on the phone demanding the whereabouts of everyone too."

I don't have the energy or capacity to wonder why. I need to find Rose. "Everything is fine, Mum," I assure her half-heartedly. "Do you have enough milk for Maggie?"

"I have plenty. Danny, do not leave me in the dark."

I sigh, relenting. She'll find out sooner or later. "On the night I went after Sandy, after I found out he was the man who raped Rose . . ." When I found out he's my son's biological father. My hands turn white around the wheel. Sandy can *never* know about Daniel.

"What about it?"

"He got away."

"What?"

"He got away, Mum." I will never forgive myself for letting that happen. For going after him without thinking about it carefully. For putting myself and everyone else at risk. If Brad, James, and the others hadn't turned up, I would be dead, no doubt. And as if to remind me that I didn't walk away scot-free, all three bullet holes twinge their presence.

"Oh my God."

I take a left, still searching for my wife. "Some bodies have turned up. Russian and Mexican—all with the Black family emblem cut into the chests."

"Oh, Danny."

"My phone's been bugged, and Sandy's called me to make sure I know he's still holding a grudge." The phone crackles a little. "Mum?"

"Did you know about this?" she hisses, her voice muffled. Because she's covering the bottom with a palm. Talking to Otto.

"Now come on, Boo," he says, pacifying her. "You know we like to keep you girls away from the—"

"You should have told me!"

I shake my head, dumping the red-stained cloth on the passenger seat, wrinkling my nose, waiting for the flow to start again. It doesn't. "Mum," I say, raising my voice to get her attention and the heat off Otto. "Call me if she shows up, okay?"

She doesn't answer me, but hangs up, and I reach back to my nape, stroking it. I hit James's number on the control display. "How did it go?" he asks.

I laugh, because it's all I feel capable of right now.

"Oh fuck," James breathes.

"What?" I hear Beau say in the background, her senses not failing her. "What's going on, James?"

He hushes her. I can't imagine that will go down well. "You know," I breathe, still scanning the sidewalks as I drive, "she actually thought I was going to tell her I was fucking another woman."

"What?"

"Yep." I laugh, with zero amusement. "She thought, because she can't put out at the moment after giving birth to my daughter, that I would stray."

"Danny, she's understandably emotional at the moment."

"That was before I told her about Sandy," I yell, laughing again. "The Sandy thing was the icing on the cake. Fuck me, I can't do right for doing wrong."

"Where is she?"

"I don't know. She left the restaurant."

"And you didn't stop her?"

I shrink into my seat. "I was busy," I say quietly, full of regret.

"Doing—"

"Threatening three men who stuck their noses into my business."

"Oh, for fuck's sake."

"And now she's out there alone somewhere, Sandy's on the loose, not to mention the Mexicans, and—" I slam the ball of my palm into the steering wheel. "I can't believe she thinks I could fuck another woman!" I take a hard right and put my foot down.

"Well, that's my romantic sunset ride with my wife and our bump out on the water done with. Meet me at the club."

"You got Tank?"

"Yeah."

"And Fury?"

"With Pearl."

"See you soon." I hang up and dial Fury. "Meet me at the club now," I order, putting my foot down.

• • •

I've called her another three times by the time I get to Hiatus. I check my face in the rearview mirror, cursing as I rub the dried blood away. There's no bruising or swelling. Yet. I get out and look down my cream jacket. "Fuck it." I wriggle out of the blood-stained piece and throw it on the back seat, slamming the door and re-tucking my shirt into my trousers as I cross the road, popping another button at the collar.

"Don't ask," I say to Des and Drake when they give me concerned, questioning eyes. Des gets the door for me, and I'm about to step in when someone calls my name. I turn and see Otto getting out of one of the Range Rovers.

"Wait up," he says, striding across the road. I scan his face for scuffs or scrapes. No. That's just *my* wife. He makes it to me and cocks his head in question. "Is that blood?"

I reach up and rub at my cheek. "Rose had at me. How's Mum?"

"Pissy."

I laugh under my breath. "At least you know where she is." I look down at my phone, willing her to stop punishing me like this. I feel sick.

"Look, I don't know whether this is the right time—"

I look up at him. "If it's about you and my mother, then no, now is definitely not the right time." I'm already straddling the thin line between stable and crazy. "Don't tip me, Otto. Any luck on the phone bug?"

"Nothing yet." Otto follows me into the club.

"And Bernard King?"

"Nothing, but cameras just picked up the Escalade that hit on Brad being driven out of town."

"They're still driving it?" With bullet holes?

Otto shrugs. "And what about Nolan? What are we doing about him?"

"Right now, nothing. I need facts before I tell Brad." Because I just know he'll defend the little prick. "I need to find my fucking wife." I look down at my phone. "If you were her, where would you go?"

"To escape you?" he asks. "Hell. It'll hurt less."

I grunt and pick up my feet, looking for Brad, noticing Ringo and Goldie are in a booth. "Cozy," I say as I pass.

"Fuck off," Goldie hisses, snarling around the rim of her beer bottle. No delicate wine glass. No dress.

"Where's Happy?"

"Hiding in his office," Ringo says over a laugh, nodding toward the bar. I see two women, both wearing fancy trouser suits. Both perfectly made up. Both radiating power.

You could bite through the tension, even from here. I peek up at the glass that looks over the club from the secret office, knowing Brad will be up there, looking down, as I dial Rose again. "Come on, baby," I say quietly. "Answer."

It goes to voicemail, and I bite down on my teeth and squeeze my phone, breathing out through my nose calmly. I try again. And again. And again.

Brad eventually appears. "All right?"

"Rose has disappeared."

He steps back. "What do you mean, disappeared?"

"She's gone, Brad. Walked out. Left. I don't know what the fuck you want to call it, but she's gone." I take a deep breath, my anger and fear doubling. "I told her I had something to tell her. She thought I'd cheated on her."

Brad snorts. "For real?"

"For real." I wish Rose had the same confidence in me. "She lost it, and since shit was already flying, I dropped the Sandy bomb."

"Fuck."

"She punched me and walked out."

"And you didn't go after her?"

My shoulders drop, and I look at him. Brad knows me. I don't need to tell him.

"For fuck's sake, you have seriously got to get ahold of your fucking temper."

I pout. "Try being married to my wife."

"No thanks, I like my nose how it is," he says, eyeing mine. "Straight." Sighing, he motions to the bar, and I look to see all eyes on us. "Elsa Dove says she has information we want to know."

"About?"

"I don't know. She won't talk with Allison around, and Allison is stuck to her fucking stool."

"Meow," I purr, dialing Rose again, pacing up and down. "Fuck it," I hiss when it goes to voicemail *again*. This time, my message isn't so loving. "Fucking call me, Rose. This isn't funny."

"I'll tell Elsa now's not a good time," Brad says.

"No." I hold my hand out, stopping him from walking away. Elsa could tell us anything, and anything could be information on Sandy, and I really want information on Sandy. "Do you think you can get Allison away?"

He laughs. "Does a bear shit in the woods?"

"Let's not talk about bears."

Brad grimaces as I look across to Elsa Dove. She's got her eyes on me. Eyes that speak without her mouth saying a word. Rui De Silva *Touch Me* starts to play. I send a quick text and wander over to Ms. Dove, and she doesn't free me from her sultry gaze the whole way.

"You must be The Brit," she says, one long leg crossed over the other, her glass suspended in front of her chest. "What a pleasure."

My lips remain straight. I hope this isn't leading to where I think it is. I'm in no mood. "Brad mentioned you had information."

She falters raising her wine to her red lips. "Straight to business."

"That is why you're here, isn't it? Business."

Her lips quirk, half pouting, half smiling, as she drops her gaze down my body. "Maybe."

"Definitely," I counter, picking up the glass Anya just slid to me with my left hand, making sure my ring finger is bang in her line of her sight. Though whether I'm married anymore is up for debate. My stomach turns. A quick check of my phone. Nothing.

I look up to see Ms. Dove's eyes on my finger, and something tells me the ring there is of no consequence to her. "I've heard a lot about you," she muses.

Then she will have heard I'm married, and I'm all for my wife. Would kill for her. Die for her. "All good, I hope," I say, and she laughs lightly, head back, a tactical flash of her throat being thrown into the mix. I swig my Scotch and glance past her, where Brad's taken up a seat with Allison. She does not look happy. Brad looks exasperated. Then, he appears furious, his attention on the doorway. I look back and see Fury.

And Pearl.

For fuck's sake.

"Listen, Ms. Dove, I'm a busy man." With a missing wife. "Can we cut to the chase?"

"How formal of you." She smiles, a long, lingering smile. "Of course." Leaning forward, she rests her hand on my knee. "Maybe we should go somewhere quieter and be *less* formal."

I look down at her hand. My gut didn't fail me. She thinks fucking me will get her protection? My temper flares. "You said you have information."

"Well, less information, more a proposition."

I bet. I remove her hand. "I'm married."

"And?"

"And . . . I love my wife." *Wherever the fuck she is.*

"I don't want a lifetime commitment, Danny. Just"—she shrugs— "some fun."

She wanted some fun from Brad an hour ago. She's got fucking front, I'll give her that. Like all the whores who came and went for years. But I'm insulted. She thinks she can talk her way into my bed and blow my mind, send me dizzy with pleasure, so much so I'll deem her precious and valued enough to protect?

My phone dings the arrival of a message, and my heart leaps into my throat. I look down. It's not Rose. It's Higham replying to my message.

Elsa Dove? The FBI have connected her to the Russians. Be careful.

I swallow down the instant rage. She's still smiling, still trying to seduce me with her eyes, her smiles, her body language. The fuck?

She's already got her protection. And this is what they want in return.

Me.

I roll my shoulders, keeping a lid on my anger.

Then I feel something.

A presence.

My wife.

No mistake, it's my wife. I inhale and look over my shoulder and see her at the entrance of the club.

Staring at me.

She looks fit to kill.

Could drop every man in the club with that outfit.

She has a fucking nerve.

Elsa Dove. Another woman with a nerve. Except, this one I don't adore. Wouldn't kill for. But, actually, *want* to kill.

But . . . can't do that.

So I lick my lips, and Elsa Dove's eyes follow the journey of my tongue from one side to the other. Then my glass to my mouth. I burn holes into her with my cold stare that I've no doubt is loaded with heat.

Touch me.

Her hand finds my knee again.

For approximately a second.

She yelps as Rose yanks her from her stool by her perfectly styled hair, tossing her to the floor, removing the imposter from my personal space. I keep my drink at my lips as I watch Rose sink her six-inch stiletto into Elsa's side. *Jesus.* But before she dives on Elsa and starts throwing punches, I move fast and grab her around the waist, pulling her back. She's still delicate. And if Elsa hasn't got the message, I'll happily reinforce it with a gun to her head.

"Get the hell off me," Rose screams, going ballistic in my hold, trying to pry my hands from around her waist. "Danny!"

"Shut the fuck up, Rose." I look at Elsa on the floor. She's in a state of shock, scrambling to her feet, embarrassment rife. "Meet my wife," I say, holding on to Rose a little tighter. "I think it's time for you to leave, Ms. Dove, and I don't recommend coming back."

She frantically grabs her handbag off the bar, while Rose fights like a wild animal to get free. Elsa is understandably alarmed.

"I'm not going to be able to hold her forever," I say, smiling sickly.

She's gone like a shot, and I release Rose when I deem it safe, fully aware that I'm about to cop a load of her crazy. I lean back, just swerving her slap, and grab her wrist, yanking her into me, my face up in hers. I expected it, yes. Doesn't dull the rage, though. "Don't you *ever* fucking run away from me again, do you hear me?" I roar.

"Danny," Brad says, bravely moving in, a hand on my shoulder.

"Get the fuck off me." I release Rose, and she shoves me away, going to the bar and demanding wine. Mason looks at me. I shake my head. Not a fucking chance.

"Get me a fucking drink!" she screams.

"Calm the hell down," I warn, trying to heed my own advice. I could fucking burst. Again. I know what she's doing now, her behavior—it's fear, nothing more, nothing less. She's mad with me, I get it, but I am backed into a corner here, and I do not need her rabid temper coming at me.

"Fuck off." Rose lowers to a stool, looking exhausted. I'm with her. "Who was that?"

"We should take this to the office."

"Fine." She's up off her stool and marching through the club, arse swaying, boobs bouncing, hair swishing. Every man eyes her. God help any of them if they try their luck. God help Rose if she goads them.

She doesn't, but she looks back at me, and her eyes . . .

Fuck.

I see the same heat I saw when we met. The fear. The hatred. The desperation. Everything around me drops into slow motion, as I study my wife's long, slow strides toward the office, her head turning slowly back away from me. My feet start to move without instruction, and I follow her, people parting to let me through.

My trousers getting tighter.

And tighter.

My pulse pounding.

I make it to the office downstairs and find her standing in the middle of the room. If she stops me right now, I'll fucking cry. "Who was she?" she asks as I close the door.

"Elsa Dove. Owns the Pink Flamingo. She told Brad she had information we would want. Turns out she was trying to get into my trousers and expected protection in return for blowing my mind in bed. She would have had Brad before I got here. I told her I was married. I told her I love my wife. She didn't care. I put a text in to Higham to find out what he knows about her. The FBI have connected her to the Russians. I expect Sandy's protecting her and he's sent her in to try and seduce me. Get information. I don't know. I wanted to kill her. Couldn't. You could." I raise my eyebrows. "That's everything." I step forward. "Now I want to fuck my wife and reinforce a few things." Another step.

Her shoulders roll back. Her skin lights up. "Like what?"

"Like I'd rather cut my dick off than let another woman near it." I reach her and tug her close, looking down at her. "Get on the desk and open your legs."

"And if I say no?"

I smile. It's dark. "Try." I can smell her desire. Taste it in the air between us. "Go on, baby. Try to say no to me."

Her eyes drop to my lips briefly before she moves fast, attacking me, hands in my hair, cupping my face, her tongue owning me. Her kiss totally fucking owning me.

And I'm home.

I walk her to the desk and get her on the wood, keeping up our kiss as I rip her blouse apart and she yanks my shirt open, buttons popping and flying everywhere. The anticipation. The desperation. Fucking hell, this office could go up in flames. She starts on my belt, wrenching it open as I push her blouse down her arms, forcing her to release the belt, but she's soon back to work, her mission to get to me ruling her. I'm throbbing.

And when she reaches past my boxers and wraps her hand around me, I have to break the kiss, yelling, the pressure immense, the pleasure like nothing else. I'm fucking dizzy. I look at her smudged lipstick. Her wild hair. Her drowsy eyes. "Stroke me," I whisper, grunting when she pulls a slow caress. "Fuck," I hiss, my trousers dropping to my ankles. I need to be inside her before I come right here in her palm. I knock her hand away and push her down to the wood, pulling her leathers open and yanking them down her legs, taking her heels off with them. Hands behind her thighs, I tug her down, watching as I slide right in and she inhales. I look up at her tits. Her black bra. I know my limits. I know hers. I leave her boobs and slide out, watching intently as my cock slips free, glistening.

And I slide back in.

Out.

In.

Steady, slow, and she moans, writhing languidly. My skin tingles, buzzes. I take my thumb to her clit and start rolling it softly around to help her along—I need her with me.

"Danny," she whispers, clinging to the edge of the desk.

I see it rising in her, the heat, the pleasure, and the pressure. My balls throb, my shaft pulses. "Fuck," I wheeze, increasing my pace. "Fuck, Rose."

"Yes!"

"Rose!"

Faster.

"Fuck, yes!"

Faster.

"Rose, tell me!"

"Shit, Danny!"

Faster.

"Oh my God!"

Faster.

"Rose!"

"Yes!"

"Fuck!"

"I'm coming!"

I apply more pressure on her clit and smash into her like a depraved madman, and it hits me like a fucking bulldozer, taking me out, making my body fold over her to deal with the attack of pleasure, my chokes real, my head spinning, her screams ringing in my ears. "Jesus," I gasp, being milked dry by her muscles.

"I can't breathe," she pants, heaving beneath me, my head rolling where it's lying on her chest. "Fucking hell, Danny."

I blink, trying to clear my vision, the aftermath of my orgasm still rippling through me. I grit my teeth, the intensity not letting up, as I roll into her gently but firmly. I'm still coming, and Rose is still shaking under me. I drag my eyes up to see her sweaty face. "That's what happens when you deprive me."

She smiles, if mildly, stroking through my hair, and I shift up, framing her head with my forearms. "I'm going to find him, Rose," I whisper, not feeling I need to go into details. She knows.

"We can't lose you," she murmurs, dragging her thumb across

my lips. *We.* Because there isn't just Rose now.

I drop a kiss on her lips and slip out of her on a hiss. Rose hisses too, and I see two wet patches on the cups of her bra. "Okay?" I ask, plucking some Kleenex off the desk. I hand them over, and she accepts on a smile, wiping between her legs.

She sits up and looks down at her buttonless blouse. Then to my buttonless shirt. I'm not doing very well with clothes today. I manage to find two remaining buttons and fasten them, pulling my trousers up before collecting Rose's leathers off the floor and helping her into them. I frown at her blouse. I may have done myself over here. I take the tails and tie them, pulling each side in to cover her boobs as best I can. Not very well. Not surprising, since they're double the size they usually are. "I think I'll have to take you out the back way."

She smiles and retrieves her bag, pulling out her breast pump. And this is my life. I smile and go to her, slipping an arm around her waist and pulling her close, kissing her forehead. "You are and will always be the most beautiful woman to ever enter my orbit. You own every murdering inch of me, baby. Please don't ever doubt that."

She nods, her expression and eyes apologetic for momentarily and very stupidly doubting me. "I'm sorry for punching you."

"Which time?" I ask, chuckling. I'll always take her slaps, punches, and hits. With the freedom I gave her, I accepted she'll always fight me. If I have Rose and our family, I'll take it all like a man.

She draws a line down my scar, from my eye to my lip. Then down my neck to my shoulder. Across my shirt where the bullet wound is beneath. "Make it messy," she whispers, dipping and kissing my shirt.

I nod, backing away. "You pump, I'll pull," I say, smirking, and her eyebrows lift as she fiddles with the contraption that blows my mind daily. "Brad for a chat," I add.

"Cute."

I wrinkle my nose and leave Rose to take the pressure off, literally, closing the door behind me, rearranging myself. I bump into James. Again, literally. "Whoa," I say, stepping back.

"You're alive."

"I'm alive," I say, trying not to grin.

"For fuck's sake." James shakes his head. Obviously I failed in my attempts. "Everyone is out there worried you two are killing each other and—"

"We were ironing out a few differences." I pass him. "And now she's expressing milk."

"Sexy."

"Bet you can't wait." I smile back at him. I know he really can't. "Beau here?"

"Yes, she's here. You cut our date short."

"Sorry. Did Brad tell you about Elsa Dove?"

"He did."

"I think she's working for Sandy."

"Well, I'd say she's a dead woman now."

"Where's Brad?"

"Taking a leak and a break from the lawyer hanging off his front."

I chuckle. It stops when Nolan appears. "I want a word with you," I say, pointing at him.

"What's going on?" Brad comes out the men's, fastening his fly, looking between the three of us.

"Nothing." *Fuck*. I flash a look at Nolan. That's interrupted too when James's cell rings.

He frowns at the screen. "Higham."

"Why's he calling you?" I ask, looking at Brad. "Why's he calling James?"

Brad shrugs, and all attention is on James. I can't say I like the widening of his eyes.

At.

All.

"Yeah," he says, slowly, cautiously. "That's commendable, Higham, but I don't think you're getting away with it."

"Getting away with what?" I ask. What's the fucker done?

James's lips straighten, and he clicks it to loudspeaker. What's with that expression? "Tell him, Higham."

Higham sighs. Tired. "They've found a body in the woods off the interstate freeway. Late twenties. Blonde. Time of death estimated to be roughly six months ago. Cause of death, bullet wound."

I fall back against the wall. *Fuck, no.* But . . . is it her? "Formally identified?"

"Not formally. I'm sending you an image."

My phone dings, and I look down at the message from Higham, wincing at the decaying face.

"Ex-whore at Casa Black, yes?" Higham goes on. "Who went on to date Tom Hayley, who was running for mayor before he was murdered. Know anything about her death, Danny? Because it stinks of The Brit."

I laugh to myself. What, because I used to fuck Amber? And actually, it stinks of The Brit's wife. "I need to see you, Higham."

"Thought you might say that."

"I'll call you." Jesus Christ. Today needs to just fuck off.

Chapter 17

PEARL

I watch as Brad, Danny, James, and Nolan all appear from the corridor that leads to the offices. Danny, James, and Nolan head to the booth where the others are. Brad heads to Allison. I return my attention to the bar. I wouldn't be here through choice, but when a big hairy Viking tells you to get in the car, you get in the car. I doubt Brad orchestrated this encounter, as things seem too tense for him to play stupid games. So . . . she was here anyway. Last night, now tonight too. She knows where he lives and works. I'm surprised. And ignoring the sting.

I fiddle with the coaster. "Hey, sorry, it's busy tonight," Anya says, leaning over the bar in front of me. "Want a drink?"

"Yes," I say, with not much thought at all. "Yes, I want a drink." Bring me all the drinks. "I'll have a vodka tonic. Easy on the tonic." Anya dances off to get my drink, and I put my head in my hands. What the hell am I going to do?

"Hey." Beau pulls at my wrist. "What's up?"

"Nothing." I smile lamely and accept my drink, taking a good healthy glug, squeezing my eyes shut, blowing out my cheeks. She really did go easy on the tonic.

"Did you check her ID?" Brad asks Anya as he passes.

I grit my teeth as Anya rolls her eyes. Beau spins on her stool and glares at him. "Fuck off, Brad." She took the words right out of my mouth.

"Pregnancy's making you feisty."

"God, you're a dick." Beau swivels back. "I don't like him right now."

"Me neither," I muse.

"Mind if I join you?"

I drop my eyes to my glass. I don't want to look. I can already sense the awkwardness coming from Beau. I don't want people to feel like this around me. Around Brad and me. And now around Allison and me. God, and they don't know the half of it. But whatever they think they know, I need to squash it.

I pull a smile out of the bag and swivel on my stool. "Sure, have a seat." I reach back and pull the next stool closer. "Would you like a drink?"

Allison sits and rests her handbag on her lap, smiling. I can feel Beau eyeing me. "I'll have an Aperol Spritz, please."

"Anya," I call. "An Aperol Spritz for Allison, when you're ready." I slurp back my drink, wincing at the strength again. I'm in a sea of predicaments, struggling to swim. But really, Brad is the least of my worries. The call from the unknown number has shaken me. How did he get my number? "You look lovely," I say, taking another sip, swallowing hard, blinking. Allison looks no different to the perfect woman I saw this morning.

"Thank you."

"Welcome." My eyes catch Beau's. I avoid her interested, raised brows. And silence falls. I'm out of words.

"Allison's a lawyer," Beau says, and I nearly spit out my drink. "A criminal lawyer." She gives me a smile. It's fake. It's a *I'm-smiling-because-Allison-will-think-it's-weird-if-I-don't* smile.

"A criminal lawyer," I parrot, diving back into my drink. Brad, The American, one of the most notorious crime lords of America, probably even the fucking world, is fucking a criminal lawyer? Does she know who he is? "Nice."

Allison looks toward the offices. "Is everything okay? With Rose, I mean."

"Oh." Beau waves a hand flippantly. "Just a lover's tiff."

Allison nods, surely not convinced—she's a fucking lawyer after all—and looks at the spot where a woman just landed in a pile, courtesy of Rose throwing her there. Who was that woman? I notice Beau's thinking the same. Everyone has descended on the club, so something's going down. What? And is that why Fury has been babysitting me all day? Curious, I glance over to the men.

"Brad's got a nice club here." Allison's eyes settle on the stage where legs are wrapped around poles and tits are rubbing up the metal. Is that what she thinks he does? Just runs a strip club?

"Yeah," I muse.

"Yeah." Beau's still smiling, although awkwardly. For God's sake.

"Shame about his apartment," she goes on. What the hell has he told her happened to his apartment, because I'm pretty sure it won't be that Beau's mother blew it up? "The fire," she prompts, and Beau and I both visibly sag on our stools.

"Yeah, terrible," Beau says. "Completely destroyed. So you're from Miami?"

Yes. Change the subject.

"No, I'm from out of state. Washington, actually. I moved here a few months ago."

"Oh, so you're still getting to know the place?" Beau asks, a definite dig for information. Has Allison been living under a rock? She's a lawyer, and she's never heard of Brad?

"Yeah, I've been focused on settling into the new company, but"—she looks past me, smiling—"well, now I've met Brad."

Oh my God, she's falling for him. I look back too, finding the man himself with the others, eyes like slits, watching us. I quickly look away. "How long have you known him?"

"We've been dating a few months."

Dating. I flick my eyes to Beau as I take more vodka. For *months.* She's shaking her head mildly, in disbelief, I think. Anya sets a stemmed bowl glass on the bar and I pass it to Allison. "Cheers."

"Cheers." She taps my glass with hers and Beau lifts a can of Pepsi. "Of course," Allison says, smiling. "How far are you?"

"Four months." Beau feels at her tummy, and I smile, my happiness for her quite overwhelming. "Do you have kids?"

My smile drops, and I look at Allison. She laughs. "No." A sip of her drink as she looks across to Brad again. "Hopefully one day."

I dive back into my vodka again. I'm not sure what to feel right now. Sorry for poor, deluded, clueless Allison? Uneasy because I can feel his eyes burning into my back? Jealous? Would Brad ever want any of those things? I laugh on the inside. No. Brad's an arsehole. Allison will soon figure that out, which means their relationship has a shelf life.

"So you're English." Allison asks.

"I am."

"Have you been in the States long?"

I set my glass down on the bar, searching for my go-to story, the one I've fed everyone. I can't find it. "Not long," I say, tucking my hair behind my ear on one side.

Beau senses my uneasiness and hops in. "Hey, I saw some amazing beach huts online earlier." She dips into her bag on the bar and pulls out her mobile. "I saved the links. I'll text them to you."

I reach for my bag too. And remember. "Shit, I've lost my phone."

"Oh, how annoying," Allison says.

"Here." Beau hands hers to me. "Use the Find My App."

I stare at her mobile, scrambling for some words. *Any* words. Fuck. "I mean, it smashed. I dropped it." I smile awkwardly as Beau withdraws, head tilted in question. I look away. Fucking hell, I need to think before I speak. And remember that Beau was once a cop. A good cop.

"Ladies."

Oh, get me out of here. I swallow, feeling my heart wedge in my throat, and take a big breath, looking up at him. "Hi, Brad," I chirp, downing more drink.

He frowns. "Hi."

I feel like my face could fall off, it's aching so much from smiling, and I can feel Beau's curious attention passing around all of us.

"Hey, you." Brad slips an arm around Allison's waist and gets close to her. "Ready to grab dinner?" He smiles down at her. He's never smiled at me like that.

I want to vomit.

"Sure," she says, looking a little uncertain. "Maybe we can have a chat about my status."

Brad looks uneasy but tries to hide it. "Yes, let's talk about that." He casts a look across to Beau and me. "Maybe without an audience."

"Allison was telling us you've been *dating* for a few months." Beau stares at Brad. "You never mentioned her."

He looks like he wants to throttle Beau. But he doesn't entertain her, looking over to the men when Danny raises a hand. "Give me five minutes."

"Okay." Allison slips down from her stool. "I just need to powder my nose." Off she goes, and I turn back to the bar, finishing the last of my drink and holding up my empty to Anya.

She must sense my urgency and stress, because she already has one poured. "Here." She swaps my empty for a fresh drink and gives me a look to suggest she's feeling the atmosphere, which means I'm not doing a very good job of appearing fine.

"I hope you're charging her for that," Brad says to Anya, who falters walking away, looking torn.

"Here." I pull a twenty-dollar bill out of my bag and slide it across the bar. "And my ID," I add, smiling back at Brad. There's no ID. I have no ID. I'm just being childish. *Ironic.*

He snarls before walking off, and Beau reaches for the twenty and puts it back in my bag. "Pearl," she says, coming closer. "What the hell is going on?"

"Nothing's going on." I face her, smiling. "You know he irritates me."

"But *why* is the question."

"He's just a grouch."

"Right." She doesn't look convinced. "Let me just say this."

"What?"

"You don't want Brad."

I laugh. "Of course I don't want Brad. He's a certified arsehole." I slip down off my stool, because I need to regroup. "I need the ladies'." Wait. Allison is in the ladies'. So I'll grab some fresh air out back instead. "Back in a minute." I pull my bag off the bar and head toward the back of the club, meeting Rose on the threshold of the corridor that leads to the offices and the restrooms.

"Hey, are you okay?" she asks, throwing her bag onto her shoulder.

"Yes, are you?" I nod down at her chest. "What happened to your blouse?" It's tied at the tails, all the buttons missing.

"Oh." She wriggles and pulls at the material to get the best coverage over her boobs. "Small misunderstanding with Danny."

"I'm glad your blouse took the brunt of his rage."

She giggles, patting at her cheeks. "Do I look okay?"

"You look amazing, as always," I say as I pass her.

"Where are you going?"

"Ladies'," I call, rounding the corner and bypassing the ladies', pushing into the fire exit door and breathing in the fresh, nighttime air. Deep breaths. I reach into my bag and pull out a fresh pack of cigarettes and a lighter, falling back against a brick wall and sliding down until I'm crouching. Relishing the quiet. Breathing in the fresh air. I hold a cigarette up in front of me and roll my eyes, lighting up and taking back my first hit. A familiar sense of relief engulfs me, the pressure leaving my body with my exhale of smoke.

"Oh, that feels good," I murmur, dropping my head back. I'm not going in there until five minutes have passed. Or ten, just to be on the safe side. To be sure they've left for dinner and to discuss Allison's status. So I start counting as I smoke my way through my Marlboro, one to sixty, ten times.

· · ·

"Have you been stealing my fags, pumpkin? Wanna smoke like a big girl, do ya?" He shoves three cigarettes past my lips and lights each one. "Then smoke." I cough my guts up, my eyes bursting with water, breathing hard. "Smoke, girl!" He picks them up off the floor and puts them back in my mouth.

"No, please."

"Smoke!"

I yelp when he back-hands me across my cheek, all three cigarettes dropping to my bare feet. Two get shoved back past my lips. The other?

I grit my teeth, pain searing me.

But I manage to keep the cigarettes in my mouth.

· · ·

I look at the end of my Marlboro. I didn't want to smoke, I hadn't been stealing his cigarettes, but I did from that day forward. So that if he forced cigarettes into my mouth again, I wouldn't nearly choke to death. But the pain of being burned? My back twinges, as if reminding me. I pull on the end, taking the smoke deep into my lungs, focusing on counting.

On my sixth minute and second cigarette, I see a car turn into the alley off the main road, the headlights blinding, making me squint. It pulls over near a row of bins, the engine turns off, and the lights slowly fade to nothing. I push myself up to standing, taking one more drag of my cigarette and watching the car as I exhale, flicking the butt away. I only got to six minutes. I'll take my chances. I turn toward the door.

"Hey, lady."

"Shit!" I startle, flying around, finding a young guy, Spanish looking, his hands up, his eyes wide.

"Sorry, just wondered if I could bum a smoke."

"Jesus, you made me jump." I look down the alley toward the car as I rootle blindly through my bag for my packet. "Here." I hand one over.

"Thanks." He slips it between his lips. "Lighter?"

"Sure." I give it to him, and he lights up, flicking his head to the door behind me. "It's a strip joint, right?"

"That's right."

"You work here?"

"No." I shake my head, eyes back on the car down the alley. No one's gotten out. I feel uneasy.

He hands my lighter back. "Thanks," I say, stuffing it inside my bag and turning toward the door.

"No, thank *you*."

I frown, looking over my shoulder.

And come face to face with a flick knife.

Chapter 18

BRAD

What a night. I sit with the men around the table, half listening, half not, my attention on the back of the club where Allison went to powder her nose and Pearl followed a few minutes after. Fuck's sake, I don't want to go for dinner with Allison, don't even want to fuck her, whether that be at the Four Seasons or at the house. What I want to do is get Pearl in a room alone and find out who the fuck I killed in the men's.

"I have an address for the Escalade," Otto says. "Texting it to you." All of our phones ding at the same time. "And if that's me done for the night, I'll be heading home. *Again.*"

"Not quite," James says, stopping Otto halfway up to standing.

"Really?" Danny drones. "Because I've had it up to here today." He indicates his head.

"What are you telling Rose about the body Higham's reported?"

"I'm telling her nothing," Danny says, giving everyone a moment of his threatening eyes. "And neither will anyone else."

"Received loud and clear." I return my eyes to the back of the club, seeing Allison appear. No Pearl. "That all?"

"Wouldn't want to keep you from your date," James muses. I give him an evil eye. I wish he and Beau would fuck off on their honeymoon, but I know that's not happening anytime soon. And, really, I know we need all the deadly hands we can get right now. A shitstorm is brewing. Emotions are high. And the tension is off the charts.

"So, on the agenda," I prompt, distracted.

"I need to meet Higham," Danny says. "Otto, I need something on the bug on my old phone."

"Trying, Danny. Really trying."

"And find out where Luis is, what he's doing, and who he's seeing. Elsa Dove is connected to the Russians. I want to know if that's Sandy or someone else."

Where the fuck is Pearl?

"Brad!"

I jump, looking at Danny. "What?"

"I need you and James with me when I meet Higham."

"Fine." I rise from my chair. "I've got some shit to sort in the office before I go." I leave the men and head past the bar. "Mason, you seen Pearl?"

"She went to the ladies'." Beau looks up from her phone. "A while ago, actually."

"I didn't see her in the restrooms," Allison appears, dabbing at her freshly painted lips.

My spine lengthens. My eyes shoot toward the ladies'.

"What do you want her for, anyway?" Beau asks, her look accusing. "You have a dinner date to get to."

I'm blank, without the will to even find any excuse or words. *Where is she?*

"A date?" Rose asks.

I walk away, leaving the three women at the bar, the unease inside worsening the longer I stare at the corridor entrance and Pearl doesn't come out.

"I thought we were going," Allison calls, sounding whiny and indignant.

"In a minute," I snap, my pace increasing. I push my way into the ladies' restrooms and shove the door to the first stall open. "Pearl?" I say, as it hits the wood behind it. I shove the next one open. "Pearl, are you in here?" I work my way down the line, the bang of each door deafening as I shove them open, my heart hammering more with each stall I find empty. I swear to God, if she fucking left on her own again, I'll lose my shit.

She doesn't know about the cocky prick looking for her.

I rake a hand roughly through my hair. "Pearl!" I yell. I pull out my phone and dial her. It goes to voicemail. "Fuck."

I haul the door to the ladies' open and leave, feeling in my pocket for my car keys as I stalk down the corridor. I see Allison coming at me. "Not now," I hiss, catching sight of the door into the alley.

Ajar.

I slow to a stop, eyes on the door. "Wait for me in the club," I say without looking at her, walking toward the door.

"But—"

"Just wait in the fucking club, woman," I growl, flicking out a hand dismissively, my patience lost. I know Pearl is outside this door—I can fucking smell her—and I don't need Allison seeing the imminent showdown. Not that I care. But I don't need an injured woman on my back, because I am in no fit state to pacify her. Not now. Not ever.

I push my way outside, my mouth loaded ready to rant.

And suck back my words when I find her being held up against a wall by her throat, a hand on her exposed breast.

A flashback of her on a dirty mattress in the hangar, a tube dangling out of her arm, attacks me. "The fuck?" I roar, momentarily paralyzed by my anger. I get my shit together a few moments too late, drawing my gun and aiming. He yanks Pearl away from the wall and pulls her back to his front. Her green eyes are blank. Her mouth's open a fraction. Her hands are gripping his forearm around her chest.

The blade held at her neck glistens under the glow of the moon.

I lift my gaze from the knife to her eyes. She doesn't look scared. Appears perfectly calm.

I can't say the same for myself.

Red hair.

Red mist.

Red.

I close one eye, trying to line up my shot, but the fucker keeps dipping his head behind Pearl's. "Let her go," I grate, my voice thick with threat, my throat tight. "Or I will rip your insides out with my bare fucking hands." I've already killed one man this evening. I'd say that's enough for one day but knowing what I know, there's not a chance in Hell this piece of shit's walking away alive, whether he releases Pearl or not. I study his arm, the bend at the elbow, how far that precise part of his body is from her.

"You should have stayed in the club, man," he yells, the panic in his voice real. Warranted. Stupid fuck.

"And you should have left her alone." I aim, fire, and put a bullet in his elbow, sending his hand flying out, the knife ricocheting off the wall nearby before hitting the ground. Reaching for Pearl's hand, I yank her behind me as the fucker screams, clenching his arm, circling, yelling, crying. "Does that hurt?" I ask, changing the magazine of my gun for a fresh one. A *full* one.

The music in club changes, Woodkid coming on.

Run Boy Run.

Perfect. Let's make a show of this. I smack the bottom of my gun, smiling as he looks up at me. "Run," I whisper, lining up my shot.

"Brad," Pearl breathes, pulling at my arm. "Brad, stop."

I shrug her off. "I said . . . run."

Fear in a man isn't something I ever usually get a kick out of. If they deserve to die, I kill them. Today, though? Satisfaction with purpose licks its way up my spine. I realign my shot and shoot, catching his upper arm.

"Shit, no, please!"

"Run, boy," I say, walking forward as he staggers back. He turns, starting to jog down the alley. I stop, aim, and fire, hitting his lower right arm.

"Brad, please!" Pearl says.

He runs.

I shoot again.

"Brad!"

I smile when his shoulder jerks, and he screams some more. Wiping my brow with the back of my shooting hand, I keep walking as he staggers along, a fucked-up excitement sailing through my veins. I don't know who made a bruised mess of Pearl's breasts when I found her. In this moment, I'm imagining it's this sick fuck. I stop again, lift my hand, close one eye, and pull the trigger, aiming for his left arm.

Not his legs.

Not yet.

"Arhhh!" He trips, falling to his knees, looking back at me, his face full of terror.

"Run," I yell, walking on as he struggles to his feet. Two bullets left. I let him stumble on for a little while longer, his wide eyes constantly looking back at me as I follow casually, in no rush at all, the music fading the farther we get from the club. I can see he's going to collapse soon.

I look over my shoulder, seeing Pearl watching, and it's a fucking relief to finally detect the fear that was absent when I found her held at knife point. I'm fucking savage. What the fuck was she doing out here alone? Especially now I know this cunt's been looking for her.

And he found her. Unlucky for him, I found him too.

I return my attention to his pitiful, fleeing form, done with this game. I lift my gun and aim for his thigh, taking him out. He hits the concrete on a squeal and by the time I've made it to him, he's rolled onto his back. Dribbling. Crying. I stand over him, gun pointing at his head. "How sorry are you?" I ask.

"So sorry! I'm sorry, I'm sorry, I'm sorry."

"I'm not."

Bang.

He jerks and stills, eyes open, a pool of red instantly expanding slowly around his head. I let my gun hang limply by my side and reach into my pocket, pulling out my smokes and lighting up, exhaling all over him, taking deep breaths, cooling down before I go back to Pearl. I hardly want to admit my anger isn't only fueled by her recklessness.

I nearly lost her.

I flinch, rejecting my thoughts—dangerous thoughts—and dip, going to his pockets. I pull out his wallet and cell, pocketing them. I call Nolan. "There's a body in the alley out back. Lose it, and do not breathe a word to anyone."

"Yes, boss."

Now to deal with Pearl.

Calm.

I turn on the spot, taking one last drag and flicking away my cigarette, catching her slowly pulling her tank back into place, her face a sea of impassive beauty. I close my eyes. I can't talk to her right now. Can't look at her. I feel dangerous. This whole fucking situation is dangerous.

I reach into my inside pocket as I pick up my feet, passing her, feeling at the small baggy there. Cocaine will be my only company tonight. Cocaine and my unrelenting torturing thoughts that have got progressively worse since I took her to bed.

"Brad," she calls.

"Don't, Pearl," I warn, yanking the door open.

"You should have just let him slice my throat!"

I lose my grip of the door *and* my temper, then fly around and grab her face, pushing my forehead to hers. "Perhaps I fucking should have," I seethe. Her hand finds my wrist, wrapping around it, her small body backing up. I don't let her gain any distance. I don't let her pull away my hand. Her eyes aren't blank now. They're bursting with emotion. A bit of fear still, a lot of anger.

And need.

I heave in her face, my gaze being pulled to her lips. I fight the instinct with all I have as my anger multiplies, and I shove her away from me, smacking my temple with my balled fist, willing her to fuck off out of my head.

"You shouldn't have killed him," she says quietly.

I laugh, an evil edge to it. "Sorry, did you have feelings for him?"

"What?" she whispers.

I go to the wall and stare at the bricks, not wanting to look at her. But I really want to see her face when I tell her what I'm about to tell her. So I turn around. "Who was he?"

"I don't know," she cries, arms thrown up in the air. "He asked me for a cigarette." Her torso deflates. "He didn't deserve to die."

"He had a fucking knife at your throat, Pearl." Has she lost her fucking mind? "Is that how he always treated you?"

"You're not making any sense," she yells.

For fuck's sake. "He's not the only man I've killed today." I point at the club. "I also killed a man who came in and showed Mason a picture of you. Asked if he knew you. Said he'd heard you'd been seen around here."

Everything in her eyes disappears. Everything except fear. Now they're overflowing with it.

"So don't tell me you don't know the asshole I just found assaulting you. Who is he? An ex?"

"I didn't know him," she grates. "And in case you've forgotten, I was a fucking virgin until I caved to your *charms*."

The sting is very real, as is the shame. And doesn't that amplify the anger? So who? Is her family looking for her? No parents. They're dead. What the fuck isn't she telling me? "I don't believe you."

"Believe what you damn well please, Brad. I'm done with you." She barges past me, and instinct has me reaching for her arm, grabbing her.

"You will *never* be done with me."

She stills, staring at the air before her.

"And I'm not done with you, Pearl." I turn her, going against my common sense but following that stupid fucking instinct. She looks up at me, and something kicks in my chest.

Stupid.

Fucking.

Heart.

Her lip trembles, her eyes glaze over, as she shakes her head. I lower my mouth to hers. "Tell me to stop," I whisper, her head still mildly shaking but her mouth not speaking the word I need. "Tell me to stop, Pearl," I repeat, a whisper away from her lips, my body flush with hers. She leans into me.

"I want to," she breathes. "I want to say no so badly."

"But you can't." I know the fucking feeling.

"I can't," she confirms, brushing against my mouth, exhaling her relief, softening against me.

The door flies open, and I fly back, dazed.

"Boss," Nolan says, looking between us. "Are you all right?"

I take way too long to find my sense *and* my words. Pearl steps away from me, tucking her hair behind her ear. *God help me.*

I point down the alley, clearing my throat. "Pearl came out for some air and got mugged."

"Fuck," Nolan curses, all attention on Pearl, which is fine by me. She seems to have composed herself a lot faster than I have. "Are you okay?" Nolan goes to her, hands on her upper arms, dipping to check her face. The beast inside growls. *Jesus Christ.* I stuff my hands in my pockets to stop myself dragging Nolan off her and start pacing down the alley, my back turned while Nolan fusses over her.

"I'm fine," Pearl says. "Really."

"Brad, y—"

"Get inside the club, Pearl," I order curtly.

"Brad, that car," Pearl says, ignoring my demand.

I see it parked up the alley. "What about it?" I frown when the headlights come on. And my blood runs cold when the engine comes to life. "Fuck," I whisper, backing up, eyes on the car as it kicks up smoke, screeching as it pulls off. "Get in the club!" I turn and run back toward them, seeing Pearl backing up, but not nearly fast enough. "Pearl, get your fucking ass inside!"

"Shit, Boss," Nolan yells, pulling a gun from his pants as I feel for mine with one hand and pat around in my pocket for the magazine that I discarded earlier. I'm an optimistic man but running full pelt while trying to load a gun isn't an easy feat, especially when you've got a car speeding toward you. "Window's down," Nolan yells, aiming.

"Pearl, get in the fucking club!"

She scrambles for the handle, her panicked attention split between me and the door. I look over my shoulder. Mentally calculate the distance between me and the car and me and Pearl. I drop my gun, the magazine, and pick up my pace.

"There's a gun!" Nolan yells.

"Fucking shoot," I bellow as gunfire rings out behind me.

Nolan ducks, getting himself behind a trashcan. But Pearl? She's a sitting fucking duck, still trying to get in the club.

"Brad!" Nolan shouts.

I look back, flinching when a bullet sails past. "Fucking hell," I breathe, literally running for my fucking life. And Pearl's. As soon as I make it to her, I pull her away from the door and yank her into me a second before endless bullets sink into the metal.

"Oh my God," she gasps, making herself small in my chest as I pick her up and run for cover. I feel a sharp pain slam into the back of my arm. For fuck's sake. I look down, seeing Pearl's shoulder around the same place but on the front of my body, and in a panic, I wrench her away, checking to see if the bullet exited my arm and sank itself into her shoulder.

"Pearl," I breathe, scanning her body for blood and her face for pain.

She blinks. "You're bleeding," she whispers, automatically feeling at the wound.

I hiss, pain searing through me. "Yeah, gorgeous, don't touch it." I pull her back into my chest and look for Nolan.

And lose my breath when I see him on the ground. "No," I whisper, looking up the alley, seeing the car practically on two wheels as it takes the corner, smoke billowing up from the tires. "Get inside." I release Pearl and pull the door open, shoving her in. "Get Danny."

I run over to Nolan, dropping to my knee, scanning his body that's face first on the concrete. "Shit, no."

Chapter 19

ROSE

"Honestly," Beau says quietly. "I'm going to kick his ass all over the house when we get home." Her nose wrinkles. "As long as Allison's not with him, obviously. He's being a dick for the sake of it now. If he likes Allison, he should channel all his energy into her. I'm happy for him."

I wriggle on my stool, wincing at the achy feeling inside. But, God, we both needed that. It was fuck each other or murder each other. "Do you really think he likes her?" I look at the lawyer a few stools down, now on her phone after excusing herself. She doesn't seem as chirpy as she did when I got to the bar after Danny and I . . . my cheeks heat.

"Who knows what the hell that man's thinking these days."

"Well, she's a nice lady," I muse.

"And also a fucking lawyer, Rose."

I pout. "You and I always nag him about settling down. Maybe he's taken our advice." I take a small sip of my wine, now that my husband has permitted Mason to serve me.

Beau hums, sounding skeptical, and I can't really blame her. Brad's sudden devotion to one woman is out of the blue. But Allison seems reasonable. More Brad's age too. Yet I can't see her fitting in—accepting this life—like Beau and I do. Still . . . "And if he wants to hook up with Allison, fine, but it doesn't mean he has to be a dick to Pearl."

"He's always been a dick to Pearl," I point out. "I think it weirds him out that Pearl saw him as a hero." I slip down off my stool. "My husband soon fixed that when he gave her explicit details of Brad's bad habits."

Beau shakes her head in disappointment, turning fully toward me. "So how was dinner?"

I falter a fraction as I set my glass down. "Lovely."

"Rose?" she says slowly. "How was dinner?"

I cringe, not only because I don't want to admit I jumped to the wrong conclusion and completely embarrassed myself about my husband's fidelity, but I also don't want to tell Beau what Danny eventually confessed. How is it possible that Sandy, my son's father, the monster who raped me, is still breathing when Danny told me he'd ended him six months ago? I can't forget—*won't* forget—that Sandy tried to kill Beau when she lay helpless in hospital after she'd been shot by her bent-cop uncle and lost her baby as a consequence. My lip wobbles, the pain I feel for my best friend as real as if I'm suffering it myself. We've all been through so much. Beau's journey has been treacherous. And James's. They've both only recently been freed from their many demons, and I really don't want to be the person to tell her one is still alive. "You should talk to James."

Her eyes widen. "Don't make me tell your husband that you're hiding a razor behind the toilet."

My mouth falls open. "You wouldn't."

She snorts, looking over to the table. "Hey, Danny."

"Beau!" I hiss, outraged. "You call yourself a friend?"

"And *you* do?"

I scowl at her. "Fine." God damn it. "Sandy's not dead."

"Oh."

"Oh?" I parrot, studying her, seeing her obviously contemplating something. "That's all you've got to say? *Oh?*" Is she high?

"I had a feeling."

"A feeling about what?"

"The night Danny went after Sandy and came home with a few too many bullet holes in him."

"What about it?"

"I saw Sandy arrive. There were six of them. The paper reported only five bodies in the shooting."

"And you didn't think to share?"

"No," she says over a laugh. "Not until it was confirmed. I tried plying Higham but got nowhere." Her hand goes to her tummy. "Look, Rose, I'm not stressing out over something that will be dead before the end of the week."

I blink, surprised.

"You shouldn't either." She nods at my chest. "One hint of worry and your boobs spring a leak."

I look down. Exhale my exasperation. "I need to get home." I drop a kiss on Beau's cheek. "Coming?"

"I'll wait for James," she says, looking past me to the boys around the table. Calm. God, she's so together.

"Creative meeting soon?" I ask, yawning, tiredness catching me. It's been a long day, and I'm functioning on next to no sleep.

"Sure." She smiles. "Pearl's really into this project."

"I know. Maybe it's the distraction she needs." I make my way over to the men, frowning when they slowly rise from their seats in unison, all attention pointed past me. And when I look over my shoulder, Pearl's by the corridor, a disheveled mess, eyes brimming with tears. *What the hell?*

"It's Brad," she says. It's all she needs to say. The men fly out from the booth like bullets and race across the club, rage leaking from every pore of their bodies.

"You stay exactly where you are," Danny orders, giving me a look I would never dare challenge.

"Right there, Beau," James grunts as he stomps past.

I hurry over to Pearl and take her arm, bringing her to the bar and sitting her down. "Anya," I call. "Vodka. Neat." Poor thing is shaking like a leaf.

Mason springs over the bar and runs out to join the men as Anya slips a drink toward Pearl. I don't have a chance to put it in her hand. She grabs it and throws it back. What the hell is going on?

"Oh my God!" Allison is soon with us, eyes wide, looking at Pearl. "What happened?"

Pearl turns her stare onto Allison, swallowing her drink hard. She doesn't say a word. Just stares. Shock? I don't know, but I do know Allison the lawyer definitely should not be here. I take her elbow and lead her away, and she looks back constantly, both to Pearl and to where the men all just ran. "You should probably get out of here."

"Where's Brad?" she asks. "Is he okay? What's happened?" She appears panicked, truly worried for him, as she struggles to free herself from my hold. Fucking hell. I should be comforting Pearl, not battling with Brad's new lady friend, who has absolutely no idea who we are. That's Brad's problem to solve. Not mine. I look back and see Beau with Pearl wrapped up in her arms. My worry worsens.

"Brad's fine, but he said to tell you to go home."

"Rose, will you please just tell me what's happened?"

Fuck. "He's been having issues with dealers in the club," I blurt out, scratching around for more. "Pearl just encountered one in the restrooms. Quite an unsavory sort. The men are just dealing with it."

"Drugs?"

"Yes, drugs." I take her elbow. "The police have been called. It's all fine, but I'm sure you don't want to get mixed up in it. Brad's going to have to rearrange your dinner date." I guide her out the front of the club and find Des and Drake looking edgy. "Taxi for Allison," I quip, smiling like a crazy woman, telling them all they need to know with my awkwardness and an urgency I'm trying to play down. "He said he'd call you."

Allison nods, letting me hand her over to Des, who raises one of his beefy arms, hollering a taxi.

"Hope to see you again soon," I say, sounding genuine. I'm not. I go to Drake. "Whatever you do, do not let her back in the club."

A nod. "What's going down?"

"I have no idea," I answer, hurrying back inside, worried.

Chapter 20

DANNY

I'm the second to make it outside after James, my dress shoes skidding to a stop when I see Brad on his knees next to a body. "Fuck," I whisper, recognizing the suit. The blond hair.

"Nolan." Brad looks up and down his body, his face a picture I hate on him. Horror. Problem is, I'm worried his concern is wasted. This kid has a lot of questions to answer.

Or . . . had.

I look down Nolan's body, searching for movement, reaching for Brad's shoulder. "Turn him over, mate," I say, bracing myself for the damage, along with everyone else.

"No need." Nolan rolls over of his own accord on a wheeze, and Brad falls back on his arse on a gasp. "Fuck, that hurt."

I stare, flummoxed. Has this kid got nine fucking lives? "For fuck's sake, Nolan." I reach down and grab the lapels of his jacket, hauling him up to my face, raging. "I'll fucking kill you myself one day."

"Whoa, easy," James says, seeing my predicament. I seriously want to grill him. Can't do that.

"Fuck, Danny," Nolan yelps, and I drop him, scowling, looking him up and down. "You shot?"

"No, I was fucking hit by a fucking car." His face creases in pain as he struggles to sit up. Brad's still on his arse, staring at the concrete.

"Hey."

He looks at me, and I recoil.

"What happened?"

He seems to shake himself to life, wedging a palm into the concrete and pushing himself to his feet. "Drive-by." He looks down the alley, and I follow his stare, noticing a body splayed out. "Got caught in the crossfire," Brad explains, as I wander toward the dead man.

I stop and stare down at his body. "He certainly did." What a fucking mess. "Did you get a registration?"

Brad shakes his head. I look at Nolan. He shakes his head too.

"And what were you doing out here?"

Brad raises his eyes but not his head, warning me off. I heed the warning. He looks on the edge of lunacy right now. He lifts his arm and looks under it. "Fuck's sake."

"You're bleeding." James moves in and takes a look. "Flesh wound. You should get it checked out." He goes to Nolan and pulls him to his feet. "A trip to the doctor for you too, my boy."

"I'm fine," Nolan grumbles, hobbling away.

"It's not up for negotiation," Brad grates, storming through us all, back into the club. "Close the club and get the mess cleaned up," he barks at Mason as he passes. "I'm going home."

I give everyone the nod and they all disperse, leaving me and James alone in the alley. "He's not telling us something," I muse quietly.

"I'm worried about him."

"Yeah," I say, scuffing my shoes on the concrete. "I think we should take this opportunity to have a chat with Nolan." Let's get that little issue resolved, cross it off our list of things to do. "I'll meet you in the upstairs office. Make sure Brad's gone."

I head inside, seeing Nolan limping into the men's. I check the coast is clear and follow him in. "This way," I say, taking his arm and leading him right back out. "We need a friendly chat."

"What? What about?"

"About *your* friendly chat with a cop." I turn my impassive face his way, and the terror is instant. Speaks volumes. I can only imagine the menace in my expression.

"I don't know what you're talking about."

And he lies? I curl my lip, enraged, and shove him through the office door. "Get the fuck up the stairs now."

"Danny, please."

"Move!" I roar, kicking his leg. Is he the mole? Did he bug my fucking phone?

"Danny, I haven't been talking to any cop."

I ignore him and lose my patience with his slow limp across the office, pushing him on roughly. I smack the code into the pad and thrust the door open.

"Danny, I'm loyal, you know that."

I snort. "You're also fucking stupid, Nolan." I get him up to the office and, God, I so want to tear him a new arsehole. I slam him down on a chair and he yelps, straightening his leg out, holding his thigh. Great. That's where I'll start when I torture the information I want out of him. "Sit there and shut the fuck up." I pour myself a drink and neck it. I want to find calm. Can't.

The door opens, and James walks in. He nods. Good. Brad's left the building. Let's get on with this. I go to Nolan and rest my palms on his thighs, squeezing.

"Arhhhhhhh," he squeals. "Danny, please!"

"You're talking to a cop."

"No, Danny."

I squeeze some more.

"Arhhhhhhh, Danny!"

"The name Bean ring any bells?"

I can feel James watching me lose my shit, silent.

Nolan shakes his head, spit trickling down his chin. But the brave little fucker doesn't cry.

"I've had a really shit day, Nolan. *Really* shit." I pull my gun and aim it at his head. "Talk."

He inhales, eyes wide, and looks at James.

"He won't help you."

"Talk, boy," James orders. "I can't stop him pulling that trigger."

"He's blackmailing me," he blurts in a rush. I hear James's inhale. Feel mine. "Bean's fucking blackmailing me."

"What's he asked you to do?"

"He's asked me for all the footage from the club." He looks at me, eyes glazed, but still no tears. "I've been stalling, trying to think of a way out of it."

"And he's blackmailing you with what?" I ask. "What does he have on you, Nolan?"

He looks between us, hesitant, and I fear the worst. What the fuck has Nolan done? What the hell has Bean got on him that means Nolan might bend to his will? Betray us? Risk his fucking life, because he knows I won't hesitate to kill him if I find out he's turned us over. And Brad will accept that.

Nolan swallows, and I brace myself.

"It's Brad," he says.

"What about Brad?"

Another swallow.

"Nolan, what the fuck is it?" I bellow, wedging the gun into his forehead.

He breathes in.

I breathe in.

James breathes in.

"He's my dad."

My gun drops like lead, my body moving back. "What?" I stare at the kid, flummoxed, not sure I've heard him right, as he shifts in the chair, looking small and uncomfortable, refusing to look either of us in the eye.

James moves in, crouching before Nolan. "Did you just—"

"Brad's my dad." He looks defeated. "He's my fucking dad."

James grabs his face and forces him to give us his eyes, and the moment I see the pain in them, I know he's not bullshitting us.

Fucking hell.

"Bean knew my mom. Took care of her, if you know what I mean. He said he'd have you all killed if I didn't give him something to lock you up. He said he has endless shit on me to get me locked up too. And he said Brad wouldn't accept me. He'll make sure of it. That he'll probably shoot me. I don't want him to know . . . about me," he whispers. "I don't want this to change things." Now, his lips trembles, and God damn my black heart, it cracks slightly. "I don't want him to reject me."

I stare, stunned, eventually turning my eyes onto James. He's displaying a similar shade of shock.

Fuck. Me.

Chapter 21

BRAD

The girls protested when I insisted that I was leaving Hiatus on my own. Except Pearl. She couldn't even look at me, just stared at the bar while Beau rubbed at her back and glowered at me. She might recant that attitude when she finds out what happened. *If* she finds out. *I saved her. Took a bullet.* I've unintentionally fueled Pearl's misconception of me.

I'm no fucking hero.

I sit outside the house for an age, hands on the wheel, staring at the windshield, my phone ringing off the hook. I feel lost. Hopeless. The men and I are back in a time when we all need to be functioning on a full tank of energy and alertness, no distractions. We're vulnerable. Danny's vulnerable. James is vulnerable. Now I feel vulnerable too. And we're making everyone else vulnerable.

I slide out of my car, feeling so fucking heavy—heavy with guilt, heavy with tiredness. Heavy. I pull my phone out as I walk up the steps. Ten missed calls from Allison. A text from Danny asking if I'm home. Nothing from Pearl.

She told me she didn't know the creep in the alley. I haven't a clue what to fucking believe but, unbelievably, it took Pearl to remind me that she was a virgin, therefore an ex seems unlikely. Why didn't I think of that before? That's the state of my mind right now. The fact that she was a virgin escaped me as I put bullet after bullet in that sleazebag. Sending his ID to Otto confirmed it. He was a nobody. An opportunist. Not connected to anyone I should be worried about. So, again, who the fuck is looking for her?

I text Danny back and ignore Allison, opening the door. Esther is coming down the stairs, Maggie in her arms. She stops and looks me up and down. "What's happened?" she asks sharply.

"We're fine," I assure her. "Everyone's fine." I'm far from fine. "They're on their way back."

I see her deflate, her feet picking up and meeting me at the bottom. "Tea?"

I smile mildly. Esther's tea fixes everything, apparently. If only. "I need something a little stronger." I look down at Maggie in her arms. She's wide awake, her face rounder than when she was born. She's found her voice, kicking her legs, flailing her arms. I reach for her chin and tap it with the tip of my finger, looking at her properly for the first time. Oblivious. Beautiful. Innocent. "She's—" I retract my hand. "Did she just smile?"

"Yes, she's full of them tonight." Esther lifts her and nuzzles her face in her neck. "She needs a bottle."

"Ah, here's the wounded soldier." Doc appears at the top of the stairs in his PJs with his bag. "Let's have a look at you, then."

"In my room," I say. I don't want everyone fussing over me when they get home. "I'll meet you there. I need a drink."

"As you wish."

Doc reverses his steps as Daniel emerges in his pajama pants, rubbing at his eyes. "What are you doing up?" I call up to him.

He frowns at the blood on my shirt. "You're hurt?" he asks, taking a couple of steps down, stopping when I hold up a halting hand.

I look at my clothes. Blood. Everywhere. "It's just a graze. Get your ass back to bed."

"What happened?"

"Uncle Brad's lost his shit," I mutter.

"Huh? Pearl said you'd got your shit together."

I look at him in question.

"When she met your new girlfriend this morning."

Got my shit together? I sigh. "Your dad's on his way back. Be in bed when he gets home." I flick my head, sending him on his way, and take myself to the office, pouring a large Scotch. I don't hang around, heading straight upstairs.

Before I see her.

Doc's waiting outside my room when I make it there. "Sorry for getting you up." I open the door and let the old boy lead the way. He puts his bag on the chair next to the bed and starts rummaging through as I set my Scotch on the nightstand.

"It's no bother. I've been feeling rather redundant lately. Wondered whether you'd send me into early retirement."

I laugh as I unbutton my shirt and shrug it off. "Early?" The old boy should have hung up his stethoscope years ago. Did, actually, until James pulled him into our world. "You like it here, Doc?" I ask, lowering to the edge of the bed.

He smiles as he turns my arm to see the damage. "It beats wasting my days playing bridge or golf with fellow retired colleagues."

Purpose. Doc's a part of this fucked-up family. A vital part. But he's not only here because he's handy with a needle and thread. Everyone is fond of him. But he's just that. Old.

I hiss when he wipes my wound. "It's a bit more than a graze, my boy." He holds a swab over it while he dips into his bag. "Breathe."

"What?"

"I said, breathe." He replaces the swab with a wet pad, and I nearly go through the ceiling, this sting a fucking killer.

"Fuck!"

"It needs cleaning."

I grit my teeth, the sting now burning. "Jesus, Doc."

"You'll have a lovely dent," he says, lifting the pad and checking. "The bullet's taken a chunk of flesh with it."

"Nice." I take a look and grimace at the crater in my arm. "Another scar to add to the collection."

Doc chuckles and checks my shoulder as he unwinds a length of bandage. "It's healed well."

"Yeah."

"What about up here?" He indicates my head with a nod of his. "The girls have been worried about you."

"I'm fine."

"Sleeping?"

"On and off."

"Did you try the pills I gave Beau?"

I scowl at his hands working around my arm, wrapping it in the bandage. "Not yet." Neither have I tried the potion she forced on me. Dare not open it because . . . lavender.

"Try them. And let me know if you need any more."

"Will do." I won't. He knows that. But should I? I can't fuck Allison, not tonight. I can't fuck Pearl. *Ever.* Scotch only works temporarily. Coke *definitely* won't help. It all begs the question . . . should I try the pills?

He hums, finishing bandaging me up. "Keep it dry and clean." He pops a bottle of solution on the bedside with another bandage and some cleaning pads. "Want any painkillers?"

I smile and reach for my Scotch. "I'm good."

On a nod, he packs his bag and leaves quietly, and I'm alone. The silence screams at me. I pull out my phone, putting on a random playlist to kill it, then I find my smokes and light up, wandering out onto the terrace, looking back, listening when a track starts playing. The lyrics. I stand, absorbing them, unable to laugh at the irony. I definitely feel like I'm walking a tightrope. I'm *definitely* struggling to breathe.

I drop heavily into a chair and slump back.

Smoking.

Listening.

Thinking.

And when the song's finished, I play it again. Listen again. Stare up at the sky.

Red.

Chapter 22

Pearl

I let Doc check me over. Accepted the cup of tea Esther put in my hand, and swapped it for a vodka when I left the kitchen, stepping out in the garden to smoke. I lower to a step. Alcohol has taken the edge off my shock. But I'm still shook up. Not only by the weirdo in the alley, but by the words Brad yelled at me. That man in the alley wasn't the first man he'd killed today? I don't know who turned up at the club looking for me. A private detective? Certainly not an ex. For God's sake. I can't even be grateful that Brad killed whoever it was before he had a chance to leave the club and report his findings. And now Brad knows there's someone. Some*thing*. And I'm . . . uneasy.

I can't go back.

How much longer can I shirk the truth? I should go before they find out who I am. Where I've come from. But before I even consider exiting the only safe haven I've known, I need to know exactly what happened between Brad and the man who was looking for me. Or do I? There's only one person on this planet who would want to find me.

"Hey."

I look back. Beau's stepped out, arms wrapped around her body. "Everyone's going to bed."

I hold up my drink. "I'll just finish this."

She nods. "Are you okay, Pearl?"

I see the questions past her eyes. So many of them. I truly wish I could give her the answers. I wish I could stay here with her and Rose and everyone else, but I'm slowly accepting that I can't. So I pull a smile from deep down. "I'm good."

She accepts, although I can see it's reluctant, and backs up into James's body. "Night."

"Night," I whisper, swallowing down the lump in my throat. James nods, short and sharp, and I quickly turn away from them before they can see the tears falling. My shaky hand brings the cigarette to my lips, and I pull hard, feeling my tears soaking into the butt, Brad's words—again—going over and over in my head.

And I'm not done with you, Pearl. Tell me to stop.

He needs to be done with me.

I need to leave. To run. Leave the family I've found here.

I look at the gardens, exhaling and stubbing out my cigarette, rising to my feet. Brushing at my cheeks, I head inside, taking the stairs quietly to collect some things. I pass Brad's room and slow to a stop just past it.

Keep walking. Get your stuff and get out of here.

I can't risk his hatred and disgust if my truths come out. I wouldn't survive it if any of them spurned me. My eyes well up again, and I look at the door, something powerful pulling me toward it.

Him.

I take the knob and turn it, pushing my way inside, going against every ounce of sensibility in me.

He has Allison now.

The curtains billow in the breeze.

He doesn't want me to want him.

The room is dimly lit. The terrace outside dark.

I'm leaving.

There's music playing, a slow, haunting track. I'm ruined.

I swallow, padding toward the open terrace doors, the music getting louder.

I can hear the lyrics.

"Oh God," I whisper, chills rippling through me, so much so, I hug myself, coming to a stop on the threshold of the terrace. Standing. Listening to Tamer sing *Beautiful Crime*.

I lose my breath when I see him shirtless in a chair, staring into space, the smoke of the cigarette resting in his limp hand on his knee gusting messily in the breeze. Messy. This whole situation is messy. And if I don't turn and walk out, it will get messier.

His elbow is wedged into the arm of the chair, his fingertips on his forehead holding his head up.

Despair. Despondency.

Regret.

It's pouring out of his weary body.

Because of me.

Leave.

I swallow back the renewed emotion climbing into my throat,

trying so hard not to snivel and disturb him.

I fail.

He slowly cranes his head back, his eyes lifting to mine.

And something slams into me. Something powerful. Something I'm incapable of describing. He holds my eyes for an eternity, looking at me like he both loathes me and admires me. I don't know what's happening. Where this insane connection came from. I didn't ask for it to happen, it just happened, and despite everything I know—and much I'm sure that I don't know—I'm struggling to fight it. Resist it. When he was worshipping me, the world as I knew it no longer existed.

And that's a dangerous feeling for me to have.

My eyes begin to burn from staring at him for so long, and I see his shoulders lift with an inhale as he finally breaks the deadlock, turning away, taking a drag of his cigarette.

Leave.

And yet my legs refuse to take me away.

I tentatively move closer, the breeze wafting his cologne toward me, the heavy, familiar, manly scent mixing with his cigarette smoke and swirling around my head, making me dizzier. Intoxicated.

Leave.

Rounding the chair, I stand before him, my breathing quick. He doesn't miss it, his gaze on my chest—watching me struggling to be near him—before his eyes slowly climb my neck to my face. I see the wave of contempt drift across his face. But I stand firm. I don't wilt.

"I would say thank you," I say quietly, "but I know you won't appreciate my gratitude."

His lip lifts at the edge. Not in a smile. A sneer. "You can thank me, Pearl," he whispers, taking his half-smoked cigarette to his mouth and pulling hard, exhaling slowly as he leans forward, his eyes dangerous slits, "when my face is between your legs licking that sweet cunt until I'm drunk on it and you're screaming for more."

I subtly breathe in my hurt, but I remain stoic. Unmoving.

"Only then will I truly appreciate your gratitude."

I won't give in to his need to be a bastard. To treat me like an object. He's obviously forgotten in the heat of his anger that I've experienced him at his best, and his best was the worst he could have given me. Because I liked him, and I know everything else I see now is an act. "You don't shock me, Brad," I murmur, seeing the confusion he's trying to conceal behind his steel façade.

"What would it take to shock you?"

"You admitting that you can't stop thinking about me."

"No," he growls, showing nothing but disgust.

"No, you won't? Or no, you don't think about me all the time?"

"I don't care about you, Pearl."

"You're a liar."

"Come here and say that to my face," he grates, flicking his cigarette away angrily, leaning forward some more. Threatening. But he doesn't get up from his chair. I can't help but think he's trying to anchor himself. Restrain himself.

He's a fucking joke.

So I go to him, the fronts of my legs touching his. I look down at him as he tilts his head far back to look up at me. "You're a liar," I whisper.

The mixture of anger and defeat on his handsome face twists it, and he slumps back in the chair. I step back, giving him space to absorb his unspoken confession. I still don't know what I'm doing, but I can't stop myself. Can't seem to find it in myself to walk away from him. From this.

I push my hair over my ear on one side, biting at my lip ring as he pinches the bridge of his nose, sucking air through his teeth. He looks like he's going to explode, cursing quietly under his breath over and over.

I back up some more until I'm against the glass pane of the balcony, reaching back and holding on, if only to stem my shakes. And I watch him, something inside willing me to see this through to the end.

Whenever the end may be. No matter *how* it ends.

His fingers grip each arm of the chair, then ball into fists.

And he looks at me.

Every inch of his face softens, and with it, I soften too, relaxing, seeing the fight leave him and free me. With no prompt, I approach him, bending and resting my palms on his thighs, lowering to my knees between his legs. He looks down at my hands and places his on them, lacing our fingers, squeezing, watching, before sitting forward and hooking his arm around my shoulders. He pulls me into him, his face hiding in the crook of my neck, his breath hot on my skin. My body comes to life. I feel life in him too.

I move my hands onto his bare chest, feel my way around his back, and hold him tight. Get us as close as physically possible.

It's quiet but so fucking loud. And despite knowing I could be walking into an absolute nightmare, I can't help but feel like the nightmare will be worse if Brad isn't there with me.

Chapter 23

BRAD

I'm so done with this fight. I'm out of restraint. Out of energy. And as she clings to me, relief drowns me. I listen to her breathe, listen to the track for . . . God knows how many times it's been. I clench my eyes closed and slide my hand into her hair, gripping it hard. I can't ignore the ache inside anymore. Can't cast it aside as nothing. It's something.

"I can't stop thinking about you," I whisper, my mouth at her ear, my grip of her hair getting harder. "I just can't stop."

She doesn't speak, only nods, telling me she understands, as she strokes her way across my back, feeling me. I revel in the new, pleasurable feeling of a woman's warm, soft hands on my flesh. Welcome it.

Enjoy it. *Because it's her. Only her.*

Securing my hand over her nape, I encourage her out. Her eyes search mine. For what? Hesitation? Like I said, I'm done with this fight. "Get off your knees," I order gently, helping her to her feet, resting back on the chair and pulling her onto my lap. I never want her on her knees for me. Begging for me. Subservient to me. Not like every other woman I've had. Pearl's different. She triggers feelings—feelings I've not had before. Something beyond physical pleasure. So young but so strong. I know I have to ask her questions. She knows she has to answer them. But right now, I just need this moment of clarity. Of acceptance, because I'm experiencing the same level of relief I felt when I first succumbed to this madness.

Pearl straddles me, and I cup her ass, pulling her closer, resting my head back. She eyes the bandage. "What do you want to do, Pearl?" I ask, my voice gruff and loaded with unstoppable need.

Her chest expands, her gaze flicking to my room, and I clench my eyes closed. "The sheets haven't been changed." Regret and shame grip me. I'm not putting her in a bed where I fucked a nobody last night without at least changing the sheets. I open my eyes and find a faint smile curving her lips, and it's fucking stunning. "I'm sorry," I whisper, framing her face with my hands, pulling her closer as I sit up. Up until this moment, there have been two people in this world I've never wanted to disappoint. My mom. And my uncle.

Now there's three.

"Don't be sorry," she murmurs, rolling her body into mine, forcing me into controlled breathing. "I know who you are, Brad." She kisses me, her chest pressing into me, pushing me back into the chair.

And I'm lost. Floating.

I know who you are, Brad.

No judgment. No malice.

Just . . . understanding.

I no longer feel heavy, but . . . light.

I wouldn't say I'm particularly damaged. I'm sure a therapist would disagree given both of my parents' deaths, given where I am now, what I do, how I do it. But as I kiss Pearl, drink her in, appreciate the light, I realize I've deprived myself over the years. Depended on our status and work to distract me from my tragedies. Almost felt guilty grieving, because I had Danny and I had Carlo, and they were without question the most stable things in my life.

Danny still is, but he has his own family now.

And I have never felt . . . this.

I drop my head back to accommodate Pearl's height on me, sliding my hand into her hair, surrendering to the chemistry. There's not a chance I'm going to be able to keep myself from the mind-bending pleasure I know she gives me, and as our kiss deepens, firm but slow, all I can think about is watching her—watching her while I slide into her, this time knowing I am literally going where no man has gone before. Only me.

Blood rushes into my cock. "Shit," I breathe, gripping her hair, biting at her lip ring, tugging. I pull her in and stand, holding her to my front, dizzy with anticipation and desperation to relive the most intimate experience I've ever had.

I walk us inside and put her down by the bed, reaching for the comforter and tugging it off, along with the mattress cover before I pull the pillows from the cases. I get the throw off the chair in the corner and cover the mattress, then unbuckle my belt as I return to Pearl, her body pulsing, mine tingling as I drag the belt from around my waist and loop it over her head, using the two ends to pull her close. Her hands wrap around the leather on either side, her eyes darting across my face.

"I'm trembling in my boots, Brad Black," she murmurs, and I smile, pushing my mouth to hers. The belt's dropped, and I snake an arm around her waist, lifting her and pressing her to me as I walk us to the bed, growling, groaning at the feel of her fingers dragging across my head, pulling my hair. I lay her down and strip her slowly, addicted to the sounds of her impatience, of my heart, of her face as she watches me worship her, kissing a different part of her body each time I remove something, until she's naked and I'm painfully solid behind the fly of my pants. I have never been so desperate to be inside a woman.

I take her hands and place them over her breasts, and she exhales, long and loud, massaging herself as I stand and remove my pants. I reach into my boxers, feeling the dampness of my leaking cock. Fucking hell, I'm going to have her in every position known to man, teach her everything, discover her pleasure—what she likes, what she doesn't—and I'll be the only man to ever see her face like this. I push my boxers down my legs and watch her eyes fall straight to my jutting dick. In this moment, I wish she was the only woman to have ever touched it. Felt it.

Kneeling on the bed, dropping my ass to my heels, I slip on a condom under her watchful eye. Then I take her hand, pulling her onto my lap, holding my breath, feeling her tense when I skim her entrance. "Relax," I whisper, taking her hips. "Lift a little." Her leg muscles tense, her ass peeling off my thighs to allow me to reach beneath us. My mouth lax, my vision hazy, I level up and swallow, preparing for the insane pleasure coming. "Lower slowly." It's a gentle order, as I take her hips again, helping her. This is categorically the best view I've had—her lust-filled eyes, her wet lips, her pink cheeks. The feel of her shaking, her scent overwhelming me. And the feel of her tight pussy taking me inch by inch?

"Fuck." I exhale the word, keeping a close eye for discomfort. "You okay?" I ask, and she nods, breathing in, clenching her eyes closed briefly. I firm up my grip of her hips, stopping her taking any more. "Pearl."

"It's okay," she says, fighting me. "I'm okay."

"Stop," I order.

"Brad, I'm—"

"I said, stop," I snap, my voice raised. She relents fighting my hold and stops trying to push herself down. I know what she's doing here. I lift, slipping out of her. "What's the rush?" I tuck her hair back for her, kissing the corner of her mouth. "We've got all the time in the world." I won't be able to push her away after this. Not again.

She nods, her arms going around my neck and holding on, leaning back, giving me an eyeful of her chest. I raise a brow. She smirks. I drop my mouth to her nipple and flick it lightly with my tongue.

"Oh God," she whispers, her chest concaving.

"Is that good?" I ask, taking my mouth across her chest to the other, repeating.

"Bloody hell, yes."

Again on the other side.

"Brad." Her hands fist my hair.

"I think I could make you come just doing this," I whisper, tickling each bullet in turn, biting at her flesh, licking around her nipple.

"Oh God," she breathes. "Oh God, oh God, oh God."

I look up and see nothing but ecstasy on her face. Sensitive nipples. Perfect. I reach between her thighs and rub gently across her hot, wet clit. "Shit!" she yelps, grinding down onto my hand. Her green eyes swirl, her hair swishing around her face. I hold it back, needing to see her come every time I make it happen tonight, continuing my assault on her body. She becomes rigid on my lap. I keep my eyes on her, lowering my face to her breast and sucking it deep into my mouth as I plunge a finger inside of her. Her body jacks, her muscles tighten further around my fingers, and she cries out, the strain on her face beautiful as she rides my hand, takes the pleasure. I release her boob, giving her nipple a quick bite first. She jerks, too out of breath to yelp, her forehead falling onto my shoulder. I give her a few moments to recover before pulling my fingers out and taking her hair, easing her away from my shoulder.

"Open your mouth," I order gently. She does without question or hesitation, and I slip my fingers in, kissing her at the same time, helping her lick up her sweet essence. "Let's try again." I lift her, holding my aching dick at the root. The tip scuffs her pussy, and I inhale, as does she.

"I'm still tingling," she whispers.

"You're going to be tingling all night, gorgeous." I take her hips, she takes my shoulders, and she starts to lower onto me, every fraction of my length she takes, draining me of breath until my lungs have shrunk to nothing. A breathy gasp escapes, her mouth falling open when she comes to rest on my lap, her short nails digging into my shoulders. I start to shake with her, forcing back my body's demand for release. Fuck no, I'm going all night. I just need to get past this initial urge. I grit my teeth, tense every muscle. "Don't move," I say, panting.

"Are you okay?" she asks.

I smile into my darkness. "I'm fucking incredible," I admit. "I just need a moment."

I take my moment, breathing through the rush, the temptation to take the release almost getting me more than once. I open my eyes. Blow out some air. Encourage her hips round slowly. Her nails instantly scratch my upper arms. "Brad," she gasps, shaking her head, biting her bottom lip.

"Stop that," I order, watching her teeth latching on. Fuck me, I'll come here and now.

She falls forward, and I bark out my pleasure, hitting her deep. "God, you're so fucking tight." It's making me dizzy. I roll up, grind hard, removing Pearl from my chest, taking her throat and holding it softly as she instinctively starts to circle on my lap. She swallows, eyes flitting all over my face, her nails persistent in their mission to shred me. She starts nodding, her hands grappling, catching my wound. I hiss.

"Sorry!" she blurts, head rolling. "Oh God, Brad."

"Take it," I growl, rising to my knees, my thigh muscles instantly burning. "Take it, Pearl. Claim it."

"Shit!"

I growl, my hips piston, and her body's a slave to the pleasure. Her spine cracks straight, she yells, and I roar, still holding myself back, on the brink of exploding. But I won't. I'll watch her a few more times before I'll allow myself to come, because it is truly the most incredible vision I've ever had. I want more.

Head dropped back, she heaves in my hold, arms straight and

braced against my shoulders. I look down at my chest—it's red raw—and smile to myself, placing a hand between her breasts and dragging it down the center of her body to the apex of her thighs. "And again," I whisper, taking her to her back, still buried deep, and pinning her arms over her head. I kiss her nose, her cheeks, her chin. "Let's give my skin a break." I thread our fingers, holding her hands, slipping back into her, and she groans, gripping my hands hard. I find her mouth and push my tongue past her lips, rolling slowly, thrusting gently.

"Brad," she mumbles into my mouth. "You feel so good."

Fucking hell, she should feel what I'm feeling. And that's with a condom. I want to rip the fucker off and go bareback, feel her skin on skin, let her feel me. *Fuck.* I bite down on my teeth, hating that I can't. Pearl isn't on birth control—*virgin*—so I have to be sensible here. It's hard when she makes me stupid.

I feel her moves become chaotic again, her kiss harder and more frantic. "Is it coming?" I ask, grinding into her, lifting to see her face.

Her cheeks balloon, her hands squeezing, her eyes darkening.

"Go on," I whisper, watching her. "Again, gorgeous."

She yells, lifting her head, stilling, tensing, and I slow my pace, feeling it take her. She flops back to the bed on a gasp, and I smile on the inside. A little on the out.

"Look at you, all sweaty."

She laughs through her exhaustion, closing her eyes briefly, her chest pulsing with her fitful breaths. I dip and kiss her wet cheek, withdrawing on a suppressed hiss, and turn her onto her front. I put my mouth all over her back, her shoulders, her ass, her thighs, and she sighs constantly as I indulge in her, working my way back up to her neck. I see the scar at the base and circle it. "What is this?" I whisper, studying the mar on her creamy skin, the wound not old enough to be silver yet, her damaged flesh still tinged red.

"Chickenpox," she replies quietly as I rest over her, my dick wedged between her thighs. I look up at her profile, thoughtful. Not convinced. But now isn't the time. I slide a hand into the crook of her knee and pull her leg up, bending it so she's not quite front down. "Okay?" I ask, nudging at her entrance. She nods, sighs, and pulls in air as I enter her again. Her arms slide up the mattress, her face turns out, and I study her profile as I get to my knees and lift her ass a little, stroking over each perfect, firm cheek, nudging my way into her.

Fuck. Me.

I stop, swallow, breathe in, go a little farther. Her fists ball. Her ass lifts some more with no help from me. "You like that?" I ask, easing in and out, resisting the intense urge to slam into her. No. Not yet. She needs a lot more breaking in before I fuck her hard, and I'm going to enjoy every moment.

But for now?

Now, I'm going to give in to my body's demand for release and come really fucking hard.

I pick up my pace, keeping my moves firm but not too brutal, and it soon claims me, assisted by Pearl's body rolling, accepting me, her cries consistent and fucking glorious.

My body quivers, my jaw tight, blood rushing to my head as I chase my climax. She hits the mattress. "Fuck, Pearl!" I yell, eyes fixed on her face, her eyes squeezed shut. "Open your eyes." I release one hip and lean forward, fisting her hair and pulling her head back so she looks at me. And the moment I have her eyes, I come so hard, the pleasure slamming into me and knocking me from this world into another.

A world where I'm not Brad Black.

I'm just hers.

Chapter 24

Pearl

I don't know how many times he sent me to heaven throughout the night. I lost count. He's sleeping soundly, has been for a few hours, and I've watched him the whole time. Fascinated. Mesmerized. Curled on my side, feeling an uncomfortable sense of safety. My eyes skate down his chest and each of his arms. Red. Scratches and raised skin dominate the expanse of his perfect body. A scar mars his shoulder. A bandage covers his latest wound.

And yet, he's still perfect.

And I am in more trouble than I ever dreaded I could be.

I edge to the side of the bed and get up, every muscle pulling. It's a strange mix of pain and satisfaction. I've never been touched and wanted to be. I've never silently begged for more of a man's hands on my body. Because their touches were never touches. They were grabs. Gropes. Violent and uncaring. Brad's a big man. Tall, lean, strong. But tender. Each time he touches me, a small piece of "me" is revived.

I get up and check between my thighs. No blood. I check the makeshift sheet he put on the mattress. It's bunched up. I can't see any blood. I slide his packet of cigarettes off the nightstand and find my knickers, slipping into them, before going out onto the terrace. I stand and inhale the fresh air, looking at the sun rising in the distance. It's early, but I know this house. Someone will be up and about. So I take myself to the back corner and lower to my arse, leaning my bare back against the rough bricks and pulling my knees into my chest. I take a cigarette, light it, and breathe in, holding the stick up in front of me, looking at the ember burn as I blow out a plume of smoke, trying to analyze . . . everything. Only Brad can help me unravel it all. But I know that with time will come the questions. Questions I can't answer. What would he say? What would he do?

My breath hitches, my next pull on the cigarette urgent. I'm not stupid. Not naïve. Passion, pleasure, it makes people say things they don't mean. Makcs people behave in ways they wouldn't under normal circumstances. Men especially.

You're beautiful. I could fall in love with you in a minute. What did I ever do without you? I'm going to worship you. I heard it all from every one of the girls I was kept with—the things men said to them.

Didn't experience it firsthand myself.

Because no one was allowed to touch me like that.

One man did.

He paid with his life.

I flinch the memory away, my stomach turning, as I pull on my Marlboro. *Think of last night.*

A noise stirs me from my thoughts, and I look to my left. Brad towers above me, naked, scanning the terrace.

"Over here," I say, pulling his attention to the corner where I'm tucked away. Hidden. He looks relieved. Padding over on his bare feet, he slowly crouches before me. My lip slips between my teeth, my cigarette resting between my fingers, a trail of smoke drifting up to the sky. He looks at my lip. Looks at the Marlboro. Reaches for it, plucking it from my hold, and slips it between his lips. I pout. He smirks.

My eyes fall down his bare chest to his legs. To his long, semi-hard manhood hanging between his thighs. I pull at the ring in my lip with my teeth. Without a word, he reaches under my arms and stands, lifting me to his front, and carries my right back into the bedroom, flicking my smoke away. He walks up the bed on his knees and settles me on my back, stroking between my boobs before caging me in beneath him, gazing down at me, his sleepy, sexy eyes dizzying. I cock him a questioning look. He raises his brows.

And then he starts dotting kisses across my chest, slow, soft presses of his lips against my skin, over and over. "I want you to stop smoking," he says, taking a small break before going back to worshipping my flesh.

"Maybe," I whisper, sliding my hands into his hair.

He pulls his face from my skin and cocks a brow. "The answer is, yes, Brad."

I nibble my lip, restraining my smile. "Yes, Brad."

"Oh, how you please me. How sore are you?"

"Very."

"Me too."

It's me cocking a brow now. He's used to all-night sessions. Usually in hotel rooms. I wince at the thought. I need to forget that. "Really?"

"Yes, really," he murmurs, taking a lock of my hair and rubbing it between his fingers. "Because you're so tight."

I press my lips together when he peeks up at me, his mischievous smirk adorable. He slides down and starts nipping at my nipples, and the pleasure shoots straight down to between my thighs. I breathe in some restraint.

"I want to keep you this tight, but I also want to break you in over and over."

"What a conundrum you face."

"Isn't it?" He keeps his eyes on me as he sucks my boob into his mouth, watching me come undone. "What should a man do?" He sits up and grabs a condom off the nightstand, ripping it open and sliding it on while I watch. Planting his fists either side of my head, his eyes dart across my face. "Well?"

"I don't know."

He swivels his hips and plunges deep, and I suck back air, my nails automatically clinging to him. "Seems I want my cake, and I want to eat it." He pumps, his face a sweaty, tense, beautiful mess.

"Then have it and eat it," I say quietly, my overworked internal muscles flexing.

I've never seen Brad Black smile.

Not properly.

Until now.

And, my God, it's magical.

He rolls his hips, driving deeply, and I whimper my pleasure, unable to take my eyes off him, hypnotized by him. By this. By us.

My body feels trained, and I'm so grateful it's him who's trained it. I flex my torso up into his chest, and he rises, bracing his arms, grinding. It's coming again, that incredible surge of energy that wipes me out but brings me to life. His brow glistens, beads of sweat rolling down his temples. I hold my breath, and I'm ambushed from every angle, hijacked by the pleasure, the pressure bursting out of me on a burst of air.

"Fuck," he gasps, falling to one elbow, his head hanging, his body beginning to shake. "Fuck . . . fuck . . . fuck."

I let my arms fall to above my head, trying to catch my breath while I let him find his. Our breathing is noisy. Our skin wet. I feel overcome once again.

"I don't know what's happening," I say without thought, silently cursing my runaway mouth.

Brad stills, and I cringe further, turning my face into my arm, hiding. I eventually feel him move.

"Look at me."

"I don't know if I want to," I say.

"You do, Pearl. So look at me."

I turn my face out, and he spends a few precious moments, his eyes tender, studying me.

"I am the only man in this world who ever has and ever will touch you." He brushes my hair from my cheeks with both palms, holding my face.

I swallow. "Ever again?"

"Ever."

I bite my lip.

"Don't do that, Pearl."

I'm doing it to stop my smile. "Why, Brad? Why shouldn't I bite my lip?"

"Because this happens." He thrusts his hardening dick into me, and my eyes widen.

"But you just—"

"Had you, I know." He starts moving again, circling deeply. Insatiable. Both of us, and I'm lying beneath him wondering . . . why me? This capable, powerful, virile man. Why me?

It's a question for another time, because when he's inside me, my brain is mush. My body a slave to the need. My mind not my own. My muscles start to harden, dulling the ache momentarily while the pressure builds again, and I look up at him in wonder as he stares down at me. He drives in, circles deeply, withdraws slowly, over and over, the flesh between my legs throbbing and heavy. His jaw becomes tight, his eyes dropping to his arm where I'm clinging to him. "Down a bit, gorgeous," he hisses, growling when I move my grip away from his bandage.

I lift my hips, murmuring some inaudible words, clenching and releasing both with my inside muscles and my hands on his arms. He closes his eyes briefly and jerks, and that one sharp move puts pressure where I need it, and I burst beneath him again, drawing him into me.

And he goes too, his head becoming limp again, his dick expanding inside me, his groan deep. "Shit," he gasps, collapsing on top of me, panting, our chests pumping. My throat's sore. My muscles are screaming. Between my thighs feels deliciously raw. I close my heavy eyes and sink into the mattress, arms splayed above my head. I wince when Brad slips out, closing my legs, and he falls onto his back on a huff, one of his long, muscled legs bending at the knee, his palm on his broad, pumping chest. He's drifting off.

I roll away from him, onto my front, and stare across the room. *Why me?* And what now? I feel his fingertip meet the top of my arse and drag slowly up my spine, making my shoulder blades pull in. He stops on my scar, and I subtly inhale. He doesn't believe my lie about where it came from.

"Are you ready to talk?" he asks softly.

I close my eyes, feeling my time ticking away fast. "No."

He pinches my bum, and I yelp, but I remain front down on the bed, looking across the room. "Who was that man?"

"The one in the alley?"

"No, the one in the club flashing pictures of you around."

"I don't know."

On an impatient huff, he takes my hip and pulls me over onto my back. "Who would hire someone to find you?"

"My family."

He frowns, eyes a little narrowed. "You lost your parents in a burglary."

Give him something. *Anything.* "It's complicated," I say.

"Try me."

"I knew you'd say that."

He pinches my boob in warning, and I yelp on a buck. "You know, I like that more than I don't."

"Pearl," he says lowly, warningly.

"I'm just saying, you'll need to find another form of punishment if you want it to be effective."

"I'm sure that can be arranged." He moves so fast, the room is a blur.

"Brad!"

I'm spun onto my front, he slaps my arse, really fucking hard, and spins me back. "Talk."

"Fuck, that hurt," I yell, the sting biting.

"You want me to go again?"

"No," I grate.

"Then talk, gorgeous." He straddles my stomach and tickles his way from my armpits to my wrists, his fingers moving in delicate, feathery circles across my skin. Then he pins me to the bed. Trapped. But free. I can feel his soft dick lying on my lower stomach. Can see the demand in his lazy eyes.

Talk. I have never talked to anyone about anything. I'm not sure I should start now. "I didn't lose my parents in a burglary." I shrug, apologetic. "It's just an easier story to tell than the truth."

"And what's the truth?"

"I lost my mum when I was thirteen." I'm aware of the lack of emotion in my voice. I won't bother trying to fix it. I'm no actress.

Brad flinches on a blink, releasing my wrists. "I'm sorry."

I smile sadly at how uncomfortable he is right now. But . . . he asked. "Don't be."

"Your father?"

"Died when I was ten." I have no idea if he's buying this. I mean, there's an element of truth to it, but I'm being economical. Not only because his expression is hard to look at now.

"So why would your family want to find you? And what family?"

I shrug noncommittedly. "Dad owned a lot of land. I expect his siblings want it, I don't know, but I don't want to see any of them."

"Land?"

"In England."

"Your parents were wealthy?"

I nod. "And his family were not. The land's just sitting there. Wasted."

"So you lost your father when you were ten, your mum when you were thirteen."

Another nod.

"So who looked after you?"

"I was taken into care." I feel my voice crack and fight to get it under control, because I will never cry over that situation again. And that right there was a bare-faced lie. I don't want to lie to him.

"How did they die, Pearl?"

"Dad drink driving," I whisper. "My mum killed herself."

I have to look away from Brad's tense expression, hating that I can't give him the complete picture. Hating that I'm exposing him. Exposing everyone I love just by being here.

Which is why I should leave.

"In the end," I whisper, "she chose death over me, and I couldn't even be angry with her for it." I swallow down the lump in my throat, and Brad blows out his cheeks, pulling a hand through his hair. "Fucking hell."

"Yeah," I reply.

"My mum killed herself." He frowns down at my stomach. "She killed herself because Uncle Carlo killed my dad for fucking around behind her back."

"What?"

"She loved him so much, despite everything he did to her. She couldn't live without him."

I breathe back my shock. But she *could* be without Brad. That's what he's thinking but not saying. He felt abandoned. And I'm possibly one of the few people who truly understands how that feels. Because Mum chose death over me too.

Brad tilts his head, his face a mass of concentration. "I always thought she was a strong woman. Dad was a player, a fucking asshole to her, and she always thought she could change him." He laughs under his breath. "She always said behind every good man is a good woman." He looks up at me, and the pain in his eyes would put me on my arse if I wasn't on my back. "She chose to be with him in hell and left me here wondering what the fuck I *didn't* do to make her choose me."

Oh . . . shit, I cannot sob on him. I can't believe what he's shared, and as I watch him, frowning to himself, I know he can't believe he's opened up to me too, especially when I haven't asked him. I haven't pressed. We're the same, and yet so different.

"I've never told anyone that before." He laughs, uncomfortable.

"Never?" But he and Danny are so close.

"Never."

"Does it feel better to get it off your chest?" I ask, trying to inject a bit of lightness. "My hourly rate is very competitive."

His nose wrinkles as he comes down, laying his body on the length of mine. "They won't find you if you don't want them to."

Oh. And now we're back to me. "I don't want them to," I whisper.

"Then they won't."

Hope. Is it wasted? "Thank you."

"Welcome." He dips and kisses me deeply, and I soak up his affection, my fears chased away. Just for now. "I need to take a shower." He gets up, pulling the condom off and dropping it in the bin by the dressing table.

I push myself up on my elbows, watching him stride to the bathroom, his arse cheeks like rocks, his back sharp, his legs long, his thighs thick. I grin mildly, just as he looks back, catching me admiring him.

"Get that fine ass in the shower now," he orders.

My grin widens, and I shuffle off the bed, hurrying over, wincing at the constant pull of my muscles. I pass him. Yelp when he spanks my arse. "Fuck!"

"I have a bar of soap in here somewhere," he grumbles, tackling me from behind, snaking an arm around my waist and lifting me off my feet. I yelp my surprise as he carries me into the stall, lowers me, and pushes me up against the tile, looming, his erection wedged against my stomach.

"Your bandage," I whisper, full of lust.

"You can play nurse when we're done." He slips his hands behind my thighs and lifts me, pressing me into the wall. "Hold on."

And we go again.

Chapter 25

BRAD

In the shower. Without a condom. *Dick*. But, fuck, it felt fucking amazing. I pulled out, of course. It was the hardest thing I've ever done. And I feel guilty. Worried. It's the biggest turn-on knowing she's only ever known me in her body. And I have . . . been in many bodies.

I watch as she carefully wraps my arm while I sit on the edge of the bed, Pearl kneeling between my thighs. I know I said I'd never have her kneel for me. But this is nice. Being taken care of. Taking care of her. Being inside her. Jesus, it's like nothing I've had before, and not just because she's tight. I don't have an urge to fuck like an animal to get my kicks. Weirdly, her pleasure is more important than mine. I want to take my time with her. Absorb every detail of her face, feel every tiny thing there is to feel. It should make me uneasy. Has for months. But I can't deprive myself of her anymore. I'm at peace with how I feel. Which is . . . what? How do I feel?

"What?" she asks, peeking up at me through her lashes as she finishes.

"Nothing." I dip and kiss her in thanks, helping her to her feet before grabbing my shirt off the bed and shrugging it on.

"May I?" She nods at the buttons, looking a little shy.

"You want to button me up?"

She moves in, starting at the bottom and slowly working her way up. I watch her with a mild smile. "Tie?"

"It's not a tie kind of day," I say, kissing her in thanks again. It's a casual shirt kind of day for a casual, relaxed man. Shoot-outs, Russians, and Mexicans aside. I take my jacket and swing it on, casting my gaze down the towel wrapped around her. "I've been thinking," I say, rolling over how to say this. Her head is tilted, her eyes interested. "Maybe we should think about protection."

Her mouth opens, and I'm not sure if it's because she was going to speak or because she's surprised.

"I can wear a condom," I go on. Hate it, but I'll do it. "But, you know . . ." I shrug. Fuck me, I feel like a douche. "It was nice. In the shower."

Her lips twitch. "Should I talk to Doc?"

I smile. "Talk to Doc."

"Okay." Easy as that.

I kiss her gently. "Anya's going to ask where you were last night."

"I'll tell her I slept in the TV room."

"That won't wash forever."

"What do you suggest?" She puts it straight back on me. I haven't got a fucking clue. I honestly didn't expect to be in this situation. What I *do* know is that I'm a grown man, and I am not sneaking around to see her. I also know the fact I'm sleeping with Pearl is going to go down like a concrete balloon. I need to think about this. And, strangely, I have the capacity *to* think today.

"I have nothing right now." And business to sort out, for which I need to be on my A-game. "Let's talk about it later." I slip a hand onto her cheek, needing one more feel, one more kiss. Her wet hair tickles the back of my hand.

"Later?" she asks.

"Do you have plans?"

"Do you?"

"I might be killing a few men, but other than that, I'm all yours."

She laughs, and it's wholly inappropriate. But I'll take it. I like making her laugh. "Call me," she says, and then frowns.

"What's up?"

"I smashed my phone." She shakes her head. "Dropped it."

"Speak to Otto. He'll sort you out a new one. Ask him to load it with everyone's numbers." Most importantly, mine. I step into her, tilting her head back. "Kiss me."

"Or else?"

I reach under the towel and grab her ass, and her eyes pop, the green greener, brighter. "Anyone would think you like me spanking you." I raise a hand and bring it down in a stinger of a slap, knocking her into me. She grunts, her hands coming up and grabbing the lapels of my jacket as she peeks up at me and lifts on her toes, opening up, taking my tongue deep, sighing her happiness. "That's better, gorgeous."

"Call me by my name."

"No."

"Then I'll have to think of a pet name for you."

"Whatever you want." I break away and slam a hard kiss on her cheek before walking away. "Just make sure it's not *daddy*." I cringe as Pearl bursts out laughing, but a knock on my door soon shuts her up. For fuck's sake. I look back and indicate the bathroom, opening my bedroom door a fraction. "Doc?"

"Just checking up on you."

I slip out.

"You look much better," he says. "Did you have a good night's sleep?"

I laugh under my breath as we start walking down the corridor toward the stairs. "Yeah. I was going to come see you."

"Did you try the pills?"

"Not exactly." I stop and look left and right, checking for company. How the fucking hell do I put this? Yes, Pearl can take the contraceptive pill, but that only protects her—us—from pregnancy. What about the endless times I've been . . . careless. Or maybe the condom's split. "I need you to do something for me."

"What?"

I shift, awkward as fuck. "Tests."

"For what?"

Jesus, someone help me. "Things."

"What things?"

"Fuck me, Doc. Read the room."

He frowns, looking me up and down. "Ohhhh," he breathes. "*Tests.*"

"Yes." I exhale. "I just want to, you know, make sure everything is . . . clean." Fuck, this is awkward.

"I'll need a urine sample. Should probably take some blood if you want to be thorough."

"I do." I never want to wear a condom with Pearl again, especially after our shower. I stop walking, thinking, pulling at the collar on my shirt. "You free now?" Let's get this done.

"Give me ten minutes. James has ordered a scan on Baby Enigma in an hour. I just need to set up the machine." He cocks me a wry smile, and I laugh. Then stop.

"Wait, Beau's okay, right?"

"Beau's fine. You know how it is. A shoot-out, a scan. An argument, a scan." He wanders off toward his room, and I take the stairs down to the kitchen. James is mixing that green shit he and Beau love when I enter.

He looks up as I pull a coffee cup down. "You need to make peace with Beau," he says, grumpy as hell. "She's stressing about you, and I don't need her stressing about anything at the moment."

Oh. So the scan is because of me? "She doesn't need to stress about me, I'm fine."

James stops chopping fruit and glares at me. "Tell Beau that."

"Fine." I laugh, going to the coffee machine. "I will." I stab at the button and stare at the timer as it warms up, drifting into a daydream. I'm not sure what happened this morning. I had no intention of pointing the conversation onto me, but hearing how Pearl lost her mom really got me. I've buried that shit for years. I feel like, along with all the other feelings that are unfamiliar to me, I'm getting a hard dose of delayed heartache. Mom was a firecracker. Beautiful, confident.

And my dad ruined her.

I can't blame Uncle Carlo for butchering the bastard. But back then, I thought my dad really had left. What I would love to know is if Mom did too, or if she knew what Carlo had done. All answers only a dead man can give me. Danny's pops didn't know that by killing my father to save his sister, he would actually end her. But that's on Mom's head. Not Carlo's. She chose to leave this world behind. She chose to leave *me* behind. It doesn't matter that I had Uncle Carlo. She chose *him*.

I vividly remember the day Uncle Carlo sat me down and told me that Mom had been involved in an accident. I don't remember exactly when I figured out Uncle Carlo was protecting me. It didn't matter by then. I wouldn't have insulted him by confronting him about it.

He only ever did right by me.

Doesn't stop the dormant ache inside from rising though. What the fuck is with that?

I blink, the buzz of a blender whizzing ringing in my ears. "Fuck." I grab my overflowing cup of coffee and set it on the side, snatching a towel off the handle of the stove and mopping up my mess.

"You okay?" James asks loudly over the blender.

"Fine." I lift my cup and take that first, amazing sip, turning as I do. My cup stills halfway down from my lips when I find Beau in front of me. *Here we go.* I'm about to be given an earache when she grills me or back ache when she kicks my feet out from beneath me. "Please don't hurt me," I say, giving her a cheesy smile. Then I register her sorrowful face. I cock my head. She pushes her bottom lip out on a pout.

"How are you?" she asks, reaching for my wounded arm and rubbing just south of the bandage beneath my clothes.

"Fine," I say slowly, looking at James. He's watching Beau too. Frowning. Am I missing something? The last time I saw her, she was scowling at me. Don't tell me after sleeping on it, she realizes she was out of line. That she's worried about my injury. And I know no one's told her about what really went down in the alley because no one fucking knows except Pearl, Nolan, and me. Which reminds me, I must call Nolan.

"You sure?" she asks, stepping closer. Is she about to hug me? I lean back as Beau leans in, but with the counter behind me, I'm going nowhere. She flings her arms around my neck and squeezes me, forcing me to hold my coffee up and away from our bodies. What the fuck? James is shaking his head in despair as he drinks his green juice. I'm stiff as a board in her arms, not that she's noticing how uncomfortable I am. Or confused. "I love you," Beau says. "I just want you to know that." She breaks away and wanders off, taking her juice as she passes James.

"Hormones," he mutters when she's gone.

"Right." She's all over the place, hating on me one second, loving me the next.

Danny walks in, wriggling the knot of his tie. I frown at his impeccable suited form. "Since when does meeting Higham warrant a full-blown three-piece?"

He goes to his cuffs and starts fiddling.

"With cufflinks," I add, looking between him and James, who's in his running shorts. No T-shirt. "Are you wearing a suit today with all the trimmings?"

"I never wear a suit with all the trimmings." He throws Danny an exasperated look. "Unless I'm getting married or taking my wife to the opera."

"You need cuffs for that too," Danny says, getting himself a coffee.

"And an AK47," I add, smiling when James places his glass down with a bit too much force. "Do I need to change?" I motion down my casually suited form.

"You look gorgeous, darling," Danny quips.

I roll my eyes and take a seat opposite James, sipping my coffee and pulling my phone out, dialing Nolan.

"Anyway, it might not happen," Danny grumbles, glancing at his watch.

"What?"

"The meeting with Higham."

"Why?"

"Because I can't get hold of the fucker."

I cut the call when Nolan doesn't answer and start texting him. "Anyone seen Nolan this morning?"

Silence.

I look up from my cell. "Well?"

Danny shakes his head. James shakes his head. "Brad!" I jump at the screech of my name, spilling my coffee on my hand.

"Fuck." I shake off the wet just in time for Rose to pass Maggie to Danny before she dives at me. I catch her, and she hisses.

"Shit, my tits."

My eyes widen at Danny. His jaw rolls.

Rose pulls out and takes both my cheeks in her palms, her face coming close. "Are you all right?"

"Yes," I say through my squished lips. "Fine." *My cock's red raw, but I'm fine.*

She comes nose to nose with me, searching my eyes. Fuck me, it's like she has a sixth sense. I feel my face flame, and all I can smell is Pearl.

Pearl, lavender, and sex.

"Are you sure?"

"Rose," Danny warns.

"I'm sure." It was a flesh wound. That's all. Why all the concern? I've had worse.

She releases me. "I love you, I want you to know that."

"What the fuck's going on?" I ask, looking around the room.

"Nothing," all three of them say in unison, and then very quickly glance at each other awkwardly.

"Right." Fuck me, is this something to do with everyone thinking I'm on the edge over Pearl? Or are they happy because they think I've moved on to Allison? Jesus. I get up. "Let me know if you reach Higham." I leave my coffee and get the fuck out of there, meeting Otto as he enters. He stops, his hairy face an unusual shade of pity. He puts a hand on my shoulder. Squeezes. "If you tell me you love me," I say, "I'm going to rape your ass with Rose's breast pump."

He nods mildly, unfazed, as I look back into the kitchen. Everyone is watching. What's going on? And why the fuck hasn't Otto got up in my face for making such a threat? I'd demand answers. But I won't. Their unnecessary pity is better than their suspicions or interrogations.

I dial Nolan again as I take the stairs, nodding to Tank and Fury as I pass. They don't even look at me. This fucking house. Nolan's phone goes to voicemail. I try again. Nothing. Since I'm passing his room on the way to Doc's, I give him a knock. "Nolan, you in there?" I take the handle and push it open a fraction, seeing him lying on the bed, eyes closed. His toned chest is bare, a few scuffs and scrapes on his flesh—nothing major. But his leg? A huge bandage covers his thigh. A gash? Ouch. Doesn't look like he'll be walking properly on that for a while, which means I need to make arrangements at the club.

I pull the door closed and continue toward Doc's, texting Mason to let him know Nolan's out of action.

"Oh!"

I ricochet off a body, and my arm explodes with pain. I drop my phone. "Fuck."

"Sorry!"

Her voice slides under the material of my suit and licks my skin. Pearl drops to the floor and grabs my cell, handing it over. I don't take it, caught in a trance. The smell of her overwhelms me, and the sight of her? Her high-waisted jeans hug her hips, her cropped T-shirt showing a slither of skin on her stomach, her red hair freshly blow-dried, the thick locks pinned half up, her green eyes without the veil of hair that's always falling across it. Shit, she looks divine.

"Here," she says, reaching for my pants pocket and slipping my cell in. I gulp, her face close to mine.

"Why would you do that?" I whisper, feeling a flurry of activity in my boxers. "Jesus, Pearl." I look over my shoulder and past her, checking the coast is clear, before walking her to a wall and pinning her there.

"Brad," she gasps, hands on my chest, looking each way.

"Fuck." I release her and move back, just as Doc swings his door open.

"Ah, there you are. Do you want to see me now?" He looks between me and Pearl, and I cringe, knowing she's wondering why I would want to see Doc.

"Pain meds," I say, walking off, giving Doc the eye.

"Hey, Doc, mind if we talk later?" Pearl calls, making me stop in my tracks.

"Of course. Looks like I'm a busy man today, huh?" He chuckles, and I chuckle too, as he wanders into his room. I look back over my shoulder, eyebrows high. She's not wasting any time. Fine by me.

She blows me a kiss and backs away, her eyes dancing. Fuck, she's beautiful.

I follow Doc into his room, and he points to a chair where a needle has been placed on a cloth beside a pot. "Blood first, or pee?"

"Blood." I take my jacket off and roll up my sleeve, lowering to the chair.

"Wow," Doc murmurs, taking in the scratches. "You have been knocked around."

I look down at the endless marks. Feel them on my back. Smile on the inside. "How long for the results to come back?"

"I know a man who will do anything quickly for the right price."

"Drop by the boatyard. I'll let Leon know you're picking up some stock."

"Guns or money?" he asks, and I smile.

Chapter 26

DANNY

"For God's sake, Rose," I hiss, lifting Maggie onto my shoulder.

"What?"

"I told you to act normal."

"I tried." She shows the ceiling her exasperation. "What do you want me to do? Ignore him? Shit, Danny, he's going to—" She frowns. "I don't know, but I haven't got a good feeling."

"It'll be fine," I say for the sake of it. I honestly don't know how Brad's going to take the news. He seems so volatile lately. But this morning? Definitely a bit lighter. Maybe a second brush with death was what it took to bring the old Brad back.

"I hope so." She sighs, thinks for a moment, then goes to the freezer, pulling out some milk and transferring it to the fridge.

"Just try not to smother him."

"Beau did exactly the same," James pipes in.

"I'm sure Esther will too," Otto says, not looking up from his laptop.

"Great." The poor bloke looked confused as fuck, especially since the girls have been up his arse recently about every little thing. I didn't sleep a fucking wink last night, and it wasn't because Maggie was playing her usual nocturnal games. Nolan? Brad's son? We've had some shockers in this family, some curveballs thrown, but this floored me. I did the math. He was fourteen. Some girl from the other side of the tracks, a no-hoper who was an easy lay. She died of an overdose when Nolan was fifteen and he fell into the system. Poor fucker didn't stand a chance. Until he found Brad. And the more I looked at him while he spilled his miserable, shitty life, the more I saw Brad. I pull my phone out and text Otto. He looks up at me in question when his phone dings.

See what you can dig up on Bean.

I haven't told Rose some of the finer details of our latest revelation. Like Nolan being blackmailed and who's blackmailing him.

"Where's Beau?" she asks. "I need her help with the spa's color palette." She smiles wide. "The spa that's going to be finished anytime so we can decorate. Right?"

I ignore her, having a little natter with Maggie while I walk up and down the kitchen, winding down, thinking calming thoughts. Before I go out and kill a few men.

"Right?" she prompts.

"I thought you'd be distracted by the new land you've obtained," I mutter. "Permits, plans, fancy furniture."

"It's all in hand, dear."

I growl at her as I hand our daughter over. "You look delightfully fucked this morning."

She smirks. "When are you telling him?"

Kill my buzz, why don't you? I feel a stressed sweat coming on. "I don't know." Of all the shit I have to deal with, I'm looking forward to that problem the least.

"He needs to know," James says, checking his watch.

"Agreed." Nolan doesn't win that fight. "But for now, we need Brad's head on straight." I drop a kiss on Rose's forehead. "Where's the kid?"

"Showering. He should be at school." She sighs. I agree. He should. "He wanted to see Barney. I said no."

"Come on, Rose. Give the kid a break."

Her indignance is fierce. She sees any intervention as me questioning her mothering skills. "He threatened to stab a kid, Danny." She pushes her face close, her eyes as fierce as her indignance. "With your shiny gold letter opener."

"Such emphasis put on *yours*," I reply, making sure she sees my fierceness. "Is it my fault?"

"No."

"Is it the kid's fault?"

"No."

"No, it's Preston Bean's father's fault."

"And you're leaving that situation well alone. Right?"

"You're firing a lot of *rights?* this morning, baby." I push my face into her cheek. "I told you not to worry. I've got other shit to deal with at the moment."

"Like shoot-outs."

"Exactly." I turn her and pat her bottom. "Have a lovely day, dear." I give Tank a nod when he immediately falls into position like the mind-reading robot he is.

"Right." I give my attention to James and Otto, frowning to myself. "Okay. My office. Now." I march out across the foyer and down the corridor, pushing my way through the door and doing what I always do when I enter—breathe in my old man and his lingering scent that's still embedded into every thread of fabric. Minus the rug that's been replaced a few times.

"What bright spark thought I could retire, eh, Pops?" I sit at the desk and open the drawer, pulling out the letter opener, smiling at the blade as I spin it. Then the photo of Pops. He thought he took the secret of Brad's parents to the grave with him. He should have given Brad more credit. Bombshell after bombshell. And where the hell has that Russian fuckhead put his body? "I'll find you, Pops." I slip the photo back into the drawer when the men file in. And Goldie. She looks around. "Where's Brad?"

"Going to the club."

"Alone?"

"No, not alone." I point to the couch. "Sit."

She lowers, but not without her usual attitude.

"I've got Fury on him." I rest back in my chair. "I need him *not* to be here while I get a debrief." So much has happened the past few days, I've forgotten who I'm supposed to be killing.

"I have something," Otto says, winning the attention of everyone in the room, naturally.

"Go on."

"I picked up on a sale of a derelict warehouse by MIA."

"Okay."

"It was paid for by wire transfer from a bank in Moscow." He taps away at his keyboard so casually. "Naturally, such activity promoted me to investigate further."

"Naturally," I murmur, noticing James shaking my head in amazement.

"And I found another unit half a mile up the dirt track that's been paid for by wire transfer from a bank in Mexico City."

My mouth falls open. "That's kind of convenient."

"I thought so too." He snaps the lid of his laptop closed. "So, given the evidence, I'd say the Russians and the Mexicans, both of which have beefs with us, might be joining forces."

"Funny, I was thinking the same," I say, thoughtful. "That's quite a force." There's familiar worry on everyone's faces. "And to add to our problems, we've got Bernard King as the possible supplier of their weaponry." I smile. "Fabulous. Oh, and let's not forget the few drive-bys and the fact that Amber Kendrick's body's just turned up." For fuck's sake. "I need some breakfast." I get up and go to the bar, pouring myself a Scotch, necking it. "And in addition, Daniel's school principal threw him out as a direct result of a cop called Bean who's been trying to blackmail Nolan for information on us in return for keeping his mouth shut about the fact that Nolan is Brad's kid." I exhale, smiling. "Everyone clear?"

"Clear," everyone grunts.

"And I've somehow got to convince my wife to go back to St. Lucia."

Goldie sighs. "God, you poor, delusional fuck."

I glare at her. "Don't come back here with your attitude on steroids after stuffing ice creams." I get up in her face, and she grins.

"Sorry, boss."

I'm not stupid, she's humoring me. And she's also right. I'm fucking delusional. I look at James, ready to ask what he plans on doing with Beau, but he's staring across the room, his mind obviously spinning.

"Oi," I yell. "What are you thinking?"

"I'm thinking . . ." he hums.

"James, for fuck's sake, what are you thinking?" I need more brain power, because mine's knackered.

"I'm thinking we break this down into small, manageable pieces."

"The fuck?" I breathe, as Goldie and Ringo chuckle. "You been taking parenting classes?"

He stands, tall, intimidating, and pissed off, and I step back, wary. "We'll start with Bean."

"He's out of state on a training course," Otto pipes in.

"How the fuck do you know this shit? Where?"

"That, I can't tell you."

Which means it's some police secret shit. Is he trying to move up the ranks? "When's he back?"

Otto peeks up at me tiredly.

He can't tell me that either. Fabulous. We're making fucking strides.

"No one says anything to Brad about Nolan. Act normal." Until I know how I'm going to break it to him, and when. I would have kept it between me and James, but Otto walked in on us, followed by the others, and I couldn't hide my shock. Even when I got home, I had to tell Rose. Had to. *Fuck, I need a cuddle.* I feel like we're getting precisely nowhere. "I'm going to find my wife."

"Danny, wait," Otto calls, pulling me to a stop halfway down the corridor.

"What?" I ask, facing him.

"There's something else?"

There's more? "What?"

"I want to marry your mother."

I sneer at him. I know I can't say no. I know he's being honorable. I know Mum, God help me, loves this big, hairy beast. And I know Brad's right. I should want her to be happy.

But still . . .

I pull my fist back and deliver a stellar right hook to his jaw, knocking him back ten paces until he hits the deck outside the open office door. Everyone comes to investigate while I shake my hand. *Motherfucker.* "Fine," I snap like a child, getting on my way. "But if you hurt her, I'll ram Rose's breast pump up your arse."

"That breast pump sure is going places," James says from the door. I grunt, throwing my hand up, annoyed, irritated—stressed—that the world's back on my shoulders. Except now the responsibility feels so much worse. It's not just me, my name, and the family reputation. It's everyone in this family. Because despite the arguments, the digs, the physical tussles sometimes, we *are* a family.

And it needs protecting.

I try to calm myself down as I take the stairs, breathing deeply, needing to be stable. I approach Nolan's door, straightening my tie. What the fuck am I doing?

"What are you doing?"

"Brad?" I blurt. He hasn't left? I frown, looking up and down the corridor. Brad's room is that way, but he just came from the other way. "Where have you been?"

He shifts, looking instantly uncomfortable. "Doc's," he says, just as the old man comes out of his room with a bag in his hand. And a pot of piss in the other.

The old boy slips it into his bag, embarrassed, and passes. "Good day to you," he says.

"Good day," I muse, returning my interested attention to Brad. "I didn't know dressing wounds required piss samples."

"Fuck off," he spits, barging past me. "He thinks I have a UTI."

"Oh," I muse, not stopping him from storming off. Not so light now. "You ready for shit to fly?" There are plenty of feathers to ruffle, just as soon as I've ruffled Bean's feathers. Can't take Brad for that.

"Yes." He pulls out his gun and holds it up as he carries on down the corridor, and I smile at the sight of my wingman back to his bloodthirsty self. But for how long? I don't know what he was doing in that alley with Pearl. Or am I being dumb?

No.

Pearl wouldn't, and Brad *definitely* wouldn't.

He would literally be taking his life into his own hands. The girls would skin him. And she's . . . so young. Like the same age as Nolan. *His fucking kid.*

Jesus. I return my attention to the door and knock.

Silence.

I push my way inside. He's lying on the bed, still and quiet. "Nolan?" I close the door and pad over to the bed. He opens one eye. "Pretending?"

"Brad came in."

Of course he did. "Listen"—I rub at my forehead with the tips of my fingers—"he has to know." I pull a chair over to the bed and lower into it.

"No, Danny, pl—"

"I can't take this to the grave, Nolan. It's too fucking big, and it's not fair to Brad."

"I want things to stay the way they are," he grates, returning his eyes to the ceiling.

I smile at his naivety. "It ain't gonna happen, kid."

"What if he rejects me?"

"I won't let him."

He looks at me, and the hope I see in his eyes gets me in the gut. I've given him that hope and, honestly, I really don't know how Brad's gonna handle this. He's not dealing with anything very well these days, and this might be a push too far. But I'll fucking try.

"What about Bean?" Nolan asks. "He said he has loads of old shit on me. Things that'll have me put away for a long time, Danny. And he'll get you all killed."

"I'll deal with Bean." Just as soon as he's back from training camp. The delusional fuck. "You don't have to worry. How's your leg?" End of discussion.

"Doc said I've strained a few muscles." He feels down his thigh. "Feels like I've fucking broken it. There's a gash, nothing major. A few stiches fixed it."

I nod mildly. "I'm sorry for . . . well, torturing you."

He laughs under his breath. "No problem."

"What happened in that alley, Nolan?"

He keeps his attention on his thigh, stalling a moment too long. "We saw the back door open. We checked it out, found Pearl smoking."

"We?"

"Me and Brad."

"And?"

He shifts, leaving another beat of silence I'm not sure I like. "And Brad lost his shit with Pearl."

"Standard."

He smiles. "The car was parked at the end of the alley. Came at us fast."

I nod, thinking. It's plausible. And Nolan would be a fucking fool to try me right now. I stand, pushing the chair back into the corner. "I've got some things to deal with."

His eyes shoot to mine.

"Not that. Not yet. I need Brad on the ball while we figure a few things out. But I *will* be telling him, Nolan."

He nods, defeated but accepting.

"You need anything?"

He shakes his head.

"Rest up." I give his shoulder a reassuring squeeze and leave, answering a call from Higham as I close the door.

"Finally," I breathe. "Meet today?"

"Yeah, no."

I frown at my mobile. "What?"

"I'm out of town."

"What?"

"My wife surprised me for my birthday, Danny. What the fuck could I do?"

"Say no."

He laughs. "I'm lucky I'm still married."

"What about the woman that was found dead?"

"They're still identifying the body so don't panic."

I laugh. Easy for him to say. "I'm not happy."

"Me neither. But here we are. I'll call you when I'm back in town." He hangs up.

"Fuck," I curse. But it's not like I haven't got enough to keep me busy. I check my watch as I wander down the corridor. Nine. It's going to be a long day.

Chapter 27

DANNY

It's been a long fucking *week*. A week of silence, no action, no calls, and no more shoot-outs. I'm not relieved. I still haven't broached the subject of my wife and children leaving for St. Lucia, there's nothing happening at the warehouses that were bought by the Russians and Mexicans, Bean is still at training camp, and Higham must be having a merry old time on holiday because the fucker isn't answering my calls and hasn't let me know when he's back. The one thing that hasn't happened that I am grateful for? Otto doesn't appear to have popped the question to Mum. I hope he's bottled it. Realized she's too good for him. Unlikely because, fuck my life, he's very good for her.

I wriggle the knot of my tie and leave our room, sending a prayer for answers today. I bump into Pearl halfway down the stairs. "All right?" I ask, stopping, telling her she should too.

"Yeah, just getting my bag. We're going to the spa."

Great. I'll expect a call from Alan soon. "Take Tank."

"Yes, Danny. We're taking Tank."

I look up and down the corridor, preparing to ask what I've been wanting to ask for a week now, but have stalled, perhaps because I'm a little worried about what I might hear. "Tell me what happened in the alley that night," I order softly, watching as Pearl's smile falters.

"What?" she breathes.

"You didn't hear me?"

"Yes, I heard you."

"Well?"

"I went out to smoke."

"You shouldn't be smoking."

She rolls her eyes. "I'm a—"

"And? What else happened?"

"Nolan came out. I left the door ajar."

Nolan went out? Alone? What about Brad? "And?"

"And we were just chitchatting."

"Chitchatting," I muse. "And?"

"Then Brad came out and ranted, as per usual Brad."

"Standard."

"Yes. And then it's a bit of a blur. Screeching tires, guns firing."

I nod, slipping my hands into my pockets and carrying on. "I'm glad you're okay." I'm sure I've left a frowning face behind. "Enjoy your day," I call back, heading for the kitchen, thinking.

There's no breakfast laid out. I feel the coffee machine. Cold. I wander over to the laundry room. Empty too. And the washing machine is silent.

This is . . . odd.

I wait for the coffee machine to warm up, pondering my day, and watch as it spits out my caffeine, then answer a call from Otto. "Where are you?" I ask.

"In the kitchen."

I look around for him. No Otto. "*I'm* in the kitchen."

"Oh."

"So where are you?"

A beat. A sigh. "I'm in bed with your—"

"Okay," I blurt. "Why the fuck are you calling me when you're in bed with—" I can't say it. "What do you want?"

"Bean's back."

"Got a ring to it, hasn't it?" I take a sip of my coffee. "Anything else?"

"The Escalade that pulled the drive-by on Brad was seen back in Lake Harbor last night."

Great. "Now get out of that fucking bed. We've got shit to do." I hang up and shudder, pouting to myself, wondering if Otto's bottled it. Changed his mind. Or did Mum say no and he doesn't want to admit it? I send a quick message to James to meet me outside with the others.

"Morning, stud."

I look up and find Rose in the doorway, Maggie half concealed under her tank. Give me strength, my daughter feeding from my wife should *not* turn me on. "Come here," I order, resting back against the counter, taking more coffee. Bean's not only getting a visit from The Brit today, he's getting a visit from The Brit high on caffeine.

Rose comes straight to me and leans up, giving me her lips. I drop a kiss on them. Damn it, I am *not* looking forward to reining in her freedom. She can have today. After that, I have to brave telling her she's going back to St. Lucia.

"You look beautiful."

"I just woke up." She nuzzles my nose and kisses my scar.

"You look beautiful." I repeat. Her hair's piled in a messy bun, strands falling down here and there. "Really beautiful."

"What are you doing today?" she asks, moving back, checking on Maggie. She knows shit's about to hit the fan. She's asks me every morning what I'm doing today.

"This and that."

"Telling Brad about Nolan?" Her eyebrows rise as I down the rest of my coffee.

"Not until I've sorted a few things out."

"Like . . ."

I drop a kiss on Maggie's forehead, her eyes rooted on me as she suckles. Fuck, she's a beauty. We created this. Two fucked-up humans made something pure and untarnished. It defies reason. And it blows my mind every minute of every hour of every blessed day. "See you later." Another kiss for my wife before I leave.

"Aren't you going to ask what *we're* doing?" she calls.

"I know what you're doing. You're going to the spa."

"And you're okay with that?"

"Not really, but I know my limits, Rose." I reach up to my nearly fully recovered nose, and her lips straighten. "I've put a gun in your purse and there's a baby carrier in the trunk of Tank's car. Use it."

She inhales deeply, but she doesn't argue.

"Just be vigilant, okay?" There's no question—if I didn't trust Tank with my family, they wouldn't be leaving the house. I need to get this shit dealt with so normal life can resume. I laugh to myself as I head through the entrance hall. Normal life? What the fuck is that?

I open the door and step out, finding Goldie, Otto, and Ringo in one of the Mercs, waiting, and James perched on the bonnet on the Range Rover up front. No Otto. I mutter my disapproval under my breath as I walk down the steps, seeing Brad's Merc pulling out of the gates down the driveway.

"Did he say anything?" I ask, approaching the car.

"Not a thing. Just slipped into his car and left."

Weird. He's absent again, although definitely not as grumpy.

Maybe this thing with the lawyer is working out. Still, he's supposed to be present, and he's definitely not that. So he walked out of the house, saw all the men in the car, and didn't think to ask where we're going? I hum to myself, watching Fury pulling off to tail him. We shouldn't be out on our own, and I can't be bothered with a disagreement over that with Brad. So Fury's just . . . there. At the club, at the boatyard. And we can't take Brad to where we're going. "You can drive," I say to James, getting in the passenger seat. "Bluetooth?" I ask, prompting James to go to the screen.

"I'm connected. Wait up." He disconnects his phone and connects mine. "You're good."

I call Ringo, resting my arm on the door. "Danny," he grunts. "What's the plan?"

"Today, Ringo, we kill lots of people."

"I'm excited."

I smile. "I want you three to drive up to Lake Harbor and check out the Escalade situation. And I mean, just check it out."

"You said we get to kill today," he grumbles.

"Patient, child," I muse, as James laughs under his breath. "We need information first." Like why the fuck a retired cop's vehicle was involved in a drive-by on us. "We're going to pay a little visit to Bean and then check out the factory units again." I look out of my window, seeing Otto coming down the steps, a laptop in one hand, his jacket in the other.

He comes straight to my window, and I hit the button to let it down, glaring at him. "What?"

"Bean. He has three phones."

"Oh?"

"One work, one personal, and one—"

"Very personal?"

"I'm checking the records."

"Let me know what you find. I'm hoping Higham's back from his inconvenient holiday soon." I've got to talk to him about Amber's body, along with a few other things, the kind of things you don't want to talk to a cop about over the phone. I raise the window and exhale, looking at James as he pulls off. "What do you think happened in the alley the night Nolan got hurt?"

He turns a frown my way. "Why?"

"Something feels off."

He laughs a little. "Probably because something is always off. What's off?"

"I don't know. My brain's always fucking aching lately. What do you make of Brad and Pearl?"

"I think she was momentarily enthralled by a big, bad-arse mafia boss saving her. Then she found out he's a cunt."

I chuckle. "And Brad?"

"I think he finds Pearl attractive."

"Who wouldn't?" I ask.

"You *shouldn't*."

"I'm just saying. She's a woman. A beautiful young, smart, strong woman."

"Something I'm sure hasn't escaped Brad's notice, either." He pulls a left at the gates. "But the fact is, she's twenty-one."

"He wants to fuck her."

"But he won't because that's *all* he'll want to do, and Brad's not dumb. He doesn't get caught up in anything complicated. Hence hookers and hotels."

"So how do you explain this lawyer woman?"

He sighs. "I don't know, I'm not a psychotherapist."

I hum and lay off the questioning. It's not like I have the brain space to spare, and Brad's certainly going to have more problems than wanting to fuck Pearl when he finds out his long-lost son's been working for him for over a year.

• • •

We sit at the end of the road in a leafy, respectable suburb across town, watching Bean's house. A woman comes out with a young lad, and they get in a car and pull away.

"How lovely," I say, watching them pass. "Little Preston's going to school." I open the door and slide out, James following, both of us checking the backs of our pants.

"Is there a plan?" he asks as we cross the road.

"Let's see how it pans out."

James pulls out his cell when it rings. "Otto." He puts it on speaker, holding it between us.

"The third phone," Otto says. "He calls one person."

We look at each other, moving in closer. "His shrink?" I ask.

"Officer Mandy Leeson," Otto says. "Image sent to Danny's phone."

I open the message and hold it up, and we both lean in, taking in the image of a very striking young woman in blues. "Ohhhh," I breathe. "Bean's been a bad boy."

James chuckles. "Bean's *being* a bad boy. Thanks, Otto."

"I love it when a plan comes together."

James strides up the front yard path to the solid wooden front door, knocking it with his massive fist.

"You're keen," I muse, following.

"I want to go on my honeymoon."

I laugh, but I know it's no joke. James wants to get this mess fixed so he can pick up his pregnant wife and get her back to St. Lucia. I bet he has better luck than I do.

We wait, listening for any movement inside. "Work?" I ask, wandering to the corner of the house and looking up the drive to the garage. A Lexus greets me, answering my question. "Maybe he's having a morning coffee and natter with his bit of stuff now the wife and kid's left." I say. "I'll take a look round the back." Wandering up the driveway, I look up and see a security camera mounted on the back corner. I reach over the gate and feel around for a latch, find one, and pull the lever. When it creaks open a fraction, I remain on the threshold, pushing it open some more, craning my neck to see into the back garden. There's a sliding door on the side of the house leading into the kitchen.

Open.

"Tut, tut," I say quietly, wandering in and looking around. Breakfast dishes, bread, jam, and cereal have all been left on the counter, and there's a half-empty coffee pot, steam rising from the spout. "Don't mind if I do." I find a cup and pour myself some, going to the fridge for some milk. No milk. "What kind of café is this?" I mumble, settling for black. I pad quietly through the house, pushing every door I pass open a fraction, peeking inside. There's the distant sound of a shower running when I reach the bottom of the stairs, but the knocking on the front door distracts me, pulling me there. I open it. Smile wide.

"For fuck's sake," James mutters, stepping inside, pulling his gun.

"He's in the shower." I point to the stairs with my cup.

"Black?" James questions, throwing my coffee a look as he passes.

"Like my soul," I whisper menacingly as I follow him up, looking around the space. "And my name, ironically." There are clothes strewn over the banister, some on the floor. "The kitchen was a state too. Messy fuckers."

"Your mum would have a fit."

I chuckle, taking some more coffee. "This is good coffee though."

"Not as nice as Esther's tea, surely?"

"Never," I reply, disgusted. Nothing beats Mum's tea.

James stops at a door, pushing it open a little, and the sound of running water gets louder. He looks at me, flicks his head, and I take his prompt, walking into the bedroom. The bed's unmade. It's a lovely house, but mess everywhere. Have they no pride in it?

I walk toward the bathroom and peek into the steam-filled room. The shower screen is fogged, giving me only a silhouette of Bean, nothing clear. But I can hear him *very* clearly.

Grunting.

Moaning.

I look back at James, my eyebrows probably blending with my hairline. He's mildly shaking his head, disbelief a blanket on his face. I lower to the toilet seat, coffee in my left hand, gun in my right, and cross one leg over the other, while Bean continues to grunt and . . . squeak. He's fucking squeaking.

"Are you wanking off, Bean?"

"Fuck!" A collection of clatters rings around the bathroom, and I wince when an ear-piercing bang sounds. Bean taking a tumble. He lands on his back, his head, conveniently, at the right end to see me.

I lift my cup. "Morning."

"Jesus Christ." He scrambles to his feet, not reaching for a towel, but instead reaching for his gun belt on the sink. The gun belt that has no gun in it. My smile widens as James lifts Bean's weapon, his finger in the trigger ring, making it dangle.

Bean's face falls more, and this time he opts for a towel, snatching one down from the heated rail and covering himself. He's a bit soft around the middle. Receding. Pushing fifty. A poor excuse for bristle. As ugly in the flesh as he is in the photograph. He doesn't ask who I am. There's no need, so I skip the introductions. "Tell me, Bean," I say, remaining on my arse, still enjoying my coffee. "Were you jerking off to your wife or Mandy?"

His face.

It's faces like these I wish I could collect. "Fuck," he whispers.

"Let's have a little chat." James steps back from the door rather than manhandling Bean's wet, naked body into the bedroom.

"Off you trot," I sing, smirking at James when he looks at me tiredly. "What?" I've missed this fun. "Sit your arse down."

Bean flops onto the bed, arranging his towel. His dignity is the least of his problems. "How's your boy getting on at school?"

"Oh fuck, please. Leave Preston out of this."

"Tell that to my son. He's currently polishing my lovely gold letter opener." I kneel, all amusement gone, my face twisting with utter contempt for this piece of shit. "You got my kid thrown out of school. I should rip your fucking guts out." I rise and swipe at his face with the handle of my gun, sending him to his back on a blood-curdling crack. "That was mistake number one." I smash the coffee cup on the edge of the nightstand and pick up a jagged blade of porcelain. "Nice cups, by the way. Look expensive."

"Shit, please, no." Bean scrambles across the bed minus one towel, and James walks around, meeting him on the other side.

"Don't make me touch you," James warns, pushing his gun into Bean's forehead. He scrambles back to the middle.

"The grass isn't greener over there, my friend."

"Look, I'm sorry, okay? I'll back off. Please, please don't hurt me."

"Mistake number two," I say, holding my makeshift blade up and inspecting it.

"Danny, please."

I turn my stare away from the blade. "You may call me Mr. Black." I grab his ankle and haul him toward me, slamming the blade into his thigh, just shy of his main artery. I'm not an unreasonable man. I know I can't kill a cop in his home and get away with it, but I can torture the fucker and get away with it. Because I can guarantee he won't utter my name ever again. I also have Mandy as a backup. Today's going well.

"You've been in touch with someone very dear to me, Bean." I twist the makeshift blade, and he chokes more. "My nephew."

He stills, looking at me with wide eyes. "What?"

"You thought you could force information out of him for your silence?"

"No, I—"

"Bad, bad move, Bean." I pull the blade out of his leg, spiking a suppressed scream. "How would your wife feel knowing you *looked after* Nolan's mother? And your department. Bet they'd love to know."

"Oh, Christ," he mumbles, sniffing, wiping at his nose.

I throw him the towel. "Cover yourself up. I can't concentrate with your limp dick staring me in the face."

I peek at James, and he looks familiarly stoic. Dark. Deadly. "Anything to say before I tell Bean here what's going to happen?" I ask, wondering if he wants a piece of the action.

"Yes."

"What?"

James takes the lamp off the nightstand and clouts Bean around the head with it. "That's all."

"Lovely. So, yes, as I was saying." I frown at Bean as he falls back, eyes closed, and my shoulders drop. "For fuck's sake," I mutter, kicking his leg. "You knocked him out."

"Oops." James tosses the lamp aside and walks out, leaving me, open-mouthed, watching him go. "Your games get boring after a while."

"I thought you loved my games." I lean down and give Bean a few slaps around the face, bringing him round. He blinks up at me. "The Enigma just saved your life. Not many men can claim that. Do I need to explain what happens next?"

He shakes his head, blinking.

"Good." I leave him, catching up with James on the stairs. "You're no fun anymore. I remember the days when you used to chop limbs off and talk dirty to your prey." I pull out my cigarettes and light up as we walk out into the sunshine.

"You won't say that when we find Sandy." He fires the fob at the Range Rover. "Who next?"

"We're picking up Brad." I get in the car and roll the window down. "Mind if I smoke in here?"

"Yes." He starts the car and pulls away.

I take a drag and do my best to exhale out of the window. "We need to take the girls out for dinner. I miss our double dates."

"You took Rose out last week."

"That was last week."

"Does she still think you're having a fling?"

I laugh. Yeah, I'm fucking my way through Miami in between insomnia and murdering all the fuckers that refuse to let us have our peace.

Chapter 28

BRAD

For the first time, Ella isn't on me like a wolf when I enter the club, as she has been each time since Nolan had a fight with a speeding car, asking if he's okay, when he'll be back. She's worried. She can't fake that. She briefly looks up at me from where she's sitting in a booth on the other side of the club before quickly giving her cell her attention again.

"Is she okay?" I ask Mason, stopping at the bar. Oh Jesus, don't tell me Nolan's broken the bad news and finished it with her. I demanded it, I know, but I haven't got the capacity to replace her at the moment.

Mason peeks up at me, eyebrows high. "She's not happy."

Dare I ask? "Why?"

Nolan appears at the door on a pair of crutches.

"That's why," Mason says. "She told me to send him home. I told her I don't have the authority to do that."

"As of now, I give you the authority. What the fuck, Nolan?" I say, looking up and down at the shorts and T-shirt he has on, a sneaker on one foot.

"I couldn't get my suit on."

"You shouldn't have got *anything* on." I follow his path as he hobbles past. "Nolan," I call. "Get your ass home."

"I'm fine."

I look at Mason, astounded. He shrugs and gets back to counting the float. From Ella's expression, I can tell she's had this row with him. I'm ignoring the fact that feelings are involved if she's insisting on him resting. For fuck's sake. I go after Nolan, trailing him into the office. "And what the fuck do you think you're going to do here?"

"Work."

"Doing what?"

"I don't know. Something."

"Nolan, I said—"

"I'm fine!" he yells, wobbling on his crutches, nearly putting himself on his ass.

I withdraw, shocked, and he starts breathing through his nose, obviously trying to cool himself down. He looks . . . really fucking troubled. What happened has really got to him. "It's all part of the job," I say, giving him space rather than getting up in his face, giving him soft rather than the usual tough love. He looks like he'd break if I let loose on him.

"I know."

"But if you want out . . ." He'd be a great loss, but I can't have fairies around, crying over a few flying bullets and a hit-and-run.

His eyes widen. "No, I don't want out. Never." He drops into a chair.

"Then get your shit together, boy."

"I'm fine." His face bunches, his hand going to his thigh.

"As you keep saying. What has Doc said?"

He looks up through his lashes at me. "He said I'm fine."

For fuck's sake. "How did you get here?"

"Taxi."

"On your own?"

"No, with a taxi driver."

Oh, he's pushing it. I go to him, taking his arm and manhandling him back out of the office, his crutches flapping around as he tries to fight me.

"Brad, leave me here, I can't sit around at home in bed. It's driving me insane."

"Mason," I yell as I enter the club, reaching into my pocket for my keys and tossing them to him when he looks up. He catches them with one quick hand. "Take this dipshit to the boatyard." I thrust Nolan toward a stool. "Sit." He does. Fast. "There's fuck all point you being here, so if you insist that you don't want to lie around the house, you can go play shop at the yard." Fury appears. "What the fuck are you doing here?"

He shrugs.

"For fuck's sake." But I can't bitch. I wouldn't want Danny out on his own at the moment. I put my hand out to Mason, who passes my keys promptly. I throw them to Fury. "Take Nolan to the boatyard."

"But—"

"Danny's picking me up now." So Fury doesn't need to worry

about my well-being. I leave them behind, calling Leon. "Fury's bringing Nolan to the boatyard. Put him at the cash register in the store."

"Sure, B-Boss."

I hang up and leave the club, lighting up outside, looking up and down the street for them. No sign. "Fucking headache," I mutter, glancing at my phone when it dings.

Morning.

And the stress? Poof. I exhale, relaxing back against the wall. The snatched moments, the stolen nights. It's getting painful to let her out of my bed.

Morning.

The dots across the top of the screen bounce. Stop bouncing. Bounce. Stop bouncing. I sigh, dialing and taking my cell to my ear. "You know, we could just talk," I say when she answers.

"Okay," she whispers.

"Why are you whispering?"

"Because we can't *just talk*," she says quietly, and I smile. "Beau and Rose are five meters away from me."

"What are you doing?"

"Watching Rose be all passive-aggressive with the project manager at the spa."

I laugh under my breath, flicking my ash. "She's learned from the best."

"Where are you?" she asks.

"Missing you." What the fuck just came out of my mouth? I clear my throat. "At work," I say, my voice deep, and she laughs. The sound goes straight to my dick, and every moment from last night marches through my memory. And the night before. And the night before that. All stolen moments. But there's been no penetration without a condom. Apparently, fuck my life, the contraceptive pill isn't immediately effective. It takes seven days. Seven fucking days. It's been the longest seven days of my life. On the plus side, I still haven't got my results back from Doc, so even if the pill was instant protection, I'd still be wearing a condom until I know beyond doubt that I'm clean. That I won't . . . contaminate her. Which reminds me: I need to pick up some more condoms. "What do you want to do tonight, gorgeous?"

"I don't know, Daddy."

I jerk, coughing over my smoke. "Pearl," I snap, making her laugh again.

"What do *you* want to do?"

I know *exactly* what I want to do. Right after Doc tells me I'm all clear. Fuck me, how long do a few tests take? Fast, he said. "Let me think about that."

"Okay," she agrees easily, leaving a few beats of silence hanging between us, until she eventually says, "Brad?" Her voice is quiet and unsure.

"What?"

"Did you mean it?" she asks. "When you said . . ." She leaves more silence. "When you said—"

"When I said no one would touch you again except me?" I ask. I've seen the question in her eyes since that night. She's wanted to ask and has finally found the courage. "I meant it, Pearl." For my fucking sins, I really fucking meant it.

I hear her relief down the line. "So what happens now?"

James's Range Rover pulls into the street. "You're gonna have to let me think about that," I say, pushing my back from the wall. I know they all think I'm incapable of anything but fucking. I know the girls will take some convincing. I know they think I'll hurt Pearl, and truth is, deep down, I'm worried I will too. This is new to me—the possessiveness, the pleasure, the fierce protectiveness I'm feeling. My instinct. As for the men? I wince. She's twenty-fucking-one. Only just legal to drink. "I've got to go. Danny and James are here."

"Where are you going?"

I smile as I take one last puff of my Marlboro and flick it into the gutter. "There are things you'll need to know, and there are things you *won't* need to know. This is one of the *won't* need to know things." I hang up as James pulls over, and I frown when Danny gets out the passenger side and climbs into the back. "What are you doing?"

He falters. "Getting in the back."

"Why?"

"Because I want to get in the fucking back."

I exhale heavily, climbing in the passenger seat. "You been smoking in here?" I ask, getting a waft of nicotine.

"Yes, he has," James says, unimpressed, pulling off fast. He looks at me. "Good morning?"

"Fine. You?"

"Lovely," they say in unison.

"So where are we going?"

"The two disused factories that have been bought near MIA," Danny replies.

I turn in my seat. "There been some activity?"

"Nope."

"And the Escalade?"

"Ringo, Goldie, and Otto are on their way to the address in Harbor Lake as I speak. Jonathon Dresden is back from his holiday. You ready to talk about the other night yet?"

I still for a moment, before facing the front again. "What night?" He's asked a few times. I've shirked him. I get a tired look from James. "Oh. That night. I already told you." Fuck, I'm once again trying to recall if I splurged bullshit that night amidst the chaos. I can't.

"You've told us fuck all since you stomped off from the scene."

For fuck's sake, won't he just drop it? My fists clench, my impatience building. "I'd been fucking shot."

"Flesh wound."

"Fuck off, Danny."

"What's up with you?"

I swing around in my seat. "Why the fuck have the girls gone from being up my ass to kissing it?" It's unbearable, not least because I feel more attention on me than there should be. I unconsciously slam my fist into the arm rest. And there's the very reason Danny got out and sat in the back. I can't reach him to knock him out.

"They're worried about you. So what happened?" he pushes, raising his brows when I turn and give him a death glare.

I need to shut this down. "I saw the back door ajar," I say, facing forward again, so he can't see the lies in my eyes. "I checked outside and found Pearl smoking."

"Naughty girl."

James coughs, and I press my lips together as he divides his attention between me, the road, and Danny in the rearview mirror. Probably wondering if he's going to have to make an emergency stop to split us up.

"I told her to get inside," I go on. "Nolan came out when he saw the door open."

"So you went outside first?"

"Yes. A car came at us. It all happened fast."

Danny nods, accepting.

I don't feel any relief.

"So how's it going with the lawyer?" he asks. "I haven't seen her since her sleepover a week ago."

Allison. She's been calling. Every-fucking-day. Texting. Checking in. I'm surprised. Especially after Rose told me she got her a cab and sent her home with news that my establishment was being used as a local dealing shop. "She's great," I murmur.

"I'm happy for you," he says, sounding truly genuine.

"Me too," James adds.

"Thanks." Reaching for the volume, I turn the music up. New Order, *Blue Monday*. I settle back and look out the window, listening. Thinking. They're happy for me. Translated: they approve of her age and the girls won't cut off my dick. The problem? I may not be convinced that I'm the best choice for Pearl, but I certainly won't mistreat her. *I'll worship her.* Just like Danny does Rose, and James does Beau.

Would they ever believe I'm capable of that?

I look out the corner of my eye, seeing James's hand lightly drumming the wheel. Look over my shoulder to Danny in the middle of the back seat, bobbing his head to the beat. I notice my foot tapping as James looks at my bumping knee and frowns before he looks at his hand tapping the steering wheel. I laugh, reaching for my smokes and lighting one up, passing them back to Danny.

"Fuck it," James mutters, holding his hand out for them. Then he turns the music up, winds the windows down, and continues his drumming of the wheel.

And laughs with me.

· · ·

We checked out the factories. Nothing. "Where are we going?" I ask, as James heads across town.

"It's a surprise," Danny muses. "Nearly there."

"Where's *there*?" I ask as James pulls over. I look up at the building. "Seriously?"

"Seriously." Danny replies.

I sigh, dragging myself out of the car. "I don't know whether to be excited or worried for you." We stride toward the gate in a row, and I feel Danny's eyes on my profile. I turn to find him smiling mildly at me. "What?"

"I miss this Brad," he says, shoulder bumping me. "The sarcastic fucker who constantly states the obvious."

"Jesus." I move away. What's got into everyone lately?

"No, honestly," he goes on. "I feel like you've been absent."

Me too. "I'm fine."

"You'll always be fine." Danny reaches for my nape and squeezes as we come to a stop. "'Cause I've got you."

I give him a questioning look. "Is there something you're not telling me?"

"Otto asked me if he can marry Mum."

Recoiling, I search for the murder on his face. "And what did you do?"

"Punched him."

"Of course you did." I roll my eyes and return my attention to the gate. I get it, he felt screwed over by his mom for years, and I know deep down he's done resenting her. Wants her to be content. He's aware of how much she suffered, and Otto makes her happy. He's lucky there's a man around to want to make her happy. Someone except him.

"After I said he could," he adds. I shoot him a look, and Danny smiles, proud of himself. "I think she's said no or something, though, because nothing's been mentioned since."

"Or she's scared to tell you."

"Otto would *definitely* tell me." Danny squeezes my shoulder again. "See how I took your wise advice?"

"There's a first time for everything."

"I hope I can return the favor soon."

When James turns toward me, I ask him with my eyes if he has any fucking clue what the fuck's gotten into Danny. "Are we here for therapy or blood?" I ask.

"Blood," Danny says, losing all lightness and switching on the crazy. "Let's go."

Chapter 29

ROSE

"Yes, Rose," Alan says. "Of course, Rose." He smiles when I narrow my eyes in question. "Anything else?"

"Alan," I sigh. "You keep reassuring me this is going to be finished in a matter of days"—I glance round at the building site—"but I'm struggling to see how."

"You just leave that to me." He starts walking toward the exit, and it's an obvious hint I've overstayed my welcome. I remain exactly where I am. "How much is he paying you?" I ask.

He laughs. I've seen and heard enough nervous laughs from men since I met The Brit to know one. "I don't know what you're talking about."

"Sure," I murmur, setting my bag on a nearby workbench. And quickly removing it again, dusting it off. "I know my husband can be scary, Alan."

He coughs.

I smile. "But I can be scarier." I reach into my bag, and Alan flies back, hands up. I pause. My God, did he think I was about to pull a gun on him? I mean, I have one, but I'm not unreasonable. I slowly pull out my cell, glancing at Beau across the room. She's casually flicking through a design magazine, her smile poorly restrained. "My son is here, Alan," I say, pointing to Daniel in the corner, who looks bored out of his mind, scuffing his sneakers across the dusty concrete floor, kicking up plumes of dirt. "But if my son wasn't here?" I let him ponder that. Poor guy's caught in the middle—I feel bad for him, of course—but if I'm going to beat my husband, I need to play him at his own game. And unfortunately for Alan, that means using him as a pawn, because if Danny has his way, this spa will never be open and I'll be at home being nothing but sex and milk on tap. "I know Danny's been paying you cash." I smile. "I'm sure the IRS will need some evidence of your earnings and tax liabilities." One raised brow. "So I'll transfer you a payment for the works." I call my bank. "I need to make a payment. It's Mrs. Black."

"Oh, how lovely to hear from you. Let me put your through to your personal bank manager."

"Thanks." I smile as Alan's shoulders drop, defeated. "My husband won't kill you," I say, my hand over the microphone on my cell. "I promise."

He laughs—the nervous laugh again—obviously not believing me.

"Trust me, Alan. I know exactly how to handle The Brit."

"You must be the only one on this planet who does."

"I am," I assure him. "Which is why you should definitely make me your best friend, and you know how to achieve that, don't you, Alan?"

He flashes me a huge, fake smile. "We'll be out of your hair by Friday." Clapping his hands, he walks off, throwing orders around to all of the workmen, and I get back to my call, satisfied.

• • •

I walk out with Daniel dragging his feet behind me and Beau laughing. "That's that sorted," I mutter.

"You're such a hardball."

I smile, happy with myself, and take Maggie from Pearl. "Hey, my girl."

"I think she's hungry," Pearl says. "She nearly swallowed my finger whole."

I look around the street, seeing a café not too far away. "Coffee?" I chirp. "While we still have a little freedom?"

Daniel groans, head dropped back, looking at the sky. "I'm so bored."

"Zinnea called," Beau says, giving Daniel's head a pacifying ruffle. "She wants to meet us." She goes to the car and opens the trunk, reaching in to get Maggie's stroller.

"What are you doing?" Tank muscles Beau out of the way on a scowl and pulls it out, putting it together in record time. "You don't want to use this?" He holds up Maggie's carrier.

"No, I don't." I throw it a dirty look. For Christ's sake, it weighs more than I do. I lay Maggie down in the stroller and drape a blanket over her. I don't have a chance to push her though, as Tank takes the handles. "She's hungry," I call, preparing him for her scream.

"Her eyes are heavy," Tank calls back.

Oh? My boobs are grateful. I grab her bag and join Beau, Pearl, and Anya, all four of us watching the Viking wander down the street with Maggie. "He looks so cute," Anya says on a laugh, prompting the rest of us to turn an interested look her way. She quickly wipes the awe away.

"Why does Zinnea want to meet us?" I ask Beau.

"I don't know, but I do know she spent the night with Quinton again."

"Oh my, do you think she's bringing him?"

"Come on," Tank yells back, stalling at the crossing with Maggie, looking impatient. Always does when we're not either in Hiatus, at Byron's Reach, or in the house.

"Coming," I call, getting us all moving, pushing Daniel's heavy body on.

"I hope so," Beau muses. "And I so hope this is the start of something amazing for her. She deserves it after . . ."

I give her arm a gentle rub, telling her I get it. She shouldn't have to say that man's name ever again. Beau flashes me a smile, nodding to the back of Daniel's head, giving me eyes I understand, before she walks on with Pearl and Anya, and I hover back with Daniel. "Hey," I say, putting an arm around his shoulder. God damn it, he's now overtaken me, my eyes level with his when I look at him. "I thought we could look at private tuition later." He needs to get back into the learning groove before his education suffers.

"Really, Mom?" he drones. "Can't I just go back to school?" He looks at me, hopeful, and I drop my head onto his shoulder, sighing.

"Well, not really. Believe it or not, Principal Tucker has this thing called morals."

"Preston Bean thinks he's better than us because his dad's a cop. It was none of his business getting into my family business. Dad's given that school so much money for projects to better the facilities. Now some kid's telling tales, and they seem to have forgotten all of that."

My face bunches at thin air before me. My boy has a point. Problem is . . . "Well, Preston wasn't telling tales, was he?"

"It was between Preston and me. The shitbag was all mouth in front of his buddies. When I got him on his own, he crapped his pants and went snitching to Principal Tucker."

"You weren't on your own. There was a witness."

"My bad. Next time I threaten someone, I'll make sure it's his word against mine."

"Daniel—"

"And do you know what sucks most, Mom? Preston Bean is at school being all macho, telling people he kicked The Brit's son's ass."

The little weasel. I have a good mind to pay a visit to Preston Bean's parents and give them a subtle, polite warning to tell their son to back off my boy, and to tell the dad to back off my husband. I stop and turn Daniel into me, taking the tops of his arms, shaking him so he looks at me. "We can't control other people's actions, but we are in charge of our own."

"Dad would sort it if you'd let him."

"Oh my God, Daniel, you can't go through life threatening people to get what you want."

"Dad does."

Fuck it. "Dad's set in his ways." What the hell am I saying? "I mean—" God damn it, how do I approach this? "Your dad doesn't go around shooting people for fun, Daniel. He's got a reputation"—a deadly one—"and a lot of money and power."

"I thought you had all the money?"

I roll my eyes. "That's besides the point. Unfortunately, when you have a reputation like your father's, there are people who want to ruin it. When you have power like your father, there are people who want to take it. The world is full of megalomaniacs, darling. Your father is simply protecting what's his, including us."

His ever-widening shoulders drop. "I know that," he says. "I just miss school. Miss Barney. Miss soccer and football, Mom. I even miss algebra!"

Oh my heart.

"We'll figure it out," I say. "I promise."

"Rose!" Tank yells.

"We'd better catch up." Daniel puts his arm around my shoulders. Because he's the biggest of us now. "I know you worry about me, Mom."

"Always. I don't want you to face prejudice or discrimination." Because that's what'll happen if Daniel returns to school now everyone knows who he is. And *everyone* includes his teachers. There's no way they'll remain impartial. So, as much as he thinks he can handle it, I'm not certain Principal Tucker and Daniel's teachers will make his re-entry easy.

"I'm a big boy," he says quietly.

And he also knows where his father's gold letter opener is kept.

I know he's right—he's a big boy.

But he's still our little boy.

• • •

"How do you think he'll take it?" Beau asks quietly, aware that Pearl and Anya aren't privy to the latest bombshell news about Brad and Nolan.

"That's anyone's guess." I'm worried. Worried for Brad, for Nolan. For us.

"He might surprise us and embrace it," Beau muses.

I look at her, smiling, even if I'm doubtful. Brad has been a little unhinged lately. Lost. I doubt finding out he has a kid over twenty years too late is going to force him into levelheadedness. Although, admittedly, he's been a bit perkier this week. "Do you know if he's seen the lawyer since last week?"

"He said he was, but he seemed unenthusiastic about it. I don't know if she's right for him. We'll see, I suppose."

"We'll see what?" Pearl asks, joining the conversation too late, thank God.

"Nothing. Just some family politics. Don't worry." I lift the muslin and peek down at Maggie. She's fallen asleep on my boob. I grit my teeth as I slip my finger between her mouth and my flesh, breaking her latched lips. "Ouchy," I whisper, letting my top drop into place over my chest as I ease her off.

"Here," Beau says, gently taking her from my arms so I can make myself decent.

"How did Zinnea meet Quinton?" Pearl asks, stirring her macchiato. She's gotten over the incident last week well, thankfully. Poor thing was utterly traumatized when she stumbled into the club.

"That's a story for Beau to answer," Esther says, passing around napkins.

"They're old friends." Beau smiles fondly. "Quinton manages a hotel I stayed at—"

"When she'd performed one of her disappearing acts," I pipe in.

"When I needed some space from the chaos," Beau says slowly, giving me a playful scowl. "He and Zinnea knew each other from the circuit, but Zinnea was married to Dexter at the time."

"Oh, Dexter." Pearl muses. "The—"

"Corrupt cop who shot me and helped my mother fake her own murder," Beau says so matter-of-factly. It's such a pleasure to see her light indifference after so long immersed in the darkness.

"What happened to him?" Pearl asks innocently.

James butchered him. I watch Beau shrug nonchalantly. "He's on the run."

"God help him if James ever finds him," Pearl says, dread overcoming her.

I smile, awkward, as does Esther.

"I wouldn't want to be Dexter," Beau says, looking down at Maggie asleep in her arms. She hasn't had a panic attack for months. It's not down to meds, it's down to her inner peace. Even now, when we've learned Sandy isn't dead and is threatening to pop our bubble once again, she's so fucking chilled out. It's the baby. She's taking care of herself, her mind, and her body.

I check on Daniel, seeing him sitting in the window with Tank. The big guy is tucked in close to him, talking. A pep talk. Some wise words from one of the many men in his life.

"Oh my God," Esther breathes, rising from her chair.

My heart instantly thrums. "What?" I follow the direction of her stare to the window. "Esther, what?" I stand, as does Anya and Pearl, and Beau with Maggie, all of us trying to see what's got Esther's panicked attention. Is it panic? I check her face again. She's smiling. Not panic. Thank God. But what—

I gasp, seeing Zinnea flouncing across the road, her rainbow Pride wrap flapping in the wind, her zebra-print sequin pants glistening under the sun. And attached to her hand, another hand. "Is that Quinton?" A well-dressed man with a moustache in a herringbone tweed three-piece as tall as Zinnea—and she's wearing skyscraper platforms—strides along beside her, his chest puffed out proudly, his shoulders back, his smile broad. "What a force," I murmur.

"Quick, sit down," Beau orders, dropping back to her chair. "Don't make a big deal of it."

"But it's massive," I say.

"So is his moustache," Pearl whispers. "Wow, that's impressive."

"It's new," Beau says. "He never had that when I saw him months ago."

"Hey, Beau," Daniel calls back. "Zinnea's here, and she's brought a man with a walking stick."

"It's a cane," Beau replies. "A fashion accessory."

"He looks like he's from England," Daniel says. "Doesn't he, Pearl?"

Pearl chuckles. "Right out of a manor house, kid."

We all watch through the window as they approach, and I see the handlebar moustache and round rimless glasses. What a character. Zinnea flings the door open, walks in, and throws her arms out wide. "Darlings!"

"Shhhh," Beau hisses, making Zinnea slap a hand over her mouth.

"Oh, darn, the beast is asleep."

And Maggie starts screaming.

I deflate. "*Was* asleep," I moan, waving off Zinnea's sorry eyes. "It's fine." I stand and take her from Beau, starting to bounce her lightly.

"Everyone," Zinnea whispers, pulling Quinton into her side. "It's my pleasure to introduce you to Quinton." She looks at him with love hearts in her eyes. "Isn't he wonderful?"

"Wonderful," Beau says, standing and being the first to greet him with a hug. "Good to see you again, Quinton."

"And you, Beau. And I believe congratulations are in order. How wonderful."

"Thanks."

"Wonderful," we all murmur, every one of us smiling like idiots, fascinated by the duo that is Zinnea and Quinton.

"This is Esther," Zinnea says as Beau goes back to her seat. "She's Rose's mother-in-law and the family matriarch."

"I thought that was *your* title, Zinnea," Esther says, standing and hugging Quinton as Zinnea chuckles. "Lovely to meet you, Quinton."

"And you, dear."

"And that is Rose and the beast." Zinnea sweeps out a flamboyant arm as I edge out and give Quinton a one-arm cuddle. "Pleasure," I say, holding Maggie up for him to see.

"Hello, beast," Quinton coos, dipping and smiling at Maggie. She screams in his face, and Quinton recoils.

"Sorry, she's grouchy today."

"Give her here," Esther says, holding out grabby hands. "Come to Grandma." She takes her and wanders off up the café, hushing her.

"Colic?" Beau asks, and I shrug, feeling a bit defeated by the whole situation. Feeling like I'm doing something wrong. I need to talk to Doc again.

"This here is Pearl," Zinnea goes on. "There's Anya, and over there we have Rose's son Daniel, and that's Tank."

Quinton looks at Tank, wide eyed, and Tank smiles, trying to look friendly. I laugh, lowering to my chair. "Do you want a drink, Quinton?"

"I'd kill for a chai tea latte."

"No need to kill, darling," Zinnea quips, laughing lightly, flashing us all round eyes. "We're all friendly around here."

I press my lips together and look at Beau, who is equally amused.

"So," I say, relaxing back. "When are you introducing Quinton to the men?"

Pearl snorts, Anya chuckles, Beau knocks her coffee cup on the plate, and Zinnea laughs harder.

• • •

It was so lovely to drink coffee, chat, just . . . be. I almost forgot how tired I am. As Tank loads the stroller into the car, I watch Daniel, my heart becoming heavier. His despondency. His missing sparkle. God damn it, I can fix this. Or try my hardest. I look at my cell. School's out in an hour. I dial Lennox, walking a few meters away from Tank, but not so far he'll give me earache for it.

"Hi, Rose."

"Hi." We haven't spoken since he told me he knew exactly who my husband is. In fact, I'm surprised he's taken my call. "I wondered if you'd mind Daniel coming over to see Barney." I'm certain Danny won't approve, but I can't stand by and watch my kid be miserable.

Lennox is silent for a few, uncomfortable seconds. "We'd love that. We've missed him."

I sag. "Thank you. I'm going to the school to see if I can appeal to Principal Tucker's reasonable side." And perhaps to gently remind him—as Daniel reminded me—that Danny's funded a hell of a lot of projects in the short time Daniel's been a student there.

"As you should," Lennox says. "And I'll happily vouch for your family, Rose."

"You would?" I ask, stunned.

"Of course I would. Daniel's an asset to that school. He said something silly in the heat of the moment."

Fucking hell. My lip wobbles, and I suddenly feel so terrible for coming down so hard on him. He's right. Daniel is a credit to them. "Thanks, Lennox. It means a lot."

"No sweat. Do you want me to come with you to the school?"

I look back to the car. "We have to drop everyone home, then I'll get Tank to bring us over, but I can't leave Daniel without Tank. Plus, Danny will go spare if he finds out I went anywhere without one of the Vikings." Damn it, where's Fury?

"Well, I have my own Viking now."

"What?"

"It's a long story."

"Oh?" I say warily.

"It's nothing like that. No men out to kill me." He laughs, awkward as hell. "Barney's mother's been in touch. I don't trust that woman as far as I can throw her, so I've hired Sid."

"Sid?"

"Yeah, Sid. Former CIA. Scary fucker."

That feels extreme. "You think she'd take Barney?"

"I don't know. We've not heard from her since she went to Sri Lanka with her new man. She's showed no interest in Barney, and now all of a sudden she wants custody. It doesn't make any sense to me. I'm just being cautious."

Very cautious. "I'm sorry to hear that."

"It's fine. Anyway, my point is, Tank can watch the kids, we can take Sid. Or vice versa, whichever you're comfortable with."

"I think I want to meet Sid before I make that decision."

Lennox laughs. "Fair enough. See you soon."

• • •

I opted to leave Tank with the boys. Yes, Sid is a scary fucker, as per Lennox's words, but Tank knows the boys, and Tank's a scary fucker too. I'm just used to him, so the impact has worn off. I can still appreciate it, though.

Pearl and Anya asked if they could stay at the café to hang out, so

Tank called Fury in, who was kicking his heels around the boatyard after being relieved by Brad when James and Danny picked him up. Naturally, my mind wonders what they're doing. Who they're killing. Threatening. Paying. Supplying. It's actually been so . . . unusual. The quiet of the last six months. Well, five if you include the last month of *loud* thanks to Miss Maggie's entrance into the world. But I've enjoyed the quieter side of Danny. The less secretive, less . . . volatile side. And I never thought I'd think that.

After dropping everyone home, leaving Maggie with Esther, expressing to relieve my chest—again—and leaving a few extra bottles, Tank and I went to Lennox's.

I hopped into Lennox's four-wheeled drive Volvo and made small talk from the back while figuring out how to approach this in between the brief silences on the journey.

I couldn't hide where I was going—Daniel's not stupid. Where else would I go with Lennox? So the pressure is on to fix this and get Daniel back into school, but more importantly, get his sparkle back.

Sid pulls up. "You can wait here," Lennox says, slipping out and opening the door for me before I've had a chance to unclip my belt.

"Thank you."

"Welcome."

I look up at the impressive building as we walk side by side up the well-kept lawn . . . that's been cut with the new ride-on lawnmower Danny paid for. I press the buzzer and announce myself, and, to my surprise, I'm let straight in. The kids have all gone, so I enter the reception and see Mrs. Carnaby. She looks a little pale today. "I'm here to see Principal Tucker."

Without even looking at me, she points to the door, offering us to go straight in, as if she was expecting us. I frown at Lennox. He shrugs. Then I wander to Principal Tucker's door, knocking before pushing it open.

And stutter to a stop, my mouth dropping open, when I see my husband perched on the desk.

Holding a gun to the temple of a terrified-looking Principal Tucker.

Chapter 30

Danny

I look up and see my wife on the threshold of the office. "Well, this isn't ideal," I say quietly.

"Oh hell," James murmurs.

"She's gonna fucking raise it," Brad adds.

"What the fuck?" Rose yells, eyes bouncing between me and the end of my gun.

What the fuck? Yes, what the fucking *fuck*?

I slowly relieve Tucker of my gun and just as slowly rise from the desk, feeling my blood beginning to burn. "What the hell are you—" I lose my line of thought when someone appears behind her. Lose my breath. Lose my fucking mind.

Benson stops and takes one step back. One step? He'd better get his fucking arse on a rocket and fuck off to the moon.

"Are . . . what . . . " I can't even form a sentence. But my mind can think, and it's telling me to kill the fucker. I aim my gun at him, though the damn thing shakes, meaning Benson could strike it lucky when I *might* miss his forehead.

"Danny." His hands come up.

Kill him.

I can't fucking kill him. Daniel will never forgive me for popping off his best mate's dad. "What the fuck is he doing here?"

Rose flies around and pushes her palms into Benson's chest, trying to push him out. "You should go."

"And you *touch* him?" I shriek.

"Oh Jesus," Brad breathes. "Danny, come on."

I re-aim my gun at him. "Shut the fuck up."

"Danny," James warns quietly.

I turn my gun onto him. "And you. Both of you shut the fuck up." Wisely, they raise their hands in surrender, sinking into their chairs. I point my gun back at Benson.

Kill him.

Can't.

Can.

Rose turns as I pace slowly toward them. "Danny," she implores gently, appeasing me. She's got more chance of her husband cheating on her. Zero possibility.

"Move."

Kill him.

She remains between Benson and me, blocking my path to him. I sneer at her. She comes here against everything I've told her, and she brings him? Him to help fix a family issue? Him *at all*? "I'll deal with you later."

"Excuse me?" Rose coughs, instantly outraged. I haven't even got the energy or inclination to apologize for my manner toward her. She's bang out of line, and Benson here is going to pay for it. I physically pick her up and place her to the side.

"Danny, calm down," Benson says, hands up.

"Calm down?"

Kill him.

Can.

Can't.

Fuck!

I drop my gun and swing at Benson, my fist sinking into his face on a satisfying punch, sending him staggering back into the reception area.

"Danny!" Rose yells. Fair played, he remains on his feet. So I go again, an upper cut this time, snapping his head back. And just as I'm about to deliver a left hook, he surprises me with a shot that catches me on my recovering nose, knocking me back. I still, shocked, my nose throbbing. Then I feel the warm sensation of blood trickling. I sniff, dragging the back of my hand across my upper lip, tasting the coppery flavor. I look at Benson. My bleeding nostrils flare. He did *not* just do that. On a bellow, I dive at him, tackling him at the waist and taking him down to the carpeted floor. We both grunt, Rose screams, Brad and James curse.

"You sly fucking snake." I straddle him and punch him repeatedly in the face, but once again he catches me off guard, spinning and reversing the roles, slamming me down on my back and returning the favor.

"You need to calm the fuck down," he yells, breathless.

Says he who's currently delivering punches to my face like a machine gun delivers bullets. And calm down? I roar, lifting my upper body and nutting him. His nose explodes, Rose yells some more, and we roll around, punching, kicking, headbutting.

Bang!

I jump, and Benson ricochets back.

"The fuck?" I wheeze, looking up from where I'm on my back, seeing the mirror on the wall shattered. I drop my gaze. Rose is standing over me, a gun in her hand.

"Get up," she hisses.

I snort my thoughts on that. Stupid me.

She fires again, this time a foot away from my shoulder, and I bring my hands up over my head protectively. "Are you fucking kidding me right now?" I yell.

"Do I look like I'm fucking kidding?"

I growl, getting to my feet fast, and grab her arm, and in a few fast, expert moves, disarm her. I get up in her face, and she gets up in mine, very à la Rose. "I think we need a chat when we get home."

"Can't wait."

I hiss, looking at Brad and James, who are still relaxed in their seats. But I register their expressions. *Too far, Danny.* Principal Tucker, however, looks like he's seen the devil. "Daniel will see you in the morning." I lead my crazy, maddening, reckless wife out of the office, snarling at Benson as we pass. "I was having a great day until you ruined it," I growl, marching her on. "And that fucking gun was for protection, not to use on the love of your life."

She laughs dementedly. "And I was having a great *life* until you kidnapped me," she spits back. I hold my breath and my tongue. Basically, she's saying being beaten, raped, and whored out is better than being my wife. And it hurts, even if I know that's exactly what she wants. To hurt me. And you can bet your bottom dollar she'll take sex off the menu for fuck knows how long. Which sucks majorly because she only just put it back on the menu, and I was planning on indulging.

Fuck my fucking life.

Chapter 31

Pearl

I tap out a message and delete it. Five times. Seems ridiculous to ask him if he's having a good day. I know Brad. I know Danny. I know James. They might be having a great day, but whoever is on the receiving end of them won't be.

Missing you.

I cringe at myself, deleting it. If I cringe, I definitely shouldn't send it. Send nothing. Don't be needy. Is it needy to want to hear from someone? And he did say he missed me. And probably cringed, I'm sure. I pull my lip ring between my teeth, laying my phone on the table and my hands on either side of it. But then it pings, and I swoop it up, my heart in my mouth. My God, I'm pathetic.

It's been a day, gorgeous, and we're not done yet. Can't promise tonight's gonna happen. Will call you when I can.

I smile, despite myself. *It's been a day.* What's he been doing? I scrunch up my face. Killing? And who? Would he kill for me?

"You came to bed late again last night," Anya says, pulling my attention away from my new phone. She's fiddling with her glass, trying and failing to look casual.

Think. "Oh, I fell asleep in the TV room." I smile, awkward, and wrap my lips around my straw.

"Again." Her eyebrows raise as she, too, has a sip of her drink. "But I checked and you weren't in there."

"You checked?" I sound so defensive.

"I was worried."

"Maybe I was in the kitchen getting a drink."

"I checked in there too."

"Maybe I was using the bathroom."

She smiles. "Checked there too."

I direct my stare to my drink. "Maybe I was—"

"In Brad's room?"

I still, my eyes widening on my glass. *Shit.* "I—"

"Pearl, I am not stupid." Anya gives me a tired look, turning on her chair to face me. "What are you doing?"

"I don't know," I admit, giving up on my lame bullshit excuses.

"You hate him."

I laugh to myself. "I did," I admit. "For a while."

"So what happened?"

My self-restraint snapped. That's what happened. I sigh, giving Anya my full attention. "I know what I'm doing," I say. That's not true at all. I have no idea what I'm doing, all I know is that I tried to leave and I couldn't, and one week later, I'm in really fucking deep. He doesn't know who I am. No one does. The shit won't only hit the fan, it'll slap it, hit it, kick it, and punch it. I want to hope Brad might step in and save me from the repercussions. *No one will ever touch me again. Except him.* It sounds too good to be true, because it probably is. But the past week? It's been incredible. I've followed his lead and discovered my body along with Brad. And the cuddles in bed?

Safe.

Anya's mobile interrupts me, and she sweeps it up. "Mason," she says, getting up and walking away. I watch her, sighing, and finish my drink. My eyes fall onto Anya's handbag on the table—or something poking out of a side zip. I tilt my head, trying to see it. Is it a driver's license? I don't know. Definitely not American issued, the writing foreign, so perhaps Romanian? Pursing my lips, I look at Anya. She's near the back of the café, her back to me. I walk my fingers across the table and push a fingertip into the card, dragging it out a little. Anya's face greets me, looking a little younger than she does now. Her heart-shaped face, her hair a bit shorter. She's so unique looking, it's no wonder she was taken. The only thing I can read is her name, and I laugh at how ridiculous it is that I didn't know her surname. "Anya Dimitri," I muse, pushing it back in her handbag. "Pretty." I get back to my phone and reply to Brad.

Anya knows I was with you last night. And every other night. I tried to lie. Turns out I'm not very good at it, and Anya is a master sleuth. I'm sorry.

Kiss? No kiss?

I roll my eyes to myself, adding a kiss. Because that's who I am. And Brad is a professional killer.

Oh dear.

I frown, my fingers working fast across my screen.

What does that mean?

The dots pulse across the top, my attention split between them and Anya on her phone.

It means I don't get to keep you a secret for as long as I'd like.

Oh?

You want to keep me a secret?

Yes.

I scoff.

Charming.

Because once Beau and Rose know, they're definitely cutting my dick off. Will you still want me if I'm dickless?

I smile, and I know it's stupid and goofy.

It's not you, it's me . . .

You'll pay for that. Signing off. Danny's about to kill Rose.

I frown, checking the time. She couldn't have gotten to the school, dealt with what she wanted to deal with and gotten anywhere else by now.

Rose is at the school

And so is Danny. With his gun.

"Oh fuck," I breathe, hearing the proverbial fireworks going off all over Miami.

"What?" Fury asks, moving in, sipping from his takeaway cup.

"What?" Anya asks, joining us.

Should I say? I'm sure the whole house will hear when we get home. "Danny was at the school when Rose got there."

"Oh, fucking hell," Fury breathes, going straight to his phone, undoubtedly to call his brother and get the finer details. He doesn't need to do that. I can tell him. But then it occurs to me . . .

Fuck.

Fury frowns down at his phone for a few uncomfortable moments, obviously thinking, then looks up at me. "How did you know Danny was at the school?"

Shit, shit, shit. "Beau," I squeak. "She was checking in. We should go." I get up and grab my bag.

"I have to go to the club," Anya says, shrugging her jacket on. "Mason doesn't have Nolan, and Brad's not there."

"We can drop you off before Fury takes me home."

We all walk out together, my worry for Rose real. As is my worry for Danny. Those two can't half go when they're pissed off with each other. I step out into the afternoon sun and immediately shield my eyes from the glare. "Quinton seemed nice," I say as we walk to the car together, Fury tailing us, still on his phone, endless fucks coming at our back.

"Yeah, really nice."

"I was sur—" I swallow my words, jarring to a stop, my heart crawling up into my throat, suffocating me, as I watch a man get out of a car down the street. "No," I whisper, as Fury crashes into my back. I slip into a nearby doorway, struggling to breathe, staring at the bricks, blinking, shaking my head.

It's him.

Huge, menacing, a constant leer on his lip, a cigar hanging from his mouth, a ridiculous fur coat. *Terrifying*.

"Pearl?" Fury appears, and I look at him with wide, blank eyes. "What's up?"

"I feel faint," I whisper, my gaze dropping to my feet. "I'll be okay in a moment." *Breathe, breathe, breathe*.

He's here.

In Miami.

How did he . . .?

I inhale, thinking . . .

Oh no. The man that Brad killed. He must've followed the scent. And now he's here to get me. Here to claim what's his.

And, suddenly, I don't feel safe anymore.

Chapter 32

BRAD

How those two aren't dead at the hands of each other, I don't fucking know. Danny bundled Rose in James's Range Rover and screeched off, leaving us hanging around waiting for Tank to pick us up, and Tank couldn't leave Lennox's until he got home with the ominous creature he's hired to tail him. Something about a messy custody battle. I'm not so sure. Daniel naturally asked what happened to Lennox. We, naturally, fed him some bullshit about a fall down some stairs. Other than that, the journey back to the house was silent. The kid's not stupid, he knows Lennox didn't fall down any stairs. But he didn't press.

James pulls through the gates of the house, raising his hand out of the window to Len as we pass the gatehouse. I see his Range Rover parked haphazardly, the doors open. "Jesus," I breathe to myself, looking toward the back where Tank and the kid are. "Straight to the TV room."

Daniel nods, looking at Tank. "You go," Tank says, reading the silent order in my eyes. "I'll be two minutes. I've got to help Uncle Brad with something. Go set up the Xbox."

The kid returns his eyes to me. "Am I allowed to go back to school?"

"Yeah, kid."

"Yes!" He hops out and runs through the doors, and I pray Danny and Rose have taken their argument upstairs. I look at Tank in the rearview mirror, filling the entire back seat apart from the small space Daniel just vacated. "What were you thinking?"

"I was thinking Rose is scarier than Danny these days." He rubs at his beard, looking a bit shook up. "She was going to that school whether I agreed or not."

I can't skin him. He literally has the toughest job in the world. "Go make sure the kid stays out of their way until they've ironed this out." Tank gets out, and I turn my wary gaze to a silent James. "You're quiet."

"Otto just texted me. The Escalade they found in Lake Harbor has been cloned."

"Fuck off," I breathe, rubbing at my forehead. "They—whoever they are—cloned a retired cop's vehicle?"

"People who clone vehicles don't dive deep. They find a car—same make, same model—and steal the license plate."

"Major faux pas. So, chances are, the clone is still in Miami."

"Dumped somewhere I expect. Burned out. It was full of holes after you and Tank opened fire on it. They'll have another vehicle by now."

"For fuck's sake."

"Agreed." James opens the door, sliding out.

"Where are you going?" I'm going to need some backup when Danny emerges. *If* he emerges.

"I'm going to see my wife. Where are you going?" He slams the door and paces around the front of the car, closing the doors of his Range Rover on his way. "The lawyer?"

"Yeah, the lawyer." I sigh and get out, following him into the house. "I'll call her." I don't call Allison, but call Doc instead. He doesn't answer. Since when does Doc not answer? He said this testing business would be quick. It's been a week.

As I pass through the entrance hall to the kitchen, I listen for the sounds of murder. Nothing. Esther's got Maggie in a travel cot by the island. She looks up but doesn't say a word, going back to chopping zucchini. She doesn't want to know.

"Have you eaten today?" James asks Beau.

"I thought you weren't back until later," she says, pulling some plates out of the dishwasher. "Or have you just popped home to check up on me?"

"Answer my question."

"I had a ham and cheese croissant and a bag of chips."

"No vegetables? No fruit?"

I smile as I lower to a stool, watching James go to the fridge. He starts pulling out all the things he needs for the green stuff. "She's going to turn green soon," I say, helping myself to the pot of tea on the island, dialing Doc again. I want the results of those tests. I want to take Pearl tonight with nothing between us. I can't ask anyone if they've seen the old boy, that'll raise too many questions.

Beau pauses stacking plates and looks at me with soft eyes.

"What?" I ask, my gaze moving between my tea and Beau.

"How are you?"

"Traumatized," I quip, lifting my cup to my lips.

"Are you seeing Allison tonight?" she asks, and my eyes naturally flick to James.

"Yeah, might do."

"What the hell happened?" Esther asks, deciding *she* does want to know. "His face was a bloody mess."

"That wasn't Rose," James says, as he juggles his ingredients to the island and lays it out on the chopping board Esther's just placed down, along with a knife.

"It wasn't?" Beau asks, so shocked.

I laugh. "Jesus, Beau, she's popped him in the chops a few times, but what you saw wasn't the work of a woman."

She scowls at me.

"No disrespect intended."

"Then think before you open your big trap."

I smile over my rim. "It was Benson." There's a collection of gasps, and both James and I nod. "He went to the school with Rose to talk to the principal. We were already there."

"Oh God." Esther rests her elbows on the island and buries her head in her hands.

"On the bright side, Daniel's going back to school." I give Beau a grin when she balks at me. "Actions speak louder than words." My cell rings in my pocket, and I pull it out, getting up and stepping out into the garden, expecting to see Doc calling me back. It's not. "Higham?"

"I'm trying to get hold of Danny."

"He's busy murdering his wife."

He huffs. "I know how he feels. I thought I'd be home today. Turns out my wife's invited half of Florida up to the lake house for a barbeque tonight."

"Don't worry, we've got plenty of other shit to keep us occupied."

"And I don't suppose you know anything about the breaking and entering and subsequent assault on Officer Richard Bean, do you?"

"Who the fuck is Officer Richard Bean?" I ask, hearing a car pull up the drive. I walk to the corner and see Fury following Pearl into the house. "Higham?"

"Sorry, I lost you for a moment," he says, as I study Pearl's face, not sure I'm liking what I'm seeing. She looks . . . dull. "I'll be in touch when I'm back."

"Yeah, I've got to go," I murmur, going back into the kitchen. "Higham's not back tonight," I say, eyes on the entrance. "Something about a barbeque." I lower to a stool and slowly and blindly reach for my tea. Eyes still on the entrance. Fury enters. No Pearl. "Wh—" I just about hold my tongue. "All right?" I ask instead.

Fury looks around. "Where's Tank?"

I frown. He looks worried. "Playing on the Xbox with the kid."

"He's still alive?"

I nod, Fury leaves, and James starts the blender, but the noise does nothing to drown out my thoughts. Pearl's face. I wonder if I'm reading into things. She didn't look happy at all. In fact, she looked shook up.

"Brad?"

I jump when Beau snaps my name. "What?"

"Are you okay?" she asks, her hands wrapped around her green juice.

"I'm fine." I force a smile, trying to reassure her. "I need a shower then I'm . . . going out with Allison." I walk out, looking up the stairs as I pass through the hallway, heading for the TV room. I find Daniel sandwiched between the Vikings, Fury watching while Daniel and Tank wave around their controllers. "Okay?" I ask all three of them, getting three different pitched grunts in return.

Tank and Daniel are engrossed in the TV, so I jerk my head for Fury to join me. He struggles to get his body up off the low couch. "Everything okay, Boss?" he asks.

"You brought Pearl back."

"Yeah, I watched them while they hung out at the café. You didn't say anything about staying with Nolan so when Tank called me to watch them, I assumed it was okay."

"Yeah, yeah, it's fine," I assure him. "Watch *them*?"

"Pearl and Anya. You want me to go get Nolan?"

"Yeah, please." Fuck, how do I get to what I need to know without raising questions? "All good today?"

"All good." Fury passes me, leaving the room. "I've got to talk to

Beau. Is she still in the kitchen?"

"Yeah." I frown at his back, following him back that way, curious.

"Can I have a word with Beau?" Fury asks James, who has his wife firmly wedged between his thighs with no sign of letting her go.

"Sure," he says, turning Beau to face him. "Go ahead."

Yes, no chance of letting her go. Fury looks uncomfortable for a moment, and my curiosity goes through the roof. "Sorry to bring this up," he says, taking a seat.

"Tea, Fury?" Esther asks from the crib, checking on Maggie.

"No, thanks." He gets straight back to Beau, and in an attempt to look like I'm not hanging around to listen in, I step outside again, pulling out my cigarettes. Close enough to hear but just out of sight.

"Sorry to bring what up?" James prompts.

"Your panic attacks," Fury says. "What were they like?"

"Why the hell are you asking that?" James asks, sounding annoyed.

"It's fine," Beau says, placating him. "Why do you ask, Fury?" I can hear the worry in Beau's voice. Worry for Fury. I know how close they've become since James first appointed him chief guard of Beau.

"I think Pearl had one earlier."

I still, smoke billowing up into my face, my lighter hovering at the end of my Marlboro. *What?* I pull it from my lips and exhale, moving closer to the door.

"You do?" Beau asks. "What happened?"

"I don't know. I was walking her and Anya back to the car to take Anya to the club before bringing Pearl home, and everything was fine, they were chatting, but Pearl went quiet, froze up, like she'd been stunned."

I move closer to the door, looking in, seeing Fury circling a hand in front of his chest.

"She started breathing heavily, shaking, and her eyes were a little . . . I don't know. Wild."

"Yeah," Beau says quietly, thoughtfully. "Is she okay?"

I move back, my mind racing.

"A bit quiet."

"I'll go check on her."

"No," Fury says, rushed. "She didn't want me to say anything and cause a fuss." I hear the legs of the stool scrape the floor, Fury getting up. "I'll tell her to see Doc, but just letting you know to keep an eye on her."

"Thanks, Fury."

"No sweat."

I wander farther into the garden, puffing away on my Marlboro, lost in thought. I knew she didn't look right when she got home. A panic attack? About what? Naturally, my mind goes to the man looking for her at the club. Has she seen something she didn't want to see? Not told me something?

Churned up inside, I discard my cigarette and walk back into the kitchen, not speaking to James, Beau, or Esther, just passing through, my usual non-talkative self as of late.

I want some answers.

I take one step up the stairs and stop when I see Danny coming down them. I take in his face, the red scrape on his cheekbone over his scar, his shadowed eye. I know Lennox will look worse. Brave fucker. I don't ask if he's okay, it's obvious—his eyes are ice, and his lips straight. "Higham's not back tonight as expected," I say. "Said he'd be in touch."

"Fine." He passes me, heading toward the office. He's going to drink.

I leave him and take myself upstairs, checking over my shoulder constantly for company as I approach Pearl and Anya's room. I knock lightly, not expecting to get an answer. And I don't. "Pearl?" I call through the wood, trying the door. Locked. If I hadn't seen her come in the house, I'd question if she was here at all. But I did. Not that Pearl knows. So she doesn't want to see me? Or anyone? I pull my cell out and dial her, not taking it to my ear but listening for it ringing in her room instead. When it does, I knock the wood again. "Come on," I say. "You've been found." I cut the call and rest a palm on the doorjamb. I hear the door handle shift and it opens a little, just enough to tell me I'm not getting an invite inside.

"What are you doing?" she whispers, looking up and down the corridor.

"What are *you* doing?" I force my way in with care, and dip, getting her on my shoulder.

"Brad!"

I turn back around and march to my room, entering and lowering her to her feet. Where the hell do I start? "What happened?" I can't drop Fury in the shit. Don't want Pearl to think she can't trust him. "When you got home, you looked worried."

"I'm fine."

I can see her walls coming up like iron, bulletproof shutters, her eyes avoiding mine. Fuck it, I'm not going to get anything out of her. So yes, I can drop Fury in the shit. "You had a panic attack outside the café," I say.

Her mouth falls open.

"Pearl, those big hairy fuckers that follow you girls around all day are there to make sure you're all okay. If you're not, they're contracted to report it."

"Contracted?"

"Under threat," I say. But that's not the reason he told us. "He shared because he cares, Pearl. You've worried him, and now I'm really worried too. What happened, gorgeous?" I detect a definite wobble of her lip, a glaze of her eyes.

"It's nothing."

Oh, come on. She's infuriating. I move into her, my palms resting on her upper arms, my body hunkering to make eye contact. "Tell me."

She winces, swallows hard. Fucking hell. What the hell did she see? I move to the chair and lower, pulling her down onto my lap, and like a scared, fragile animal, she curls into my body, hiding, arms clinging on around my neck. I needed this. Needed her to trust me, even if only physically.

"Tell me," I encourage softly, stroking her hair.

"I saw a man," she whispers, pushing herself farther into me.

"What man?"

She's quiet for a beat. Finding the courage to share. "A man on a gurney."

"What?" I ask, confused. "On the street?"

"He was being wheeled to an ambulance. He had a wire in his arm, they were holding up a bag of fluids, and it just . . . triggered something. From the hangar. The line in my arm, the drugs so close to making it into my veins."

"My love," I whisper, holding her tighter.

"What if they find me?" she asks, her voice ragged. Her fear is very fucking real.

I'm stiff as a fucking board, my teeth about to pop from the force of my bite. "It's over," I grate, willing my body to relax.

"I know." She frees herself from my chest and finds my face, her eyes scanning mine. I remain still, paralyzed by the need staring back at me.

Purpose.

A man without it is merely a shell with a heartbeat and no soul.

I pull her in for a hug, holding her tight, reinforcing her safety. And with her this close, all the stupid things that have kept me from her seem inconsequential. This whole situation has knocked me on my ass. Come from left field. What's happening, it can't be wrong, because it feels too fucking right.

I've been waiting for her.

"What's wrong?" she asks, withdrawing, worried.

I reach for her cheek and stroke it with the back of my finger. "I said we'd do something tonight."

"Does that mean you can't?"

"No, it doesn't."

"So what do you want to do?"

"I want to take a bath with you."

She exhales, unsure. "What?"

"A bath." I stand, placing her down. "With you."

"I thought you'd . . ." She pauses. "Well, I thought we would—"

"Fuck like rabbits all night?" Fuck me, we can't because, dumb me, I forgot to pick up some condoms and Doc's nowhere to be found.

"A bath," she says, looking at the door into the bathroom. "You want to have a bath."

"Yeah."

"With me?"

"With you." What's going on? She looks stunned by the suggestion.

"I'm not sure I can."

The uncertainty I see in her gaze hits me in the gut. She's not sure? It's just a bath. "Pearl, you can do anything in the world," I whisper, directing her backward steps into bathroom, my face close to hers. I place her on the vanity unit. "I've got you." I kiss the corner of her mouth, lick her lip ring, and inhale her lavender.

"You've got me," she replies, looking like she's turning that statement over in her mind as she stares at the tub. I leave her on the vanity and flip on the faucets, adding bubbles and lavender, inhaling the potent hit of my favorite scent. I'll talk to Beau, get her thoughts on this . . . situation. I know she'll hear me. And threaten me. I don't plan on hurting Pearl. Doesn't mean it won't happen though.

When I face her again, she looks like she's in a trance. "Look at me," I order, frowning. Fuck me, that man she saw on the street has hit her hard.

She tears her stare away from the tub.

"I've got you," I say again, moving in, crowding her. "Always." My eyes flit across her face, blood trickling into my dick as she starts to breathe heavily. *Fuck . . . me.* I reach for the small gold ring and circle it with the tip of my tongue, ensuring I only touch the metal.

She moves fast to catch my lips. "I want you," she murmurs urgently, cupping me over my hardness. And clearly, I want her too. But I am not putting myself inside her without protection until I've got the okay from Doc. Period.

I take her hand and remove it. "I don't have any condoms."

"It's been seven days."

Fuck. "I think we should hold off one more day." I need to distract her. "To be certain." I start to strip down, her attention acute as I build a pile of clothes next to me until I'm naked, reveling in her awe. "Your turn." I lower to the edge of the tub as her eyes dart to mine in question. "Take your clothes off." I spread my thighs, feeling the engorged, pulsing head of my cock dripping with need. I circle myself at the root, inhaling. Pearl's eyes fall to my lap, her breath lost on an audible, sharp hitch. I am not going to need much friction, my dick already locked and loaded. I draw my fist up my shaft, taking my spare hand to the edge of the bath for support, and she watches, engrossed. "Pearl." I strain her name, gritting my teeth before I draw back down. She reaches for the bottom of her dress and pulls it up over her head. And my eyes cross at the sight of her curves, her breasts bulging against the lace material of her bra. I draw back up. Breathe in. Eyes fixed on her chest as she reaches behind her and unhooks the catch. Her bra falls into the crook of her arms, and I look at her as she blows a strand of hair from her face. Bites her lip.

"Oh, you know exactly what you're doing, don't you?" Killing me fucking gently. "Drop it." I start a slow thrust of my fist, up and down, the rate manageable. But not for long. Her bra hits the floor. "Jesus." I squeeze myself, holding back my release, and stand, taking a few breathes to find my control again. I'm sweating. Reaching for her nape, I pull her close and swap my hand for hers, staring down at her. "Slow," I order, starting to guide her hand up and down as I trace the edge of her panties. Her green eyes explode with anticipation. When she's got her rhythm over my cock, I leave her to work alone, holding the back of her head, tilting it, absorbing the lust emblazoned all over her face. I push a finger past the seam of her panties, and her rhythm falters for a second before she finds it again. "Concentrate," I whisper, making her blink rapidly before closing her eyes. I watch her face in fascination as I push a finger into her sex, the soft, warm, spongy vessel throbbing around me. Her lips part, her hand starting to shake as she strokes my raging hard-on. I add my thumb to her clit and she croaks her despair, starting to shake before me.

"Brad, stop."

I stop.

"No, don't stop," she yells, squeezing my dick a little too aggressively.

I smile, fisting her hair, introducing another finger. Her eyes pop open, and I watch as she fights to keep them on me, my massaging thumb slipping beautifully around her swollen nub of screaming nerves. "Easy," I whisper as her face twists, her hand becoming clumsy as she tries to concentrate on me *and* herself. Her nails drag down my chest, my teeth gritting to sustain the pain, her face too beautiful to stop this. "Are you coming, my love?"

"Oh God." She collapses forward, forcing me to pull her back out by her hair. She looks high on ecstasy, her head dropped back, her hand on my shaft beginning to hurt more than pleasure me. I knock it away, walk her to a wall to hold her up, and take over myself. Her eyes snap open, her hands grabbing my biceps. I hiss, and she quickly releases her clench around my wound. I feel beads of sweat start to trickle down my temple as I work us both to the finish line, my jaw beginning to ache. One Pearl becomes two, and in a moment of pure euphoria, I hear only her pants, see only the glint in her green eyes, feel only the intense sensations rippling through my body.

Everything else disappears.

I come all over her stomach as she comes all over my hand, we both cry out, and I collapse forward, squeezing myself, hissing at the intensity as she grips and releases my fingers, gasping for breath. *Fuck.* "Okay?" I wheeze, my eyes on the floor. I slowly pull my fingers out of her pussy and her panties, and pull my head back to look at her. This look on Pearl? Incredible.

"My legs feel wobbly."

I can feel her heart hammering along with mine. "Weak at the knees for me?"

She peeks up, unable to hide her smile. And I just have to kiss her. Softly. Slowly.

"I needed that," I whisper, finally letting go of my dick.

Pearl looks down her front to the mess I've made, my spunk trickling down her leg. I grab a cloth and kneel, catching the trail and wiping up to her stomach, around, and across her boobs. "It went nowhere near my chest," she says, giving me a playful dirty look.

"It didn't?" I pout, reaching for one and cupping it. "And I thought I was a good shot."

She bursts into laughter, forced to reach for my chest to hold herself up, and I can do no more than support her while she falls apart, smiling. Because her laughter, her smiles, bring me immeasurable contentment. "You done?" I ask, looking down at her head, feeling her body jerk.

"Yes," she says, assertive, moving away from my chest. I admire the beautiful mess of her face—her hair stuck to her wet cheeks, her nose red, her lashes wet and sticky. Gorgeous.

"You sure?"

She's off again, collapsing forward, laughing her fucking tits off as she clings on to my front. I snake an arm around her lower back and look at us in the mirror. Me holding her up. Supporting her.

No longer alone.

"I'm sorry," she wheezes, out of breath, attempting once again to face me, the odd giggle escaping. She's sorry? "I'm okay now." Her lips press together, trying to hold back an encore of laughter.

"Shall we have that bath?"

Her nod is jerky, her lips becoming white, her cheeks red. She's going to burst a fucking blood vessel soon.

"Let it out," I order, and she breaks out all over again, complete, uncontrollable laughter. It's a vision, a sound I adore, but it also makes me wonder when the last time she laughed so freely was. I hold her, reaching for the tub and feeling at the water, wincing when freezing cold water hits my hot skin. I look at the tap, seeing I've turned the damn thing the wrong way. "Shit." I reach for the plug to drain it as Pearl laughs like a hyena in my arms, but I pause for thought, looking down at the back of her head. I smile. Leave the plug where it is.

Pick Pearl up and lower her into the water.

Her intake of breath is ear-piercing. "Oh my God, Brad!" Water splashes everywhere as I release her and get out of the way of her flailing arms and legs. "Fuck!" She shoots up and I briefly admire the puckering of her nipples before I've got freezing cold water being splashed at me.

My arms come up, like they can protect me from her attack. "Pearl," I yell over my laugh. Fuck, that really is cold. "Pearl, stop it."

"You arsehole!"

I move in, seizing her around the waist, and she screams as she falls over my shoulder, sending more water everywhere.

"Brad! Oh my God!"

I jolt when she slaps my ass. "Calm down." I chuckle.

"I'm so cold!"

I face the mirror, lowering her to her feet, and turn her toward it too. Her eyes find mine as I crouch behind her and drag her wet panties down. She lifts one foot. Then the other. I slide my palm up her inside thigh, watching her chest expand. Slipping two fingers into her sex, I smile playfully. "Not so cold here." The heat of her sucks me in for a moment as I rise and free her of my touch.

Her lips roll, her eyes mischievous. "That was mean."

I reach for her breast and squeeze her nipple. "I'm sorry."

She slaps her hand over mine. "Are you?"

"Yes."

"Prove it."

"How?"

I expect a demand to pleasure her, touch her, or kiss her. She looks at the bath, and I smile, crowding her and kissing her, pinning her naked body to mine, warming her up. "You want me to get in the cold tub, gorgeous?"

"Yes."

"Fine." I release her and get in, lowering into the water. It's nothing. I've been out on the water at the crack of dawn in every month of the year. She pouts. "Come," I say, offering my hand. "It's mind over matter."

She looks doubtful, but it speaks fucking volumes that she takes my hand. I love the trust she has in me. She steps in, breathes in, and curses under her breath. "Hurry up," I beg. "My balls are shrinking by the second."

She releases a sharp puff of laughter with her outward breath, losing her footing halfway down to her ass. "Brad!" She's once again laughing, and she lands on her ass with a thud and a splash, soon snapping her from her latest bout of hysterics. "Shit."

"Mind over matter." I arrange her legs over mine so she's mirroring my position opposite me. "Lean back," I whisper, drifting down to my back. She watches me. Just me. "Good girl." I wrap my palms around her ankles. "Okay?"

She nods, settling, relaxing. Enjoying the stone-cold bath. Watching me. "Are Danny and Rose all right?"

"They will be," I say, starting to stroke up and down her calves. "They've always been the same. Fight. Fuck. Adore. Repeat."

She smiles, nodding mildly, using both hands to push her wet hair back from her face.

"Where did you live in England?" I ask, trying and failing to sound casual. Ever since she opened up about her parents' deaths, I've been curious. I want to look her family up. Maybe warn them off. Whoever they are.

Pearl looks at me with a wary eye.

"What?" I ask, guilty.

"No," she says, firm and serious. "Whatever you're thinking, no."

"It'll just be a polite request to back off." *Or die.*

"No," she affirms. "You mustn't. Promise me you won't get involved, Brad."

I recoil, taken aback by her instant, rising panic.

"Promise me," she demands.

"Promise," I whisper, watching her on the cusp of a full-blown panic attack. Again. *What isn't she telling me?* I reach for the faucet and turn it on to warm the water up, but Pearl shoots a hand out and turns it straight back off.

"I was going to warm up the water."

"It's fine," she says, her gaze on the faucet.

"It's freezing," I point out, watching her on the brink of another attack. Seeing her like this? Painful. "Come here." I hold my hand out and she studies it for a moment before tentatively taking it. I pull her onto my body, holding her against my chest, hugging her hard. "I promise," I assure her again, feeling her nod into me.

"Okay."

"Okay," I breathe, settling.

Feeling.

Adoring.

Chapter 33

DANNY

I'm three drinks in and still hurting everywhere. My face. *Jesus*, my face. I reach up and press gently into my swollen lip, sucking back air. The touch upsets the clotting blood there, and it starts bleeding again. "Fucker." I lick it away, creaking up from the chair and raking a hand through my hair. I need to fucking sleep. Rest. But there's no chance of that. Or I could drink. I look at my glass and knock it back. I can drink myself into a coma. I pour another before leaving the office to stretch my legs, tired of sitting there, thinking of all the reasons Rose and I are bad for each other. Toxic. Damaging. Dangerous.

But fucking perfect.

I step out into the nighttime air and light up, following the path through the garden. Past the patio, past the pool, all the way to the back. "Cindy, Barbie," I call, putting my Marlboro between my lips as I dip to pick up a ball. "Good God," I moan, my muscles screaming. The girls appear from around the back of the summer house, running at me, as I creak my way back up from crouching. "Heel." They both sit at my feet. "Fetch?" They're up again, that one word telling them it's time for some relaxing.

I spend half an hour wandering the grounds, sipping my Scotch, smoking, the dogs flanking me, waiting for me to throw the ball for them. Each time I do, they dash off, barking. Cindy always returns with the ball.

I circle the back of the house and stop in front of a bed full of roses. All kinds—climbing, reds, whites, yellows. "Pretty," I murmur, for the first time taking notice of the beautiful, established rose bed. Pops would be proud. He loved his gardens.

I light up another cigarette and turn my head to blow the smoke away from the roses, frowning when I hear a high-pitched, shrill yelp of a woman coming from Brad's room. I look up at his terrace. The lights are on.

"Brad!" she yells.

I can just about muster the energy to be happy for the miserable fucker. Even if his choice of outlet is a fucking *lawyer*.

"You dick," I mutter as I carry on my way, dawdling, smoking, now kicking the ball for the girls so I don't have to stop and dip, saving myself a little discomfort. I could do with a massage. "Yeah, not happening," I say, laughing but not. I come to a stop below the terrace for our bedroom, hearing Maggie crying, and I sigh, bracing myself for another night with no sleep. I don't rush to the bedroom to try to help Rose. She made it clear I'm not welcome in the marital bed. Then *I* made it clear that the day we don't sleep in the same bed is the day I die. I scrub a hand down my face, finish my smoke, and head to the house. "That's enough for tonight, girls," I say. "Release." They dash off, up the garden, abandoning their ball, back on duty.

Mum's in the kitchen when I get there, sitting at the island, reading a magazine. She looks up at me when I come to a stop in the doorway. I can't even muster the strength to tell her I'm okay. Tell her not to worry.

"Look at the state of you," she breathes, closing the magazine and coming to me. She holds me still, a hand on either side of my neck, turning my face slowly each way to check the damage. "Why haven't you been cleaned up?"

I take one of her hands and pull it away, making her automatically release the other. "My wife's not in the mood to tend to me, and I don't know where Doc is."

"Sit." She goes to the cupboard and I do as I'm told, dropping heavily onto a stool at the island. "Doc's gone out for drinks with a lady friend."

"What?"

She nods, eyebrows high as she carries a box back over. "A nurse he used to work with." She flips the box open. "Twenty years younger than him."

"The rampant old git."

"He bumped into her while he was out and about." She soaks a pad in some liquid and comes in close, starting to wipe me up.

I wince. "Where does Doc go *out and about*?"

"I think it was at a clinic." Mum dumps the used pad and gets a fresh one. "Maybe he's moonlighting."

"We pay him too much," I mumble. "Ouch!"

"Shhh," she murmurs, holding my chin as she dabs at my cut lip.

"He was carrying piss around last week," I say.

"What?"

"Brad's piss. Doc had a sample. Brad said something about a water infection."

"Really?"

"Yeah. He was obviously lying."

"So why would Doc have Brad's piss?"

I have absolutely no brain space to devote to that. "Fuck." I shy away from the pad. "Shit, that stings."

"I'm sorry, my baby boy." She wrinkles her nose and pops a kiss on the end of mine, squeezing my jaw in her hand. I curl my lip and growl to make a point, and she laughs. "You don't scare me, son."

I grin, pulling her hand down, watching her faff like she loves.

"What?" she asks, getting a tube of something from the box.

"I love you, Mum."

She tries to hide her surprise, squeezing a bit onto the tip of her finger and moving into my side, dabbing at my lip. "What's got into you?"

"I want you to be happy."

"Okay," she says slowly. "I *am* happy."

"The happiest you can possibly be."

"Danny, why are you talking like this?" she asks, withdrawing. "I don't like it. Is something about to happen?"

I smile, hearing a couple of cars pulling up outside. Otto's not asked her. And I know that because she will definitely say yes. She loves him. I'm slowly accepting that. I stand and kiss her cheek. "Something's always about to happen, Mum. Goodnight."

"Night," she whispers, unsure, letting me wander away half cleaned up. I make it into the entrance hall and meet Otto, Ringo, and Goldie. "Good evening," I quip, because it's far from good. I try to smile and feel it pull on my lip, opening the wound again. *Fuck it.* I latch on and suck it clean.

"Fucking Christ," Otto mutters, taking in my war wounds.

"Mine's better than yours." I point to his quite pathetic swollen nose, and he shakes his head. "How did you get on?" I ask, willing someone to take my mind off my woes.

"You've not spoken to James or Brad?"

"No, I've been busy bleeding." *Face and heart.*

"The Escalade we checked out has been cloned. The ex-cop is an eighty-year-old charity worker with a wholesome wife, two-point-five children, five grandchildren, a retriever, and a lake house."

"Perfect."

"And heads-up," Otto says.

"What?"

"James overhead a call Brad took from Higham."

"What's he calling Brad for?"

"You were busy."

I huff, vaguely remembering Brad mentioning Higham's trip's been extended. "When's he back in town?" I need to find out what's going on with Amber's body.

"Don't know. But that's not what you should be concerned about."

"It's not?" Amber's body feels like a big deal.

"No. Higham mentioned Richard Bean to Brad."

Shit. "How does Higham know about Bean? He's on holiday."

"I'd say ask Brad, but I'm not sure you want to go there yet."

Fuck, I don't. My fucking head is ringing. I sigh, going to Otto and resting a hand on his shoulder, squeezing, not looking at him. "Make her happy," I whisper so the others can't hear.

"Don't insult me."

I look out the corner of my eye, smiling. And the overgrown, pierced, mean motherfucker smiles right back. "Goodnight."

"Night," he says quietly.

I climb the stairs on heavy feet and drag my tired bones down the corridor, my despondency increasing the closer I get to our room. And the louder Maggie's cries get.

When I reach the door, I take the handle, resting my forehead on the wood, taking a moment. *Breathe. It's just one more night. It'll get better.* I open the door and find Rose standing at the end of the bed.

Floods of tears streaming down her cheeks.

Maggie's in the middle of the sheets screaming the fucking house down—a high-pitched, distressed cry.

Rose sees me, her red, blotchy face a picture of equal distress. "She won't stop," she sobs, beaten. "She just won't stop crying." She points at our baby accusingly, like . . . look at her. "What's wrong with her?" she cries, hands covering her face. "I've fed her, changed her, burped her. I don't know what's wrong with her."

Even when I fucking hate my wife, I can't bear to see her cry.

I push the door closed and go to the bathroom, quickly scrubbing my hands, brushing my teeth and unbuttoning my shirt halfway down before pulling it over my head and tossing it aside, the screaming continuing, making me work faster, more urgently, my mind spinning, my head ringing. I pull my phone out of my pocket as I pace back into the bedroom, opening the Sonos App, frantically stabbing at a track, any track, just give me music.

Love & Hate by Michael Kiwanuka fills the room, not too loud, but loud enough, and I scoop Maggie up off the bed, looking down at her little red face, her tongue quivering as she screams, gasping for breath. "Shhhh." I hush her, rocking her gently, going to Rose and hooking my spare arm around her neck, pulling her into me, kissing her temple over and over as Maggie squawks and Rose jerks over her sobs. I clench my eyes closed, looking up at the ceiling in so much fucking pain. Not from my injuries, but because my girls are distraught. Both of them.

I swallow, feeling Rose's hot tears on my chest, and breathe deeply, starting to rock us all, moving slowly in circles, hushing, whispering soft words of comfort. *Holding them.* Maggie persists. Rose continues to sob and shake against me.

But I don't give up. *Never will.* Not until I've made everything okay.

"I love you," I whisper in Rose's ear, pressing my sore face into hers. She nods, snivels, shifting her arms to cling on to me, as she follows my moves, turning in constant, endless circles. "We've got this, baby." She clings tighter, calming, but Maggie still cries, although not as violently, the ear-splitting sound slowly melding into a more tired cry, as the track plays on and we continue to turn on the spot in the middle of the bedroom. "It's okay," I whisper. "We're okay." I kiss Rose's temple again, tasting the saltiness of her tears in her hair, feeling the aftermath of her sobs. Her breathing is becoming steadier. Her body settling.

I peek down at Maggie. She's stopped crying, inhaling shakily every now and then. Looking up at me. My fucking heart cracks, watching her little lip wobbling. "Daddy's here," I whisper, raising her to kiss her forehead. "Always here." Closing my eyes, I keep them in my arms, peace finally finding us and chasing away the chaos. I tighten my hold on Rose, feeling her stroking across my bare back with her warm palm, her feet tucked between mine, her body guided by my slow moves.

And I don't stop holding them, moving them, keeping them close, safe, until the track's finished and we turn to absolute silence, scared to stop. Scared they'll get upset again.

I eventually breathe in and peek down. Maggie's asleep. Calm. I release Rose, keeping our baby close to my chest, and take her to her crib, lowering her gently on a held breath, carefully releasing her and tucking her in.

I only breathe once I'm standing and she's not stirred. Oh God. And now look at her. Peaceful. Oblivious to the bedlam around her.

I turn to Rose. She's holding her breath too. It's been the worst day. I help her undress, strip out of my trousers, and put her in bed, turning her back to me and crawling in behind her, my body curving perfectly around hers. I kiss her back. Lace my fingers through hers where her hand rests on her tummy. "You're mine, Rose Lillian Black," I whisper, pulling from our past to remind her of who we are. "You're fearless, I'm fearless." I kiss the back of her head. "Don't cry, baby, it doesn't suit you." I hug her closer, feeling the last of her sobs leaving her body on air. "The only thing we're scared of is each other." I smile, but it's sad, because that's not true anymore. Both of us are terrified of the little thing in that crib and her big brother down the hall. The love you feel for your children is crippling. It's a different kind of love.

And Rose and I are both in agony over them.

Chapter 34

BRAD

How the fuck I stopped myself from putting my dick inside her I don't know. I've snoozed occasionally throughout the night. Half hour here, half hour there. Then my mind would wake me up and shit would happen that I couldn't stop. I can't get enough of her. I woke her up endless times with my head between her legs, or my fingers inside her, or by moving her hand to my begging cock. I'm a glutton for her, and despite having her over and over throughout the night, I'm not sated. Not satisfied. Because I couldn't be inside her. "Oh Jesus," I whisper, feeling my cock waking up too. I'm just going to have to accept that when she's naked and close, I'm going to be in pain.

I look down at the mess of red hair splayed across my chest, my arm holding her close to my side. Covered in scratches. I hum, finding one of her hands and lifting it to see her nails. Short, straight nails. Not short enough to be harmless, obviously. I should leave her to sleep. My face screws up in pain as my dick starts to throb.

What's the time, anyway? I reach for my cell on the nightstand. Six. I groan, dropping my head back. She didn't go back to her room. If I got two hours during the night, I'd be surprised. If I wasn't indulging in her, I was thinking about what she might not be telling me.

But back to the matter at hand.

My overused, greedy cock.

Let her sleep. Get a few more winks yourself.

I close my eyes.

And snap them back open again when I feel a wandering hand creeping across my stomach. She's awake? I look down at the back of her head. Well, now I don't feel so guilty. "Morning," I whisper hoarsely.

She doesn't reply but instead circles my dick in her small, dainty palm. I moan, dropping my head back, as she slowly starts to work me, her pace lazy and steady, perfect for this time of day. I hum my praise, my hips starting to thrust upward, my eyes closing. That feels so good. I smile into my darkness, but it drops when she releases me. I don't have a moment to protest. She's straddling me in a second, her generous, wonderful boobs in perfect view, her beautiful, wild, red hair a mess across her face. She lifts and reaches between us, and I cough and seize her hand. She sags, disappointment invading her fresh face. Can't say I like disappointment on my girl.

"Why?" she asks, not pouting but close. "We've not had sex all night." Poor thing looks so mystified. "Is something wrong?"

My hard, black heart melts. I can't tell her why I refuse to put myself inside her. "You've done nothing wrong," I assure her, circling her waist with my hands. "I already told you, I'm out of condoms."

Her semi-pout transforms into a full-on, sulky pout. "That wasn't a problem in the shower last week," she whispers, lowering her chest to mine, forcing me to breathe in when she presses into me. *Shit.* She frames my face with her arms, eyes a fraction from mine, her hot breath sending me even wilder. Harder.

"That was a momentary lapse of focus on my part."

Her nose bunches. "I like it when you have a momentary lapse of focus." She grinds down, and I curse to high heaven. "Have one now."

"Pearl," I warn, squeezing my eyes closed, resisting. *Resisting, resisting, resisting.*

She nuzzles at my ear. "Please," she whispers, sending bolts of pleasure directly into my groin. "It's been eight days now, I'm sure it'll be okay."

"Oh God."

Another grind.

"Pearl, come on," I plead, making no attempt to stop her.

"I want you."

Fuck.

I spin her onto her back and blanket her body with mine, not entering her, but rubbing her in just the right place for both of us. Dry-fucking-humping. I'd be mortified if it wasn't so nice. "You want me, do you?" I ask, dipping and kissing one cheek. Grinding. Kissing the other cheek. She whimpers, those fucking nails finding my back. "You like me inside you with nothing between us?" Why the fuck am I goading her? It isn't happening.

I roll my hips and she yelps a resounding *yes!*

"Oh, gorgeous." I grit my teeth, gaining momentum, feeling it coming. I look down at her face, seeing she's with me. I push up on one forearm and lower my mouth to her nipple, sucking, flicking, kissing as I gyrate my hips into her.

"Shit, Brad." She moves with me, building, building, building.

I grunt at the feel of her nails down my back.

"Oh God. It's coming."

"Shhhh," I growl around her nipple. She'll wake the whole fucking house up.

"Oh God!"

I reach up and put a hand over her mouth to shut her up, the pressure about to leave me. I hold my breath, bite at her nipple, looking up at her, seeing she's about to come when—

My bedroom door flies open.

"Fuck." I fly up, yanking the comforter over us at lightning speed as Pearl yelps and I lay a hand over my dick to dull the instant pain. I blink, trying to gain some focus through my pre-climax state. I find Danny in the doorway in his boxers. "The fuck?" I instinctively look over my shoulder to the bed, seeing Pearl covered by the sheets, but they're rising and falling with her heavy breathing.

For fuck's sake. "Doesn't anyone knock around here?" I snap, giving Danny deadly eyes. I've been caught red-handed. It's time to confess. "I—"

"Get dressed," he says, not paying any attention to the hidden woman next to me.

"What?"

"We're going—" He looks past me to the bed. Scowls. Then points to the bathroom, going there, obviously wanting me to follow. I sigh, peeking under the covers to Pearl. Her cheeks are a beautiful shade of pre-orgasm.

"Did he see me?" she whispers. "Oh God, I can't face him." Slamming her eyes closed, she pulls the covers down onto her face.

I drag myself out of bed and go to the bathroom, my hand over my groin, closing the door, bracing myself for the showdown. His face looks a fucking mess. "I just got a call from Benson," he says.

"What?"

"Someone broke into his house last night."

"What?"

"Killed that Sid bloke."

"What?" I blurt.

Danny throws his hands up. "Am I speaking Chinese this morning?"

"Fuck."

He tilts his head, like, yes, you heard me right. "That's exactly what I thought." He pulls the door open and leaves. "Get dressed." He stops at the bedroom door, looking back at the lump in the bed. "Morning, Allison," he says, sarcastic as fuck, before slamming the door behind him.

What?

The covers fly up, as does Pearl, her face a picture of indignance.

"You want me to go out there and tell him you're not Allison?" I ask.

"Yes," she says, pointing at the door.

I laugh, going to the dressing room and getting some boxers on.

"Fine," she calls. "I will."

I frown, leaning back to see into the bedroom, my boxers halfway up my legs. She's marching across the bedroom. Naked. What the fuck? "Pearl," I yell, yanking my boxers up the rest of the way as I run after her. I seize her at the door and haul her back to the bed, throwing her on it. "Seriously?"

"I'm not Allison."

"You're also not thinking straight." I kneel on the edge of the bed and dip. "I said you have to let me figure out the best way to approach this." And that, just then—Danny barging in—is exactly why I need to speed things up.

"I know," Pearl relents, shuffling forward and circling my shoulders, kissing me chastely. Then she looks at me for a moment, and I see the swirl of thoughts in her eyes. "Are you sure—" She chews her lip. "I mean, Allison is"—she rolls her eyes—"experienced."

I chuckle, enchanted. "She's also not you." I hit her with a hard kiss as the door is hit with a hard fist.

"Hurry up," Danny yells through the wood.

"Coming." One more kiss. "I'll call you later." I break away and pull on some jeans and a T-shirt, stuffing my feet into some brown leather boots and leaving the laces untied. I look back at her curled on her side in my bed, the sheets all bunched and held to her front, her red hair spread across the pillow. It's a sight for the mental archives.

"You look gorgeous."

"Don't get shot."

I smile and leave her.

Danny's pacing the foyer when I get there, and James is motionless by the door. "Just the three of us?"

Danny scowls at me. "Is Allison Edward Scissorhands in disguise?"

"What?"

He points at my arms, and I look down at the fresh red lines on my tan skin.

"Are we going or what?" I ask irritably, marching between them and heading for my car. "I'll follow you." I have a few calls to make. I slide into the driver's seat and start the engine, slamming the door.

The passenger door opens and James gets in, his face blank as he looks at me. Danny gets in the back. "Oh, no." I laugh, getting out and opening the back door, reaching for his T-shirt and dragging him out.

"What the fuck are you doing?" he yells.

"If you insist on riding with me, you're going within punching range." I put myself in the middle of the back seat as Danny laughs his way into my driver's seat. I curl my lip at the back of his head and get my phone out. And smile when I see a text from Pearl.

Tie your laces or you'll stand on them and trip.

I look down at my boots.

Yes, boss.

I quickly text Nolan to ask how he's doing and drop my phone on the seat, reaching down to tie my laces. I'll have to call Otto later. I need to think about how to get the information I want without him asking why I want to know it. Because why the fuck would I care if Pearl has family looking for her?

"So what's the situation?" I ask as James pulls down the sun visor and flips up the cover of the mirror so he can see me. "Missing my face?"

His eyes go back to the road as Danny turns onto the freeway. "Lennox called Danny. He heard something outside around two. Checked his CCTV. Saw nothing. Went to bed. Woke up to a man in his bedroom."

"And the kid?"

"Don't know," Danny says quietly, obviously wondering too. And worrying. "All I know is the guy he hired to protect them is dead and he's asked for our help."

"So there's more to it."

"Definitely. Did either of you know Doc went on a date last night?" Danny asks, doing a complete one-eighty on subject matter.

"Oh, behave," I say over a laugh. "Doc on a date?"

"I'm telling you," Danny says, eyes between me in the rearview mirror and the road. "He met an old colleague while *out and about* and they reconnected."

Great. So I got no penetration because the old boy was getting some himself?

Danny looks up at the mirror at me with high eyebrows. "Mum said he met her at a clinic. I expect that's where he took your piss sample for testing."

My mouth opens to tell him to fuck off, and my fist bunches ready to punch him. James looks at me in the mirror of the sun visor. "What's wrong with your piss?"

Jesus Christ. "Doc thinks I've got a water infection." Both of their brows hitch higher. *Oh for fuck's sake.* "I've had some tests done, okay?"

"Why?" they both ask.

"Just because." I slam my back into the seat, silently daring either of them to laugh.

"You cover up, though, right?" Danny asks.

"Of course I do." I grimace. There's been the odd occasion when alcohol or plain lust has got in the way of condoms, but I always made sure birth control was in place. *Always.*

"Really?"

"Look, I'm a thirty-five-year-old man who's . . ." How do I put this?

"A manwhore that needs to check the lady whores haven't left anything behind?"

That's it. I launch my fist into Danny's bicep, and he swerves into the next lane, getting honked at by a truck.

"You fucker," he yells, abandoning the wheel and practically throwing himself into the back between the seats. I'm pinned to the leather, his psycho face up in mine, his teeth bared. "I've got a dead fucking arm." He pulls his head back and headbutts me.

"Fuck!" I yelp, water bursting from my eyes, blood from my nose. "Jesus Christ." I grab his arms and haul him into the door, extending my leg fast and kicking him in the gut.

He instantly retches, holding his stomach. "You wanker," he says, coughing. "That was uncalled for."

"Stop pissing me off," I mutter, my breathing labored, running the back of my hand across my bloody nose. I look up and find James has somehow managed to get his big body over the center console into the driving seat. "You could have killed us all."

Danny huffs, settling back on his side of the car. "I already feel dead from lack of sleep."

"Another bad night?" James asks, looking at us both in the rearview mirror.

"It was better, actually," Danny says. "After I'd rocked her for fifteen minutes. Turns out she's a Michael Kiwanuka fan. She slept for five hours straight."

"And Rose?" I ask, daring to go there.

"Rose is Rose." He smiles to himself, looking out of the window at the freeway whizzing past. "Brilliantly strong while being heartbreakingly fragile."

I smile. Sounds familiar.

"So you're having a sexual overhaul to make sure you're clean for the lawyer?" Danny asks, snapping out of his wistful musings of his wife and turning his attention back to me.

"Sounds sensible," James pipes in.

Okay. Enough about me and my recently born consideration for the woman I'm sleeping with. "When's Otto popping the question?"

"Don't know," Danny replies quickly. "So, answer me this."

"What?"

"Has the lawyer pushed for these tests?"

"What?"

"Am I speaking Chinese again?"

I look at James, like he can help me, but he appears interested too. "No, she hasn't. I don't know why you two are making such a big deal of the lawyer. I'm fucking her."

"And when are you planning on telling her you live life one step away from America's Most Wanted list?"

"Did you invite me along just to piss me off?"

He grins. "Always."

"I'm just fucking her." What the fuck am I saying? I should be speaking some truths. Tell them it wasn't Allison in my bed this morning.

"And your little crush on Pearl isn't a thing anymore?"

I look at him in horror. *Speak!* "It was never a thing," I grate, incensed. Crush? Fuck, would I love it to be just a crush.

"So you don't want to fuck her anymore?"

Fuck, yes, I want to fuck her every minute of every day. "I'm going to smash your fucking face in again, Danny," I warn, and he holds his hands up.

"Just checking." He goes back to James. "Do you think you could convince Beau to go to St. Lucia?"

I exhale, the heat off. What the fuck am I going to tell them? I'm just fucking her? No. It's more than fucking. I *think*. Is it? I frown to myself, my hand automatically going to my heart and rubbing. It's like an innate something that's ordering me to devote myself to her. Is this—

Oh fuck.

"Probably," James says, and I blink.

"You think?" Danny asks, surprised.

"Yeah, I think. Pregnancy's brought out a reasonable side to her." He smiles at the mirror, and I laugh under my breath.

"Still thinks she's fucking Lara Croft, though."

"All the girls should go," Danny declares.

"I think Otto would agree too," James says. "Zinnea might be harder to convince."

"Why?"

"Beau said they met Quinton yesterday while they were having coffee. She's smitten."

"There's nothing stopping Quinton getting on the plane too," Danny says.

"I know everyone will get on that plane, Danny." James turns off the freeway. "But Beau might think twice if Rose doesn't."

I cringe, knowing that to be one hundred percent true. There's no way Beau would leave Rose behind.

"Rose will go," Danny says, sounding unsure. As he should.

"So we're sending all the women and children to St. Lucia until this is sorted out." What would I do if Pearl was hurt? An uncomfortable ache in my heart gets me. "How did you two know you were in love?" I blurt, surprising myself *and* the boys. They both look at me like I've flashed some fangs.

James blinks a few times. "Umm . . ."

"The fucking lawyer?" Danny looks disgusted.

"I'm not in love with the lawyer," I answer tiredly.

"Then why are you asking?"

"Because it blows my mind every day how you both can love something that drives you to distraction."

They laugh. "Us too."

Then silence falls for a while, and I mull over the questions turning in my mind. The new feelings. The instinct I can't control.

"You could never comprehend it," James says quietly, pulling my gaze up to his eyes in the mirror. He's not looking at me. "Unless you feel it. It's"—his lips roll, his eyes squinting, thinking—"like a bomb going off in your chest. But it's quiet. Like a shift in something you didn't know was inside you. Dark becomes light."

"Purpose," Danny adds quietly.

"Yeah, purpose," James says. "Purpose and an uncontrollable instinct to kill anything that threatens their happiness and safety."

I stare forward, slightly dazed, a lot worried.

"Let's have a drink later," Danny says. "Just the three of us. Maybe go out on the water for a few hours."

Sounds good to me.

I could do with a race.

And twenty Scotches.

It's like a bomb going off in your chest. But it's quiet. Like a shift in something you didn't know was inside you.

I rub at my chest.

Fucking hell.

Chapter 35

DANNY

The plan was to tell Brad about Nolan this morning. Benson has fucked with my plan. Part of me is pissed off. The other part is relieved. How the fuck do we tell him who Nolan is? And in some fucked-up turn of events, I find out *now* that he's suddenly all worried about possible breached condoms?

Jesus.

On top of that, Higham's been saying things he shouldn't be saying to Brad, but since Higham doesn't know about the situation with Nolan, I don't suppose I can hold it against him. Neither am I in a position to go ape shit on Higham's arse, since I'm calling in all the favors he owes me and is ever likely to owe me in order to keep my wife out of prison. What I do want to know, though, is how Higham knows about Bean? What's Bean said? Why did Higham ask Brad about it? Surely Bean's not dumb enough to throw our names out there. And yet Brad hasn't mentioned the call from Higham or asked who Bean is. I'm putting that down to the hour. He's probably not woken up yet. Which means I need to figure this out fast before Brad comes at me with his questions.

But first, let's deal with this mess.

We pull up outside a flashy, modern house in a suburb on a tree-lined street on the west side of town. I pout up at Benson's house. "Mine's bigger than yours," I muse, slipping out of the back, rolling my shoulder, my arm still fucking numb. I throw a scowl back at Brad as he gets out, rubbing his nose. He's lucky I'd never kill him.

James checks his gun as he joins me. "There's tire marks in the road back there," he says casually, making me look back.

"This doesn't look like the kind of street a resident would break any speed limits." I cast an eye across the larger-than-average driveways. "Or park on the road." I make my way up the path to the door, looking at all of the windows, Brad and James following.

Benson opens the door before I can knock, peeking out at us, his relief obvious. The state of his face makes me feel a bit better about my own. "I didn't know who else to call." He opens the door wide.

"I'm touched," I say, stepping inside, looking up the stairs. "Where's Barney?"

"In bed still. He was up until midnight playing on his Xbox with Daniel over the headphone things they use. He won't stir until I drag him up for school." He motions toward the back of the stairs. "Through there."

Brad overtakes me with James and enters the room. "Jesus," he breathes, as I follow behind, Lennox tailing me.

I walk in and find Brad crouched by the body of Lennox's new hire. "I'd say he's fired," I muse, joining James standing over him. I grimace at the knife sticking out of his neck. "Accurate."

"Not really," James says. "Frantic and lucky."

"Why'd you say that?"

"Because if you're trained to do the job properly, you'd remove the knife." He dips and yanks the knife out, and blood splashes from the blade, nearly catching Brad's jeans.

"Fuck's sake, James," he yells, standing and stepping back. "Control your urges."

Benson retches and turns away, and I smile. Got a better stomach than him too, although mine's definitely aching after Brad booted me in it.

"There's more," Lennox says, his voice muffled from his hand over his mouth.

"More what?" James asks.

"My bedroom."

James is off, Brad following, both their guns ready to fire. Curious, I follow them up the stairs, poking my head around a few doors on my way. I see Barney spread-eagled on his front, mouth open, dead to the world. Thank God.

I make it to the bedroom. "The fuck?" I breathe, stepping in.

"We have a live one," Brad chimes, kicking the boot of the man propped in the corner holding his stomach. Bleeding out. Sweating. Brad crouches. "Now, who would you be?"

He dribbles and slurs, his chest pumping fast, his heart trying hard to pump what blood's left around his body. He wouldn't be able to talk if he wanted to. I look at the shot gun on the bed. At the footprints on the carpet. The blood everywhere, on the sheets, the floor, the doorframes. It's a forensics dream. "Who are they, Benson?" I ask, facing him as he hovers in the doorway looking at the mess.

A sharp woosh and a click sounds.

Lennox flinches, and I look back to see Brad rising, unscrewing the silencer from his gun, the unknown man now with a hole in his head too, though arguably not as big as the one in his stomach.

"I owe money," Lennox breathes, sounding beaten. James sighs, Brad curses. "A lot."

"How much is a lot?"

He hesitates, and I cock my head in impatience. "Five million."

I can't contain my baulk. "What the fuck do you owe five million for?"

He swallows, looking past me. "Can we go downstairs and talk about this?"

Bless him. The dead man's making him feel sick. "Fine." I breathe out my irritation and motion with my gun for him to lead the way. Obviously, we don't go into the kitchen. We go into the lounge. Benson lowers to the couch, head in his hands. James remains by the door. Brad goes to the window.

"Barney's Mom," Lennox says. "She wanted custody of Barney. Or money."

"Well." I laugh, unstoppably irate. Not with Lennox, weirdly, but with his ex. "She's put her kid and money in the same sentence of things she'd like one or the other of?"

"Yes, she wants money." He drops back in the chair. "She already financially raped me in our divorce."

"Bitch," I mutter.

"She has a habit."

"Drugs?"

"Gambling. The guy she's with now is the same."

"So they've spent all your money and want more, or she'll take Barney." She won't take Barney. She doesn't want Barney.

"In a nutshell."

"So you borrowed five million to pay her off."

"No, I borrowed two."

Oh. Interest. Late payment fees. It soon adds up. And now the debt collectors are calling. "You didn't have two million?"

"Not liquid cash, no. It's tied up in this place and St. Lucia."

I hum, looking around the lounge. "You should have come to me. I would have given you a better interest rate."

He laughs, rubbing at his head. "Hindsight, eh?"

"My question is, who did you borrow from?"

Lennox looks up, hesitant, and I just know I'm going to hate the answer.

"Russians," James says.

He has his phone held up, an image of the dead man upstairs on the screen. "Otto."

I breathe in my patience. "You borrowed two million from the Russians?" Lennox can't possibly know our connection to the depraved cunts. "How the fuck did you know where to get two million from fast?"

"I work for a private bank, Danny. It wasn't hard to find out who to ask in Miami."

I can't believe this dickhe— "Wait." My spine straightens, and I glance at Brad. He has a similar expression on his face as I know I have. Wary interest. As does James. There's only one Russian big bod in this town. "Are you telling me you looked up a client on the system, got his name and address, and popped by to ask him if you could borrow two million?"

His head in his hands again, he sighs, "No. That client isn't the kind of client our bank would take legitimate details from."

"So the bank's corrupt."

"It's owned by an Estonian businessman, Danny."

"Oh." Well, that's a turn out for the books.

"There are certain clients on a certain list that are looked after by certain people."

"And you're not one of those people?" I can't believe what's transpiring here. I fucking hated Lennox Benson. I think I might love him now.

"No. I'm not one of those people. I deal with legit, high-wealth clients. Those with a lot of cash to invest."

"That side of the business obviously doesn't pay enough."

"Not when you've got an ex-wife with no morals and a nasty gambling habit, no."

"So how did you know about this non-legitimate side?"

"I'm not stupid."

"But you're also not a mind reader. How did you know where to go?"

"I hacked the company system."

I recoil. "You did, did you?" Otto better up his game. "And . . .?"

"And found the fraudulent details of various Russian clients. Fake names, fake addresses. But the contact number was always the same."

"Do you have that number?"

"On my cell." He pats at his lounge pants and pulls it out.

"Call him."

"What?"

"Call him." I get up and start pacing, my fucking head reeling. I give Brad and James a *can you fucking believe this?* look as I pass them. I hear Benson's phone ringing, and I move closer, listening. The moment someone answers, my heartbeats increase.

"Do you realize what you've done?" the Russian accent drawls. "You killed my men?"

Poor Benson looks white as a sheet. "I was defending my home. My family."

"If you don't pay, you *pay*. You have two days. I have more men. They'll keep coming." He hangs up, and I slowly turn to face James. The Enigma doesn't show much emotion at work these days. His anger has subsided . . . tamed. His face now, though?

Utter shock. "Fuck . . . me," he whispers.

"Sandy?" Brad gasps, doing what Brad does best. Stating the fucking obvious.

"Well, would you Adam and Eve it," I say, laughing to myself.

"Wait, you know him?" Benson asks, standing, his eyes jumping around the room.

"Old enemies." I smile, taking his mobile out of his hand. Oh, how I would have *loved* to interrupt that call. I check the number. Not surprisingly, it's different to the one I have.

"Of course." Benson drops back to the couch, head back in his hands. "Jesus Christ."

"Listen up, friend," I say, lowering next to him and smiling. Because now I am *definitely* Benson's friend. "I'm going to fix this mess."

"How? You're going to pay off my debt?"

Brad chuckles, James smiles, and I huff, unimpressed. "No, Benson, I'm going to kill them."

"Oh fucking hell."

"Don't feel bad. They've had it coming for years." I stand, looking around. "You can't stay here anymore."

"Yeah, I know that, Danny." He rolls his eyes, exasperated by me.

"I think I need a coffee," I muse, heading to the kitchen. "You got a machine?"

"I can't cope," I hear him mutter, following me. "Here." He steps over the body and pulls a few cups down. "Anyone else?"

"Please," Brad calls from the lounge. "No sugar."

"No sugar," James grunts.

I grin when Lennox looks at me. "Black." I wander away, leaving Benson to distract himself from his situation for a few moments playing barista. James and Brad are by the window when I get back. "I feel like Candid Camera is gonna pop out of the fireplace at any moment and tell us this is a cruel joke."

"Are you thinking what I'm thinking?" Brad asks.

"I don't know, Brad, because I never know what the fuck you're thinking these days."

"Me neither," he mutters to himself, winning both James's and my attention.

"I think I know what you're thinking," James says, a definite hint of glee and excitement in his eyes.

"Coffee," Benson says, entering with four cups split between two hands. He passes them around and I take my seat again, as do James and Brad.

"No reports of gunshots last night," James says, holding up his phone.

How, I don't fucking know. I saw the shotgun. But the police didn't show up and here we are.

I look around Benson's lovely Miami property. "We need to burn this place down."

He coughs over his coffee. "What?"

"Don't worry," Brad says, going straight to his phone. "Our pal Ringo is an expert arsonist. He'll be in is element."

"And the bodies?"

"No issue," James muses. "We know where the sharks play."

The poor bloke looks dazed as he takes some coffee. "Mind if I smoke?" I ask, and he laughs.

"Danny, you do whatever the fuck you like."

"Thanks." I light up and throw my packet and lighter to Brad, who follows suit. James declines this time. "So in return for sorting out this mess for you, there's something you can do for me."

Benson takes a few deep breaths, bracing himself for what I might demand. "Go on."

I can't say I like the fuckhead. True, he's good in a fight. Has raised a good kid. Drew the short straw on wives. I don't want him anywhere near Rose, but he could solve the problem of Daniel. Yes, the principal acquiesced—*sort of*—and allowed Daniel back into the school, but to what end? It won't be made easy for the kid, no matter what threats I toss around, and I really don't want to expose Daniel like that *or* put him in a position where he has to threaten people with Pops's gold letter opener. Will Rose worry less if he does some distance ed? "You can go back to St. Lucia," I say, feeling Brad's focus on my profile. "It shouldn't raise too many questions given your house in Miami just burned down." I smile. Benson exhales his disbelief. "And take Daniel with you."

Dubious, he watches me as I slowly sip my coffee. "That's it?"

"You can use my private jet. It'll be ready to leave in a day or two. You should get Barney up." I go to the fireplace and flick my ash in there. "You're coming to stay with us."

"What?" Benson blurts, recoiling.

I look at Brad, exasperated. "No, seriously, am I speaking Chi-fucking-nese?" For fuck's sake. "You. Are. Coming. To. Stay. With. Us." I take one last puff of my cigarette and throw it in the fireplace. "But, I swear, Benson, if you even *look* at my wife in a way I don't like, I'll—"

"I get it." His hand comes up, stopping me from finishing my threat. "With respect, Danny, your wife is a beautiful wom—"

"Stop."

"She's stunning, b—"

"Shut up, Benson."

"She's not my type."

I recoil, insulted. "What the hell do you mean, she's not your type?"

"I prefer redheads."

A choking sound comes from across the room, and I look back to see Brad juggling the coffee cup, the hot liquid all over his hand. "Fuck, that's hot."

I roll my eyes and get back to Benson.

"Like I said, she's beautiful, b—" He finally registers the crazy in my eyes. "I'll shut up."

"I highly recommend it," Brad whispers menacingly from behind. "Can we get home now?"

"You in a rush?" James asks.

"Yes," he grunts, stomping out.

James shrugs. It's probably best Brad's in a bad mood. I'd hate for him to be in a good one and then have to ruin it with the news I'm about to give him.

Chapter 36

ROSE

I walk down the stairs with Maggie in my arms, feeling a lot fresher than I have for days. The post-baby high was certainly an adrenaline rush keeping me sane and human for a while. The adrenaline has worn off. I'm exhausted. Danny's exhausted. Yet last night, our daughter slept for a few hours . . . *in a row*. It's insane what a few hours of sleep can do.

As I reach the bottom, the front door opens and Leon walks in, a bag in his hands. "Mrs. B," he chimes, dropping the bag and coming straight at me. "Aww, she's getting chubby."

"What are you doing here?"

He steps back. His chin raises. "I'm fulfilling the request of one of the bosses."

"Which one?"

"Oh come on, Rose, don't do this to me." He grabs the bag and heads for the kitchen. "Any breakfast on offer?"

I follow him, placing Maggie in her crib, watching as Leon dives into the pancakes piled on the island. Esther smiles, offering him syrup and bacon too. "These are so good," he says, his mouth full.

"Have you got the munchies?" Beau asks as I join her at the island.

He chuckles, powering his way through the pancakes. Leon spends half his life high. But he's a good kid.

"Hey," she says. "Fury mentioned Pearl may have had a panic attack yesterday after we left them at the café."

"She did? She seemed fine."

"She did," Beau muses. "But Fury described all the signs, and . . . well, I know." She shrugs, and I reach for her hand. It's been a while since Beau has been captured by an attack. I hope those days are long gone for her. "She didn't want Fury to tell us, so"—her finger meets her lip—"let's just keep an eye on her."

"Okay." I frown at Leon, prompting Beau to too.

"Jesus, Leon," she says. "No one is stealing the pancakes."

He suddenly straightens, wiping his mouth with the back of his hand. "Morning," he mumbles, swallowing.

Pearl wanders in, taking a stool on the other side of the island. "Morning," she says quietly.

"Hey." Leon gives her a goofy smile. "You look nice today."

Pearl lifts a brow as she butters some toast, surprised, then glances down her front. "Thanks . . . I think." She smiles a little, not a lot, sinking her teeth into her toast, then she seems to drift away with the fairies, lost in thought. I look at Beau. She nods. We *definitely* need to keep an eye on her.

Leon excuses himself and slips out. With that bag. I watch him go with a narrowed eye. "Anyone seen my husband?"

"He's—" Pearl coughs, patting at her chest. "Sorry."

"He's?"

"The gym maybe?"

"Maybe," I muse, looking back at the door when Leon disappears. Beau's hand on mine pulls me back. She shakes her head, like . . . leave it. I nod, reluctant, and she indicates to Pearl with a flick of her eyes in that direction. I fiddle with my coffee cup, turning it in circles. "Are you okay?" I ask.

Pearl nods around a bite, half smiling. It's a lame attempt to convince us.

"Tea?" Esther asks, holding up the pot, her face hopeful.

"No, thank you," Pearl says. "I'm just going to see what time Anya's starting today."

"Call her," I say, pointing to her new cell.

"I need . . . a shower." She dashes off, and I eye Beau who's watching her go.

"Excuse me," Esther says, hauling a basket of laundry off the counter. "Deliveries to make." She disappears, and the moment she has, Otto appears on the other side of the room. I frown. "You just missed her."

"Where's she gone?"

"Making deliveries," Beau singsongs, going to the fridge and collecting her green juice ingredients. I smile. She's so compliant and reasonable these days. "I want to know all the details," she says.

"About what?" Otto places his laptop on the counter.

"Stop." I lean in. "We know," I whisper.

"Of course you fucking know," he grunts.

"So why haven't you asked her yet?"

"I'm waiting for the right moment."

I put my hand on my heart. "So, what's the plan?"

"The plan?"

"How will you ask her?"

"I'll ask her."

Beau laughs and then yelps. "Shit!" She pulls her finger in protectively, her face screwing up.

"Be fucking careful." Otto takes her finger and looks, and Beau pouts. "Maybe leave the slicing and dicing to your husband," he suggests.

"Are you going to pass out?" I ask.

"No, it's nothing." She goes to the cupboard and pulls out the first aid box and a Band-Aid.

"Good." I return my attention to Otto. "The plan."

"I told you, I'll ask her."

"But *how* are you going to ask her?"

"With words, Rose. How do you think?" Poor man is completely exasperated.

And so am I. "Otto, let me help you out."

"Let her," Beau chimes in, concentrating on wrapping the end of her finger.

"You have to be romantic."

"Me?" He balks, looking down his front, to the black jeans and black T-shirt, while I take in his hairy, pierced face. "I can't be romantic."

"Yes, you can, *Boo*," Beau teases.

I titter under my breath, while Otto becomes increasingly uncomfortable. "I could help. What are you doing this afternoon?" I ask.

"Getting rid of evidence," he mutters, grabbing his laptop and leaving, obviously not interested in any proposal advice. He meets Daniel at the door, my boy all ready for school.

"Morning," Otto says as he passes, patting him on the head.

"Hey, Grandpa."

"Don't fuck with me, kid."

I laugh as Daniel smiles, and it's a sight to behold. He's happy to be going back. *I'm* happy he's going back. I'm not so sure about Principal Tucker. The poor man. *Did he have nightmares last night?* I'd say three mafia men invading his space, threatening him at gunpoint, wouldn't have been expected. And Danny's insane and irrational reaction to Lennox? What was with him? Although, I guess my reaction to his "news" in the restaurant was equally fucked up. Do we really not trust each other? "Look at you." I smile and straighten the collar of Daniel's polo T-shirt. "So handsome." He grimaces but lets me at him. "I'll take you to school."

"I don't think I'm going to school." He turns and wanders off.

"What?"

"I'm going to play tennis with Barney. He's just taking a shower."

"Barney's here?"

"Yeah, Mom, that's what I said. Barney's here."

"Barney's here?" I face Beau. "What the hell is Barney doing here, and why is my boy so cool about not going to school? What's going on?"

"They are all very good questions," Beau says, her Band-Aid-covered finger held up. "And I don't know the answer to any of them."

I get up and leave the kitchen, following my feet to the office. I barge in. Find Danny, Brad, James, and Otto.

And Lennox. His face is . . . I wince. "What the hell are you doing here?" I ask him. Of course, he doesn't answer.

"Morning, darling," Danny says, infuriatingly cool.

I give him the death stare. Please don't tell me he's threatening Daniel's best mate's father. Then I see the bag Leon brought here on the table. Open. I step forward and look inside. "What's that?" I ask, looking at James. He's silent, unwilling to answer. So I try Brad. He shakes his head. Lennox won't look at me at all.

I glare at my husband.

"That's five million dollars, baby." He smiles and comes to me, kissing my nose, like he's getting ready to pacify me. "Lennox is taking the boys to St. Lucia."

"What?"

"And you're going too. He's into redheads."

I stare at him, flummoxed. Am I hearing him right? "What?"

Danny looks at Brad, exasperated. "I think I'm going to learn Chinese."

Chapter 37

Pearl

I take the stairs up to our room, unable to be around anyone, fearful I'm a walking red flag. I had the opportunity to share. I didn't take it. I should have known Fury would tell someone about my . . . episode. Out of worry, like Brad said. And maybe a little because he's obliged to divulge everything. My confession hung on my tongue, so close to falling out of my mouth. But instead, I lied. I bottled it. And then when Brad—a merciless, cold-blooded, supposedly unattached fucking machine—comforted me, hugged me, it took strength I didn't have to resist that sense of safety. The sense of belonging. But I have to tell him. Tell him everything. I'm putting him, everyone here, in danger. I feel like I'm clinging on to hope. Praying I mean enough to Brad for him not to abandon me. Or kill me.

I walk into the room as Anya comes out of the bathroom, her hands in her hair, tying it up. She stills, taking me in. "Yes," I breathe. "Yes, I was in Brad's room."

She looks at me like she feels sorry for me. "Pearl, I am a good listener."

I know she is. Problem is, I'm not sure I want to hear what anyone has to say about my predicament. "I'm going to take a shower." I shut the door and flip it on, my mind in overdrive as I strip down. He's here in Miami. It's only a matter of time before he finds me. He's already so close. *Too* close.

But I'm safer here than out there on my own. Or . . . am I? Because my heart feels terribly at risk right now. Am I naïve to hope this could be forever? Undoubtedly. But Brad says all the right things. Treats me with tenderness but sureness. Am I in . . . "Oh my God," I breathe, frustrated with my spinning head. I step under the water and wash my hair, washing away Brad from my skin.

When I'm done and drying myself, I go to the mirror and have a mental pep talk with my reflection. *Tell him.* My heart beats faster as I secure the towel, tucking it in around my chest, and I sweep my hands through my hair, pulling it back off my face. "Tell him," I say to my reflection. I grab my mobile and open the bathroom door.

And meet a chest.

"Oh." I move back, my phone slipping out of my hand. "Fucking hell."

Brad tilts his head, his expression disapproving.

"You frightened me," I breathe as he dips and picks up my mobile.

A slow, sexy smile appears. "Oh, so you *are* afraid of me?"

He has no idea. "Where did Danny drag you to at the crack of dawn?"

"I've told you, there are things you should know, things you shouldn't."

"Right." I crane my head to look past him, pulling in my towel. "You *shouldn't* be in here."

"Who says?"

I shoot my eyes to his. "Everyone except you and me."

"But we're all that matters." He casually leans against the doorframe, spinning my mobile in his hand, one jean-clad leg crossed over the other. *Stunning man.* My wild heartbeats ease off, and I melt. When I look at him, I feel a warmth that's been absent for years. I look at him and want to be in this world so long as he's in it with me. I look at him and want to rip his clothes off.

I look at him and forget everything for a while.

Escape.

I have to believe everything can be all right.

So tell him!

My thighs quivering, I launch myself at him, kissing him manically, eating him alive, wrapping my arms around his neck and my legs around his waist. *Ravenous.*

"Whoa, easy," he says, laughing around our kiss, walking backward into the bedroom. He returns my kiss, hard and hungry, continuing to the door. He opens it, drops my mouth, and peeks out, and then throws me onto his shoulder and practically runs to his room. I'm suddenly on my back, my hands with a mind of their own, reaching for his jeans and unbuttoning the fly. I feel him, hot and ready, a long, low growl rumbling in his throat.

"Jesus Christ, I don't think I'll ever get enough of you." He pulls my towel away and removes my hand from his cock, his mouth falling to my boob, kissing around the flesh, before he sucks and bites his way toward my thighs.

The moment his tongue licks through me, my body arches, the euphoria instant. "Brad." I throw my hands up to the headboard. I can feel my climax looming already. It's too soon. "Brad, stop."

He pulls away immediately, looking up at me, his eyes drunk, his mouth wet.

"Inside." I reach down to pull him up my body. "I want you inside me," I whisper, feeling between us for his hardness, desperately wanting him to cool the burn and ease my uncertainties.

He shakes his head, pushing his lips to my neck, licking. "I don't have a condom."

"You didn't get any?"

"I've been kind of busy, gorgeous."

"Pull out."

"No."

"You did it in the shower last week."

"Do you know how hard that was?"

"Please." I squirm beneath him, feeling him pushed into my thigh.

He ignores my pleas, working his way back down my body again, and when he kisses me between my legs, tickling the end of my clit with the end of his tongue, nibbling, licking me from front to back across my opening, I nearly lose my fucking mind. "Brad!"

He moans against me, feasting on my flesh. I slam my fist into the mattress. Close my eyes. Tense beneath him.

No.

I pull away from the temptation and reach down, pulling him back up my body.

"No, Pearl," he grates.

I slide my hands onto his bare arse, pushing him down into me. "Please," I whisper, kissing the corner of his mouth. He grunts under his breath, his head hanging.

"Don't beg me. I don't ever want to hear you beg."

"Then give me what I want."

"No."

I'm so fucking confused. "Why?" I ask. I won't ask if he doesn't want me, because I can feel his want. I won't ask if he's struggling with my recent sexual status. Recent until he solved that problem for me. We've been at it all week. "Brad, I don't understand." I push into his chest, hearing him sigh. "Look at me." Lifting his heavy head, he lays his forearms on the mattress and gives me his eyes, laughing under his breath, blinking lazily, his lashes too pretty for a killer.

"I'm looking at you, Pearl," he says quietly, dropping a kiss on my lips.

"What is it? What's wrong?"

"Oh, for fuck's sake." His chest expands with his deep inhale. "I wanted to have myself checked out."

"Checked out?" I ask, my mind obviously dragging.

He peeks up at me. "I've been with a lot of women, gorgeous."

"Ohhh," I breathe, clicking.

"And you have been with no one. I didn't want to risk spoiling you."

I press my lips together, so stunned but equally happy. He cares.

"It felt so good in the shower," he whispers, scanning my face, taking a lock of my hair and twirling it. "I've never cared enough before to go down that rabbit hole."

"You care?" I whisper.

"Yeah, I care." He drops my hair and drags his finger across my bottom lip, kissing it. "I really fucking care, Pearl."

My inhale is shaky. "I really fucking care too."

He smiles, sinking his face into my neck, and I wrap every limb around him, squeezing, hoping to stick myself to him forever. Because he cares.

I've never cared enough before to go down that rabbit hole.

For someone so brusque and hurtful a few weeks ago—*a week ago*—he's thoughtful and caring now. For me. *With me.* And it makes me pause and consider what this blissful emotion that I'm feeling is.

It's more than simply fucking caring.

I've never been in love before.

But I'm sure it must feel like this.

Chapter 38

BRAD

I don't know what the fuck is going on here. But it feels good. I don't want to leave, but there's shit to deal with as soon as Danny has pacified Rose. It's a full-time job these days.

"I've got to go," I whisper into her neck, and she nods but doesn't release me. "I've got to go," I repeat softly. Another nod. "Pearl, my love, I've got to go." She squeezes harder, and I smile against her skin, sucking her flesh into my mouth, probably marking her. Don't care. I fight against her resistance to keep me close, pulling away. "What are you doing today?" I take in every detail of her face.

"I haven't thought about it," she says.

"Good. Don't."

"Why?"

"Because you're not leaving the house," I say, ripping the Band-Aid off and getting off the bed. Should I tell her she's going to St. Lucia? I fasten my jeans, pouting at her nakedness. Let's see how the land lies with Danny and Rose first. It'll be easier to tell Pearl she's going if she's going with a willing Rose. I plant my fists into mattress and lean down for a kiss.

"Why can't I leave the house?" she asks. There's no indignance, only interest.

"Because I said so."

On a sigh, she crawls up and kneels, resting her ass on her heels, taking my face in her palms and kissing me gently. "Okay."

This is good. Compliance. It's what I need right now.

"Can I use your shower?"

"You just had one."

"Want to join me?"

I scowl at her tactics and break away, leaving before I succumb to temptation, heading to Nolan's room. I knock, poking my head around the door. He's sitting up in bed and Doc's checking his leg. When he sees me, his eyes widen. He thinks I'm here to tear him a new asshole again. Doc looks back. "Morning, Brad."

"How's he doing?" I ask, wandering to the bed.

"Getting there." He pops some painkillers on the nightstand. "I don't want to see you without those crutches."

Nolan nods. Eyes on me.

"You going to the boatyard again today?" I ask.

He nods.

"I've given Ella the night off."

Wide eyes again.

"That's not a green light to overexert yourself," I add, picking up Doc's bag for him. I've seen Ella's worry. Seen Nolan's despondency. Who the fuck am I to stop two people from being together? I don't like seeing him like this, and if Ella can fix that, so be it. Because I obviously can't. "She can give you a hand at the boatyard."

Nolan's face is a picture of confusion as he nods mildly. What's with him? Did he hit his head when he was run down? I cock him a questioning look, wondering where his gratitude is, as I take Doc's shoulder and walk him out.

"I was just going to call you," he says as I close the door behind us and he takes his bag.

"I heard you've been busy," I quip, raising my brows. "Be careful, Doc, that ticker of yours isn't as strong as it once was."

"You're a terrible man, Brad Black."

I laugh to myself. "I know."

"Anyway"—he looks up and down the corridor—"the results."

I swallow, bracing myself, my stomach flipping. Fuck, am I nervous? "What about them?"

"All clear." He walks off, and I turn, following him with my eyes.

"Completely?" I ask, not daring to believe it.

"As a whistle."

I sag on the spot. Then straighten, my lips pressing together, my steps reversing back up the corridor, my dick singing its happiness. I push my way into my room and follow the sound of running water. She's under the spray.

Wet.

Naked.

My cock weeps. I pull her out of the stall and throw her over my shoulder.

"Oh my God," she gasps.

"It's about to be oh my *Brad*." I toss her on the bed and rip off my T-shirt and jeans before laying myself all over her.

She laughs. Holds my face. "Hello, again."

"Hello," I whisper. "I just saw Doc."

"Oh?" She bites at her lip. "And?"

"And . . ." I shift up her body and fall into place between her legs. "I'm all yours, my love." I push forward and sink into her slowly. And the feeling? It's inexplicable. "Fucking hell," I whisper, closing my eyes, the pleasure starting at my toes and rippling up through my body. I have to hold still. Absorb the feel of her tight muscles wrapped around me. "Good God, Pearl." I'm fucking shaking with the exertion to pull myself back from the edge, my breathing controlled, and when I release myself from my darkness, I see her more clearly than I ever have before.

Red.

Mine.

"What?" she asks quietly, her gaze unsure as she studies me. "Are you okay?"

"I don't know," I admit, lifting my upper body, needing to see all of her as I drive deep, pump slowly, grind firmly. I do know. *I do fucking know.*

Fuck.

She looks incredible, her body accepting, absorbing me.

Kiss her.

I fall to my forearms, claiming her lips, kissing her deeply, with more feeling and passion than I've ever kissed a woman.

"Brad," she murmurs.

Coming.

"I've got you," I whisper. "Always got you."

But has she got me? Because I have never been more terrified of anything in my life. She's the difference between existing and living. Loving and hating. Killing and reviving.

I stare down at her as I make love to her, watching her as she watches me, both of us studying each other so carefully. What is she thinking? "My love," I whisper, my body sinking into hers over and over, my heart kicking more with each drive. Not in exertion. No. I fucking love her, and it's truly fucking with my head.

"My love," she says quietly in answer, a silent, mutual

understanding passing between us.

The moment is intense.

So beautiful.

She whimpers, jerks, and her release triggers mine, everything I have pouring into her in long surges, my shakes now out of control.

My heart exploding.

Her mouth becomes harder on mine, our kiss deeper, while I hold myself inside her, pulsing, releasing, absorbing her quivering walls, relishing the feel of her constricting around me, milking me.

I endure the sensitivity until I have to stop moving, my cock twitching in the aftermath. "You're shaking," I say, my voice rough. She pushes her face into the crook of my neck, gasping for air, clinging on. She doesn't speak. Doesn't show herself to me.

Is she feeling what I'm feeling?

"Pearl?"

"Brad?"

"You okay?"

"I think so."

I settle on top of her, nudging her face from my neck, and she gazes up at me, her eyes on fire. She's *definitely* feeling what I'm feeling. I encase her face with my palms. "I *know* I am," I say, and she swallows, nodding her head, albeit jerkily. "I'm really okay." I blanket her and feel her arms stroking across my back, the moment calm. Quiet.

Until my cell rings. I groan, putting my forehead on hers. "I have to go."

"Don't get shot," she says quietly, giving me an extra squeeze before releasing me.

Engaging my stomach muscles, I get up, grabbing my cell out of my jeans pocket. "I'm coming," I say.

"Where the hell are you?" Danny snaps.

"I said I'm coming." I hang up and pull on my jeans.

"Can we go for dinner tonight?" she asks. "Just me and you?"

Dinner. Like a couple? "I'll do whatever you want me to do." I'd walk to the end of the earth for her, I swear, and probably step off the edge of it. "I don't know what time I'll be back."

"I can wait." She shrugs. "I know this life is unpredictable. Someone may pop up that needs killing."

I laugh lightly. "Yeah." One every fucking hour at the moment. "I'll try my best," I say. I really will, because soon she'll hopefully be on the jet to St. Lucia, and it's going to be fucking painful watching her go.

"Okay." She gets up and grimaces, looking down her body, and I see the inside of her thigh slick with my release. "I need another shower."

"Call you later." I place my palm on her nape and pull her forehead onto my lips.

Then I leave.

And it hurts. Because that was the best fucking thing I've ever experienced. The connection.

"Fucking hell." I scrub my hands down my face as I walk down to meet the men. Danny looks like he wants to punch me when I get outside.

"Anytime today," he mutters as I pass him, going to the Range Rover.

"I'm here."

"Where have you been?"

"Checking on Nolan." I look at him, irritated. "You got a problem with that?"

"None at all."

"Good, let's go sort this shit out." I get in the passenger seat next to James, and Danny gets in the back. Ringo, Otto, and Goldie are in a car behind with Lennox. "How's Rose?"

Danny huffs. "Pissy."

I smile to myself. "And she's still not going?"

"No. I'll try again when my nose can take it," he muses, feeling at the bridge. "You said anything to Beau yet?" he asks James.

"Not yet. Probably don't need to now, do I?"

Danny laughs sardonically. "Probably not."

I'm not worried about telling Pearl she's going to St. Lucia. Whenever that might be. Sooner rather than later, obviously, but . . . well, that depends on Danny's nose. My apprehension about telling everyone I have feelings for her? Yeah, not looking forward to the backlash *at all*. Or the insults that'll come at me. I know what they'll say. "How's Lennox?" I ask, pushing that dilemma back for another day.

"Shitting himself," James says.

"He made the call?"

"Not yet. Best from his house in case they spring any surprises."

"Like showing up promptly to collect?"

"Exactly."

"Stating the fucking obvious again," Danny mutters from the back. "Why the fuck isn't Higham answering my calls?"

Which reminds me . . . I turn in my seat to face him. "Who's Richard Bean?"

"I don't fucking know," Danny snaps, hitting the screen of his phone. "If he answers, I'll ask him."

Higham's phone goes to voicemail again and Danny curses, sinking back in his seat, thoughtful. James looks up at the rearview mirror as he slows to a stop outside the gates. He's thinking what I'm thinking.

The start of a fractured relationship between a criminal and a bent cop is the bent cop avoiding the criminal.

• • •

We pull onto Lennox's driveway as the garage door starts to rise. James tucks his Range Rover to the left, leaving Goldie room to park beside him. No one gets out until the doors slide back down. Then Ringo goes to the door into the house, unlocking it as he pulls his gun from the back of his pants, right as we all check ours. It's a tense few minutes until he appears at the door and signals the all clear, before he starts pulling canisters of gas out of the trunks of each car.

"Let's go," Danny says, getting out and leading. Lennox follows, not surprisingly looking apprehensive. Danny dumps the bag of money on the coffee table in the lounge and takes a picture on Lennox's phone. "Only send the picture if they ask for it," he says, handing the phone to him. He nods and sends a text, and a second later, it chimes. He looks up. "He wants proof. Send the picture?"

"Send the picture." Danny lowers to the couch, and I perch on the arm while Lennox does as he's bid. His phone chimes again. "He's sending someone to pick it up."

"There will be more than some*one*," I muse. "How long?"

"I don't know." Lennox shakes his head, lowering to a chair. "Do I invite them in?"

"No, we'll torture the fuckers on your front lawn." I stand, feeling restless. "Of course invite them in." I start to pace. *Don't get shot.* I laugh to myself. I've taken more than my fair share of bullets. "Anyone bring any vests?"

"Since when do you want a vest?" Danny asks.

"Since now."

"Here." Goldie appears, holding up a bunch of them. She hands them out, finishing with Ringo. "Don't argue with me," she says, and he doesn't, starting to strip his upper body with the rest of us.

"Got a spare one of those?" Lennox asks.

"I think it might raise suspicion if you answer the door in a vest." But the last thing any of us want is to have to go home and explain to a young lad that his only decent parent is dead. So I nod to Goldie, who throws him one. "Make sure it's covered properly," I say.

Half an hour passes.

An hour.

Two.

Everyone is restless, James is standing back from the window, checking past the blind constantly. "Game of cards?" Ringo asks. "Poker?"

I laugh under my breath, as Danny smiles to himself.

"What's so funny?" Lennox asks.

"The last time I played poker, I won my wife."

"What?" Lennox blurts. "You're serious, aren't you?"

"Deadly." Danny starts pacing.

"Come on," Ringo whines. "I'm dying of boredom here."

"I don't have any money on me," Danny muses, as everyone looks at the bag of cash.

"Here we go," James says from the window, his gun coming up. Everyone in the room stands, alert, weapons being pulled from everywhere. "Two cars."

"Two?" Lennox asks, his eyes batting between us all. "Why the fuck have they sent two cars?"

I go to him, taking his hand and putting my gun in it. "Don't hesitate," I say, pulling another from the back of my jeans. "Just make sure the bullet doesn't land in any of us." I go to James and Danny by the window.

"There're two in each car," James says. "The two men from the first car will come in. The other two will stay outside." The first car slows to a stop just past the driveway, the second stopping directly across it. "Lennox will answer the door. I'll be behind it, so you all wait in here."

I nod, Danny takes a casual seat on the couch, looking comfortable as James faces Lennox. "Where's the gun?" he asks. Lennox taps the back of his pants. "You open the door onto me, stand back, not letting go of the door, and let them in. Close the door and draw at the same time." James wanders out to the front door, leaving Lennox looking bewildered. "And don't drag this out," he calls back. I think he's talking to me and Danny. "It's a nice neighborhood. It's only a matter of time before someone notices the two X5s on the street."

"Yes, sir," Danny says, stoic, his gun resting on the arm in his loose grip. He looks at me. "Don't drag it out," he says, passing the baton. Happy days.

"You're not in the mood for bloodshed?"

"My wife's provided enough bloodshed recently." He turns a cold stare onto Lennox.

"Like I said," Lennox murmurs, looking toward where James just disappeared. "I prefer redheads."

I feel Danny's eyes on me, but I don't entertain him.

"Ready," Goldie says from the window.

"Armed?" I ask.

"Yep." Of course they are. And extra vigilant, I expect, after Lennox pulled a James and went all Rambo on Sandy's messengers. Goldie holds up three fingers. Then two. Then one. Everyone falls silent, and the doorbell chimes.

"Jesus," Lennox murmurs, leaving the room.

"Be cool," I order as he goes, listening, hearing the door open. No talking. The sound of boots on the wooden floor. Then the door closes and a flurry of rushed foreign words are spat. Russian curses. We all watch the entrance of the lounge until two wide black-covered backs appear, hands up. "You stupid man," one drawls. "You'll be dead within twelve hours."

"Welcome," I sing, and they spin around. Their faces when they realize how outnumbered they are is quite amusing. Ringo moves in and pats them down, pulling backup guns from their pants. "Take a seat." I point my gun to the couch opposite. "Enjoy our hospitality."

James appears behind them, Lennox beside him, looking surprisingly comfortable, as both the Russians shuffle across the room and tentatively lower to the couch, like they're worried it could explode the second their asses meet the soft, luxury fabric.

I put myself on the coffee table before them, forearms resting on my knees, casual, and light up. Some cigarettes you enjoy more than most. Like the one you have with your first Scotch of the day. Or the one right after your dinner. I'm going to enjoy this smoke.

One of the Russians looks at Lennox, his lip curling. "How do you know these men?"

"Oh, my apologies, how rude of me." I look back at Danny, laughing, and he smiles darkly. "That there is The Brit." I'm wasting valuable time, I know that. And when I look at James, he gives me tired eyes, expressing his impatience. But this is what we do. We perform. "Over there is The Enigma." I point my gun at the window. "That's Ringo."

The big, ugly fucker grins. "Pleased to meet you."

"That beauty is Goldie."

"Pleasure." She nods.

"And that's Otto." Otto doesn't greet them. "I believe you know Lennox." I pull on my Marlboro and rise to my feet, ensuring I have the best range, as I screw the silencer onto the head of my gun. "And I believe I'm affectionately known as The American these days." I aim. "And you are?"

They stare at my extended arm. "You will kill us whether we talk or not."

"True. But only you can decide how painful it is."

"Fuck you."

I smile. "Speaking of pain, do you know where the most painful place on the body is to be shot?" They stare up at me, their chests beginning to pump faster. "Pass?" I look around the room. "Any offers?" Everyone remains silent. I know James will have the answer to this. He won't spoil my fun, though. "It's the pelvis," I say, tapping my hip with my gun. "Right about here." I bend and get up in his face. "Now, you both have a bit more meat on your bones than I do, so it could be hit or miss." I push the gun into the biggest of the two fuckers' waist area, and he pushes himself back into the couch. "Fancy talking?" I put more weight behind me. "No?" I pout. "Okay." And pull the trigger.

His eyes bulge so much, I'm certain for a moment they're going to pop out of his head.

"Ouch," Danny says behind me.

Right before the pain kicks in and Ringo gets a pillow over my victim's face to stifle his scream.

I turn to his mate, who's looking on in horror. "Do *you* fancy talking?" I ask as muffled cries of pain fill the room. I push the gun to his hip. "Where the fuck is Sandy?"

"I don't know."

James, his patience non-existent, moves in and clouts him over the head with his gun. "Fucking talk."

"I don't know!"

"So where were you taking the money?" I ask. "Because it feels pretty fucking pointless having two fat cunts like you two collecting cash for him if you're not gonna drop it off." So he's fucking lying. We're getting nothing out of them. That much is obvious. I aim at his forehead. "It was nice knowing you." I sink a bullet in his skull as Ringo lifts the pillow on the other guy, giving me access to his head too. I pull the trigger and sigh. "Waste of fucking time that was." I point to the window. "What's going on out there?"

"I think they're getting impatient," Goldie says from the window. "One's gotten out."

"So we have one more stab at this," Danny says, smiling as he pulls a hunting knife from his jeans.

"Where the fuck did you get that?"

"A friend."

"Chaka," I say, rolling my eyes. "You moving to the jungle to wrestle snakes and tigers?"

He bashes his fists on his chest. "Me Tarzan. You—"

"Fucking cunt," James mutters, going to the window as Ringo chuckles. "The other's out."

"Good." Danny checks out the window too. "It's my turn." He faces the room, wandering back to his seat.

And catches his foot on the leg of the coffee table. "Fuck!" He hits the carpet with a thud and in the process manages to fire his gun. "Oops."

"For fuck's sake," James snaps, immediately pulling back his elbow and sending it sailing into the window, smashing it. He aims and fires, and the two guys coming toward the house are soon running away from it. I run to the dead guys and feel through their pockets, pulling out the keys for the X5 that's blocking the driveway, therefore blocking our cars.

"Good plan," Danny says, jumping to his feet as James jumps out the window. Danny watches him disappear. "Fuck that." And runs to the door, yanking it open.

I opt for the conventional exit too, following him out.

And here we go.

Don't get shot.

Chapter 39

DANNY

James is on the lawn, motionless, aiming at the first X5 as it screeches off. "Fuck." He lowers his gun and paces toward the other.

"Who's driving?" Brad asks.

"Me." James gets in the driver's side. "I'm not trusting that clumsy fuck behind the wheel today, and you're a better shot."

"Me?" I blurt, outraged. "Clumsy? I didn't see the fucking table." I climb in the back, and Brad gets in the other side, laughing. "Fuck off." I hit the button to get the back window down as James pulls off, throwing us both back in the seat.

"The good news is I can see them up ahead," James says.

"The bad news is, I only have three bullets," Brad adds.

"Five," I mutter. "Would have been six but a coffee table fucked me over."

James throws something over his shoulder. Two magazines. "See what you can do with nine and eleven."

"You've got to get in front of them." Brad switches his half-empty magazine for the full one. I'll stick with five for now.

"Is there a jet pack on this vehicle that I didn't know about?" James asks.

"Don't be sarcastic," I muse. "It's beneath you." James looks at me in the rearview mirror, and I give him a dashing smile. "We'll try to shoot the back tires out."

"Please do." He takes a hard left, and I fly into the door, smacking my head on the frame, as Brad flies into me.

"For fuck's sake, James," I yell, rubbing at my head. "My face is fucked up enough."

"Sorry."

"Perhaps tell us when you're on a straight."

"Okay." A hard right, and we're flying across the car again. Brad grunts on impact, and again when I land in his lap.

I shuffle up and get back on my side of the car, reaching for the handle above the door. "I don't think I've ever been in a car chase before. You?"

"Yes," James grunts. The sound of screeching tires rings, and the smell of rubber burning invades my nose.

"Of course you have." I tighten my grip of the handle and tense my muscles, keeping myself on the right side of the car.

"Straight."

"Great." Brad sticks his head out of the window.

"But watch the bus."

"Fuck!" He dips back inside, his hair wafting as the bus passes. The poor fuck looks like he's been stunned, his wide eyes staring forward, and I howl with unstoppable laughter. "Any fucking buses?" he grates.

"You're good."

He double-checks, poking his head out tentatively, before hauling his body up, getting the whole of his torso out of the window. "You're more flexible than I thought," I yell, mirroring him on the other side. "Jesus Christ," I breathe, struggling to catch my breath in the high-speed wind blowing in my face.

"You first," I yell across the car to him as he aims, his jaw tight, his straight arm jerking too much to get a good shot.

"Fuck," he hisses.

I hit the roof of the car with the handle of my gun. "Slow down," I yell.

"What?"

"Slow the fuck down!" Stability wins over distance. Always. And Brad is a fucking master shot. A few more meters won't faze him.

James takes his foot off the gas, and Brad's wobbling arm settles just enough for him to get the shot. He squeezes the trigger, jerking when he fires, and the X5 swerves.

"Bullseye," I whisper, watching as the vehicle hits a curb and flips, spinning in the air countless times, the wheels flying off, the screen shattering, before it lands on its roof. James hits the brakes, forcing Brad and me to cling on for dear life. We come to a stop, but the X5 continues gliding down the road on its roof, sparks flying everywhere.

I look at Brad across the car.

"That wasn't supposed to happen," he admits. "Fuck."

There will be no torturing for information now. I get back into the car, meeting Brad on the back seat, and watch as the X5 comes to a slow, creaking stop. "They've gotta be dead, right?" I take in the mangled car.

Just as it explodes.

Fuck! We all bring our arms over our head protectively, being blinded by the blaze roaring in the middle of the road, smoke billowing up into the air, pieces of metal flying far and wide. "I'd say so," Brad says quietly.

"Shit," I breathe.

"We've got company." James says, and we look out the rear window seeing blue lights heading this way. "Put your belts on."

I comply, naturally, as James screeches off.

"The good news is, we're not in a car registered to us," he says over his shoulder, yanking the steering wheel to the right, sending the car skidding up the road before he speeds off down a side street.

"What's the bad news?" I ask.

"There is no bad news."

"There's always bad news when someone says the *good news is—*"

"Anyone would think you want some bad news." Brad chuckles, doing the window up.

"Call Otto," James orders. "Tell him to meet us at the place Beau drove Nathan Butler's car to when the cops were pursuing her."

Brad's the first with his mobile out, and he quickly relays James's instructions.

"Tell him to bring the two dead Russians."

"What?" Brad asks, his phone limp at his ear.

"And a tracker."

"Did you get that?" Brad says to Otto, grabbing the headrest in front when James swerves. He hangs up and holds the headrest with both hands, looking back. "Two more."

I laugh under my breath, very fucking close to breaking out in a nervous sweat. "Fuck, the sirens are making my head ring." I dive forward and turn the stereo on. Then drop back. Listen. Smile. "Perfect."

Bloc Party *Flux* starts blaring from the speakers, and I laugh as the car constantly flies from one side of the road to the other, the stench of burning rubber starting to irritate my nose. A cop car skids out of a side street and joins the convoy, and I shoot back in my seat, out of sight. "Company on the left," I yell over the music, prompting James to very quickly and very efficiently swerve and smash into them, sending them up the curb into a streetlight.

"Good move."

"Right," Brad shouts, sending James across the lane. The car jars, and James fights with the steering wheel to get us back under control. I look back to see the police car slow, smoke coming up from beneath the hood.

Fuck. We have five of the fuckers chasing us. I crane my neck to look up to the sky out of the sunroof, highly expecting to see the choppers out in force. It won't be long. "You need to lose them, James," I shout over the music, reaching forward and slapping his shoulder but flying back when he hits the gas. "Looks like we have a jet pack after all."

Brad cheeks blow out, like, fuck, this is close. I couldn't agree more.

A sharp left.

We lose one.

A right.

One more down.

Three remain, keeping up.

"Fuck it." I undo my belt and hit the button to let the window down, turning around so my back is against the front seat.

"Don't let them see your face, Danny," Brad yells.

"No, just the end of my fucking gun." I put my arm out of the window and fire randomly.

"One more down," Brad says, joining me, both of us firing with little to no aiming out of the window.

"I'm turning," James warns, and we both wedge our hands into the seats as he slams on the brakes and sends the car into a side glide, which would be the equivalent to a good old-fashioned handbrake turn if cars still had good old-fashioned handbrakes. "Done."

I put my arm back out and look out the rear window, firing just as the cop car skids into the street. It crashes into a trash can, the hood flipping up. "Boom," I whisper, waiting for the next car. We make it to the end of the street. No cop cars appear. We lost them?

James turns off the music, and we all listen. No sirens.

"Fucking hell." Brad turns and slumps back down into his seat, head dropped back.

James doesn't slow down.

Not until we make it onto a deserted track past the marina.

He pulls in past some overgrowth and turns off the engine, bracing his arms against the wheel.

"Good driving, bud," I breathe, looking over my shoulder when I hear tires across stones, seeing Otto pulling up in James's Range Rover. "Oh look, here's Otto with two dead Russians." He gets out and rounds the front of the car, reaching under the offside wheel arch on the X5 and nodding. A tracker.

I slip out the back, stretching my muscles, and rub at my head. It's beginning to pound. "And now for a workout after the shoot-out," I muse, opening the trunk of James's car and sighing at the sight of the two massive Russians. We all drag the bodies to the X5, putting one behind the wheel and one in the passenger seat. "What if the police find them before Sandy?"

"Then the police find them first," James says.

My phone rings, and I look at the screen, laughing loudly. "Higham, your timing is impeccable."

"Why? What's happened?"

"Don't ask." I sigh, walking away from the others. Just another mess for him to pretend he doesn't know we caused. "Where the hell have you been?"

"Don't ask."

"What's the situation with the body?"

"Still not officially identified."

I grit my teeth. "And the unofficially unidentified body's cause of death?"

"Gunshot. As soon as they identify her, we'll launch a murder investigation."

"Fuck."

"What's going on, Danny?"

"Too much to explain, especially over the phone. When can I see you?"

"Ah, well . . ."

"What, Higham?"

"My wife surprised me with a post-vacation vacation. I'm at MIA."

"Then get the fuck out of MIA."

"Give me a break, Danny. I'm trying to fix my marriage."

"Aren't we all." I grimace as I rub at my sore lip, wandering back over to the others, getting questioning looks. I wave a hand at them dismissively.

"What do you know about Officer Richard Bean?" Higham asks.

"What do *you* know about Officer Richard Bean?"

"I know his wife reported a break in."

"I didn't break in. The doors were wide open."

"What the hell, Danny?"

"Why would you think I've got anything to do with this?"

"Because I took some time over a Scotch while my wife was in bed and did a little digging, and do you know what I found?"

"What did you find?"

"I found out his son goes to the same school as your son."

"What a coincidence."

"And footage from a Ring doorbell sent in by a resident shows you and James approaching the house."

"Footage? You sure?"

He sighs. "Jesus, Danny."

"Oh shut up, Higham. I don't need your bitching in my ear. When are you back? I need to talk to you about the unidentified body."

"Listen, these things take time, so I have time for a few extra days' vacation, and you have time to think about if you'd like to tell me what happened to Officer Richard Bean."

"I don't need time for that. I didn't stab him and James didn't knock him out with a table lamp."

"For fuck's sake."

"I did you a favor. Richard Bean is an immoral fuckhead." I still in my seat when I realize what I've done, and James's eyes confirm that I am, indeed, a clumsy cunt today. I can feel Brad's eyes on me. "Call me when you're back." I hang up and every part of me tenses, waiting.

"Bean," Brad says, looking between us. "Who the fuck is this Bean guy?"

Shit. "It's nothing." I wave a hand flippantly.

"Danny, who the fuck is Bean and why the fuck are you stabbing him and James knocking him out with a table lamp?"

"He's the dad of the little shite that had Daniel kicked out of school."

"And why didn't I know you went to have a friendly chat with him?"

"Because you've been a miserable fucker recently, and I didn't want to burden you with my family politics."

"I *am* part of your family."

I pout. "Fancy a beer?"

"Yeah." He scowls. "Seems like we've both got shit we want to share."

"We have?"

"Yeah." Brad gets in the Range Rover and rests back in his seat. "But I need a drink first."

Sorry, cousin. You'll be needing more than just a drink with the bomb I'm about to drop on you.

Chapter 40

BRAD

The ride to the boatyard is painfully quiet. Danny thinks I'm pissed off with him. I would be if my mind wasn't pre-occupied with how the fuck I tell them about Pearl. I'm taking her out tonight. Not sneaking her out. *Taking* her out. And everyone will watch me. Accept it. And when we get home, she'll be coming to *my* room and getting in *my* bed.

I get out and immediately light up, my eyes following two jet skis across the water. "Beer?" Danny asks.

"Yeah."

He and James stride off together side by side, talking quietly, and I'm about to go after them and find out what the hushed whispers are all about, but stall when my cell rings. I answer to the contractor who's working on my apartment. "Brad," he says, his Texan accent thick. "Quick update for you. We should have everything done and be out of your hair in a few weeks."

"Thanks, Barry." I hang up as Tank pulls up, and the flash of red in the passenger seat flips my stomach. I told her *not* to leave the fucking house.

Pearl gets out and glances over at me briefly, and maybe a bit cautiously. I give her an expectant look. She shrugs. Rose gets out the back, and Tank helps her get the stroller from the trunk as Pearl lifts Maggie out of her infant car seat. I frown when Fury pulls up too, Beau and Esther getting out. And Anya. And Zinnea. What is this, a family reunion?

What the fuck's going on?

Beau looks me up and down as she comes to me. Checking for blood. "How did it go?"

"How did what go?"

She looks at me tiredly. "Come on, Brad."

She's a gem. "Beau, babe, how long have we known each other?" I drop my cigarette on the ground and try to waft the smoke away as she gets closer.

"Not that long, actually."

"Feels like centuries," I mutter, chuckling when she whacks my arm.

"Oh my God," she gasps. "It laughed."

"If you weren't pregnant—"

"Don't let that stop you." She moves in, getting her face up in mine.

I snarl, then scrunch my nose and kiss her cheek. "What are you all doing here, anyway?"

She links arms with me and starts leading me toward the cabin. "Just hanging out."

I look down at her, suspicious, as she peeks up at me. "Just hanging out?"

"I wanted to feel the sun on my face." She directs it up to the sky, closing her eyes.

Tank passes, carrying Maggie's stroller, Rose following with the others. "If I'd known today was a family trip to the beach, I would have bought a bucket and spade, maybe some games."

"Oh my God," Beau blurts. "We should absolutely get some games. Volleyball, beach bowls." A gasp. "Water polo!"

I stare at her, bemused. Yeah, that sounds like a perfect wind down after a torturing session and a car chase. "Where's Daniel?"

"He's at home with Barney on the Xbox. Lennox had some work to do."

"Beau, what's going on?"

"Nothing." She beams at me—totally fake—and hurries up the steps to the cabin. I trudge after her, scanning the café when I enter. Rose and Danny are by the beer fridge, whispering angrily at each other. "What the hell are you doing here?" he growls at Rose, swigging a beer.

"Moral support."

I reach between them and they both quit their fight briefly, giving me enough time to get my beer. "Don't let me interrupt," I muse, seeing Nolan out on the decking, his bad leg up on a chair, his good leg supporting the ass of Ella. I grab another two beers and wander out, and the moment he sees me he tries to move her. "Leave her," I say, lowering to a chair, placing the beers down and unscrewing the caps. I pass one to Nolan. One to Ella. He looks shocked. I expect Ella is too behind her shades. I hit my bottle with theirs and rest back. "Have you called things off with your boyfriend?" I ask Ella.

She swallows, nodding, tentatively taking a sip of her beer.

"Yes, she told him." Nolan reaches for her shades and tries to pull them off her face, but she fights him.

"Nolan, please."

Nolan wins their little wrestle, and I recoil when he reveals a shiner of a black eye. Ella immediately covers it with her palm.

"He did that?" I ask.

"It's nothing."

I look at Nolan. I see the anger he's struggling to hide. I can feel it myself. He gives Ella her glasses and she quickly slips them back on. How many times has she told people it's nothing? "She's got nowhere to stay," Nolan says, awkward. I laugh, but it dries up when I see Pearl go through the shop area toward the ladies' changing rooms and restrooms.

"You better speak to Danny," I tell him, eyes on Pearl's back as she disappears through the door. "I've got to go check . . . something." I stand, leaving my bottle on the table, and Nolan looks back into the café.

"Why's everyone here?" he asks.

"Family fun day at the beach," I murmur, leaving the lovebirds to nurse each other, looking around before passing through the shop. I text Pearl.

Where are you?

Peeing

I hover outside the ladies' making sure the coast is clear, trying not to look like a sicko loiterer, before I back my way in, wandering down the line of stalls. I knock the only closed door.

"I'll be just a minute," she calls.

"Okay," I reply.

"Brad?"

She flushes and opens the door, flinching when she sees me on the other side. "What are you doing?"

I push her back into the stall and slam the door behind me, picking her up and crushing her to my front. "I told you not to leave the house."

"And Rose told me we were coming to the boatyard. Did you want me to tell her I couldn't because Brad specifically told me not to leave the house when we were in bed this morning?"

I roll my eyes. "I've missed you."

She breathes in, pressing her lips together, hiding her smile. "That's sweet."

I scowl playfully, gently kissing the corner of her mouth, breathing her goodness into me. "I don't want to keep you a secret anymore."

"Okay," she mumbles, pushing her tongue into my mouth, swirling.

"Okay." I feel down to her ass and squeeze. "I'm doing it now."

She withdraws, stunned. "Now?"

"Yes, now."

"In front of everyone?"

"Yes." I laugh. One stone, a dozen birds. There will be no grand, romantic announcement. I'll sit Danny and James down, tell them how it is, and leave them to process the news. I take a lock of her hair and twirl it. "Then I'll take you for your first lesson."

"Lesson in what?"

I hold her nape, loving her cheeky half-smile. "Oh, gorgeous, the things you will learn from me."

"Can't wait."

"Me—"

The door to the ladies swings open, and Pearl sucks back air. I quickly cover her mouth with my palm, a finger to my lips. "Pearl?" Beau calls.

My face bunches. *Fuck.* I release Pearl's mouth and nod for her to talk. "Yeah?" she calls out.

"Oh, you're in here." Beau's voice gets closer, and I look down to see her shadow on the floor. "Have you seen Brad?"

Pearl's green eyes are like saucers. "No, why?"

"James is looking for him."

"Oh." Pearl pouts, mischief invading her green eyes. "He's probably bitching to someone about something somewhere."

I raise my brows. Pearl raises hers.

Beau chuckles. "I thought he seemed perkier the past week."

"I wouldn't know. I avoid that miserable bastard at all costs."

Is she for real? Slighted, I flick her nipple, giving her a warning glare.

"Check the workshop!" she practically yelps, rubbing her boob and scowling at me. "I thought I saw him heading that way."

"Okay." The restroom door opens and closes, and I take Pearl's cheeks in my hands, squeezing.

"You got something to say?" I ask.

"Kiss me."

That'll do. I slam my mouth on hers and kiss her hard, and she's all in, crawling up my body, clinging on, giving me all the sounds. I give her just enough to keep us going for a little while longer. Until I don't have to hide this . . .

What is this?

Pulling away, I put my face in her neck and soak up the glorious smell of her. "Go get your wetsuit on," I order, releasing her from the side of the stall. "The right way this time."

She laughs lightly. "Okay."

I pull the door open.

Freeze.

"Hi," Beau says, arms crossed over her chest.

"Oh fuck." I take one step to the left, like I can hide who's behind me. "Don't look at me like that," I warn.

Beau's brows lift.

"Or like that."

Her head tilts.

"Beau, stop it."

"I knew it!" she hisses.

I feel Pearl's hands rest on my hips from behind, guiding me out of the stall, and I reluctantly let her. She steps out from behind me. Smiles awkwardly. This is exactly what I didn't want. I'm a grown fucking man sneaking around, and now I'm a grown fucking man standing here like a naughty schoolboy waiting for a lecture.

No.

Beau looks at Pearl, all pouty. "I can't believe you've kept this from me."

"I . . . it was a mistake."

I cough over my disbelief, and Pearl looks at me in apology.

"I said, *was*," she points out.

"And it's not now?" Beau asks, her disbelief rampant.

"Well . . . I don't . . ." I listen to Pearl trip up all over her words, trying to explain herself.

Absolutely not. I get myself behind her and cover her mouth with my hand. This is not going down like this. Beau looks up at me in question. I can see it in her eyes. The accusations. The assumptions. I lean into Pearl's ear. "Go get your wetsuit on," I order gently, releasing her mouth and taking her shoulders, leading her to the door. I'm not having her standing here under the spotlight like she's committed an outrageous crime. "Go." I open the door and she turns to me, looking worried and guilty. "Go," I reiterate softly, and she relents, turning and walking away quietly. I close the door and face Beau.

She looks pissy. Here it comes. "She's quite obedient, isn't she?" she snaps.

But of course she'd go straight there. "You've got it all wrong."

"So you're not fucking her?" she asks, her expression angry. "Brad!"

"I do not have to explain myself to you." I brush past her, incensed by her extremely low opinion of me. Even if it's fair. I pull the door open, Beau chasing my heels.

"You do have to explain yourself, Brad. You really do."

"I really don't, Beau."

"She's young."

"I know how old she is."

"What can you offer her?"

"Who are you, her mother?"

"I'm the closest she fucking has." She reaches for my shoulder and yanks me to a stop, and because it's Beau, and only because it's Beau, I let her. Taking some calming breaths, I face her. She looks annoyed, disgusted, and worried. "You're old enough to be—"

"Do not fucking say that," I warn. "Because I'm not old enough to be her father, for fuck's sake."

She slams her mouth shut and backs up. "She's young and naïve, Brad."

"You need to give her more credit." I led this. I pushed for it. Or the stupidly crazy chemistry did. Pearl is arguably more mature than I am, and I don't mind admitting it.

"So she knows you're just fucking her, does she?" she asks. "You've made that clear?"

It takes everything in me not to explode. "Yeah, she knows I'm only capable of fucking, Beau," I hiss. "I'm going to talk to James and Danny." To tell them. There will be no more lectures. No warnings. "I would appreciate it if you keep your thoughts to yourself around me." I storm off, furious, and find Danny and James on the decking with Nolan.

No Ella.

Nolan's trying to get up. Danny gently pushes him back into the chair. And there's another something I need to tell them.

"A word," I say when I get to the table. "Alone." Nolan looks fucking terrified. It only pisses me off more.

Danny and James both regard me, nodding, before Danny returns his attention to Nolan. "Stay put." Then he points to a table on the corner of the veranda. I make my way over and the moment we're all in our chairs, I start getting shit off my chest. "I've dealt with Nolan." They both look at each other. "If he wants to see Ella, that's his call. They're both adults." Neither protest nor point out that the dancers have always been off limits.

"Okay," Danny says, waving for some beers. They land on the table before he's found his Marlboros in his pocket. He holds the packet across the table, and I take one, leaning in when he ignites his lighter. James passes.

Right. Now I'm armed with a beer and a smoke, let's get this shit on the table. "I—"

"There's something I've not told you," Danny says, taking on an edge of discomfort, shifting in his chair, fiddling with his bottle. It's not a look I've often seen on The Brit. If ever. I cast my eyes to James. He looks serious. A very familiar look.

"What's going on?" I ask, reading the signs and concluding quite quickly that I don't like them.

"The cop Higham mentioned on the phone. Bean."

"What about him?"

"He's been"—he clears his throat, shifting again—"talking to someone. Trying to get information on us. Someone we know."

I feel my hackles rise. "Who?"

"Blackmailing them."

"Who?" I grate, my hand tightening around my bottle.

"I've dealt with it."

"Who?" I demand, getting more and more worked up. James takes on an unfamiliar shade of really fucking awkward, sending my patience down the fucking drain. I rise from my chair, my breathing out of control. "Will you fucking tell me who?"

"Nolan."

My mouth goes lax, words escaping me. Nolan? I look across the terrace toward him. Still shitting himself. *The fucker.* No wonder he's been so quiet lately. After everything I've fucking done for that kid? I drop my beer and my smoke, and take one step, enraged, my fists flexing.

"Wait." James dives up, grabbing my arm.

"Get the fuck off me." I shake him off and quickly have both of them on me, forcing me back down to the chair.

"Why the fuck haven't you dealt with him?" I laugh, looking between them. "What? You think I'll have something to say about it?" I slam my fist on the table. Yes, I've always looked out for the kid, always shielded him from Danny and James's wrath when he's fucked up, but all his fuck-ups have been learning curves. This? This is different. This is outright betrayal.

"There's more," James says, hands up, a silent indication to keep calm.

More? Jesus, I already want to kill him. Don't make me want to do it slowly. "What?" I grab Danny's smokes and light up again, puffing through it urgently, needing calm. And it occurs to me. "What were they using to blackmail him?"

Silence.

I look between them. Serious. So fucking serious. My blood chills, every one of my senses telling me I am not going to like what I hear next. "What?" I ask quietly.

"There were using information they have on Nolan against him," Danny breathes, rubbing at his forehead.

He exhales as I slowly lift my smoke back to my lips, drawing hard on it, every muscle I possess tensing. "Spit it out, Danny."

"He didn't share anything about us." Danny looks me square in the eye. "And there's a reason why he wouldn't."

I stare at my best friend. My cousin. "Why?"

"Because he's your son, Brad."

I cough, letting out a disbelieving laugh. "What?"

"Nolan's your son."

"That was a rhetorical question."

"I'm not fucking with you."

I laugh, taking my beer and swigging. "Shut the fuck up." Nolan's looking this way. Expressionless. And my laughter dries up. "He's not my son." The cool of my blood disappears. It begins to heat. He's fucking twenty-one. He *cannot* be my fucking son. "Is that what he's told you?" I return my eyes to James and Danny. "You stupid fucks." I stand abruptly, my chair flying back, and I'm reminded as I look around the terrace that everyone is here. "What the fuck is this?" I ask, giving every single one of them a moment of my eyes. "Did you all know about this pack of lies?" I laugh, and it's fucking demented. "You all believe this bullshit? Are you fucking stupid? He's been found out and spewed some shit he thinks will get him off the hook, and you dumb fucks all believe him?" Wait. I breathe in, something coming to me. "How long have you kept this from me?"

"We found out last week." Danny fidgets in his chair, uncomfortable.

"A week?" I bellow. "A fucking *week*?" I lose it, throwing down my bottle and smoke, stalking over to Nolan and grabbing his T-shirt, hauling him up out of his chair. I can feel him shaking in my hold. Good. He fucking should be. "You lying piece of shit," I snarl in his face, feeling like my head could pop.

"I'm not lying, Brad."

"Fuck you." I shove him back down and face everyone. "Fuck you all." I kick a chair across the room, all eyes on me, watching me lose my shit. I can't stand the judgment. The pity. No. I stalk out, raking a hand through my hair, my vision blurry from my rage, and as soon as I'm out of sight, I roar, slamming a fist into the wall. "Fuck!"

The door to the ladies' changing rooms opens. Pearl appears, her hand over her back pulling up the zip of her wet suit.

Smiling.

It falls when she registers the state of me.

Twenty-fucking-one.

I clench my teeth and back up, ripping my eyes away from her and turning.

Leaving.

I make a call as I go.

Chapter 41

Pearl

I silently watch him walk away, wondering what the hell has happened between the ladies' bathroom and now. I don't know, but his expression, his persona, the way he looked at me like he hates me, tells me it's over. I know it didn't really start, it's only been days, but . . .

My love.

My heart sinks. My hope sinks. What did Beau say?

I pick up my feet, determined to find out, but the moment I walk out on the veranda, I sense the unease, and when I scan the faces of everyone here, I note a solemnity I don't like.

"I told you," Nolan yells, his voice shaky as he tries to stand. Ella backs off, wary, withdrawing her helping hands. But Nolan's not shouting at her. He's shouting at Danny and James. "I fucking told you not to tell him." He wobbles, grabbing the table for support, reaching for his crutch that's leaning on the side of it. I watch, astounded, as no one moves in to help him. They just look on, silent. Sad.

I hurry over and help him. "I'm fine," he snaps, startling me, abandoning his crutch and limping away, cursing constantly.

Ella puts her hand on my arm, winning my attention. She takes her glasses off and wipes the tears from her eyes. "What the hell happened to your eye?" I ask, and she shakes her head.

I look around at all the men. "What's happened?"

They all disperse, and I stand like a clueless idiot on the veranda in my wetsuit. Beau collects me and leads me to a table, sitting me down. "There's something you should know."

"What?" I ask, my attention split between her and everyone else, searching their faces, my uneasiness doubling. "What is it?"

"It's Brad."

My eyes shoot to hers, my worry very real, and there is nothing I can do to hold it back. "What about him?"

I hate the breath of bravery she takes. The swallow of dread.

"It's Nolan. He's Brad's son."

"What?" I look toward the doors where Brad just escaped. "He never said. He never—" Oh God. *He never knew.* "Oh my God," I whisper. "He didn't know?" She shakes her head, her eyes sad. "He just found out?" A nod. A swallow. "And everyone knew?" I ask, casting my eyes around the terrace. Everyone, it seems, apart from me and Brad. "How long? How long have you all known?"

"A week. The guys didn't know when best to tell him." I can see she's torn. She wants to go to Brad, but she won't. She'll give him the time he needs to process this. And he will. He has no choice.

"Nolan's twenty-one, Pearl." She looks at me, as if willing me to connect dots that don't seem connectable. But if Brad is thirty-five . . . *oh.* "Nolan's the same age as I am," I whisper, my heart breaking. That probably explains the look of disdain just thrown at me. I'm the same age as his son. Beau just nods, because what else can she say? And that look of distain? It wasn't for me. It was for himself. I just hope he didn't think I, along with everyone else, knew who Nolan was. "His son?" I whisper. *His twenty-one-year-old son.*

And that has compounded Brad's problem.

And ended the only good thing that's happened in my life. I breathe in the strength I need and face Beau. "Have you told anyone?" I ask. She shakes her head. Good. "Brad's got enough on his plate right now. He doesn't need a headache from you or the others about"—I swallow, beg the pain to fuck off—"about . . . me."

She smiles, nodding, and I hate that she can see the hurt and disappointment I'm trying so hard to hide. I hate that she's silently concluding that she was right. That I would be an idiot to expect more from the emotionally detached, fuck machine Brad Black. Because I'm young and naïve and stupid. I won't correct her. I didn't expect a thing from Brad. Not at first. I was simply answering to the chemistry that caught me off guard. He was the one who came back. He was the one who told me no other man would ever touch me again. He was the one who claimed me as his. And I was so fine with that.

My love.

So I *am* an idiot.

Because the bastard made me fall in love with the forbidden, dangerous, cold but passionate beast. He made me see past the shallow, cool-hearted arsehole who used women to scratch his itches. And I can't even be mad with him for making me feel wanted.

Because I wanted him to want me. I wanted him to want me so much, he would think twice about casting me aside—or worse—when he finds out who I really am.

"I'm sure he'll come round," I say, putting on a brave face and standing. Because, truly, I have faced worse than this temporary heartache. "He probably just needs some space to get his head around it."

"I hope so."

"He'll be fine," I assure her. I know they're close. I know Beau worries about him. "I should get back. I want to wrap up on the—" What the hell do I need to do? "The architect wants some final details for the drawings on Winstable."

"Sounds like things are moving in the right direction."

"Yeah, and then we have to go through the permit application, and all that, so . . ." I blow out my cheeks. "Busy, busy, busy." I turn before my face betrays me or my voice becomes wobbly. "See you at home."

Home.

That's what I'll be leaving. The home I found here with people fucked up yet beautiful. Wrong yet right.

Where Brad was mine. Momentarily.

My legs take me to the changing rooms to get dressed, and then I manage to use words to ask to be taken back to the mansion. All the while, I beg my tears to stay back. For my heart to hold it together, just for a little longer. Because the moment I don't have an audience, everything will fall.

My face.

My tears.

My heart.

Chapter 42

BRAD

I slap a wedge of cash in Jeeves's hand as I pass him, and in return he slips me a keycard. "The suite is suitably stocked, Mr. Black."

"Good man," I grunt, hitting the elevator call button aggressively. I pull out my cell and check to see if tonight's lay has arrived. Some nameless, faceless someone who is going to help me escape. One ordered every day for the next three days.

I step into the elevator when the doors open and hit the button for the twenty-ninth floor, nodding to Jeeves as he discreetly slips the handful of bills into his top pocket. As soon as the doors meet in the middle, I drop my head.

And breathe.

I'm hot. Suffocating. I start to pace up and down in the small box, watching the dial count up the floors.

So fucking slowly.

My heartrate increases.

I close my eyes, leaning back against the back wall. I see Uncle Carlo dragging me out of a hotel room. I see him putting a gun to my head. I see the girl I was fucking running scared. I was twenty-one.

So young.

So fucking clueless.

Women cloud your judgment.

Uncle Carlo only ever had my best interests at heart. He loved my mother. Thought he was saving her. He couldn't save her. But he saved me. I've always hung on every word he said. So did Danny.

Until Rose.

Ding!

I blink as the doors slide open, but I don't move. *Twenty-one.* I bite down on my back teeth and push off the wall, pacing down the corridor and entering the suite. I let the door close behind me, seeing a mound of white powder on the glass coffee table in front of the couches. A bottle of Scotch next to it. And, fuck my life, a pile of condoms.

I laugh under my breath and approach with caution, lighting up. Condoms. I pour a drink and neck it, topping it off immediately. I leave the mountain of cocaine untouched and drop to the couch.

My son.

I snort my disgust and snarl around the rim of my glass, taking more Scotch.

Fighting away the memories.

The girl.

Shit.

We were fourteen.

She was the kind of girl who gave it freely and every fourteen-year-old kid wanted a piece. I thought I was being sensible. Laughing under my breath, I remember the clumsy affair. My less than impressive dick that slipped around in the condom like a toothpick in a tunnel.

The girl disappeared a few months later.

No one asked why.

No one cared.

I close my eyes and see me. A kid. Then like some torturous, fucked-up nightmare, my face blends into Nolan's. I'm slightly darker than he is. His mother was blonde.

He's mine.

I don't want to admit it, but I know he's mine.

I yell and throw my glass across the room, caught between a conflicting feeling of calm and unhinged.

Calm because he's mine and I accept that. Will make up for that.

Unhinged because with my son entering my life, someone else has to exit. I drop back against the couch and stare up and the ceiling. Why didn't he tell me? Why the *fuck* didn't he tell me?

He was scared of this. My reaction.

My cell rings. I ignore Allison's call. It rings again. I ignore Beau's call.

The door to the suite knocks.

I get up.

Answer.

The smile that greets me makes me want to slap it off her face.

Long, blonde hair. Blue eyes.

Not Pearl.

I throw five hundred bucks at her exposed chest and slam the door.

I can't have Pearl. I'll *never* accept that.

Doesn't mean I have to be a cunt.

Chapter 43

PEARL

I can't lock myself away in my bedroom and hide. It would look odd. So I must endure peopling, sitting in the kitchen, pretending to work, while everyone comes and goes. He's been gone for two nights. Everyone knows where he is, but no one is going to save him from himself. No one is intervening. Perhaps they're giving him the space they think he needs to deal with this bombshell. With cocaine, women, and alcohol. Because that's what Brad Black does. That's what he turns to, even when Brad's simply being Brad. But when he's in crisis? How much worse will one of his binges be?

I know I'm an added layer of complication to this complete and utter clusterfuck in his life. It's easy to eradicate me. Not so much his son.

I stare down at the keyboard of my laptop. At the screen with drawings and furniture stores.

"What are you doing there, Pearl?" Esther asks.

I look up, blank. What am I doing? "I'm . . ." I register her body. Her face. "Wow," I breathe, taking in her glowing complexion and her body encased in a beautiful cherry-red wraparound dress, with gold piping on the edges and hem. "You look so lovely, Esther."

She smiles, almost shyly, her hand at her ear putting an earring in. "Otto is taking me out."

"I hope you enjoy."

"I'm sure she will," Rose says, sitting next to me at the island with Maggie in her arms and flipping me a wink that I'm sure should be discreet.

"Anyone heard from Brad?" Esther asks, brushing her hair back off her shoulders.

Rose shakes her head. "He's not answering anyone's calls."

"We've got to give him time." Esther pulls her handbag toward her and finds a lipstick. "Anyone checked in on Nolan?"

"He's in his room. Quiet."

Esther nods and applies. "I made him some pancakes and bacon.

It's in the fridge when he's ready." She comes to Rose and fusses over Maggie for a few moments. "Do you think you and my son could refrain from ripping out each other's throats while I'm gone?"

"We'll try," Rose quips, her smile cheeky. "I've forgiven him, anyway."

"For which bit?"

"All of it. The jet's ready. Daniel's packing for St. Lucia."

"And you're not?" Esther asks, her eyebrows arched. Rose shakes her head, and Esther exhales.

"You look beautiful, Mum," Danny says, wandering in with a Scotch in his grasp. "Enjoy." His nose scrunches and Rose obviously tries to hold back a grin.

"I will." She plants a kiss on his cheek. "Isn't it a bit early?" she asks, indicating the drink in his hand.

"It's noon." He takes some of his drink, eyes on Rose.

"Ready?" Otto asks, appearing at the door. I blink my surprise. He's in trousers and a jacket.

"Ready," Esther says, joining him. He takes her in as she wanders over, his eyes lighting up, but he doesn't tell her how stunning she looks. He doesn't need to. His face says it all as he slips an arm around her shoulders and leads her out.

Rose immediately turns to me. "Otto's proposing."

"Oh, that's great," I smile, trying to inject some enthusiasm into my words.

"I'm delighted," Danny says dryly, abandoning his drink and taking Maggie from Rose's arms, putting her on his shoulder.

"I can tell." I look at my mobile. Would Brad answer if *I* called?

"Oh, are these the revised drawings?" Rose drags the laptop toward her and looks at the screen.

"Yeah. A few tweaks still needed I think," I say, absentmindedly. Should I call him? "I'm thinking maybe we should pinch a few more feet from the sunbed area for the beach bar." I can't stand this. Sitting around waiting for him to emerge from his splurge on all things forbidden. I know it's over. I accept that.

But . . . do I?

I feel like I'm depending on someone to tell me my destiny.

It's driving me insane.

"Excuse me," I blurt, getting up. "I need the bathroom." I turn the laptop fully toward Rose. "There are some lovely lounger pods which would look amazing in the bar area. Take a look." Everyone's carrying on like normal, pretending they're not worried Brad has gone AWOL.

"Sure."

I exit the kitchen and hurry up the stairs, rushing down the corridor and knocking on a door. Fury pulls it open, a towel wrapped around his waist. I divert my eyes up. I don't know how to approach this without getting a flat refusal. "I need to go to the club," I say. "Mason's had to take over for Brad, and Nolan and Anya are struggling to get everything done for opening."

"Give me five minutes."

I nod and go to my room, quickly changing into some denim shorts and a white linen shirt before heading downstairs. "Anya needs some help at Hiatus," I say.

Danny looks across to me as he pulls a sterilizing bag from the microwave. He nods. No objection. Nothing. "Get one of the Vikings to take you."

"Okay." I back out of the kitchen and wait at the bottom of the stairs for Fury, pacing, twitchy.

As to his word, he appears in five minutes, suited and booted. "Let's go." I leave the house and slip into the front of his car, putting my bag on my lap. He climbs in.

I wait until we're on the main road before I talk. "Fury," I say, facing him.

"Pearl."

"I want to go to the Four Seasons."

"I had a feeling that was coming." He slows at a red light, tapping the wheel with one hand, stroking his beard with the other. Thinking. Weighing up the pros and cons.

"I'm worried," I go on.

"Me too." He looks at me. "But if anything happened to you under my watch, I'd feel pretty bad about that."

"What could happen, Fury?" I ask. "You take me to the hotel, I check on Brad, we leave."

"What could happen?" He laughs. "Pearl, you sweet thing. You aren't in the normal world anymore."

I've never been in a normal world. "I know that, Fury."

He regards me with a curious eye, and I wilt in my chair.

"I'm worried," I repeat. "Nothing more."

"He'll be fine." He pulls off from the lights, and I deflate, resisting protesting. "Brad does what Brad does. And he's doing it now. He'll come out of it when he's ready." Except they don't know *everything*. I know Fury would never knowingly put any of us in danger.

I bite at my lip, glancing down at the cup holders between us where Fury's dropped the keys for the car. It wouldn't be his fault if I gave him the slip.

I bide my time, looking ahead at the road, watching for cabs. I see one in the distance, and like they know I need it, the lights up ahead change to red. Fury slows down, and the moment the car's stopped, I reach for the button on the dashboard to turn off the engine then grab the keys, jumping out.

"Pearl!"

"I'm sorry," I whisper as I dash across the road, waving an arm for the cab to stop, praying it's free. My heart leaps when I see the blinker come on. He pulls over and I hop in. "The Four Seasons," I blurt, slamming the door. I look back as the cab pulls away, seeing Fury in the middle of the road, arms up in the air, a face full of . . . fury. And today I learned why Fury if known as Fury. Murderous. "As quick as you can," I say, resting back, staring at the screen of my phone as Fury's name flashes angrily at me. I don't ignore him. "I'll be okay," I say when I answer.

"I'm pissed."

"I could see that."

"Pearl, my car is at the lights, abandoned, and I have no way of moving it."

That was kind of my point. To buy myself some time. Fury knows that.

"With a trunk full of guns."

"Oh," I breathe, cringing.

"I need those keys, Pearl, and I need you to get your ass back here under my watch."

"Okay," I say, if only to appease him. I hang up and send a mental prayer to the skies that the police don't stumble upon Fury before I can get the keys back to him.

• • •

Ten minutes later, the cab pulls up, and I lean forward, handing the driver triple the fare and Fury's keys. "I need you to take these keys back to where you picked me up from."

The cabbie frowns as he accepts the money and the keys. "And give them to who?"

"There's a big, angry-looking Viking by an abandoned Mercedes. You won't miss him." I hop out and look up at the tower. My heart speeds up. I take the steps and enter the vast lobby, glancing around as I wander through.

"Can I help you?"

I turn toward the voice, finding a mature man in a pristine gray suit. He's looking me up and down. Concluding that I don't belong here. "I'm here to see Mr. Black," I say, making my voice strong and my back straight.

He blinks, surprised, and takes me in again, from head to toe. He's thinking I'm not Mr. Black's usual type. "Oh, I see, a guest of Mr. Black's." He clears his throat and looks around the lobby, before smiling brightly and sweeping an arm out. "This way, miss."

"Thank you." I let him guide me to the elevators, call one for me, and hold the door while I step inside. He presses the button for the twenty-ninth floor. "Enjoy your stay, miss."

I stare at him, my heart heavy. I'm a part of the process. How many women has he shown up to the twenty-ninth floor in the past forty-eight hours? I rest back against the wall, closing my eyes to stop the building tears from escaping.

Part of the process . . .

• • •

"Look pretty, my darling girl," Mother says as she buttons up my cardigan. "Look pretty and smile." She pulls the collar of my pale blue-striped dress over the top and pats it down. "That's what we must always do."

"We smile when we're unhappy?" I ask, mystified by this. Mother's hands falter on her sweeping up-do as she smooths it with a palm spritzed with hairspray for the hundredth time since she pinned it up an hour ago.

Then she laughs lightly. "My darling, I am very happy." She comes to me, crouching to get her face level with mine. She taps the end of my nose with her fingertip, her red lips stretched wide. "You are too curious for a little girl. We must control that."

"Yes, Mother." I smile at her necklace, reaching forward and touching the creamy stone. A giant pearl surrounded by small rubies.

"One day it will be yours, my darling. Now, then. Go and say hello to your father and his guests. Then you must go to your bedroom and play quietly. We must not interrupt your father's poker evening."

"Okay," I say, not asking what Mother will be doing. She will be sitting quietly beside my father, smiling on tap. Laughing when prompted. Being the perfect, silent wife.

She takes my shoulders and leads me into the drawing room. It always confuses me why we call it a drawing room when I am never allowed to do any drawing in it.

I enter the large, elaborate space and immediately feel all eyes on me. "Ah, here they are." Father pops his fat cigar in his mouth and smiles at us. "Come, come, say hello to my friends."

I look at father's friends. All men. All with women by their sides who appear to be mute. And young. All so young. I know Father is older than my mother, but whenever I have asked, Mother has always told me not to be curious, as curiosity is troublesome. Especially in women.

The men will play cards. The women will sit in a square and sip champagne. "Hello," I say when presented to them. I get endless plumes of rancid cigar smoke breathed all over me as they all look me up and down.

"Beautiful like her mother," one says.

I feel my mother's hands tighten on my shoulders, and I look up at her. She nods. Instruction. "Thank you," I say as Father claims me from Mother's hold and wraps one of his big arms around my shoulders, pulling me in close.

He drops a kiss on top of my head, sniffing, and sits, pulling me down onto his knee, and Mother takes that as her cue to join the ladies on the other side of the drawing room. "Tell me about the deal," he says to a friend, pulling on his fat cigar.

His friend looks at me.

"She's ten, Frazer," Father reminds him. "Speak freely."

He nods, sitting forward, rubbing at his nose. "We have reached mutually agreeable terms."

"Excellent."

I gaze around the room as Father chats with his friends about things that don't sound very interesting at all. I see something white on the table. A straw. A gold little card. "Why is it called a drawing room if I can't draw in here, Father?" I blurt my question and everyone in the room falls silent. Looking at me. Father eventually laughs, glancing at my mother. "You must control her curiosity, Ruby. No one wants a wife with too much to say." He stands me up, and Mother is soon collecting me.

"I'm sorry, dear," she says quickly, leading me away, and the moment I'm out of the room, she dips and gets her mouth to my ear. "Pearl, my darling, children must be seen and not heard." I look up at her. "And women should be graceful and quiet." She straightens my collar again. "Off to your room."

I do as I'm told, closing the door behind me and settling on the carpet next to my doll's house. I play with it for an hour, rearranging the furniture, making sure there's a table by the chair in the . . . what will I call this room? "The drawing room," I say to myself. After tidying the library, I get up and put a few more pieces in my jigsaw puzzle, looking over the building picture of the English countryside.

When I hear a car door close, I go to the window and look down onto the driveway. Father's seeing his guests off, shaking hands while all the ladies wait, quiet, smiling their goodbyes. I watch all of the fancy cars drive away, then hear mother's steps coming down the hallway. I grab a book and sit on the chair in the corner as she enters. She smiles, happy I'm reading, and goes to the window, pulling the curtains closed. "Supper and bed."

"Okay, Mother." I close my book and set it neatly on the bedside table ready to read myself to sleep as she fixes the closed curtains just so, brushing down the velvet material.

She pauses when the sound of a car coming down the gravel driveway drifts through the window. Her face. I never know how to decipher her expressions. She opens the curtains again. "Oh, no."

"Ruby!" Father bursts through the door, his cigar hanging from his mouth. "Get her in the cupboard. Now."

• • •

Ding!

I blink myself back to the present as the doors slide open, and on a swallow, I step out. *Okay, Mother.* Never heard. Hardly ever seen.

I walk around the corner and come to a sharp stop when I spot a woman walking toward me. She has long, black hair. A short, tight little black dress. Her chest is exposed. Her heels sky high. She's counting money, a smile on her face. A guest of Mr. Black's? This early in the day? My heart hurts.

I follow her strut as she passes, all the way to the elevator, and watch her step inside. She smiles at me as the doors close. I somehow convince my legs to walk, taking me to the door. I knock. Breathe in some strength. Mentally tell myself to be strong. Be heard. Be seen.

The door swings open. Brad takes one look at me and steps back, his face impassive. He has a Scotch in his hand, only a pair of boxers covering him. I make sure I keep his eyes.

He knows I will have passed his latest fuck leaving the building. But I didn't need to see it happening to know it was happening. Imagining it was tough. Seeing the evidence leave?

"Why are you here, Pearl?" he asks, leaning on the door with a hand. He's not drunk, no slur to his words at all. I'm surprised.

"I was worried about you," I tell him. Somehow, Brad being stone-cold sober while he fucks me out of his head is so much worse than him being blind drunk. I'm so easy to replace. To look past. Nothing has changed. His words of forever meant absolutely nothing after all. "Do you have company?"

He frowns, looking back into the suite. "No."

"Then can I come in?"

He's quickly looking at me again. Maybe confused. Maybe curious. I don't know. He's thinking really hard about whether he should let me in. He eventually releases the door and steps back, and I walk into the room. The first thing I see is the pile of white powder on the table in front of the couches. Not drunk but high on cocaine? Naturally, I look for residue around his nose, listening for the tell-tale sniff. Nothing. And, actually, the pile looks too perfect to have had any dragged away. There's no line. No card on the table. No rolled-up note.

Brad looks at me, watching me measure him. "Sit," he says coldly. I assess the seating options. The couch? Too cozy. The occasional chairs by the far wall? Too formal.

I go to one of the armchairs and drop to the cushion, feeling him behind me. He passes, and my eyes fall to the backs of his thighs as he goes to the couch opposite and slowly lowers. He doesn't rest back, instead taking the edge, forearms on his bare knees.

Eyes on me.

The silence that falls is painful as I search for the right words and Brad waits. Has he nothing to say? "I know about Nolan," I say.

"Everyone knew about Nolan. Except me."

"I didn't know before you." I wouldn't want him to think I'd hold that kind of information back. Not that it matters now. "Beau told me after you left the boatyard." He watches me falling all over myself trying to explain. I don't know why I'm bothering. But I care that he'd believe I'd betray him, which is ridiculous considering the situation I'm currently in. But still. Two wrongs don't make a right.

He doesn't tell me he believes me, perhaps because he doesn't. Again, what does it matter now? He's already done what I hoped he wouldn't. And if he hadn't, was I hoping to stop him? Save him from himself? "I don't know if I'm a contributing factor to this," I say, motioning to his semi-naked body and the pile of drugs before me. "Or if it's just the fact you've found out Nolan's your son."

"A bit of both," he says flatly.

I nod. "I understand why it would mess with your head. Me. My age." I look back at the door. The woman who just left can't be that much older than I am. But definitely not young enough to be his daughter, and now, what with the revelation of Nolan, it's confirmed that Brad really is old enough to be my father. And that sucks.

"It messed with my head before I found out about Nolan," he says, showing absolutely no emotion at all, and that's screwing with *my* head. No anger, no regret, no anything.

"I accept it's over," I whisper. "Whatever it was between us."

He looks away, his face showing the first sign of an expression. Twisted. "It was nothing."

"Okay," I say. "It was nothing." A moment ago, I was a significant piece of the reason he's here. And now I'm nothing. Fine. Whatever he wants to tell himself. "But you're better than this, Brad."

"God, you're so naïve."

"Better than being a fucking child."

"You *are* a fucking child!" he yells, his eyes wild. "A bit of fun, something to do."

I stand, suddenly needing to leave. I can't be around him, knowing he's lying to himself, and I'm once again wondering why the fuck I came. If he's going to self-destruct, no one can stop him, and I was foolish to think I could. And even more foolish to let a tiny part of me cling onto hope.

He's a coward.

"You can walk away from me, fine, but not your son." I head to the door. "We've both lost our parents, Brad. Both been without that love. It's fucked us up, whether we admit it or not. Don't let him down like you've let me and yourself down." I pull the door open and still, feeling his eyes on my back. "I never wanted the fairy tale," I say, refusing to give in to the need to take one last look at him. "But I did want a man who isn't pathetic and weak." I leave, closing the door behind me, holding back my tears. I hate him for showing me his soft side. I hate him even more for being a coward. I hate him for making me fall in love with only one version of himself, not Brad in his entirety. Because young me can't change a man like The American.

I go to the elevator, press the call button, and step inside in a haze of grief, feeling profound loss for something that was only briefly in my life. So *I'm* pathetic too.

The doors start to close.

And a hand appears, stopping them from meeting in the middle. I move back as Brad forces them open again and steps into the opening, in his boxers, a hand on each side of the doors. "You're right about so much," he says, his lazy eyes hooded and low, pinning me in place. He's looked at me like this before. I can't control myself when he does. But I must. "But wrong about one thing."

My hammering heart is making breathing tricky, so words are almost impossible. "What?" I ask, sounding as shaky as I feel.

"You said I can walk away from you." He releases the door. "And I can't. Get in the bedroom."

"What," I breathe, fighting to maintain my steady head. Is he joking? "So you can fuck me like one of your whores?"

"No, Pearl," he grates, jaw rolling. Angry. "So I can fuck you like you're *mine*."

I lose my breath, taking another step back. Away from him. "But I'm not yours."

"Oh, you're mine." He takes my arm, yanking me into his chest.

"Brad, stop it." I cannot let this happen. I cannot be with a man who turns to another woman when he's in a mindfuck.

He tips my chin up, scanning my face. "Look at me."

"No." I wrench my face from his hold. "I will not give myself to you."

"You already did, Pearl," he whispers, rolling his hips into my tummy, showing me his condition. I grit my teeth and shut off my sense of smell. "Which means you now belong to me."

My mouth falls open, shocked, disgusted. "And in between your indecisiveness—I'm yours, I'm not, you want me, you don't—I have to accept you'll fuck a few whores in the presidential suite of the Four Seasons while high on cocaine and Scotch?" I'm suddenly outraged. Suddenly thinking fucking straight. I do *not* want this man. "Get the fuck out of the elevator," I yell. "Get the fuck away from me! You're no better than your father!"

He flinches, injured. "God damn you, woman," he hisses, grabbing me.

"Get off!" I fight him, tussling in his hold, but I'm no match for him. He throws me over his shoulder. "Brad!"

"Shut the fuck up, Pearl." He marches back to the room and kicks the door shut, carrying me through the suite into a bedroom. I drop my bag to the floor while trying to free myself, smacking at his naked back.

"Let me go!"

"Shut up."

The sheets are strewn on the bed, and I look away, incensed. Brad kicks another door, and the loud bang of it hitting the wall behind makes me jump. He dumps me on my feet and grabs something from the sink, squeezing my cheeks, holding something up in front of me. Soap. "I swear to God," he seethes. "I will clean your mouth out of curses."

"Make sure there's some left to clean your cock," I hiss, making him draw back. Blink. "And even then, I'll never let it near me again."

"No?" He drops the soap and pushes his front to mine. My stupid heart pounds in my chest. I know he can feel it.

"No."

His fingertip meets my exposed skin past the open collar or my shirt. I inhale, and Brad pauses with his dragging touch, watching me react to it. "No?"

I close my eyes and fight the desire steaming forward. "No," I whisper.

He cups me between my thighs and my pussy throbs into his hand. His mouth moves to my ear, his teeth grazing my lobe. I whimper, grabbing his bicep and clawing my nails into his flesh. "No?"

"No," I breathe.

"Okay." He drops me and moves back, hands up, and I heave where I stand, gulping down oxygen. "Now who's the one pretending?"

I pass him, making sure I give him a wide berth—no touching—and snatch my bag up from the floor, making my escape before I do something stupid. Like give myself to him again. I'm not his. I'm not *anyone's*.

Never again.

"I didn't fuck anyone," he calls to my back, his words rushed and urgent.

I stop running, my bag clenched to my chest, and stare forward.

"I've not touched another woman, Pearl."

My eyes drop like rocks to the carpet, darting. "The woman I saw leave," I say quietly.

"I sent her away."

His bare feet appear in my downcast vision, and I allow my eyes to creep up his naked legs and chest. He looks so . . . contrite. "I called a few women," he says, his voice thick. "But I couldn't do it. I didn't *want* to do it. I didn't want them."

"But—" I want to believe him. Desperately. "Her hands were full of money."

"Her pimp would have something to say if I didn't compensate her for wasting her time." He reaches for me, but I retreat, and he holds his hands up in surrender. "I made the arrangements. I sent the first woman away. I didn't cancel the others."

Why? In case he changed his mind?

He holds his hands out. "These hands. I don't want them to touch any other woman ever again."

My head's a mess. *It was nothing.* That's what he called us. *Nothing.* "You said we were nothing."

"You will never be nothing." He reaches for me again, but I lean back. "Please believe me. I only want you, Pearl. Forever, only you."

Forever?

"Forever is a really long time."

He nods, stepping closer, and this time I don't stop him. He gently takes my bag from my chest and dips, placing it on the floor. I look up at him, holding my breath as he scans every tiny bit of my face, watching his fingers as they brush my hair back. And then his gaze falls onto my mouth, and he slowly brings his lips down to meet mine. The moment they touch, I jolt, as if life has just been injected back into me, my heart kick-starting. I open up to him and accept his soft tongue. His kiss is reverent. Slow. Tender.

Loving?

My hands go to the back of his head, my fingers in his hair, and he picks me up, walking me out of the bathroom across the suite as our mouths indulge, a familiar heaviness falling between my legs. Throbbing. The bed he lays me on is freshly made. No strewn sheets. He blankets me, his tall, built body cocooning me, his arousal throbbing against my leg. And he kisses me, bites my lip, I bite his, he pecks, I peck, and then he plunges deep, hands everywhere.

He tears his mouth away and sits back on his heels, pulling me up to sit. My arms lift to help him get my shirt off, and I'm wriggling out of my shorts quickly after. He tosses them aside and reaches behind me to unhook my bra, his mouth on my neck and shoulder, the tingles becoming too much. I drop to my back the second he's rid me of my bra, lifting my arse to let him get my knickers down.

I watch with bated breath as he gets off the bed and pushes his boxers down his thighs, kicking them off before grabbing my ankle and yanking me to the bottom of the bed. He falls to his knees and puts his mouth on my sex, and my spine snaps into an arch, my fingers clawing into the sheets and bunching them, as he kisses me between my legs like he's just kissed my mouth. Deeply. My hips grind up into him, his forearm lying across my stomach to keep me from bucking. I'm on the cusp immediately, and the constant cries of pleasure tell him so.

"Too soon," he rumbles, releasing me from the wicked talents of his mouth.

I cry out and grab his biceps, pulling him down onto my body, taking his mouth urgently. He rolls us, holding me to his front, his fingers clawing into my bottom, his hardness pulsing against me, teasing me. I feel and yank at his hair as he rolls us again, caging me beneath him, kissing down to my breasts, swirling his tongue around each nipple, his hand stroking down my body and dragging through my wetness. I throw my head back, insane with pleasure. I feel like I'm permanently tinkering on the edge of that inconceivably incredible fall.

And he's not even inside me.

Just kissing. Mouths and body.

I stretch my arms above my head, rolling my chest up onto his mouth, closing my eyes and exhaling, feeling peace crawl across my skin with every kiss he places on me. Goosebumps invade every inch of me, my smile small as I writhe beneath him, listening to his pleasure from pleasuring me.

He crawls up farther, breathes into my neck, and I bring my arms down, holding him for a short time before he pulls away and sits on his heels, helping me up onto his lap. He holds me by my nape, kisses me, then lifts me, positioning himself at my entrance, and kisses me again as I slowly sink onto him, filling my lungs as I do until I'm full of him and exhaling, remaining still for a minute, getting used to him inside me, my face in his neck. He's patient, still, his hands stroking across my back softly, his mouth kissing my shoulder.

I tell him I'm ready with one brief peck beneath his ear, and he encourages me out of his neck, slipping an arm around my waist, his other holding the outside of my thigh. I lock my ankles around his lower back, my arms around his neck, and begin to move on his lap. His chest concaves, his jaw ticks, his eyes never leaving mine. I circle, tense, feeling him the deepest I ever have. But it doesn't hurt. It just feels . . . right.

I move in to kiss him, but he turns away from it, shaking his head. Then realigns his eyes on mine, and my heart bucks, feeling a beautifully poignant shift between us as we watch each other, connected so deeply, so intimately, his moves helping mine, my pleasure pushing his. I've never been looked at so closely before.

He stifles a moan as I whimper, gripping every muscle around him, and he stills for a moment, takes a breather, as do I, before he slowly guides me back up and lazily rotates, plunging deeply. Eyes fixed on me.

I'm mindless on pleasure, totally swallowed up by him. I want to kiss him, but I want to watch him more. How he's looking at me now. How he's guiding me on his lap, controlling our pleasure, unhurriedly working his way in and out of me, steadily building us both up.

I start to wobble on the edge of release, sharp bursts of air escaping as I try and hold myself back. Brad maintains the tempo, and I begin to shake with the effort to not let go. Then he raises to his knees, holding me under my arse, and I know I'll never resist the ecstasy. I cry out, grappling at his neck, watching as his eyes smoke. And then he kisses me, and I surrender to the pull, letting it take me, his drives carrying us both to the finish line.

I fall off the edge with a relieved exhale, shaking around him, my arms and legs aching, and he bucks, grunts, and breaks our kiss, panting into my shoulder on a quiet curse as he spills himself into me. I absorb the throbs of his cock, laying my head on my arms around his neck, staring across the room.

Dazed.

"My love," he whispers, kissing my shoulder. "Forever."

Chapter 44

BRAD

I lower to my heels, holding her to my chest, fighting for air. I could never accept not having her in my life. I could never accept not being able to love her. Something has happened to my heart, and I need to acknowledge it. The way she looks at me. The way I feel when I make love to her.

"Shall we talk about it?" I ask, unable to leave the unspoken hanging heavy in the air with the potent scent of sex. I feel her nod against my shoulder, so I pull back, but keep myself deep inside her, her bare walls feeling too good against my bare cock to give up. I hold her face, taking in every perfect piece of her. I've never seen anything more clearly.

Hearing the words she spoke—watching her walk away from me—was the shove I didn't need. I already knew what I needed. I already knew what Pearl needed. And Nolan. I have so many wrongs to right.

I brush her hair out of her face as she looks at me. Nibbles at her lip ring nervously. Her naked skin is beautifully flushed. "Do I need to warn you not to fall in love with me?" I ask.

She nods, so mildly.

"I can't," I admit. I want her to love me. Her love feels good on me. I realize she's not biting at her ring because she's nervous. She's trying to hold back her tears. "Why are you sad?"

"Because I'm scared."

My heart squeezes a little. "Don't be scared, my love." I surrender her warmth, pulling out and moving to the edge of the bed, tugging her over. She climbs onto my lap, pinning her front to my mine, and I cuddle her. "Can you warn *me* not to love *you*?" I ask.

She shakes her head, and I force her back to look at me. She's let go of her tears, her big eyes like green glass balls. "Then I will love you."

She inhales, searching my eyes. Speechless? Me too. But I'm a man of a certain age and I'm not fucking stupid. And no longer in denial. "I love you." I say it again, the words sounding sublime. I think I loved her even when I hated her. "I love you." I kiss her wet cheek. "I love you." Her other. "I love you." Her forehead. "I love you." Her nose. "I lo—" She seals our lips and swallows the words, sniveling in between the soft swirl of our tongues. I fall back to the bed with her, lost, floating. Respite.

This is what Danny and James have had all this time, and now I can appreciate it. Because I have it.

Purpose.

"It hurts, Pearl," I whisper around her lips. "And I don't know how to control it."

She sits up on me, her palms flat on my stomach. "I don't think we're supposed to know how to control it."

I smile, placing my hands on her thighs and gripping, thinking. "You haven't said it," I whisper. Am I being needy?

Her head cocks, a small smile tickling one corner of her mouth. I am. I'm being needy. "The day you need me to tell you I love you is the day I stop showing you well enough." She falls to me, taking my face in her hands. "I will never stop showing you." And kisses me deeply. And my God, I feel it. Her love. And then she holds me with a formidable strength. I feel her love in this hug too. And we don't let go. Not for a long, long while.

I squeeze her a little harder, hearing my cell ringing in the distance, but I have no will or inclination to answer it. I'm not prepared to surrender this feeling. Then it stops. And another phone begins to ring. The landline by the bed.

"For fuck's sake." It's time to stop ignoring everyone. I exhale and lift, keeping Pearl attached to my front as I reach for the phone and take it to my ear.

"Mr. Black," Jeeves says, sounding anxious. "I have a man in the lobby claiming to know you."

"Who?" I ask, automatically hostile. It can't be Danny. He'd come straight up with Jeeves's blessing, a keycard, and a Glock. I frown when Pearl burrows deeper into my chest, her body tense. What the hell has she done? I didn't think about how she got here. Until now.

"He goes by the name Fury. No surname, sir. He said you wouldn't need one."

"I don't," I say flatly, prizing Pearl from her hiding place and giving her a very scornful look. "You'd better send him up." I place the phone in the cradle. "Guess who that was."

"My fairy godmother?" she asks, looking cute when she half-smiles.

"What did you do?" I grip her ass and squeeze threateningly.

"Stole his car keys so he couldn't come after me when I ran." She presses her lips together and shrinks on my lap.

"With a trunk full of weapons in the middle of Miami?"

"That part didn't occur to me at the time."

"I'm mad," I say, slapping her ass and lifting her off my lap. "Fury sounds even madder."

She groans, falling to her back as I pull on my boxers. God damn her, the trunk full of weapons is the least of my worries. There are too many men out there wanting to get to us, and I've just added Pearl to their list of targets. "You'd better get dressed." I grab her panties and lean over her reclined body, dropping them on her face. "I'll let Fury in."

"Please don't," she pleads, leaving her panties exactly where they are.

"Get dressed." I pass through the suite and grab a trash can, taking it to the table and dragging the pile of coke to the edge and into it, dusting off the remnants from the glass before quickly washing my hands. *I don't need you anymore.* I don't need that kind of fix now. *Freedom.*

The door knocks, and I open it to Fury. He looks down my semi-naked front. Then beyond me into the room. "She's getting dressed," I say, opening the way for him. "Come in."

He looks startled. Not because of me and Pearl, but because I've not denied it. "I'll be telling the others later," I say, and he nods.

"Good to see you're okay." He links his hands in front of him.

"Thanks." I go to the coffee machine and slip a cup under it. "Want one?"

"No, thanks. After the day I've had, I think I'd like something stronger."

I laugh under my breath, pointing to the bar behind him. "Help yourself."

"Not while I'm on the job. Am I still on the job?"

"You're still on the job," I confirm as the machine spits out some caffeine. "And Pearl just reached Rose and Beau status."

"She wasn't before?" he asks, making me raise my brows. "I mean before you finally admitted you have feelings for her?"

I smile around the rim of my cup as I take a sip of my coffee and Fury looks past me. I turn to see Pearl in the doorway, looking sheepish. "I'm sorry," she says, trying to look cute.

"Not accepted," Fury grunts, flicking a cautious eye to me, checking I'm cool with his scorn. I'm totally cool with it. She's been reckless, and anyone in this family who pulls her up for being reckless has my blessing.

I toast thin air with my coffee. "Have at her," I say, taking another sip, smiling on the inside when she gasps at me, outraged.

"Don't you ever give me the slip again," Fury fumes, wagging a fat finger in her face. "Christ, Pearl, I can't believe how stupid that was. I can't cope with another Beau."

I cough over my coffee. No, we definitely do not want another Beau dashing off all over town.

"I know," Pearl breathes, truly looking remorseful. "I—"

"And all because you wanted to—" He pauses, looking my way. "See Brad."

"Actually, I wanted to tell Brad he's an arsehole." She smiles across to me.

"But you ended up in bed with him instead?" Fury says over a laugh. "You sure did tell him."

"Oh, fuck off," she spits, and I chuckle, amused.

"Take her home," I say. "I've got some business to deal with." I go to Pearl and lead her to Fury. "Don't let her out of your sight."

"Yes, boss."

I dip and kiss her cheek from behind, and she turns into me quickly, looking up at me. "Can we have dinner together?" she asks.

"Sure," I say, handing her over to Fury, trusting him to do my job. Just for now.

As soon as he's gone, I call Otto. "I need you to find someone for me."

"And?"

"And put him in the green container at the boatyard."

Chapter 45

PEARL

Fury's giving me the silent treatment, and it's screaming as we wait for the elevator. "I'm sorry," I say for the hundredth time. "It was reckless and stupid, and I feel bad." I'm sure Brad, Danny, and James would have figured out how to get Fury out of jail—blackmail, threats, murder—but it would have been a stress no one needs.

"Do you?"

"Yes."

He gestures to the elevator doors opening, and I wander into the cart, Fury following. "Okay, I might forgive you."

"Might?" I nudge him with my shoulder, rolling my eyes. He doesn't budge an inch.

"I'll think about it."

I see his hidden smile when I stare up at the big beast as he hits the button for the lobby. Everything worked out in the end. I smile at the door, a little giddy. A lot sore between my thighs. He loves me. I never thought Brad would ever admit loving anyone. He's conditioned not to.

But he has. And not only that, he's embraced it.

I'm floored.

And so fucking happy. Perhaps naïvely so.

On that thought, my contentment wavers, and I'm brought back down to earth. Dinner tonight. I'll open up. Be honest. Between now and then, I need to think about how the hell I explain. I'll start from the beginning. Make him understand.

"Pearl?"

I blink and look up at Fury. He points to the open doors. "Oh, sorry, I was daydreaming." I step out, smiling. "Did you know Otto has taken Es—" My smile drops, my words fade, and my heart jumps into my throat. The whole world spins around me, my past world and my current world, melding and blending into one, the sounds of the hotel lobby blurring into an unbearable white noise of screams from my other life.

He's.

Here.

He's here, and he's sitting in a chair, one leg crossed over the other, watching the elevator doors.

Watching me stepping out.

Casual.

Thoughtful.

He knew I was here. How? Did he follow me? Track me? I wince, an old pain returning, and I reach up to my nape, rubbing at the scar.

• • •

I look back at Father as my mum hurries me around the landing. "You must be silent," she says, her heels clicking on the wooden floor as I blindly stumble along behind her, my arm stretched out to keep hold of her hand.

I look through the wooden spindles and see my father swing the front door open. "Leave," he demands.

"Or what?" He steps into the hallway, shoving Dad aside, looking around at the luxury. "Am I interrupting one of your cigar smoking, Scotch-drinking poncy parties?" He plucks the Cuban from Dad's hold and sucks on the fat stick. "Why am I never invited?" he asks.

"Because you're not, you immoral piece of shit." Dad growls.

"Of course. You think I'm below you. You think I'm unworthy of the expensive smokes and swanky liquor." He takes the crystal tumbler from Dad's hand and knocks back the rest of his drink, including the ice cubes. Then he crunches hard and drops the glass to the marble floor. It shatters, making me flinch, as Mother gasps, dragging me on. "Oops." Then he walks along the hallway, his arm stretched out, swiping all of Mother's Royal Dalton figurines off the antique French cabinet.

"Get out of my house!" Dad roars, stomping toward him. His face, enraged, is the last thing I see before Mother tugs me through a doorway.

And the last thing I hear is her distressed whimper as she shuts me in the cupboard.

• • •

I lose my balance, wobbling, reaching for Fury's arm. The monster smiles, as if knowing what I'm thinking, his chest expanding—an inhale of satisfaction.

"Pearl?"

I cough, tearing my eyes away from the man in the chair. "I tripped."

Fury looks down at the smooth, even floor, and I walk on, feeling his eyes following me. I don't breathe easy when we make it outside. I don't breathe easy when we're in the car. Not even when Fury's driving me away.

"You sure you're okay?" He looks across the car to me. "You look really pasty."

"I'm fine."

"Is this another panic attack?"

I swallow, feeling at my neck again, my windpipe closing. "Honestly, Fury, please, don't worry." I flex my clammy hands. "I've not eaten yet today."

Fury expresses his disappointment, shaking his head, his attention still split between me and the road. Too much on me. "I think Brad might have something to say about that. Breakfast, Pearl. Always eat your breakfast."

I smile meekly, looking in the side mirror. He's come out the hotel and is getting in a black Audi. Following me.

Which confirms everything I knew.

He just wants me.

Not Brad, Danny, James, or anyone else.

He just wants *me*.

"I'll make you something to eat when we get back," Fury says, getting his phone out of his inside pocket and checking it. "Since Esther is out with Otto."

"So you know," I say, trying not to keep my eyes constantly on the mirror.

"Everyone knows except Esther. Do you think she'll accept?"

I rub a palm into my chest. "Of course she'll accept." I peek at the mirror again, seeing the black Audi a few cars back.

Breathe.

I focus on taking in air steadily, constantly checking the mirrors, making small talk in an attempt to convince Fury I'm okay.

The Audi remains two cars back the entire way to the house. The gates open, and I nearly have a heart attack when I come face to face with Danny, James, Ringo, Goldie, Tank, *and* Len, all aiming machine guns at us.

"What the hell?" I exhale, pushing back in my seat as Fury pulls through the gates and cuts the engine.

"Stay in the car."

He jumps out, catches another big gun that Tank throws his way, and all of them move toward the gate. "A black Audi," Fury says. "Spotted it about two miles back."

"Oh my God." I turn in my seat, watching the line of deadly killers move out onto the road, and all hell breaks loose. I cover my ears, watching them fire at the Audi as it picks up speed, screeching away, swerving, tires screaming and burning.

I return forward, staring at the house. What have I done? Why did I lead him to the mansion? I should have told Fury. I should have had him drive away from their home.

I startle when Fury drops back into the driver's seat. He doesn't say a word. Just starts the car and drives me calmly toward the house. "Get something to eat," he orders, getting out.

I open the door and slowly drag myself from the car, looking back down the driveway. The gates are now closed. Everyone is walking back toward the house.

Danny comes to me, rubbing my shoulder. "You all right?" he asks.

The guilt flares. "Yeah," I breathe. *Lie.*

"I got the license plate." James is on his phone. "Sending it to Otto."

I walk into the house, stopping and listening to the noise coming from the kitchen. Rose. I walk to the door and see her fussing over Daniel. "Call me when you land," she says as he rolls his eyes. "And school work before jet skiing or Xboxing."

"Yes, Mom."

I back out and carry on to the stairs, seeing Danny and James with Barney's dad, words being spoken quietly, hands being shaken. "She will leave you both alone now," Danny says.

"Dare I ask what you did?" Lennox asks.

Danny smiles, and it's wicked. "I heard your house burned down."

"Oh Jesus," Lennox breathes. "You framed her?"

"You're welcome." Danny's smile falters as he spots me at the bottom of the stairs. "You sure you're all right?"

I nod and head to my room, and finding the biggest bag, I stuff it with as much as it will carry and as much as I can manage.

My lip wobbles the entire time.

It's over.

He's found me.

Chapter 46

BRAD

I brush down the front of my new suit. "Pay five thousand fucking dollars for a suit, and it's covered in lint?" I mutter, scowling at the lapel as I walk through the hotel lobby.

"Mr. Black, can I help with that?" Jeeves asks, coming at me with a lint roller.

I look at him, exasperated. "What the fuck's going on with this?" I ask. I feel like a magnet for every bit of dust in the air.

"It's the material, sir," he explains, rolling up and down my sleeve. "Static." He moves back and smiles at my finely clad form. "Very smart, sir. Special occasion?"

"Yeah, I'm meeting my son," I say quietly, sinking one hand into my trouser pocket and walking away. *And telling everyone I'm in love with Pearl.* I might kill someone too. "Thanks, Jeeves."

"Anytime, Mr. Black." *But perhaps never again.*

I text Danny to let him know I'm on my way to the club.

Oh good. You've left the pity party. You missed a shoot-out, and I'm pretty sure Maggie chuckled for the first time

What was she chuckling at?

Daddy's machine gun

I believe it.

And the shoot-out?

Fury had an Audi tail him back to the house.

I skid to a stop on my dress shoes. With Pearl in the car? "The fuck?" I breathe, my thumbs hovering over the screen, not knowing what to say.

Who?

That's a negative. Where are you?

"Fuck," I hiss, squeezing my cell, lifting it to my lips and biting at the corner.

Heading to Hiatus.

I've just dropped Benson and the kids off at the airfield. Meet you at the club.

I call Otto. He doesn't answer. So I call him again. Nothing. And again. "Come on," I snap, texting him, telling him to fucking answer or die. I don't have a chance to call him again. He calls me.

"I'm kind of in the middle of something here," he growls on a whisper.

"What?" What could be so important he wouldn't take my call when I'm dialing him off the hook? Wait . . . "Oohhh," I breathe. "Did she say yes?"

"I don't know because I haven't fucking asked her yet, because every fucker in the world keeps interrupting me, this time you. Danny with his bratty protests, Rose wanting to know where the washing powder is, the waiter wanting to know what we want to fucking eat and drink."

"Tell me one thing before you go back to your romantic date."

"What?"

"Did you find him?"

"Yeah, I'll call you when I'm done." He hangs up, and I ponder who the fuck was following Fury?

"Brad Black?" someone says, pulling my attention to my left. I look the guy up and down, not sure I'm liking what I'm seeing. Tall. Smart and clearly trying to be. "Or should I call you The American?"

"Who's asking?"

He sniffs, wiping his nose with the back of his hand. "I heard you're looking for a supplier."

"From whom?"

"Does it matter?"

I step into him, serious. "It really fucking matters." I feel my gun against my back, my hand twitching to pull it. I get away with a lot around here, thanks to Jeeves. Brandishing a gun in the lobby? I think glossing over that is beyond his concierge abilities. "Who the fuck told you I'm in for a supplier?"

He hesitates, and doesn't that amplify my concern and heat my temper.

"Listen to me," I whisper, up close to his face, seeing white residue around his nose. "You need your tongue to talk, and since you're choosing not to talk, I think I might just cut the fucker out."

"Mr. Black!" Jeeves sings, coming between us. He laughs, nervous as shit. "Now, now, no need for a scene in the lobby."

I wave a hand at the creep. "Do you know this dickhead?" I ask, my patience lost.

"Yes, Mr. Black, he helps with certain requests that our guests may make."

Guests like me.

"This is a friend. Horris."

"Right. And who does your friend work for?" I ask, discreetly pulling my gun and folding my arms with it in my grasp.

"Oh, Mr. Black." Jeeves shakes his head, looking around nervously.

"It's okay, Jeeves. I'll only kill him if he doesn't answer my questions."

The guy's hands go up in the air pretty speedily. "I don't want any trouble." And the sleeves of his cheap suit jacket nearly ride up to his elbows. For fuck's sake. At least there's no lint on his two-piece, though.

I look at Jeeves. "Where did you find this prick?"

"I—"

Horris is suddenly gone from before us and, naturally I'm quickly aiming my gun at his back as he makes a mad run for it. Jeeves, brave fucker, pushes my arm down. "No, Mr. Black, please."

"Fuck," I growl, watching the slippery little shit run off in his cheap suit. I slide my gun back into my trousers. "Jeeves," I say, fixing my lapels and brushing off yet more lint. "I don't think you'll be seeing that dude again."

"Oh, don't worry, I will find someone else."

"Don't bother." I start to leave. "I won't be staying here again." I look back. "But if you need anything, you know where I am."

Jeeves nods, and I break out into the sunshine, slipping on my shades, feeling like a new man. I text Pearl while I wait for my Mercedes to be brought up from the parking garage.

What happened on the way back from here?

Let's see what she has to say, because I have a horrible feeling in my stomach. A shoot out. If it was her family, I expect they'll abandon their mission to get the land. I want to believe her, yet something isn't stacking up. Tracking her down in Miami for a bit of land in England?

I get no reply to my text, and she doesn't answer when I call. My car pulls up thanks to the valet, and I slip him a twenty, getting in and waiting for my Bluetooth to connect. I call Fury. "You okay?" I ask when he answers.

"Yeah, good."

"And Pearl?"

"A little shook up."

"But she's there? At home, I mean?"

"Yeah, she's here."

"And the Audi?"

"Otto's got the license plate number."

And Otto's busy on his romantic date. "Thanks, Fury."

"You shouldn't be out on your own."

I roll my eyes. "I'm heading to the club." I hang up, tapping the steering wheel, my mind working harder than it has for a while, which is why my head is probably aching.

We're going out for dinner tonight. Maybe then she'll open up. And if she doesn't?

I exhale, raking a hand through my hair.

• • •

I let myself in the back of Hiatus and find some of the girls practicing on the stage when I get into the main club. Ella is one of them. I go to the foot of the stage and she slows her shimmy down the pole when she clocks me. Thankfully, she's semi-dressed so there will be no need for me to tell her to cover herself. I check her eye. It's concealed with a thick layer of makeup.

"Does Nolan know you're here?" I ask.

She nods. "He said he had some accounts to sort."

I look toward the office, nodding. "You know you can't dance anymore, don't you, Ella?" I say, giving her my eyes again.

Her face drops. "Nolan hasn't said I can't."

"He won't. Because that's what your ex did. He told you what to do. And backhanded you if you didn't do it."

She flinches. "This is all I'm good at. It's the only way I can make money."

I nod, seeming to accept, and walk away, taking a call from Danny. "We're upstairs," he says, before hanging up. I look up at the vast expanse of glass that stretches across the club, nodding.

"Looking smart, boss," Mason says as I pass the bar.

"It's an important day." I push my way into the office, and Nolan looks up from his place at the desk. Worried. His eyes drop. Like he might turn to stone if he looks at me. Or I might attack him.

And there's the biggest kick in the gut I think I've ever felt. He didn't want me to know. He thought I wouldn't accept him.

I've let us both down.

Going to the desk, I perch on the edge, and he struggles up from the chair. "You want this chair?"

"Sit down."

He virtually drops to the seat, unable to hold himself up, glancing up at me briefly, before diverting his gaze away. And then the silence that falls is awkward. I don't want it to be awkward.

"Clearly I'm not old enough to be your father," I say flatly. He peeks up at me, the uncertainty in his eyes killing me. "But I know I am," I add.

His body softens in the chair. And my fucking heart splits.

"I'm sorry for how I reacted," I say softly.

He swallows, his eyes glazing. "I didn't want you to know." His voice is as small as I've ever known it. "I was worried—"

"Things would change?"

He nods.

"Things *will* change, Nolan. That's a fact none of us can control."

"I don't want you to look at me differently."

"You *are* different," I say over a small laugh. "You're my son."

He blinks, as if hearing it is odd. It is. "Do you remember her?" he asks.

I can't lie, it catches me off guard. I'm not prepared for this conversation. What do I tell him?

"I remember her," I say. "But I was fourteen, so you probably have better memories."

"Not really." He shrugs, like it's nothing, and I just know it is absolutely everything. "She wasn't around much."

"Working?" I don't know why I'm asking. Even at fourteen it was obvious his mother wasn't going far in life.

Nolan smiles up at me. "If that's what we should call it."

I inhale, nodding, hating myself right now. "How did you find me?" There must have been dozens of possibilities.

"She talked about many . . ." His lips twist. "Boys."

I huff. Yeah, I was a boy. Stupid. Inexperienced. Cocky.

"She talked about you most, though," he adds.

"She did?"

"We have the same hands."

"What?" I look down, turning my hands over, frowning. I've never really taken any notice of my hands. They're big. Capable. Can fire a gun with expert precision. And they can punch . . . hard.

Nolan holds his hands out, laying them on the desk. "Obviously we're kind of alike in features," he says. "But when I saw your hands, I just knew."

I stare at his hands on the desk, then at mine, back and forth. The width of our palms, the length of our fingers, the shape of our thumbs. "Well, I'll be damned," I whisper, taken aback. I look up at him, and he smiles. How the fuck did I not see this before? Even his teeth are the same as mine. His smile. The cheeky glint in his eyes. "You're a lot like me when I was your age."

"I am?"

"Yeah." I stand. "Fucking stupid." I pick up a pen and throw it at his head, and he ducks too late. It ricochets of his forehead and hits the desk. "We need to work on your stealth skills."

"I'm incapacitated," he protests, outraged, rising from the desk with too much effort. So I help him, and he stands on one leg before me, his gaze lifting up my chest until he has my eyes. I see tears in his. Feel them in mine.

Fucking hell.

I swallow down the lump in my throat and reach for his cheek, cupping it, nodding mildly. "Hey, son," I say quietly. "Nice to meet you."

Tears run down his cheeks, a small snivel escaping. "Hey . . . Dad?"

Dad? Fuck, I never thought I'd get that word tossed my way.

I haul him into my chest and hug the shit out of him, making sure he knows he's wanted, feeling an incredibly intense instinct to protect him. And an insane feeling of peace mixed with sorrow. I missed the first twenty years of his life. How will I ever make up for that? I've always had an inexplicable soft spot for the kid. Now, I can't help but think it was the universe talking to me. "You good?" I ask, keeping hold of him.

"Yeah, I'm good." He eases away from me, and I roughly wipe at his cheeks.

"Sit the fuck down," I say, pushing into his shoulder, watching him struggle to remain standing on one leg. He falls to the seat, and I prop myself back on the desk, lighting up as I answer a call from Otto.

"How'd it go?" I ask.

"You should buy a hat."

I smile. "Congratulations. What do you have for me?"

"I'm on my way to the boatyard. I'm dropping him off and leaving, okay?"

"Thanks." I hang up and get back to Nolan. "We need to talk about Ella," I say, blowing out the smoke over his head. "You know she can't keep working the stage, don't you?"

"I can't make her quit."

"You can and you will."

He looks up at me, alarmed. "It's all she knows."

"It's all she *knew*. Now she knows you, and you are my son. I can't have clientele drooling over my son's girlfriend." I stand. "Pearl's quit the bar, so Ella can fill for her."

"What? You'd do that for her?"

I study him for a moment, thinking. Then lower to the desk again. "You're serious about her?" I ask. "Because in this world, Nolan, you only take a woman if you're serious about her. And when I say serious, I mean a lifetime. Forever. You would die for her. Kill for her. You pull a woman into our world, you vow to protect her from it."

He nods, his face straight and serious, and I return it, rising from the desk again. "Don't go far. We have somewhere to go." I walk over to the door that leads up to the hidden office.

"Where?"

"It's a surprise. Now go get Ella off that stage." I push in the code and make my way up the stairs, the small space filled with clouds of my smoke. I relish it, pushing the door open. Danny's on the couch, a Scotch in his hand, James is at the window with a vodka, looking down on the club, and Ringo and Goldie are playing chess. Fucking chess. They both look up, hunched over the board.

Danny nods mildly, impressed by the state of me. I go to him. "Stand up."

He frowns, flicking questioning eyes to James, before slowly rising to his feet. I remove the glass of Scotch from his hand, holding it out, and James is quick to take it. "What the fuck are you doing?" Danny asks. "I was enjoying that."

I swing at him, cracking him on the jaw, trying to aim for an undamaged part of his face, but that's easier said than done given what his face has been through recently. The noise is piercing. He flies back, landing on the couch, his arms sprawled out, his face a picture of shock. "You ever lay a finger on my son again," I say calmly. "I'll fucking kill you."

He stares at me, slowly taking his hand to his mouth and wiping, licking his lip, tasting the blood. I've upset the old wound. He laughs under his breath in disbelief, then looks at me, and the slow formation of a smile spreads across his evil face. I put my hand out, he takes it, let's me pull him to his feet, and then drags me in for a manly hug.

"I'll take that on the chin," he says. "Literally."

James nods, showing rare happiness with a mild smile as I break away from Danny and sit. James's phone rings. "Otto." He answers and starts to roam the office. "Got it." He cuts the call. "The X5's been picked up."

I sit up straight. "Please don't say by the police."

He shakes his head. "The Russians. Otto's tracking it."

"Fuck, yes," Danny yells, taking his Scotch off the desk and necking it. Then his phone rings. "Higham," he says cheerfully, switching to loudspeaker. "Tell me you're back."

"I'm back."

"Excellent. I'm in a really good mood. Don't spoil it."

"I'll try. I'm at the boatyard. Just watched Otto manhandle some poor confused bastard into a green container."

"Who?" Danny asks, then turns his attention onto the room. "Anyone know who Otto's put in the green container?"

I raise my hand. "We'd better get to the boatyard."

• • •

We pull up and find Higham sitting on the hood of his car. He looks tired. Really fucking tired. "You're not looking like you've had much of a vacation," I say as I pass him.

"Who's in the container, Brad?"

"Yeah, who's in the container, Brad?" Danny asks.

"No one. You're seeing things, Higham." I point to the café. "I'll be there in a minute." I take Nolan's spare arm and help him toward the green container, looking back, seeing Danny's questioning face following us. But he doesn't demand an answer.

"What's going on?" Nolan asks, hobbling along next to me, using my arm for support.

"I have a gift for you."

"What?"

I open the container door and usher him inside, flicking on the lightbulb before closing the door behind me. I see the piece of shit on a chair, wrists and ankles bound with tape, his mouth gagged. He looks between us. Confused. I walk over and pull his gag down.

"Who the fuck are you?" he gasps.

"Don't worry about who I am." I pull my gun and point it at Nolan. "The cripple over there is who you should be concerned about."

Nolan looks at me, and I see the penny drop. "Oh," he breathes.

I nod, moving back, letting him take the stage while I screw the silencer onto my gun. "Have fun," I quip.

The poor fucker in the chair bats his eyes back and forth between us. "What's going on? Who are you?"

Nolan lifts his crutch and pushes the end into the guy's throat, forcing him back in the chair. "I know your ex."

His persona changes in an instant, a sneer crawling across his face. "She's not my ex."

"She has to be," Nolan says, smiling. "Since she's my girlfriend."

"What?"

"You heard."

"Fuck off. She's mine. She wouldn't dare."

I smile, unable to help myself, and pull my phone from my pocket, bringing up the video of Nolan fucking Ella. I can't watch it myself, can't even listen, so I turn the volume down—it felt wrong even before I knew Nolan was mine—and hold it in front of Ella's ex, just to torture the fucker, just to prove beyond all doubt in his stupid fucking mind that Ella is, in fact, not his. "You've got the moves, son," I say, amused when Nolan's eyes widen at me. A mild shake of his head. I pass him the gun. "Let's not drag this out."

He accepts, wedges it in the slime ball's kneecap, and blows it out. Poor thing screams to high heaven, looking like he's having a fit in the chair as his restrained body tries to cope with the pain. "Come near her again, I'll kill you," Nolan seethes.

"Not sure he'll be able to walk after this, son."

Nolan blows out his other knee and hops back, putting his weight on his crutch. Satisfied. Ella's ex dribbles and cries, yelps and screams. So I gag him again before someone comes to investigate the noise—namely the FBI agent outside.

I bend, looking at him. He's going to pass out, his head hanging, so I grab a fistful of his hair and pull his head up. "Bet you're full of regrets now, aren't you?" *Fucking bully.*

He can't answer.

I step back. "Finish him."

"What?" Nolan looks at me, shocked.

"Did he lay a finger on your woman?"

"Yes."

"Then kill him," I order, seeing a steeliness wash over Nolan's face. Understanding. I slap his shoulder and walk away, leaving him to finish the job, breaking out into the sunshine.

Dad.

Fuck. Me.

I wave Leon over as I delete the video from my phone and try to delete it from my head. "Clean up when he's done."

"Yes, B-Boss."

Going to the café, I grab a beer from the fridge, stalling when I see Ella sitting in the corner. I go over, take note of her eye, now not concealed with makeup. I lower to a seat. "He's a bit busy at the moment."

"Should I go?"

"No, stay." I point to the counter. "Get a drink, he won't be long."

"Where is he?" she asks, looking around.

"He's dealing with someone in the green container."

"Dealing with someone? Who?"

I tilt my head, and she inhales. "Cody, was it?"

"Yes."

"I'll tell you the same as I told my son," I say. "Once you're in this world, you don't leave it."

She sits back, her eyes resolute. "I love him."

I nod. "Give him fifteen." Getting up, I slurp my beer as I head to the others. "What did I miss?"

"What did *we* miss?" James asks, interested.

"A little father and son bonding by the sounds of it," Danny says. He's obviously called Otto.

"Something like that."

Danny's phone rings, and he rejects the call. "So, Higham, le—" It rings again. He rejects it again. "Let's get—" *Ring, ring.* "For the love of fucking *God.* Hello, darling," he says, sarcastic as fuck, a strained, gritted-teeth smile on his face as he gets up and starts to wander. His face falls. "What?" Then his eyes dart, and I feel an awful chill slither through my veins. "Okay." Danny hangs up, and we all look at each other, waiting. "Pearl's missing," he says quietly. But, my God, it's like someone screaming directly into my ear.

"Missing?" I say, hardly able to breathe. "What do you mean, missing? She was at home. Fury took her home."

"She's packed and gone."

My body won't move, my brain is struggling to compute this news. Gone. Packed and gone.

Why?

I get up, sit back down. *The Audi.* The black Audi.

Standing on unstable legs, I walk away, calling her cell. She doesn't pick up.

"You need to see this," Higham says, pulling my attention back to the table. He throws something down, and James picks it up, his face deadly. An envelope. He pulls something out, studying it.

I don't know what, and I really don't care right now. I walk up and down, trying to call Pearl. Nothing. No answer. *Fuck.* I dial Rose, lighting up, puffing anxiously. "Are all of her things gone?" I ask when she answers. "Everything?"

"No, not everything."

"So you might be overreacting? Worrying over nothing?"

"Then where is she?"

I don't know, but I'll be fucking savage if she's out in the city on her own.

"Brad," Danny says, his attention on the table.

"Wait a minute," I snap, going back to my call with Rose. "Can you go—"

"Brad," James yells.

"I said, wait! Rose—" My cell is suddenly missing from my ear, and I swing around, fuming. "For fuck's sa—" I slowly register everyone's expressions.

James inhales, sitting back in his chair, eyes on a picture on the table. "Bernard King," he says quietly.

I snatch my cell out of Danny's hand and walk over to the table, looking down at the image of the notorious London gangster. My heart slows. "What the fuck?" My cigarette hangs from my mouth, smoke billowing up into my face. It doesn't hamper my view.

Red.

I look up at the men. Then back down at the image to check I'm not seeing things. Bernard King. With Pearl.

How the hell—

What is she—

But . . .

She said she loved me. Why the fuck of all the things I could be thinking about am I thinking about that? *Because it was a lie.* Yet she never actually said those words.

No, she said she'd show me with her actions. She never *said* anything.

Lies.

All fucking lies. Everything starts to click into place. The Audi was him. She brought him to the mansion . . . the shoot-out . . .

That he got away from.

Her cue to get the fuck out of here? And she has.

What the fuck has she been feeding him?

More thoughts hit my brain. The drive-by. The incident out the back of the club where I thought I'd lost Nolan. *She wasn't hit by any of the bullets.*

My blood boils dangerously. I feel like I'm going to explode.

Leaving the men, I stalk into the changing room, feeling their eyes following me. *Breathe, Brad.* "Fuck!" I punch the locker repeatedly, and I only stop when my knuckles split and blood starts smearing the metal. "Fuck, fuck, fuck!" She's played me.

Made me look like a total fucking mug.

Gone.

And she's took my fucking heart and any scrap of sanity I had left with her.

Chapter 47

DANNY

I hear the sound of a fist meeting metals doors over and over and eventually stand to go stop him before he destroys the whole place.

I still when James reaches for my arm to halt me, shaking his head mildly. I don't listen to many people. James is one of the few I do. So I sit back down, eyes on the changing room door.

"How did you get these pictures?" James asks Higham.

"British intelligence. They're keeping an eye on King and want to know what he's doing in Miami."

I hum as another collection of bangs ring out from the changing room. "Thanks, Higham," I say quietly, looking at him. He doesn't want to be here for the next conversation. "Don't go far." He nods and leaves the table.

James raises a hand, frowning down at his phone. "The X5 has been taken to the warehouse bought by the Mexicans."

I shoot him a look. "Well, that settles the question mark hanging over that. The Russians and the Mexicans *are* collaborating."

"To take us down," James says, eyes like lasers on the table. "And they're getting their stock from King."

"And Pearl, fucking Pearl, has been sitting pretty here feeding them information on . . . what?" I close my eyes and inhale as more bangs come from the changing room. "I can't fucking think." Shooting up, I stalk away and barge into the changing rooms, and the moment I see him, I suck back the barrage of abuse that's loaded and ready to fire. He's on the bench, head in his hands. "What is this?" I ask. "The extreme reaction?"

Brad looks up at me, aghast. "She's a fucking mole."

"Or a honey trap," I muse, eyeing him. "Did the bee take the honey?"

His face screws up in disgust. "Fuck, no." He stands, hands in his hair, and I watch him walk circles around the changing room, sporadically cursing and hitting the lockers. James enters, obviously wondering why Brad's still hitting things when I came in to *stop* him hitting things.

I shake my head. I don't know what the fuck is going on. Brad's so fucking mad, and I have never seen him like this. Ever. I know he wanted to fuck Pearl. Fought his compulsion. Maybe that's why his head's spinning. He nearly took the bait. "Look, Brad, we have a few important problems to solve right now, and none of them include fixing your damaged ego." I see it coming a mile away.

His fist.

Toward my face.

I lean back, swerving it, and dive at his waist, taking him to the floor. "The fuck?" I roar, straddling him and firing a few right hooks. They should knock him out. Not Brad. His eyes demented, he launches himself upward and nuts me straight on the nose. Jesus Christ, not again. The pain radiates through my head and fogs my vision, and I fall back, cupping my bleeding face. "Fuck."

"Okay, I'm stepping in," James says, out of patience. He drags Brad up and pins him against the dented lockers, his finger in his face. "Do not make me go all Enigma on your arse, Brad. My mood's slipping by the minute." He slams him into the metal and turns his attention onto me. He doesn't have a chance to deliver the same warning. I hold my hand up in surrender, using my other to push into the floor and get myself to my feet, blood pouring from my nose. "Get your fucking shit together," James barks. "We've got the Russians, Mexicans, and now a power-tripping British psycho all plotting our demise, so your focus would be fucking appreciated." He storms out and slams the door.

Silence.

Except for our heavy breathing. I go to the towel cupboard and grab one, holding it to my nose and plonking my arse on the bench. "Sorry," I grunt.

"Sorry," Brad mutters back, dropping his arse next to mine. His cigarettes appear in my sight—his peace offering—and I accept, slipping one between my teeth. I wince, the cut stinging like a bitch. Brad lights us both up, and together we sit there, quiet, smoking our way back to calm.

I look across at him. His cheek is swollen, his eye already on its way to black. "Any idea what she's shared with them?" I ask.

"Why'd you think I'd know?"

I shrug. "Just asking." Getting up from the bench, I stub my smoke out in a nearby sink and drop it in the trash. "I have the small matter of Amber's body turning up to deal with."

Brad nods, distracted. Then he stands too. "I've got something I need to do." He walks out, and I follow him, frowning.

"Now?" I ask, catching the door before it shuts in my face. "What could you possibly need to deal with now?" He ignores me, keeping up his pace. "Brad! We kind of have a life-or-death situation here." I chase his heels out of the café and watch, astounded, as he gets in his car and drives off. "What the fuck is he playing at?" I march back into the café and dump my arse on a chair. "Amber," I bark at Higham.

He sighs. "Danny, listen to me."

"I'm listening, Higham." *So make it something I want to hear.*

"I cannot make a gunshot wound disappear from a dead body."

I snarl, tempted to grab his head and slam his face down on the table. But even I know a cop can't make a gunshot wound disappear. "Then what do you suggest?" I ask, drumming the table with my fingertips.

"I suggest you hope very hard that forensics can't find anything."

"Higham. That dead body will lead the police this way whether they find any evidence or not. She was the in-house whore my men used to fuck before she got herself a fiancé."

"From whore for mafia men, to fiancé of candidate for mayor? That's some leap up the status scale."

I glare at him, my eyes surely black.

"Sorry," he mutters.

"Tom Hayley is Beau's father, who was married to Jaz Hayley, who, as you know, just had more murders pinned on her than the Mexicans, Russians, Poles, and Romanians put together." I take a breath. "Don't know if you've noticed, but Beau Hayley leads to The Enigma, since she recently married him, and the police really want him, as well as me and Brad. So, Higham, I'm sure you can appreciate why I'm feeling . . . tense about this situation."

"So who killed her?" he asks flatly. I can only growl my warning. That, he will never know. Unless forensics can prove it, of course.

"It doesn't matter. They'll try to make anything stick."

He laughs. "Danny, if there's one thing I've learned about you, it's this—"

I raise my eyebrows, waiting.

"You're Teflon."

Maybe. But my wife isn't.

"May I?" Ringo asks, raising a hand. I nod, so he continues. "Do you have access to the body?"

I look at Higham, seeing his reluctance to answer. He inhales. "I do."

"Then I have the answer to your problem. Might kill two birds."

I cock a questioning look at Ringo, and James moves in, interested. "Go on."

I listen, nodding. Piecing it together. I'm also wondering where the fuck Brad has gone.

Chapter 48

PEARL

I drop my bag to the floor, rolling my aching shoulder, as I scan the screens in the station. Platform one. Leaving in twenty minutes. I look down at the bag at my feet that virtually contains my whole life. It's as heavy as my heart feels.

I hoof it up and trudge outside to have a cigarette before boarding.

Leaving.

Nowhere to go, no idea where I'm sleeping tonight. But at least I'll still be alive. And Brad, the men, the girls, and the children will all be safe from the repercussions of unknowingly harboring me for months.

I pray.

I walk to the end of the building and drop my bag again, lighting up and leaning against the wall, sliding down the concrete until I'm crouched. The heat kicking off the stone behind me is intense. So intense, I'm forced to stand again and move away.

I pull my phone from my shorts pocket, contemplating texting him. Apologizing for deceiving him. For lying. But what's the point? I can't be with Brad and no apologies or words will change that. It was a dream. Story of my fucking life.

I slip my phone back into my pocket but freeze when something occurs to me. "Idiot," I whisper to myself, pulling it back out and staring at the illuminated screen. "Stupid, *stupid* idiot." I scan the area in front of me, spotting a Chevy waiting by the pick-up area, the rear window open. I approach and dip, smiling at the driver, a friendly looking lady with long, blonde curly hair and green-framed glasses. "Hi. Do you know how far it is to MIA?"

"Oh, maybe a half hour on the bus. A bit faster on the train." She smiles past me. "Elise!"

"Mom!"

I turn around, seeing a young girl running toward the car.

Dragging a backpack. I put my hand behind me, tactically keeping my back to the car while the lady jumps out of the driver's side and runs around the front, embracing the girl. Mother and daughter.

"Oh, how I've missed you," she sobs into her daughter's neck. I can feel the strength of her hug from simply observing. And feel my heartache at the same time. I never had the chance to grieve the loss of my mother. I was too terrified, too focused on staying alive. Avoiding pain as best I could.

Then Brad Black found me, and for the first time since she died, I felt safe. Cherished. The mother and daughter before me blur as my eyes well. But I can see they're still cuddling.

• • •

I turn the doorknob, pushing my way into the bathroom, the sound of running water now deafening. I step in, looking down at my bare feet on a frown. Water. The whole floor is an inch deep in water. "Mum?" I say quietly, an odd uneasy feeling swirling in my tummy. I find the roll-top, claw-foot tub in the bay window. Water is pouring over the edge, the tap still running. I step through the water, lifting my nightdress up from my ankles, slowly getting closer to the tub. But something inside holds me back from taking that final step to see over the edge. My heart pounds, so much I'm sure I might cough it up.

I inhale some bravery, moving forward. Inside the tub slowly comes into view.

Her face isn't one I will ever forget. Eyes open. Staring up at the ceiling. Completely submerged.

"Mum," I whisper. She's naked.

And in her hand beneath the water, is her necklace.

• • •

I blink, holding up my unfinished cigarette, then I look over my shoulder. The lady and her daughter are still hugging. I drop my phone into the back of the car and go to a nearby bench, lowering. Finishing my cigarette.

• • •

"You want to have a bath?" I ask, instantly troubled. "I'm not sure I can."

"Pearl, you can do anything in the world that you want to," Brad says gently, sitting me by the sink. I look at the bath with narrowed eyes, hearing the sound of water pouring over the edge. "I've got you."

. . .

He's got me.

I had a bath for the first time in eight years. I listened to water running from a tap and made myself sustain it. Because he was there.

I hardly have the strength past my sob to take one last drag of my cigarette. But I try. Tasting Brad Black, Scotch, and his skin. I flick the butt away, my shoulders jumping from the effort to suppress my sobs, My eyes sting. Every single face I've come to know and love flashes through my mind, one after the other. Even the bloody dogs.

I sniff back my sadness, my reel of reminders finishing on the clearest face of all.

My love.

Chapter 49

Brad

"What's happened?" Otto asks down the line as I speed away from the boatyard. "Jesus Christ, I take a few hours off, and all hell breaks loose."

"I'll fill you in soon." I overtake a truck that's chugging along at a painstakingly slow speed. "I need you to get your laptop out and check the tracker on Pearl's phone."

"For fuck's sake, Brad, I'm trying to create a romantic, memorable day for Esther and all I've done is serve as your bitch. I just got back from dropping your last request off at the boatyard."

"Please, Otto," I beg. "It's important." I want answers, and I want them from Pearl. Her words, her mouth. I hear him muttering and cursing, a few thuds, a door closing, a lock engaging. He's in the bathroom. Probably naked.

"She's at Miami Station. Why is Pearl at Miami Station, Brad?"

"I said I'd fill you in s—"

"No, wait. She's moving away from Miami station."

Fuck! "Find out which train."

"I don't think she's on a train. In a car, I think. Or on a bus."

"Why would she go to Miami Station and then drive away from Miami Station?"

"I don't fucking know, Brad. I have a tracker on her phone, not a spy camera."

I should've had him put a fucking spy camera on her phone. "I'll call you back." I hang up and call Pearl, swerving through the traffic.

"Hello?" someone says, someone I don't recognize.

I frown. "Who's that?"

"This is Geraldine."

"Why do you have . . . my friend's phone?"

"I don't know!" She laughs. "I just found it on the back seat when I stopped for some gas outside the train station."

I glare at the windshield.

The little fucker.

Chapter 50

PEARL

I wrestle with my bag, trying to push it up onto the overhead rack, puffing and panting.

"Want some help?"

I look back, arms still in the air, bag still wedged against the edge of the rack, a few inches shy of actually being *on* the shelf. A tall guy in sports pants and a baseball tank smiles at me, reaching up, and he practically flicks my bag into place.

"Thanks," I say, smiling awkwardly and shuffling into a seat at a table.

"Mind?" he asks, motioning to one of the chairs opposite.

I smile again, not engaging. I don't want to talk or smile. I look across to the double seats. I should have taken one of those, leaving minimal scope for chatty strangers to bother me. I'd look really rude if I stand now and move. Do I care? No. But the man pulls out an iPad and some earbuds, getting himself set up, and I settle again when he opens a can of Pepsi Max. The hiss melds with the sound of the doors of the train closing. I look at them, then up at the speakers as the driver announces our departure, settling back in my seat, turning my gaze to the platform outside the window as the train starts to pull away.

Goodbye, Miami.

Goodbye, freedom.

Goodbye, Brad.

I sniff and wipe my nose, my body heavy in the seat. It's for the best. I have to keep telling myself that. Leave so he has no reason to bother Brad or any of the others. All people I've become so attached to. Love. I swallow down my emotion.

"Excuse me," a man says.

I shoot my eyes toward the voice, my heart racing up to my throat.

Brad's standing in the aisle, suited, my phone in his hand. A mild sheen of sweat coats his forehead. His face is a mess of bruises. What the hell happened? And why the hell is he here? "You dropped this."

He smiles. It's not a smile I like. "Through the back window of an old Chevy outside the station." He places it down carefully on the table. "Oops."

I stare at my phone, my mind a blank mess.

"You don't mind if I take your seat, do you." It's not a question, and I peek up at the guy opposite me. He's staring at Brad, his eyebrows arched.

"You're welcome to join us," he says, motioning to the two empty seats in the group of four.

Brad seems to inhale some patience, and I will the stranger to be wise and just move. "I don't think you heard me right." Brad reaches to the back of his trousers, and I shrink down into the seat, worried, anxious, stressed. He pulls his gun and scratches his temple with the end. "Move."

"Whoa, dude, I'm out of here." The guy laughs over his words, scrambling up and not only leaving his seat, but leaving the carriage too.

I watch Brad lower to the outside chair, pull the tails of his suit jacket out from under his arse, and shuffle across the small space so he's in the window seat opposite me. I can see the unbridled rage he's trying to keep a lid on. "Going somewhere nice?" he asks, laying his gun on the table. It's so fucking passive aggressive.

"Are you going to kill me?" I ask frankly, my jaw tense as I look at him. Steel in my expression. Strength in my voice. He told me he loved me only a few hours ago, although it feels like weeks since I was in bed with him this morning. And now he's going to kill me?

He flies across the table, the gun in his hand, and pushes it into my forehead, breathing in my face. Out of control. Completely.

"I will fucking kill you, Pearl."

"What for?" I ask calmly. "Lying to you? Or for sleeping with you? Or," I murmur, my eyes searching his, "will you shoot me because you love me?"

He scoffs, easing up on the pressure of his gun on my skin. "I don't fucking love you."

Child. "Of course. Because the big, bad Brad Black can't love anyone, least of all a twenty-one-year-old virgin."

He slams his fist down on the table, and I jump, despite expecting his anger. "You lied to me!"

"Just let me leave, Brad," I say quietly. "Trust me." I can make this right as long as no one knows about Brad and me.

"Trust you?" His gun is thrust forward, and I lean back in my seat, looking at the end of it. "I just saw a picture of you with Bernard fucking King, and you want me to trust you?"

I try to hide my surprise. Why would anyone show Brad a picture of me with him? And how the hell does Brad know who he is? My mind spins.

But my mouth remains closed. Brad will never get the truth from me. I will never be that pathetic to him.

"So you're a mole," he says with nothing but pure venom in his voice.

"What? No!"

"Don't lie to me!" he bellows, sending me farther back in my seat, shocked.

Even at his grumpiest, his cruelest moments, he has never looked at me like he's looking at me now. As if he despises me.

"I'm not a mole, Brad." I shuffle across the seat to get out and get precisely nowhere.

Brad dives over the table and holds me in place. "Stay where the fuck you are."

I blink, stunned, faced with a very different man to the soft, gentle, patient guy I've encountered recently. His fleeting look of shame doesn't lessen my hurt.

"Was it him who sent the guy looking for you at the club?" he asks.

I don't say anything, because nothing I say will change anything. "Just let me go," I beg. "He doesn't want you or Danny or James. He only wants me."

Brad blinks, a million questions staring back at me. "What the fuck aren't you telling me?" he asks. I swallow, looking away. "Pearl, answer me."

I don't answer him. I never want to share that part of my life. Truly, I would rather die, so whether he shoots me or not is of no consequence to me. If Brad knows, he will without question cut his losses and send me back.

"God damn it, talk! What the fuck were you doing with King?"

"Let me leave," I whisper.

"Pearl, fucking look at me." He reaches across the table and grabs my jaw, yanking my face toward his. I hold my tears back and bite my tongue. "What the fuck is wrong with you?" he whispers as I stare at him, empty. Disconnecting. I have no choice.

"Excuse me, sir," a man says quietly, as if making a point of Brad's noise level.

"What?" Brad slides his gun off the table and aims. The poor man backs up, hands up, and falls back to his seat a few rows down before scrambling up and dashing off to the next carriage. "God help me, Pearl."

"Let me go," I whisper.

"No."

"Yes," I croak. "I—" My mobile rings on the table and my eyes drop to the screen. A private number.

"Answer it." Brad stares at me. I shake my head, and Brad growls, snatching it up and accepting the call, switching to loudspeaker, remaining silent.

"Hello, pumpkin." The voice sends shivers down my spine, has me closing my eyes and swallowing. I can't stop my shakes. And when I open my eyes, Brad is watching my silent meltdown.

He cuts the call. "King?"

I just stare at him, the chain of events about to unfold truly terrifying me.

"Talk to me!" Brad's expression goes from angry to psycho in a heartbeat. He stands and moves to the aisle, yanking my bag off the shelf above.

"What are you doing?" I ask as he grabs my hand and pulls me out. "Brad, stop, just let me go."

He doesn't speak. Just pulls me through the carriages toward the front.

"Brad, please."

His grip tightens.

"Brad!"

He walks on, dragging me with him, and I feel the train starting to slow down. I stagger forward, and Brad catches me in his side, holding me by the nearest doors, and the moment the train stops, he hits the button to open the door. They slide open on a hiss, he steps out, pulling me out too, and then he looks down at me.

"I'm going to kill him, Pearl, whether you tell me anything or not. Don't make me kill you too."

"Then kill me." Because death is certainly better that returning to my hell. And that's exactly what's going to happen when Brad and the others find out the truth.

I'll be sent back.

My calm order seems to ramp up his anger. "Maybe I fucking will."

My time is up.

Chapter 51

DANNY

Higham drops a small, clear bag on the table, and everyone leans forward to inspect the contents. "Is that a lump of hair?" Goldie asks, grimacing.

"With a bit of scalp attached," Ringo says, pointing to the small chunk of flesh on the end of the strands.

"She wasn't a natural blonde," Goldie adds.

"No shit," Ringo muses, truly blown away. "I always thought she was."

I look up at the pair tiredly. "Are you two done?"

They both sit back, and Higham leaves. "Just let me know where the evidence will be," he calls.

I slide the bag over to Ringo. "Make sure you don't contaminate it and put yourself in the frame."

"Don't worry." Goldie whips out a pair of rubber gloves. "I've got his back."

James smiles, raising his phone to his ear. Growls, cuts the call, and dials again. "God damn it."

"What?" I ask.

"All I ask is that she answers when I call her." He starts bashing out a text. "Did Rose lose the ability to answer her phone when she was pregnant?"

I chuckle, leaving James to try and get hold of Beau as I dial Brad again, wandering out into the sunshine. He doesn't answer. "Where the fuck is he?" I dump my arse on a chair and light up.

"Here."

I look over my shoulder and find *him* on the threshold of the veranda.

With Pearl.

And she's alive.

I slowly stand, eyes batting back and forth between them, smoke leaving my mouth on my exhale. Is either of them going to speak? Apparently not, but Brad jerks his head, an order to go inside. So I go. Curious. "Goldie," Brad says, looking at Pearl, a silent order to watch her. He thinks she'll bolt? He lowers to a chair at the table, joining James and Ringo, looking as stressed as I've ever known him to look.

"Where did you find her?" James asks, appearing unusually worried.

"On a train heading out of Miami." Brad picks up the packet of Marlboros on the table and lights up. "She's not saying much."

"And you haven't tortured her for information?" I ask.

He lifts his eyes while he holds the flame at the end of his smoke, sucking. He's warning me. I'll take it. "King called her on her cell."

"The cell Otto supplied?" James asks.

"Yes."

"The one you had a tracker put on?" I ask casually. Because how else did he find her?

"Yes, that one."

"And why did you have a tracker put on Pearl's phone?"

He snarls. "Because I was suspicious."

"Why?"

"Because a man showed up at the club looking for her."

"Who?"

"She said her family sent him. Something about her father's estate. Her parents weren't murdered in a burglary. Her father died in a drunk-driving accident."

"So she lied?"

"Yes," he grates, every question being thrown at him being answered with a tight jaw.

James's hand appears in midair before us, distracting us both. Winning our attention. "Can we ask how King got Pearl's mobile phone number if Otto gave her the new phone?"

I raise my brows. Brad maintains his fixed glare. "What happened to her old mobile?" I ask.

"She said she dropped it."

I rest back, wondering, thinking. "Why won't she talk?"

"Is she scared?" James asks.

"Of whom?" I ask. "King?" That infuriates me. "She should be fucking scared of *us*." I rise slowly from the table, and Brad's eyes follow me up. "If she's set us up, she has to die. Simple. So are you going to fix this, or am I?"

Brad stubs out his smoke on the tabletop and gets up. I take that as his answer, and he stalks off toward Pearl.

"What's he not telling us?" I muse, not liking his lack of talking or emotion.

"What did I miss?" Otto asks, breezing into the café, all smiles. Makes me want to knock it off his face.

"Pearl ran," James says. "But you already knew that, because Brad called *you* to track her." Both of us hold Otto in place with accusing eyes. It doesn't faze him. "King called her on her cell after Brad found her on a train. She won't talk." At that moment, a bang rings out, and we all look toward Brad and Pearl, seeing his fist balled on the table and her back pressed into the back of the chair. Fuck, he looks livid. Good. So am I.

"How'd King get her number?" Otto asks, opening up his laptop.

"That's what we'd like to know." It could be as simple as Pearl gave it to him. It would be pretty fucking dumb of her, but I've got nothing else. "Anything on the bug on mine?"

"Nothing."

I pout across the table at him. "Do I get to call you Stepdaddy yet?"

"Fuck off."

James smiles, getting up and going to the fridge, collecting some beers. Beers and brainstorming. What the fuck is going on? "We pulled her out of a hangar at Winstable, for fuck's sake," I mutter, my head hurting.

"Could have been planted to get in on the Poles," Ringo muses.

"But why?" I scowl toward the decking.

"Or maybe she was planted to get in on *us*," he adds.

"What does King want with us?"

"If he's working with the Russians and Mexicans, maybe Pearl was his in. Someone on the inside to feed information to King who in turn feeds it to Sandy and Luis."

"His *in* is supplying them. He doesn't need Pearl spying on us. She needs to start talking."

"Or else?" James asks, looking at me expectantly. "For fuck's sake, Danny." He slams a beer down and pulls his phone out when it chimes. "Ah. She knows I'm alive." He scowls. "They're at the salon."

I growl. "What does my wife not understand when I say *don't* leave the fucking house?" She better not argue with me when I put my foot down about St. Lucia. I check out on the veranda. "How long do we give them?" I ask, getting up and going to the doors. Brad's sitting opposite Pearl, arms on the table, looking way too patient for my liking. I give him a gesture, like, well? He shakes his head. "For fuck's sake." I go back to the table and sit. Be patient, be patient.

"Hello, hello," Ringo says. "What's he doing back?" We all look over our shoulder. Higham's marching across the café. I don't like the expression on his face.

"Did you miss us?" I ask as Brad appears at the door, interested in Higham's unexpected arrival too.

Higham doesn't answer, coming to a stop at the table. I lift a beer. He looks like he needs one. "You have a problem."

I glance at James. James glances at me. Brad keeps his eyes on Higham. "I'm not sure I like the use of the word *you* in that sentence," I say. Why not *we* have a problem?

"And what's the problem?" Brad asks.

"The redhead in the picture," Higham looks between us. "I assume, given your reaction to the photo of her with King, you know her."

"She was one of the girls we got out of Winstable," James says, as the tension around the table grows. He points to where Pearl is sitting, and Higham looks.

"Oh Jesus," he breathes. "You still have her?" He laughs. Then blows out his cheeks. "Fucking hell."

"Talk, Higham," Brad says, his body rolling with his forced deep breaths. "Or I'll rip your fucking throat out, I swear to God."

"King sold her to the Poles," he says, raking a hand through his hair. I look at Brad. His eyes are black. *Sold* her? "For one hundred million dollars."

"The fuck?" I blurt.

"One hundred million?" James asks, and Higham nods dementedly.

I release a disbelieving puff of air, falling back in my chair.

"Jesus. That's some price tag."

"Look, I do not need this shit in Miami, boys," Higham goes on. "So just give the girl back to King and let him go on his merry way back to the green pastures of England."

"He sold her," I muse. What does he care where she is now? It doesn't make any sense. "Do we know if King's *actually* had any contact with Sandy or Luis?" We've assumed. We could be wrong.

James shakes his head as everyone else looks at each other, waiting for someone to confirm whether there's hard evidence. Have we been barking up the wrong tree?

"What does it matter?" Higham laughs, the sound full of panic. "Everyone wins. The Russians and Mexicans won't take you on with no arms, will they? And they can't get any arms without King. So Miami remains peaceful." He claps. "The end."

Send Pearl back to King. The end, except it goes against everything I stand for. Just ask my wife. James rolls his eyes. Brad remains a statue by the door. "Okay," Higham says, looking at us all. "Okay. Great. I'll leave you to make the arrangements. I'll be off."

Higham leaves, and no sooner is his arse out of the cabin, James's phone is ringing. Unknown number. We all stare at it for a few moments before he hits the accept button. Silence.

Then a low, booming British accent. "Good evening, I'm wondering if you can help me."

I frown to myself. "I'll try," James says.

"I'm looking for The American one."

We all look at Brad.

"And The Brit."

All attention points my way.

"And The Enigma."

Then to James.

"Who's asking?" I lean over the phone, noting Otto working furiously across the keys of his laptop. Trying to locate the caller.

"Me. I'm asking," he says, laughing lightly. Lightly but psychotic. "Because I understand you have something that belongs to me."

"And what would that be?" I ask.

"Pretty little redhead. You see, I made a deal with someone, and because of your interference, the deal has gone tits up." *Interference.* We took the girls from the hangar. "I haven't been paid. The buyer is waiting for their bride."

Oh fuck, he's not got his money. *That's* why he's here, and I bet Sandy and Luis have taken the greatest delight in telling King where he can find Pearl. Struck a deal with him that gets them the guns they need to take us down, while getting King his pretty little redhead back.

"Bride?" James coughs.

"Yes, bride. Give her back, and I might not supply your Russian and Mexican friends with enough ammunition to kick off a world war."

And there we have it. He's their supplier.

"Is that where you got my number?" James asks. "From our *friends*?"

King starts laughing. It's a knowing laugh. Can't say I like it. "Return her."

"I'm curious," I say, assessing Brad again, seeing a man on the edge. "One hundred million?"

"Rich, depraved men with too much money will pay up to two hundred," he drawls, "for a virgin."

What the fuck? The temperature in the room drops to sub-zero, all eyes bugging.

"They like to get a lead on them, you see," King goes on. "Train them young. Make sure they know who their master is. Break them in just right."

I can't talk. Can hardly swallow.

"You don't want to fuck with me," King says candidly. "I eat men like you for breakfast. Return my virgin." He hangs up, and I slump back, astounded.

"She's a virgin," I breathe, looking at Brad. *Fuck.* I didn't see *that* coming.

Brad seems to come round from his daze, looks at us all, then walks off, going into the men's changing room.

James gets up and follows him, and, of course, I do too. I walk in behind James, and we find Brad on the bench. I know what's running through his head. "I bet you're thanking your lucky fucking stars you resisted temptation, mate, because I don't even want to consider the consequences if King doesn't get his one-hundred-million-dollar virgin back." We could take on the Russians, even the Russians and the Mexicans together, but add King, his arsenal, and his love of explosives into the mix? Yeah. I don't mind admitting that we'd be biting off more than we could chew. "This is fucked up," I say, laughing. "Everything we believe in, my own personal integrity, being put into question, but I don't see what other options we have." I look at Brad. I've never seen his eyes so fucking wild. "It's Pearl or it's all of us."

Chapter 52

BRAD

James and Danny are watching me. Assessing me. Trying to figure out what the fuck is going on in my head. They'd never guess.

He doesn't want you or Danny or James. He only wants me.

Leave.

I should get Pearl and leave. But I know if I did that, the whole family would still be exposed. In danger. For the first time in our lives, we are out of our depths. And I can't even be sorry. Would I change things if I knew then what I know now?

No.

Not a thing.

"It could be worse," Danny quips, almost laughing. It's a nervous laugh. One I have never heard on The Brit.

"How?" I ask, looking up at him. "How could this be any worse, Danny?"

"Well, you could have fucked her." He laughs louder, uneasy, and looks at James. He's not laughing. I'm not laughing. And when Danny registers that, his amusement slowly fades until his expression is nothing but worried. "Brad," he says quietly. "Tell me you haven't fucked her." There's an unmistakable pleading edge to his tone. "*Please*, tell me you haven't fucked Pearl."

I inhale and drop my eyes to my feet. "I can't."

"Oh fuck," he breathes, dropping to his ass to the nearby bench.

"Shit." James turns into the lockers, pushing his head to the metal.

"You fucked a virgin?" Danny asks, the disbelief in his tone cutting.

"I didn't fucking know." I grind the words out, my fists balling.

"She didn't tell you?" He gasps. "That's need-to-know information. She fucking tricked you." He stands. "She fucking led you on and got the small issue of her virginity out of the way so King wouldn't want her back, and you, you dumb fuck, fell for it!"

I'm up like a rocket, and I slam him into the lockers, snarling in his face, but before I can swing at him, James is between us, arms extended, keeping us at a safe distance from each other. "Enough," he yells.

"You're talking like it would make a difference if she wasn't a virgin," I seethe. Has he forgotten how he met his wife? "Either way, we are not sending her back to him." Over my dead fucking body. And that's possible.

"Yes, we fucking are," Danny bellows.

"No, Danny. We're not."

"For fuck's sake," James roars. "Cut it out!"

"Why, Brad?" Danny shouts, fighting James's hold to get to me. His scar is so fucking deep, his temper lost. "Why aren't we sending her back?"

"Because," I roar.

"Because what?"

"Because I fucking love her!" I yell, shoving James away and staggering back a few paces. "Because I fucking love her, and it's fucked up, and my head is fucking spinning, but I fucking love her." I take a few breaths, exhausted by my outburst, raking a hand through my hair, stressed. She told me she wasn't a mole. I didn't believe her. *Couldn't* because I was so filled with rage. But mixed with that rage was a burning love. I wasn't letting her run away from me without an explanation. I would *not* be made a fool of. Manipulated. But now? I feel sick. So fucking sick. "I fucking love her," I breathe. "And I can't change that. So, no, we are not sending her back." I take a few deep breaths, try to appear calm amid this absolute carnage. "We have to find another way."

James observes me sweating and shaking, and Danny straightens himself out. Curls his lip at me. "Of course we find another fucking way, you dumb fuck." He pushes James aside and hauls me into his chest, hugging me. "For fuck's sake. How the fuck is she a virgin at twenty-one?" he asks himself. I don't even want to know. But I know I need all the information I can get. Danny shoves me away and starts to pace. "For the record, do not try to keep shit like this from me again."

Well, that won't be happening because I don't plan on falling in love with anyone else. What a fucking mess. But my relief? I should have trusted Danny and James. Trusted they would hear me. And he *knew*. "I need to speak to her," I say, backing out of the changing rooms.

"You need to get her to talk," James says.

Except she's mute right now. I need to get my head on straight and start figuring some shit out. I leave them and go back to Pearl, sitting opposite her, placing both of my hands on the table. She studies them for a moment before she looks up at me, her eyes full of tears. And past the tears, fear. And past the fear? Resignation. She's sat here doubting me. And I deserve it. Doesn't lessen the pain, though. "I know Bernard King sold you to the Polish," I say. "I know virgins get higher prices, and I know he hasn't been paid because we took you from Winstable." She just stares at me. "Pearl, please, fill in the blanks for me."

"Are you going to send me back?"

"God, no. No, never. Do you think I would? Is that why you ran?"

"I realize it's not only you in this family, Brad. I'm just little me and all your problems will be solved if you send me back."

"They wouldn't be solved, Pearl, because if I send you back, I lose you. And that is *not* an option."

Her lip wobbles. I can't stand seeing her like this. It's the young woman I found on the dirty mattress all those months ago. But more scared. More vulnerable. I stand, moving around the table, and pull her up from the chair, cocooning her in my arms. Her heart pulses into my chest. "I knew I had to leave here," she says into my shirt. "But I didn't want to leave you."

"You should have trusted me. Talked to me." I kiss her hair, clenching my eyes closed, knowing I'm going to hear things I'm not sure I can deal with.

"I was going to tell you at dinner. But then he followed me and Fury, and I was so scared. I know he just wants me, his money, his deal, so I-I—"

"Shhhh," I say.

"I thought if I left it would solve the problem."

I pull her away and hold her by the tops of her arms. "You're not going anywhere."

"But . . ." she whispers.

"Over my dead body," I grate as she stares at me, her face an unbearable picture of anxiety. "You need to talk to me, Pearl. Tell me everything." I don't know much right now. But I do know that Bernard King is going to die a long, ugly, painful death.

Chapter 53

DANNY

"That was really fucked up," James says.

"Quit complaining." I know Brad. He's his own worst enemy. I got the information we needed. My God, this day, though? "I need another beer. And a smoke." And when I get home, a really big cuddle. My phone rings, reminding me that my wife isn't at home waiting for me. Of course she isn't at home waiting for me. "Alan?" I answer in question.

"Yeah, hi, Danny." He sounds tentative. "I don't know how to tell you this."

I roll my eyes. "What's she up to now?" God love that woman, she's a trier.

"The spa just blew up."

My smoke stops halfway to my mouth, and I feel the blood physically drain from my face. "What?"

"I just got here. Hardly had one foot out of the car. I'm telling you, the explosion knocked me back ten feet."

"Alan." My Marlboro drops from my fingers, my collar tight around my neck. "Can you see Tank's car in the parking lot?"

"I haven't looked."

"Then fucking look!" I bellow, raking a stressed hand through my hair.

James is up in my face like a shot, his psycho eyes demanding answers. "The salon just blew up."

"Fuck, no," he breathes. "No!" He rushes out of the café and down the steps, and I follow, my heart beating frantically.

"Baby?"

I skid to a stop.

Turn.

See Rose on the shore, Maggie held to her front. She looks me up and down. "We're paddling," she says quietly.

I see Beau beyond, up to her knees in the water, her face worried. "What's going on?" she asks.

"Oh my God." My phone slips from my hand, my legs failing

me, and I fold to the floor in a heap of relief as James wades into the water and claims Beau, taking her in his fierce hold. My head hangs. My skin is cold. "Fuck," I whisper, trying to calm my shakes. I should have manhandled her onto the fucking jet.

I eventually look up at Rose. She's staring at me with an expression that I hate on my wife. Knowing. Preparation. She pulls Maggie in closer and kisses her head, eyes on me. A silent message.

She's had her freedom. She better not fight me on what she knows is coming.

I get up and go to her, wrapping an arm around her and walking her into the café.

"What's going on?" Brad asks, appearing with Pearl tucked into his side.

"The spa just blew up," I say, feeling Rose's shocked eyes hit me from her place under my arm.

And when my phone rings, my recovering heart drops again. Unknown number. He's called Pearl. James. Now me. But my phone rings off before I can answer, and another rings. Brad's. Then that stops and another rings. I turn my eyes onto Beau as she looks down at her screen.

"Unknown number," she says.

Rose's phone starts ringing from her bag. "Who is that?"

"Jesus fucking Christ," Otto mutters from his laptop. He's thinking what I'm thinking. My number, James's, Brad's, yes. But our wives? How the fuck did he get those numbers?

Ringo's phone starts, and Brad moves in, holding up his hands for Ringo to pass it. He throws it, and Brad catches and connects the call. "You've made your point," he says in answer, holding the phone out for us all to hear.

"Have I?" King asks. "You mean the salon and the musical ringing tones worked?"

"It worked."

"Oh, then I suppose I should have left your son alone."

Every face swivels in various directions.

Looking for Nolan.

Where the fuck is he?

"Like I said. I want her back. Virginity intact. Then you can have your son." He hangs up.

Chapter 54

PEARL

My hands go to my mouth, my lungs burning with the sudden effort it's taking to breathe. "Send me back," I demand. "Send me back, send me back." I feel the tears coming, and I look around at the people who have shown me nothing but kindness. The women, mothers, and Beau's pregnant. I can't allow this. "Send me back!" I turn into Brad, fisting the front of his suit jacket with my hands. He's a statue. Blank as he looks down at me. This is all my fault. I shouldn't have stayed. I should have left sooner. I should never have accepted their shelter, their safety.

Brad blinks, his long eyelashes fluttering. And he seems to come back into his body. His soft, vacant gaze slips away, and in its place, a terrifying expression. Fearsome. Apoplectic. He blankets my fists with his hands and detaches them from his suit, and Beau moves in, taking me from him as the men fly into action. Brad takes his phone to his ear, a wrathful scowl on his face. "Nolan's been taken. Get everyone out of the club now and take all the stock to the house. Guns *and* money." He hangs up. "Where the fuck is Ella?" he yells, walking out onto the veranda. I watch him look across to the containers. "Fuck," he curses, dashing back through the cafe, James following.

Danny goes to a stunned Rose. "Home," he orders in a tone she'd never challenge. She nods and Danny goes after the others as Beau walks me down the steps to the cars.

"Fuck!" Brad roars, disappearing inside the green container. He appears a few seconds later with Ella draped across his arms.

"Oh my God," I whisper, trying to break out of Beau's hold.

"No, Pearl, we have to go," she snaps, hauling me on, her strength far greater than mine, even pregnant. And of course, I don't fight her because of that. "She'll be okay."

"She's breathing," Brad says, carrying her to a car. "Someone get Doc on standby." Fury opens the back door to a Mercedes and helps Brad place Ella in the back as Rose loads Maggie into the other car. Beau gets her phone out and makes a call, walking my useless, dazed body to another car.

"Doc," she says urgently. "We need you back at the house." She helps me into the back of the car and closes the door, running back to James and taking his forearms, looking up at him. I don't know what she says. But the way he's looking at her? Anger. Love. Hate. He dips and lets her kiss his cheek before turning her around and sending her back toward me. Danny's quiet. Observing. A face that's frankly terrifying as he pushes bullets into the magazine of his gun, a cigarette held between his lips. All of them. Like robots. A button pressed. No longer husbands, friends, and fathers.

They're killers.

Unlawful Men.

And I'm scared.

Brad rejoins the others, and James smacks his back lightly, talking. He looks back at me sitting in the car, stares hard. And yet it's soft. "I love you," he mouths, and my heart cracks, my hand taking on a mind of its own and opening the door. I get out and go to him, and he turns, giving me access to his chest, letting me walk into his body and bury my face under his chin, unconcerned by the spectators.

"I don't want this," I whisper.

"You don't want me?"

"Yes, I want you," I say, remaining in his neck, the smell of him, his heat, soothing me. "I don't want everyone put at risk because of me. I love you all too much. Give me back to him." I feel Brad's body solidify. His chest expands.

"Didn't you hear him, Pearl? Virginity *intact*. So even if that was an option and, to be crystal fucking clear, it really *fucking* isn't, it's not happening." I close my eyes. "I took your virginity, Pearl." He pushes his face into my hair, and I hear a collection of quiet gasps behind me.

"I gave it to you," I grate. "He'll never know."

Brad pulls me free of his body and cups my cheeks, getting his face close to mine. "What did I tell you?"

"That you love me?" I ask as he looks into my eyes, his thumbs stroking across my cheeks.

"I do love you, but not that." He pushes his mouth to my forehead and breathes onto my skin. "I told you no one else would ever touch you again."

Such glorious words. I want to believe them. A huge part of me knows that if there is anyone in this world who can keep me safe from that monster, it's Brad. It's these men. But at what cost? He's taken Nolan. Blown up the spa. "If you run," Brad says. "I'll bring you back, Pearl." He looks up over my head, and I stare at his rough neck. "Take her back to the house."

"And what about you? What are you doing?"

"Take her."

Urgency pumps into my blood. "No." I don't like this. "What are you going to do?" Brad releases me, and I feel so pathetic without him holding me up. Holding me at all.

"Pearl, come on," Beau says, encouraging me away. Short of clinging to Brad's suit and begging him, I have no choice but to go. "It's going to be okay."

How can she say that? How? I search Brad's face as I'm guided back to the car. It's no longer soft. There's no love.

Only hate.

And I am the most terrified I have ever been.

I drop into the back of the car and stare at the head rest.

Pumpkin.

• • •

I feel his rough hand rest over my nape, holding me, as I stare at my mother's coffin being lowered into the ground. Birds tweet. The leaves on the trees rustle in the breeze. It's a sunny day, whereas it feels like it should be raining. Dark. Desolate.

Like how I feel.

Why did she do it? How could she leave me?

"Don't be sad, pumpkin," he says, his cigar smoke making clouds before me. "She's with your daddy now."

"And what about me?" I ask, almost scared to know. For three years, Mother protected me from him. She was the barrier between him and me.

And now she's gone.

"Now," he says, directing me away from her grave by my nape, "I look after you."

I reach for my neck, feeling at Mother's necklace, hating that this is all I have left of her.

Chapter 55

ROSE

Esther is on the steps when we pull through the gates, waiting, Doc by her side. I get out and unclip Maggie's seat, passing it to Tank. Esther meets him at the bottom of the steps and takes over, and Tank returns to help Fury with Ella.

I'm reeling. The information I have is sketchy, but I am completely reeling. A virgin. She was a virgin. *Was* being the operative word here because Brad took her virginity. But more shocking than that, he loves her. And he didn't mind who heard him say it.

This is serious. Not just Brad and Pearl's situation, but the *whole* situation. My question is, though, who does she belong to? Because that's what this is. Ownership. Someone, the man who called all of our cells, owns her. Controls her. And he wants her back. And if my obliterated spa and Nolan's kidnapping is anything to go by, he'll do anything. I shudder. She's been here for over six months. Praying to never be found. Or found out. Did her naïveté put us all in danger?

Pearl gets out of the other side of the car, her face vacant, her movements robotic, as if she's going through the motions. I glance at Beau, just as she glances at me. I can see we're both thinking the same thing and, frankly, we have a nerve to think it. But Pearl has *got* to pull herself together. Curling up into a ball of anxiety isn't an option in our world.

I go to her, slipping an arm around her shoulders. "I know you probably won't believe me when I tell you this," I say gently, "but it will be okay."

She looks at me, and I can see clearly that I'm right. She doesn't believe it. "What if they don't find Nolan?" she asks. I have no answer for that. I just hope for everyone's sake they do, because I would not want to be in Brad's way. "It will be because of me."

"They will find him," I say surely, despite the horrible feeling in my bones. This is all unexpected, and the men weren't prepared. God knows what could blow up next. The house and its grounds. It's been targeted before. Another shudder. "Come on, we have things to do." Distract her. I don't know who I'm trying to kid. I've been in Pearl's shoes, more than once. And I'm here again now. Distraction doesn't work. But strength and faith do.

"I never spoke to him," Pearl murmurs. "I never shared anything about anyone here." I hush her, believing her, as we follow the Vikings up the steps. I drop my bag by the door.

"Nolan's room?" Tank asks over his shoulder, Ella lifeless in his arms.

"Yeah." Beau runs ahead and opens the door, standing back, and we all follow them in. He lays her down on the bed, and I move in on one side with Beau, while Doc assesses her on the other side to determine what we're dealing with. Doc takes her pulse. I check her head. Beau's cell beeps, and her thumbs work across the screen before she slips it onto the nightstand and starts scanning Ella's body. "Brad. He was checking that we're back."

Pearl sits on a chair in the corner, watching. "Her pulse is good," Doc says, moving to her head. I give him space. "Whatever she was hit with, it was blunt. There's no blood."

"His fist," Pearl says quietly. Beau and I turn toward her. "He would have punched her in the side of the head. It's the quickest, most effective way to disable someone."

I stare at Pearl in horror. How almost blasé she is about it. And I remember the exact same numbness as I look at my arms. The scars.

"No, Rose," Beau says quietly. "No."

I shake myself away from those memories. Away from the punches in the gut, the constant times he forced himself on me. Nox Dimitri was pure evil. But he's dead. And I'm not. I'm living. Sometimes my life feels like a psychological thriller, but I'm living.

Ella stirs, her eyes clenching even though they're already closed. Relief gets me. "Ella," Beau says, getting closer, holding her hand. "Ella, it's Beau, can you hear me?"

Pearl comes to the bed and joins us, taking Ella's other hand while Doc continues his assessment. "Ella," he says. "How are you feeling?"

"Like a boulder hit me in the side of my head." She reaches up and winces, touching the side of her head, and Pearl flicks a look at me. Then Ella seems to register where she is and with who, and her eyes snap open, looking around. "Nolan," she says. "Where's Nolan?"

"They're looking for him," Pearl says. "Everyone is looking for him."

"Why? Where is he?" She tries to sit up. "Oh my God."

"Easy now," Doc says gently, encouraging her back down to the bed. "Tell me if anything else hurts."

"Where is he?" she murmurs, her eyes welling.

"What can you remember?" Pearl asks, eager for information. "Tell me."

Ella scowls at thin air before her, straining to remember. "Brad said Nolan was in the green container, to give him fifteen minutes." A shake of her head, probably to clear the fog. "I waited thirty and was getting worried. It was dark, and I called for him, but he didn't answer." She turns a watery gaze onto Pearl, her lip trembling. "So I used my cell to see. My ex was in there. Shot. And Nolan was on the floor. That's the last I remember."

Her ex? What? I look at Beau, and she shrugs. I have to pull myself together. These girls, too young to be here, are depending on us. I clear my throat and move in, but before I make it to Ella, before I even try and attempt to reassure her, Beau intercepts me and jerks her head toward the door. I go with her, letting her close the door behind her. I exhale, my palm on my forehead. "What the fuck is this nightmare?" I whisper. "Have you seen Pearl's face? How fucking terrified she is of that man, whoever the hell he is." I start pacing, breathing, shoving back the wretched memories that I honestly thought I had under control.

"Rose, I know what's going on up there," Beau says, pointing to my head. "You have to stop letting this fuck with your head." I laugh but stop when she gets up in my face, her expression stern and determined. "Nox Dimitri might be dead, but he's winning every second you give your mind to him." She squeezes my hands. "Do not give your emotions to a ghost. I need you to focus."

I don't have a chance to listen to Beau and work on that focus. We both hear the sound of ringing. Both look at the door. I burst in and see Pearl staring down at a cell. Not hers. Brad has that. Beau's.

"Is it him?" I ask.

I've never seen a woman shake so much. She latches onto her lip ring, and the scale of her trembles might rip the damn thing out. Her glazed eyes turn to us, her nod jerky. "Withheld number."

"Who?" Ella asks, forcing Beau to go to her and settle her.

"Do not answer." I claim the cell from Pearl and give it back to Beau, taking her in a hug and trying to squeeze her shakes away. I can't bear seeing her like this. All vibrancy lost. Happiness in the gutter. "You need to take my word for it, Pearl," I whisper. "Everything will be fine." I release her, wiping her tears.

"I need to talk to Brad." She snivels over her words. "Tell him everything."

"He doesn't know everything?"

"We started to talk but news of the spa exploding and Nolan being taken—" She shakes her head. "I don't think he'll release Nolan even if he gets me back."

God, I can't even consider that. "You must tell Brad everything. Every little detail, no matter how unimportant you think it is." *Fucking hell.* I remember Danny's face when I shared my dismal past. Murderous. I can't imagine Brad will feel any different. He loves her. I'm so fucking happy for him, but at the same time, terrified. We're all fucked up. Some more than others. He'll struggle to accept the terrible things that have happened to Pearl, and it'll affect their relationship. But he will have to get past it. Or just pretend to get past it.

"It's ugly, Rose," Pearl whispers.

"He'll take it," I assure her. "But you must be patient with him." Brad's never loved a woman before. And I know the whole virginity thing would have fucked with his head. My question is, did he know she was a virgin? And is that why he was so fucking tetchy for so long? His moral compass must have been spinning. "I remember when I told Danny about Dimitri," I say, his name like tar on my tongue. "I saw the monsters inside him stirring, his mind conjuring up all the ways he would kill him. Brad will be the same because he and Danny are so similar." I smile softly, but it falters when Pearl blinks, her forehead crinkling. "Pearl?"

"Dimitri?" she whispers.

"Yes," I confirm, every hair on my body standing on end. She knows the story. I've told her. "He was the man who bought me."

Her eyes drop to the carpet and dart, and Beau is soon with us, obviously sharing my deep unease. "You never told me his name."

I didn't? "Pearl?" I press. "What is it?"

"Anya," she breathes, looking up at us. "Anya's surname is Dimitri."

My loss of breath causes me to stagger back, forcing Beau to catch me. "No."

"I saw. On an ID card or foreign driver's license. Anya Dimitri."

"Fuck," Beau whispers.

No.

Tell me that's not true.

"Anya Dimitri," I say quietly, and in a complete haze, I walk out of the room.

"Rose!"

My pace increases steadily as my mind computes the information until I'm in a full-blown sprint, racing down the corridor.

"Rose, stop!" Beau yells behind me. "Rose, please!"

I burst through Pearl and Anya's bedroom door and scan the space, pacing to the bathroom. Empty. My eyes fall to the cupboard under the sink. The panel on the front. It's hanging down on one side. Has been put back in a rush. Disbelief turns into anger. So much fucking anger. I back out, hurrying to the terrace doors, and push my way out, scanning the gardens below. And I see her, hurrying through the garden.

Carrying something.

"No," I whisper, my blood running cold.

My baby.

"No!" I scream, making her stop. "Anya, no!"

"Rose," Beau breathes, seeing what I'm seeing. "Oh my God."

My heart literally falls out of my chest as I turn and race back out of the room, nearly taking Pearl off her feet as I do. I dart down the stairs, seeing my purse by the door. I kick my sandals off and rummage through urgently, pulling out the gun Danny gave me, then I fly out of the front door, running around the side of the house, my legs like pistons, adrenaline fueling them.

"Rose!" Beau screams.

I see Anya on the side of the driveway heading toward the cars. She sees me.

Her pace increases.

"Anya, don't run!" I yell. "Anya, please!"

I see the headlights of a Mercedes blink. "Anya, stop!"

I keep running. Just keep running. But I'm judging the distance. *I won't make it.*

"Anya, please, stop!" My lungs burn, but I keep going. I will never stop. I will run to the end of the fucking earth. "Anya!"

And from nowhere, Pearl appears, much closer to her than I am. I slow to a stop, my heart clattering, and watch Pearl gain on her. Anya's unaware of her closing in, her attention on me. I send a million silent prayers to the heavens, willing Pearl on. "Please," I beg. "Please, please, please."

"Cindy, Barbie!" Pearl yells, breathless.

I gasp on a wracked sob when she catches Anya, grabbing the handle of Maggie's car seat and wrestling with her hold. Anya's not giving up, and neither is Pearl. But it's the dogs that force Anya to release Maggie. They come charging around the corner, barking as they run.

"Oh my God," Beau whispers, holding on to me—holding me up. The sneer Anya fires at Pearl tells me everything I need to know about Anya.

She's the enemy.

How the hell didn't we see that?

Pearl backs away calmly with Maggie, and I raise my gun, as Anya runs toward the Mercedes and jumps in, getting the door closed just before Cindy and Barbie reach the car. They jump up at the side, barking, snarling, as Anya starts the engine. I begin to move again. Running. No. She does *not* get away after trying to take my baby. I yell for the dogs, and they dart back, coming to me.

"Rose!" Beau yells. "Oh, God, Rose, please don't!"

I pick up my pace, my feet pounding the concrete to make it to her, Cindy and Barbie now flanking me.

Anya pulls off, heading for the closed gates. "No, Len," I whisper, seeing daylight break through the middle of the two wooden panels. They're opening. "God damn it," I yell, slowing, knowing I'll never make it to her. I look back, seeing Pearl handing Maggie over to Beau. I come to a stop. *She's safe.*

I send the dogs back to guard Maggie as Fury and Tank barrel out of the doors, taking in the scene, both of their huge, muscled bodies pulsing. Apprehension. Anger. Disbelief.

"Stay where the fuck you are, Rose," Tank warns.

I slowly turn my gaze back to the fleeing car, making a mental vow to find Anya. Find her and make her regret she ever stepped foot in my house. But I frown when the car starts to slow until it finally come to a standstill just short of the open gates. *Why has she stopped? Has she seen sense? Has she surrendered?* I start to walk toward her, looking back when I hear Tank calling me.

"Stay where you are!" He pulls his gun, taking the steps faster than his body should allow, his brother by his side. "God help me, Rose."

I hold up a hand, telling him I'm fine, and return my attention forward.

"No, Rose!"

The reverse lights come on. The wheels screech, and the car comes speeding toward me.

"Move, Rose!"

I freeze, my brain not working fast enough to tell me what to do.

"Rose!" Tank bellows.

I blink, smoke from the tires bursting up into the air.

"Rose, move!"

What is she doing? Why is she doing it?

"Rose!"

Air gushes into my lungs, waking me up from my trance. The car's too close. I'm frozen by shock. And suddenly flying through the air like a ragdoll, landing in a heap on the grass to the side of the driveway.

I cry out, dazed, disorientated, struggling to sit up.

And my heart jumps into my throat when I realize it wasn't the car that hit me.

It was Pearl.

"Pearl!" Beau screams, as I take in her lifeless body on the ground, her eyes closed, blood seeping into the hairline cracks in the concrete, her arms and legs splayed unnaturally.

"No," I choke, scrambling up to my feet, dizziness capturing me, making my path to Pearl's lifeless body a clumsy zigzag. I drop to my knees next to her, my hands patting hesitantly at her body. "Get Doc!" I yell, looking at Beau, seeing Esther taking Maggie. "Get Doc now!"

I stare down at Pearl, stunned, and at the back of the Mercedes when it pulls away again. I stand up, watching her drive off. And on autopilot again, I pick up my gun and start walking down the drive after her as she drives toward the closing gates.

"Rose," Tank yells. "For fuck's sake, Rose, what the hell are you doing?"

I don't stop.

She will pay.

Chapter 56

DANNY

We pull off the freeway, and I check behind us, just as Phil Collins hits the speakers with *In the Air Tonight*. I cough over my smoke, casting an ironic look James's way. He shakes his head mildly, looking up at me in the rearview mirror briefly before returning his attention to the road, raising his own smoke to his lips and pulling. He's given in to the lure of a relaxing cigarette again. I can't blame him.

Brad remains silent in the passenger seat, his focus set on the world passing, the air from the open window breezing in, mixing the track with wind. I look at the weaponry surrounding me. On the seat, in the trunk, on the floor, on my lap. We're loaded. Literally. The whole fucking bunker is split between the cars as we drive back from the boatyard in a convoy of four. I'm certain not one of us without some kind of stressed sweat going on. Brad's not murmured a word. James is pensive. Goldie and Ringo were without their usual irritating banter as we loaded the cars, and Otto obviously hadn't found anything that could help us because he was persistently silent too. Even Leon read the room and remained mute as he and Jerry helped. Bernard King, or someone associated with him, had been at the boatyard. Too close for comfort. So close, they got one of our own.

We all need a drink. We all need a moment. A fucking plan. My God, Pops will be turning in his fucking grave. If he had one.

James pulls onto the road that leads up to the mansion, checking his mirrors to make sure Ringo, Otto, and Leon are all still behind. I look back and see them. "We unload then meet in the office," I say as James slows toward the gates of the house.

"I'm talking to Pearl first," Brad murmurs, his tone flat, without emotion, but his entire persona radiating threat. I won't be challenging him. I've been in his shoes. Worst shoes I've ever stood in.

"Of course," I reply. "I'm here if—"

"Fuck!" James slams the brakes on, and I'm suddenly flying forward, my arms shooting up to save me from being thrown into the front. "Fuck, fuck, fuck!"

I catch sight of a Mercedes crashing through the gates before James yanks the steering wheel to the left to avoid hitting it, sending us skidding sideways up the street.

I'm tossed around on the back seat, my fucking legs in the air, guns flying, and fight to right my sprawled body. *What the fuck is going on?* "Shit," I yell, as my head meets the window and the Range Rover comes to a jarring stop.

"What the hell?" Brad murmurs, unclipping his belt and getting out of the car. I follow urgently, as does James, all of us walking around to the other side of the Range Rover. The hood of the Mercedes is buried in a bush on the opposite side of the road, the engine still running.

"That's Tank's car." James starts walking toward it, pulling his gun, leaning forward to try and see in the driver's seat.

"Be careful," I say, drawing my gun. "It's—" My attention is caught by my wife walking calmly through the destroyed gates. *What the fuck?*

"What's going on, Danny?" Brad asks, uneasy, pulling his gun too, as Rose picks up her pace toward the Mercedes.

"Rose," I yell, a sliver of fear running through my veins. She doesn't hear me. But as I gage the look on her face, I realize Rose won't be hearing anything right now. She's got that vacant, determined, haunted expression I'm too familiar with. And my trepidation multiplies.

"Rose!" I bellow, jogging toward her.

"Danny, what the fuck's going on?" Ringo yells, coming after me.

"I don't fucking know!" Rose is running now, set to make it to the car before any of us. "Rose!" I overtake Brad as she reaches the driver's door and yanks it open.

"Get out!" she screams.

I jump at the volume and hatred loaded into her voice as she starts wrestling with whoever's in the driver's seat. "Get the fuck out now!"

I slow to a stop when Anya falls out of the car, her body landing on the road with a thwack. Rose kicks her in the stomach.

"What the fuck?" Brad breathes, coming to a stop next to me.

"Jesus." James flanks my other side, and I hear the shocked gasps of the others from behind as we all stand like useless cunts while my wife beats the shit out of Anya, repeatedly kicking her, punching her, screaming. Absolutely unhinged. I know she's got this in her, but . . .

Fuck . . . me.

I come to my senses when Rose rams a gun under Anya's chin. "Jesus, Rose," I gasp, running over, but I skid to a stop, arms up, when she aims it my way, her eyes wild. Warning me.

I back up. "Okay," I say, appearing calm but really not feeling it. "Rose, baby, what's happening?"

"Tell him!" she screams. "Tell him your name!"

Anya does something that shocks me more than Rose aiming a gun my way. She spits in Rose's face. "The fuck?" I blurt, my voice high. And what the fuck is Anya's name?

I don't know, but I need to defuse this fucking pronto before the police show up and find our whole fucking arsenal in the cars. "Rose, baby, can we take this inside?" I take one step gingerly toward her and stop when I hear Brad curse.

I look back, seeing his attention pointed up the street. I turn to see he's looking at a van. Tires start screeching, and Brad starts running after it, firing at the wheels. He takes the back one out, sending it into the curb. It bounces off and starts rocking, and I flinch as I watch it go up on two wheels. "It's going," I whisper, the van tilting precariously, leaning, until it eventually drops onto its side with a deafening crash.

"No!" Rose yells, falling to her arse as Anya bolts.

Bang!

I raise my arm over my head, flinching, the whole scene too much for my brain to process. My wife, armed, Anya making a run for it, Brad heading for the van.

"Jesus Christ," James says, obviously experiencing the same level of *what the hell is happening?* as I am.

I go straight to Rose and disarm her.

"What are you doing?" she screams, getting up in my face.

"Taking control of this fucking madness." I take her elbow and squeeze, fighting her fighting me, as James catches Anya, immobilizing her with an arm up her back, and Brad drags out a man from the driver's seat of the van.

"Get the cars inside," I yell. "And someone call the fucking gate company to repair them." *Again.*

Tank walks through the debris of splintered and broken wood, his gun poised, his eyes crazy. So crazy, even I'm wary. "You stupid woman," he yells, furious, going in on Rose.

"What's going on, Tank?" I ask, breathless.

"I don't fucking know," he shouts. "But I do fucking know I gave her clear instructions to stay fucking put and she fucking didn't!"

I swing an incensed look onto Rose. "What the fuck is going on?"

"Anya," she says, her breathing labored. "Her name is Anya Dimitri."

I feel like someone just pressed high voltage into my body. "What?"

"What?" Brad gasps.

Something in Rose shifts, adrenaline making way for emotion now. "Pearl," she whispers, looking back toward the house.

Brad steps closer, dragging the man with him. "Rose?" he says, slowly, warily. "What about Pearl?"

"Anya ran her down."

Brad's gun hits the floor. "No." He stands motionless for far too long, forcing Ringo to dive in and claim the man before he gets away. "No!" He sprints through the destroyed gates up the long driveway toward the house, and I follow, seeing Fury and Beau huddled around something. "God, no," I breathe.

"Pearl!" Brad breaks through them and nearly coughs his heart up when he sees her on the ground.

Unmoving.

I cover my mouth with my hand as Brad slowly lowers to his knees next to her, taking her in. Pale. So fucking pale.

Then I see the pool of blood.

Fuck.

The dogs are sitting nearby, whimpering, their paws treading the ground as they watch Brad huddle round Pearl's broken body. "Pearl?" he begs. "Pearl, wake up." He looks up when he hears the crunching of shoes on the stones. His eyes are glazed. His face everything I don't know on Brad. *Agony.* "Do something," he whispers when Doc comes rushing out of the house. "Please, Doc, you have to do something."

My heart, which only ever usually softens for my wife or kids, tears in two.

Chapter 57

ROSE

I go straight to Maggie, scooping her out of Esther's arms, checking every square inch of her. She's crying. But she seems unharmed. I bury my face in her neck, hushing her, rocking her, trying to find my calm. Needing distraction from my rage. She eventually quietens down, and I stand at the kitchen window and watch the men drive all the cars in, including Tank's mangled Mercedes and the van that tried to get away. Goldie has taken Anya and the man to Danny's office. I'm itching to go there. Smash her to pieces. But they need information first. And I need this.

I take a seat at the table, and a cup of tea slides in front of me. I notice the ring on Esther's finger. "Congrat . . ." I can't get the word out, breaking down, my adrenaline drained.

"Oh, Rose." She crouches, trying to hug us both. "She's okay."

"But Pearl isn't," I whisper, looking down at Maggie. She's now calm, trying to focus on her arms flapping in front of her, mesmerized by the movement. But all I see is Pearl's face. Her closed eyes.

"Mum, take Maggie." Danny stands at the entrance to the kitchen looking like he could explode.

I don't protest, giving our daughter up to her grandmother. "She probably needs her diaper changed," I say, standing.

"I've got it." Esther disappears, and I face my husband, bracing myself for the show. I've no doubt it'll be epic.

He strolls across the kitchen and opens a cupboard, pulling down a bottle of Scotch. He pours two glasses. One for me? No. He necks both. Faces me. "I'm so fucking mad I don't even know where to begin."

"Then I will," I say, sitting. "Ella seems okay, but she can't remember much from the boatyard. She used her cell to see in the container because it was dark. She saw Nolan on the floor. And her ex. Why was her ex in the container?"

"He knocked Ella about. Brad brought him to the boatyard." His nostrils flare. "A gift to his son."

"Right," I say, taking in more air, ready to go again. "That's the last Ella remembers before she was struck. Pearl said it was a fist. I expect because she was victim to that fist a few times herself. I told her repeatedly things were going to be okay, and she didn't look like she believed me, so I used my own history as a source of evidence that even in the darkest, worst times, you can find your way to the light." I get up and go to the counter, pouring myself a glass, since my husband's lost his manners. I down it, gasp, and slam the tumbler down, returning to the table. "I mentioned Dimitri. Pearl blanched. I pressed her and she told me Anya's surname was Dimitri." I show the ceiling my palms. "There's foreign identification, apparently, and when I went to find Anya to question her, she had already left. I found her running to Tank's car. With. Our. Baby. So if you're mad, fine. I'll happily bear the brunt of your rage." I take a breath, trying to stabilize my voice. "Pearl got Maggie back." His eyes widen. "Anya got in the car and tried to run me down. Pearl knocked me out of the way and took the force of the car."

An inhale, long and deep. Calming. "You're quite good at debriefing."

"I learned from the best." I stare at him, my face as straight as his. "So what are you going to do about Anya fucking Dimitri?" I ask.

"I'm not going to do anything." Danny's cell chimes and he lifts it, looking at the screen, his eyebrows slowly arching as he reads whatever he's reading. What the fuck *is* he reading?

"You're doing nothing?"

Danny pushes away from the counter and walks out, and I watch, astounded, as he leaves me alone in the kitchen. "No." I go after him, following him to his office. Tank and Fury stand either side of the entrance. I expect to be blocked, but they let me pass. And Danny leaves the door open for me to enter.

Anya is on a chair, Goldie guarding her, and the other guy is front-down on the rug, Ringo standing over him. I notice there is no Brad. He'll be with Pearl. I swallow down the tennis ball wedged in my throat. *Please be okay.*

Danny sits on the edge of his desk and drags a gun off the wood. "*I'm* not going to do anything," he repeats, looking at me, holding the gun out. "You are."

I accept the gun, half shocked, half thirsty for Anya's blood, as

Danny folds his arms. "This is Stefan Dalca." He nods to the guy on the rug. "He's the dumb fucker boyfriend of this sweet thing," he says quietly, looking at Anya. "Nox Dimitri's baby sister."

My mouth falls open as I look at Anya. She has a sneer on her face still. She is *not* here because she has been forced to be here. She's here because she wants to be.

Danny pulls a cell from Anya's backpack. "The code."

"Du-te dracului," she hisses.

"That sounds like a no." He sighs, throwing the cell to Otto. "Well, given King asked for his virgin *intact*, I'm going to assume news that Pearl is no longer a virgin hasn't made it to him yet."

"How did you come to be with the Polish?" I ask the obvious question. She doesn't answer.

But Danny does. He stands and smiles at Anya. "Mind if I give my wife a bit of background information?" he asks, as I peek across to Otto. He's on his laptop. A constant, real-time stream of information.

"Your wife betrayed my brother!" Anya screams. "She is a whore!"

Danny laughs lightly, a worrying edge of psycho laced through it. I wouldn't blame him if he backhanded her. But he won't. Even The Brit has limits. He turns to me. "You gonna let her speak about you like that?"

I step in and crack Anya across the face, the connection stinging and deafening, the mark on her cheek instant.

Then I step back before I get carried away.

"There was a time many months ago," Danny begins casually, "when The Russians and the Polish were working together quite nicely under The Bear, AKA Beau's mother, who, as we all know, met quite the spectacular death at the hands of her daughter, our very own little ninja, or, as her fellow cops knew her, Lara Croft." He smiles. It's dark. Then he turns it onto Anya. "The Poles and the Russians. Friends once upon a time. That soon went to shit when egos, power, and money got in the way. And us. *We* got in the way." He pouts. "You're not talking, but Brad's confirmed you knew about him and Pearl, and, like I said, King *doesn't* know, so something tells me you might be batting for Sandy. There is only you and that cunt over there." He looks at the man face down on the rug. "You couldn't very well take us down on your own, so to get revenge for your brother, as well as information for Sandy, who is passing *select* information on to King, you went to places you completely underestimated, didn't you, you sick little bitch? To earn your stripes, maybe earn some cash, and reinstate your family's name and reputation." He leans down. Smiles. "Am I right, or am I right?"

She spits in Danny's face and shouts a whole load of Romanian as he slowly wipes his cheek.

"Did you really think Sandy would ensure your safe departure from this situation?"

"I will help anyone to make sure you get what you deserve for what you did to my brother."

Danny rests his hands on the arms of the chair and gets his sneering face up in hers. "You mean when I sliced off his depraved, bald, ugly head?" he asks. Anya can't conceal her shock. "You know, the sound it made when it hit the ground was like a rugby ball plopping into wet mud. And it rolled a little way too."

I'm not looking at my husband right now. I'm looking at The Brit.

"One swing. One swipe. One . . . *chop*."

"Fuck you!" she screams in his face. And my husband? He smiles, lighting up and blowing the smoke in Anya's face. She coughs. He takes another drag. Blows that in her face too.

"You know what upsets me most in this world, Anya?" he asks. "Pass? Okay, let me tell you." He dips, clearing his throat. "When my wife is upset. And she's upset now because *you* have upset her." He smirks. Deadly. "And you know what I love most about my wife? Pass again? Okay, I'll tell you. She's a lioness, and you, you stupid, deluded *fuck*, dared bring our kids into your silly mess. A token? A pawn to earn you a pat on the back? No. Bad move." He stands up straight. "So now my wife will kill you." Then lowers back to the desk. Looks at me. Nods. And without much thought at all—because I know The Brit wouldn't kill a woman—I aim and fire, doing the job for him. And I hit her straight between the eyes.

Her head drops back, her mouth falls open, and blood sprays the air.

Done.

"Your aim's improving, baby," Danny muses, satisfied.

I go to him, hold out the gun, and he takes the end, using it to pull me closer to him, getting my face close to his. He scans my eyes.

"When I tell you to jump in future, you're going to ask me how high." The swirl of anger in his gaze is very real. The threat.

"Never," I retort calmly, pulling my grasp off the gun and leaving his office to find my daughter, call my son, and get back to being a mother.

Chapter 58

BRAD

I stare at her closed eyes, willing them to open, as Doc quietly moves around the bed and the machinery. Her heartbeat is stable. Good. That's what Doc keeps telling me. Her blood pressure satisfactory, her blood loss not worrying. But her brain? He can't see that, so Doc has advised us to allow a specialist to come and assess her. It's only been an hour, if that, since we returned to the house and found all hell had broken loose, but Doc's not taking any chances. And I'm fine with that. Anything. Losing her isn't an option.

Doc was a gentleman while I cut Pearl's clothes off her broken body so he could see exactly what he's dealing with, turning his back. I honestly couldn't have cared less what he saw. I was too worried. Endless grazes. A few cuts, one particularly bad one on her thigh. I know all the sweet spots. It's not far from a main artery. Her arm is broken. Maybe a few ribs.

I sat there and listened to him detail the damage, and with each injury to her delicate body he listed, I felt my blood boil that little bit more. I don't know the exact details of what's happened yet. I'm almost scared to find out.

I flex my neck, and it clicks, sending a shockwave into my skull. It's an effort to breathe easy, to not feel like I'm constantly out of breath. All the air in my lungs is draining, and the longer she remains unconscious, it's getting worse. As is the anger.

I cup one of her limp, dainty hands in both of mine and lay my head on them, taking a moment to rest my eyes. "You have to wake up," I whisper. "That's an order."

Red.

The day you need me to tell you that I love you is the day I stop showing you well enough.

Red.

And then as if the universe thinks now is the perfect time, the red merges into Nolan. My son. One love of my life lying lifeless on the bed, the other . . . where?

I sit up and check my phone again. Nothing from Otto. I curse under my breath and go back to Pearl, feeling so fucking useless. I need to be out there getting my son back. Tearing the bastard that sold Pearl limb from limb. But even in my unbalanced state, I appreciate no move should be made until we have all the facts. All the information. Everything in place. We've cleared the boatyard. The club. The only place we are all permitted to be is here, at the house, and that is only because Otto has been through the fucking place with a fine-toothed comb to check for bombs and bugs. Our safe haven. Infiltrated.

Anya?

"Brad?"

I cast a heavy gaze toward the end of the bed where Doc is standing. "Yeah?" My voice is cracked. Broken. A lot like my body and my heart.

"I'll leave you for a few moments. I should check on Ella again, and Danny wants me to check Maggie over."

"What's wrong with Maggie?"

Doc shakes his head, looking troubled. "Anya tried to take her."

"What?" I breathe. *Jesus Christ.* She's a dead woman. And she won't be alive long enough for me to do the honors.

I nod, and the old boy pads out quietly, leaving me alone with Pearl. I look at her. Silently beg her to wake up.

I flinch when I feel a hand on my shoulder. *Beau.* I don't think I can take her pregnant female emotions on top of my own. I'm close to breaking. To exploding and taking out anything and everything in my path.

"My cell," she says, holding it out. "He called it . . . before Pearl told us Anya's surname."

"How did she know Anya was a Dimitri?"

"She saw a foreign card in her purse."

"She was carrying ID? How? We pulled them out of that hangar with nothing."

Beau shrugs. "I dread to think where she's been and who she's seen since she's been here. Rose mentioned Nox Dimitri to Pearl. It spiraled from there."

"Anya took Maggie?"

She nods. "Pearl got her back. Then pushed Rose out of the way of the car Anya was driving."

I drop my head. God damn her. But if not Pearl, then Maggie or Rose. Either Danny or I would be sitting here praying. "Get Otto to check your phone." I order. "You can sit."

Beau drags a chair close. "How is she?"

"Battered."

"And you?"

I still, looking at Pearl again. "I get it now," I whisper. "I understand." I look at Beau. My fiery little ninja nutter. "How James feels about you. How Danny feels about Rose. I totally comprehend it. The level of their love." I smile, returning my eyes to Pearl's motionless form. "The unbridled hatred." I clear my throat, feeling water building in my eyes. It spills over, rolling down my cheeks, and I roughly wipe the tears away. "I understand. I just hope it's not too late to show her how much I love her."

Beau seizes one of my hands, moving closer. "She will wake up," she says. "And when she does, you will show her."

I squeeze her hold, flinching when a bang sounds in the distance. We don't race out to see what's happening. We remain in our chairs watching Pearl, because we both know that bang was the end of Anya. And we both know Danny won't have pulled the trigger. The second gunshot, though? That's his.

"Would you . . ." I start. "Can you watch her? I need the bathroom."

"Of course."

I drop Beau's hand, kiss Pearl's before resting it gently on her tummy, and go to the bathroom, closing the door quietly behind me. I have to press a palm into the wall behind the toilet to hold myself up, and the opportunity to close my eyes for a brief moment while I take a piss is too hard to resist. I let my head hang too.

Red.

"Brad!" A bang on the door startles me, and Beau bursts in.

I jerk, pissing up the back of the toilet. "Fuck." I grab some toilet paper and start wiping up my mess. "Jesus, Beau, you scared the shit out of me."

"She's awake!"

I turn to face her. "What?" And frown when she slaps a hand over her eyes.

"Brad, put yourself away."

I look down at my groin area, finding my dick hanging out.

"Shit." I quickly fix myself, walking out of the bathroom as I do. I wasn't there when she opened her eyes, damn it.

"Wash your hands," Beau snaps, turning me straight back around and taking me to the sink. She flips on the faucet and shoves my hands under for me, rubbing soap into my skin as I crane my neck back to try and see into the bedroom. Try to see Pearl.

"Am I done?" I don't give her a chance to answer, shaking my hands as I rush into the bedroom. Pearl's squinting at me. "Oh Jesus," I gasp, bending over the bed, getting as close as I dare, trying so hard not to apply pressure where it might hurt. Which is basically everywhere. I kiss her forehead, her right cheek, avoiding her left because . . . damage.

"Shit," she whispers, her voice rough. "Bloody hell."

I move back, scanning her. My relief is unspeakable. Seeing her eyes open, hearing her voice. "What hurts? Where hurts? Tell me what's hurting, my love." My stupid, useless hands hover over her body, gliding up and down in thin air.

"Are you trying to make her levitate?" Beau asks, laughing a little as she joins us by the bed. I frown at my big hands and stow them away. "How are you feeling, Pearl?" Beau asks.

"Yes, how are you feeling?" I lean down a bit, narrowing my eyes, waiting for her to answer.

She seems to push her head back into the pillow, thinking, her forehead creased. "Oh," she eventually whispers, looking at me. "Maggie? Rose?"

"Are fine." Fucking hell, I can't even be furious with her for putting herself in danger like that. "What about you?"

"Felt better," she murmurs, holding her arm up, looking at the brace Doc's put on. Then she inhales and hisses, feeling her torso. "Ouch."

"Doc thinks you've got a few broken ribs," I say, reaching for her fractured arm and lowering it to the mattress.

"Do you need anything for the pain?" Beau asks. "Or some water, perhaps?"

"Yes, Advil?" I ask. "Water?" Why is Beau thinking of all the important things? My brain has short-circuited. "Where's Doc? Someone should get Doc. Beau, go get Doc."

"Brad," Pearl breathes, sinking farther into the bed on a wince.

Fuck. "She's in pain. Go get Doc."

"Brad, stop!" Pearl snaps. "Jesus, let me breathe. Just give me some space."

I stand up straight, wounded, my face, I'm sure, if Beau's half-smile is a measure, indignant. "To be clear," I say, trying and failing to force the scorn from my voice. "You never get space ever again." Pearl's eyebrows jump up, and I move in and crowd her, making my point. "I nearly fucking lost you." I frame her head with my forearms and get my face close to hers. "Which means any chance of *space* ever again is really fucking slim, do you understand me?"

She nods, looking quite startled, so I kiss away her surprise, dotting pecks everywhere I can put my lips. And she doesn't protest. Doesn't demand space. Much better. I finally pull away and catch Beau's soft, knowing smile. I flip her a scowl. She can judge all she likes. Could give a fuck. Don't.

"Oh, she's awake." Doc enters, happy to see his patient has come around. "How are you feeling, Pearl?"

"Like I've been run down by a Mercedes."

Beau snorts, chuckling. I do not. This is not funny. I cast Beau a warning look before giving my attention to someone who *will* take this seriously. "I think she needs some pain relief. And some water."

"And a pee," Pearl adds, pushing her good hand into the mattress, trying to move.

I swoop in, blocking her. "What the hell are you doing?"

She exhales, going heavy on the bed again, giving her sleepy eyes to Doc. "I think it's too early for visitors, Doc."

Beau snorts unattractively again, and Doc joins her. So I'm surrounded by fucking clowns now, am I? "Tough," I grunt. "And I'm not a visitor."

"Then what are you?" Beau asks.

"A walking bad mood, so I recommend *not* fucking with me." I round the bed and pull the blood pressure machine forward, taking the band and helping myself to Pearl's arm. "What's ideal, Doc?" I ask. "One-ten over seventy?"

"Around there, yes." He takes over the controls and checks Pearl's blood pressure again, the consistent whirring and pumping of the machine filling the silence for a few moments as I watch the digits. I nod, satisfied, when it reads a good one-fifteen over sixty-eight. The ripping sound of Velcro as Doc removes the band from Pearl's arm makes her flinch.

"Did that hurt?" I ask, moving in, checking her arm. "That hurt. She needs pain relief."

"Or Brad relief," Pearl grumbles, not quietly enough for me not to hear. Beau's laughing again.

I open my mouth, ready to launch into a lecture on acceptable levels of humor and appropriate times, but when I catch a sparkle in Pearl's eye, my scorn fades and everything other than that in this moment feels inconsequential. She smiles. That only adds to my wonder. "Chill out," she breathes, probably exasperated by my fussing.

"Chill out," I mutter, dropping to a chair next to the bed, forcing her to turn her head on the pillow to see me. Such a young thing to say. "Pearl." I shift closer, taking her hand. "I thought I'd lost you."

"I'm okay."

I laugh under my breath. Okay? Look at her. There's not one inch of her body without a scuff or mark. "You will be."

"Please stop stressing out."

"Never. You could have died."

I can see she wants to roll her eyes, but she won't. Instead, she squeezes my hold. "At least I wouldn't have died a virgin."

"We need to have a discussion about your humor."

"Okay. But can I pee first?"

I look at Doc. "Doesn't she have one of those bag things?"

"I hadn't got around to a catheter." Doc rummages through his bag. "And now she's awake, we don't need one."

My head retracts on my neck. "You're surely not suggesting she walks to the bathroom."

"That is exactly what I'm suggesting, Brad."

"Are you insane?"

He laughs, as does Beau. For fuck's sake. I turn to her. "Does pregnancy bring out the inner hyena in you or what?"

"Chill out," she says, her tongue in her cheek. "Want some help?"

"Please," Pearl replies, shaking off my hold and starting to shift up the bed.

"What? No." I stand, looming over her. "This is madness." I glare at Doc. "You can't allow this."

"I encourage movement, Brad, or her muscles will seize up. The longer she remains on her ass, the longer it'll take to recover."

"She has an *arse*," I snap. "*I* have an *ass*, and you can kiss it." The whole room erupts into laughter. I don't join in.

"I'll give you some privacy," Doc says, leaving the room.

I gawk at him. "You're leaving?"

"I think she's in capable hands, Brad." He drops his head, looking over his glasses.

Capable? I feel capable of murder. Not much else.

"I'm going to check on Rose." Beau disappears too.

For fuck's sake. I scan up and down Pearl's body, wondering where to start. "Come," I order, wrapping my arms around her waist and helping her to sit up. I get a much-needed waft of her lavender scent as I do, and it's glorious. "You good?"

"Yeah." She sucks back air through her teeth too many times, until she's sitting on the edge of the bed, legs dangling. I reach for one of my T-shirts on the back of a nearby chair and stretch the neck, putting it over her head, then pull the arm down so she can thread her braced arm through the hole. Once her other arm is through, I pull it down her body, covering her. I should carry her, but that would defeat the purpose, I guess, and I can't see how I could do that without causing too much pain. She's covered in cuts and bruises. Absolutely covered. Broken ribs, a broken arm. I grit my teeth. Anya got off lightly. "Ready to stand?" I ask, holding her elbows as she grips the inside of mine and shuffles her ass to the edge of the bed. "Easy," I whisper, watching her place her feet down and pad them a few times into the carpet. "Go slow. You might get a head rush." She slowly brings her body to standing, gripping me harder.

"Yep. Head rush." She sinks into my chest, her forehead under my neck. I feel her lashes ticking my throat past my open collar.

"Sit back down."

"No, no, no. I'm good."

Good?

She breaks away and peeks up at me. Smiles a little. It's an opportunity to drink her in, and I don't pass it up. "You need a hair tie," I say, holding her red waves back.

"You need a trim." Her eyes scan my bristle. "Or maybe not. I like you a little overgrown. And overprotective. And over the top. All the overs."

I laugh lightly and turn her away from me, taking her shoulders and walking her to the bathroom. I shut the door and let her hold on to me while I pull her panties down her thighs, lining her up to the seat. "You're good," I say easing her down, crouching to keep myself level with her. She closes her eyes, her nose wrinkling, and exhales, sagging when she releases her bladder. Not shy. No drama about me being here while she uses the toilet. I'm setting the standard, and she's not protesting my standards. We're getting off to the best start. Pearl opens her eyes, chewing on the ring in her lip, and reaches for my face, feeling my cheek.

I cover her hand with mine. "I never wanted to be," I murmur.

"Be what?"

"Your hero."

Bursts of sparkles light up her green eyes.

"But I do now," I add, pulling her hand away from my cheek and kissing it. "If you'll still have me."

"Have you as my hero?" she asks.

"Or whatever you want to call me." I rub my scrunched nose with hers. "Just not *daddy*."

She chuckles, and I stand while she wipes before helping her up. "Hands," I say, taking her to the sink and washing them. "Dry." I smother her hands in a towel and pat off the wet, being careful of her broken arm. "What?" I ask, feeling her studying me.

"Considering you've never done this, you're quite good at it."

"Washing hands?" I ask, my smile wry.

"Yeah," she whispers, but I know she doesn't mean that specifically. *Looking after her. Being gentle. Loving.*

She lets me lead her to the bed and get her back under the sheets, and I tuck her in, feeling her watching me still. "Water?"

She hums her yes and lets me put the straw past her lips, and I watch her take half the glass before releasing the straw. "Are you okay?" she asks, and I laugh under my breath.

"I'm fine." I set the glass on the nightstand and perch on the edge of the bed.

"Want to get in?" she says, lifting the sheets with her good hand.

I raise my brows. Not in interest, but in warning. Any kind of intimacy isn't happening for a while. But that's okay. I can wait. In the meantime, I get to appreciate her.

Love her.

This. Taking care of her. It feels like what I've been waiting to do. This and be a father. I swallow and push back that particular edge of anger until I can unleash it. Right now, I need a level head, and I need some information.

"Are you ready to fill in those blanks?" I ask, and she nods, her happy smile faltering. I take her hand and hold it. "How did you come to be in Bernard King's possession, Pearl?"

She swallows, her eyes darting. "Because—" Her voice is noticeably tight. "Because he killed my dad."

I recoil. Her dad didn't die in a drink-driving incident? "Because he wanted you?" I ask.

"No. He killed him because he hated him."

"Who was your dad, Pearl?"

Her stare remains on her lap, and I allow it. Anything she needs to make this easier. "He was Bernard King's brother."

I jerk, jarring her arm. It's not her broken one, but she still flinches. "Fuck, I'm sorry. He's your uncle?" I question, stunned.

She peeks up, and I see eyes so fucking terrified. What the hell did he do to her? "Bernard hated my dad because he was everything he wasn't. Successful, respected, self-made. A tyrant at times too, but he could control his temper. Bernard couldn't. He was a bully. Jealous of what my dad had made for us. My mother and I were my father's trophies. Another facet to his achievements, and Bernard wanted to take away everything Dad had achieved." She shrugs, biting at her lip.

"My God." I rub at my forehead. "He's your fucking uncle?"

"He was always there on the periphery of our lives." Her hand flexes in mine, not to release it, but to cling on that bit tighter. "Trying to upend everything. Scare my mum, force my dad into losing his temper. There was a time when he wasn't around." She smiles. "He joined the forces. I heard Father tell Mother that it satisfied his need to hurt people. But then he came back when I was ten and my mum was back to being anxious again. Father back to being angry." She blinks, and I move closer, catching the tear that rolls down her cheek, truly petrified to hear the rest of this story. But I need to know everything.

"Go on," I whisper.

"He showed up at the house," she continues after a deep breath. "And Mother hid me in the closet. I was there for . . . I don't know. Hours. I came out, scared, because my father would be annoyed if I hadn't done what I was told. I saw my uncle putting my father in his car. His body was floppy."

"Bernard's car?"

"My father's car."

"Drunk driving," I breathe.

"Yeah." Her eyes drop to the sheets. "He moved into our home after that. Said he needed to look after his brother's family." She laughs at her lap. "He didn't look after us. He terrorized us. Treated my mother like a slave, hit her if she did things wrong, forced her . . ." She swallows.

"My love," I whisper through gritted teeth, struggling to hold it together.

"She tried to run once. He broke her legs so she couldn't run again."

Fucking hell.

"He never touched me, though," she goes on. "I think Mum hung on to that. Which is why she decided to leave this world too." Her glassy eyes find mine. "She left me with him."

"And his punching bag was gone."

"So I became his . . ."

I cough over my shock, my sweat intensifying. "Oh Pearl."

"He never...well, you know."

Virgin. I reach for her mouth and put my finger across her lips, staring at her. And that's the part of her story she shared with me before today that's true. Her mother chose death over her daughter. Uncle Carlo was an immoral man, granted, but he had my back. Guided me. Looked out for me. Loved me in his own fucked-up way. Pearl had a man who resented her. Despised her. *Fuck me.* What has she endured since she lost her parents? "You were thirteen," I say. "When your mum died."

"Thirteen and three months."

"You didn't try to get away?"

"Once. He made sure I couldn't run again, but he didn't break my legs like he did my mum's." She indicates the scar on her nape, and I move back in my chair.

"No," I breathe. "He put a tracker in you?"

"I tried to dig it out."

I withdraw. "Wait—"

"The Polish men removed it. My uncle didn't tell them about it. But I did."

Jesus Christ, so even for a payday of one hundred million, he still couldn't let her go? I can't form any words. I also need a break from the horror movie playing in my mind. So I hold my hand up, and I feel like a complete asshole calling for a timeout. I get up and start walking around the room, trying to walk off the rising fury. I can't wrap my twisted mind around such cruelty. Couldn't if Pearl was a perfect stranger. But she's not a perfect stranger. She's mine, and knowing what her life was before I found her fucking kills me.

"So between the ages of thirteen and twenty, you were in his sole care?" I ask. *Care.* It's the wrong word. "You were—"

"His?"

My jaw twitches. "You were kept by him."

She nods.

"And . . ."

She must see my struggle to ask the questions because she starts talking without me asking anything specific. "My father was a wealthy man, Brad. Our home was . . . impressive. I realize now his businesses weren't legitimate, but when I was a kid, I thought he must have been the most powerful man in the world." She smiles. "He looked after my mother. Adored me. When I found my mother—"

"*You* found her?"

She nods. Fuck me, Carlo spared me the mean mercy of finding my mother dead.

"I hadn't seen her for a whole day," she says. "So I went looking for her. She was in the bath."

My eyes widen. "The bath."

She smiles a little. Knowingly. "The bath," she confirms.

Fucking hell. "And you had no other family? No one to check up on you?"

"My mother's parents were dead. My father's parents were terrified of Bernard. They were very old. Mum and Dad's estate was left to me, but it's in a trust until I'm twenty-five. Bernard had to wait until then for me to sign it over to him."

"Or he could have killed you too."

"Would look a bit suspicious, wouldn't it?" she says, so candidly, and I know she probably considered death to be more appealing.

Like her mother. "He got away with killing my father. Mother killed herself and saved him the trouble. Me too? His pumpkin? Why risk it when he could live like a king on my father's twenty-million-pound estate anyway, and then force me to sell it when I turned twenty-five?"

Christ. I feel like I need another timeout. "Pumpkin?" I ask, tentative.

She reaches for a lock of her vibrant red air, and I look away, holding up a hand again, digesting all the information. What the fuck is this madness? He was going to keep her until she was twenty-five. Torture her. And something tells me that even if he got the twenty-million-pound estate, he wouldn't have freed Pearl. *Kill me now.* I don't know how much more of this I can bear, but she's on a roll, looking strangely lighter with each word she shares, but heavier too.

"I learned to keep out of his way." She pats the covers around her thighs, as if getting herself settled for more of the horror show. "I only angered him. One time, I went a whole week without seeing him. But I heard him. The parties, the drunken men, the guns, the explosions. He liked fishing in my father's lake too. Would blow the fish out of the water." She bites at her lip ring, tugging it.

Fuck. Me.

Please, God, surely he didn't . . . her lip . . . *no.* She peeks up at me, finding me staring at the piercing. "You don't need to hear the rest."

"Tell me," I demand, giving her my eyes. They're surely full of lethal intent. "I want to know."

"Brad—"

"Tell me," I snap.

"He would . . . put a hook . . ." Pearl bunches the sheet in her good fist, and I swallow. "You don't need to kn—"

"I need to know." I lower to the chair and brace myself. She endured it. I only have to *hear* it.

"If I didn't go to him, he would put a hook in my lip and reel me in. Punch me in the side of the head." She winces and reaches for her right temple, as if feeling one of those punches right now. "Put a leash on me and make me crawl like a dog. Put me in a cage outside. Naked."

I bury my face in my palms, my fingers clawing into my cheeks. How the hell do I help her put all that behind her? *It's why she's so fucking strong.* Why she tolerated my hostility, seemingly unaffected. How she "accepted" Allison when I used her as a shield. *Fuck me.*

I wasn't physically as cruel to her as her uncle, but I certainly didn't show her any grace. And yet, she forgave me. Loves me.

"When he told me he'd sold me," she says, almost wistfully. "I was happy."

I blink into my darkness. Happy? Jesus Christ, she has no idea that she was heading for worse. Because she wouldn't only be beaten . . . but raped daily too. And I haven't got the heart to tell her.

"Then you found me."

I still.

I found her.

"He hasn't been paid the money for you, Pearl," I remind her, braving looking at her. I'm a fucking coward. She's sustained all of that, and I'm struggling to even keep eye contact while she tells me her miserable story. "Because you never made it to your new owner. Because we took you."

She stares at me. "How did he know *you* took me?"

"There aren't many people who would take on the Polish. We did. Your uncle has made a point of being friendly with our enemies." I'm sure Pearl knows many things about Sandy, the girls talk, but I'm not going into details. "King's made a deal to supply their weaponry. He won't if—"

"I heard the rest," she says, looking away. "Intact."

What I can't figure out is why a private detective would come looking for her at the club if King knew where she was the entire time. So . . . when did he find out Pearl was here with us? We know he landed in Miami a few months ago—Otto confirmed that. But Pearl's been with us for six months. And another thing . . . "Kennedy?" I ask.

"It's my mother's maiden name. Dad changed our surname. He said it was more fitting."

And not the same as his psycho brother's.

Pearl looks at me, frowning. "Anya knew I was sleeping with you," she says, panic rising. "If she's reported that information back to my uncle, he'll know I'm not—"

"It doesn't matter." I hold a hand up.

"He saw me at the hotel. With you." She frowns. "I don't know if he knows I was with you. Maybe he—"

"It doesn't matter." King asked for Pearl intact. That tells me he can't know about me. It also tells me that Anya wasn't working for

King, or he'd have that piece of crucial information. Danny's figured that much out too. She was working for Sandy. But does *he* know, and, if so, why hasn't he told King? I go to Pearl, dipping, getting close. "I have to go talk to the men."

She shakes her head mildly as I nod mine. King has inflicted unthinkable atrocities on her over the years. So bad, she's still terrified, even now when she's safe here with me. And unlucky for King, that just enhances my unbridled hatred and anger.

I press my mouth to hers. "Don't be scared. That's an order."

"He has Nolan."

"He has a target on his head, Pearl. That's what he has." I plan on hitting that target.

First time.

Point-blank.

Chapter 59

DANNY

"I liked that rug," I mutter as Goldie rolls it up. "Definitely not salvageable?"

She pauses rolling, points a filthy look my way.

"Okay." I surrender, hands up, before lighting up. "The rug goes."

"I have a spare," she mutters.

"You do?" I ask, surprised. I don't know why. I've made a lot of messes in this office. I wander over to the Picasso hanging over the fireplace, taking a moment to admire it. It's been too long since I have. I still don't know if the damn thing is real. "Is it, Pops?"

"I think it is."

I look over my shoulder. James is in the doorway. "I don't know." I motion to it with my smoke, pointing at the signature. "It looks . . . off." I tilt my head, pouting. "Pops took it as payment from a bad debtor." He killed him anyway. *No second chances.*

"He would have had it authenticated, surely."

I hum, going to my desk. We have more important things to worry about, and I'm itching to get on and deal with them. "Brad emerged yet?"

"No. Give it time." James goes to the cabinet and pours us both a drink, one for Brad too. So he's expecting him soon. Good. James lowers into the chair opposite me and slides my drink across the leather top. "Are you wondering what I'm wondering?"

I laugh, taking a swig of Scotch. "My head's a bit busy right now. What are you wondering?"

"I'm still wondering who took out the two Russians and Mexicans and carved your family emblem into their chests. Because the two prime suspects, King and Anya Dimitri, are, or have been, working with Sandy."

"And Sandy wouldn't order the deaths of two of his own," I muse.

"And Sandy and Luis are quite friendly."

I hum, turning my glass, thinking. "Do you know what I'm wondering?"

"What are you wondering?"

"I'm wondering how the fuck we get out of this mess and get Nolan back, because it sounds to me like King will only take Pearl *intact*"—I shudder—"and she's no longer that, thanks to Brad."

"Brad mentioned someone looking for her at the club."

"Yeah," I say quietly, my head getting busier.

"King wouldn't be so stupid to send someone into our club looking for her."

"Yeah," I breathe.

"So who did?"

My eyes narrow on my desk. So many fucking questions. The door knocks, and Beau pops her head around. "She's awake." Then there's a high-pitched shrill *cooeee* coming from the hallway. "And Aunt Zinnea just arrived."

"Great, I need a bit of color in my life right now." I rise from my chair as James collects Beau and leads her out of the office back into the hallway.

"Darlings." Zinnea claps her hands, but her painted lips purse when she obviously reads the room. "Is now a bad time?" she asks, reaching back and dragging forward a man. He looks like he's stepped off Phileas Fogg's hot-air balloon. So this is the one I've been hearing about.

"No, now is the perfect time." I step forward and offer a hand, smiling like a madman. "Danny Black. Welcome to Hell."

"Umm . . . Quinton," he says, pushing his glasses up his nose as he accepts. "Lovely house you have here."

"Yes, beautiful, isn't it?" I reply, just as Goldie passes carrying a new rug on her shoulder.

"Doesn't look much like hell."

I laugh, head thrown back. "You just got here, Quinton. Give it time."

"He's just playing," Beau says, muscling me out of the way.

"Am I?"

She rolls her eyes as Zinnea, still reading the room and concluding a shitstorm is brewing, takes Quinton's arm, clearly ready to haul him out of here.

"Quinton, this is my husband, James." Beau points to James. Problem is, he isn't James right now. He's The Enigma. I chuckle when Beau jabs James in the ribs and he forces a smile. "The others are in the kitchen. I'll take you there, introduce you."

"No, no, no." Zinnea starts moving toward the front door with Quinton hanging on to her arm. "It's obviously a bad time. We'll get out of your hair. I just thought it was about time he met the men."

"You're not going anywhere, Zinnea," I say, taking the handrail on the stairs and leaning on it, crossing one leg over the other. "We're on lockdown."

"God damn it," she says, quickly looking at Quinton and apologizing for her blue language. "What's happened?"

"Nothing," Beau rushes to tell her. "Everything is fine."

"Yes, except someone just tried to kidnap my daughter, kill my wife, someone *has* kidnapped Brad's son, Pearl's upstairs with endless broken bones, the spa's been blown up, and Brad fucked a virgin worth one-hundred-million-dollars, which might mean the Russians, Mexicans, and a psycho cunt from England could attack us imminently." I take a drag of my cigarette and finish my Scotch. "But other than that, everything is tickety-fucking-boo."

"Good Lord," Zinnea murmurs, as Quinton blinks repeatedly, and Beau scowls at me.

I bare my teeth at her, and she flings me a look to suggest I should pack it in. It's fine. I'm done.

"Brad's son?" Zinnea asks. "A virgin?"

"I'll explain." Beau gives me one final scowl before ushering her aunt and the boyfriend off into the kitchen.

"Where the hell is Brad?" I ask, looking up the stairs.

"Esther cooked. You should eat." James follows Beau, and I trudge after them, scanning the room when I make it there. No wife. No daughter. I find Mum spooning stew into a bowl and passing it to the Vikings. I can see the guilt still lingering in them. Mum nods toward the garden, so I head there. I find Rose at the back near the summer house pushing Maggie in her stroller, a Doberman flanking each side. Guarding her. They sense the looming danger.

I stand watching her for a while, remembering the first time she encountered my dogs. When she was my *guest*. After I'd held her hand against a burning hot toaster. She didn't feel pain back then.

She does now.

As do I.

Excruciating, crippling, debilitating pain.

She reaches the end of the path and turns, the dogs turning in a perfect circle with her, stopping for a moment, before walking on when she starts pushing the stroller again. And when Rose sees me and stops, the dogs stop too, sitting. I take one step toward my wife and daughter.

And they growl, teeth bared.

"Heel," Rose says calmly. They lie down. "I needed some fresh air."

"I needed some love." I approach with caution. I don't mind admitting I'm a little wary of being mauled by Cindy and Barbie. They've learned to protect the women and children before anyone else.

"Away," Rose says, a wry smile on her face, and they dash off.

I hook an arm around her neck and pull her in, pushing my face into her hair. I don't tell her everything will be okay. I don't tell her not to worry. And I definitely don't tell her to be strong for me. All pointless, wasted words. She's been with me long enough to know the drill. I peek down at Maggie as she sleepy snorts, pulling the blanket across her face. To think she was almost taken. My stomach turns, but I tamper down the anger. I need a level head. I need information.

"I'm not going to ask what you're planning," Rose says, her words muffled.

"If you did, I'd tell you."

She pulls out and looks up at me. "I'm tired of worrying."

I feel at her cheek. "And I'm tired of killing." Dipping, I kiss her gently, seeking entry with my tongue. She moves in closer, her front pressed to mine, and our kiss soon becomes unstoppably firmer, more desperate, her hands in my hair, my palms holding her face. My dick swells, rubbing into her, and I groan, taking one hand to her arse and pushing her farther into me. Rose and I have always been similar. It's what pulled us together in the first place. Dangerous lust. Unthinkable pasts. A fucked-up connection neither of us could control. Today, she killed a woman for messing with her family. And true to our fucked-up relationship, it turned me on. *No second chances.* It's been a stark reminder. Trust no one.

Fuck, I need her.

Now.

I rip my mouth away and gasp in her face, and she reads my eyes in a heartbeat. We both look down at Maggie in the stroller. Sound asleep. "I mean," I pant. "It's just the same as her being asleep in the bedroom." I start walking Rose to the summer house, taking her around the side and pushing her against the wood. "The last time you had your back up against this wall, it was the dogs keeping you there."

She smiles, yanking my belt open as I lift the skirt of her dress and rip her knickers off. She gasps, pulling me out of my boxers and stroking, licking across my lips. I close my eyes and slow my breathing, absorbing the feel of her soft hand working me for a few moments, taking the calm, before I tackle her mouth, bat her hand away, and pull her leg up to cradle my hip. I stare into her eyes. Thrust forward. Inhale as I slide into her. "Fuck, that feels good." I cast a quick look over my shoulder, checking Maggie. I ignore my conscience telling me how debased this is. I'm too desperate for a release of pressure. My head's full, my balls are full. One's got to give.

"God, this is so wrong," Rose whispers, kissing me between her words. Moving with me, taking every drive. "We should stop."

"I'll think more clearly if I come." I fist her hair with my spare hand, squeezing her leg.

"Okay. If it'll save your life."

"It could."

"Then fuck me."

"With pleasure."

I slam into her hard, moving my hand to her mouth to muffle her yell. The pressure builds. "Fuck." I start to sweat.

"Danny."

"Fuck, fuck, fuck."

"Danny!"

I thrust harder, watching her eyes mist, cloud with desire. My neck muscles strain, my teeth ache from the force of my bite. I bang into her more, she slams her head against the wood, bites my palm. "Shit!" I move my hand and replace it with my mouth, attacking with force. It's coming. Her walls are clenching. Her moves are less controlled, clumsier, an obvious sign she's close. I pull back, assess her, and up the ante again.

Closer.

Faster.

Closer.

"Danny!"

Faster.

Closer.

"Oh my God." She exhales over the words and starts twitching against me, and my dick detonates, my knees go weak, giving, and I slump forward, pinning her to the wood.

"Fucking hell."

She pants and gasps, arms holding my shoulders, head dropped back, looking up at the sky. I take her chin and direct her face back down. Kiss her far more gently than I just fucked her.

She feels my face, her fingertip dragging from my eye to my lip across my scar. "Come back to me," she whispers, still a little short of breath.

"Where else would I go?" I turn my face out slightly, latching on to her finger, and suck it into my mouth. Maggie stirs, and I laugh under my breath. "Hard and fast has a whole new meaning these days," I whisper, slipping out on a suppressed grunt. I look down at Rose's chest. "As does getting you wet."

She pouts down at her leaking boobs as I pull my jeans up and button the fly.

"Sore?" I ask, the strain of them against her dress making me wince on her behalf.

"Not as much." She pulls her dress back into place and wanders over to Maggie as I follow, doing up my belt. "Hey," she coos, leaning over the stroller. "Is someone hungry?"

"Starving," I mutter, one hand claiming the handle and pushing Maggie back to the house, the other claiming Rose's hand.

Brad's coming down the stairs as we pass through the hallway, and I stop, evaluating his persona. I fucking hate what I conclude. White-hot rage. "The office," he says as he stalks past, his thumbs working across the screen of his phone. "Everyone."

"How's Pearl?" Rose calls.

"Alive."

"I need to thank her," she says quietly, looking down at our baby girl. I can't even let my mind go there. It would be Armageddon.

"Mum will watch Maggie."

"I need to feed her first before my boobs burst."

"Or *she* bursts," I say dryly, looking toward the office, kind of worried about what I'm about to find out. I remember all too vividly the emotions that flooded me the day Rose shared her past with me. She'd been sent to seduce me. Sent to get information, set me up. Get me killed. We can't argue Pearl was serving a similar purpose for the enemy and Brad took the bait. No one sends a fucking virgin to loosen a man's lips with her power of seduction, for obvious fucking reasons. Pearl was here because she was terrified of the alternative. Brad's simply an additional layer to the messy situation. He's not going to be in a good place.

I walk Rose to the kitchen and nod to the others, who all get up and follow me to the office. Brad's arms are braced against the drinks cabinet, the glass James poured for him empty.

"You'd better sit down," he says, facing the room. Everyone, quiet, apprehensive, looks at each other as we all find a seat. "I'm going to give you the shorter, less graphic version, because I don't think I can hear it all out loud again."

My heart thuds hard, and I shift in my chair, trying to get comfortable as James flicks wary eyes my way.

"Pearl's father was Bernard King's brother."

"He's her uncle?" James breathes.

"What was her father's name?" Otto asks.

"He was known as Arnold Kennedy. Before that, he was Arnold King. He changed his surname."

"Why?" I ask.

"To try and disassociate himself from his brother."

"Why?"

"Because his brother's a sadistic, psychopathic fuck who terrorized him and his family. A bully. A thug. Pearl's father wasn't exactly a legit businessman, but he was smart. Wealthy. Bernard King is a loose cannon. No one wants to do business with him. Be associated with him."

I cock my head, watching as Brad tries and fails to restrain his anger. "The Russians and Mexicans do. And that speaks for itself."

Brad eyes me briefly. He agrees. "King killed Pearl's dad in a rage when she was ten. Made it look like a drunk-driving accident. Her mother ki—" It looks like he's shaking something out of his head while clearing his throat. *Jesus fucking Christ, please don't say what I think you're going to say.* "Her mother killed herself and left Pearl in the sole care of King when she was thirteen."

Everyone looks both engrossed and really fucking worried, and they don't even know Brad's mother committed suicide. *Jesus Christ.*

"Her father's twenty-million-pound estate was left in a trust fund until Pearl turns twenty-five, so King had to wait until then to force the sale."

"Or kill—"

"He'd gotten away with one murder and a suicide. It was too risky." Brad's head drops. "He did . . . things."

"Like what?" I ask, feeling everyone's shocked eyes shoot my way.

Including Brad's. "Don't make me say it."

"I need you to say it. I need everyone here to know and understand the gravity of your burning anger right now." I stand. "I need everyone to know what we're dealing with and how gruesome King's death will be."

Brad's breathing becomes heavy. "He put a tracking chip in her neck so she couldn't run away. He put a fishing hook through her lip so he could reel her in to him." Sweat starts to bead on his forehead. Pearl's piercing. *A fucking fishing hook?* "He punched her in the side of her head because he simply felt like it. Knocked her out. Put her in a crate and fed her from a bowl like a dog. Your average, everyday child abuse. Depending on his mood, of course. On a good day, he'd lock her in the outhouses in the dead of winter with no clothes."

Jesus fucking Christ.

Goldie's head goes into her hands, Ringo's cheeks balloon, and Otto strokes at his beard, his lips straight. James is expressionless. But utterly disgusted.

"He lived like a lord on Arnold Kennedy's estate. Parties, shootouts, blowing things up. He kept Pearl as a pet. Then, I assume, he was introduced to the dark web and hit the one-hundred-million-dollar jackpot." Brad laughs, a little manic, a lot in agony. "And do you know what's most fucked up?" he asks the room. "Pearl wanted to go. She thought she was getting away from the evil fucker. She thought it would be better with her new owner." He laughs harder, his fists balling. He's going to explode. "But it wouldn't have been, would it? It would have been the same, but with the added bonus of being raped every day." He swings around and punches the wall. "Fuck!"

I don't go to him. I stay well clear. I'm wondering how the fuck he's still here and not on a manhunt.

"And now he's not been paid, he wants his pet back, *intact*, and the fucker has my son too." He falls back against a wall and looks up at the ceiling. Sweating. But I can't let him focus on his anger and hurt for too long. It'll eat him up inside—he needs to trust me on that. I'm sure James is thinking the same.

"The guy who came to the club looking for her," I say, my plan working, Brad's attention piqued instantly. "He had nothing on him?"

"A phone. It was empty."

"Odd."

"I gave it to Otto." Brad looks at him.

As do I. "You knew about this?"

"I was given a phone," Otto says. "I looked into it. Came up with nothing. I didn't know I had to run everything past you."

I feel my lip twitching to curl. Now is not the time to pick a fight with Otto. Or is he picking a fight with me? Feels like it. "Where's the body?" I ask, slowly tearing my eyes from Otto to Brad.

"Nolan got rid of it."

"Oh, so Nolan knew about it too?" I ask. "The fuck, Brad?"

"What did you want me to do, Danny?"

"Talk to me!"

"Oh, like you talked to me when Rose got inside *your* head? Like you talked to me when you fucked off to Winstable to meet the Romanians on your fucking own?"

I back down instantly. *Fuck.* I was protecting Rose. Protecting *him*. God, how is that nearly four years ago? I remember Brad looking like he was having a fit on the driveway as I drove away. I push my lips out, sulking. "Rose was planted. I was worried you'd kill her if I told you all the sordid details."

"Well, Pearl wasn't planted. She was seeking fucking asylum. Safety."

"You didn't know that then."

"No, but something wasn't adding up. I also knew she was twenty-one, and I'm a lot fucking older than twenty-one."

"And you didn't know she was a virgin?"

He reaches for his nose, pinching the bridge, inhaling. "No, I already told you that. Not the first time."

"But the—"

"Second, third, fourth, fifth time?" He throws his arms up. "Yes. I found out after the first time. Am I on trial?"

"Just trying to understand—"

"I have something." Otto gets up from the couch and walks across the office with his laptop open, taking it to Brad. "The guy who turned up at the club looking for Pearl. Is that him?"

Brad frowns at the screen. "Yeah, that's him."

Otto appears dazed. "That's Hector Gillingham. Abductor and contract killer."

"Excuse me?" Brad looks at me, like I can confirm what Otto's said.

"The image you sent me wasn't great after you'd made mash potato out of his face, so I started scanning face shapes in the system."

"What the fuck?"

I couldn't agree more. "How did you get that information?"

"I have my ways." Otto goes back to his laptop, tapping furiously at the keys.

"Are you joking?" Ringo laughs. "Is there some kind of online store you browse when you're in the market for a killer?"

"Hire a killer dot com," I say dryly, seeing James holding back a smile. Because he knows. Of course he knows. "Were you verified, James? Did you have a blue tick to confirm you were legit The Enigma and not someone posing as you?"

"Do the killers offer guarantees?" Ringo goes on, astounded. "This is a joke, right?"

Goldie's also holding back a smile. Because she knows too. "No joke," she says.

"Someone hired him to kill Pearl?" Brad asks. "Then why the fuck would he be asking after her at the club? Sounds like a pretty stupid thing to do if you're planning on killing someone."

"Not if you don't care," I muse, my brain about to explode. "And why would he? He's a ghost. We only found out who he is because James is a former member of hire a killer dot com."

"I wasn't a member, actually."

"Were you too expensive?"

"I didn't charge."

No, because his mission was personal.

"Fuck this." Brad laughs over his words as he heads for the door. I rush over and block it, shaking my head, and his lips twist. "Screw your head on straight," I order.

"Fuck!" He swings around and yells at the ceiling.

I cast a worried look James's way. He agrees. He's getting too emotional. "We've got this," I say, laying a palm on his shoulder and squeezing. "Sit down." I guide him to the chair and push him down, pouring him a drink and putting it in his hand.

"King wouldn't have hired a hitman," Brad breathes, taking his drink. "He needs Pearl alive."

Right. God, my head. "The questions we need answering," I say, getting myself a top-up.

"Who killed the Mexicans and Russians and engraved the Black family emblem on their chests?" James kicks things off.

"Not a fucking clue," I answer.

"Who did the drive-by on Brad?" he goes on.

"Maybe King." I take a swig of my drink.

"Why?" Brad asks. "It doesn't make any sense. Why bother with the Russians and Mexicans if he's going to try and take us down himself?"

"Who hired Gillingham to kill Pearl?" James continues.

"Or kidnap her," I add. "In which case, it *definitely* could have been King. Abduction isn't killing."

"Again, doesn't make sense," Brad mumbles. "King went to Sandy and Luis. Promised them guns in exchange for their back up. He knows he can't take us on alone, so why suddenly start trying?"

"He can take us on if he's got Nolan," I say, putting that out there. Brad gives me the eye.

"Do Sandy and Luis know King's got Nolan?" James asks. "And if Anya knows Pearl's not a virgin, why doesn't King? Surely she told Sandy." He gives his attention to Otto. "Anything on her phone?"

"Working on it," Otto replies, not looking up.

"The guy in the alley who mugged Pearl?" I prompt, like there's not enough fucking unanswered questions.

Brad snorts. "That's a question I *do* have the answer to."

"Oh good," I quip. "Hit me with it. I was beginning to think we're stupid."

"He was a nobody. A chancer." Brad says, looking at Otto again.
I recoil. "You had him check that out too?"

"Don't start, Danny."

I breathe in some patience. Right. Losing my shit will get us
nowhere. *Think*. "How did King know Pearl was in Miami?"

Brad strokes his nape. "The tracker King put in Pearl's neck. He
didn't tell the Poles about it. Pearl did. They removed it."

Fucking hell. "Does that mean King knows Pearl's been in our
care for the past six months?"

James narrows his eyes, thoughtful. "He's only been in Miami a
few months."

So is that a no? So many fucking questions. So many answers
needed. Fuck, this feels like a bastard of a brain-teaser. I knock back
my Scotch and pour myself another, but freeze when a phone rings.
Everyone's looking around the room, waiting for who claims the call.

Brad lifts his arse and feels at his back pocket. Pulls out a mobile.
"Pearl's," he says, staring at the screen.

"Be cool," James warns, going to him.

He laughs under his breath and connects the call. Doesn't speak.
I don't think he can. He's struggling to breathe.

"My instinct tells me I've not come through to my darling niece."

Brad shifts in his chair, while we all watch, on edge, all hoping
and praying he handles this delicately. Wisely. "You're a smart man."

"I want her back."

The atmosphere thickens, all eyes on Brad as he stands abruptly
and starts pacing. "I'm sure you've heard, you immoral piece of shit,
that we're famous for having issues with men who abuse, rape, and
traffic women."

"Ah, yes. I've heard. Something to do with The Brit's wife, yes?
My Russian friend did mention you may be averse to returning what's
rightly mine. Hence, I took your boy." He pauses, and I lower my
arse to the desk, willing myself to stay put. "Sandy also alluded to a
certain fondness for The Brit's wife."

Oh, he did not. I'm across the office like an arrow, swiping
the phone from Brad's hand. "You listen to me, you—" It's quickly
removed, and Brad's got a palm pushed into my chest to keep me at
arm's length.

King's torturous laugh down the line fills the room. "I'm hitting nerves left and right today. Where's The Enigma? Is he there? I don't want him to feel left out. My Russian friend sends his regards. Wants you to know he's looking forward to a little one-on-one time with the ex-cop once you're dealt with. I've told him I'll lend him my fishing kit."

Fuck. Me.

I blow out my cheeks as James sinks deeper into his chair, silent. But the evil splashed across his face? Does this piece of shit know what he's doing? Who he's dealing with? For the first time Brad appears together, while James and I restrain our rampant rage. He pulls his phone out of his pocket while keeping Pearl's at his ear. Stares down at the screen.

He walks to my desk and pulls a pad out of the drawer, writing something and holding it up.

We need to talk to Richard Bean.

I feel my forehead bunch but still hold a hand up to Ringo, who quickly leaves, Goldie in tow.

"What do you want, King?" Brad asks, going to the couch and lowering next to James.

"Are you deaf? I want my niece."

"I think you want money more."

He hums, laughing lightly. "I am partial to a dollar or . . . two hundred million of them."

I balk at Brad. He remains impassive. "Two . . . hundred million?" he repeats.

"That is correct."

"I thought the deal with the Poles was for one hundred million."

"That was before you caused me this inconvenience. And now I have your son *and* you don't want me to supply the enemy."

"Two hundred million," Brad says calmly. "For the girl, my son, and no supplies."

"Two hundred million," King confirms.

Two hundred fucking million? I blow out my cheeks. Start sweating.

"I want proof of life," Brad says.

"You got it," King replies in a shitty American accent. "I want to see my pumpkin."

"Absolutely no deal."

"Fine, no deal." There are a few rustles. He's hanging up?

"Wait," Brad barks, every inch of him stiff. "Why? Why do you want to see her?"

"I have something for her. A goodbye gift."

"What?"

"She'll know. Besides, I would like to see her one last time. Say goodbye. We became rather close since her parents died."

"I'll send you the arrangements." Brad hangs up and chews the edge of Pearl's mobile for a few moments, thinking, while we all wait. Impatient.

"Brad?" I snap, palms facing the ceiling. "What the fuck? Two hundred million?"

"Yes, two hundred million."

I laugh and pull the pockets of my trousers out. "Everyone empty your pockets. Let's see how much we can scrape together."

"Pearl's laid up," James says, standing. "She can't go."

"I know," Brad grates. She wouldn't be going even if she wasn't lying battered and bruised in Brad's bed. "I'm thinking." He scowls at the rug.

"Let's just tell him she's not a virgin anymore. She's not worth shit to him, so why the fuck would we pay him?"

"And risk pissing him off?" Brad barks. "He has my fucking son, Danny!"

I hold my hands up in surrender, and Brad takes a breath. Yes, King might be pissy, but I think two hundred *fucking* million would ease the sting. *Fuck.*

"And the last thing we need is King handing over the guns that Sandy and Luis need to take us down." James adds, reminding me of that little issue too. "We need to remember why King went to them in the first place."

Because he can't take us down on his own. But now he's trying. Why? Why not just get his money from us, give Sandy the guns, and fuck off back to London? "If money's all he wants, he could get it from Sandy for the guns," I say. Brad's right. This isn't making sense. Now he's trying to do a deal with us, no Sandy or Luis involved.

Pearl's phone dings and Brad opens the message, his jaw tight. "The fucker," he breathes, turning away, holding the phone out. I take it from his hand and look at the screen. Nolan. Gagged. Battered.

God damn that dipshit, he put up a fight. I give the phone to Otto, and he gets straight to work. "Get Leon," Brad says. "Tell him to start getting the cash together."

My shoulder drops. Fucking hell. "Brad, I don't know if we have that much to hand."

"Doesn't matter. He's not counting two hundred million on the spot, is he?" He throws a hand up, walking up and down.

"And Bean?" James asks. "What's the deal?"

"Uncle Carlo went through a fishing faze once, didn't he?" Brad asks, swerving James's question, going to the office door and leaving.

James and I look at each other like *what the fuck*? "Did he?" James asks.

"Yeah, about fifteen years ago." I get up and go after Brad, James flanking me. "It lasted two weeks. He didn't catch anything, and the peace he was promised eluded him."

The front door is open when we make it to the foyer, and we break out into the late afternoon sunshine, seeing Brad heading around the side of the house toward the garages. "What the fuck is he doing?"

We go after him and find him rummaging through the shit piled high at the back of the garages. All shit Pops bought during one of his peace-searching missions. "Found it," Brad pants, knocking some buckets and a jet washer out the way. He holds up a rod and a case, and marches back between us. "Let's go fishing."

Chapter 60

BRAD

James's and Danny's bewildered expressions were understandable as they followed me back into the house. They're still watching me now, an hour later, as I divide my time between the fishing hooks and my Scotch, while Otto remains on the couch analyzing the footage King sent through. I hold up a hook. "Rusty," I muse, laying it on the desk.

"Think I'll have another drink," Danny says.

"I'll join you." James pulls a chair over and sits, watching me lay out the fishing hooks meticulously.

"Brad, what the fuck are you doing?" Danny finally asks, dropping down into his chair and passing James his drink.

"Have you got Leon sorting the money?"

"Yes," he answers shortly.

"Anything?" I ask Otto without looking.

"Nothing."

I grit my teeth, looking at my work. Then I relax back in my seat and ponder . . . everything, unraveling it all. And James and Danny let me. Waiting. Showing patience but clearly not feeling it. Thank fuck they trust me.

The door swings open and a man staggers into the office, blindfolded and gagged with thick duct tape, Ringo helping him along with a solid boot up his ass. Goldie steps forward and rips off the tape. "Fuck," he curses, reaching for his face and feeling where his brows once were. "You don't know who the hell you're deal—" His mouth snaps shut when he clocks me, Danny, and James around the desk.

"Dealing with?" I say, smiling, feeling an edge of psycho take over. "Oh, you poor, delusional fuckwit." I get up and seize his shoulder, pushing him into a chair as Ringo and Goldie leave.

"What are you doing? I'm a cop! You'll get the lethal injection!"

I get down in his face. "They need to determine a crime was committed, and to determine a crime was committed, they need a body." I smile. "I don't plan on leaving any evidence."

Bean leans back, panicked eyes jumping between the three of us, and Danny smiles. "The American one is in a far worse mood than we were when we called for coffee the other morning," he says.

"Awful," James adds. "How's your leg?"

I look down at Bean's thighs—I know Danny Black—then rest my palms on both, squeezing. He screams. "Still sore, I'd say." I muse, making Danny chuckle. "Now back to business." I clap my hands but still when I hear the distinct sound of water hissing. I frown and glance underneath the chair that Bean's slumped on, seeing piss trickling down the legs.

"Anyone else hear that?" Danny says quietly. "Leaking all over my new fucking rug." He picks up a paperweight and throws it with force at Bean's knee, and he yelps in pain.

I slide a hook off the desk. "Would you mind?" I say, and James gets straight up and circles Bean, taking his arms and holding them back.

"What are you doing?" he yells, horrified eyes on the rusty hook as I lean in. "No, stop!" His head thrashes, hindering me.

I stand tall and sigh. "More hands."

"Oh, I'm good with my hands." Danny's soon holding Bean's head, allowing me to shove the hook through his tongue.

"Arhhhhh!"

"Perfect," I muse, looping a fishing line through and trailing it back to the desk. I take a seat, giving the hook a little tug, jerking Bean's head. It's an effort to stop mental images of Pearl in this situation from sending me over the edge. Bean does *not* want me to tip the edge. Not yet, anyway. "Now we're all comfortable." I take my Scotch in my spare hand. "Let's get on with the show." I look at the boys. "Get *some* of these fucking questions answered."

"Wh-what do you want?" Bean stutters, struggling to talk. "I'm sorry about blackmailing your son."

I give the line a warning tug, making him yell, more in fear than in pain. "Are you, Bean?" I ask. "Are you really?"

"Yes, yes I am!"

I snarl and yank the line, pulling just enough to rip his flesh a little. A bead of blood trickles down his chin. "You know the thing that pisses me off most about bent cops?"

"What?" James asks.

"They're greedy?" Danny volunteers.

"Exactly." I swig my drink and slam the glass down, making Bean jump, making the line pull again. "Now *that* was your fault," I say, getting up and walking toward the Picasso. I come to a stop when the line pulls taut and look over my shoulder, seeing Bean's head jutting forward, James still holding him in the seat. I smile and take a step back. "How do you know Bernard King, Bean?"

"I don't."

Liar.

I sag where I stand, dropping my head. "I'm disappointed." I take one more step toward the fireplace, feeling the pull on the line as I look up and admire the painting. "Mind explaining how he would know the Black family emblem? Because he'd only get that from us or the cops." I face him. Stupid fucker will fall flat on his face if James lets go. "And he definitely didn't get it from us." I feel Danny's interested attention on me. "It was you, wasn't it, Bean?" I ask, smiling, sounding excited. "Did you show him some photos from the archives?"

He shakes his head, if only mildly to avoid the pull. So I fix that, moving closer to the painting. He's breathing so heavily through his nose, snot is flying out.

"Any of this jogging your memory?"

"Anything at all?" Danny asks. "I mean, I'm enjoying the show, but I'm really fucking hungry, and my mum's made her signature stew." Danny rubs his belly, and James rolls his eyes. "We have a lot of mouths to feed in this family. I'd be most fucked off if it was all gobbled up before I make it to the kitchen."

"No one likes a hangry Brit," I say quietly.

Tug, tug.

"Fuck, fine, yes, it was me." Bean practically whimpers. "I showed him."

"Of course it was you, Bean, and do you know how I know?"

His eyes get progressively wider. "How?"

I feel Danny and James watching me carefully, quietly curious. "Because King's got my son, and the only person in Miami outside my family who knows Nolan is my son, is you."

"Fuck," Danny breathes, slamming the heel of his palm into his forehead. "Of course."

"Oh God." Bean dribbles and shakes, realization hitting him hard. "You must understand, he threatened me. My family."

"Oh . . ." I jut out my bottom lip. "You were cornered."

"Yes, yes, I was cornered."

"And blackmailing my son," I ask, "Did King make you do that too?"

"What?" An extra layer on panic arrives on his face.

"Am I not speaking loudly enough?" I ask James as I go to Bean, fisting his shirt and yanking him up to my snarling face. "When your plan to pin the murders of the Russians and Mexicans on us went to shit, did King make you blackmail my son?" I bellow.

His head shakes, more snot flies, more dribble mixing with the trickles of blood down his chin. "No."

"No, he didn't. That was all you. Because you're a greedy fuck, aren't you? You want to get yourself noticed by the FBI, don't you?"

"Oh, you'd hate being an agent," Danny says, grimacing. "We kill them even more gruesomely."

"So you gave King what he needed to frame us—fuck what his motive was—and thought you'd swoop on in and claim the murders of the two Russians and two Mexicans solved. Except it didn't work out, did it? Because our friend Agent Higham raised the fact that the emblems were carved by someone *left*-handed." I tug the line again with my *right* hand, hearing Danny and James's huffs of comprehension. "And Higham just confirmed it was *you* investigating those crimes. *You* trying to nail us for the murders King committed. So, with that plan fucked—because you couldn't very well arrest King, could you?—you resorted to blackmailing my son for information on Danny. Because one unlawful man is better than none, right?"

"I feel targeted," Danny grunts.

"I feel insulted," James adds.

"Problem is, Bean, you dumb piece of shit, you neglected to see past your own agenda to make it into the FBI, and now you've contributed toward a huge fucking shitstorm in Miami. You've stalled us, sent us on a wild fucking goose chase." I thrust my face in his. "And King has my son and is using him to blackmail us!"

"I didn't . . . I never—"

"Do you know what King used to do to his niece?" I ask, suddenly calm.

"His niece?"

"Yes, his niece. He abused her for years. Sold her to some rich, depraved rapist. She happens to be my woman now."

"Oh, God, please." He leans back, and I yank on the line. "Arhhhh!"

"This. This is what he used to do." Another sharp tug. "Not nice, is it?" *Tug, tug. Yelp, yelp.* I walk toward the fireplace. Look back when the line pulls. "Oh dear," I whisper. "It appears we've reached the end of the line."

"No, please!"

I yank it with force and rip the hook out of his tongue, provoking a blood-curdling scream as James keeps him in his chair.

"Ewww." Danny grimaces at Bean's flapping tongue. "That's fucking gross."

The office door swings open. "Ah." James releases Bean. "Speak of the devil and he shall appear."

Higham watches Bean hit the floor. "Oh, for fuck's sake." And walks straight back out, Tank following him.

"That was a flying visit," Danny muses, just as Higham pushes his way back in and takes in Bean on the floor again, like he's hoping he walked into the wrong room and will find a completely different scene.

"What the hell is going on?" he asks, looking at each of us in turn, like a principal giving a group of boys an opportunity to explain before their punishments are laid down.

I point to Bean. "I'm kind of in the middle of something here, so do you mind waiting in the kitchen?"

"Fucking hell, you three will be the death of me." He backs out and slams the door.

"Don't eat all the stew!" Danny yells to the door.

Bean rolls onto his back, spitting blood, mumbling inaudible prayers. I go to him, get down on one knee, and hold out my hand. A gun lands in it swiftly. "I will rip the tongue out of every man who has ever worked with Bernard King, helped him, associated with him." I push the end of the Glock into his groin and fire. "And blow their balls off too." He goes limp, and I toss the gun aside, fetching myself a fresh drink.

It's silent while I enjoy it, Danny and James giving me a moment. Then I face them.

"So King killed the Russians and Mexicans?" James asks.

"Yeah. Like I said, only Bean knows who Nolan is to me. That's how King knows Nolan's mine. That's how he got the Black family emblem. He's been talking to Bean."

"Fuck." Danny curses, looking at the piece of scum on the rug.

"And Nolan's face confirmed it." I point to Otto, who's still happily working in the corner, unperturbed. "There's more damage to the right side of his face."

"Left hooks," Danny breathes.

I drop into a chair and take a breather. "And Pearl indicated the right side of her head when she was telling me what he used to do to her."

"The fucker." Danny lights up and takes a few puffs.

"King was promised the money from the Polish after Pearl's safe delivery to her new owner. As we know, she didn't make it to her new owner." I blow out my cheeks as all the puzzle pieces begin to slot into place nicely. Or not so nicely. "The polish removed the tracker from Pearl's neck. Must have been at Winstable, so that was her last known location and it brought King to Miami. King made a point of getting pally with Bean at golf, made a few threats. The rumor was, *we* took the Polish out, so finding his virgin started with us. King knew he couldn't take us on alone, and he'd heard the Russians and Mexicans were in the market for some weapons, so he went to them."

"Jesus," Danny breathes. "He really wants his money."

I hum. "And he needed the Russians and Mexicans to want us dead if he was going to get his virgin back, hence he killed their men and framed us."

"Waste of his fucking time," Danny mutters. "Sandy and Luis want us dead without that added incentive."

"Maybe, but it's an effective incentive, yes? A good way to renew the hatred."

"I suppose. And the hitman at the club?" James asks. "King?"

"No, I think it was Sandy who sent him. But not to kill Pearl. What use is Pearl to King if she's dead?"

James's frown is impressive. "What? Sandy sent someone to

abduct Pearl? Why?"

"Sandy needs King's guns, but he doesn't trust him. No one does. I think he was going to use Pearl as a bargaining chip to get his arsenal."

"Fuck," Danny breathes.

"Do we know if Anya told Sandy about Brad and Pearl yet?" James asks Otto.

"She told him," he says, holding Anya's phone up. "By text."

"What does it say?" I ask, getting up, my heart banging.

"That she's sleeping with The American."

"So why wouldn't Sandy tell King?" James asks.

"Because Pearl's worthless to King if she's not worth one hundred million. Sandy needs King to have some skin in the game."

"Jesus Christ," Danny breathes. "And now King's got *two*-hundred-million-dollars' worth of skin in the game, *and* he has Nolan, *plus* he doesn't need to do business with the Russians and Mexicans."

I stare forward, thinking. That's a lot of enemies to make.

"But, again," Danny continues. "What does it matter to King if Pearl's not a virgin anymore? He's bagging a cool two hundred million."

I don't know why it would matter to King, but something tells me it would. And to Danny's point, why didn't King just take money from Sandy for the guns if that's all he's interested in? *Because it wouldn't have been two hundred million?* I sink into my chair, uneasy. "There's not a chance in hell I'm taking Pearl to the exchange," I say quietly, but loud enough for everyone to hear me. Like Sandy, I don't trust that fucker King. "Has Sandy tried to contact Anya?"

"Yeah, he's tried." Otto replies. "Texts and calls."

"Should we reply?" Danny asks.

"No," I say resolutely. "Anya was spooked, hence she ran. She could have called Sandy to say she's leaving. She might not have had time. As far as Sandy's aware, she could have simply bailed. I don't want him to know that we've exposed her."

"Fucking hell, I need to eat," Danny moans, holding his aching head as he leaves the office, James not far behind, going to get their stew. And to appease the FBI agent who's dropped by.

But Otto remains on the couch. He looks at me, jerking his head, prompting me to go over. "Can you see what I can see?" he asks, as I study the footage of Nolan with him.

"I see it."

"And this," he says, switching the screen.

Fuck, yeah, I see it. "Thanks. Get Leon to clean the mess up." I get my phone out and make a call. He answers fast, as I knew he would. "Are you on your way?" I ask, following the others.

"Just looking for my American passport."

I smile. "I'm having a welcome party for you."

"Shall I bring a bottle?"

"Bring a crate."

Chapter 61

PEARL

I don't realize I'm holding my breath until I release it, tentatively letting go of the chair and taking cautious steps toward the edge of the terrace with no support, no one to hold me up. I feel like someone is constantly stabbing at my lung with a fork, the pain cutting. I watch as the glass gets closer and at the same time seems to get farther away, each step more painful than the last. "Come on," I say through gritted teeth, pushing the pain back because, really, it's nothing compared to what I've endured in the past. Nothing at all. I bite down harder on my back teeth, holding my side, my face screwing up. It's not nothing. It's everything. My pain now feels more acute, more real. Now, I have every reason to fight for relief. To not curl up into a ball and give up. To numb myself. Hide. I have something to live for again. I can't be weak. "I can do it." I stretch my hand out, trying to reach the rail.

Nearly there.

Just a few more steps.

"The fuck?"

I jump, hiss with pain, and fall forward, missing the rail. Brad catches me, just before I face-plant the glass. "Ow," I whisper, clenching his forearms as he eases me upright.

"I'll give you fucking ow," he mutters grumpily, slipping his arm under my knees and scooping me up. It hurts to get my arm around his neck, too, and my newly cast arm feels like lead where it rests on my chest. But my view?

I study his profile as he carries me back to the bed, marveling at his beauty. Even now, when he's stressed and scowling. So beautiful. He lowers me gently. "What the fucking hell are you doing?" he snaps.

"Doc said I should move around," I argue. "And my arse was getting sore from being on it for too long."

"I'll give you a sore ass too."

"You sure are in a giving mood this evening."

His warning look makes me smile. "Are you hungry?"

"Rose brought me some stew." I point to the bowl on the bedside, and Brad looks.

"You've not touched it."

I shrug, easing back against the pillow. Truth is, I was hungry. Then I foolishly asked Rose some questions. I didn't like the answers. "She's worried."

"Rose is always worried." He picks up the bowl and stirs the stew, cocking a leg and sitting on the edge of the bed. He's going to feed me.

"*I'm* worried," I add, watching for his reaction. He doesn't give me one, just keeps his focus on his task and scoops some vegetables onto the spoon, bringing it to my mouth. And because I don't want to add to his grumpiness, I take it. I don't like this. Not the stew, the situation. I chew and swallow as Brad gets more onto the spoon. "What are you going to do, Brad?"

"You know what I'm going to do." He peeks up, his eyes on my lip. He doesn't see a dainty little ring anymore. He sees a fishing hook. He sees a victim. He blinks and looks away, directing the spoon to my mouth. "Open."

"No."

"Eat the stew, Pearl."

"I don't want the fucking stew!"

The spoon clangs in the bowl, his face outraged. *Fuck* not adding to his grumpiness. He looks at my mouth again. And quickly looks away.

"Stop it," I order. "Don't make me that girl again."

His jaw is spasming as he stares at the bowl. "I'm sorry. I just—" His body lifts with his inhale. "I need some time to get my head around it." He smiles meekly.

I feel my throat clogging up, my panic rising. And what if he can't get his head around it? What if he can't see me as anything but that girl? What if . . . what if he doesn't want me? "I can't be her to you." My voice cracks, and I hate myself for it.

He watches me try to hold on to my tears. "Stop," he orders, placing the bowl down and getting up on the bed, on all fours, his knees and fists buried into the mattress on either side of my body. Caging me in. But not touching me. I look up at his face hovering over mine, his hair falling forward into his eyes. "You'll never be anything but a fucking hero to me, Pearl. A fighter."

"Then touch me," I whisper, begging him to hear me.

"You're too delicate."

"Touch me," I grate, and he shakes his head, his eyes dragging down my broken body.

"I'll never be the cause of your pain. I will never hurt you."

"You're hurting me now," I tell him, making him wince as I reach for his face and feel his stubble. His eyes close, his face turning into my touch, breathing in.

"I love you," he murmurs, "but I can't touch you." He turns a kiss onto my palm and gets up off the bed, pulling his T-shirt off, like some kind of sadistic arsehole. His chest looks pumped. Smooth. His bullet wound shimmers. I struggle up to sitting as he walks into the bathroom, taking the bandage off his arm as he goes, shutting the door. He can't touch me. Now or never?

My eyes dart across my bare knees. No. No, he is not making me a victim. I swing my legs off the edge of the bed on a suppressed, pain-filled grunt, and stand, cradling my arm to my chest as I walk slowly to the bathroom, each step sending shockwaves up my body into my ribs. I'm breathless by the time I make it there, and when I push the door open, Brad's in the shower. I make sure there's enough swing for it to hit the wall behind, alerting him to my presence. His hands are on his head, halfway pulling back his wet hair, his body naked and drenched.

"Are you kidding me?" he barks.

"I am not," I confirm, taking the doorframe for support.

"Get your ass back in bed." He snatches a towel down and covers himself, fastening it.

"I have an arse, Brad. And you can kiss it." I frown, and Brad jerks like he's been shot. Then his feet are slapping the tile floor, coming at me. "You're acting like my father," I yell, stopping him dead in his tracks, his expression injured. I take a moment to breathe, to gather my temper before it puts me on my arse. Not my ass, but my *arse*. There's no calm to be found. "I did not sign up to be bossed around and . . . and . . . and . . . parented!" I yell. "I signed up to have you. I signed up to be touched and it not hurt. To be loved and love back without being terrified my love would leave me. I signed up not to be abandoned and left alone, scared and lonely." My anger makes me stagger forward, and Brad catches me for the second time in a few minutes. Pain sears me, but it's nothing compared to the pain in my heart. I stare at his chest, my head low, my eyes low. Until Brad takes my throat and forces my face to his. I'm immediately lost in his lazy gaze. Immediately rocked by the level of love I feel for him. He's the only person I've given my whole heart to—all my trust and hope—and I'll be destroyed if I lost him.

"To be picked up when you fall down," he murmurs, pushing his mouth gently to mine, stopping my lip from quivering and breathing life back into me again. I melt into the tenderness of his lips on mine, the gentle swirl of his tongue, the heat of his mouth. And my world rights itself once again. It's a long, slow kiss. The best kind. I need him to kiss me every day like this. It goes on forever, but it still feels like too soon when he brings it to a gradual stop, pecking my lips gently and letting his face fall into the crook of my neck. "I've got you," he whispers, pressing light kisses across my throat. "I've got you."

I sigh, leaning on him. In every way. "I didn't mean to yell."

"I didn't mean to make you feel like I don't want you," he replies, his voice raspy. "It's—"

"A lot."

I feel him nod. Take a few breaths. "He wants to see you."

My body stiffens, and it hurts again. I think I expected that, if only because he's a sick bastard who thrives on the fear he sees in people. He's not seen that fear in me for a long time. Because he simply hasn't seen me. The moment in the hotel was brief and not enough to feed his kicks. But if one more time means never again. And, actually, if he's demanded it, there's only one right answer. Especially if we want to get Nolan back. "I'll do it. I'll see him."

Brad's quickly out of my neck, his face a picture of incredulity. "What?"

"I said I'd do it."

He laughs, not in humor, releasing me before quickly reclaiming me when I wobble. His face straightens. "It's a hard no."

"He won't return Nolan."

"He will for two hundred million."

I baulk at him. "You're paying him?" *Two hundred million?* "Wait. Does he know I'm not . . ." Did Anya tell anyone?

Brad shakes his head. "He doesn't know, and he has Nolan, Pearl. I can't risk pissing him off."

"But Anya knew."

Brad puts a finger over my lips. "Need to know," he says quietly.

"Oh my God, Brad." I blink, astounded, feeling incredibly wobbly again. "You can't pay him that." But what did I think was going to happen? My uncle would return Nolan, accept he wasn't getting me, and that would be that? Of course I didn't. But that's an insane amount of money.

"Shhhh," Brad hushes me, feeling at my face. "He's never coming near you again."

"My uncle doesn't bargain, Brad. He makes his demands and people meet the demands or—"

"Or, what?" he asks. "He kills them? Pearl, my love, you're not in the English countryside anymore. You're in Miami. You're in The Brit's mansion." He takes my neck and massages gently. "You're in my heart." It may be a completely unfitting time to swoon, but it happens nonetheless. "You have to trust me."

Trust him. *My God.* I nod halfheartedly—because what else *can* I do?—and let him smother me with kisses, fearful that he should be trusting *my* words. I know Bernard King. He shouldn't be underestimated.

"He said he has a gift for you," Brad says quietly. "Do you know what it is?"

I take in air. It could be only one thing. Something so precious to me. "My mother's necklace."

"A necklace?"

"My dad brought it for her when I was born. It's a pearl surrounded by rubies." I swallow. "Pearls for me, rubies for mother."

"Her name was Ruby?"

I nod. "She said it would be mine one day. He took it after I buried her."

"We'll get it back," Brad says, sounding sure, and definitely angry. "Come on, back to bed."

Bed? I'm sick of being in bed. "Can't I go downstairs for a while?"

A tea and a cigarette sound dreamy right now.

"You're too—" His body deflates when I give him a tired look. "Fine," he relents. "*Just* for a little while."

"Okay, Daddy," I breathe, and then yelp when he squeezes my arse before he sits me on the bed and pulls some jeans on. I blink back my awe as he picks me up and carries me downstairs across his arms. "Let me walk a little bit," I plead as he nears the bottom. I need to build up my strength, and Brad carrying me everywhere isn't going to help, even if it feels nice.

When he reaches the bottom, he dips and places me on my feet gingerly, watching my face for discomfort, so I work hard not to show it. "Okay?"

"Okay," I breathe, feeling his arm snake around my back. He walks me into the kitchen, and all of the chatter dies when everyone sees me. "Oh gosh, everyone is here," I say over an awkward laugh, all attention pointing my way. Faces full of sympathy. Oh, I don't like this. It was a mistake. They all know what's happened to me. They all know who I am. I start to back up, feeling resistance from Brad. I look up at him. "That's enough for one day," I whisper.

"I've got you," he says quietly, taking me toward the table. Fury jumps up and pulls out a chair. Then looks around the room, frowns, dashes off, and everyone watches him go, the big beast of a man moving fast. He appears a few moments later with a cushion from the TV room. Puts it on the chair. Pats it.

"I haven't got piles, Fury," I say, prompting a few snorts from the crowd that eases the atmosphere marginally. Brad helps me down to the chair next to Beau. She reaches for my hand and squeezes. Ella smiles weakly. Rose comes up behind me and hugs me gently around my shoulders. Esther places a cup of tea in my grasp and kisses my head before going back to the stove, dishing up a bowl and giving it to Tank. Danny flips me a wink. James nods mildly. Goldie, Ringo, and Otto all smile, more gently than their hard faces should allow. Even Zinnea and Quinton are here.

"All right, chick?" Mason asks.

I look to the corner of the room, where Mason is leaning against the counter, a beer in his hand. "All right." I smile.

Then Leon and Jerry walk into the kitchen. "All done," Leon says. "But the rug can't be saved. Pearl, my girl." He comes and gently hugs me from behind, and I peek at Brad. He rolls his eyes.

Jesus. Literally *everyone*.

"My darling," Zinnea sings, shoving Leon aside and cupping my face, smiling. "We should meditate."

"Zinnea," Quinton sighs. "Let the girl breathe."

"Are we done?" Brad asks the room, his face stern. And that's that. Everyone gets back to themselves, eating, drinking, and talking. Not much laughing. No Nolan. No Anya. This is a lockdown. Because of me.

Brad seems vacant now, lost in thought, and I'm not sure I like where those thoughts are. "Hey," I say gently, disturbing him. He blinks and gives me his attention. "Where were you?"

"Just . . . piecing a few things together."

"Like . . .?"

"Like nothing for you to worry yourself with." He dips and kisses my forehead, looking to Danny and James. This is the part when they disappear to plot.

"I'll be back," he says, leaving me at the table. Rose checks on Maggie in her crib—obviously not willing to let her out of her sight—and then lowers to a chair beside me, and Beau squeezes my hand again. How many times have they done this? Watched their men leave to make their battle plans? Watched their men leave and wonder if they'll see them again.

"Am I invited?" a man asks. I recognize him. He's been at the boatyard.

Brad laughs, not answering, and leaves.

"I guess I was never here, then," he calls.

"You guess right," Brad says over his shoulder. "Take care, Higham."

"Who is that?" I ask, considering the suited guy as he watches all the men and Goldie file out. Even the Vikings, Mason, Leon, and Jerry go.

"That's Agent Higham," Beau says, so casually.

"What?" I squeak. "Police?"

"FBI." Rose stands. "I'll see you out, Harold." She links arms with him and walks him out of the kitchen. "Always lovely to see you."

I shake my head in wonder and lift my tea, sipping, checking Ella across the table. I don't know her very well, but I hate how worried she seems. "Excuse me," Beau says, standing and leaving, following the cop and Rose.

I stare at a packet of cigarettes on the table, wanting one so badly. To breathe normally, even if it's polluted air. Long breaths. Not short, sharp, panicked ones.

Doc enters the room, his bushy eyebrows raising when he sees me. "You okay there, Pearl?"

"Brad carried me down," I say, making sure he knows that.

"Of course he did. Here, try these. Much stronger." He hands me two pills, and I waste no time knocking them back with some water. "Two every four hours," he says, putting a pot on the table. "It should keep on top of the pain."

"Thank you, Doc."

"Stew, Doc?" Esther asks.

"Yes, please." He rubs his tummy and settles next to Ella, checking her over as he does.

"Here." Esther sets a bowl down, and Doc gasps, grabbing her hand.

"Well, would you look at that whopper."

She blushes terribly and becomes flustered. "It still feels a little odd."

"Congratulations, dear."

"Thanks, Doc. You want some bread with that?" she asks, getting an enthusiastic nod. "I'll get some."

"Congratulations, Esther," I say around a smile.

"Thank you, Pearl."

"I think I'll just get some fresh air," I say, pushing myself to my feet. "Not too far." I point to the door that leads to the garden from the kitchen.

"You want some help?" Zinnea asks, volunteering Quinton by pushing him forward.

"No, no, I'm okay." I hold up my good hand.

"She can walk in short spurts," Doc says, vouching for me.

"Tell that to Brad," I mutter.

"I have." He takes a big mouthful of stew and hums his happiness, and I take the moment he's got his eyes closed to pick up the packet of Marlboros, taking small manageable steps to the door, forcing my face not to show my pain. I make it outside and sit on a low wall, lighting up.

And wait.

Because my vicious, inhumane uncle always gets what he demands.

Chapter 62

BRAD

I don't think there's ever been so many people in this office. All attention on me. It's time to fill *everyone* in. "Has Higham gone?" I ask.

"Rose was seeing him out." Goldie's staring at the rug, pissed off.

"Nolan's being held in a motel," I tell them as Otto sets his laptop on the desk and turns it to face the room. The image of Nolan tied to a chair fills the screen. Proof of life. But he's black and fucking blue. My teeth grit. "The X5 that Otto put a tracker on stopped at a shitty motel off the freeway near MIA."

"I got this CCTV footage from Target's parking lot," Otto says as we all lean in and see the X5 driving through the lot, then soon after, a truck pulling a jet ski. I point at it. "That's King. I expect he was driving this truck pulling *that* jet ski when he took Nolan from the boatyard."

"Because no one would question a truck pulling a jet ski at the boatyard," James grunts.

"Correct." I drag my pointed finger to the X5. "That's Sandy." And then a Lexus comes into view. "And that there is Luis."

"Fuck me," Danny breathes.

Otto changes the screen, and we all watch two men dragging an unconscious body from the trunk of the X5 to a door. "King took Nolan from the container. Sandy has him now." Thank the Lord for Otto. Quite honestly, I'm not sure how Danny and I got through our debased, criminal lives without his tech genius brain. "Nolan's an insurance policy. We know Anya was working for Sandy. Anya knew Pearl and I were together, and she told Sandy, but King asked for Pearl intact, so we know Sandy hasn't given King that information."

"Wait," Ringo says, a halting hand held up.

"Let me finish," I say flatly, and he backs down.

"We also know King took up golf and got friendly with Bean to track down Pearl."

"Or two-hundred-million-dollars," Danny grunts.

"We know Anya bugged Danny's phone and gave Sandy the cell

numbers of our women. Sandy gave those numbers to King. We *think* Sandy tried to have Pearl abducted so he could use her as bait to ensure he gets what he wants from King. Guns. Because he doesn't trust him."

"So now can you wait?" Ringo's hand comes up again. "And don't tell me you're not finished."

"I'm not finished."

"Tough. I need to know. Why the fuck wouldn't Sandy tell King Pearl's no longer a virgin? It's the perfect way to turn King against us."

"Because then she's worthless to King," Danny pipes up.

"Sandy needs King to have some skin in the game," I go on. "Something worth having. No Pearl, no money, no skin. He needs King's guns and can't risk him leaving town without supplying them. Money is King's prize, we are Sandy's." Fuck me, my head could fall off it's so full.

"If money's King's prize, why the fuck isn't he simply taking Sandy's money for the guns?" Ringo asks.

And that's the unanswered question. "It could be as simple as Sandy hasn't got what King wants." *Two hundred million.*

"Could be," James muses, thoughtful. I'm not the only one doubting that.

"So this is the plan," I say.

"Great," Danny sings. "There's a plan. And there I was worried we were going in blind." He goes and lines up a dozen tumblers and tips a bottle, running it up and down the row of glasses a few times, haphazardly filling them. "Anyone want one?"

A collection of mumbled *yeahs* fill the room, and a flurry of bodies move in and claim a drink.

"The deal is two hundred million for Nolan, Pearl, and no guns for Sandy and Luis." Many cheeks expand in disbelief, but not James's and Danny's. They remain thoughtful. "I don't trust King to return Nolan in the exchange. Sandy has Nolan, and Sandy won't release Nolan without getting his guns or us. King won't supply the guns until he has his money from us. If he supplies the guns at all. There's nothing to say he won't fuck off once he's got what he wants. Basically, no one trusts anyone, and they're both covering their arses."

"King's trying to get what he wants without giving Sandy the guns?" Goldie asks.

"It's looking like that, yes."

"That's good for us, right?"

You'd think so. "I'm not taking any chances. I don't trust King." I say quietly. "Chaka's going to move in on the motel where Nolan is being kept at the same time I'm meeting King in a location yet to be agreed." Because I've no doubt he'll want to call those shots. "I'll need you all to have my back *if* I need it. We have to let King think he's in control. Where he wants to meet, I'll meet him. What time he says, I'll make it work. Any demands he makes, I'll accept." He won't risk two hundred million for the sake of *seeing* Pearl. "I'll transport the cash to a designated location. Again, King's choice."

Danny nods and points to Pearl's phone on the desk. "Only one more thing to do."

I nod, staring at the cell for a few beats, willing myself to remain in control. I pick it up and dial him. "We have the money."

"Exciting," he says. "I'll call you with details of where and when within the next forty-eight hours."

"Okay. And Sandy and Luis?"

"This is our little secret, my American friend."

I look at Danny. He doesn't believe it either. "And you have my son?"

"I do."

"Good," I say quietly. *Fucking liar.*

"And my niece?" he drawls.

I can't. I just *can't.* "I already told you, she's not included in these plans. You get two hundred million. You don't get to see the girl too."

"So *you* get to keep my pumpkin?"

"No. I just get to save a young woman from the depraved clutches of a rapist."

"That's very gallant of you."

"I call it principled."

"For two hundred million?" He laughs, and it's like razors on my skin. "That's an expensive principle."

"You don't need to worry about the cost of my principles."

"But I have a necklace to return."

"She's not coming," I grate.

"Then I'm afraid I must change the terms of our deal, supply some guns, and kill your son." He hangs up, a collection of gasps rings out around the room, and my heart drops into my stomach. I breathe out on a long breath, feeling all focus on me. Watching me being slowly backed into a corner.

I have a horrible feeling King doesn't only want to see Pearl. He *wants* her. It explains why he's not taking Sandy's money. He wants his pet back, *and* the money. Happy days. He gets the best of both worlds, plus in four years when Pearl turns twenty-five, he gets her father's twenty-million-pound estate too. *Fuck*. His death is going to be really fucking slow. "Fuck, fuck, fuck," I hiss, calling him back, my back firmly up against the wall. He answers with silence. "I'll wait for your call." I hang up and bellow at the ceiling before slumping into a chair, hot and sweaty. The silence is excruciating.

"Give us five," James says, opening the office door and ushering everyone out.

I light up, puff urgently, head resting back. I was the one who said we do what he wants us to do. But that? *Fuck!*

"Doesn't sound like money is his only motivation, Brad," Danny says quietly.

"There must be another way." I take another drag and blow the smoke skyward. "Chaka needs to get Nolan out *now*, and then we make our move. No Pearl involved."

Danny's cheeks balloon. "It's risky. Sandy will have men watching the motel."

"But we don't have any other choice." James pulls out his phone. "Am I making the call to Chaka?"

I nod and James dials. "Move in," he says simply, before hanging up.

And the next ten minutes feel like ten years, all of us smoking, waiting, drinking, and pacing. I constantly check my watch, the clock, my cell.

When James's phone rings, my heart crawls up to my throat. He connects. "Nolan's not here," Chaka says. "They've moved him."

"Fuck!" I yell, kicking the chair across the room and throwing my tumbler at the wall. It shatters loudly, but we all still hear the sound of gunfire from down the line.

"Chaka?" James says, as it continues—bullets, explosions, and yells. "Chaka, can you hear me?"

The line goes dead.

Silence.

A long, lingering, tense silence.

It's broken when Pearl's phone rings. I close my eyes and breathe in, connecting the call. "Oh you thought our Russian friend had your son? How disappointing for you. Don't fuck with me." He chuckles. "I eat men like you for lunch, too. Wait for further instructions. And you *will* bring my niece. Just you, Pearl, and my money."

The silence that follows once he's hung up is torturous. "Fuck!" I drop the phone and leave the office, walking back to the kitchen. "Where is she?" I ask the room. Everyone looks to the door. I go out and find her sitting on a wall. Smoking. Waiting for me.

She casts her eyes my way.

I don't want to say the words.

But I don't need to. She nods, looking down at her cigarette, thinking.

I hate that she knew this was coming.

Chapter 63

ROSE

The following evening, I walk into the TV room with Maggie and find the Vikings, Leon, and Jerry stacking bundles of cash on the coffee table. I stare at the piles, and they all look up, hands mid-placing a bundle of cash. "You're gonna need a bigger table," I say, blasé, leaving them to it, hearing Tank chuckling as I go. I meet Beau on the threshold. "The room's occupied," I say.

She frowns and peeks in. Doesn't bat an eyelid. And isn't that a sad situation for us to be in? Bombs, ransoms, kidnappings. All just a day in the life of this family. I still need a drink, though. Just a small one.

Beau heads into the kitchen, and I look out of the window by the front door, seeing the workmen fitting new gates. How long before those ones are destroyed too? I sigh, backing up to take Maggie upstairs to change her diaper but stop at the first step, listening to the men in the office. They've been in and out of there all day. And then I hear the door open and quickly get my backside in gear, taking the stairs.

"Rose?" Danny calls, and I look back over my shoulder. "You putting her to bed?"

"Yeah, she's tired. Needs some quiet."

"Don't we all," he mutters, taking the stairs, coming up to us. He has that look about him. The calm before the storm look. The look that tells me I'll hear the words *I need you to be strong for me, Rose* anytime soon. The look that tells me all hell will be breaking loose imminently. "Drinks on the terrace?"

"Drinks on the terrace?" I parrot. "Are you joking?"

His face remains straight, his eyes lasers on me. "Whenever have you known me to joke when I'm talking about devoting time to my wife?" He catches a potent waft of Maggie's ass. "Christ alive."

"I'm not feeling neglected, if that's what you're worried about." He's talking like he's not planning a mass crime at any moment. "And haven't you got things to do?" Like pay a ransom and get Nolan back? "I can't sit down and have a few lovely drinks with my husband knowing what I know."

"What do you know?" he asks, interested.

"Enough to know I don't like this."

"Which means not a lot."

I huff, indignant. "Basically, yes, but that is something I'm used to, being married to you."

"Said with such venom and emphasis on *you*," he muses, taking my arm and walking us to the bedroom. "Let's put our little girl down, then I'll help you out with the information you're clearly pissy about not having over a nice, cold drink."

Oh? "You're going to tell me everything?"

He shrugs. "Most of it. I'll leave out the stuff that'll turn your stomach."

I flinch. He's talking about Pearl. What she's endured. Danny takes Maggie from my arms and lays her down in her crib. "She needs her diaper changed," I say.

"No shit."

"Yes shit," I counter, grabbing her changing things off the cabinet. "Lots of it, actually." I pass them to Danny and smile sweetly. "I'm going to take a quick shower."

"How wonderful for you," he mutters, pouting at our girl. I leave him to it, but I don't turn on the shower when I get to the bathroom. I stop at the door and watch him. Listen to him. "I've killed many men, baby girl," he says quietly, pulling the tabs of her diaper. "Many were quite disgusting deaths." His head pulls back, the crook of his arm covering his nose. "But none of them turned my stomach like you do. Good *God*." He turns his head and takes a breath before going in, his big hands working fast. "That's quite an achievement."

I smile, resting against the doorframe.

"But you'll never know that man," he goes on, wiping her butt and taking her ankles, lifting her and quickly slipping a clean diaper under her. "I hate that your brother does." My smile falters. I hate that too. "This will all soon be done." Danny inspects her peachy skin. "That looks sore." Then grabs the cream. "I can fix that." He dips his big finger in the pot and scoops out way too much, dabbing it across her bottom. "I can fix anything," he says, fastening her diaper as she gurgles her agreement. "Yes." Scooping her up, he holds her in front of him. "You could be the most beautiful thing I've ever seen," he whispers. "Don't tell your mother."

"I don't mind," I call softly from the door, making him turn.

He rolls his eyes and goes back to Maggie. "She says she won't mind, but what your mother says and what she means are two different things. That's what us men need to contend with."

"You're priceless, Danny Black."

"Shut up. Go take a shower."

I smirk and push my weight off the door, going to the shower and flipping it on. I strip, tie my hair back, and get in. It's not long before he joins me. A prelude to our romantic drinks on the terrace. He walks in behind me, sliding his hands onto my stomach, and kisses my shoulder. "We have a lot of catching up to do, Mrs. Black."

"Then you'd better come home alive." I push my ass back into his hard-on, inhaling at the feel of the stiffness against my soft butt.

"I can't die," he whispers, his lips traveling across my wet back slowly. "Even Hell won't have me."

My head drops back as he slides his palm down to my pussy, inserting one, thick finger. He pushes high, then withdraws, adding another. "You'll wear a vest," I say. I'm not asking. I don't know what's happening, but I do know it'll involve guns.

I groan, reaching for the tiles as he fucks me with his fingers.

"Whatever you want, baby. Turn around." He pulls his fingers free, spins me and takes me under my thighs, hoisting me up to his body. I sink slowly down, pushing his wet hair back. He shakes. His face strains.

His calm before his storm.

• • •

I set the monitor on the table and Beau turns it toward her, smiling. "I know you're not here for the drinks, so you must be here for the information," I quip, lowering to my chair.

She quirks a brow. "How much do you hate this?"

I look over my shoulder, seeing Danny and James heading this way, drinks in hands. Talking. Quietly. "Are we about to hear the truth?"

"It'll be economical, I expect."

The men reach the table, and both Beau and I sit back in our seats, waiting. They place the glasses down. Take their chairs. Get comfortable.

"We thought we'd found Nolan." James kicks things off, clearly not wanting to drag this out. I peek at Danny, not liking his stoic expression as he watches James. "Chaka moved in. Reported Nolan wasn't there. We heard gunfire break out. Chaka's off grid."

"You mean dead?" Beau says.

"We can't reach him."

"He's got kids," I blurt. *Hundreds of them!* "And a wife."

Danny turns his glass slowly on the table. Just that move tells me he's about to say something we won't like. "King wants to see Pearl."

Beau starts laughing but stops when the men stare at us across the table, their expressions serious. "You're not seriously entertaining that request?" she says.

"We have no choice, Beau," Danny replies. "It's delicate."

"He's her uncle," I whisper, shaking my head. "What kind of animal is he?" The worst kind. I can tell by how tense my husband is.

"He doesn't know Pearl's no longer a virgin." James goes on. "He has Nolan. He wants two hundred million, and he wants to see Pearl. If not, no Nolan, and the Russians and Mexicans get what they need to try and take us out."

My God.

"Where's Brad?" Beau asks, shooting up from her chair.

"He's with Pearl. He's okay."

Okay? We all know Brad will *not* be okay.

I look between The Brit and The Enigma. I can tell they're not confident about how this is going to go. A nasty feeling comes over me, and I just know Beau feels the same because her back straightens as she lowers back down to her seat.

And then I see Tank and Fury emerge from the house and that nasty feeling amplifies. "What's going on?" Beau asks calmly, spotting them too.

"The jet's waiting for you," Danny says, his face impassive. "You can go quietly or make a noise. The former is preferable."

I stare at my husband as he stares at me. Safety in numbers.

Support. Maybe hope that at least one of us will see reason. That person is guaranteed to be Beau. "I'm going nowhere," I declare assertively.

"Wrong," Danny says. "Would you like to finish your drink and enjoy this time on the terrace before you go, or not?"

"I've not even started my fucking drink," I snap.

Danny leans forward, his scar glowing. "Then start it."

I swipe the glass up, stand, and throw the drink in his face. He closes his eyes, takes in air, settles back, and picks up a cloth napkin from the table, wiping his face. "You're still going," he muses.

James's eyes are on Beau's hand on her stomach. She won't put up a fight.

"I fucking hate you," I hiss at Danny, pivoting and storming away, Tank on my heels. "I'll go," I yell back at him. "No need to brace yourself for a fight." I stomp through the house, up the stairs, and into our room. Two suitcases have been placed on the carpet. Maggie's in her car seat. Esther is looking quite sheepish beside them.

"You know it's for the best," she says, coming to me, arms outstretched. And I burst into tears. "Oh, Rose." She takes me in a hug. "He just wants to protect you and the kids. You always said you're a mother before anything else. That includes The Brit's wife."

"I should never have to leave his side."

"We all know he needs full focus. He can't have that with you and the kids around. Come on, now."

He. Needs. Full. Focus. He has children, just like Chaka does. *Did.* If Chaka was sent in and was killed, it means that King is one step ahead.

I hate this.

I hate Danny.

I hate this fucked-up world we live in.

"Mum." Danny's voice drifts into the room, and Esther looks past me.

"I'll get the rest of my things ready," she says, collecting Maggie and leaving, probably knowing the volume is about to be cranked up.

"I don't want to leave on bad words," he says quietly.

"Why? In case we never see each other again?" I ask, going to a drawer and pulling it open, taking out some more clothes. I roughly fold a sweater and dump it on the bed.

"We *will* see each other again."

"Have you had all of the razors removed from the villa?" I ask, pulling out another sweater and dumping it next to the other. "In case I have a wobble? In case I spiral and feel helpless and unstable?"

"Don't, Rose."

"What about Doc? Who does he go with?" I yank out another sweater. Stare at it. My Union Jack sweater. And burst into tears.

"Baby, don't cry." He sighs and comes to me, taking my hair and pulling it hard. Reminding me of who I am. His wife. "You will meet me on the beach in St. Lucia."

I've been here before. Many times. I've had this feeling of dread, waited for the words *I need you to be strong*, to come, but it doesn't get any easier, and I can't control my knee-jerk reaction to fight it. Because my fear is a different fear since Danny took me. I'm scared of losing him. Terrified. He can say he's immortal. He is to an extent. But this time feels different. And how many times can a man be shot before it's fatal? I thought I'd lost him six months ago. I also thought I'd lost him four years ago. I feel like he's pushing the law of probabilities. "What if you don't come?" I whisper.

"There's only one person in the world with the ability to kill me, and she's going out of town, so I'll be safe from Death's claws." He kisses my lids. "Come on." He dips and collects the sweater, wiping at my face. "The jet's waiting at the airfield." He gets the cases and leaves me, and I watch his tall, capable frame go. My husband. The Brit. *Be safe.*

I turn one full circle of the room, swallowing and sniffing. I hoped it wouldn't come to this, but it has. So I must do what I must do. I walk to the bathroom and wash my face, pulling myself together. I don't know who I'm kidding. I look distraught. Disturbed. Apprehensive.

I sigh and head downstairs. James is loading the trunk, and Otto has Esther in a hug.

No Pearl. Because she must stay with them.

"I need to get Maggie's milk," I say, diverting to the kitchen. And say goodbye to Pearl. I see the door to the outside open and find her sitting on a wall smoking. I go over, lowering, and she smiles with effort. I don't tell her everything will be okay. I'd be a hypocrite.

"Here." I hand over my cell. "So we can reach each other. Call Beau's, okay?" She nods, I give her a kiss in her hair, and leave her, going to the kitchen and finding a cooler bag. I open the freezer and start loading my milk supplies inside, hoping it keeps until it makes it to the other end.

Hope that it lasts as long as I need it to.

Chapter 64

PEARL

The house is like a huge box of tension, everyone quiet. I watch from the window as Rose and Beau are put in a Range Rover with Maggie. James gets behind the wheel, Danny in the passenger seat. Ringo and Goldie are up front in a Mercedes. Otto, Esther, and the Vikings at the back in another. All are armed. The girls are being sent to St. Lucia. Sent away from the danger. I know it both pains and enrages Brad that he can't put me on Danny's private jet with them.

I watch the cars until they pull out of the gates where a car is waiting. Blue lights flash once. An unmarked police car. An escort. The FBI agent? Higham? I pop some more pills and swallow them with some water. Now the house is quiet. The kitchen's empty, but there's a mug by the sink. Esther wouldn't have that. Moving slowly, my pain far less cutting since Doc prescribed those wonder painkillers, I swill the mug under the water before tugging the dishwasher open and setting it on the top rack. I close it and look across the work surface. A few smears mar the shiny top, so I take a cloth and dampen it, wiping them away. Then I rinse the sink. Straighten the tea towel that's hanging on the stove handle.

Distracting myself.

Killing time until the men get the call they're waiting for. There will be no time for them to plan. And that's the point. I reach to my back pocket and pull out the mobile Rose gave me. I know she's worried about me, worried for everyone, but I also know she and Beau need to know what's happening here or they'll go crazy. I send Beau a message.

I didn't know police escorts were available to hire for criminals ☺

When you're our husbands, you can get anything. Keep in touch xxx

I slip the phone back into my pocket and pad through to the entrance hall. Quiet. I go to the office. No men. A few sounds from the TV room catch my attention, so I head there and find Mason, Leon, and Jerry.

Counting cash.

An obscene amount of dollar bills. The ransom. My price tag. "Have you been here all night and day?" I ask, lowering to a soft chair on a mild wince.

Mason huffs, dropping a bundle. "We had a few hours off to catch some winks. The boss wants it double-checked."

"We're short eighteen million," Leon breathes, falling back on the couch. "Definitely eighteen."

"They just have one-hundred and eight-two million dollars lying around?" I ask, stunned.

"All waiting to be cleaned."

I frown. "You mean laundered. That money's not been cleaned?" I ask, and Mason nods his head. "I have no idea how my uncle plans on cleaning it himself. He has no businesses, he's British in the States, and he's got to get home with it." He was a bully, a thug, a monster. A businessman? No. My father was the respected businessman, and that added another layer of hatred.

Leon chuckles. "Pearl, babe, I don't think your uncle should be concerned by how he's going to clean this cash."

I catch Mason toss him a warning look. "I'm talking hypothetically," I go on. "Are you saying he should be more concerned by . . . what?"

"It sounds like too much talking is going on in here." Brad appears at the door in his workout shorts, his T-shirt around his neck. His accusing eyes are on me.

"I was just helping," I say, scowling at Mason when he smiles down at the cash.

"They don't need any help."

"I was keeping them company."

"They have two-hundred million dollars for company."

"You're short eighteen million, actually," I say, immediately realizing I've put my foot in it. I give Leon an apologetic smile, and he rolls his eyes.

"I think that's enough business for you for one day," Brad says, coming to the chair and holding out a hand. My appreciative gaze travels up his muscly, wet chest to his sweaty face.

I place my good hand in his and let him ease me up slowly. "Is Leon saying it doesn't matter how much money is in there because they're going to kill him before he has a chance to count it?"

"Throw me under the bus why don't you?" Leon mutters.

Slipping an arm around my waist, Brad walks me unhurriedly out of the TV room. "I said, enough."

"Right," I murmur, scolded. How am I going to handle seeing him? That probably explains the uncomfortable twinge in my gut. I'd love to show him he doesn't scare me anymore, but that would be poking him. Besides, it's not true. I'm terrified. And Bernard King *loves* being provoked and feared. Now? The choice has been taken away because he's demanded it. Strangely, I believe he wants to see me. I also believe he wants to thwart any plans Brad and the others may have had to double-cross him. The men won't put me in the middle of a shootout, and my uncle won't kill me. *Because living is more painful.* Especially living with him. You can't suffer when you're dead. "He's not a businessman, but he's smart, Brad. He will cover all his bases. Trust me, I know." I look up at him when I get no reply or acknowledgment. His face is constantly passing from irritated to relaxed, as if he's permanently working on keeping his emotions in check. Which I know he is. Brad's more than capable. He's disgustingly deadly. God, they all are. And I truly hate that I'm worried, but this unease inside me is too familiar. A constant feeling of dread, just waiting for the explosion that is Bernard King. Bracing myself for the damage he can do. "Say something," I push, his silence unbearable.

His mouth remains shut, and when we reach the stairs, I expect him to carry me up them and put me back in the bed to rest, but he doesn't. He diverts to the kitchen and takes me out to the garden. He stops for a moment, leaving me standing on my own, and lights up. "Can you walk?" he asks.

"Yes, I can walk," I breathe, exasperated. He's not going to talk about anything.

"Then let's walk." He offers me a hand, and I take it, a little uncertain. "I'll go slowly." He starts down the path to the main garden, ambling casually, me in one hand, his Marlboro in the other. Silent. I can't stand it.

"What are we doing?" I ask, seeing Cindy and Barbie in the distance. They stop, look this way, and continue their patrol. Like they sense there's no fun to be had here. I can't throw their ball. And danger is afoot, so they must be alert. Ready.

"We're walking."

"Why?"

He looks down at me. "Well, you're not in any fit state for me to take you to bed, so I must take you for a walk instead." He takes a drag of his cigarette and blows it out over my head, the corner of his mouth tipping a fraction.

I shake my head in dismay—and disappointment—watching my feet as I take each step across the gravel path. "Maybe he'll let you off the eighteen million because I'm defective now."

His hand tightens around mine. "Pearl."

"And no longer a virgin."

"God help me," he mutters.

"Sorry." I sigh heavily, bringing my cast up to my chest, the weight and blood flow uncomfortable.

"Where's your sling?" he asks, noting my discomfort.

"I left it in the bathroom."

"Here." He stops us and slips his cigarette between his lips, pulling his T-shirt from around his neck, ripping it clean down the middle. I watch him, mesmerized, a cloud of smoke between us as he ties a few knots, a few loops, and slips it over my head, taking my arm and settling it in his makeshift sling. He nods, satisfied, and I reach for his mouth and pluck the cigarette from between his lips. His scowl is playful, but he lets me take a drag. Just one. He reclaims it, and I turn my head, blowing the smoke away from his face. His hand slips onto my neck and eases me toward him until our lips meet, his mouth opening, his tongue seeking entry.

He says he can't have me, and yet he does this?

Dread drains from my body as my good arm hooks around his neck. So gentle. But so deep. I taste nicotine and pure, manly Brad. And I smell his clean sweat. I see his eyes open, looking at me as he kisses me. I feel his hardness against my lower belly, and the new, warm sensations gliding through my veins. "Shit," he mumbles around my mouth. "I wish I could take you to bed."

"You can." I push myself closer to him, enticing him, and a deep, needy rumble vibrates at the back of his throat. On my back. Still. I can do that. I need that. Closeness. Escape for a short time before we face our reality. "Please," I whisper, nibbling at his jaw.

He pulls back, scanning my face, his eyes hungry. Mine are

matching, I'm sure. I can see the mental debate he's having. The need, the resistance, the want, all fighting against each other.

Need wins.

He flicks away his cigarette and gently picks me up, carrying me back into the house, up the stairs, and into his room. He lays me down on the bed and scans me from head to toe. "How the fuck am I supposed to do this without hurting you?"

Frustrated by my injuries, I hit the mattress with my elbow. "Fuck!" I yelp, an awful, extreme pain shooting up my arm. My stomach instantly turns, nausea overwhelming me.

"Pearl." My name is full of scorn as he scowls down at me. "That was a bit idiotic, wasn't it?" He sighs and lies down next to me, propping himself up on his side with his elbow, resting his head on his hand. "Okay?"

"No," I breathe, dropping my head to the side to see him.

"Tell me."

"How I feel?" I ask, and he nods. "Frustrated. Uncertain. Scared."

He nods mildly, slipping a hand past the waistband of my loose shorts. "What can I do to take your mind off things?"

My body lights up, all pain forgotten. My chest starts to pump, and he doesn't miss it. The anticipation. "What about you?"

"I can multitask," he whispers. "Lift."

I ease my arse off the bed and let him push my shorts down to my thighs, and then he slips his thumb across my sex, smiling when I breathe in deeply.

And wince hard, the stab at my lungs dizzying.

"No, this isn't happening," he says, withdrawing his touch, and I can't even be sorry. The pain is excruciating. "When did you last have some painkillers?"

"Just now," I grumble. "They've probably not kicked in yet. We can try again in half an hour."

His smile is fond. I know we won't be trying again in half an hour. He eases my shorts up and settles for stroking across my tummy. He's quiet. Thoughtful. I don't disturb him, but his phone does. He reaches into his pocket and pulls it out, but it's not his phone. It's mine. He makes sure the screen is facing away from me as he reads the message. I try to gage his face but can't.

"What is it?" I ask. Was that the message he's been waiting for from my uncle?

"I need to talk to you about a few things," he says, facing me, cupping my cheek with one hand.

"Okay," I reply tentatively.

"About the arrangements."

I nod, seeing him struggle. Whose arrangements? My uncle's or Brad's?

"You will not engage with him," he says sharply. "Don't even look at him. You will accept your mother's necklace and stay close to me."

"And at what point are you killing him?"

He blinks. "I'm not putting you at risk."

Does that mean he's *not* going to kill him? "Brad, he doesn't play fair."

"You'll be wearing a vest." He dips and kisses me gently, ignoring me. "And remember, stay calm, no matter what."

Chapter 65

BRAD

I stand at the top of the steps by the front door watching Mason, Leon, and Jerry loading the bags of cash into the back of my Mercedes. Getting as prepared as we can with no location or exact time. "Any word from Chaka yet?" I ask no one in particular.

"No word," James says as he passes, wedging a machine gun into the driver's footwell in his Range. "Anything else from King?"

"No." I dip and stub out my smoke in a plant pot, just as Pearl's cell dings. Everyone stops what they're doing and looks this way. "He wants to meet me at the boatyard," I say. "Now." He knows we've abandoned it. Cleared it out of all supplies.

"He'll have a boat waiting," Danny muses, joining me on the steps. "Clear getaway."

"And I'll let him go."

Danny nods, accepting. Pearl coming changes everything. The fucker has us cornered, and our backup—Chaka—is missing in action. James goes to the trunk of his Range Rover and pulls out a vest, approaching, holding it up and nodding to indicate something behind me. I turn and find Pearl at the bottom of the stairs dressed for a workout—leggings and a tank, a hoodie tied around her waist.

"Is it time?" she asks, taking in the atmosphere.

"It's time." I snatch the vest from James and go to her, checking her over. "How are you feeling?"

"Okay," she says, immediately taking my forearm when I'm close enough, telling me otherwise. "I needed to stretch my legs." She looks past me to Danny and James outside. Both are loading handguns.

"It's a precaution," I say. "Come." I lead her to a chair by the window next to the front door and sit her down.

She eyes the vest in my hand as I lower to my knees before her, and remains quiet as I remove her sling before ripping the side straps of the vest open. "We'll go over your head," I say, lifting it and lowering it to her shoulders, saving her feeding an arm through. I feel her studying me, I see her heart beating hard. "Tell me what you're not going to do," I order as I get her vest into position.

"I'm not going to look at him."

I nod, pulling one of the side traps round and fastening it. "Or?"

She breathes in from the pressure on her ribs. "Talk to him."

I take the other strap and fasten it, flicking my gaze up to her, checking the level of her discomfort. "Keep your eyes low." I gently pull at the vest, checking the fit. It doesn't cover enough of her body, nowhere near.

She nods, eyes on mine. "It's lighter than I thought."

I see her apprehension, her fear, even if she's trying to hide it with idol chitchat about her armor. "Look at me," I demand. Her eyes lift. Big, green, expressive eyes. "It's going to be okay."

"Is it?"

"Yes."

She nods, swallowing, and remains still when I lean in and kiss her, not accepting, but not refusing either. I stand from my knees and pull her up, unraveling the hoodie from around her waist. I can't save her arm with this, so I stretch the material as much as I can. Which isn't enough. So I cast it aside and pull off my own, taking my baseball cap with it.

"What about you?" she asks as I put it over her head and pull the sleeve hole away from her body. She eases her arm through, holding her breath.

"Worried I'll catch a chill?"

She wants to smile. Can't.

"I'll wear yours," I say quietly as I get her sling back into position, resting her arm in it.

Now, she smiles, and it's just what I need. "Don't be ridiculous."

I dip, collect my baseball cap, and slip it onto her head, tucking her hair behind her ears as I do. It'll help keep her eyes low. I kiss her again. This time she participates, holding her lips on mine. "I love you," I whisper, and she nods again, her face disappearing into my neck for a few, precious moments. I hold her, silently sending prayers to the heavens, hoping they are heard. I can't lose her. *My love.* "Come." Let's get this over with. I straighten her baseball cap, claim her hand, and lead her out to my Mercedes, helping her into the passenger seat.

Closing the door, I go to Danny and James.

"We'll come in from the east." James watches me. As uneasy as me. "We'll only move in if you give the signal."

I don't plan on giving him the signal. Get what I want, give him what he wants, get the fuck out of there. I just pray King will meet his end of the deal, give me Nolan, and not try to take Pearl, because the signal will mean a shootout that I really don't want Pearl in the middle of.

"You're loaded," James goes on, motioning to the Mercedes. "He'll sniff them out."

Leaving me an unarmed, sitting duck, so Danny, James, and the others better be on their A game if I resort to the signal.

I catch the keys James tosses and go to the car, stalling at the door when Pearl's cell rings. I pull it out, see the screen. Turn it to face the others, showing them who's calling. *Unknown number.* Every man before me looks as stiff as I feel, wondering . . . what now? I answer, walking closer to the others so they can hear.

"I've changed my mind," King says. "Bring your friends. It's probably best I have them in plain sight." The line goes dead, the cell held out in my limp hand.

"Fuck," Ringo breathes, saying that one word we're all thinking. "What now?"

I tamp down the red-hot blood climbing to my head before it explodes out of me. "Now why would King outnumber himself like that?" I muse, seeing the rage rising in Danny and James too. "Move the cash to Leon's jeep," I order, and they all fly into action. "Let's go." I help Pearl out of the Mercedes and move her to James's Range Rover.

"What is it?" she asks, her fear escalating. "What's happened?"

"Slight change of plan."

The American, The Brit, and The Enigma, all in a row.

All of us unarmed, *all* sitting ducks.

Only one man would be behind that.

Sandy.

• • •

The drive is quiet and tense, as you'd expect. I can't look at Pearl. Every time I do, that little bit more crazy seeps into me. I hold her hand though. On the seat between us. Tightly.

As we pull off the main road onto the stone track that leads to Byron's Reach, memories invade my mind. Danny, Rose, and Winstable Boatyard. His face when I showed up with Rose. How he must have felt. My stomach turns.

I get it.

"They're everywhere," James says, eyes on the track as we progress slowly.

"I'm seeing it," Danny confirms as I cast my eyes across the dense overgrowth, clocking men evenly spaced, all bases covered. We were right.

"He's got support," I muse quietly, feeling Pearl's hand in mine shift as my phone dings. I look down at the message. Smile.

"Who's that?" Danny asks, finding me in the rear-view mirror. I don't answer. And he doesn't push. *Trust me.*

As we reach the end of the track and the boatyard comes into view, I take in every man gathered around the cabin—all armed.

And King, Sandy, and Luis.

Chatting like friends.

Fuckers.

It's not the best start to what I hoped would be a straightforward exchange.

This is our little secret, my American friend.

King, the cunt. But did I trust him? No. It sets the standard going forward.

There's a boat on the shoreline. A jet ski. Getaway options?

"Cozy," I mutter, releasing Pearl's hand and lifting my ass from the seat. I pull my Glock, check the magazine, the safety, all under Pearl's watchful eye.

James pulls to a stop and turns off the engine, hands on the wheel where they can be seen. Danny follows his lead and holds his up. I can feel the anger radiating from them both as Sandy slowly lifts his machine gun and jerks his head in indication for his men to move in.

"So they have *some* guns," Danny mutters as his door is opened. He turns a smile onto the bald tower of a man. "Evening."

I turn to Pearl. "Remember?"

She nods jerkily as her door is opened by another goon. She turns in her seat, giving me her back, and I lean over, pulling her hoodie over her vest. "Don't touch her," I warn the Russian, who wisely moves back. I shift across the back seat and get out the same side, raising my hands, keeping close to Pearl. More men move in on Leon's Jeep behind us, ushering them all out of the car, and more go to the Mercedes up back. Goldie steps out, hands up, Ringo, then Otto.

"Move away from the vehicles," King yells, and just the sound of his voice causes Pearl's shoulders to rise. He has a wicked sneer on his face, his mouth heavier on the left, making it look like he's trying to smile. His bald head is riddled with scars. His suit is cheap. I laugh on the inside at his attempt to look important. Distinguished. A big player. *Fucking joke.*

I flick a look to Danny as he closes the gap between him and Pearl. Endless men move in and clear our cars of all arms, carrying them to an X5. I peek down at Pearl, seeing her head dipped, eyes on her tennis shoes. "Good girl," I whisper.

"The money," King yells.

Pearl's face lifts a little when she jerks.

"Face down," I say quietly.

She drops her head.

Danny, James, me, and the others are patted down. They find nothing on us, and a dozen men lift their weapons and aim at Leon, Jerry, and Mason, prompting them to start transferring the cash onto the boat. Every bag is checked. Not counted. Just checked.

"Kellan James," King muses. "How did you end up on this side of the track?"

James doesn't answer him.

"Tragic thing that happened to your family. Tragic. And Otto! How's ya belly, mate?"

Fucking hell.

"You've made a new friend," Danny says to Sandy and Luis, stepping in before James starts amputating limbs and making this mess messier. "How sweet."

"Fuck you, Black," Luis spits. "You fucked me over. I lost dozens of men because you failed to deliver."

"I was kinda busy," Danny retorts calmly, turning his attention to Sandy. "Dealing with the results of broken friendships." A smile, dirty and malicious. "Take note, King. Sandy's the kind of friend you need when enemies are sparse."

"You're just pissed because I fucked your wife," Sandy drawls. I tense on Danny's behalf. Jesus Christ, if he was armed, Sandy would be dead on the spot, fuck the consequences.

"You raped her, you sick fuck." The Brit is here. "When she was fourteen."

Sandy waves a dismissive hand, Luis looks truly disgusted, and King bursts into laughter. "Fourteen? Fucking hell." He chuckles. "People claim *I'm* a sicko." He looks at James. "And he tried to kill your girlfriend."

"Wife." James grunts.

Danny's itching to kill. James is twitching. This could go south very quickly.

Then King turns his attention to Pearl, and my blood begins to simmer. "What happened to her arm?" he hisses, sounding oddly outraged that she's injured. It doesn't sit well. Fuck, he definitely intends on taking her. Selling her again? Doubling his money?

"She fell," I say, biding my time, locking down every muscle to remain where I am.

"Fell?" King dips, trying to see under the peak of Pearl's baseball cap. I breathe in. Keep my mouth shut. "Did you get tired of the hook, Pumpkin?"

"Where's my son?" I ask, stepping to the side, half concealing Pearl from King.

"Bring him out," King yells, and one of Luis's men appears from behind a container. My heart drops when I see the state of Nolan. *But he's here.*

"Fucking hell," James says quietly, Danny parroting him, all of us watching as Nolan limps along, being guided roughly. His face is so swollen, his eyes black. Definitely more damage than the footage. They've disfigured my boy. "You fuckers," I hiss under my breath as Nolan's half-closed eyes find me. I feel my nostrils flare. I can't look at him. It'll tip me. "Where's the necklace?" I turn to King, and he pulls an envelope from his back pocket.

"Here." He tosses it down on the dirt, and I see Pearl peek up. Breathe in.

I step forward and scoop up the envelope, looking inside. I don't find a necklace. Instead I find a photograph. I close my eyes and turn my face away from the image of Pearl curled up on a bed as King barks his laughter. Naked. She's a vessel. A shell. No emotion on her face. Nothing.

God help me.

One of King's men moves in on Pearl, and I step in front of her, blocking his way. Pretty fucking useless unarmed, but still. "I don't think so."

King laughs more, amused. "Okay, okay." He checks the boat. It's full of cash. "Let's move this along."

Yes, let's.

Nolan gets shoved forward, and he falls to his knees. "Choose," King grunts, waving his machine gun between Pearl and Nolan.

My throat tightens. "What?"

"I said"—his lips stretch—"choose."

Is he telling me to do what I think he's telling me to do? "Choose between"—*don't call her by her name*—". . . her and my son?"

"Yes."

"Choose her," Nolan murmurs.

"What?" I blurt, outraged, spinning to face him. "Shut your fucking mouth."

"Choose her," he repeats, robotic, all life kicked and punched out of him. Pearl's head is still low.

"Come on, Mr. America," King sings. "Choose."

"Fuck you," I hiss, my heart hammering.

James's hands start discreetly pressing against thin air. *Calm down.* But then Pearl appears in front of me. Walking to King? *The fuck?* "Pearl," I yell, reaching for her. And get countless guns thrust in my face, forcing me back. "Pearl, what the fuck are you doing?"

King smirks. "Oh, how the moral compass is tested. Your long-lost son or a helpless little virgin?"

Virgin.

I throw a look Sandy's way. Observing. Still keeping his filthy mouth shut. He fucking knows. But King doesn't. "A few facts for you," I say, facing King. He can't hide the falter of his sneering smile. "Your Russian friend here tried to have your precious virgin abducted."

"You speak lies," Sandy hisses. "Why would I do that?"

"To use her as a pawn against King." I smile. It's a fucking effort. "Why? Because you don't trust him? You shouldn't. He's a fucking lying, immoral cunt."

"Fuck you," King bellows at me before swinging outraged eyes to Sandy. "You tried to abduct her? Use her?"

"And his pretty mole also tried to kill her," I add. "*That's* why her arm's broken and she's covered in cuts."

"What?" King barks.

Here we go. *Uncontrollable rage.*

"And King murdered your men." I go on, relishing Sandy's frown. "Because he needed help getting his precious niece back from us. Needed *you* to have a reason to want to back him." I raise my brows. "So he offered you the guns."

"God," Danny exhales dramatically. "I'm so tired of being the scapegoat around here."

Luis looks across to King, scowling. "You killed my men? My brother?"

King brushes it off casually. "It was for the greater cause." He looks at Sandy. "You tried to abduct my niece! Look at her! Broken! How the fuck do you think I will sell her now?"

Fuck. Me.

Danny laughs wickedly. "Christ, who needs enemies with friends like you three, eh?"

"And one last thing," I say, feeling James and Danny glance at me. "The guns King promised you."

"What about them?" Sandy asks, unable to conceal his unease.

"There aren't any."

"What?" Sandy barks.

"What?" Danny whispers.

"He. Has. No. Guns." I spell it out. "Because he sold them all to the Irish six months ago."

And suddenly the three of them are in a triangle, guns swinging between each other, and their men surrounding us are thrown into a muddle. Who to kill. Who to aim their guns at. Who to trust. I release a slow burst of amused breath. "What a fucking circus."

"Makes a change from a zoo," James says, all of us unmoving, and still fucking unarmed. I look back at the others. Their faces are a picture. I shake my head, telling them to remain where they are until I get Pearl back. But King has hold of her wrist.

"Anyone got any popcorn?" Danny asks.

"A hotdog?" I add.

"I prefer Haribos," James muses lightly, but I detect his unease, and Danny's, and every one of our men behind us. I have not one fucking clue how this is going to play out, and Pearl's removed herself from my reach, God damn her.

But then . . .

I quickly check Nolan again. He's with me. Sees the opportunity. *His father's son*. I flick my eyes to the nearby container. He nods.

"Well, none of us anticipated this," King says over a laugh. "I thought we were friends, Sandy."

"Your niece has been fucked," Sandy hisses, waving his gun at Pearl.

Oh fuck.

I feel James and Danny tense with me.

"Your virgin isn't worth shit." He laughs.

I see it. The complete, catastrophic rage that bangs into King, his body jolting.

"Let's get ready to rumble," James murmurs.

"This true?" King's gun is suddenly pointed at us. "She's been fucked?"

Fucked. I've never fucked Pearl.

"Over to you." Danny's physically shaking with the effort to remain where he is.

"Yeah, about that."

I clear my throat, all attention on me.

Fuck.

Chapter 66

Pearl

I can smell him. The stench of cheap, heavy cologne that used to waft through the manor. That smell would tell me if he was near. If he'd been somewhere close by.

I peek up from under the baseball cap. Brad, Danny, and James look so fucking calm, but I can feel their fury. I don't know what Brad saw on the envelope he threw to the ground. Knowing my uncle, it was heinous. Vulgar, like he is.

"Your virgin isn't worth shit," the tall, foreign man hisses, and I flinch when he points his gun at me.

My uncle swings his gun toward Brad. "This true? She's been fucked?"

I inhale sharply, consumed by dread, my mind chasing in circles.

"Yeah, about that," Brad says. "Do you want the good news or the bad news?"

My uncle's chin lifts.

"The bad news is, she's no longer a virgin." Brad flicks his eyes to me, and I will him not to goad my uncle. "The good news is, it was a nice experience for her." He smiles. I know Brad's smiles. They're light, his lazy gaze twinkly. There's none of that. "Or is that bad news for you? And good news for . . . me?"

I can't see my uncle, won't look. I keep my eyes on Brad.

"You?" he barks.

"Me," Brad confirms.

"Well, that explains everything." My uncle laughs, the manic, uncontrollable laughter turning my blood to ice. "Why else would you pay two hundred million for her? What do you think this is? Try before you buy?"

"What does it matter? You're getting your money."

"What does it matter?" he asks. I hear it. The frenzy rising. "You made a fucking fool of me, that's what matters!" I watch Brad, feeling the gun that he tucked into my leggings as I climbed out of the car pressing into my back. I wasn't supposed to move away from him. I wasn't supposed to move out of his reach. Nolan or me. Brad would never have chosen. So I had to. Because my uncle's here for me. Virgin or not.

And now it's over.

Chapter 67

DANNY

I don't like the look on Pearl's face. I don't like the defeat. I don't like the darting of her eyes as she thinks. *Don't do it, Pearl. Leave the gun exactly where it is.* "Look at me," Brad whispers under his breath, desperate for her to see him. She doesn't look up. Her hands twitch. King is making sure he's keeping her close even when his attention is pointed elsewhere.

"You. Fucked. My. Niece!"

"I'm surprised it's a surprise," Brad says, casual. *Jesus Christ, what is he doing?* "Since your friend knew."

"You knew!" King barks, aiming his gun at Sandy again. "You knew my Pumpkin had been fucked!"

I look at Brad, nervous. We are in way over our heads, and I don't mind admitting it. So why the fuck does he look so calm?

"Fucking hell," James whispers.

"Well," King barks, and then he starts laughing out of the blue again. *Psychotic. Unpredictable.* "I suppose now she's worthless, I'll keep her for my own pleasure."

Fuck, no.

Brad inhales harshly, as does James. *Shit.* King takes Pearl's arm—her broken arm—and pulls her closer, and the sound of her yelp nearly has *me* diving at King, so fuck knows how Brad feels. I have to throw a forearm out to stop him moving forward.

"Danny, tell me you've got something up your fucking sleeve," he says quietly.

"Pretty please," James adds.

"I'm not wearing any fucking sleeves," I mutter. "What about *your* sleeves?"

"Chaka was up one sleeve," Brad murmurs. "And he's fucking disappeared. The gun I tucked in the back of Pearl's pants was up the other, and she's now out of reach."

"Fucking hell." I'm beginning to sweat.

"If I don't go home alive, Rose will kill y—" I hear the sweet sound of something in the distance. "Wait," I say quietly, listening.

"What's that noise?" James asks.

"Sounds like a chopper." Brad doesn't look up to the sky, his eyes unmoving from Pearl. "Is that a fucking chopper?"

"Police?" I ask, seeing King and the others looking up at the sky too, just as a helicopter appears from over the trees and bullets start to hit the water. "Fuck!" Men scatter like ants, including us, everyone diving for cover, but not Brad. He goes straight to Pearl and pulls the gun from her pants, handing her over to Nolan before he fires, hitting a Russian by a tree. Then he runs into the water toward the jet ski. "What the fuck are you doing?" I yell, checking the coast is clear before making a run for it, going after him, James on my tail, all of us dodging bullets. Brad flips the seat up of a jet ski.

He starts pulling out guns, throwing them to us. "I had the boys load all the fake jet skis when we cleared out and had them put at the front of the store," he yells over the gunfire. "If he was going to use one as an escape backup, he'd pull out the easiest."

"You crafty fuck," I breathe.

And then laugh, firing on a demented roar.

Chapter 68

BRAD

Danny's laugh is off-the-charts manic as he showers bullets left and right.

I spot Nolan behind the door of the container, and nearly whimper my relief when I see he has Pearl behind him. "Good lad. Fuck!" I jump when a bullet hits the water at my feet and quickly get myself behind a low wall by the café, peeking round. "I see you, you fucker," I whisper, watching Sandy dash for cover.

"Who the fuck is in that chopper?" James stands tall over me, almost goading the enemy, firing a few shots before lowering and reloading. "Friend or foe?"

"I haven't a fucking clue, J—"

"My friends!"

I frown at the happy yelled greeting, looking at the sky, seeing a ladder dangling from the helicopter as it comes in low, practically skimming the water as it coasts past.

"Fuck me," Danny laughs, as Chaka, in full tribal garb, hangs off the ladder, one hand clenching it, the other brandishing a machine gun.

"What happened to the boat and jet skis, Chaka?" James yells.

"I brought those too!" He laughs, deep and throaty, head thrown back, then lets off a few more rounds across the boatyard, taking down more men. He releases the ladder and drops into the shallow water, and someone is soon replacing him on the ladder, coming to join the party. Chaka, the bloodthirsty fucker, needs to be in the thick of it.

"Village life in the middle of the jungle getting boring, Chaka?" I ask, making him chuckle as he goes off, firing all over the fucking place. What a fucking hero.

I lift, turn, and shoot, taking out two more men, but we have a way to go. Between Luis and Sandy, they have an army. We have a village tribe. I do a quick reccy, checking everyone's positions. "They won't have much ammo," I say, reloading.

"They have what they took from our vehicles," Danny pants. "Fuckers. I'll take Sandy," he says, gathering his breath.

James doesn't challenge him. "I'll take Luis," he counters calmly.

"And I get King." I look over at Otto. At Goldie. At Ringo. Silently wish everyone safe. "Your timing is impeccable, Chaka," I call as he pops off a few more Mexicans.

"I have to be home for dinner or Mrs. Chaka will blow my brain out."

"What the fuck happened at the motel?" I yell.

"Oh, I hired new recruits for that mission." He fires. *Bang, bang, bang.*

"Who?"

"Naughty little drug dealer boys who think they're bad ass gangsters." *Bang, bang, bang.* "Suffice to say, they've changed their career options." *Bang, bang, bang.* "Well, the ones who walked away." *Bang.*

I smile and move out, my target the café where I saw King flee. I take out a trigger-happy Russian on my right, a few Mexicans on my left, and keep moving forward, my ears ringing with the sound of bullets firing. I get to the café, kick the door open, and scan the space, dipping back behind the jamb when I'm fired at. "You're cornered, King," I call.

"No one fights like a trapped animal." He laughs and fires again, taking a chunk of wood off the doorjamb.

I flinch and wait for a few moments before edging around the veranda quietly, listening for movement inside, watching. It's hard when an all-out war is happening a few feet away.

Which would explain why I don't see the fucker when he dives out of a window and tackles me around the waist, sending us both crashing through the wooden balustrades onto the dirt. I hit the stones with force, coughing, and King lands on his back next to me, giving me the advantage. I move fast, straddling him, and punch him repeatedly in the face, dazing him, before pulling my Glock from my jeans and wedging it in his forehead. I have not one second to consider pulling the trigger. He bucks, knocking the gun from my hand, and I fall back, coughing when I get a size-fifteen boot in my gut. "Fuck," I wheeze, clenching it as I roll onto my back, blinking. I come face to face with the end of a machine gun.

My eyes widen as he leers down at me. "You fucked my niece." Then he jerks, and his ear literally flies right off his head.

"Arhhhh!" he yells, clenching his temple.

I lift my head and see Danny, sarcastic fucker, blowing the end of his gun. "Welcome."

He can fuck right off. I have saved his skin more times than I care to remember. I search the ground for my gun and spot it by a nearby rock. James kicks it over to me, dips, rises, fires, turns, fires again.

"Fucking robot," I mutter, grabbing my gun and scrambling to my feet. I look for King. "Where the fuck is he?" I yell at no one, turning on the spot, firing a few times when necessary.

"He went toward the woods," James yells. "But we have another problem."

"What?" I look around and mentally count everyone off my list of men to account for. Except— "Where's Danny?" I check the area again, searching for him, hearing the screeching of tires. Sandy's making his getaway, and Danny's running after the car, bellowing his threats, firing like a madman. "For fuck's sake," I hiss, checking around him, the woods, the road, the cabin. "I haven't got time to save his life right now." I aim my handgun, close one eye, and fire, shooting my best friend, taking the dumb fucker down with a bullet in his calf.

"What the fuck are you doing?" Goldie hisses, falling against her back next to me, breathless.

"I'm stopping the stupid fucker from getting himself killed."

James joins me behind the wall, and I peek round, seeing Danny propped up against a tree holding his leg. "Luis has fled," James says. "We have one fat King and a few stray heroes left." One of those stray heroes moves in on Danny at the tree and gets blown away with one sharp round of Danny's machine gun. "Goldie, go get him in the car. I'll cover you." She's off, doing what she's bid, and James fires here and there, protecting her as promised.

"Fuck my life," Danny bellows when he sees Goldie moving in to save him.

"I'm going after King." I get up and run to the loaded jet ski, reloading and helping myself to a few grenades. I hear James yell after me, hear Danny bellowing his threats, but I ignore them all, my focus unmoving.

Until I hear more screeching tires, way too close.

I turn.

Just as a car plows into me.

I'm thrown ten feet into the air, the sound of curses following me, and when I land, I grunt, rolling onto my back, coughing my guts up, pain searing me. *Jesus.* "Brad, move!" someone yells.

Move? *Not fucking likely.*

"Move!"

I blink, hear tires again.

"Move!"

I look above my head. See the car coming at me again. See King behind the wheel.

"Fucking move!"

I try to roll out of the way. Can't.

Bang, bang, bang!

I flinch at the sound and watch as the car sails past my ear and smashes into a tree trunk, sending the hood flipping up and smoke billowing toward the sky. "Fuck," I breathe, my ears ringing as I'm grabbed on each side and pulled to my feet. "Ouch." I try to shake them off, stand on my own, and once I've found my balance, I grab James's gun, the one that just saved my life, and limp round to the driver's door.

It's open. The seat is empty. "No." I back up, heading toward the container, my gut, my instincts, my heart leading me there. "Fuck, no!" I go as fast as I can, the feeling of dread getting heavier the closer I get. I arrive, limping. Out of breath. No Pearl. And Nolan is face down on the metal floor, blood pooling his torso. "No!" I roar, falling to my knees beside him, turning his limp, broken body over. "No, no, no." I shout the words repeatedly, like he might hear me. Listen to me. "You fucking hear me, boy," I yell. "Fucking hear me!" I pull his shoulders onto my knees and scan his face. "Nolan!" I yell, getting nothing from him, his eyes remaining closed. "Nolan, fucking hear me!" My voice cracks. My heart splinters. "Fucking hear me," I murmur, feeling his pulse. Weak. Too weak. I stand, my bones cracking, and pick him up, hoofing him onto my shoulder and carrying him to the nearest car, easing him onto the back seat. "Hospital," I order, feeling everyone behind me. "Now!" I find my gun.

"Brad, no." Danny moves in front of me.

I push him out of my way. "Get him to the fucking hospital." I stalk away in a haze of ruin, fear, and anger, my limp harsh, sweat dripping from my body.

Murder.

"Brad!"

Pearl?

Her voice infiltrates my blinding rage, clearing my vision, and I spin on the spot searching. I find her being dragged onto the boat by King. "No."

"Use my boat!" Chaka yells, finishing one more man who's face down in the dirt.

Danny jogs past me toward Chaka's boat, his own limp hampering him, and I follow, catching up, the pair of us struggling. But determined. James falls into stride beside us, keeping our pace, his eyes flicking over to King's boat with Pearl onboard and now pulling away from the shore.

"Brad!" Pearl screams, the terror in her voice cutting.

"Fuck," Danny whispers, hearing it too. And then King clouts her around her face, putting her on her ass. I don't think I've ever felt anger so deeply rooted as I do now. My injuries forgotten, my pace picks up, as does Danny's and James's, all of us running toward Chaka's boat.

And we get blown back twenty paces when it explodes.

Heat licks my skin, fire blinds me. I blink, shaking my daze away, and watch as King races away from the shore.

With Pearl.

Chapter 69

PEARL

My head rings, the throb on my cheekbone adding one more layer of pain to my already broken body. I tremble—cold and utterly terrified—my knees clenched to my chest with one arm as I'm constantly jarred by the boat hitting the waves. The shore is getting farther away. My freedom.

Brad.

A choked sob escapes as I look around at the bags of money. He's got his compensation for me being ruined. And now he has the best of both worlds. Millions of dollars and his plaything to torture and tease for . . . ever.

No.

I look over the edge of the boat into the murky darkness of the water as tears stream down my cheeks, and then I reach for the side to pull myself closer with my working arm, peeking over my shoulder. He's laughing at the horizon. Manic. I crawl up onto the edge and watch the water kick up the edge of the boat. Take a breath.

Roll in.

The pain when I hit the water is excruciating, and I try my hardest to ignore it as I frantically kick my legs to stop myself sinking. I break the surface and gasp, searching around me. His boat's slowing. "No," I pant. "Keep going." But he won't. He can't lose. The boat circles, and I turn in the water, as if I might find somewhere nearby to swim to, to escape, before he makes it to me.

I'm going nowhere.

"No," I murmur, exhausted already, hearing him getting closer, slowing, searching the water for me. I take a deep breath and go under, counting in my head, releasing just a little bit of breath to sink. My lungs begin to scream, the stabbing constant in my ribs. My heart throbs in my ears. *Just a little longer, a little while longer.* My chest burns. My natural instinct to take a breath nearly gets the better of me. *A few more seconds.*

Fifty-four.

Fifty-five.

Fifty-six.

Lightheadedness gets me.

I need to breathe.

I see my mother's face in the darkness. Submerged. Eyes open. *Not breathing.*

I kick my feet and break the surface, gasping as quietly as I can. No splashing.

I see the shore in the distance.

Turn.

"Well, this could be fun," he muses, holding a fishing rod, the hook dangling not too far away from my lip.

Chapter 70

DANNY

That's how much he wants her. He would risk everything—his life *and* money—to go back to get her out of the water after she jumped in. Fuck, we underestimated this sick fucker.

My body screams as my jet ski bombs across the water, Brad up front, James to my side. King's seen us coming, so bullets are sailing past rapidly—it's pure luck they're missing us. But they miss us.

Then I see something land in the water up ahead of me. It takes a few too many seconds to register what. "Oh fuck." I yank the steering to the left and get thrown from my ski, landing in the water with a slap, just as the grenade explodes.

"Danny!"

I throw an arm up, showing I'm all right, and see another land in the water near James. He spots it too, and dives off, sending his jet ski straight into the danger zone. Another explosion, and James's jet ski is blown to smithereens, shrapnel flying everywhere and landing around us.

"Jesus fucking Christ."

Brad's still racing toward the boat, looking back. His engine doesn't slow, and the grenades keep coming, explosions going off all around us as we bob in the water, absolutely defenseless. And my fucking leg stings like a bitch. I hiss as James swims over, reaching down to apply a bit of pressure. "God help the fucker who shot me if I find him," I mutter, my eyes on Brad, willing him to be wise.

Don't act rashly.

Think this through.

King will have a better aim the closer he gets.

"You good?" James asks, his attention split between me and Brad.

"I'm good."

"Fuck!" He slaps the water with his palm. "What now?"

"Fuck knows." For the first time in my life, I feel utterly up shit's creek.

Chapter 71

BRAD

Nothing would stop me. Not even the endless grenades coming at me.

But they might. If they hit their target.

I move in on the back of the boat, zigzagging through the water, until I reach it and start circling closely, torn between checking on Pearl and keeping my eye on King as he fires his gun, throws a grenade, alternating constantly. I can't fucking think with all these bullets and grenades coming at me.

I pull back, gain some distance, and find Pearl on the back of the boat, sopping wet, terrified. *Keep it together, my love. Stay alive.*

"Brad!" she screams.

Something plops into the water before me.

And the sky lights up.

My body becomes weightless.

Blackness.

Chapter 72

DANNY

"Fuck, no," James says, taking the words right out of my mouth.

I don't tell my arms and legs to start moving, but they move fast. I swim toward the boat, my heart racing, all pain forgotten, not sure what I'm going to do when I get there but needing to get there. *Get to him.* I can hear Pearl screaming. I can also hear King laughing, the psychotic fuck.

"Take a moment, Danny," James puffs from beside me. "He thinks we're dead in the water."

"I'll think when I find Brad." I increase my pace, and when we're fifty or so yards away from the back of the boat, I break into breaststroke, minimizing the movement in the water. But my breathing is loud and out of control. "Can you see him?" I ask, scanning the water, searching.

"Nothing," James says, and I curse quietly, hearing the boat engine start. "Shit," James hisses.

And then I see Brad—hanging off the side of the boat, his face bloody. My heart lifts and sinks all at the same time. "James," I whisper, nodding to the stern as I start to swim to the boat, hoping I can make it before King hits the throttle, although what the fuck we can do all hanging off the back of a boat, I don't know. I split my attention between King at the helm and Brad on the side, moving in and holding on to the edge with him, James the other side. "You could look a bit more pleased to see us."

Brad breathes out. "And what the fuck are we going to do now?"

"Not a fucking clue." I don't mind admitting it.

James looks back toward the shore, probably looking to see if anyone is coming after us. We took the jet skis. One boat has blown, the other we're currently clinging to. I don't mind admitting we're fucking fucked. Where's that fucking chopper?

Think! I frown when a shadow creeps over us.

Slowly look up.

My forehead meets the end of a gun, his big, meaty face smiling as he leans over the edge, a Glock in each hand. "God, won't you three just fucking die?"

I won't lie; my life flashes before my eyes as I stare down the barrel of his gun. The amazing bits. The shitty parts. Everything.

This really is my time.

I start thinking stupid thoughts. How I wouldn't want to die with anyone else. How it's been a pleasure knowing these two madmen. *See you in hell*, I think, closing my eyes.

Bang!

I blink my eyes open, looking for Brad and James. Which one did he take first? But they're both still hanging on to the edge of the boat, looking at me. I peek up, cautious. No King. "What the fuck?" I whisper, using all my strength to haul myself up along with the others. King's staggered toward the helm, his hand on the throttle. *Shit.* "Pull yourselves up," I hiss, fighting the pain and exhaustion to haul myself up the side of the boat.

"Fuck," Brad curses, struggling.

I spot Pearl in the corner looking utterly traumatized, her hands shaking. No gun, because Brad took it from the back of her leggings. So who the fuck shot at King?

The engines roar. "Whoa!" All progress I'd made goes to shit, and I slip down the side of the boat, barely holding on with the tips of my fingers.

"Fucking hell!" James is clinging on with one hand, dangling, Brad too, trying to clear his face of the sprays of water coming at us now as the boat gains speed.

Bang!

"Who the fuck's firing?" I yell, spitting out salty water.

"Just hold on," Brad bellows.

"Yeah, I'm struggling." James's face is a picture of strain. "Fuck!"

Bang!

The throttle suddenly dies, the boat slowing, and Brad and James manage to grip the side of the boat with both hands. Brad rushes to scramble up again, us following, and we peek into the boat. Pearl's still frozen in the corner, and King is standing near the edge of the boat, his eyes frantic as they scan around him. I hear the sound of a boat in the distance getting closer.

"Don't move," Brad says to Pearl, using his upper body to haul himself up. King spots him, turns his gun our way.

"No!" Pearl stretches a leg out, straining, and kicks him. She pays for it too. He turns and cracks her around the face on a bellow, then kicks her in the side. My own blood burns, so I can only imagine what Brad's is doing. He must feel like a volcano inside.

"You fucking cunt," Brad roars, slipping back down, clinging on before he starts hauling himself up all over again.

The boat closing in gets louder, and the water starts swelling as it circles around the back of us. Someone appears on the bow. They aim, fire, and King hits the deck, but the big, steel fucker gets back up again, aiming his own gun, but with too many options to fire at, he loses a few seconds. Enough time for the mystery shooter to take another pop.

Bang!

His shoulder jars, and he staggers back toward the edge of the boat. But then comes forward again. "Fuck me," James breathes. "Is he fucking bulletproof? And who the fuck is on that boat?"

I crane my neck, trying to get a better look, frowning.

Bang!

King staggers toward Pearl. He's going to use her as a shield. *Fuck.*

Bang!

The shot gets him in the back, and the fucker finally hits the deck, and this time he doesn't get up. The air that leaves all three of us could whip up a hurricane. Brad falls into the boat and pulls me up before he hurries over to Pearl, taking her face, checking the damage King's done. I see him blink back his rage as I help James up, breathing rapidly.

"Come here," Brad says, sitting and easing Pearl onto his lap. "What hurts? Tell me what hurts."

"He blew you up," she says, wiping his face of blood.

"He tried."

"Who the fuck is that?" I pant, dragging myself to my feet. The boat bobs at the side of us, the shooter nowhere in sight now, and I look to James and Brad, waiting for them to declare that this was up one of their sleeves. Both look as confused as I am. This isn't anything to do with us. So, again, who the fuck is it?

"Stay there." Brad gets Pearl off his lap and away from King, and quickly gathers up the guns and checks him over, giving him a bonus boot in his gut. He doesn't move. Bloods pissing out of him everywhere. Brad joins us, handing each of us a gun, and an uneasy feeling comes over me, as we all search for the gunman. "Where did they go?"

"Don't know," James says quietly, eyes running up and down the length of the boat, his gun poised.

Then the shooter appears, coming to the edge, and we all aim. He reaches for the cap on his head and pulls it off.

My eyes pop out of my head, my aim lowering.

"The fuck," James sputters, his gun dropping into the ocean.

I can't help it—I think I might be in a euphoric place of shock—but I burst into fits of laughter as Beau shakes out her long, blonde hair before running a hand through the waves and resting her eyes on her husband. "Thought you might need a hand," she says, all casual, cocking a booted foot up on the side of the boat.

James's face. I could never describe it. But I want to box it up and pull it out whenever I need a laugh. "Is this some kind of joke?" He blinks. Scowls. "You're fucking pregnant!"

"And my kid might not have a dad right now if its mother hadn't stepped in."

My laughter is out of control.

"Fuck off, Danny," James hisses, stomping his way to the edge of the boat. "Come here," he orders Beau. "Now."

"You'll have to ask my driver to bring me in closer."

"Who's your driver?" he asks, looking toward the helm. "Who have I got to kill?"

Rose's head pops up. "Me." And she grins, all toothy, a lot nervous.

"Oh, boy," Brad breathes, as my laughter slowly dries up, my eyes like saucers.

"Rose?"

"Hi, darling." She waves tentatively, but she's definitely smug.

"You're in St. Lucia."

"Yeah, Tank might be quitting." She comes to the edge of her boat and leans over, trying to see into ours. "Where is she? Is she okay?"

I glance back. Pearl looks guilty. "Wait. Did you have something to do with this?"

She nibbles her lip, remaining silent, as Brad glares at her in disbelief.

"She may have enlightened us on a few details," Rose says.

I can't fucking believe this. "I'm fucking furious!"

"Yes, thought you would be." Rose takes one step back.

"Nolan?" Brad murmurs, his shock and anger subsiding for a moment.

"He's conscious," Beau says, holding her mobile up. "Goldie's driving him to the emergency room."

Relief. It's rife. On all of us. But I'm still fucking savage.

"You're in so much trouble," James growls, reaching for the boat and pulling it over. "So much fucking trouble, Beau Kelly, I can't even talk."

"You sound like you're talking just fine."

"Pregnant!"

"I'm okay," she breathes. "And so are you."

Jesus Christ. Okay, she's right. But still. "I'm mad at you too," I declare. The ex-cop in her will never go away. Our Lara Croft.

"Do you want a ride or not?" Rose asks. "It's a really long way back to shore."

My lip must look deformed it's so curled.

"Fuck it, I'm swimming," James mutters, jumping in.

I look at him in the water. Feel my exhaustion. My pain. But . . . *brothers.* I dive in after him, and once Brad's helped Pearl onto the girl's boat—where the fuck did they get that boat?—he's not far behind.

"They're all grounded," I declare.

"Forever," James grunts. "And beyond that."

"They've gone too far this time," Brad says, tossing a filthy look back at the boat as we start a leisurely swim back to the shore while the girls chug along beside us. "Rose and Beau are rubbing off on Pearl. Not acceptable. Sort your women out."

"Just let us know if you want to climb onboard," Rose sings.

Oh, they'll be sorted out. "Fuck off, Rose," I pant.

"There's no need to be like that."

"We had it covered." I spit out some water.

"Sure you did."

"We had it fucking covered!"

"I'd save your energy. It's still quite a way to shore."

"I'm going to kill her," I mumble. "It'll be slow. Painful."

And that's what I do the entire way to shore. I plan her punishment. What the hell was she thinking?

Chapter 73

BRAD

We make it to the shore, virtually crawling up the sand, and find the others looking pretty sorry for themselves with various injuries. "Any fatalities?" James asks, looking around at all the bodies lying around. "Any of ours?"

"None of ours."

Leon appears—God love that kid—with a tray of beers and a pack of smokes. He's limping. "You okay?" I ask.

"Just a graze, B-Boss," he says, nodding. "The girls just took Pearl to the ladies to try and clean her up."

Try. I nod. It's probably wise they took her. I feel like I might explode with the pressure of my anger. I need to cool off before I take in *more* injuries. "Thanks." I swipe up a bottle and drop to the sand, lighting up and swigging. This cigarette. My God, it's glorious. And the beer? The salt in my mouth is washed away with each swig.

James lowers to my side, his face still twisted, and Danny on the other, his scar deep. I won't tell them to chill out. I lost my shit when Pearl took a trip to an ATM alone. This is beyond my comprehension.

We look at King's boat bobbing in the distance.

"He was definitely dead, wasn't he?" Danny says, exhaling.

"That crossed my mind too," James muses.

"I checked," I tell them.

"You checked his pulse?"

I frown. "No." I didn't have time to check his pulse.

"Rule number one," James says. "Always check the dead man's pulse." Something appears in front of us, held up by James.

"What's that?" Danny asks.

A small click sounds.

And the boat blows up in the distance, lighting up the sky, forcing me to shield my eyes. "Well, there's definitely no need to check for a pulse now," I muse, taking a swig and a drag.

"Did anyone think to move the money off the boat?" James asks as what looks like a swarm of butterflies flutters in the air around the boat in the distance. Dollar bills. *Pretty.*

"Yeah," Danny says dryly. "While being shot at, blown up, and discovering my wife's moonlighting as a getaway driver, I remembered the money."

"What a shitter," I muse.

"A real shitter," Danny agrees, stretching out his leg and wincing. "How the fuck did you know King sold all his guns?"

"Higham. British Intelligence. It wasn't making any sense why King didn't just get the money from Sandy for the guns. Turns out, he didn't have any guns to sell. He offloaded his supplies when he thought he'd cashed in a virgin for one hundred million."

"Thank fuck for Higham," Danny chuckles. "We need to buy him a drink. I don't think Sandy and Luis could have raised two hundred million, anyway."

"Neither could we," I chuckle. "And the cunt wanted Pearl back anyway." *To sell again.* I shudder. "So where do we stand?"

"Luis scarpered, as did Sandy," James says. "One out of three ain't bad."

"I had Sandy," Danny gripes. "Until some fucker shot me."

"Sure you had him," James grunts. "Since when has your top speed been one hundred miles per hour?"

"When I'm fucking."

James chuckles. "Anyway, you should talk to Brad," he says, pointing my way. "I think he knows who shot you."

The fucking traitor.

Danny swings his face my way. "Who?"

I scowl at James as he smiles his way through his smoke. "It was me. I fucking shot you."

"What?" he blurts. "Why?"

"Because, to James's point, you can't run as fast as a BMW, and you would have got yourself killed. Remember last time you went after Sandy alone?" I ask? "When we all had to chase you down? You were shot three times, Danny."

He pouts. "Bad luck."

"Yeah, I feel like we're operating on luck these days." And luck won't do. "And now our women are stepping in to save the day. I think it's time to hang up the guns."

"Not until I've killed Sandy and Luis," Danny mutters,

struggling to his feet. "And my wife." He wobbles off as Beau and Pearl approach, both sheepish, especially Beau.

"Forgive me?" she purrs.

"No," James snaps. "I can't tolerate that level of recklessness."

"So what are you going to do?" she asks. "Divorce me? Okay, my lawyer will be in touch." She pivots and walks off, and James, of course, is soon making chase.

"I want my honeymoon first." He scoops her up into his arms, carrying her to the café while she laughs loudly. I cast my eyes over to Danny and Rose and chuckle.

"You're really showing her," I call as he kisses Rose hard, holding a finger up in the air to shut me up.

I look up at Pearl. They *tried* to clean her up. It will be a while before the scuffs on her face fade. And my anger. I sigh and spread my legs, and she lowers gingerly between them, plucking my Marlboro from my fingers. I don't challenge her. Never again. She can have whatever she wants, whenever she wants it. Within reason.

She exhales. "Thank you for rescuing me."

I push my face into the back of her neck. "Anytime." I reclaim my smoke and take one last drag before flicking it away. "Are you hurting?"

"Not really. All I can feel is relief right now."

I smile. I'd like to feel *only* relief. "Come on, let's get you home." I stand and pull her up, making her face me while I ease her arms out of the wet hoodie and lift it over her head. I go to toss it on the ground, but she claims it, smiling mildly. She wants to keep my hoodie? "Want me to make you a mix tape too?" I ask, and she rolls her eyes. I release the side straps and lift the vest off. That, I *do* toss aside, turning her and pulling her back into my front and hugging her gently, looking out at the ocean, my chin on her shoulder. "It's over," I whisper, kissing her cheek. That's not strictly true, Sandy and Luis are still out there, but for Pearl, it's over. I reach into her pocket and pull the necklace out, holding it up.

"Oh my God," she breathes. "How . . . when?"

"He was wearing it," I whisper, taking it to her neck. "I put it in your pocket when I got you onto the other boat." My big fingers struggle with the delicate catch, fastening it. "There," I say quietly. "Where it's meant to be."

She reaches up and feels at the stone, quiet. "I love you, Brad," she says, as I nod and put my face in her neck, holding her from behind. "And whether you like it or not, you will always be my hero."

I smile into her skin. "I'll be whatever the fuck you want me to be, my love."

She laughs. "Well, th—"

"Fuck!" Danny roars.

I quickly pull out of Pearl's neck as James comes running out of the cabin, and confused as fuck, I watch him take in the scene, pulling his gun. My heart starts pounding as my eyes slowly drag across the boatyard, seeing every one of our men aiming a gun at a guy who's on his knees in the dirt, looking half fucking dead. *Russian*. He's armed.

And pointing his gun my way.

"Fuck," I breathe, as Danny and James start to fire at him, along with everyone else, sinking hundreds of bullets into his body as I turn Pearl away, using my body as a shield, my eyes clenched closed, my arms tight around her.

Bang, bang, bang!

My body jolts.

Fuck.

But . . . no pain.

The gunfire stops, silence falls.

And then Pearl suddenly feels heavy in my arms. I turn her, scanning her face, watching as her eyes widen, looking straight into mine. Ice glides through my veins. "No," I whisper, seeing blood on her tank. She slumps forward into me on a rattly gasp. "No," I say, catching her, holding her weight. "No, no, no, no, no, no!" I find her face, holding her head up. "Pearl?"

Her eyes slowly close.

"No!"

Chapter 74

BRAD

I have no fingernails left. My son in one room, my love in another. One conscious. One not. One alive, one—

I grit my teeth as I rake a hand through my hair, naturally scanning the room for something to hit. I don't know if my swollen hand will sustain another punch of a wall. "When the fuck will they let me in?" I growl, sitting down, standing back up, then pacing some more.

"Brad, you're making me dizzy," Beau murmurs quietly, reluctantly. If any one of the boys passed such a comment, I'd launch them into outer space with my damaged fist. But Beau? No.

I stop at a wall and lean into it front forward, resting my head on the plaster. "I feel like I'm going insane." She's been in surgery for hours. I don't have specifics on blood loss, but I saw the car seats when I climbed out with her. And I can see myself now. My jeans are bloodstained. Visions of Pearl's bloody torso, her pale face, her blue lips, all plague my mind.

"The surgeon said he'd come to talk to you immediately," Beau says, right before I feel her hand on my shoulder. "She'll be okay."

I close my eyes and wish for it. *Be okay, be okay, be okay.* "What if she's not?" I saved her from her tormentor and couldn't protect her for more than a half hour. *Pathetic.* This feeling inside, the overwhelming pain in my chest, it's making breathing hard. I won't be able to breathe at all if I lose her. My heart starts beating faster, my pulse throbs in my ears, and my breaths become short and fast. As if demonstrating what life will be like without her—a struggle to breathe.

I turn, stressed, panicky, and Beau sees it, reads all the signs. She pulls me to a chair and shoves me down, forcing my thighs apart and pushing my head down between them. She crouches in front of me, holding my hands as I concentrate on my breath. Not saying anything. Just being there. Patient. Waiting for me to realign myself. It takes a solid five minutes, and by the time I'm breathing less rapidly, my lungs hurt, and my drying clothes are damp again.

Beau turns my hand over, inspecting the damage. "This needs seeing to."

"It's fine."

"It's double the size." She sighs and rises, sitting on the seat next to me, checking the cut on the side of my head. "I'll get a doctor."

"I don't want a doctor."

She exhales her impatience. "Then let *me* clean you up."

"If you must."

"I'll be back." She goes to the door, meeting Rose on the threshold. She's carrying an overnight bag.

They exchange one of those god-awful sympathetic smiles and a few quiet words. "I've brought you some clean clothes," Rose says, putting the bag on a chair and pulling out some fresh jeans and a T-shirt. "The nurse said there's a shower room down the hall you can use."

"I don't want a shower." I stand and yank my T-shirt over my head and push my jeans down my legs. "The surgeon might come."

Rose doesn't argue, covering her face with my T-shirt while I get out of my boxers. "Your hand needs looking at."

"You mean with all those words you and Beau whispered at the door, she didn't tell you she's gone to get supplies to clean me up?"

She lowers the T-shirt slightly so I have her eyes. "We're worried about you."

"Don't worry about me. Worry about Pearl. Where are my clean boxers?"

"Oh." Rose turns, kneels, and starts rummaging through the bag. "I know I put some in."

"Any time today," I mutter, placing a hand over my dick.

"Damn, where are they?"

"Rose, babe, I'm feeling a little vulnerable here."

She looks back, remembers herself, then quickly looks away again. "Are you sure they're not caught up in the jeans?"

I frown and pick up the jeans from the chair, shaking them out.

Just as Danny walks through the door. His eyes pass slowly between me—standing butt-naked, a pair of jeans in my hands—to his wife, who is kneeling in front of me. His eyebrows rise. "Your wife forgot my boxers, so looks like I'm going commando." I step into the jeans and pull them up, grabbing the T-shirt from Rose's limp hand.

"I didn't forget them," she says, matter-of-factly, rising to her feet. "I might have given them to Nolan."

"Why would you give them to Nolan?" I ask.

"Well, not intentionally. Maybe they were caught up in his pajama pants." She smiles awkwardly, straightening her lips when Danny stares at her in that way he does. Like he wants to kiss her and strangle her all at once. "I'm going to fetch some drinks. Want anything?"

"I'm good." I stuff my feet back into my wet boots as Rose collects up my dirty clothes. "Thanks."

"Take Tank," Danny says as she walks to the door. "Oh, wait, you can't. Because he's in St. Lucia. Where *you* should be."

"Okay, you've made your point," Rose sighs.

"And be prepared for some backlash from my mother, too. She's been ringing me off the hook. And Zinnea's pissed with Beau, so you'd better warn her too."

"Yes, boss."

"Don't push me, Rose. Where the fuck did you get that boat?"

"We hired it. Don't worry, I used a fake name and paid with your dirty cash."

Danny growls and Rose makes her escape.

I sigh and lower to the chair, my head going into my hands. "Give it a rest," I mutter. I don't need these two bickering in my ear when I'm sitting here praying for Pearl's life. My hand throbs, and I flex it as I look over the bruised mess.

"Sorry," Danny relents, lowering to the chair next to me. "How you dealing?"

I turn tired eyes onto him. "I want to kill." *Truth*.

"Any news?"

"She's still in surgery. How's your leg?"

"You mean after you shot me?" He scowls and rubs at his calf. "Missing a chunk."

"You've had worse. Where's James?"

"Don't know."

"You don't know?" I ask, shocked.

"I think it's this place," he says, looking around. "Bad memories."

I swallow, nodding. Pearl's injuries were far too serious for Doc to handle. We all knew that. A bullet in the leg, fine. The arm, Doc to the rescue. A stomach? I look at my watch. Another hour gone. Another hour of surgery. I stand. "I need to check on Nolan."

"I'll come." Danny follows me to Nolan's room, and I walk in to find Ella on the bed with him. She scrambles to get up. "Stay," I order, lowering to a chair by the bed.

"No, it's okay, I need the restroom," she says, dropping a kiss on Nolan's forehead.

"Rose has gone to get some drinks if you want to help her," Danny says, pulling another chair over and dropping to it.

"Sure." She leaves.

"That felt like a subtle hint to scram for a while." I give him questioning eyes, and he shrugs. I haven't the energy to read between Danny Black's lines right now, so I return to Nolan and check him over. Black eyes, swollen cheeks, his jaw looks a bit out of line. "How—"

"How's—"

I laugh a little. "How are you feeling?"

"Peachy." He shifts, grimacing. "How's Pearl?"

"Still in surgery." I reach for the jug of water and fill a cup. "Want some?"

"I'm good."

I down the whole cup, wishing it was Scotch. Lord knows I need a stiff drink. But . . . no. Clear head. *What a fucking joke.*

"What did you do?" Nolan nods at Danny's extended leg, and I inhale my patience, waiting for him to start bitching about it again.

"Wounded in the line of duty," he mutters. "What can you tell us about King?"

"What?" Nolan asks, his barely-open eyes squinting.

"Was he alone when he took you from the boatyard?"

"I was—"

"Did you see anyone else?"

"I don't—"

"Can you remember—"

"Shut the fuck up," I snap, my head ringing, my angry glare on Danny. "Give the kid a second to breathe, will you? What the fuck is this?"

Danny wilts in his chair, pouting, backing down. "Just asking."

"We'll deal with that shit when I know my boy and Pearl are out of the fucking woods, okay?" My thirst for blood is as potent as Danny's right now. But I have other priorities. I get it. King's dead. The man who abused my love for years is dead. The man who raped Rose and tried to kill Beau is still out there. Danny and James will want Sandy on the end of their gun or whatever torture device they choose ASAP. Not to mention Luis. But they'll have to wait, especially if they want three killers instead of two.

"Okay," he says, relenting. "I hear you."

"Good."

The door opens and a man enters. "Mr. Black?"

I'm up from my chair in a second. "Doctor." My heartbeats go wild. My skin clammy. "Is—" I can't ask what I need to ask.

"I'll be in the family room down the hall." He looks at Nolan and Danny, then steps out again, and all air drains from my lungs. My legs refuse to take me there.

I look down when I feel a hand squeeze mine, then up at Nolan on the bed. He doesn't say a thing. I squeeze his in return, taking it and laying it on the mattress by his hip. "I'll be back," I say, nodding to Danny, finally convincing my legs to move.

I walk, eyes forward, to the family room and enter, leaving the door open. Danny follows me in, limping to a chair and lowering.

I can't sit down. The doctor does, though. He's still in his scrubs. Now, my mouth won't work either.

"I've removed a bullet from Miss Kennedy," he says, his voice grave, his face grave, his whole fucking persona grave. "It grazed her bladder and lodged itself in some tissue near the lower abdomen."

My legs wobble, forcing me to lower to a chair, waiting for what comes next. "She has a broken arm and some ribs, but I'm told they were sustained in a previous accident."

I nod.

"She's lost a lot of blood but she's stable."

"Stable."

"We're monitoring her closely. We hope she'll come around very soon."

"And she'll be okay?" I ask, breathless.

"It was touch and go. Her heartbeat was erratic, and we were forced to shock it back into an even rhythm so we could continue with her surgery."

"Jesus Christ," I whisper, looking at my shaking hands. "She flatlined?"

"We intervened before that, Mr. Black. Like I said, it was touch and go. She'll be in recovery for a while. I'm confident she'll make a full recovery, but rehabilitation will be intense. Frustrating. Especially given her condition."

I look up. "Condition?"

"The baby."

I cough, dizziness attacking, forcing me to sit back and hold on to the side of the chair. "What?"

"She's pregnant, Mr. Black. You didn't know?"

I stand. Sit back down. Look at Danny. His face, I expect, is exactly the same as mine. I don't think shocked quite does it justice. "Pregnant?" I shake my head. "How?"

"I'm sure I don't need to give you a lesson in the human mating ritual, Mr. Black." The doctor laughs lightly, standing. "Does Miss Kennedy know she's pregnant?"

"I don't know," I mumble. Does she? Did she keep that from me? I instinctively look at Danny. He's holding out his smokes. I take them and light up.

"Mr. Black, this is—" The doctor looks between us. Sighs. "Never mind."

I suck hard, blow out, walk up and down. *I can't believe this.*

"It could be she didn't know," he goes on. "She's a few weeks, perhaps. And thankfully."

"Thankfully?"

"Any further along in her pregnancy, I can't promise the baby would have survived. Organs in the body move as the baby grows, to make space, and the bullet would have likely hit something vital to the baby's survival." He smiles. "This may be one of those rare occasions when the father gets to let the mother know they're pregnant."

I must look like a fucking goldfish as I stare at him, taking drags of my Marlboro as I try to process what I'm being told.

"Miss Kennedy has been very lucky," he goes on. "But, like I've said, it's going to be a long, grueling road to recovery. Add a pregnancy to that . . ."

"Okay," I murmur. Another drag.

"She'll need to be closely monitored throughout."

"Okay."

"I recommend she doesn't return to work."

"Okay."

"And regular scans during the first trimester especially."

Another drag. "Okay."

"I think I'll leave you to your thoughts for now."

"Okay."

He holds out a card, and I look down at it for a beat too long, making him pass it to Danny instead. "I'll be overseeing Miss Kennedy's care while she remains in the hospital. Once she's discharged, I'm available day and night. Any worries, anytime, you just call me." He nods and leaves, and I stare at the closed door. Frozen.

Pregnant?

I turn my wide gaze onto Danny.

And see it.

"Don't you dare fucking laugh."

Air seems to burst from every orifice he has, his arms clenching his belly. If I had it in me, I'd punch the cunt. But I don't, so I drop to a chair and stare at the floor, in a mindfuck to challenge all others, while Danny falls all over his chair. I'm speechless. I light up another cigarette, smoke my way through that pretty fast, Danny's laughing dying down until he's watching me walking circles around the room again. Pregnant? Jesus Christ, she's on birth control! How the fuck has this happened? Jesus, it was the shower. *I thought I pulled out on time.*

I take another drag and drop the butt into a cup, listening to the sizzle of it going out.

And then the door opens, and the doctor appears again. "I just got word she's coming round."

"Coming around." She's coming round and I'm not there. I dash out of the room, running aimlessly.

"It's this way, Mr. Black," he calls, making me skid to a stop and run full pelt back the other way. "Last door on your left."

I burst through, causing the staff to startle, and nearly fall on my ass when I see her on the bed, flat on her back, machines bleeping all round her. "Oh my God," I breathe, walking to the side of the bed, taking in every inch of her. The odd mix of anger and relief is too much.

"Here." Danny pushes down on my shoulder, and I lower, not checking there's anything to sit on.

"Sir, it's one person at a time, I'm afraid." The nurse looks over her glasses at Danny as she fiddles with one of the lines into Pearl's arm.

"It's okay, Lyn," the doctor says, appearing on the other side of the bed. "So long as they don't get in your way."

"I thought you said she was coming around." I stare at Pearl's eyes, seeing total stillness. And then, as if she's heard me, they open. The greenness I love looks directly at me, and she blinks, before gazing around at the rest of the room. "Jesus, Pearl," I whisper, moving in and taking her hand, careful of the canula on the back. "You scared the fucking shit out of me."

I see her swallow, flinching as she does, trying to wet her mouth to talk. It's painful just watching the effort it's taking. In the end, she sighs and settles, without the strength to speak.

"Give her time," the doctor says, wandering around the bed and machinery, checking everything. "It's an exhausting business being shot." He glances at me and Danny in turn. "Something tells me you're familiar with that."

"Oh?" Danny says. "What's that something?"

"A friend."

"Who?" The animosity reeks from Danny.

"Fred Boot."

"I don't know no Fred Boot."

"No," he says, unaffected, still smiling. "You all know him as *Doc.*"

I shoot him a shocked look. "You know Doc?"

"Fred Boot?" Danny blurts.

"He mentored me in my early career. He called me to make sure you were taken care of."

"Oh." Danny pipes down.

"He's a very good man."

"I know," I whisper, looking at Pearl again. She's watching me. Listening. Definitely smiling a little. I want to ask her if she knows. But if she doesn't, she's too fragile for that kind of a shock. Fuck me, in the space of a few weeks, I've found myself a kid, a woman, and a baby. "My love," I whisper, moving in.

She strains a smile, closing her eyes again. Resting. She needs it.

The door opens and Beau's head pops round. "There you are." Her eyes go to Pearl on the bed. "How is she?"

Pregnant!

"She's good," I say, realizing in this moment that this news could hit Beau and James really hard, and a quick look at Danny confirms he's on the same wavelength. Beau was in Pearl's situation in the past. Shot. She lost that baby.

Beau holds up some swabs and wound cleaner. "Can I clean you up?"

I look at the doctor, and he nods. "Sure. Like I said, let the nurses work."

"Of course."

Danny goes to the doctor and helps himself to the pen in his breast pocket, writing something down on the papers he's holding. "In case you're looking for a good retirement plan."

The doctor laughs lightly. "I'll bear it in mind."

Danny's gesture is a stark reminder that we're still on many wanted lists. And our resident Doc isn't getting any younger.

Beau perches on a chair next to me and sets herself up, checking the cut on my head before motioning for my hand. I give it to her on a sigh. "What was all that about?" she asks, nodding to the doctor's back.

"Nothing," Danny and I say in unison.

"Don't let me interrupt you." Her tone is loaded with sarcasm.

"We're never talking about *anything* business around any of you women ever again." Danny sits forward in his chair, getting his face closer to Beau's. "*Ever.*"

She cocks her head, unaffected, and returns to my hand, holding it while she dabs at the endless cuts. She won't poke the bear.

"How's James?" I ask, diverting the conversation as Danny rests back, moody.

"Fine," she says, short and high.

I frown, reading her persona. *Guilty.* He doesn't like this place. I understand. But it's just occurred to me; Beau is here, and James would walk through fire, hell, and everything in between to be with his wife. So why isn't he here? "Where is he?" I fire, and she recoils, her working hand faltering. I know Beau. Before Pearl, she was one of only two women I knew inside out. "Where is your husband?"

"He's . . . I think . . ." She growls. "He hates hospitals," she spits, dunking her swab roughly.

"Yes, but you're here."

"And?"

"Beau," I say slowly, withdrawing my hand, looking at Danny's thoughtful face. He's wondering the same now.

"Hmm," she hums, fiddling with the things on the bed.

"Beau," I snap, reaching for her face and directing it to mine. "Where's James?"

She glares. "He's—"

Danny's phone rings, and all attention redirects his way as he looks at the screen. He answers. "Higham?" His scar deepens by the second, his chest dipping with his long breath. "What?" He looks at me. "Where?"

I sit up straight, listening, watching Danny's expressions, hating every one of them. He eventually hangs up, rubbing at his chin, looking disturbed.

"What is it?" I ask. "Is it Sandy? Luis?"

"No," he breathes out, looking at me. "It's King."

My back straightens, my eyes going to Pearl. Sleeping. "King?"

"He's alive."

"What?" I breathe, standing up, shaking. "How?" I watched him go down. Saw the boat blow up.

"The Coast Guard pulled him out of the water a few hundred yards offshore." Danny stands, twitching. "He was brought in. Unconscious."

"He's here?" I ask, already heading to the door. Jesus *fucking* Christ. In the same building as Pearl while she was lying on a fucking operating table?

"Brad, wait," Beau calls.

"Fuck that." I swing the door open and walk face first into James. "Where the fuck have you been?" I bark. "King's still fucking alive. Move."

"No."

I slam James against a wall with force, my anger and panic feeding my strength. But he doesn't retaliate, his face annoyingly impassive.

"Calm down," Danny says, massaging my shoulders until I release my hold of James.

"Calm down?" I clench my hair with my hands. *Kill him.* "Where is he?" I stalk off. "Stay with Pearl and Nolan," I yell over my shoulder, marching on, heading for the emergency room.

"Brad, wait," Beau calls.

I stalk past Rose and Ella at the café, their bodies turning as I pass. "What's going on?" Rose calls.

"Brad, wait!" Beau clips my heels. "He's not in the emergency room."

I stop dead in my tracks, facing her, my stomach bottoming out. "He's gone?"

James moves in, his phone at his ear. "Excellent. Appreciated." He hangs up and stalks off, and I frown at his back as he goes.

"Where the fuck is he going?" Danny asks.

Good question.

"Go with him." Beau pushes me on, ignoring my confused face. "Both of you." She directs Danny as well. "Now." Then she claims a bemused Rose and Ella and walks them off.

We follow James for what feels like miles, and he doesn't look back once. Because he knows we're here. The hospital gets quieter the farther we go, until the echo of our boots is all the company we have. James eventually comes to a stop. I peer at Danny, as he peers at me.

Then we both look up to the sign above the door.

MORGUE

James pushes through the door, and I step tentatively in, gazing around at the endless fridges. He goes to the one on the far side of the room and flips a few catches. He pulls the door and the slab rolls out, the sound of metal on metal deafening.

My mouth falls open.

"The fuck?" Danny whispers moving in, looking up and down the metal, taking in the bloody, naked body.

A body that is far from dead. Unconscious, yes, bound and gagged, yes, but not dead.

I step back. Rage replaces my shock. Three fresh bullet wounds and endless old scars mar his body.

"Well, this is a turn out for the books," I muse, noticing for the first time the table behind us. Laid out with every surgical instrument known to man.

James moves to the next fridge. Pulls it out.

"Fuck me," I whisper as Luis tries to yell past the makeshift gag.

"And finally," James muses, moving to the next fridge. Anticipation swirls in my gut. For Danny. For James. For me. He pulls the fridge open and takes it with both hands, bending at his knees and pulling it. I inhale, looking at Danny.

"I'm excited," he says darkly, staring at Sandy. "So fucking excited." He walks to the table and picks up one of the piles of scrubs, grinning like an idiot. "I've always wanted to try these." He tosses some to me, some to James, and we all get into them. Head scarfs, face masks, the whole shebang. And gloves. Danny wriggles his on, making a meal of snapping the wrists.

I manage one. There's no fucking way I'll squeeze my swollen hand into the other.

We stand in a triangle, all scrubbed up. "Shall we take a selfie?" Danny says over a laugh. "I feel like I need this in the family photo album."

I roll my eyes, quickly texting Beau to tell her to call me immediately if Pearl comes back around. I don't tell her where I am. She knows. And I'm not leaving this room until King is in pieces. I refuse to let Pearl wake up again in a world where he's still alive. "Let's get on with it." I pick up the first thing I can lay my hands on. A saw. I eye it as I move in on King. "Oh, he's awake," I muse, watching him coming round, squinting, looking all kinds of groggy. "Bet you didn't expect to see me again." Poor guy. He looks like he's woken up in a nightmare. He has no idea. I reach for some surgical gloves and stuff them in his disgusting gob as Danny casually peruses the scalpels, picking them up, tapping the end with his fingertip, humming as he does. "It's like fucking Christmas at the morgue," I say, looking up and down King's solid frame. Where the fuck do I start? I hold up the saw, pouting as King's eyes widen. "The Enigma's been busy."

"I've always worked more effectively alone," James says, crossing his arms. I look at him, eyebrows high, and he rolls his eyes. "Otto slipped trackers on the cars during the chaos."

I smile.

"What a fucking legend," Danny muses. "And for that, I'll allow him my mother's hand."

"You dick," James laughs.

Danny, smirking darkly, gets back to the matter at hand. "So who's first?" He wanders over to Sandy, admiring his scalpel. Then he looks down at Sandy's dick.

"Oh fuck," I breathe, wincing as Sandy starts bucking and shaking his head, my saw poised on King's trembling leg. Poor Luis will be last. But he'll get the best show.

Danny raises his brows. Pulls the tape off Sandy's mouth. "You got something to say?"

"Yes, yes, please!"

"What?"

"I've told him where your father is," he pants, sweats, shakes.

Danny, shockingly, puts the scalpel down. "Oh?" he breathes, looking at James, who nods, confirming.

Sandy's breathing is so fucking panicked, it's thrilling. "Winstable. He's at Winstable."

"Winstable?"

"Yes, yes, Winstable."

Danny smiles. "He would have liked that," he says, weirdly reminiscent. "He really would have liked that. But how do I know you're telling me the truth?"

"He's twenty paces to the left of the hangar," he says, rushed. "Fifteen paces back."

"He's lying," James says quietly.

"What? No!" Sandy yells, outraged.

"It was twenty paces to the left of the hanger, *seventeen* paces back, actually."

I stare at James, surprised.

"You dug up my pops?" Danny asks.

He shrugs. "I wanted to be sure."

Danny smiles down at Sandy and the Russian prick relaxes, smiling nervously back. "Now, *that's* a friend," he says, happy, before he slams the tape back over Sandy's mouth and picks up the scalpel. Sandy goes wild, as I chuckle and James shakes his head. "I don't think I can bring myself to touch it." Danny sneers at Sandy's flaccid cock.

"Let me help you out." James picks up some pliers and tosses them over, and Danny catches them.

"Thank you, James." Danny returns his attention to a truly terrified Sandy. "While The Enigma works most effectively alone, The Brit works most effectively with an assistant." He puts the pliers around the very tip and pulls Sandy's limp cock up toward the ceiling, forcing him off the metal bed. "Sliced or diced?" he asks seriously.

"Definitely sliced," James says flatly.

He smiles and goes in, and the others watch in horror as Danny slices through Sandy's dick an inch at a time . . . waiting for their turn, as Sandy bucks and screams, the sound muffled, but oh so delightfully bloodcurdling.

I look down at King.

Drag the saw once through his thigh.

Delight in the sight of his eyes bulging and the sound of his stifled squeal.

"You shouldn't have fucked with me," I murmur. Another drag. "I eat men like you for breakfast, lunch, *and* dinner."

Chapter 75

BRAD

I drop my scrubs in a pile, keeping my eyes on the four drawers full of blood and body parts. You could say we've gone that extra mile to ensure no one's coming back from the dead.

"Who's cleaning the mess up?" I ask, jumping when the door swings open and a little old man wanders in, all smiles. "Who the fuck are you?"

"What's that, son?" he yells, his hand at his ear.

"I said—"

"He's deaf." James smiles at the old boy. "Good to see you again, Arnie," he yells as he goes to the fifth fridge, yanks it open, and pulls out two sports bags, dropping one at his feet. "And thanks."

"Don't you worry about a thing." He goes to the tables and looks them over. "Any organs to be donated?"

"All," I answer. "As long as it's not their ticket out of Hell."

"What's that, son?" Arnie yells, hand at his ear again, as Danny chuckles and James smiles.

"Maybe get yourself a new hearing aid with your paycheck, Arnie."

"Maybe," he muses, smiling. "Close the door on your way out."

We all wander out together. "Who the fuck is Arnie?" I ask, checking my phone. Nothing.

"Old boy who owns the funeral home downtown. And a furnace."

"Handy to know," Danny muses. "Where the fuck did you get that money?"

"From the house," James says, blasé.

"All the money from the house—fuck, all the money from *everywhere*—was on King's boat."

"The money on King's boat was counterfeit."

I gawk at him. "Where the fuck did you get nearly two hundred million in counterfeit notes?" I ask, stunned.

"From Benson."

"Serious?"

"Fuck me," Danny says, head thrown back, laughing. "I hate that I like that bloke."

"Fuck, James, that was—"

"Risky?" he says. "That's what we do, Brad. Take risks. And adapt if they don't work out."

"Hey boys."

I turn, laughing a little, but it dries up when I see who's found us. "Higham?"

He cranes his neck, peeking back at the door to the morgue. "Isn't there a proverb that says an artist's last work is his best work?"

"Is that a hint?" Danny asks, brushing off his killer hands.

"A big hint." Higham's eyebrows raise. "The Amber Kendrick case."

Danny withdraws. "What about it?"

"Forensics found an item of clothing at The Pink Flamingo. It had traces of Kendrick's blood on it. They're looking for the club owner, Elsa Dove."

Fucking hell, Ringo sure did sort that problem.

"Elsa Dove?" Danny muses, nodding, smiling mildly. "You know, Dove is a massive flirt. Not much of a lady's lady. I'm not surprised. I bet it was over a man."

"Sure," Higham muses. "You?"

Danny smirks as the other sports bag lands at Higham's feet. "Happy retirement," James says, and Higham wastes no time picking up the bag and throwing it over his shoulder.

"Where will you go?" Danny asks.

"Far, *far* away from you three." He turns and leaves with a certain lightness around him, and we walk off in the opposite direction, all of us silent. Thoughtful.

All of our enemies. Dead. We're . . . what? Free? Able to live *normal* lives? Peaceful lives?

"It's the oddest feeling, isn't it?" Danny says as we walk. "No one left to kill."

"Really odd," I admit. Like something's missing from our lives.

"Can I go on my honeymoon now?" James asks, and I laugh, along with Danny. "You can come."

"We're not going anywhere for a while," I muse, smiling on the inside.

"At least nine months," Danny adds.

"What?" James stops, looking between us.

"Pearl's pregnant," I say easily.

He laughs. Stops. "Really?"

"Yeah."

James is silent, barely suppressing his amusement.

"You can laugh," I say tiredly, looking at Danny, seeing he's ready to burst again, too. I roll my eyes. "And you."

I head back to my love, leaving behind two British assassins falling around the corridor, hysterical, crying with laughter.

And I smile.

So fucking wide, my face hurts.

Chapter 76

PEARL

Did I imagine him here? Dream it? I move my eyes but not my head, looking at what I can. I'm still in the room with loud machines and hazy strip lighting. I see the doctor in the corner, writing notes.

"My love."

I breathe in and wince, the pressure on my chest hurting.

"Easy," Brad whispers, appearing above me. His smile would knock my socks off if I had any on. I return it as best I can and settle, trying to lift an arm to reach him but failing. He takes my hand, sitting on the edge of the bed. "I wish I could cuddle you."

I smile again. I wish that too. I fight to clear my throat, feeling like a tennis ball is stuck there.

"Thirsty?"

I nod again, and Brad brings a straw to my mouth, his face twisting when I try to drink. I literally have nothing in me.

Pained, he sucks some water up through it, holding it in the straw and coming down to me. His lashes flicker, his eyes dancing, his stubble on the longer side of perfect. I open my mouth, and he releases, letting it trickle past my lips. It feels delightful, cold and refreshing. "More?" he asks, and I nod, so he goes again, sucking, holding, releasing until the glass is empty. I mourn the loss of his face so close, when I can study every gorgeous bit of it.

"What have"—another cough—"you been up to"—and one more—"while I've been away?"

He laughs lightly. "Don't ask." He dips and kisses my lips, and I hate that I can't return it. "Is there something you need to tell me?" He pulls back and scans my face as I frown, thinking.

"I don't . . . think so."

"You sure?" he asks, head tilted.

I clear my throat again, forcing the lump and dryness away. "Well, I've been un . . . conscious for—"

"Six hours."

"Feels like six . . . years."

"I know the feeling." He raises his brows. "Are you sure?"

"About what?"

"About having nothing to tell me."

"What's going . . . on?" I ask, getting agitated, shifting on the bed and regretting it. "God . . . damn . . ."

"Keep still."

"Fine." I'm out of bloody breath already. Useless. "Tell me what's . . . going on."

His lips roll, his forehead becoming heavy. I don't like that look. "You're pregnant."

I still, staring at him as he obviously watches for my reaction. "Pardon . . . me?" Is he trying to be funny? Because I haven't the capacity to laugh.

"You're pregnant."

"I heard you . . . the first . . . time."

He laughs. "Then don't ask me to repeat myself."

"I can't be preg . . . pregnant," I grate, straining with the effort to remain still. "This is a really stupid"—*Breathe*—"joke."

"I'm not joking." He smiles softly, taking my hand. "You're going to be a mom."

"I'm too . . . young to be a . . . mum."

"And I'm old enough to be a dad?"

"Maybe *too* . . . old," I wheeze.

"Thanks."

"Pregnant?"

He nods, very slowly, very seriously. I turn my wide-eyed stare up to the ceiling. Frown. *Wait.* "And the baby's . . . okay?"

"The baby is fine, but you're on strict bed rest and watch."

"Sounds fun," I mumble. *Fucking pregnant?* "Can't"—I wince—"wait."

"If I had access to your ass, I'd spank it."

"Oh . . . Brad," I say, breathless. "Stop with the . . . daddy talk."

"Jesus, Pearl."

I laugh, it hurts, so I stop.

Oh my God.

Pregnant?

Brad seems so together. Accepting. He's okay with this? "Are you . . . here out of duty?"

His face. Oh, his face. "Shut the hell up, Pearl."

"Okay." I bite at my lip, sorry, and Brad sighs. I'm bloody pregnant. And he's okay. But me? Am I? I sag into the bed, even more exhausted, without the ability to truly process this news. I'm not sure how I should feel. Shocked? Happy? Scared? "How's . . . Nolan?"

"In a better state than you."

"So, not pregnant?"

"Ha ha," he says dryly. "Jesus." He collapses onto the edge of the bed and holds my hand. "Are you ready to do this?" he asks.

"No."

"Me neither." His lip quirks. "But you know what, my love?" Dipping carefully, he kisses my lips gently. "I thought I'd lost you. Turns out I've gained even more." His lip quivers, and with it, mine does too.

"Will you still be The American?" I whisper, truly knowing the answer to that.

"Always," he says, sniffing. "But before everything, I am yours." He lays a light palm on my stomach. "Both of yours."

"Oh my God," I breathe.

"Oh my God," he whispers back, smiling.

"My hero."

He laughs lightly. "You're going to be so fucking fed up with me by the time this baby arrives."

"Can't wait." I really can't. Spending every moment of my life with Brad? Sign me up. I'd really thought I'd lost him as my uncle sped away from the beach. And then the explosion. I don't think I've ever been as scared as I was in those moments. But Brad didn't give up. He didn't abandon me. Leave me.

And now . . .

Now I get forever.

I exhale, settle, and just watch him as he relaxes, and it's the first time I've truly seen him do that. Relax. He reaches into his pocket and pulls out my mother's necklace. "Doctor," he says over his shoulder as he fiddles with the clasp, "what's your thoughts on taking Pearl away to recuperate?"

"Sun, sea, and relaxation?" he says. "Sounds like a winning combination to me." He peeks up from his notes. "As long as you take a professional medical team."

"Team? Not one professional medic?"

"I recommend two."

Brad smiles, kissing away my frown. "Let's put this back where it belongs," he says, gently feeding it around my neck and fastening it.

And weird as it is, as broken as I am, with Brad here, his baby—my God, I'm pregnant—growing in my tummy, and my mother's necklace around my neck, I know this is my destiny.

The necklace was always supposed to be mine.

As was The American.

Epilogue - Part 1

BRAD

There's sand between my toes, the sun on my back, and I'm surrounded by the smell of the sea. It feels good. And for once, there's no lingering sense of foreboding. Nothing on the peripheral of our peace threatening to infiltrate it.

Except, of course . . .

I smile, looking back at our villa when I hear the distant cries of—*fuck me*—my daughter. Ruby Beatrice Black. Named after Pearl's mom and mine. Born by caesarean section eight weeks ago today. It was a long, grueling pregnancy, Pearl spending most of it on strict bedrest. The site of her wound didn't have enough time to heal before Ruby grew and applied pressure to the healing area, causing pain and a risk of rupture. Pearl's been under the close eye of all of us. The docs left her as long as they deemed safe within reason before having her admitted and delivering Ruby. It was an opportunity to check the bullet wound was okay. It wasn't. They had to perform further surgery to repair the area before they sewed her up. There's only one other time in my life I've felt so helpless. When Pearl was shot.

But now Ruby is here, and I'm praying Pearl can get back to normal soon. She's on her feet. Slow but on her feet. The lingering guilt still sits heavy. I saved her from being a prisoner, and she's been a prisoner to her injuries since. But worshipped rather than mistreated. I will always worship her. Express my love and appreciation for her every day for the rest of my life.

I have purpose. A woman, kids.

Life.

I start back up the beach to the villa, Ruby's cries getting louder. When I enter, I find Pearl in the rocking chair in the corner by the window that looks out onto the ocean, Ruby settled now, feeding from a bottle. It's Pearl's favorite spot, looking out at the endless space. She should be bored of it by now. She claims she'll never get bored. Fine by me. We're not going anywhere.

She knows I'm here—she would have watched me walk up the beach—but I leave her for a moment, getting some water.

I wander over with my glass and stand behind her, looking at what she's looking at. Water. Still, calm, peaceful water. "My love," I whisper.

"My love," she says on a sigh, tilting her head back to look up at me. Her smile is small. It doesn't take away from how happy I know she is. "She was hungry."

I dip and kiss Pearl's forehead before rounding her, and she takes her feet off the footstool in front of her, letting me perch, her eyes lingering on my bare chest. Intimacy has been . . . tricky, to say the least. No penetration, naturally. I know I speak for both of us when I say it hasn't been easy. In time, I tell myself, reaching forward and resting a finger under her chin, lifting her head and her eyes. The green blinds me. I narrow an eye playfully. She nibbles at her lip. "Behave," I whisper.

"Okay, Daddy." She smirks, and I roll my eyes, setting my glass on the floor and taking Pearl's feet, putting them in my lap and massaging them.

"How do you feel?"

"Good," she says, nodding to the table nearby where there is an array of prescription meds. "The docs said I can lower my dosages."

"That's good." I rub at her feet, my attention constantly passing between Pearl and Ruby. She's going to be a redhead too, the signs already showing. Fire red. I hope she's as brave and resilient as her mommy too. Not that she'll need to be brave. Not with me shielding her and her mother from . . . everything. It's a vow. "How do you feel about later?"

"I'd love to go," Pearl muses, nodding. "I don't know how long I'll last, but I want to see everyone together, not in dribs and drabs as they stop by to check on us."

"Whatever you want." I check Ruby. She's stopped suckling. "Is she done?"

"Little and often." Pearl muses as she pulls the bottle away, breaking the latch, and there's no fuss about it from Ruby.

"Here." I rise and take her from Pearl's arms and settle back on the footstool, gazing down at the wonder that is my little girl. Fuck me, I get a lump in my throat every time I look at her. I don't care what anyone says—all babies are ugly when they're born. Not mine. I don't think my eyes will ever be blessed with anything so perfectly beautiful in my life. Except for her mother, of course.

I lift Ruby and push my lips to her forehead, closing my eyes.

Uncle Carlo wouldn't be turning in his grave. He'd be spinning.

I get her onto my shoulder and push my palm into her back to straighten her out, holding my breath, waiting for it. She burps, and I exhale, smiling as I start to pat her, hoping for more.

"You're a pro," Pearl says around her smile.

I chuckle. "A pro at burping her?"

She shrugs, only very mildly. "At being a daddy."

"Who would have thought?" I muse, turning my face into Ruby, smiling. Truth is, I didn't get much of a choice. I've gone from no kids to two in months. But it came so instinctively—the love, the purpose, as if someone turned on a button and that was it. *Who would have thought?* Not me. Not in a month of Sundays. I'm Dad, boyfriend, and protector. And you know what? Nothing has ever felt so natural. Being Pearl's. Being Nolan's. And now being Ruby's.

She lets out another burp, this one smaller and airy. Always the same. One big, sharp belch, followed by a breathy release. She's done. And no spit-up. I'm winning.

"Here's Nolan," Pearl says, nodding out of the window.

I turn and see him jogging up the steps from the beach to the villa, wearing the loudest Hawaiian button-up. "Jesus Christ," I murmur. "He definitely doesn't get his dress sense from his daddy."

"His daddy doesn't wear clothes most of the time," Pearl muses, taking another greedy fill of my chest.

"You complaining?"

"Never."

"Didn't think so."

"Okay, stud." She chuckles as Nolan comes through the front door, his eyes coming straight to the chair in the window, as always. He nods at me, and I return it, as he wanders over and dips, kissing the top of Pearl's head. "Hey, Mom."

"Fuck off, Nolan." She snorts, as she always does when he teases her, and I give her a warning look. "Sorry." She presses her lips together, and Nolan chuckles as I stand, transferring Ruby into the crook of my arm. "What are you doing here?" she asks, looking up over her head at him.

"Oh." His amused eyes come to me. "I came to ask Dad if he wanted to go out on the jet skis." *Dad*. Yeah, not going to lie, that took a while to get used to. We did discuss it, and I had been happy for him to continue to call me Brad. But it was my wise girlfriend who explained that Nolan's never had a dad, never been able to call another man *Dad*. So, it stuck.

"Why wouldn't you call him instead of coming all the way over here?" Pearl asks.

Nolan's panicked eyes land on me. "Oh, ermmm." He looks at Ruby in my arms. "I wanted to see my little sister before I take Ella out on the water for another lesson." He moves in, crowding me, and gets up in Ruby's face, making stupid baby noises.

"You're annoying her," I say dryly. "I'll meet you on the shore soon. Go get the jet skis ready."

"I thought he was going out on the water with Ella," Pearl says.

Fuck, this is hard work. "He is. I'm supervising."

"I'm a little rusty. And Dad's a pro." He flips me a terribly obvious wink before backing up, waving at Pearl.

"What's gotten into him?" she asks, half smiling, half frowning, as he closes the door behind him.

"Who the hell knows?" I offer a hand to Pearl. "Come," I say, and she smiles, taking it, letting me ease her up out of the chair slowly. "Okay?"

"Good." She brushes down the front of her white sundress and drops the muslin cloth on the chair.

"Up for a little wander down the beach?"

"Yes," she breathes, reaching for Ruby's little sunhat and popping it on her head before draping the muslin over her exposed legs.

"Can you manage?" I slip an arm around her waist and walk us to the door.

She laughs a little. "I can manage."

"Lean on me."

"I am leaning on you."

"Lean on me more," I demand, feeling her press into my side, one arm around my lower back, the other resting on my bare chest.

It's slow progress, but we make it down to the shore step by small step, until our toes are submerged in the sparkling water. I can sense her peace against me as she constantly looks from the horizon, to our feet, to Ruby, to me.

I don't particularly want to bring it up now, but I want Pearl to know she's able to move forward without it hanging over her head. I hired a lawyer in the UK to contest the trust. We had a strong case, given the circumstances of Pearl's parents' deaths and the ten years Pearl suffered at the hands of King. The only catch? She must pay various taxes, including inheritance taxes. It's a non-issue. "The sale on your parents' property has closed." I look down at her, seeing her biting at her lip. I don't think she knows how to feel about it. I know she's torn between guilt and relief. She could never go back there, but that place was her childhood home before it became her prison.

"That's good." She swallows, nodding, reaching for Ruby's hand and playing with her fingers.

"So you're a wealthy young woman, Miss Kennedy."

"I'm rich enough without any money," she muses, smiling mildly. "When do you think we can get her in the water?"

That's it. End of *that* conversation. Which is fine by me. "Two to three months," I say. I asked the docs. Anything earlier is too risky, infections and whatnot. "So soon."

"I don't want her to be scared of water," Pearl says quietly. "I don't want her to be scared of anything. Except her daddy, maybe, when she's a tearaway teenager kissing all the boys."

I blink. "Jesus, Pearl."

"I don't want her to be suppressed," she goes on. "Scared of the world."

"She doesn't have to kiss all the boys, though." Let's get that straight. It would be carnage.

Pearl looks at me seriously. "I want her to have all the experiences I didn't. School, field trips, her first crush, prom, her first kiss, driving lessons . . . everything."

I smile, but it's sad. If Pearl had not missed out on all those things, I wouldn't have her now. And that fucks with my head so much. Because I couldn't be without her now. And yet I want to erase her past. "She'll have everything, my love," I promise. "All the things." But all the boys? No. I've got a few years to try and curb the knee-jerk reaction I have to *that* thought. Can't promise I'll succeed.

Pearl nods, accepting, and kisses Ruby's cheek. "I won't let Daddy kill all the boys."

I laugh, looking over my shoulder to the umbrella wedged in the sand. "Come," I order, walking her over. I get us in position and take Pearl's cheek with my spare palm, kissing each one as she holds my wrist, breathing in.

"I love it here," she whispers.

Everyone who comes here does. "You want to stay forever?"

"Yes." Breaking away, she takes me in, studies me. I've watched her do it endless times. Sometimes wondering what she's thinking. Not today. Today I see the love in her eyes. The appreciation. The peace.

I turn her toward the sea. "Oh, look at that," she says, moving forward a little, forcing me to too.

"What?"

"An oyster." She holds her hand out for me to take, and I watch as she lowers slowly, collecting it out of the sand.

"Mommy's found an oyster," I muse, checking Ruby's protected from the sun. She's wide awake. Alert, looking up at me. Happy. I help Pearl back up as she shakes the shell free of sand.

Something rattles inside, and her eyes shoot to mine. "Oh my God, do you think there's a pearl in here?" Her excitement nearly puts me on my ass.

It might be Pearl on her ass soon.

My stomach does an unexpected flip as she inspects the shell, starting to pry it open. Her gasp is endearing. "There is. There's a pearl." God love her, she reaches inside and plucks the pearl from the shell, holding it up between us. Her smile falters. Some lines appear across her forehead. "And there's a ring attached." She looks at me. "Brad, there's a ring attached to this pearl."

"There is?"

"Yeah, look." She thrusts the ring forward for me to see, and I smile, shy, slowly dropping to my knees before her with Ruby snug in the crook of my arm. Poor thing looks lost. "What are you doing?"

I pluck the ring from her hand, and she retracts like she's been bitten. "I need that."

I check our daughter is still awake. She is, gurgling. She approves. I take a deep breath and look up at a dumbstruck Pearl.

"Brad?" she whispers, stepping back.

"I know you're young," I say, frowning, the specific words I've been planning over the weeks disappearing in a puff of nervous smoke. "And I'm not."

She slaps a hand over her mouth. I'm not sure if it's to stop her laughing or crying. Both? I look at my love, searching for those words. I'm coming up empty. What the fuck is wrong with me? I have a brain blockage, as well as a mouth blockage. I clear my throat. "Fuck," I whisper, dropping my ass to my heels, feeling a bit overcome. Her hand appears in my vision, and I look up at her, taking it. She joins me on the sand, our knees touching. And suddenly it all falls into place.

Red.

I stare at her, watching the breeze whip her hair round her face, watch her push that one side over her ear, her smile small but still fucking blinding. "I don't only want to be your hero, Pearl," I whisper, releasing her hand, showing her the ring. "I want to be your husband, your friend, your lover, your protector, your confidant. I want to be your everything." I feel the lump in my throat grow. "Because you're *my* everything."

One single tear rolls down her cheek.

"I will never let anyone hurt you or our little girl. I'll stand in the way of any danger or pain. I will kiss the ground you walk on for the rest of your life if you'll allow it." Because while Pearl thinks I saved her, it's actually she who saved me. From myself. I existed on cocaine, sex, and adrenaline. It was hollow, and yet I told myself it was what I wanted. That I didn't need anything else. *Couldn't* have anything else, not in my world. Then I found Pearl on a dirty mattress, bruised and lost. "It's all I want to do for the rest of my life."

She looks down at the ring, and I see a few more tears hit her knees as she slips it onto her finger. Feels at the pearl around her neck. Thinks of her mother. "I think I'd like that," she says, checking Ruby in my arms, her lip wobbling. She takes a deep breath and raises her eyes to mine, reaching for my stubbly cheek. "I love you," she whispers. "And I will never tell you ever again. Only show you." Lifting with some effort to her knees, I join her, our lips meeting over our baby's head, our hearts touching, connected by Ruby.

Always.

Her soft lips work mine, her tongue dipping into my mouth, and I accept, settled. Content. My daughter in one arm, Pearl in the other.

My loves.

Never to be let go.

Epilogue - Part 2

JAMES

Calm. I see it in Brad all the way from here as I watch from the decking of our villa. Both of them on their knees. It's apt. For all of us.

On our knees.

At the mercy of these women.

Reclined in the chair, my daughter asleep on my bare chest, her cheek squished, I relax and relish the sounds of the waves lapping the shore, my hand covering her back entirely. I watch the sun, anticipating another half hour before it touches this spot. She'll be awake by then. Two hours between one and three, guaranteed. It's amazing how much you can get done in two hours when you're against the clock. And fit in some intimate time too. *Essential.*

Not today, though.

Beau's gone to the salon with Rose for the first time since Georgie was born nearly five months ago. "So it's just me and you," I whisper, looking down at the back of her head, stroking over the silky dark blonde wisps of hair.

This was the end goal. Me, my girls, the sun shining on us. Through a sunhat and UV protective swimsuits for Georgie and sunblock for Beau, naturally. But we couldn't leave Miami until we knew the others were going to be okay. Now they're fine. We're all *more* than fine. All here. All happy.

Brad's just got to get Pearl through this final recovery period, and we're all here for them. Always.

I started this journey searching for the people responsible for the death of my family.

Ironically, I found myself another family.

A beautifully damaged, fucked-up family.

I smile to myself, exhaling my contentment, hearing the front door open.

I let my head drop, looking inside the villa, hearing her. Sensing her. She's back sooner than I thought. "Mummy's home," I whisper, lips resting on the top of Georgie's head as she sleepy sighs. I brace myself, waiting, and when Beau appears in the doorway, I lose my breath. Not because her hair looks amazing, but because ... my Beau. Ripped denim shorts, flip-flops, a cropped tank, her hair freshly done but still wild.

Peace.

And I want her.

She takes us both in, her palm on the jamb, smiling. "Afternoon."

I smile, jerking my head for her to come, my eyes following her light until she's perched on my knee, eyes on Georgie, stroking her silky hair too. "Has she been okay?"

"Perfect," I whisper. "We went for a dip."

"In the ocean?"

"Yeah," I breathe. "Just our toes. Then we went to the supermarket, stopped by to see Zinnea and Quinton, then came home for some lunch and our nap." I reach for Beau's hair and feel, glad it doesn't look too different from the hair I love. "Looks lovely."

She wrinkles her nose and pushes a hand through *my* hair, leaning in as much as she can without disturbing Georgie. My heart begins to thud. "More," I whisper, making her fist the strands and kiss me, another shot of life hitting me deeply. "I calculate we have approximately twenty-eight minutes," I mumble.

She smiles against my lips before pulling away and getting up. She checks our daughter, turns, and saunters away, pulling her tank up over her head as she goes. My heart and my dick kick, and it feels wholly inappropriate with Georgie in my arms, so I lift carefully, eyes on her, and carry her through to her bedroom, laying her down, holding my breath, easing up, hands held high. I grab her monitor and creep backward, tiptoeing out of her room.

I only breathe out when I walk into our bedroom. Then quickly lose my breath again when I find Beau on the bed, gloriously naked, her legs spread, knees up, her pussy visibly dripping.

Lord, have mercy on my depraved soul.

I push my shorts down, licking my lips, and pace over, placing the monitor on the nightstand before kneeling on the end of the bed.

"What's my name?" I whisper.

"Mine," she growls, hooking an arm around my neck and hauling me down onto her mouth.

And I smile against her lips, lifting my hips to let myself fall into place, and sink into her deeply on an inhale, cursing under my breath, the pleasure infinite. "My God, woman."

"Twenty-five minutes," she gasps, taking me all the way, tensing.

I take a few moments, making sure I don't come on the spot, before lifting and finding her eyes. "Twenty-five minutes," I muse, circling into her, watching her face as I do. "What I could do to you in twenty-five minutes."

She lifts her head and claims me, and I am all hers, our kiss quickly falling into the realms of manic, as I pump my hips and Beau meets every advance on endless whimpers. "Twenty-four minutes," she gasps, digging her nails into my scarred back. I grunt, slamming into her deep and high, before pulling out, making her yell her annoyance.

"Shhh," I say, putting a palm over her mouth and kissing my way down her stomach. I hook my other arm under her knee and lift it, opening her up to me, and cover her glistening flesh with my mouth, licking in one, long, firm stroke up her pussy. Her cry is muffled, her back jacked up off the bed. "More?" I ask against her skin, not waiting for her to answer, flicking the end of her clit with my tongue. She grabs my hand over her mouth and pushes it farther into her, forcing me to stifle her sounds of pleasure. "Twenty-three," I growl, lapping, kissing, biting, licking. My God, she tastes incredible, smells divine, as I lick her out, thorough, hard, soft. She stiffens, and I pull away, releasing her leg and removing my hand from her mouth, flipping her over onto her knees, taking her hair and pulling her head back. Sweating, I look down at her arse, smooth my palm over her skin. Slap it. Her shoulder blades pull in, but she doesn't make a sound.

I take my cock, gritting my teeth as I guide it to her pussy, inhaling when I sink in, looking up to the ceiling, absorbing the incredible feeling of her hot, wet walls drawing me in. I puff out my cheeks. Take her hips. And slowly start to drive into her.

She moans, groans, whimpers, her head turning one way, then the other, her fingers clawing into the sheets. I keep my pace meticulous and slow, watching her, every bit of her, her face turned out, turned in, her scarred arm.

Reaching forward, I place my fingertip at the top of her back, watching her shoulder blades pull in again as I drag it down the center of her spine. She reaches back with her hand, and I grab it, squeezing, threading my fingers through hers before releasing so she can support herself with two arms again. "Beau, baby, you look incredible."

A groan.

She's close.

And I need to see her face.

I pull out, turning her quickly onto her back, and spread myself all over her, sliding in while sliding my hands up the inside of her arms over her head, lacing our fingers, clenching, kissing her, rolling my hips.

She inhales sharply, her tongue circling mine becoming faster.

Closer.

I grind harder.

"James," she murmurs, releasing my lips and throwing her head back.

"Say my name," I order.

"James."

I pump harder. "Again."

"James!"

Sweat beads plummet from my forehead. "And again."

She looks at me, grates her teeth, reaches for my hair, and pulls my face down to her. "James," she murmurs calmly, her hips lifting, my cock plunging, and I twitch, hissing through my teeth, forcing my eyes to remain open to watch her come with me, every part of her beneath me tense as we still, watching each other sustain the intensity.

She cries out, and I gasp, releasing her hands, flexing some life back into them, still fucking coming. "Fucking hell," I whisper, closing my eyes briefly as Beau pushes my wet hair off my face. I exhale, collapsing onto one forearm, head hanging, my breathing labored. It takes me a few moments to find the energy to pull out and roll to my back beside her, the cool air hitting my front welcome. I drop my head to the side and reach for her breast, circling her nipple. "I love you," I whisper hoarsely.

She smiles, turning onto her side, and starting at my shoulder, she drags light fingertips down my chest. "Broken, fixed, happy, sad," she whispers.

"Are you okay?" I ask, shuddering under her touch, loving the smudge of mascara under her eyes from her sweat.

"No," she breathes, crawling up my chest and straddling me. "I'm perfect." She dips and kisses me, just as Georgie yells from her bedroom. I drop my head to look at the monitor. She's kicking, thrashing, has woken up full of beans. And I can't wait to get my hands on her again. I take Beau's hips and move her to the side, getting up and pulling on some boxers, pacing through the villa to her room. The moment I'm looming over her crib, she stills and finds me. Takes me in.

"Hey there, princess," I say quietly.

And she starts thrashing again, arms and legs. I laugh and scoop her up, getting her in the crook of my right arm. She immediately latches onto my bicep, dribbling all over me. Definitely teething on the way—everything within range goes into her mouth.

I take her back into the bedroom. Beau's got her knickers on, propped up against the headboard, her phone in her hand. She drops it the moment Georgie and I arrive, arms up, making grabby hands. "That's Mummy," I muse. "Remember her?"

Beau snorts. "Give her to me."

"No." I prop myself next to her and bend my knees, laying Georgie on them. Beau tucks herself into my chest.

"Make her laugh," she demands, prompting me to reach for the squeaky ball on the nightstand. This two-dollar piece of crap from the beach is the funniest thing since sliced bread according to our daughter.

"What's this?" I gasp, holding it up. Georgie stills, anticipating the sound, her eyes jumping from me to the ball. "Are you ready?"

She kicks once.

And I slowly squeeze, forcing the most obscene sound from the ball, something between a squeak and a fart. Georgie breaks out in fits of gurgling giggles and, I swear, the sound is life. My wife falls apart next to me too, both my girls beside themselves, Georgie over the ball, Beau over our baby girl's uncontrollable, addictive laughter. I could watch them all fucking day.

I lean down, a small chuckle falling past my lips, and push my mouth to the top of Beau's head.

She's no longer full of hate, only love. My darkness has always been her light, and her darkness has always been mine.

I didn't think Beau Hayley could get any more beautiful.

Turns out Beau Kelly, mum and wife, is beyond that.

She's no longer toxic, but she'll always be my balm. And I'll always be fatal, but to Beau and Georgie, I'm life.

Husband and Daddy.

Killing our enemies didn't free us.

Georgie did.

She's the brightest light.

Epilogue - Part 3

DANNY

"Rose, darling, this is"—I scan the spread, the marque on the terrace, the balloons in the pool—"a lot."

"It's a special day."

"Yes, but you know Brad and Pearl. They don't like too much fuss." I round the corner of the villa, still in my wetsuit, Maggie sitting on my forearm still in hers too, following Rose as she hurries off with a tray of canapés.

"It's not too much," she protests over her shoulder. "Just a little party."

"Jesus Christ, Rose," I blurt, coming face to face with a balloon arch off the door from the dining room. "Where the hell did that come from?"

"It was erected while you took Maggie out on your jet ski with Lennox and the boys."

She places the tray down on the tall table by the arch. Next to the other tall table laid out with champagne. Not too much? Then she marches off again, brushing her hands off.

Maggie's palms slap my face, squeezing, and she pushes her nose to mine.

"Dada telling mummy off," I say peeling her clawing hands off my cheeks. "Watch." I go after Rose and enter the kitchen.

"Out!" she yells, making me jump and step out onto the patio again. "Oh, for God's sake, Danny, look." She points to the small puddle just inside the door before getting the mop and angrily wiping it up.

"Dadadadada!"

I flinch when Maggie's hands land on my cheeks again, squeezing, her face coming close, her eyes blinking against mine, our lashes tickling each other's. "You giving me angel kisses, my girl?" I wrinkle my nose, bat my lashes, and she breaks out in laughter, bouncing in my arms. Then something catches her eye—I know what—and she yells, excited. I look back and see Daniel traipsing down the path, his surfboard tucked under his arm.

"Where are you going?" I ask. We just got back.

"Me and Barney want to catch the evening waves."

"Not a chance!" Rose yells, appearing. Daniel exhales his exasperation. "It's Brad and Pearl's party."

"They don't know it's a party," he points out. "Uncle Brad wouldn't even *want* a party."

"Don't you start." Rose disappears back inside on a huff of indignance. "It's been too long since we were all together."

"Here," I say, giving Maggie a quick kiss before passing her to Daniel. "Take your sister."

He doesn't argue and, of course, Maggie is delighted, screaming her joy, giving Daniel lots of angel kisses too. "I'll take her to build a sandcastle."

"Okay," I call. "Make sure you put sunscreen on her face and keep her wetsuit on." I go after Rose, finding her in the kitchen. Under a massive fucking banner wishing Brad and Pearl a happy engagement. Jesus Christ, they'll walk straight back out.

"Danny!" she yells, coming at me.

I let her, catching her wrists and holding her in place.

"You're dripping everywhere."

"Deal with it." I nod to the banner. "Not too much?"

She pouts, shoulders dropping. "I'm just excited."

And who am I to spoil my wife's fun? For fuck's sake. I relent on a sigh. "Just tone it down a little, okay?"

"Okay," she agrees.

"Hey, you might have gone to all this trouble for nothing. She might have said no."

"She didn't say no."

"How'd you know?"

She falters, thinking, going back to the island and picking up a knife, chopping a few tomatoes. "I may have stopped by the beach on my way back from the salon after I dropped Beau off." Oh yes, because my wife can drive now. She presses her lips together as she sets the knife down, and I drop my head back, exasperated. "I'm just so happy everyone is happy!" She comes to me and reaches for my shoulders, getting up on her tippy toes, waiting for me to drop my face. Her grin is impish. It's a whole new level of satisfaction, seeing this new passion in Rose.

"I'm happy you're happy," I admit. "But like I said, dial it down."

"Fine."

"Good."

She peeks past me. "Where are the kids?"

Oh? My dick twitches as I take her hand and lead it to the zip on the back of my wetsuit. "The kid took Maggie to build a sandcastle."

Her blue eyes dance, pulling my zip down, allowing me to wriggle out the top half of my wetsuit. "Now who's dripping?" I ask, losing my hand under her skirt, inhaling at the wetness I find. "Did you miss me this morning, baby?" I ask.

She attacks, and I lift her up against me, walking us out of the kitchen toward our bedroom. "Watch my hair," she pants, yelping as I throw her on the bed. She frantically strips as I get out of my wetsuit, falling on top of her, my hair falling down into my face, my dick on the cusp on breaching her entrance. I plunge in, head dropped back, quivering.

"Oh yes," I breathe, taking the pleasure, my arms braced, my torso stiff. "God, you feel good."

She flexes her hips. "Move."

"Wait," I breathe, reining myself in.

"Move!"

"Wait, Rose."

"Move!"

Fucking hell. I quickly gather myself and start pounding hard.

"Faster!"

"Fucking hell, Rose, what's the rush?"

"My cake," she pants. "Needs to come out of the oven."

The fuck? I stop moving, staring down at her in horror.

"What?" she wheezes.

"You baked a cake?"

"Yes, I baked a cake."

"An edible cake?"

She gasps and smacks my arm, and I laugh, pulling out of her and getting her off the bed. "What are you doing?" she snaps. "Danny, it'll burn if—"

I spin her and get her against the wall, front forward, crowding her, taking her hair. Fucking cakes, parties, having sex by the clock.

"I think we need a little reminder of who we are, Mrs. Black," I hiss, reaching to between her legs and stroking through her arousal. She tenses, looking over her shoulder, her dark blue eyes darker.

"Make it bloody," she whispers, and I grin, slamming into her on a grunt, fucking her hard and fast against the wall like the very first time we came together. It's loud, it's hot, it's chaotic, and when we both come, it's with force, both of us collapsing to the carpet, breathless, wet, and fucking knackered. I pant, dropping my head to see her splayed on the floor next to me, her salon-fresh hair a beautiful mess. Still deadly gorgeous. "I fucking hate you."

She finds some life and sits on my stomach, dipping and kissing my scar, my lids, my nose. I sigh and sink into the hard floor, happy to let her kiss me back to life. "I think I ruined your hair, baby," I wheeze, panting up at the ceiling.

"Never mind," she says, easygoing, moving down to the bullet wound on my pec. "I love you."

"I love you too." She gets up and saunters off to the bathroom, my tired eyes nailed to her arse. She stops. Looks back. "And I'm pregnant." She disappears quickly into the bathroom, slamming the door.

What?

I stare at the wood for an age, frowning. "Rose, baby," I eventually call, not moving.

"Yeah?"

"I think I heard you just say you're pregnant again."

"You did."

"Oh." I rest my head back on the floor. "My fucking God," I whisper, slapping a hand over my face. "When?" I call. Love how she drops *that* bomb and takes cover.

"You remember that day we went for a romantic beach picnic?" she yells through the door. "When your mom and Otto watched Maggie after they got back from their honeymoon?"

"Yeah."

"Then."

"Oh."

The door opens and she peeks out at me still lying flat on my back on the floor. "Are you mad?"

"Furious," I say dryly. *Fuck me, please give me another boy!*

"Wait." I sit up, resting back on my elbows. "Mum and Otto got back over two months ago."

"I know."

"How long have you known?"

She shrugs.

"Rose, how long?"

"Four weeks."

"Four?" I blurt.

"And it's twins." She flashes a wide, toothy, nervous smile and slams the door, hiding again.

I stare at the wood. Just stare. *Twins?* Did she say, *twins?* "Rose, baby."

"Yeah?"

"I think I just heard you say it's twins."

"You did."

"Oh." Twins? I peek across the bedroom when I hear my phone ringing. I get up and wander over to the nightstand, frowning, looking over my shoulder to the bathroom door as I answer. "Hey."

"She said yes."

"Of course she said yes," I murmur, walking out into the kitchen. "Congratulations." I don't sound very chirpy, and I won't be telling him I already knew. Privacy in this family is non-existent, despite us all having our own places on various parts of the beach.

"You all right?" Brad asks.

"Fine."

"Okay. I'll see you later?"

"Bye." I hang up and lower my phone to the island, then absentmindedly follow my feet out into the garden. I eye the champagne. Take two glasses. Down them both as I walk around the side of the villa. Daniel is coming up the path with Maggie toddling along beside him, cheering her on as she walks with the aid of his hand.

"Yeah, girl," he yells, making Maggie chuckle and squeal. "Go on, girl."

"Dadadadada!"

Daniel looks at me. Recoils. "Ummm, Dad, did you forget something?"

I look down my front. My naked front. "Yeah," I say, holding a palm over my dick. Give me a sec." I turn and go back to the bedroom, knocking on the bathroom door. She doesn't answer. I turn the handle. Surprisingly, it opens. I find her sitting on the toilet, her hands joined, her knees bouncing from her feet tapping the floor. She looks up.

"You definitely said twins, right?" I say, and she nods slowly. "Thought so." I leave her and go to the bed, collapsing onto my back, arms and legs splayed. "God," I say to the ceiling. "I know you and I haven't exactly seen eye to eye, but if you can bring yourself to help me out, I'll take all the strength and patience you can spare. Thanks."

I hear Rose chuckle and lift my head. She's standing at the bottom of the bed. And yes, she's fucking glowing. I had noticed, of course, but I put it down to the sunshine, the peace, the calm. She sighs and crawls up to me, straddling my hips. "Are you scared?" she asks.

"Nah," I say, taking her hips, eyeing her tummy. After everything we've been through, this will be a walk in the park. "You?"

"Nah." She drops her front to mine. "We're pros now."

I smack her arse. "Fucking twins." Shake my head. "Kiss me." I roll us over, letting her attack me like the lioness she is.

• • •

I sit on the edge of the terrace, a Scotch in my hand, a cigarette in the other, trying to come to terms with it. *Still.* It might take a while. So much for eternal calm and peace. I observe everyone from a distance, watching as they mingle, drink, laugh on the patio.

Relaxed.

Maggie is on Rose's hip, Georgie's in Beau's arms, Ella has Ruby, and Pearl is perched on a tall stool. She looks great. A little tired, but really great given her traumas.

I see Lennox come in, waving a bottle, his new lady friend clutching his hand. Barney dashes off to join Daniel on the Xbox, and Esther greets them. I raise a hand when he looks this way. I'll go over soon. I still need this moment.

"Oh my," Pearl had said when she and Brad arrived, her face a picture of reluctant enthusiasm.

I'd given Rose a telling look. She'd shrugged it off.

I inhale and move my eyes across to Goldie and Ringo sitting with Zinnea and Quinton. There's something there, I swear it. And

Nolan and Ella? I'm expecting wedding bells soon. I smile. How the family has grown. Mason, the Vikings, and the boys from the boatyard are chatting, beers in hands. They all came to St. Lucia and haven't gone back. Why the fuck would they? We're restructuring, rebuilding, restarting.

Never leaving.

And as for the docs? They've settled in quite well too, although we don't see as much of Fred these days. The old tart brought his lady friend along for the ride. He deserves a bit of respite. I'm happy for him. And eternally grateful for him.

Mum wanders over with a bottle, half-smiling, but half showing that old permanent look of worry. "What are you doing over here?" she asks, topping up my Scotch.

I pout, taking her hand and pulling her down. She frowns. "You and Otto are gonna be grandparents again."

"What?" she gasps, hand over her mouth. "No."

"Yep. And it's twins." I neck my drink and laugh at the look on Mum's face. "I know, right? Fucking twins." I dip and kiss her on the cheek. "Pray for me."

She laughs as I rise to my feet with her, handing my empty over. "I'm going for a stroll with the boys," I say, nodding to James and Brad across the pool. Both stand, discarding their drinks, reading the message.

They're needed.

But they don't go load their guns.

No.

The collect their daughters as I walk to Rose and take Maggie from her arms. She doesn't ask where we're going. Doesn't need to. I stop off at the lounge and pick up the urn with Dad's ashes in—let's see some fucker try to dig these up—and head out to the path that leads to the beach. The boys and their girls are waiting for me. We walk down to the shore in silence, the girls making various noises, Maggie the loudest, holding my face, insistent on angel kisses. "One day I'll teach you about spatial awareness, my girl," I say, chuckling when her nose wrinkles and she latches onto the end of mine with her mouth. "Proper kisses now?"

The boys behind me laugh, and I inhale, settling my arse on the shore just out of the reach of the water. They join me as I sit Maggie on my lap, James has Georgie between his bent legs, and Brad has Ruby on his thighs. "Look at the fucking state of us," I mumble, putting the urn down. "So fucking deadly." But the truth is, we don't need to be anymore. Never again. "Rose is pregnant," I say, and James bursts out laughing, followed quickly by Brad. "And it's twins."

The howling notches up to irritating levels, and I roll my eyes, wishing I could sock them both to the face. Maybe when the girls aren't around.

"Jesus Christ," James breathes, getting his laughter under control as Georgie takes his finger and shoves it in her mouth. "Twins."

"Man, we're moving," James chuckles.

"Fuck off." No one is ever moving. "You saying you're not having anymore?"

"Yep," he chimes quickly.

"Two's enough for me, thanks." Brad chuckles, then frowns. "What the fuck is Maggie eating?"

I shoot my eyes down, seeing her little fist at her mouth covered in some dusty powder. Confused, I take her hand and open it. "Oh fuck." I quickly check the urn. The lid's off. "Oh fuck, no." I jump up and sling Maggie under my arm, running into the shallow ocean, splashing water around her mouth. "She ate Pops!" I yell, as Maggie starts screaming to high heaven and James and Brad fall apart on the shore.

"Here." Brad chucks me a bottle of water, and I quickly unscrew it and lay her back in my arms, pouring it over her lips, hoping she takes some of it in and clears away the dust. Naturally, she screams louder, and I feel like twenty tons of shite. "Oh baby." I get her upright, seeing her spit and blow raspberries, trying to rid her mouth, more of the salt I expect. "Daddy's sorry." I stick my finger in her mouth, checking for remnants of the ashes of her dead grandfather. "Fucking hell."

"Danny!" I hear Rose yell. "What's going on?"

"Nothing, dear," I yell back. "Our daughter's a fucking Hannibal, dear," I add quietly.

I look at the boys.

Both with babies in their arms. "It's a good job we're not in the game anymore because we'd be laughing stocks."

"Would you care?" James asks.

I look at Maggie, blinking, her face a screwed-up picture of perfection. "No, can't say I would."

"Could give a flying fuck," Brad mumbles. "Don't."

I look at the urn wedged in the sand. *Pops.* Where it all began. I smile and walk over, Maggie sitting on my forearm, and pick it up, looking out at the ocean. I see me, a boy, whizzing across the waves on my jet ski.

Carlo Black in pursuit.

"Rest in peace, Mister," I whisper, turning away from the wind and tipping the urn, watching his ashes whip with the breeze, disappearing into the air. Ironically, I hear his laugh too. See him in his tanned-skin, silvered-haired glory, smoking a Cuban, supping a brandy. "Thanks for saving me."

Welcome, kid. I'm fucking proud of you.

I swallow down the unexpected lump in my throat, looking down at my girl. "Thanks for everything," I whisper.

Taking a deep breath, I turn to a quiet Brad and James. "Walk?" I say, prompting them both to work their way up from the sand.

We start to meander down the shoreline, watching the sun dropping into the ocean. "It's been a pleasure, boys," I say casually as Maggie rests her head on my shoulder. She's tired. Wants her daddy cuddles.

And I'm here for it.

"A blast," James says dryly, flipping me an ironic look.

"Wouldn't have wanted to nearly die numerous times with anyone else," Brad adds, casting a look our way.

I smile like an idiot, as he smiles back at me and James laughs.

We've always had one foot in heaven, one in hell. That will never change.

But we're no longer unlawful, just pussy-whipped instead. And that's *way* more frightening.

Unlawful men.

Over and out.

Acknowledgments

Thank you for reading.
You're the reason.

Much love,
JEM xxx

About the Author

Jodi Ellen Malpas was born and raised in England, where she lives with her husband, boys, and Theo the Doberman. She is a self-professed daydreamer and has a terrible weak spot for alpha males. Writing powerful love stories with addictive characters has become her passion—a passion she now shares with her devoted readers. She's a proud #1 *New York Times* bestselling author and *Sunday Times* bestseller, and her work is published in over twenty-seven languages around the world.

jodiellenmalpas.co.uk

*Don't miss the exciting new books
Entangled has to offer.*

Follow us!

 @EntangledPublishing

 @Entangled_Publishing

 @EntangledPub

Made in United States
Orlando, FL
16 March 2024

44833472R00355